FORGED BY LOVE AND SACRIFICE

VOLUME 1

FORGED SERIES

K. F. LETHAL

Threshold Publishing

Forged by Love and Sacrifice Volume One

Copyright by K. F. Lethal 2024

ISBN Paperback: 979-8-218-14611-5

ISBN eBook: 979-8-218-48100-1

Cover Artist: Leon Ning

Editor: Samantha Reads Spicy

Sensitivity Reader: Moss Nightwing

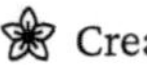 Created with Vellum

To anyone who has lost a loved one.

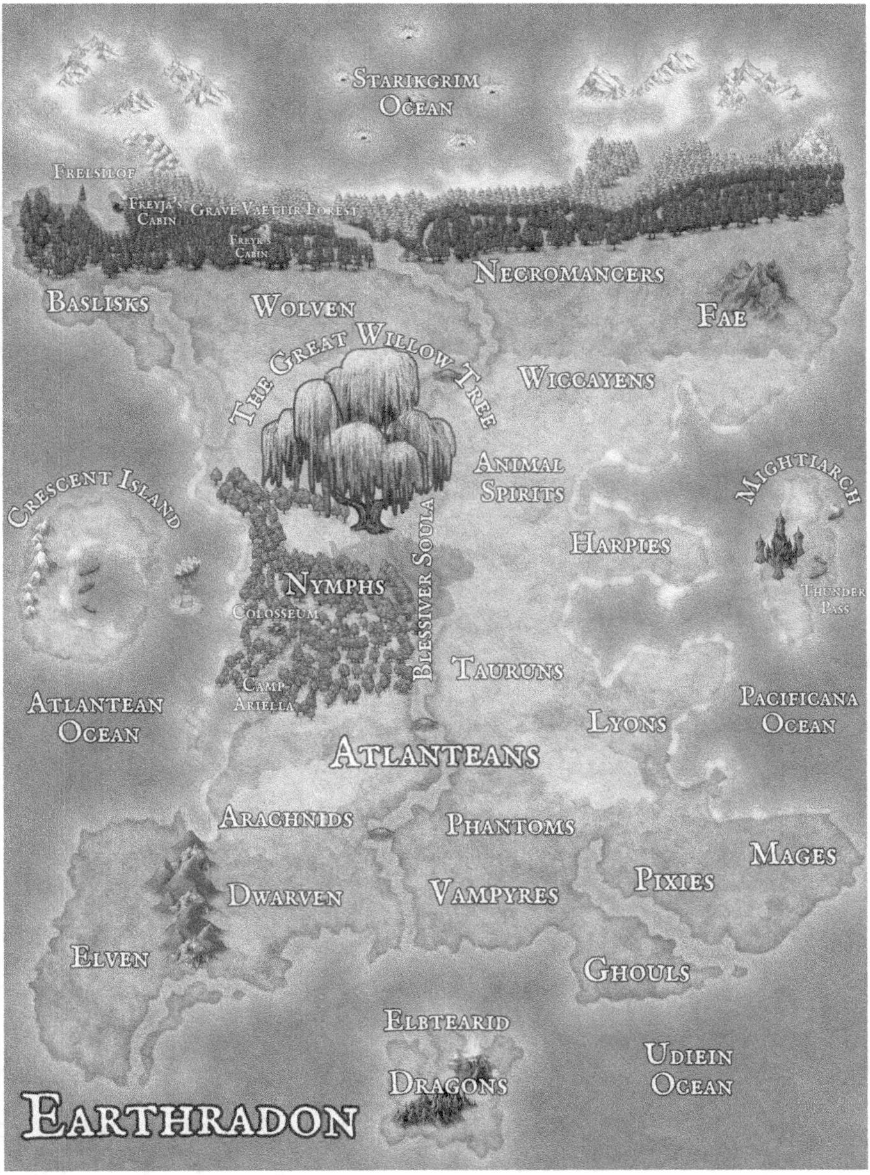

Starikgrim Ocean
Frelsilof
Freyja's Cabin
Grave Vaettir Forest
Freyka Cabin
Necromancers
Fae
Baslisks
Wolven
The Great Willow Tree
Wiccayens
Crescent Island
Animal Spirits
Mightiarch
Harpies
Nymphs
Colosseum
Blessiver Souia
Thunder Pass
Atlantean Ocean
Camp Ariella
Tauruns
Lyons
Pacificana Ocean
Atlanteans
Arachnids
Phantoms
Mages
Dwarven
Vampyres
Pixies
Elven
Ghouls
Elbtearid
Dragons
Udiein Ocean
Earthradon

CONTENTS

PART FOUR
WHY DOES EVERYONE WANT MY FEATHERS?

PRONUNCIATION GUIDE

Adom Leeater – A-dome / Lee-ate-r
Aireie – Air-e-ie
Aliith – A-li-ith
Amormatrlee Ravuletta – A-mor-ma-tr-lee / Rav-u-letta
Arganile – Ar-gan-ile
Ariella – Ar-e-ella
Arighness – A-righ-ness
Atlantean – At-lant-e-an
Aquazanite – A-quaz-an-ite
Avokyria - A-vok-yr-a

Bah Sundrae – B-ah / Sun-drae
Barighness – Bar-igh-ness
Blessiver Soula – Bless-iver / Soul-a
Bralyant – Bral-e-ant
Braxshi – Brax-shi

Carnit – Car-nit
Ceaxia – Ce-ax-ia
Cheriefi – Cher-e-fe
Churania – Chur-ron-e-a

Ciado – C-ado
Coalston – Coal-ston

Demonical – De-mon-ic-al
Drafasa – Dra-fa-sa
Dragonnira – Dra-gon-nir-a

Earthradon- Earth-ra-don
Earthradonic – Earth-ra-don-ic
Earthradonrien – Earth-ra-don-ri-en
Eirikur – E-irk-ur
Elbtearid – Elb-tear-id
Emerial – E-meri-al
Emperior – Em-peer-e-ur
Emperiest – Em-peer-e-est
Erresthralla – Air-res-thra-la
Eterna – E-tern-a
Ethasion – E-thas-ien
Excilum – Ex-ci-lum

Faetriarks – Fae-tri-arks
Falmenir Makuba – Fal-men-ir / Mak-u-ba
Fanarzien – Fan-ar-zi-en
Fleshions - Flesh-e-ins
Frelsilof – Frel-sil-of
Freyja – Frey-a
Freyr – Frey-ur
Furieyrians – Fur-ear-re-ens

Galex – Ga-lex
Galexstrials – Ga-lex-stri-als

Hafgura – Haf-gur-a
Haidion – Hay-de-in
Harcaniel – Har-can-iel
Heimdall – Heim-dall
Hornarokk –Horn-a-rock

Illyrical – Il-lyr-ic-al
Incestual – In-cest-u-al
Intergalaxiate – In-ter-gal-ax-i-ate
Iraijah – Ir-ai-jah

Kailani – Kai-la-ne
Kiani – Ki-an-e

Ladiya – Lay-d-ya
Lakonna – La-kon-na
Lanic – Lan-ic
Larvaelet - Larv-ae-let
Leifheim – Leaf-heim
Lunivium – Loon-iv-ve-um

Malvik – Mal-vik
Marcson – Marc-son
Maytower – May-tower
Maurdr - Ma-ur-dr
Melrose Gailner - Mel-rose / Gail-ner
Memoreea Fevaira – Mem-or-ee-a / Fev-air-a
Mermerrayl – Mer-mare-e-al
Mightiarch – Mighty-arch
Morgannaelmore – Mor-gan-na-el-more
Mto Ivoire – M-toe / I-voir-e
Murrdirel – Murr-di-rel

Namtar – Nam-tar
Nexurous – Nex-ur-ous
Nightnir – Night-nir
Norliska – Nor-lis-ka
Novvricken – No-vrick-en
Nymphfralo – Nymph-fra-lo

Orckrainien – Ork-rain-e-in
Orrtiereum – Or-tier-e-um

Paulyr – Paul-yr

Rawldur – Rawl-dur
Reckell – Rec-kell
Relynt – Re-ly-ent
Rhax - Racks
Rizaver – Riz-a-ver
Roareeien – Roar-ee-en

Sagerial – Sage-re-al
Serrultan – Ser-rul-tan
Serrultana – Ser-rul-ta-na
Sihotana – Sih-o-tana
Skjoldr – Sk-jul-dur
Sorbane – Sor-bane
Sothearia – So-thear-e-a
Sovrinarch – Sov-rin-arch
Spyden – Spy-den
Startikgrim – Star-tik-grim

Taurun – Taur-un

Udiein – U-di-ein

Grave Vaettir Forest – Va-e-ttir
Vahildra – Va-hil-dra
Valgorlas – Val-gor-las
Valrir - Val-rear
Vampyre – Vam-py-re
Varnus - Var-nus
Vasilis – Va-sil-is
Vianre – Vi-an-re
Virbrantrea – Vir-bran-tre-a

Wardalyn – Ward-a-lyn
Wardalyrian – Ward-a-lyr-e-an
Waregen – War-e-gen

Warrvenors – War-ven-ors
Whemida – Whe-mi-da
Wiccayen – Wic-cayenne
Wuirrls – Whirls

Yrradiant – Yr-radiant

TRIGGER AND CONTENT WARNINGS

Ableism, Age Gaps, Amputation, Anxiety, Antisemitic, Asphyxiation, Attempted Murder.
Blood, Body Fluids, Body Shaming, Branding.
Cheating, Classism, Coercion, Comp Het, Corpse, Court Proceedings.
Death Of A Loved One, Decapitation, Depression, Description Of Falling From On High, Divorce, Domestic Violence, Drugging.
Ecofascism, Emotional Abuse, End Times Rhetoric, Enslavement, Eugenics.
Femicide, Forced Sterilization.
Gaslighting, Gender Essentialism, Genocide Mentions, Gore, Graphic Depictions of Violence, Grief.
Homophobia, Humiliation.
Imprisonment, Incarceration, Incest Mentions, Infertility.
Kidnapping.
Loss Of A Spouse.
Manipulation, Marital Rape Mentions, Marital Troubles, Mass Murder, Mental Health Stigma, Mentions Of Murdered Children, Misogyny, Murder.
Near Death Experiences.
On Page Death, On Page Sexual Assault, Organ Removal Mentions.
Panic Attacks, Patriarchy, Physical Abuse, Plague Mentions, PTSD.

Race Codes, Racism, Rape Threats.
Sanism, Self Worth Struggles, Sexual Assault, Sexual Harassment,
Shipwreck, Snakes, Speciesism, Spiders, Suicide Mentions.
The Horrors Of War, The Realities Of War, Threats Against Children,
Threats of Castration, Torture, Transphobia.
Victim Blaming.
Wrongful Imprisonment.

PART ONE
DOES THIS FIRE EVER GO OUT?

ONE

SUNDOWN

I'm tempted to wake my husband with my lips wrapped around his cock. Only an hour has passed since we found euphoric pleasure together, but the more I admire my beautiful husband, the more I want him buried deep inside me again.

His wavy locks of snow-kissed hair send erotic chills down my spine as I brush strands away from his eyes. On his smooth cream skin, covered in detailed ink from all his conquests to gain knowledge, red streaks from where my nails clawed stand out on his shoulders, arms, and chest.

I suppress a giggle but allow my smile to widen as I stroke down his cheek to his full beard. The silver-gray hairs scattered throughout give him the appearance of being twice my age.

Odin reached magical maturity over two thousand years ago. Being born an immortal freezes our bodies once we reach our magical prime, but we can use magic to age our appearance if we desire. Once we alter something, there is no going back. I think I've reached my magical maturity, but I'm not sure.

As the Norse God of Wisdom, War, and Death, my husband wanted a demeanor that would earn him more respect. I'm glad the changes he made didn't impair his endurance, strength, or stamina. He could still throw me around like a ragdoll on the bed, pin me beneath him, and fuck me until I forgot who I was.

You've got to get up, Freyja.

Cuddling against my husband's body is beginning to make him sweat and should be more than enough to motivate me to move. I can never curl up with him for too long before my sweltering heat becomes unbearable for him, which is why our room has such a large bed. We can sleep on our own sides if we want, and when I'm a needy cuddle bug, I just throw the furs off of me and snuggle for as long as I can before Odin grumbles for me to roll over.

Before I received my wonderful bed sheets, I would always be in a vicious cycle of putting on and taking off blankets all night. I was always worried my tossing and turning would wake Odin. If getting a larger bed didn't work, I'd sleep in the living room after he'd dozed off. He has no trouble falling or staying asleep; he's like a rock, and he wouldn't notice my absence since I'm always up before him.

A soft shimmer draws my attention downward. I slid my hand away from him to stroke the silky star-freckled black fitted bed sheet. The fibers of the material were enchanted by star magic, so when the sky darkens, the sheet awakens with the same coolness. Our cuddle time is still only an hour, but I never overheat the bed anymore and I don't have to leave his side to sleep.

The same sheet is draped over me, and every curve of my body is caressed as if the world's softest hands were worshiping me, kneading my muscles with soothing coolness. They were an anniversary gift from my friend, Haidion. He was probably annoyed with my complaining about not getting restful sleep when we were together or went on adventures. Haidion took matters into his own hands to find a solution since I was at a loss.

I roll onto my back and stretch out, trying not to look at myself in the black mirror on the ceiling above the bed, another gift from my friend. At first, I loved the present. Over the centuries, I've become irritated at the reflection that I see most. I enjoy watching my husband's muscles flex as he fucks me and my hands gliding and clawing all over his back, but having the mirror mounted above the bed has always shown Odin is the one on top, dominating me ten times out of ten.

I give my reflection the charming middle finger before getting out of bed.

Muscular arms wrap around me before I can sit up. Odin pulls me back down to lay on my side and molds me to his slick body. One arm snakes under my neck as the other curls around my waist. His hands stop when one finds my breast and the other is buried between my thighs. *Is he wanting to have sex again?*

Odin's hold on me is too tight. I can't even turn to face him, so I turn my attention to the mirror above us. He's silently mumbling, like he always does when he's in deep sleep.

My squirming results in the hardening of his cock against my ass.

His lips brush over the shell of my ear, causing me to shudder. "I love you so much."

I become motionless. I'd never heard his deep, rustic voice beg in our almost five centuries of being together. Worry awakens, alarming my instincts.

Those comforting lips move down to kiss the sensitive spot under my ear. He kneads my breast, rolling the nipple between his fingers, and rubs my clit in slow circles. Both sensitive mounds are tenderly worshiped. He has never been so gentle with me. If my nerves weren't being stimulated to build to an orgasm right now, they'd be on high alert to figure out what was wrong with my husband.

I can no longer contain my whimpers from his affectionate pleasure or stop myself from grinding against him. *Fuck, I'm going to be late.*

"Freyja?" Odin stiffens, withdrawing his fingers, and softening against the crack of my ass.

His half-lidded eyes find me in the mirror. "Why did you stop?" I breathlessly whimper.

Instead of answering, he responds with a grunt, unwraps himself, and rolls over. Soft snores fill the silence of our moonlit room.

All the affection he fed into my needy soul and the pleasurable heat he awoke in my core ached, demanding more. But a bucket of ice water is drenched over me from head to toe, biting at my flushed skin and humiliating my arousal from thinking Odin would continue, even though I knew his behavior was odd. Tears try to break free, but I swallow them.

I should've called out to get his attention or tried harder to pull away. Maybe I disturbed him by cuddling for too long. He shouldn't have woken up after the evening we had. Since I wanted to be sure he'd be knocked out before I left after sundown, I told him to unleash himself on me. Whatever fantasy he wanted; I was willing to fulfill it.

A sensual touch of comfort brushes down my left arm, against my spiraling mind, and around my ashamed heart. Before my thoughts send me into a guilty grave from wanting Odin's tender affection, silky hands wrap around my soul and lead my mind toward a more comforting dream, promising eternal peace.

When a sigh of relief escapes me and my heart slows as if I'm about to fall into a deep sleep, my spiritual essence raises the hairs on my body, alerting my instincts and soul magic to be on guard.

The phantom energy of my spiritual essence hums in my chest and detects an intruder. My descent into slumber halts, and my desire to be lost in an eternal dream is gone in an instant. Those soft hands become sharp claws, and the soothing brushes become rough. *Fuck! Is that what I think it is?*

Before my soul magic is triggered to expel the leech from my body, a lethal wave of cold explodes in my chest, dislodging the magical parasite.

A thick, slithering mass of ink rushes out of my chest and into the air, followed by a smoky shadow monster. The two battle in silence above my head, neither taking their true form as they tumble in the air towards the open balcony doors. Once they reach the threshold, the shadow monster consumes the leech and vanishes. *What the fuck! They are real?*

Leeches were thought to be more of a mental illness an immortal could fall into when experiencing a lack of magic or hope. Only a few believed them to be creatures who feed off soul magic, like shadow monsters. Why a shadow monster was inside me as well, I don't know, and no one has been able to figure out how to detect when they are inside the body or lingering in one's own shadow.

Not caring if I wake Odin, I roll over him and place my hand on his chest. I've been experiencing a lot of uncertainty lately, but I've never reached the point of hopelessness. Odin is a saint in keeping his emotions in check. The possibility of a leech getting into him is unlikely, however I'm not going to risk leaving him tonight without checking.

His strong heart beats against my hand. After emptying the air out of my lungs, I place my other hand over my chest to activate my spiritual power. The hand against Odin's chest sinks under his skin and I'm greeted by his heart. As I've been told, if a leech was inside him, a slimy texture would be wrapped around the organ. His soul radiates heat and potent magic telling me he's not infected.

Odin is still sound asleep when I remove my hand and deactivate my power. No one can ever sense me, as if I have become a ghost. Took me centuries to only have my hand shift rather than my entire body.

My worry for my husband is soothed, and my panic sets in. Not wanting to disturb him any more than I already have, I sit on the velvety blue bench at the end of the bed, digging my short nails into the fabric as my heart rate accelerates and my breaths quicken.

Cold air wafts in from the open doors, pebbling my blush pink nipples and raising goosebumps all over my freckled, rosy-pale skin.

I'm at a loss of how I let my mind fall so far as to weaken my instincts for a leech to come in. I don't know when the leech entered my body. Since my spiritual power doesn't draw from my soul magic, I won't know if any has been stripped from me. My spiritual power comes naturally to me, as if my body was made to have it, just like a basilisk has organs to make venom.

I'm drawn to the clear night sky beyond the balcony. My evening plans are becoming more impossible without knowing if I'll have magic at my disposal. Odin is safe, and if I don't want to be disappointed with myself, I have to bottle this up before I break down. I won't allow myself to shed tears and fall victim to being weak. I'm Freyja, the Norse Goddess of Love, Fertility, Battle, and Death; I can't be anything less than mighty.

A delicate caress wraps around a sacred place in my heart, stilling me. *What now?*

When my soul warms, I put my hand to my chest, ready to check for another leech. As if a rope were attached to the core of my existence, something tugs me in the direction of the balcony, beckoning me to seek out the adventure I have planned for tonight. The caress is magical and full of life, reassuring me I'm not drained. A tear almost escapes my eye as I sigh and send a prayer, thanking the Fates for uplifting my spirit.

The oak-wood flooring nips into my bare feet when I walk off the fur carpet and into the bathroom. A black stone tub is framed in the middle of bay windows looking out to my garden and Grave Vaettir Forest. Eerie at night and lavishly green during the day.

I open the top drawer in the vanity and pull out a fire-enchanted stone from my collection. I place the stone in the water after turning off the faucet that filled the bowl. The engravings on the stone glow, and a moment later, steam rises from the water's surface.

After giving myself a bird bath, I brushed and braided my golden-copper hair into a ponytail. A giggle leaves my lips as I survey my body in the mirror. Around my neck, bruises caused by Odin's lovemaking are starting to form. He apologized before he went to sleep for being too rough, but the truth is, I wanted more.

Restricting my breathing as he pounded me into the bed wasn't enough to satisfy my dark appetite. Dropping hints to Odin about how I would like to be fucked always makes him feel inadequate and self-conscious, diminishing his libido for a couple of weeks.

Climaxing twice was not enough to control my arousal, or my "purple monster," as I like to call it. When Odin tried to pin me, I fought him in an attempt to tire him out, and I nearly orgasmed with his first thrust when he growled his victory. I'd like to see him show more of his primal side. *Now is not the time to be horny, Freyja.*

My thighs rub together, creating moan-inducing friction, as I walk over to the dresser across from the bed.

Shelves for Odin's book and journals adorn the wall above the dresser in lieu of another mirror. All through the cabin are dark cherry logs and exposed support beams, leaving most of the walls free for Odin to install more shelves or for me to build some if he asks nicely.

After slipping into a pair of black undergarments and lacing up my bra, I dress in a white tunic and a matching pair of pants, which help me see if I'm injured. When I have my black leather boots laced up, I direct my attention to the bouquet of daisies sitting in a stone-white vase on my vanity.

All who choose to worship me leave this flower at my altar as an offering to have their prayers heard. Odin collected them for me before he headed home. The bouquet on my vanity he picked himself to ensure his prayer would be heard. An ache in my lower abdomen responds. I already know the answer, but Odin hasn't lost faith. For me to get pregnant, I need magical assistance. Becoming a mother isn't my reality anymore, and after tonight, I'll know if anything awaits Odin and me after death.

With a wave of my hand, I harvest the magic from the flowers. The petals and stems wilt and transform into a flurry of pastels. The magic curls around my fingertips, followed by a phantom embrace of strength and tranquility.

I cast my magic over to my armor stand with one hand. Every piece rises off the wooden mannequin and floats over to me, hovering in place for me to step into. With my other hand, I control the strapping and belts.

My Celestial-Cyanic armor conforms to me like a second layer of skin and provides more comfort than a bath. The blue-black armor is dusted with stars and has the same effect as my bed sheets. When I fly at night, I blend in, and during the daytime hours, I glow like a ray of sunlight.

Many have offered to pay outrageous amounts of gold for my rare armor. They would have to fight an Orckrainien warrior, a vicious and barbaric race of the galaxy, just like I did, if they wanted a set.

A falcon-feather cloak completes my ensemble. Odin enchanted the feathers to allow me to fly, and when I direct my soul magic into the cloak, I can go faster.

Leaving to seek out the answer to what happens after we Gods die is long overdue. I should have done so the moment after I shot the flaming arrow into my brothers' funeral ship five hundred years ago.

I discovered the day Freyr died that our immortality only ensures us longevity, not invincibility. The hardest part was that he was so close—just a few steps away. I could have saved him if I had pushed just a little bit harder.

Even if the answer isn't what I'm hoping for, I will be less anxious if I know what will happen to my soul after this life. I desire to know if I'll ever see my brother again. When I come back at dawn, I'll be spending my last days on Earthradon in peace until the asteroid comes.

After one last look at my husband, I walk out onto the balcony.

CHAPTER

TWO

FIRST HOUR INTO NIGHTFALL

After using the last of the harvested magic to silently shut the doors, I've been gazing at a view I will never get tired of.

My brother and I built this log cabin on the cliffs of Frelsilof. One step off the balcony, and it's a vertical drop into the Startikgrim Ocean. Ahead of me are the cliffs of Hornarokk, where Thor, Odin's firstborn from his first marriage, guards the horn tower of sound and light. Both of us look after the entrance to the fjord leading into the capital city of our faith, Leifheim.

Freyr and I built a second log cabin deep in the forest near a waterfall for him to live in since Odin was going to move in with me once we were married. I haven't stepped foot in Freyr's cabin in centuries. The villagers know to stay away, and it's also heavily protected by the Sprites of Slaughter Sisterhood, a group of creatures my brother befriended. Travelers who manage to make it out alive call Grave Vaettir Forest by a more aesthetically pleasing name, Blood Bark Wood.

With Odin's second wife winning their wood castle in the divorce, he was unable to offer me a home to move in with him, which was fine because I'd rather not live in a home so massive that I'd get lost in it. Frigg's castle is partially obstructing some of the full moon as I take in the village, adding to the perception of inferiority among those who live in the shadows.

Everything is calm, from the gentle breeze making the forest behind my home sing to the ocean echoing the harmonious push and pull of the tide against the rocks below. Hearing that the Father of the Great Willow Tree, a primordial deity, is sending an asteroid to wipe out the majority of the population while only sparing a few thousand magical beings and mortals has my senses admiring everything and anything I come into contact with as if it's the first and last time I'll be able to experience them.

All the magical races on Earthradon have been plagued by the greedy desire to become stronger and a cruel selfishness to not care about how they are able to achieve it. Gods and Goddesses compete to see who has the strongest pantheon and who should be known as the King and Queen of all. And the mortals are caught in the chaos of either believing in a faith to seek the protection of the Gods; but possibly being belittled and suffering, or vowing fealty to an immortal race, which paints a target on their backs for others to attack simply because they sided with someone they don't like.

Some, like me, still try to better themselves, but the damage has been done, and the Father has ordered an asteroid to be sent from the Galaxy to wipe out the vast majority of the population. Using an asteroid to cleanse the planet of greed leads me to believe that the Father is also infected. Why can't there be a solution that doesn't lead to death? Once I have a better understanding of what awaits me after I die, I will go to the Father with my question. *Maybe if I gather all the others he told about his plan, we can all convince him to find another way to cleanse Earthradon.*

Only a select few Gods and Goddesses of each faith and the leaders of the races were told by the Father. I was one of four of the Norse Gods selected. At first, I was furious, as was everyone else. After I left, the Father's words took off the blinders I didn't know were on. I'd been so consumed with utilizing my position and influence to prevent further persecution of women's rights that I wasn't fully aware of how corrupt the rest of the world had become.

The Father had us all promise not to tell anyone. He chose to share the news with the beings he selected because he trusted us. No magical vow or brand was made to ensure we didn't say a word. And I have been racked with guilt ever since.

Odin wanting to have a baby with me hurts, and what's making the pain of keeping this secret unbearable is that I did find a way to get pregnant. I planned on telling Odin, but I was called to go see the Father, and now the biggest portion of my guilt is buried in my garden.

After speaking to some other Gods and Goddesses who have fertility magic, I learned I can decide if I want to have a cycle or not, but once I make my choice, I can't take it back. And if I want to ovulate, then I need to acquire an Ethasion stone flower from a Celestial.

Because I can't fly into the Galaxy, I asked Goddess Nyx, and now I'm indebted to her. To willingly be in debt to another goes against immortal society's norms. If I didn't trust Nyx, then I would agree. Nyx made a magical brand to seal our deal and inked it over my womb. I have the flower, and it's buried in my garden. Odin doesn't suspect anything, even though my plants are having a very promising start to the season.

The stars twinkle above, and I count them until my heart stops hammering in my chest and my guilt recedes. When minutes pass with no luck, I know of only one other way to cheer myself up. I've wasted enough time thinking and moping on my balcony.

As if trying to encourage me to break out of the mold I was told to always be, the wind picks up, tugging on the braid of my ponytail to let my wild locks free. The waves crash with the ferocity of war drums, aiding my heart to race with reckless excitement I don't often let free. Being a Goddess means I've had to lock down a side of myself that all Gods, my husband included, would find irresponsible and absurd. An image has to be kept, but all I want is to be free and fly for as long as my eternity allows me to do so.

I face my house. The life I'm expected to lead is through those doors, but for tonight, I'm free.

My heart rate finally slows as I take a step back.

When my left foot hits the air instead of the balcony, I fall into the arms of freedom.

The rush of the freefall hits, fueling the part of me I've neglected and releasing me of all my duties and burdens.

Wind rushes past my face, making my nostrils burn as I take in ample amounts of vitalizing oxygen to keep fueling my erratic soul to be free of the cage I've been made to stay in. I've been carrying so many secrets, but the one I've clung to the longest is that I'm addicted to the exhilarating rush of falling to my death.

A strong pulse comes from my chest. My spiritual essence is panicking, like she always does when I'm like this. I'm ways away from the rocky shore, and just like every other time, I'm going to have to fight off Skjoldr from activating my cloak for me. If I was born with the ability to fly, then I wouldn't have this issue.

Normally, I would trigger the magic in my cloak a healthy distance away from the crashing water, but tonight I want to push myself. I have faith that I won't be sent to an early grave, but it's clear that my spiritual essence doesn't share the sentiment.

Skjoldr acts like a Guardian since she's an entity that influences my soul and whatever source my magic derives from. Having one is both a blessing and an annoyance. She acts without my knowledge or consent, even if I object, because it is her duty to help me grow as an immortal. Some say it's an ethereal creature of the magic system living inside us, and we should take solace in the fact that anything changed is done with the best of intentions, or magic wouldn't be able to influence us.

Any day before today I would have said I'd go without her being inside of me and get her taken out. But those who believed them to protect our souls from dying by leeches were speaking the truth since Skjoldr alerted me to one tonight.

The information I've heard about leeches describes them as ghostly organisms, but that wasn't the case with the one I experienced. And by the way everyone talks about them, it seems leeches are a magical race. With the number of races inhabiting Earthradon, I'm not surprised to discover another. However, these are as unsettling as shadow monsters, since I didn't detect either one going inside me.

A thick layer of shadowy mist blows into the fjord, covering the crashing waves and rocks below me. My call to experience a thrill was answered by darkness. Every second I descend, the mass unnaturally thickens. To anyone else, this sight would be terrifying. But my excitement is heightened to another level as a stronger charge of adrenaline pumps through my veins. If I'm right, I know this darkness, and he is my friend.

Magic stirs within my chest and at the ends of my fingertips. Judging by these stronger vibrations, my spiritual essence is about ready to overpower my will and pull magic from either of my sources. Being able to generate magic from my soul as well as gather it from vegetation is a great blessing from the stars above. I love having the title of Rarity, but it also means I have to focus harder to fight off Skjoldr.

The stirring magic turns into a numbing tingle. *Oh no, you don't!*

With the slightest tilt to my side, I flip over onto my back so there is no forceful pressure from falling pushing against my chest. Activating the full strength of my spiritual power normally requires both of my hands, though there have been times I've only needed to use one hand or none at all, but that's because I'm either severely stressed or emotionally overwhelmed.

I take deep breaths and clear my mind until the pounding of my steady heartbeat fills my ears. A crisp breeze carrying the fragrances of salted air from the ocean mixed with pine from the trees on the mountainside no longer flows into my nostrils. The roaring beats of my heart consume me as the thunderous crash of the waves becomes silent.

In the distance, an orchestra of dull, fluttering beats of life sounds off, but I concentrate only on my own. As I stay focused on my heart, I place my hands over my sternum and close my eyes. Even through my armor, each rhythmic beat pulses against my palms.

Instead of taking another breath, I push out all the air in my lungs until they are empty. With my body and mind relaxed, my spiritual essence would be able to overpower me if I wasn't depriving my body of oxygen, which any immortal being needs to wield magic.

My heart rate drops, and below my hands, there is a shift in the pounding. Instead of a firm rhythmic beat, a lively entity whirls like a storm on fire. My soul.

Immortals can survive without oxygen for a short period because our souls act as fuel. I think of it as reserve magic, a hidden strength we all have but are too scared to tap into. Just like all sources of magic, I exercise this tactic to see how long I can last and what amount of harm

I can endure before causing permanent damage to my soul. An hour is how long I have, but what I'm about to do will accelerate it.

With the lightest push, my hands sink down to my skin and beneath. I don't have to delve very far to reach my spiritual essence. Skjoldr can possess me and take control, just like a Phantom. Thank the Fates that she can only control my magic and not my body.

In my grasp now is the whirling beast of my flaming soul. Even though I'm wearing the most durable metal in all of existence, my spiritual power can go through anything.

I clasp my soul, and an echo of shrills goes off around me, as if I were surrounded by dozens of ethereal creatures crying in protest at what I'm threatening to remove.

The fire of my soul, which I call my inner beast, emerges from the depths. Feather-light brushes of heat that, with a touch, could reduce anything to ash sweep across my hand, desiring to be free.

A satisfied smirk curls up the corner of my mouth when the numbing sensation goes away, telling me Skjoldr has backed down. Since she has been with me for thousands of years, I'd think she would've learned by now what I'm willing to do to have control over my magic. This is the only magic I'm able to use on myself, though. Normally, no one can use their magic on themselves.

Everyone believes that the spiritual essence can control all the magic we have, even the ones that do not require any fuel to use, like my spiritual power. I've done this trick hundreds of times, and not once has Skjoldr been able to stop me. Since the ethereal creature is a permanent resident within me, I gave her a fitting name.

I take a breath and release my grip on my soul. My senses overflow with information. The soothing smell of the sea and forest fills my nose. Salty air tingles my tongue. Cold air rushes past me, causing goosebumps to rise over my exposed skin. A ferocious chorus of waves crashes below me. I open my eyes and take in the stars, but only for a second before I'm blinded by dense fog.

With a slight tilt, I'm facing forward, but it doesn't help my sight one bit. These shadows can only be produced at this scale by one race with a high title, the Ancient Demonicals.

A spray of water splashes against me. *Fuck, I'm close.*

Each beat of my heart has been feeding my soul magic. I direct some toward my cloak, ready to take flight.

A drenching spray of water hits my face, and I activate the feathers. The shadows vanish, revealing sharp, jagged rocks inches from my face.

I'm jerked up by my cloak, forcing a scream out of me. A high I haven't felt in a long time floods my veins as a long-needed smile spreads across my face. Mountains lining the fjord echo my freedom.

Shadows pull back from the fjord, revealing the sleeping village of Leifheim. The villagers have the city all decorated for the start of spring, Ostara, also known as the Vernal Equinox to all races.

Wreaths of wildflowers adorn all the wooden doors in the log cabin village. Garlands of moss, poppies, and buttercups line the roof of the great hall. Every ship has been pulled out of winter storage and is painted with runes from the blood of sacrificed livestock, asking for blessings upon this year's crops, voyages, and the birth of their next generation. And on the beach is a pyre of stacked wood that will take days to burn through.

With a burst of magic, I shoot through the air toward the shadow mist hovering like a cloud. A homey scent flirts with my nose as I approach, but before I can take in a satisfying whiff of the aroma, the smell and the shadows rush away. Maybe he didn't see me coming at first and thought I wouldn't at least come to say hello. The mist stops a distance away, spreading out like they are lounging.

I push out another burst of magic.

Just as I get close again, the shadows sprint away and stop just out of my line of sight.

He's a fucking ass—after a second, it clicks, and I realize what my friend is doing.

A secondary high intoxicates my blood as my smile becomes one of a predator ready to outsmart its prey.

Challenge accepted. Let's play.

CHAPTER

THREE

Instead of rushing to him, I fly over casually, as if I hadn't understood his invitation to play.

The mass of shadows stays still and parts for me as I near them. His musky scent of smoke and spice with a hint of sweetness comparable to melted caramel surrounds me, and my next breath is one of relief. My nerves calm just as much as putting on my armor does.

The mist forms together, sealing me in—submerging me in darkness. Any normal being would be panicking, but his shadows both on the inside and out don't scare me.

I comb my fingers through the mist as I hover. Under my palm, the shadows purr and rub up against my hands. His wrathful servants are always friendly towards me and for my plan to work, I'll need their help.

A lighter shade of shadow comes into view.

My friend's imposing silhouette confidently strolls towards me.

One of the most respected beings in the entire plane of Orrtiereum, yet the most feared monster on Earthradon is Haidion, the Ancient Demonical of Illusion. Even though he already chose a false name to protect his true one, the non-magical race of mortals calls him Nightmare.

His power can change anyone's senses and emotions to his liking,

18

making them believe and see anything he tells them, and he can take up residence in the depths of the mind to experience everything from his prey's perspective. Once his victims see his eyes, he knows what will frighten and torment them most. If he's in the mood to play, he'll prolong their death until he's bored, and with a blink, their minds and hearts will shatter.

My friend's cleverness in nurturing what Odin refers to as my "darker side" and awakening the part of me that I'm advised to keep locked down is one of my favorite things about him. All kinds of beings would say I must have a death wish to associate with him so closely. I don't care what anyone else thinks, though I wish Odin had been more open to Haidion.

My husband told me not to befriend an Ancient Demonical, and for the first time in almost five hundred years of marriage, I didn't listen to his command. After losing Freyr, I rely on Odin to keep me strong, but I also need Haidion's friendship to lift my spirit. The only other shameful act I have committed is keeping the Father's secret from my husband.

The purring encircles my arms. Without being able to see them, I know the wisps of his servants have separated from the mass of shadows. A phantom embrace of a snake curls around my fingers and up my arms. I magically sign my plan to the wisps by rolling them between my fingers. When both rub against my cheeks, I know they understand.

One shadow wisp continues to nuzzle my cheek, while the other attempts to tickle me. My laughter prompts another to join, wrapping around my braid and tugging at the strands to free my hair.

A deep chuckle of sinister amusement alerts me to my friend's proximity. "You have them wrapped around your fingers like a queen."

My flesh becomes overly sensitive from his laugh, and my senses are in overdrive, informing me of everything he does. I've always had this odd reaction, and I haven't figured out why. Maybe because I'm always taken by surprise since his voice is as remarkable as flames dancing over water. We've been friends for as long as I've been married, and I'm still not used to him.

Time to play. "The wisps are distracting me from having my hands wrapped around something else."

A low growl from Haidion causes the shadows to thin faster and sends a thrilling shiver up my spine. The purrs of the shadow wisps change to a quieter vibration comparable to whimpers as they reluctantly disentangle themselves from me.

"Tell me, my darling Freyja, what you'd rather have your slender hands wrapped around?"

His voice is even deadlier when he brings it down an octave. Haidion could talk someone into an early grave, and they would gladly do so if it pleased him.

He starts to prowl instead of closing the gap between us. I need to be sure he isn't using his power on me before I pounce. The only way I'll know for sure is to see his eyes.

Judging by how long he takes to reveal himself, he knows I'm possibly up to something.

Time to bait him. "Where is the fun in telling you? Guess."

The tilt of his head tells me he's considering my lure. "If I guess right, will you entertain a suggestion I offer of who I think your hands should be wrapped around?" *Who?*

He's trying to bait me, and I won't let the distraction make me lose focus. If he wants to hear my honest answer, I'll gladly give it to him.

I lift my chin. "I will."

My veins are filled with a tidal wave of rip-roaring adrenaline. Being in his shadows has helped me avoid being overheated since his presence has a cooling aura, but those effects are fading as my heart pumps liquid fire throughout my body.

He halts his slow prowl around me and takes a step forward. The upper half of his face becomes visible first, as if he's leaning in to sniff and savor the meal to come.

Eyes of sparkling amethyst break through the last layer of mist.

My attention is held to admire his eyes and I don't know if this enchantment is of my own doing or his. I've seen his eyes well over a hundred times, and they still take my breath away.

He chuckles in delight. "A throat. And my suggestion for who's throat is Odin's."

I'm boiling over now for an entirely different reason. I wish I could have my hands around Odin's throat and pin him down. My husband is always one step ahead of me. I'd blame it on his ability to obtain knowledge, but he is simply more observant than I am. By the way we wrestle, it seems he allows me to try because he knows how to tame me as if I were some kind of beast. Predictability is something I despise.

"Correct. Your suggestion will be considered. However, I want someone else right now."

He shoots me a startled blink, and I mentally cheer my success. He must maintain eye contact to sustain an illusion, if this is one. I don't need to be looking at him, and it doesn't matter if I blink. His magic will seek out my eyes if he wants to use his power on me. I only have a minute to act after his last blink before he can ensnare me.

I collide with his solid body, forcing a grunt out of him as I wrap my arms around his broad frame and direct all my available magic to my cloak so I can get the burst of speed I need. Without his shadows, he can't fly, and I only need to get him out of them so I can have leverage.

Magic kicks me in the ass as we push through the layers of shadows. His arms instantly go around my shoulders.

The dim lights of the stars and the moon welcome us before he can try to seize the magic of my cloak.

Haidion's shadows would normally follow him, but I do have them wrapped around my fingers. They enthusiastically responded to my polite request for them not to listen to their master since they take enjoyment in seeing him bested. He mistook their affectionate touches. They weren't worshiping me but were ecstatic about my plan.

My friend's whistle is dulled by us sailing through the air, but his shadows would be able to hear him even if he was submerged in water.

With a glance over my shoulder, the shadows hide in an invisible magical pocket rather than coming to their master's aid.

A throaty laugh rumbles his chest as cool, sharp teeth nip at my ear. "Maybe you are the one who needs to be taught a lesson to not touch things that don't belong to them, instead of my servants." He knows what I did, and I can't contain my laughter.

His strong hand grips the collar of my cloak, and we begin to spiral downward. I expected this move and pulled on my already-loosened bindings.

I bring my knees up, push against his chest, and twist out of his grasp. Without me in the cloak, the magical properties turn off. The enchantment only works when I wear it.

For a moment, I plummeted faster from the weight of my armor. Now, I have him right where I want him, and in this instance, I don't mind someone being above me.

I've studied the art and dance of aerial combat. One of the few books I had the patience to read. I'm my husband's polar opposite; I don't care to learn more unless it's something I want to know. The first rule was to accept that I'm not in control. The second was to respect the battlefield, and the third was to anticipate the possibility of our deaths. And oddly, the same rules apply to those who wield elemental magic. When faced with a scenario like this, I allow these facts to override my fight-or-flight instincts.

Immortal races with wings always attack from above, but after studying the Oceanic races, I incorporated their hunting style with flying to create a strike no one would anticipate because, if not done properly, I could shatter every bone in my legs.

Without needing to look up, I know he's only a couple of beats above and is probably cursing my name with a smile.

The calm ocean is coming up fast.

Energy pumps through me.

I spread out to slow my descent.

In one swift movement, I twist so I'm facing up, direct all my magic into my legs to protect them, and then deploy my gliders.

Silky leather flaps fan out under my arms, down to my ankles, and between my legs.

I lift my legs, and I nail him right in the gut with my feet.

Haidion lets out a growling grunt of agony as he clutches his abdomen.

He plummets past me as I snag my cloak back. After I use magic to tie the strings around my neck and arms, the magic recognizes me, and I'm flying down to catch up.

Damp air fills my nostrils, telling me we only have a couple of beats until I hit the water; he only has a moment.

I direct all my magic into my cloak and shoot down faster.

He's within arm's reach and about to collide with the water. *Just a little bit closer.*

Shadows erupt from his shoulders like an explosion of fire.

My front collides with his back, knocking the air out of my lungs and rattling my bones.

A rush of starlight forms the shadows into feathers, and within a breath, a wide span of wings flares out, not just outstretching from his back but down his legs.

Haidion grips the back of my knees as we shoot up to soar over the water. Both of us let out thrilling shrieks, his of amusing excitement and mine of startled terror.

I try to wrap my legs around his waist, but he tips us to the side while letting go of his hold on me. I scramble to grab his shoulders, but I roll off his back.

He grips the back of my thighs as I almost get a face full of water. My hands skid across the surface before I'm able to pull them up. A sharp burn pulsates over my hands as I grip his arms.

His wicked laugh and wide, sensual smile have me forgetting about the pain in my hands and how he beat me at my own game.

No matter what light he's in, his bronzy, brown skin has a radiant, warm glow, as if he has his own personal sun inside of him. Tendrils of shadowy-looking fire run down the sides of his body and over the expanse of feathers. The tails of his black, matte suit flap in the wind behind us. His fitted clothing is already pulling at the seams, and if he breathes too hard, his muscular form will break free.

Every swirl of purple stenciling on the immaculate fabric whirls around like a maze, going to the silver buttons clasping his coat together from his waist to his collar, to his cuff links, and to the leather strings fastening his pants. With the reflection of the light coming off the water, it makes the buttons twinkle like stars.

Since strands of his thick, silky ebony curls are already coming out from his bun, I jerk myself up and wrap one arm around his neck and pull off the piece of leather, spilling his shoulder-length hair for the wind to play with.

His powerful arms wrap around my waist, securing me to his chest. Before his thick, cushiony lips can utter a comment about outsmarting me, I slide my hands to his built shoulders, direct soul magic into them, and press down hard on his pressure points.

A growl of pain escapes him as his wings tuck in.

We begin to fall towards the water, but I direct magic into my cloak and shoot us to a nearby beach at the end of the fjord.

Before we crash-land on the sand, Haidion's wings turn into a layer of shadows, coating his backside.

We slide on the sand and come to a stop where it meets the tree line.

Both of us are groaning—me from slamming into his chest and him from taking the brunt of the impact—but he recovers faster and bursts out laughing.

I push off his chest and stare down at him. "When did you get wings?!" His continued laughter only heightens my irritation, and I wrap my injured hands around his throat. "Answer the question, Haidion."

He gazes down my arms, as if trying to believe I have my hands gripping his neck or committing this image to memory. When his beautiful eyes meet mine, his laughter subsides, but the amusement doesn't leave his face.

"Is this what you wanted?" His hands grasp my arms, but instead of pulling them off his neck, he runs his hands down and envelops mine. "To have your hands wrapped around my throat." He squeezes, and I hold back a wince.

"Answer. My. Question."

Haidion reaches up and brushes an unruly strand of hair out of his eyes. "Is someone jealous?"

"We tell each other everything." *Well, almost everything.*

I can't tell him the secret I promised the Father I wouldn't share either.

Haidion places his hands on my hips, his amusement softening. "Instead of being called an arrogant show-off for flexing my newly acquired wings when I saw you next, I thought I would surprise you while we played." *That's still considered showing off.*

"You grew wings." I look over his shoulders as if I can still see them. "Holy Aurora!" I pull him to sit up by his neck, forcing a guttural groan out of him. "Show me again, Haidion. Please!"

"I would, but you put a kink in my shoulders. And let's not forget how you almost broke me in half with your aerial shark attack." His words have a little bite to them, but his teasing grin stays. "I think you owe me a massage to soothe my throbbing muscles."

Such a baby. I know he's almost healed already. One of the perks of being an Ancient Demonical is that he can rapidly repair his body and regenerate any limbs or organs.

"And you injured my hands." I brought them into view so he could see.

As an immortal, I do heal faster. However, because my hands are tools to wield magic, a physical injury to them also affects my ability to use magic. I should wear gloves like everyone else does. It's just a hassle to put them on and take them off throughout the day.

Angry, red scrapes painted my palms and fingers. I might not be able to wield magic for the rest of the night now, but what I did to Haidion was leagues worse, and fuck, my injury wasn't even his fault.

I lower my hands to my lap. "I didn't mean that. You're not to blame for my hands."

Haidion's gaze falls to my hands. His jaw clenches, and then his nose twitches in a not-so-silent snarl.

The amusement on his face has vanished, along with his playful aura. In its place comes an emotional explosion of anger and regret, sharpening his features, darkening his skin, and weighing down his eyes.

"I'll be fine, Haidion—I'll heal. I'm sure I caused you more pain." I try to brush off my discomfort with a laugh, but he isn't buying it.

"Bullshit you're fine. Don't lie to yourself—don't lie to me." His eyes glisten as if I just inflicted the most agonizing pain he'd ever felt. "You need your lovely hands for where you are going tonight." He extends his hands to me, palms open. "I expected you to be rough with me, but the pain you caused did not affect my ability to wield magic. Me being an asshole caused this." I place my hands in his. "I'll make you feel better, Freyja."

Fire-like shadows flourish out of his palms and wrap around my hands. A soothing coolness seeps into my skin, and I let out a moan.

Haidion shifts under me, making me finally realize I've been strad-dling his hips this entire time.

Warmth fills my cheeks as I slide down onto his thighs and stare only at our joined hands. Before I can apologize, starlight coats the shadows. The magic surrounding our hands is pulled into mine, making my skin buzz. Instead of angry burn marks, they are sealed with black patches dusted with star-like sparkles.

"Freyja?" I take a brave breath, hoping my flush has gone away. "Do you still feel any pain?" His eyes search mine for the answer as if it's the most important thing he needs to know.

I flex my hands. "A little achy in the joints, but nothing I can't tolerate. What's with the stars?"

"There are some things about me I haven't shared with you yet." His hands grasp mine again. "Tell me when the pain is completely gone."

I sigh and nod. Part of me wants to be upset, and the other part is telling me to shut up and not be a hypocrite.

More of his shadowy-star magic flourishes out of his hands and into mine. Magic pervades every fiber of my tendons and muscles up to my wrist. My joints are caressed as if a second layer of protection was added to reinforce the durability.

Not only does his magic heal my injured hands, but it also seeps into my reserves, where I can store harvested magic but have never learned how.

My excitement to ask Haidion to teach me is shot down when I fully grasp that he's given me some of his magic. No one has ever done that; even if they receive a debt in return, no one ever freely gives up magic. Haidion healing me is an act of kindness, one I would show him as well with my similar power to heal the soul. But this is too much for a friend to give.

"The pain is gone, but you left your magic in me."

A chuckle has him biting his lip. "I could leave it elsewhere." Warmth tingles my cheeks. *Like where?*

Haidion's magic thins into nothing as he brings my hands closer to his face to inspect them. "Because your nerve endings are burned, it will be difficult for you to harvest and cast any magic. You have my magic to use and to aid in harvesting until you are fully healed. Wielding soul magic should be fine."

"But I don't know how to use your magic," I plead and lower our conjoined hands to my lap.

"All you need to know is that the base use of my magic is similar to harvesting. You bend the magic to your will. My magic will also act on its own to protect you if it senses danger."

"That's comforting. I would have saved myself from a bunch of injuries if my magic acted the same."

"But that's why you have me, or Existence to go on adventures with you." His wink makes me giggle.

I consider myself to be a social being, and as such I have a multitude of friends, but only two I can truly count on: Haidion and Existence. She is one of the daughters of the Father and watches over all the life on Earthradon while her sisters watch over the connecting planes of Orrtiereum and Erresthralla.

Existence is the sister I always wanted, who pulled me out of my depression when Freyr died and talked me out of using Haidion's organs and blood to fertilize my garden the day after we first met—a memory I can now laugh at.

"Seems like as of late, it's only been you and me getting into trouble."

"Existence and her sisters are busier than normal. All of them have to handle their responsibilities themselves. I'm able to delegate mine." He lifts his eyebrows, studying me. "Are you complaining about me being around more than her?"

I nod to my hands, and we both start laughing.

I do a double take when I notice my hands are tucked into his, as if they are snuggling. These little displays of affection are one of the selfish reasons why I like being around Haidion more. But everything must come to an end.

Before I pull away, I meet Haidion's gaze and take a brave breath— speaking from the heart is always difficult for me, but around Haidion, it's not as scary.

"The opposite. Having you in my life has brought me so much happiness. I hope I find out tonight that we will have an eternity of mischief to look forward to."

Haidion knows what answer I seek. And judging by the heavy

emotion in his eyes and the absence of his natural smile, he heard my doubt between the lines.

When I begin to pull my hands out of his, I'm met with a little resistance. Tenderness flushes his face, and his eyes brighten as if his soul has surfaced and pleads with me not to leave just yet. He rubs his thumbs against the back of my wrist, his tongue-tied request for me to stay a moment longer.

My heart swells with a warmth I've been desperately desiring as my soul sings a song that has never been suitably sung back to her. I shouldn't be accepting his comforting kindness since he isn't my husband.

But the painfully obvious signs I'm being shown of Haidion's unwillingness to let me go have me lowering the barrier I've kept up. Wherever this bravery comes from, it isn't from me. Maybe it's from Haidion. His hold on my hands isn't tight enough to force me to stay; he's only asking but would let go if that's what I wanted.

After taking a deep breath, I stop my attempt to move away and relax, which allows the darkness in my mind to expand. I'm embraced mentally as much as I am physically, as if the care Haidion is giving me is being extended to help soothe my mind.

A warmth powerful enough to thaw a frozen lake exudes from his aura as he brings my hands to his lips.

He kisses my palms and then the pads of my fingers.

Heat blazes to fill my cheeks, then to my neck, chest, and down my spine, making my breathing heavier and my heartbeat faster.

The shudder he triggers has me gasping while tears threaten to fall. He's never shown me this kind of affection before. And his lips are as soft as they appear.

I never imagined that having my hands kissed would lead to an intimacy I had no idea existed but now crave.

The push and pull of the waves crashing on shore has me slowly rocking closer to him. My attention drifts to his neck, and a dark notion itches my mind to imagine wrapping my hands back around him for an entirely different reason.

A gentle breeze blows through the branches of the evergreen trees behind Haidion, as if gossiping about what they are witnessing. The shadows creep out of the forest, wanting to wrap us up so no one can see the desire escaping the darkest corner of my mind.

Haidion's signature smile of wicked intent brings playful amusement back to his handsome features. "My darling, Freyja, do you want me to keep soothing you with my hands and lips?"

To keep from begging, I bite my lower lip.

I realize playing predator versus monster right after I left Odin horny and with an ache in my heart wasn't a good idea as my mind wanders into forbidden places.

I say the first thing that comes to mind as I shove the forbidden darkness away. "Do you think your magic would help me grow wings?"

He stares at me for a moment, blinks away a sliver of pain, then chuckles to himself. "So, stubborn."

"I can have patience to learn." His chuckles become fake laughter and I playfully shove him. "Stop being an asshole."

"Right over your head as normal," he mumbles more to himself.

The shadows beneath us were protecting my armor and his clothing from getting sand on them, but now the shadows are thickening.

"And no, because being an asshole makes you fight with me, and I enjoy sparring with you in any capacity." After a wink, he begins to stand.

Haidion grabs the back of my thighs as the shadows help to push him up.

I wrapped my legs around his waist and my arms around his neck before I could think better of it. A throb awakens in my core, and I mentally curse at myself. My mind and heart didn't behave, and now my body is joining the party.

He's held me either bridal style or on his back—never like this. Only a breath of space is between our faces, and his attention is locked on my neck. He doesn't put me down right away, and I begin to wonder what's got his attention—*oh, my sexy-time bruises.*

As if sensing my awkwardness, he lowers me down, and I back away to leave a healthy distance between us.

"Bold of you to assume I'm not going to be able to learn or comprehend whatever it is that's going over my head. Spit it out." I snap at him, not wanting him to bring up the discoloration around my throat.

He tucks his hands in his pockets. "Want me to bring you to Crescent Island? My shadows can get you there faster." *You're a special type of asshole today.*

Haidion's eyebrows squeeze together, and he tilts his head to the side, almost as if I were speaking my thoughts aloud, but I know I'm not. I was only trying to steer our conversation into safe terrain while I rebuilt the wall around my heart, but now he has me questioning my sanity. He can't be listening to my thoughts because I can sense when he's using his magic on or around me when he isn't in a mass of shadows.

He averts his eyes as he clears his throat and rubs his hand over his mouth.

I toy with the end of my braid, removing the leather strap since my hair is a mess. "I was looking forward to traveling there probably as much as you were enjoying the thought of dragging me out of bed if I didn't meet up with you by Nightfall."

As I detangle my hair, my skin prickles, raising my awareness of Haidion's attention back on me.

With a brave breath, I take a glimpse at him through my lashes, and my exhale gets trapped in my throat. I watch as his eyes wander down the cascade of my hair, as if my long locks were appealing to him. I'd only seen him like this while he admired the colorful dancing sky on the night of the winter solstice.

"Haidion?" My voice comes out breathless, and I'm not utterly ashamed of my tone sounding more sensual than I would allow in his company.

"Freyja." His gaze flits over to mine while he tucks his hand back into the pocket of his suit. "You have no idea what I want to do with you outside of that bed. The things I want to show you, tell you, and experience with you. All of which are inconceivably out of our reach—at least for the time being."

My adrenaline pumps more rapidly than it ever has in the three thousand years of my existence.

A normal being shouldn't react the way I do—but I don't want to be normal; I want him to break me free of who I'm told to be. Whatever journey he wants to take me on, I'm all in.

Before I can even take a breath to beg him to make this adventure within my reach, Haidion whistles, stopping the blossoming growth of the seed he planted.

In an instant, his features smoothed out—he was no longer my enrapturing liberator, but merely a friend.

His shadow servants come out of an invisible pocket. The wisps wrap around my head. Only a moment later, my hair is braided into a tiara, with strands of hair brushing my cheeks. Before the shadow servants go back to their master, they nuzzle me.

"Wow, I have never felt this pretty before." My cheeks flushed at the remark. "It's only because I'm not worthy of a tiara." *Stop digging yourself into a bigger hole.*

"You're fucking beautiful and worthy of a crown to me."

Haidion glances down at my mouth as if he wants to prove to me how true his words are. Shadow fire blazes behind his eyes as his hands tighten into fists while buried in his pockets. *I can't breathe.*

After an intense moment of us locked in each other's gazes, he looks away.

The intensity of his stare held me up, and I almost fell to my knees. I push magic into my legs to help me stay balanced until my mind stops freaking out with the possibility that Haidion looked ready to close the distance and kiss me. *I must've been mistaken.*

He pulls out black leather gloves from his pockets and slips them on. "Let me know how it goes." With a swipe of his hand, as if he were grabbing something to the right of him, a black top hat appears in his grasp. "Don't promise those organisms anything too much of value." He puts on the top hat after his shadows have tied his hair back into a bun. "Just like Odin, they value knowledge more than anything. Never allow them to judge the importance of what you're willing to give. If they don't know it, the details are most valuable."

I walk over to him and tilt his hat down the way he likes it positioned. "Talking them up like this won't change my mind about having you come with me."

"My darling, *Freyja*." Haidion purrs my name. "Am I supposed to deny that I want to watch your clever mouth outwit prehistoric creatures?" A laugh escapes me. "Also, coming with you to a new peak you've never experienced before is an added bonus I don't mind claiming for myself." He's going heavy on the flirting today. "But answer me this, Freyja." All the handsome smugness vanishes, and my friend who would kill for me surfaces. "Why isn't Odin accompanying you for moral support? He's your husband, is he not?"

I swallow down part of the truth I don't want him to know because I'm worried that if I tell him, he will come with me even if I say no. "If Odin comes with me, then the organisms will ask him to give up something to answer my question. Knowledge is power to him; he wouldn't give it away for anything, and I respect that. So, it would be selfish if I asked him to go with me."

His jaw clenches. "The exchange of knowledge doesn't work like that. Since you want a question answered, they can only ask you for something in return. Your husband may be all-knowing, but don't ever think that what you have to offer is insignificant in comparison."

Haidion seems to grow taller than his six-and-a-half-foot frame whenever he gets heated up about something.

"Who told you that's how they worked? Because it sure as fuck wasn't me."

I've seen Haidion angry before, but the focus was never directed at me. His chest begins to rise and fall faster, putting stress on the fabric. If he's anything like Odin, then it's better not to answer or react because that will almost certainly result in a fight.

If what Haidion says is true, then why did Odin tell me that the organisms are only interested in exchanging knowledge with beings like him? Something is not right; maybe I misunderstood what Odin explained to me. But even with him telling me that, I wasn't going to let it stop me from trying. I'd rather go and be turned away instead of not bothering to try because the odds were against me.

A lethal cold radiates from Haidion as his body tenses. Tendrils of shadowy-star magic flow down his back like a raging waterfall.

"Your silence answered for you." My friend has been replaced by the monster everyone has told me to fear.

He grips me by the chin and pulls me into him. "I don't care what kind of God he is. Nothing is more important than helping the ones you love. Magic comes and goes, but love is the strongest power anyone can obtain, and Odin should be fucking terrified to lose it." I try to pull away, but his grip tightens. "Your mind might have already justified his absence, but did your heart?"

With another tug, he lets go of me and takes a few steps back. "And this is why I want to go alone. Trying to make you understand something personal to me only led you to judge and try to convince me that my reasoning is absurd."

Haidion scoffs and flattens out the wrinkles in his tailored, black trousers. "And I thought you liked my honesty." He brushes off some sand still on his knee-high leather boots. "I'm only telling you the truth about what matters most in a relationship. It's not my fault you don't want to hear it."

"Get yourself a mate first, and then you can give me advice, Ominous."

The shadows in the woods retreat a little as the branches sway more from a stronger breeze.

Only when he irritates the fuck out of me do I call him by the name he chose for himself to share with others. To a Demonical, knowing their name means their power can't affect a being, and to this day, I'm still surprised that he gave me his real name and revealed his true identity only a couple of years after we met.

Haidion clenches his jaw again, and I stand taller. I won't tolerate his behavior a second time.

He keeps eye contact with me as he pulls a purple bow tie out of another pocket, slides the fabric under his collar, and knots it.

He cocks a grin. "Pissed off looks good on you. It makes your blue-moon eyes look sharper, as if you have a thousand daggers ready to shred someone into ribbons." His eyes shift into burning orbs of darkness with vertical slits of starlight, revealing the beast within him. "I wonder if my daring *larvaelet* would enjoy watching blood spill from a chained-up body too." He purrs the nickname in a tongue I don't know of, and I hate how it calms me down enough to not go beast mode on him.

Instead, I go for giving him the stern silent treatment, but trying to go up against him in this battle of intimidation we're in is pointless. His job is to not only torment, trap, and torture the names he's been paid to target but also to deliver daily punishments to the immortal inmates housed in the penitentiaries of Wardalyn and Excilum. Haidion only deals with the ones who have committed the most unforgivable crimes, where death would be too kind a punishment.

"After I'm done, go chain yourself up and we'll find out, Haidion."

His wicked grin suddenly changes into something I've never seen before on him—almost like hunger. "Is that a promise, Freyja?"

With the flick of his wrist, a stream of shadowy-star magic shoots out from under his left cuff. Thick tendrils and small wisps crawl over one another to weave into his sword-like cane. A blue, ice-like crystal is revealed once the mist thins, making up the base of the staff. Delicate strands of black metal curl around the blade like vines with thorns. Once the blade is fully formed, the magic is absorbed into the cane, like a beast locked in a cage. To form the handle, Haidion removes his right-hand glove and bites his thumb, welling up a drop of blood, then smearing it over the top. A ruby-stone cardinal forms and perches on top of the cane. As Haidion strokes his bleeding thumb down the bird's back, one ruffled feather at a time, the little beauty comes to life.

Haidion's tongue laps up the blood on his thumb before placing the glove back on. "Are you choosing to answer me when I become a monster?"

He knowingly raises an eyebrow, and a tingle of awareness begins to flush my body. Without a doubt, he noticed where I was focusing my attention.

A growl stirs in my chest. "Where is the fun in telling you. I'd rather leave you in a state of anticipation, like a pet waiting to see if their master will come home."

Whimpers float on a breeze around me from the forest's edge as if the shadows were trying to persuade me to change my mind.

Haidion produces a deep, cynical laugh, alarming my senses and telling me to run. "I adore that mouth of yours."

A glittering aura forms around his body, indicating that he is using his illusion power.

Haidion's face elongates into a diamond shape, with an unhinged jaw and hundreds of sharp teeth. The flesh making up his nose and ears is gone. His complexion pales to a sickly shade of white, then hardens into stone scales. His eye sinks in, and shadows constantly leak out of his sockets. Where his ears were, two pairs of short horns grew. And bony wings with jagged claws sprout from his back as he grows another three feet.

The glittering aura fades as the illusion becomes a reality. If I touch him, everything will feel real, but for some reason I can still see some of the aura around him, like a ghost that hasn't fully become invisible.

Haidion can transform into any monster he wants. This is his favorite, it's the one he wore when we first met.

"Being your friend, Freyja." Hearing his normal voice in his monster form is confusing my senses. "Is the most important relationship in my life, and I'm terrified to lose it because—I love you."

I'm no longer breathing as my heart swells to the size of a mountain. A pulsating fire that makes up my soul is radiating and plowing into my chest, trying to break free. My instincts are screaming at me in a language I can't comprehend. Every shred of knowledge and piece of wisdom stored in my complex mind is insufficient to help me process how I'm feeling about what he just admitted to me.

A portal of shadow fire forms behind him, resembling a spider weaving a web.

"Whatever you need, my darling Freyja, I'm here for you." He reaches up to grab the brim of his hat and bows his head to me, "You only need to call."

Haidion steps backward, into the portal. With a snap of his fingers, the magic swallows him, closing the portal and leaving me staring at the moonlit forest, devoid of the thick shadows.

My lungs force me to take in air as a sharp pain presses into my heart. I brace against my legs, as I gasp for air and dry heave. When tears try to break free from the agony, I scream.

Ever since I lost my brother, I closed my heart up, not allowing anyone inside for fear of an excruciating torment worse than another heartbreak. I'm not sure how Odin did it, but he managed to open my mind and rekindle the desire I had to marry him in the first place. And now Haidion says he loves me. All I want to do is push him away. I can't tell which pain is worse: the physical one I'm currently experiencing or the thought of a reality where he isn't in my life. It doesn't matter because I'm Odin's, and being his wife is all I'm capable of doing.

I know how much it hurts when someone you care about doesn't ever say, "I love you." I've been deprived of hearing those three words for the majority of my existence. Which is why I won't let Haidion's declaration of love go unreciprocated. But I'm not incapable of filling the words with the beautiful, warm energy they mean. The potential for our relationship to get to that point is there if we had more time and if I was able to find a cure to stop my vitality from being drained whenever I experience an emotion that isn't anger.

With a couple of deep breaths and taking in the calming melody of the waves and the dancing moonlight trees being swayed by a friendly breeze. The fragrances of Fraser fir, pine, and saltwater center my focus.

I have a task I need to focus on. Depending on what the answer to my question is, loving anyone else will be pointless since none of us will be around to nurture it.

My soul aches with regret for reacting the way I did, but I couldn't allow myself to experience the caressing warmth his words wanted to touch my heart with, or I would be closer to death. I'm relieved Haidion didn't see it because it would have crushed him. But when I see him next, he better have chains handy because he can't just drop something like that and leave.

After another deep breath, I direct all my soul magic into my cloak and shoot up from the beach and into the welcoming night sky.

CHAPTER

FOUR

FOURTH HOUR INTO NIGHTFALL

Crescent Island is in the middle of the Atlantean Ocean, southwest of the northern continent where I reside, and far away from any other land mass. It is home to the Sacred Eyes Mountain range, the Capital for the Historian Guild, Novvricken Castle, and the Domed Armory, which was built on the top of the tallest mountain, Amormatrlee Ravuletta, or as Haidion calls her, Lady Amora.

I never had the desire to come here since Odin spoke of the island as if it were his home. Being jealous of an island made me sound idiotic, so instead of telling Odin how I felt, I stayed silent as he talked for hours about all the knowledge he gained from Crescent Island.

The only time he'd spoken of meeting the divine organisms who dwell in the shorter mountains was when they offered him the chance to obtain knowledge outside of our galaxy. Odin would give anything for knowledge, and I was surprised to hear he turned down the offer. He said the price would've been a tether to his mind, allowing them to see and learn everything he had. I understood Odin's reasoning, even though a pain in my heart told me he was being selfish and greedy. Odin is an amazing God, and husband, and I am not in the position to be the judge of his actions.

I've learned about what the divine organisms were from Haidion and Existence. They obtain knowledge, but their main purpose is to watch the galaxy. I find it odd that Odin refers to them as insufferable scrutinizers, while Haidion calls them divine. Existence said nothing, leaving me to form my own opinion of them.

Ever since the Father told me about the mass culling coming to Earthradon, I have wondered what will happen to my soul. I tried to go back and ask him my question, but he never revealed himself to me. Probably because I left him in anger, cursing his name to the stars.

Existence convinced me to go to the island and seek out the organisms; they will help me get in contact with the Deity who can answer my question properly since she only has theories about what could happen to my soul.

After my brother died, I asked Odin the same question; he was intrigued as well and searched for me, spending weeks away only to discover it was unknown. That's when Odin told me about how the organisms wouldn't talk to me since I'm not a being of great knowledge.

With time to calm down while flying, I was able to process Haidion's outburst of anger. He wasn't angry at me; he was angry for what Odin had convinced me was true; about how I shouldn't think of my knowledge as anything less than Odin's. Haidion could have been less forceful, but that's how he is; he never holds back from expressing his blunt honesty.

I'm still upset with Haidion, but we will hash out our issues like we always do and be okay. As for Odin, he and I are going to have a talk in the morning. Odin has a way of pulling information out of me; maybe it's the marital brand we have linked to one another, but when it comes to the two secrets I'm keeping, I'm surprised I haven't spilled them yet.

Keeping secrets isn't the only sin I've committed. For the second time in almost five hundred years of being married, I've snuck around my husband's back. Guilt has been trying to invade my mind, telling me to turn around. The same happened when I chose to continue to see Haidion. I justified my actions because both of them are bringing me closer to peace, and I hope Odin will be able to understand that.

I also hope Haidion will understand why I only told him part of the truth about why Odin isn't coming with me because even my husband doesn't know that I'm going. Odin told me his theories a while ago, insisted I wouldn't find the correct answer, and told me it's not worth looking into because it could further break my heart.

I would hope that if I did tell Odin about my wanting to go to Crescent Island, he would put aside his all-knowing ego and support me, and then when I found out the answer, he wouldn't say "I told you so" and comfort me even though I didn't believe his word and I shouldn't have questioned his knowledge.

The night's chill does nothing to help convince me that my husband would be the rock I want and need. Haidion has me questioning my husband's love for me, and I hate how his words nurture doubt to grow in my heart. I'm grateful for the cold since my face is numbing the sensation to cry.

However, the stirring anger I have towards Haidion doesn't last long. I realize that if I were to tell Haidion the full truth about why Odin isn't coming with me, he would be the listener I need to vent about my reasonings for sneaking around my husband and then be the arms I want to comfort me after I find the answer I'm dreading. But I'm certain I wouldn't have a husband to go home to afterward.

My lips quiver at the twisted thought of Haidion justifying Odin's death as assisting me in learning about the afterlife for a God.

The crescent shape of the island comes into view. Off the shore, toward which I'm approaching, fire shoots up into the sky from the Gatekeeper's Lighthouse. Flames pulsate, signaling the arrival of a ship, while a strobe of white light spins through the thick mist creeping over the island.

My attention is drawn to the spikes of magic-infused rocks that are as tall as mountains when the beacon of light circles. The spikes are all around the island, creating a barrier, and together, they create a ward barrier. And with the intensity of the lighthouses' beacon, nothing can escape the Gatekeepers sight. It also helps that the stone structure is perched atop a mound of rocks, and the ray of light slices through the darkness in a wide span.

A bang disturbs the peaceful melody of the waves crashing.

Seagulls squawk as they fly off the roof of the lighthouse.

A figure jumps off the balcony lining the top of the lighthouse and dives into the water. Their arch is flawless, avoiding the rocky shore as if they had done it a thousand times before.

As I near the lighthouse, a second figure with wings runs out of the open door and looks towards the fog-covered island. Their attention whips toward me as I fly past. If I hadn't been looking back, I wouldn't have seen their arms waving frantically, trying to get my attention.

I tilt myself and fly back around to the lighthouse.

The winged Gatekeeper rushes to the railing, the mist parting with the flap of strong wings, revealing a Harpy.

The shade of feathers covering his entire body reminds me of a warm spring morning, but by the way his chest is heaving, and his feathers are ruffling, he is anything but tranquil.

Talons have already replaced his fingers and toes, telling me he's agitated without needing to ask. His nose and mouth are shifting to become a sharp beak, and the soft fuzz on his torso is tightening to reveal his abdominal muscles.

Star siphons of raw magic for him to use to guard and defend as a Gatekeeper glow green on his shoulders, chest, and hands.

He bows his head quickly. "Goddess Freyja. The ship is stuck on the underwater barrier near the ends of the island. Ciado just left to evacuate the ship, but he won't have enough time to get everyone off safely. I didn't know if you could help him. One of us has to remain on the lighthouse at all times."

Soul magic builds in my chest, fueling every muscle. "How much time until the ship is airborne?"

"Four minutes. Whatever the cost is for your help, Goddess, we'll pay it."

"Not necessary."

I shoot towards the island as fast as my magic can push me.

Odin's constant ramblings about the island have come back to me, and I'm very happy I was able to attain it.

The island was built so that it could be defended against Oceanic races and Pirates. A thin strip of land connects the crescent's ends beneath the surface of the water. From a bird's-eye view, no one would know there was a barrier. All the rocks on the outskirts of the island are covered in flesh-eating moss, so no one can climb onto the island. The only way to get on the island's dock without flying in is to go under the arc.

The knowledge Haidion told me also floods my mind.

Only those permitted can enter without checking in with the lighthouse first. All Gods, Goddesses, leaders of a race, and Captains with the crescent flag are waved through. Anyone else must be granted passage by the Gatekeepers, or face the consequences. The guardians of the island hunt down any who dare trespass. Following an arrest, a Wardalyrian is called to bring them down to Wardalyn. If the being manages to escape a Gatekeeper, they submit their name and identity to the Demonicals, and one is dispatched to punish the being however they see fit. When Haidion wants to "relax" or "have some fun," he accepts the task.

A Wardalyrian Warship made entirely of metal—even the sails are visible after the fog lifts for me.

They are said to be the most durable ships ever created, being able to withstand the crushing strength of a kraken and the heat of a dragon's breath without melting. Whatever this island is made of, it's strong enough to stop a warship. *Fucking impressive.*

I dive down and fly over the vessel. No one is on deck or in the wheelhouse, but there are no lifeboats in the water.

"Goddess!" A masculine shriek comes from below me.

A Siren leaps out of the water and swims like a missile to where the ship is stuck in the barrier.

I let out the magic of my cloak and descended towards the being.

My feet skim the water as a Siren emerges, bobbing from his torso up.

His scales reflect the color of the water, like camouflage. I wouldn't be able to see him if it weren't for the moon, which accentuates the black, smoky contour around his eyes and makes the glitter in his scales gleam.

"I take it you're Ciado, the other Gatekeeper."

"Yes. Thank the tides you are here. I don't know why the ship didn't slow down. Once it hit, the damage must have been extensive. All hatches are sealed, so no one can get in or out, but the evacuation doors for the lifeboats are not opening. They are stuck inside."

"Is the ship still engaged forward?"

Ciado shakes his head. "I disabled the rutters. It's wedged into the stone barrier though. Since the metal doesn't crack, it caved in acting like hooks for the stone to hold onto. I don't have enough strength to free the vessel on my own." His star siphons have lost some of their green glow.

My thoughts are racing as I consider every strategic move we can make to free the ship using our combined strengths.

"Do you think you have enough magic to make the water rise over the barrier on the harbor side and crash into the ship?" With the aid of the siphons, Ciado's power will be amplified to an unimaginable level of liberated magic.

He flexes his upper body making the star siphons twinkle. "Yes, I have enough magic for that."

"Once you send the wave crashing into the ship, I will use my magic to budge the vessel free from the barrier."

"Are you going to be able to get out of the way?"

An ear-piercing wail of metal being crushed emphasizes the urgency we are under to get the ship free.

Ciado doesn't wait for my answer and dives underwater.

I take off and hover near the ship's bow. The ship is starting to point upward. The tilt would cause the ship to slide backward if it weren't stuck. *Let's see, what can I do?*

With my soul magic, I can strengthen my hands, but not enough to free the warship. None of my abilities will be able to help me either. My only option is to harvest magic. *Thank the stars, Haidion healed me.*

Water begins to recede from the other side of the barrier as Ciado builds up the wave.

I fly over to the nearest grassy area, lush with vegetation.

More wails come from the ship as it is lifted by the barrier.

With a wave of my hand, shadowy-star magic fills my palm. *What?*

I extinguish the magic by pulling my hand towards me. Instead of the magic leaving my grasp, the shadows seep back into my hand.

I try again, aiming at a tall pine tree, and Haidion's magic comes to my palm. *Fuck. Maybe I have to tell it to do what I want.*

"Um, harvest the magic from the nearby vegetation."

Thick tendrils of shadow float to the nearest vegetation like snakes. *Wow, that worked.*

When one of the shadow snakes gets to the tree, it slithers right back to my hand, along with the other ones.

"No, harvest the magic."

All but one tendril seeps back into my skin. The other wraps around my neck and nuzzles my ear.

"Can't."

I jump when a hissing voice similar to Haidion's talks to me, more beastly and ominous. Maybe that's why he chose Ominous to be his fake name. *What the fuck am I going to do?*

The snake nuzzles my cheek before going back into my palm. If I can't harvest any magic, then I only have Haidion's to use. *Fuck, I hope this works.*

As I return to the ship, Ciado has created a massive wave. We only have one shot at this.

"Brightest star in the sky, please give me strength."

I land in front of the stuck vessel. Black stone, similar to coal, makes up the rising barrier. The ground is shaking, and it is almost impossible to remain standing. Being this close has my ears ringing from the metal shrieking. With a glance over my shoulder, the wave is closing in. I have less than a minute to figure this out.

If I push against the ship, it could cave in like it did when it hit the barrier. My only option is to make the stone crumble and crack.

A roar from the approaching wave mixes with the ships' shrieking—my final warning before I'm submerged by water. *It's now or never.*

I drop to my knees, knowing that for one, I won't be able to remain steady, and two, being in direct contact with the stone I want to will to my command is more effective.

Shadowy-star magic fills both of my hands as I wave them.

What if Haidion didn't give me much of his power? *I didn't think this through fully.*

Haidion's magic swirls around my arms. The caress of the magic cools down my racing mind, but my soul is raging as if it wants to play with the shadows.

The ground shakes more violently.

I direct soul magic into my hands, giving me the strength so I can claw into the stone to steady myself.

After taking a deep breath, I slam my hands down onto the earth and force all the magic, making the barrier quake and hopefully crumble the hooks in the ship.

My body vibrates just as fiercely as the stone beneath me, and my bones threaten to dislocate as sweat pours down my face.

A loud crack comes from under my palms. Two thick slices of coal stone fill with shadowy-star magic. The magic keeps burrowing through the stone, making more cracks like a spider's web. Soon, they reach the vessel, and a menacing wail of metal has me tucking my head into my chest to protect my already injured ears.

A shield of shadows comes over me as water crashes down. Nothing hits me, and the creaking of the vessel is dulled dramatically.

Before, I questioned if I would have enough of Haidion's magic. Now I wonder exactly how much he has given me. When he said the magic could protect me without me activating it, I didn't imagine an impenetrable force shield. Is it the fact that shadow magic is different that makes it stronger?

From where the ship is wedged in the barrier, the stone cracks and chunks fall away, allowing the vessel to be pushed back. Everything moves at a slower than usual pace, as if taking its time to make sure the ship is fully dislodged before the stone lets it go or for the water to keep pushing forward.

Shadowy-star magic comes out of the cracks, and instead of thinning into oblivion, the tendrils come back to my hands, seeping in and refilling my reserves. *Is Haidion's magic reusable?*

The vessel bounces in the water, rocking side to side while being pushed by the rushing wave.

Both the ship and the water don't go far as the barrier begins to arc, creating a suction to pull everything back into the dry harbor.

When the ship comes barreling back to the arc, the top of the sails scrapes the underside of the stone barrier. With the current of water eager to refill the bay, the ship is carried too fast toward the harbor. *I did not have a plan for that.*

A screeching caw irritates my ears as a Harpy flies overhead, his wings spread wide as he shoots toward the ship. The Gatekeepers must've switched.

Once the Harpy reaches the ship, he flies around it too fast for my eyes to determine where he is. A belt of green forms, creating a tornado of air.

The ship remains still, preventing it from crashing, as the water smashes against the docks, flooding the coastline before pulling back into the harbor.

Slowly, his tornado thins, and the Harpy comes back into view. The green glow from his star siphons dims, letting the vessel ease towards the harbor. *Crisis averted.*

A thunderous clap of stone draws my attention to where the vessel was; the stone is repairing itself.

Pressure squeezes my hands as the cracks leading to me are being sealed up faster than what the shadowy-star magic did to make them.

With grunts and muffled cries, I'm able to pull my right hand out, but my left is deeper into the stone. The magic Haidion laced around my joints won't be able to stop the force of the stone from crushing and amputating my hand.

Fuck! My only option is to use my spiritual power to get my hand free. "Please work with only one hand."

Not caring if anyone sees me, I press my free hand into my chest and concentrate on activating my spiritual power.

Even though the stone is already crushing against my hand, wanting to be formed back together, I slow my breathing and focus until the pounding of my heart fills my ears, then I hold my breath.

The world around me becomes hazy, as if it's trying to refocus and become something else. I mentally cry with relief as my power fully activates and I become a spirit.

A red glow is coming from the hole my hand was in. The stone returned to its original state before I or the ship harmed it.

Curiosity about this coal-stone barrier has me willing my body to drift down. As long as I keep my hand on my chest, I won't become solid again.

Darkness surrounds me, and a phantom caress of magic attempts to mold me into the stone.

Marks in the coal stone are revealed when they are filled with the same red glow from the cracks sealing. Magic vibrates and buzzes as if millions of fireflies peer through the engravings.

My body keeps descending, not allowing me much time to study these marks. They remind me of wards being painted with magic to protect a home, but these were used to reform the barrier and control it.

Light swallows me, and the weight of the stones' magic lifts as I'm once again surrounded by hazy night.

All the dark edges of the night being blanketed by shadows are lightened, allowing me to see. Deep, rich hues of blues, purples, reds, and greens highlight the shadows in a twilight glow.

I'm descending under the arc and towards the water. Streams of blues and greens glow in the ocean like a pulse. The stars in the sky are echoing the same beat as if the environment were a living being.

I've never used my power for this long with my eyes open. This is the most beautiful sight I've ever seen, and without knowing why, I think the colors glowing, buzzing, and pulsating are magic fueling the world I love.

A dizziness comes over me, making the colors and scenery crisper but also revealing blurbs of soft light dancing around, going to the flowing magic like hummingbirds.

Thousands of heartbeats and chirps tickle my ears.

Some of the blurbs change course and circle back to get closer to me.

My heart may be slowing down, but my soul is coming to life. *I've been in this state for too long.*

Releasing my hold relieves the sensation of slipping into another plane, and if it weren't for my cloak, I'd be landing in water, not hovering over it.

Stone cracks overhead, and the lowering of the barrier is engaged.

My spiritual essence takes over for me, pushing soul magic into my cloak. In this instance, I'm glad I have Skjoldr.

Using my spiritual power three times in one day, and each time going deeper into the unknown plane, makes me want to crash on the grass and sleep until dawn. This power, I would say, is my strongest and takes the most out of me. I've been conditioning myself to last longer, but it's always been in a state of relaxation, not exertion, for fear of being seen using it.

Only the Phantom race can become spirits, and, from what I've gathered through my research, they can travel into other planes or realms. With only two other known planes connecting to Earthradon through portals, the idea of another isn't as far-fetched as a realm.

My knowledge was only able to go so far without becoming suspicious. No other Gods have a power like mine, and only Phantoms can use soul magic to shift into spirit form, but it requires an immense amount. The fact that I just have to press my chest without using any magic should be impossible, and with me already being a Rarity, if I showed off this power, I'd be a threat. Only my brother, Existence, and Haidion know about it; I can't chance slipping up.

Luna Bay is lined with sand reflecting the sky and solar boulders to absorb the light from either the moon, stars, or sun to illuminate the harbor and provide lighting for the entire island. They also act as great barricades to prevent anyone from docking on shore.

Sunny's Market, beyond the stone docks, is filled with numerous tents of various colors. Because the island is in the middle of nowhere, away from the eyes of politics, there is no rank or judgment imposed on visitors. This is a prejudice-free island, open to all who want to learn and trade, and the only place on Earthradon where races from the galaxy can legally visit.

After the busy market, nestled between the twin oak trees dedicated to the Mother and the Father, is Novvricken Castle. The architecture captures the beauty of time and space, nature, and magic. Forest vines are intertwined with aged stone that has the same texture and color as coal, matching the stone making up the barrier. My only comparison to the height from the ground to the tallest tower striking the sky is either a mountain or a mature dragon.

Amormatrlee Ravuletta stands tall and proud in the background. A light dusting of snow covers the forest, and with the full moon, there is a soft glow. The Scared Eyes Mountains range is on the side of her and stretches out to match the shape of the island.

As I fly to the docks, I can't remember why I was never curious about this enchanting island before tonight.

The Harpy Gatekeeper is finishing securing the Wardalyrian Warship to the stone dock as I land.

"You saved our asses, Goddess." Now that he isn't stressed, there is a warmth to his tone. "I'm Paulyr." He walks over and extends his hand to me in the universal form of greeting since I don't have wings to brush against his.

Paulyr's beak has pulled back along with the talons on his hands and feet. A soft fuzz flushes his chest, and his wings are tucked in neatly. For a Harpy he is abnormally tall, almost the same six-foot height as me. The feathers around his neck and on top of his head are no longer slick back, creating the impression that he has fluffy hair and a cape draping over his shoulders.

His star siphons are all drained, and the steady rise of his breath tells me he used none of his magic to create the tornado.

With rank not being enforced, that does not mean common decency isn't still required.

I grab his hand, also fuzzy, "I'm Freyja. I think an amendment should be made to allow both of you to be out at the same time. This," I release his arm and gesture to the massive vessel, "Required two. Or maybe they should hire more Gatekeepers."

"We have been screeching our lungs out for more help." His exasperation emphasizes the truth in his statement. "If you want to." He scratches the back of his neck while averting his eyes. *Very un-harpy-like.* "You can make a complaint, but the lords and ladies would probably blame the fault on the Wardalyrians and say this situation would probably never happen again."

Lords and ladies, a bunch of high-class, snobby, mortals who were elected by the eldest God in each pantheon to rule over and make changes for the betterment of Earthradon. I know them all too well from the countless hours I've sat in their court, arguing with them that women's rights shouldn't be withheld from them until they prove useful to their race. The lords and ladies should also be chosen by the population and should be an even mixture of mortals and immortals. If anyone was asked where they think the greed started, all would point to the rulers of Earthradon, who think wearing a crown means their minds are made of gold and every idea is worth celebrating with balls and festivals.

A heated growl rolls up my throat. "The Dragons still send out scouts to monitor the Red Cursed Mountains even though the Dwarven and Elven races are extinct. An uprising to claim the mountain range is never going to happen again, but the Dragon race finds it necessary to still observe them. If the lords and ladies see the reason in that, then they will in this. If my advocating will help, then I will gladly do it."

Paulyr's lips curl up in an appreciative smile. "That means a lot. No other God would ever offer their assistance. Also…" He leans in as if sharing a secret with me. "Do you think those pricy meat sticks have the balls to command the Dragon race to do anything?"

He and I both find it impossible to control our laughter.

The lords and ladies have been called a variety of names, and while we shouldn't find any of them amusing, I'm allowing myself to partake in the enjoyment because it's in reference to the worst mortals alive.

"Though we are all entitled to our opinions, I advise you not to crow out your views of Earthradon's government while you're here." His easy-going smile takes away from the authoritative tone he attempted to express.

"You started it. Lead by example, Gatekeeper."

He caws out a delighted laugh. "A feisty goddess with a sense of humor. Fuck, why can't the one who is going to be running this place be like you?"

"A God is going to be running this island?"

His feathers ruffle as he nods. "He might not be in the official position yet, but he's allowed to make changes like submitting a work order for the Wardalyrians to be here. They are being tasked with protecting the island." He sullenly sighs. "I don't know what that means for us Gatekeepers. Maybe we will be pushed out too, like the Preserver Guild."

Before I can respond, the vessel emits an alarm, and then there is a mechanical release of pressure that sounds like several doors have opened simultaneously.

His attention is back on the ship. "Now I have to find out which Wardalyrian officer has the intelligence of a headless chicken."

"Maybe it's all of them."

Paulyr turns his head toward the stars and laughs even louder than before. "We Harpies," He clears his throat. "Like all other races, don't put our faiths into any of the pantheons, but." His predatory eyes meet mine then run down the length of my body and back up. "I might have just found a Goddess I don't mind getting on my knees for."

"I like daisies, but I wouldn't mind if you left feathers at my altar as an offering. I would weave them into my hair."

Deep, gravelly voices call out from above, but Paulyr's gaze stays on me as if he's trying to comprehend something he doesn't understand. *Take the hint, I don't want to flirt with you.*

He chuckles to himself, extends his wings, and plucks a flight feather out.

Paulyr gestures toward my hair.

"Are you proposing to me?" I do a double take from him to the feather.

He laughs once more. "A Harpy male giving a female a flight feather does mean they are asking them to be their lover, but no, it's because you deserve to be paid for helping us. We both figured either my flight feather or Ciado's tail scale would be sufficient since both have magical properties. May I?"

I nod, and Paulyr comes to my right side and weaves the feather into my hair.

Any Gods or Goddess would kill to own either a Harpy flight feather or a Siren scale. Both are only given when they are seeking a mate. If any are taken, they will lose their magical abilities.

Hopefully, Odin will realize that this gift isn't me looking for another husband. When I mention someone being friendly to me, he gets possessive, but not in a sexy way. Then he lectures me about it being my fault that males were being too nice to me.

"I strung an enchanted knot from the feather to your hair, so it will stay secured. I didn't want to ruin your beautiful braid." He presses his nose into my hair, above my ear. "If you invite me into your nest, I'll show you how I'd use this feather to worship you." He backs away with a smug look on his face, winks, and takes off towards the deck of the ship.

"Fucking, horny, feather head," I irritably grunt.

The Harpy will be plucked and roasted on a fire if he tries to come to Odin's and my cabin. Maybe if I offer the feather to Odin, he won't kill the immortal if he does figure out where I live.

CHAPTER

FIVE

SIXTH HOUR INTO NIGHTFALL

I've concluded three things.

One. If the market is busy during the night, then it is always busy. I've been focused on the castle for two hours, and I don't think I made any progress toward getting closer.

Two. I would be spending all my gold, silver, and bronze here if I'd brought more coin with me. One tent sold the ingots I would need to sharpen and strengthen my armor. Another tent sold fertilizer that could enable the growth of fruits and vegetables on an ice planet, so I would undoubtedly be able to grow the produce I've always wanted.

Three. I'm going to kick Odin in the balls for not insisting on showing me this place. If I wasn't here to seek the answer to my question, I would get a room in the tavern I saw and explore everything this island has to offer.

Strings of crystals adorn the tops of the colorful tents I pass, lighting up the festive market. Music comes from every direction, and I have yet to spot where the band is—maybe it's moving around. No matter where I look, everyone has a smile on their face, or is mesmerized by the market. The amount of joy reminds me of the days leading up to the Winter Solstice, and before I know it, my anxiety begins to spike.

I make my way through another grouping of tents selling herbs

51

and potions. With the constant music being played and the voices of happy beings filling the market, it finally dawns on me as to why I'm more on edge than usual. Being in a crowd doesn't normally bother me; however, taking in the sight of remedies heightens the pain in my ears and makes me aware of my hearing and balance both being compromised.

I brought some coin with me, but only enough for food. Eating always wakes me up, and with how much I've exerted myself already by helping the Gatekeepers, my coin isn't enough for both a remedy for my ear and a meal.

Since I don't know if I'll be walking past any other tents offering remedies, I take my chances and head towards one called *"The Maids' Wrath."* The one next to it, *"Boils and Bubbles,"* will be my second try if this one doesn't have what I need.

Orbs of warm light float around. The orange fabric walls have strung up herbs, both fresh and dried. Bottles of premade remedies litter the birch wood tables. Nothing is listed on the glass bottles, but the ingredients are on a metal card in front of them.

Anything with turmeric will help to reduce the inflammation in my ears.

The fragrances of all the herbs are overpowering to most people, but when I take a deep breath, I'm mentally at home in my garden.

As I would weed, I'd think of all the possible remedies or foods I would be able to make. I'm always up for finding a new flavor to cook with or seeing how one herb might react with another.

My garden is the closest place to peace I have, and I hope whoever stumbles upon it when my soul leaves Earthradon will find as much enjoyment and relaxation as I did.

On a breeze that is too frigid for the warmer market setting, nervous chatter and shuffling feet are carried inside the tent. The commotion coming from the entrance draws the attention of every being inside.

Shadowy-star magic seeps out of my hands of its own accord.

There might not be any rank enforcement or prejudice toward who you are, but all know shadow magic belongs to the Demonical race and shadow monsters. If anyone else is seen wielding it, they are brought to Wardalyn.

Our laws forbid not only the practice of cross-training in other forms of magic but also intermating, marriage to someone of a different race, and breeding, having children with someone of a different race. Having sexual relations is frowned upon and punishable, yet beings still take the risk. I wasn't sentenced for having two sources of magic because a few other Gods were the same, so we were given the label of Rarity to protect us. I don't know if the same is done in the immortal races, but I would hope so.

When a hush silence falls over the tent, it clicks as to why the shadows in my hands aren't going away; they are acting on their own like they did with the shield, sensing a threat or danger near me. I never thought magic could be so alive. Haidion owes me an explanation when I see him next.

The tent keeper, a being of the galaxy race known as the Zodiacs given her midnight-blue, star-freckled skin, clears her throat. "Good evening, Lord Chancellor. Is there something I can assist you with finding?"

"No. I found who I'm looking for."

A voice of smooth, cordial formality but also dry of emotion, as if he's incapable of expressing anything else but power, stops the beating of all the hearts in the tent. *I know this voice.*

"Goddess Freyja."

Tucking my hands behind my back, I turn to face the Lord Chancellor.

His tall, lean frame fills the parted curtains of the opening in the tent. He's draped in a black marbled trench coat with silver flecks. Fitted leather pants are tucked into his calf-high buckled boots. Spiked leather straps wrap his forearms like gauntlets, drawing attention to his silver gloves. Buttons of coal stone are shaped into crescents and trail up his chest, then wrap around to the left side of his hooded collar, high enough to cover his neck and highlight his dark scruff. His lips would look more attractive if he were to ever smile. Woodsy, cool skin and a sharp nose frame his rich brown eyes. As for his short hair, I'd rather he kept the curls he previously had, at least they made him look more approachable.

"Lord Chancellor, huh? You failed to mention that title. Maybe I would've opened my legs for you."

The smallest quirk of a smile on his face has the shopper's tense. "I thought Ancient Demonical of Disease would've been sufficient enough, next time."

"The name lost its luster a second ago, so no."

He takes a couple of steps toward me, making the tent keeper closest to us hold her breath. "I have one more title I'd think you would find impressive."

With a casual glance over my shoulder, the magic filling my palms seeps back into my skin. "Is it Asphyxiator?"

Everyone in the tent looks at me like I'm insane; they all pale, waiting for Vahildra's response.

A rough chuckle warms his lips, and I mentally dance and cheer my victory.

"Hi, friend." I close the distance and give him a bear hug.

All in the tent gasped and I think one passed out from the hard slap of something falling. Another chuckle, a silent one, rumbles in my friend's chest. Two chuckles in one visit—a new personal record.

The spikes on Vahildra's forearms retract as he wraps his arms around me. "Welcome to Crescent Island, Freyja." With a look over his shoulder after pulling away from me, he meets the eyes of everyone. "Before you all get ticketed for littering the tent with your bodies, I suggest you all start breathing."

A spark nips everyone in the butt as they either bring their items to the tent keeper or rush out.

I raise to his ear and whisper. "I guess you don't want them to know that you're not a walking plague unless your gloves are off."

He leans into my ear. "Only my friends are privy to that knowledge. And besides, I enjoy watching them all scatter." Before pulling away, his cool lips brush across my cheek, tingling my warm skin—his kiss is polite as well as tender. "I think I'm going to go by Asphyxiator from now on."

I raise my eyebrows. "Lord Asphyxiator?"

The warmth I generated on his face falls back to his natural somber expression. "I'm not Lord for much longer." He studies me. "Are you injured from dislodging the warship?"

I'm going to circle back to his comment, but first I need this pain in my ears to stop. "Being close to the metal screeching," I gestured to my ears. "It's dulled my hearing, thrown off my balance, and most likely my telepathic messaging is shot."

Vahildra walks to the far side of the tent with purpose. He picks up a pair of scissors and a bowl, then chops some heads off of dried flowers and leaves from fresh herbs I don't know.

If everyone kept their judgments of him to themselves, they would see that the Ancient Demonical of Disease is the greatest physician in all of Earthradon and Orrtiereum.

My friend is the only one I know who holds no bias or prejudice and treats everyone with respect unless they disrespect him, which is sadly the case for the majority of everyone who meets him. All blame the loss of a loved one, crops, and livestock on my friend. He's the most despised Demonical of all, and I'm worried about his mental well-being.

We've only recently become friends, and when we first met, he told me his real name. While I know him as Vahildra, everyone else knows him as Namtar. He claims he knows how to read beings and knew I'd be trustworthy when I didn't look at him with revulsion or hatred.

I heard rumors of the Ancient Demonical of Disease helping mortals who had become cursed to slowly wither and die from a blood-draining parasite. I went to his office in Orrtiereum to ask for his assistance. He ran some tests to see if I was physically incapable. When they came back not so good, he suggested that I ask the Gods who also have fertility magic if they suffer from a similar condition. My only other option was to undergo surgery, so I chose to seek out advice from the other Gods first.

The man might look like a reaper of life, but he's such a softy that he didn't even let me pay him; he said my friendship was all he wanted. When I told him being my friend meant finding ways to make him smile, his lips twitched, and when he explained about the surgery, I commented that I would feel more comfortable if we were both not wearing pants. He stared at me for a moment, and then I got him to chuckle for the first time.

Vahildra is a friend Odin wouldn't approve of, which is why I didn't plan on telling him until I had the Ethasion stone flower. I don't see keeping all this from Odin as a secret; I wanted the news to be a surprise, and Odin would light up knowing I did all the research myself.

But now that the culling is approaching, all I've kept as a surprise from Odin weighs on me as if it were a terrible secret. Odin and I are going to have a big heart-to-heart tomorrow.

"Freyja, I need a drop of your blood."

Vahildra moved himself to a different spot while I was consumed with my thoughts. He has claimed the entire stone table with a handful of ingredients.

He holds out his gloved hand to me and I place my hand in his. For a second, he examines my star-dust black patches, but doesn't say a word before refocusing back on his task. I internally sigh with relief for not having to explain the reasoning for them.

When a couple near us looks at the touch in disgust I bare my teeth and growl. Even though he has a title here, that doesn't stop the judgment.

Metal slashes through the air, and the couple shrieks in agony from the silver daggers that have been thrust into their shoulders.

Vahildra's hand is extended to them, proving without a doubt he threw the ghostly-thin blades, and I note some of the spikes on his forearm are missing. I didn't think he was even aware of them standing in the corner watching while he was focused on my hand.

The daggers melt, leaving clean cuts. What was once a weapon is now a substance, and it moves to wrap around their necks. Solidifying once again to become collars.

Vahildra stares them down and rises from bending over the alchemy altar, causing the couple to curse and stumble backward as they try to leave the tent.

"That was your only warning. If you disrespect the rules of this island again, those collars will take their time cutting into the skin, muscles, and bones in your necks. The magic will keep you alive until the last thread of your spinal cord snaps. Now, get those wounds stitched before you taint the air with your foul blood. The Gatekeepers will take them off once you leave."

He lowers his attention back to my hand, cleaning the skin on my wrist as the couple runs from the tent. Then he presses an oily leaf over where he cleaned, making my wrist tingle.

"Your wrist will be numb for only a moment after I extract the blood. Ready?"

I nod, and Vahildra removes the leaf and pokes a needle into a vein in my wrist. My blood fills a cylinder at the end.

After removing the needle, he presses a sticky leaf over the spot where he extracted blood and has me hold pressure while he works.

A line has formed behind us from others who want to craft their own remedies and potions instead of buying premade ones. Most are chatting, and a few are trying to peer around to get a better view of what Vahildra is doing. Even though I have a front-row seat, I have no idea what any of the ingredients he gathered are. He is more advanced with herbs than I'll ever be.

Vahildra glances over to me. "What tea have you been drinking?"

I told him many times I don't mind silence if he wants to work in peace, but he always initiates small talk. "Lemon ginger with honey and mint."

He grinds all the ingredients and adds my blood, turning the herbs into a sticky paste.

"Did you finally decide to start your cycle, or are you experiencing digestive discomfort?"

It takes me a minute to process the correlation as to why he's asking about those symptoms after telling him what tea I'm drinking. "Headaches from stress, and they're triggering other wonderful side effects. Why do you ask?"

"You can tell a lot about what someone is feeling when they share what tea they drink. Try chamomile tea with lemon, and I take it the honey is more for sweetness." I flash him a wide smile, and his lip twitches before turning his attention back to the paste. "If you are having trouble sleeping, add lavender."

"What tea are you drinking?"

He holds out his hand for mine. "I drink something that I wouldn't advise you to try."

I place my hand in his. "I shared. It's only fair."

Vahildra cleans the area where he drew blood. There is no mark or scar, my skin is moisturized and only slightly numb now.

"I drink a warm beverage called coffee. And I take it with nothing added, I enjoy the bitter taste. I don't always have a smiling face around to calm me down, so I do the next best thing: I drink coffee and try to break my record for how many organs I can remove before someone dies." *What a charming method to reduce stress.*

"I did something similar to a Basilisk once." His eyebrows raise. "I received a death prayer from a farmer whose crops were being poisoned. I laid a trap and took my time to remove each of his scales until he was skinned. Then I used magic to make him eat himself. He lasted longer than I thought."

From behind us, numerous beings dry heave. All take a step back, and a mortal faints.

"I would've liked to watch. Summon me next time when you plan on testing a body's limit, will you?"

I nod. If Haidion were here, he could show Vahildra an illusion of what happened. He sat back and watched as I did my job as a Goddess.

Vahildra holds the bowl up to me. "Chew on this until it dissolves in your mouth. You might experience some popping and bubbling in your ears along with disorientation, but the effects will go away once it's gone. I flavored it with mint, so it's at least tolerable."

There is no doubt in my mind to not trust him as I pull the slime out of the bowl.

Saliva instantly floods my mouth once the slime touches my tongue, and I force myself to swallow the revolting mixture. Immediately, there is fuzziness in my ears, followed by a pressure buildup similar to being submerged underwater.

When I try to pull out my coin, Vahildra takes my hand and places it in the crook of his elbow.

He pays the tent keeper a small bag of gold not only for the supplies and use of the alchemy altar but also for the customers he scared away with his presence. The tent keepers' impression of Vahildra shifted as a result of the gesture.

Vahildra leads me through the busy market as I continue to chew. I can't hear anything now, and if he wasn't holding my arm, I'd be staggering around like a drunk.

Everyone parts for us, and I lost count of how many women stared at me with their jaws dropped. I tried my hardest to appear normal, but the effects of the slim aren't helping. All of them probably think I've been poisoned by the Lord Chancellor.

Slowly, my hearing comes back after an orchestra of pops. The slime has dissolved by the time we reach the last few tents. I sigh in relief from all that chewing.

Vahildra leads us into a velvet-purple tent called, *"Beans and Leaves Beverages."* and buys us warm beverages.

"Can you hear me?"

I jump out of his hold because of how ghostly his voice is. His chest rumbles with amusement, and if it took me going through all this again to make him laugh, I would.

"Yes. Why was your voice different?"

He hands me a black clay mug and pays the tent keeper. "I spoke at a wavelength that only races with enhanced hearing can pick up." His voice is back to normal. "I not only restored your hearing and repaired your telepathic messaging, but I heightened your capability to pick up on voices and sounds that the normal ear can't. A mortal allowed me to experiment on her, and after the treatment, she could hear as clearly as a Wolven, and now you can as well."

Vahildra directs me over to a cosmic glass-topped wooden table with all the possible fixings someone would like to add to their beverage. Based on the chamomile fragrance wafting from my mug, my friend ordered me the tea he said I should try.

After adding lemon and honey, I take a sip and sigh from the instant comfort tea always provides me.

"I want to express my gratitude. No God has hearing like this, and I don't mind an advantage, but you should've asked before experimenting on me," I tease. *Having Wolven hearing would've been helpful centuries ago.*

"I experimented on myself before I thought of trying a more powerful magical being such as yourself. Trust me when I say you are going to need the enhancement the longer you are with Ominous. I learned from being his mentor, you need a skilled sense of hearing to anticipate his actions."

I almost spit out on my tea. "Mentor? Um, so, you two are close then?"

Vahildra remains cool and crisp and isn't the least bit affected by my reaction to the blast he just fired. "Yes and no. I've known him since he was a four-hundred-year-old *larvae*. We've been familiar with each other for almost forty-eight hundred years now."

"I didn't realize how much older Ominous is than me." *Almost eighteen hundred years older.*

"Ominous's greater age doesn't mean a damn thing. He is still a moody juvenile in my eyes. Though he is still developing as an immortal, just like you, that is no reason for him to evade his duty since he has had more time to mature than you. Time works differently where we are from in case you forgot. One year for you is four for us."

"Every time Ominous visits me, I have to remind myself that it's been longer for him."

I knew Haidion was older than me, and until now I had thought that he'd be done maturing; that was the primary reason why I allowed him to call me his darling. His growing wings make sense now.

What Vahildra said about Haidion not taking his responsibilities seriously doesn't make sense to me. Haidion has such an extraordinary level of maturity when it comes to his work as an Ancient Demonical, I know this because we took turns shadowing each other. His methods might be disturbing, and the delirious state he enters seems unhinged in everyone else's eyes, but I only see a friend who is dedicated and passionate about an occupation he truly enjoys.

"Since you technically helped raise him, I think you will always see him as an adolescent."

He nods. "My time with him was more than just teaching an apprentice how to master a trade, though he didn't..." His shoulders droop as his gaze wanders to the ground for a moment before he recovers and assumes his formal stature. "Aren't you close to reaching your magical maturity?"

I know deflection all too well, and since I don't want Vahildra to entirely shut himself off from me, I go with his change in subject.

"I'm almost at the peak of my magical and physical prime before I stop aging and gaining magical power."

From birth to five hundred years, immortals on Earthradon are physically considered to be children. Adolescence is the period between the ages of five and eight hundred, during which all immortals go through physical puberty. Once an immortal reaches eight hundred years, they are no longer considered minors.

The corner of Vahildras' mouth raises, a fraction away from being smug. "You wouldn't be able to guess my age."

"Six thousand years old? Give or take a century."

"I'm slightly insulted that you think of me as being so young." The teasingly striking smile warming his lips tells me he wasn't truly offended. "Since we are friends, every time we see each other, I will allow you to take another guess."

Being able to freely discuss age with someone allows me to appreciate their wisdom and magical growth, whereas others find the question insulting. The majority of magical beings associate their age with their level of power, which fuels their ego and self-worth. I'm the youngest God in my pantheon, while Odin is one of the eldest—at least over five thousand years old.

"Such an old man," I mutter under my breath and slip my hand back into the crook of Vahildra's elbow.

His muscles flex under my palm as he tsks. "If I'm an old man, then you are a foolish little *larvae* who thought following a bear into a cave would be fun." He leans down to my ear. "Only to find out, it's a scorpion wearing a pelt."

There is no masking my involuntary tensing as if a blade were brushing against my throat. Only when I'm caught off guard, does this phantom sensation warn me to back down.

My mind tries to recall a memory, but I don't think it's to aid me in my verbal sparring with Vahildra. Something stops my mind from wandering before I can stop it. I don't question it and return my concentration to come up with a witty remark.

Vahildra eyes me curiously, waiting to see how I'll react to his participation in verbal sparring. He told me it might take him a while to rebound my comments, only because he doesn't know how far he should take it since we've only been friends for a year.

I throw caution to the wind because I like this side of him, and I'll always press into the blade.

"Jokes on you. I like playing with stingers in the dark."

With a waggle of my eyebrows, Vahildra straightens and lets out a cough.

A couple of mortal men waiting in line try to hide their laughter as a female mortal walks around me to add fixings to her tea while snickering and taking glances at Vahildra's groin, only to pale when she realizes who she was checking out.

Vahildra takes a long sip of his coffee as he walks us out of the tent.

"Have you told Ominous about the two of us being friends?" I change the subject back to Haidion to relieve him of having to think of something clever to retort with.

Vahildra's shoulders relax. "No, I haven't." He studies me for a moment before continuing. "But he finally told me about you and his relationship. Ominous might not see me in the same way that everyone else does, but if I were to tell him about us, he'd want to know why." A troubling sigh escapes him, and he shifts his attention forward. "By how he talks about you, I know that he cares a great deal about you, but I'd rather get into a fight with him for withholding the knowledge of our friendship than let him believe you came to me because you were sick."

We walk towards a moss-covered bridge over a pond of crystal-clear water. Roses of all the colors of the rainbow are sprouting from the riverbed. All the bulbs are still sealed, waiting for the start of spring to blossom. The radiance from the full moon and the stars is bright enough to illuminate the open area.

Novvricken Castle is ahead of us, with paths on the left and right leading into the forest beyond. Being so close now, I would have to lie on my back to see the tallest tower.

A gentle breeze wafts the fragrance of roses and the faintest hint of something delicious from Vahildra's coffee.

"The aroma of your coffee is intriguing." Vahildra lowers his mug for me to take a whiff of the smooth roasted beans. "Wow." My nostrils flare from the strong smell. "That smells like adrenaline."

"You already have enough of that."

I stick out my tongue and sip my tea. "So, Lord Chancellor. Are there going to be rumors going around about you courting a drunk damsel in distress?" I tease.

He rolls his eyes and slows our pace to a lazy stroll. "No. My position is elected. Who I affiliate myself with is of no concern to the Council of Scholars here."

"And what is it that you do?"

Vahildra concentrates on the castle as if it contains a list of all his responsibilities "For the most part, I look after the operations of the island and help where it's needed. I was on my way to help with the warship when Paulyr sent me a telepathic message and told me you were here and offered your assistance."

I chew on my bottom lip before confessing to calling Paulyr a derogatory name, which goes against the rules here.

"Paulyr may or may not have heard me when I called him a fucking, horny, feather head."

He casts a sidelong glance at me, then at the feather dangling from in my braid. "Did he inform you, when he compensated you for your services, that the gift of his feather also included his company?"

"No. He flirted heavily, and I tried to redirect the conversation, but he invaded my personal space when he was direct with his insinuation of wanting to fuck me."

Vahildra fully turns his head toward me. "I'll give him a refresher course on manners, unless you would prefer to perform it yourself. I'll supervise."

"What if I wanted to watch you?"

He thinks for a moment "Counteroffer, we take turns."

His wink has me giggling like an adolescent girl whose crush finally smiled at them—or is high on stardust crystal.

I take a sip of my tea to clear my throat. "I spent my early centuries living among the Wolven to understand their race since they are judged the most for their promiscuity. I learned through them to see touch as an act of communication when words aren't good enough, especially for portraying emotions you don't know how to express. My confidence in my body improved as well, and I grasped the concept that skin is only skin and isn't an invitation for sexual advances. However, when someone doesn't take a hint and tries again to emphasize their desire, that's when I have an issue. I would have frozen Paulyr's balls, but it wouldn't have been fair to Ciado since they are already understaffed as it is, and the Harpy would've been grounded."

Vahildra clicks his tongue, and with the scrunching up of his eyebrows, he appears to be contemplating something.

He glances around, not just in front of us but also behind us, piquing my curiosity about what is going on in his mind.

When the undertone of his skin starts to tint red, I'm bouncing inside while staying calm and collected on the outside.

Vahildra might have trusted me with his real name, but that didn't make me privy to anything else personal. If what I'm speculating is correct, he's about to open up to me about something.

"I admire your confidence." He lowers his voice to a whisper, and I squeeze his arm to give reassurance when he keeps scanning around to make sure no one is tuned into our conversation. "I can't say the same for myself. Being who I am makes me believe I am repulsive."

"You are not." I go up on my toes and kiss his cheek, causing him to turn redder than before. "Do my sexual references bother you?"

Vahildra's eyes warm and gloss over as if he's cherishing the most beautiful sight he's ever seen. "No. I'm used to Ominous being the same way. I would've hoped to grow numb to the blushing by now, but I think that'll remain since I've always kept my dick in my pants."

Instead of speaking my mind on some of the amusing comments I have at the ready, I move my hand down to hold his, expressing my thanks to him for opening up to me.

He looks down at our joined hands for a moment before squeezing mine. A wide smile begins to form on his face when his eyes shadow over. Haidion does the same thing when his friends or servants are trying to talk to or contact him.

When the shadows thin, the warmth leaves Vahildra's face, but he keeps his hold on my hand. "Once I've escorted you to the Stream of Echoes, where you'll begin your journey to see a Sacred Eye, I have to go and speak with the Wardalyrian Captain. It appears that something is wrong with him."

The cool energy filling out his aura once again tells me I shouldn't press him about it. "You can point me in the right direction, and I'll be okay if you need to go."

He shakes his head. "Ominous told me you were coming, and I promised him I'd be your guide if you didn't allow him to come with you."

"He asked you to be my guide?"

"No. I told him I would be, if you allowed it."

My soul is warmed by Haidion's concern for me and his not going behind my back to guarantee aid against my consent. I wish Odin would treat me similarly. He becomes so worried that I have to roar in his face that I am capable of going on my own.

"I guess you were coming to find me in the market then?"

"Yes. I was waiting at the start of the River of Roses, knowing you'd be coming this way. When you took longer than I expected, I went to look for you. I shouldn't have assumed you knew where everything was since your husband is on the council here."

I abruptly halt, drawing Vahildra's attention away from the castle gates ahead and to me in an instant.

"He's on the council here? The Council of Scholars?"

Vahildra stares at me in silence for far too long, and my patience is wearing thin.

"Yes, you—" He blinks. "Didn't know that your husband held a position here?"

"No."

In my chest, a firestorm began to blaze.

A colder energy wafts from his body, making all the roses pull themselves under the water and the river to silence as if it were loud on purpose to fill the air with its soothing melody.

Anyone close to us walks towards the closet's exit, even if it means they have to turn around.

"I take it you don't know that he..." Vahildra's jaw clenches; his form, which I previously thought was uptight, is now rigid, and he breathes heavier. "Has been elected to be Lord Scholar of Novvricken."

My silence is answer enough as Vahildra leads us through the rest of the garden, and we turn left down the path before the castle gates.

Trees frame the brick path, and the melody of the woods must've been in contact with the river because not a sound is coming from the environment. Lampposts radiate a soft light, giving the path a romantic look if I wasn't about to mentally explode.

Only when Vahildra instructed me to breathe did I realize I was holding my breath.

He takes my mug, and I'm too preoccupied to notice where he disposes of it.

I'm bracing my thighs as I consider everything Odin has told me;

not a single thing came up about him being elected to a position of power.

I thought he only came here to gain knowledge; that is what he has told me, not that he's helping to run a city. He's here more than he is at home with our people. Odin has been coming here since before we were married. The duration of my keeping my research about us trying to have a child a secret has only been a year, while he has kept something from me for our entire union. I can't shake the feeling that this is a betrayal of my trust. *Why wouldn't he tell me!?*

Vahildra is speaking to me, but I cut him off. "I need to go." A voice more dangerously powerful than mine speaks for me.

I turn around and walk back down the path Vahildra had us take, my body trembling more and more with each step.

Vice-grip hands squeeze my shoulders, and I'm turned to face Vahildra in the blink of an eye. "Freyja, breathe before I make you!"

Tree branches shake and leaves fall from them as a result of Vahildra's raised voice, creating a rain of foliage all the way down the walkway.

The fire in my chest is raging, not allowing me to focus on anything other than finding out why my husband would keep this from me.

Soul magic fuels my cloak, ready to take off the moment I say, "Go". I'll make my own exit out of the trees.

"I warned you." Before I can fly away, he cups my cheeks and leans down.

Vahildra delicately brushes his lips over mine.

Every fiber in my body goes numb as the raging fire of my soul stops trying to fight and fly away. Instead, my inner beast is waiting to see what the magic will do. Something infinitely stronger than me has taken control of my body and locked me away. All I can do is wait for the beast to release me from the cage she's put me in—the one she has been locked in.

The cool energy Vahildra pushes off goes directly into my mouth and then down my throat when his lips form around mine. His kiss is gentle and stills the world around us as we're stuck in a trance of uncertainty about whether we are going to ascend from our bodies or not—what a first kiss should be like.

My lungs and heart are filled with a rush of magic. As a pull from

Vahildra's kiss retrieves me and forces my beast back into the cage, my soul blazes in protest—and I can finally gasp for air.

Vahildra pulls away and places his hands on my shoulders to help stabilize me while my heart races at being able to beat once again and my lungs fill to the point of pain.

I may have referred to the fire of my soul as my inner beast, but I've never experienced such a powerful possession, not just over my magic but also over my body. Since it's not my spiritual essence, then—

"What was that?" The words come out before my body is ready for me to speak and I cough uncontrollably.

"I kissed you."

Really, I wouldn't have figured that!

Since Vahildra's kiss was to help me breathe, my mind isn't automatically chastising me for being an unfaithful wife.

Unable to speak, I wave my hand, motioning for him to keep explaining.

"One of the powers I possess is the kiss of death and life. Pretty self-explanatory."

I keep waving my hand to fan myself as I force my lungs to work properly so I can ask him what that shifting sensation was.

A puzzled expression contorts Vahildra's face, then he lets out a painful groan. "Uh, well, you weren't breathing." His voice is shaking. "I freaked out. I didn't kiss you for any other reason, I swear, Freyja."

"Stop," I manage to gasp out as I place my hand over his mouth. "No." His eyes darted back and forth, trying to comprehend what I'm trying to communicate. "What was that?" I patted my chest, drawing his eyes to follow.

Vahildra and I aren't close enough for him to know I practice suffocating myself to tap into my reserve magic, so of course he would be worried. I can't fault him for that, or for kissing me.

He glances down at my hand, and I remove it. "Have you heard the theory about how our souls might be able to function without needing oxygen?"

"Vaguely."

"In texts dated before the existence of mortals, Gods, Goddesses, and Demonicals, it says one of the Father's sons, who holds the elemental power of air, slaughtered thousands of immortals, which led to the creation of the planes Orrtiereum so they could continue living if they chose since their lives were cut short. And the plane of Erresthralla where beings ascend to be at peace. The son was bound and locked up, and all who were created or born after the massacre are believed to survive without oxygen for a period of time in case that ever were to happen again. It's only a theory, but I've been doing tests, and I think that's what happened to you just now. I've only been able to remain conscious until my spiritual essence takes over after a minute, and you were going longer than that."

After another minute of heaving, my breathing finally calms down. "I was told a similar theory by a friend, but I've been able to go a lot longer without breathing." His eyes widen, and before he can attack me with questions, I cover his mouth again. "But that's not what I meant when I asked; *what was that?* I was locked in a cage, and the fire in my soul took over. Your magic pulled me out and pushed the beast back in. And I'm not talking about my spiritual essence."

I'm surprised Skjoldr didn't act on my behalf. Maybe she finally learned her lesson to not interfere when I try to push my limits.

I lower my hand once again and raise my arms above me to allow more air into my lungs.

Fascination lightens his face. "How long can you hold your breath?"

"An hour, if I'm relaxed."

His eyes dart side to side as he reaches into his trench coat and pulls out a leather journal and feather pen. "Can you tell me exactly what you've been doing?"

He starts writing frantically as if the information he's acquired will expire in his mind if he doesn't get it written down as soon as possible.

"I don't have the time to explain it all to you. Do you have any insight as to what I said happened to me?"

Vahildra's writing pace does not slow as he flips a page over. "Could be a multitude of things. All who can shift into a beast say that when they are in their humanoid form, their beast roams inside of them. But you were born a Goddess, not a race. So that can only leave to your spiritual essence taking control, which makes no sense since you should've started breathing, or...," His focus finally shifts away from his notebook. "Have you experienced deception before?" I shake my head. "There is a theory about how all Gods and Goddesses' abilities are more powerful when experiencing a strong emotion; some say they are linked, but all of you can summon your abilities as long as you have enough soul magic. Maybe you acquired a new ability when you experienced the spike of emotion a moment ago. How you describe it sounds like an astral projection of the part of yourself that is locked down, and as for the fire, that could be the magic that would've come out if I hadn't intervened."

The last one makes the most sense since I haven't reached magical maturity yet. Gods and Goddesses acquire all their abilities by the time they reach their prime. Maybe because I'm a Rarity, my maturation takes longer than most.

After another minute, Vahildra finally stops writing and puts his journal and pen away. "When you are free, will you tell me?"

I owe him; he gave me his thoughts and stopped me from possibly setting the forest on fire.

"Yes, but I need to talk to my husband first." Excitement twitches his lips, and the ghost of his kiss lingers on mine. "You're a good kisser, by the way."

He rubs the back of his neck as he tries to hide his flushing cheeks in his hooded collar. "Shall we."

Vahildra extends his arm to me, and I tuck my hand into his elbow once again.

As we walk down the path, I note small piles of ash instead of leaves. *Did I cause them to burn?*

My friend clears his throat. "There is more that you need to know about your husband, but I don't want to say it if it will upset you."

With a couple of steadying breaths, I focus my mind to calm down. Vahildra was right to stop me from going home; I would've overreacted, which never led to a productive conversation between Odin and me.

"Tell me what I need to know."

"First off, I understand if you don't want to take any of my words for the truth, but another power I possess is that I can't lie. If I could, the vast majority of all beings would be unaware that I was the one who murdered their families or stole their livelihoods."

Vahildra doesn't meet my gaze, but I don't turn mine away. "You are not a murderer or a thief."

He isn't comforted by my words, and I'd hug him, but I don't know where his limit is when it comes to physical displays of affection.

"Did you know that Novvricken Castle was the capital for the Historian and Preserver Guild?"

"Odin told me the only Guild residing here are the Historians. But Paulyr mentioned something about the Preserver Guild being pushed out."

His jaw tightens as if he bit his tongue. "It makes sense why Odin told you that. And the Preserver Guild wasn't pushed out; they chose to leave the island not too long ago. Before I continue, do you know what the Guild races are?"

I nod. Guild races, unlike Wolven, Fae, Nymphs, Dragons, etc. are ones that beings choose to be a part of rather than ones they are born into. Each Guild serves a different purpose and is given magical power specifically to perform their duty, like the Wardalyrians, who are part of the Gargoyle Guild race. They are called races because, once a person joins, the race they were born into becomes secondary to their Guild. Most run on a schedule of needing to serve for a length of time, then they are relieved from duty until their next shift. Only the Guild races of the Guardians and the Valkyries are not open to volunteers because those are selected by the magic system.

"Our current Lord Scholar, Sir Carnit, is deciding to retire. He has been around since the island was created, about nine thousand years ago. An election was held to determine who would take his place, and Odin received the most votes. He'll be sworn in at the start of the new year, but he was given the authority of his position already. His first decree was that the Governor of the Historian Guild race should be under the Lord Scholar's rule. A Governor of any Guild race is decided by who upholds the duties and responsibilities the best, but it can be decided by a unanimous vote. Odin not only won the vote of every member of the Historian Guild to replace the current Governor, but he now has the Governor position to be whoever the Lord Scholar of Novvricken is, permanently making this castle the Capital of the Historian Guild race."

"Was Odin a member of the Historian Guild?"

"No." A skin-prickling growl left Vahildra's lips. "He may have the power to acquire knowledge, but the role of a Historian, particularly the Governor, is more than that and should always be filled by someone who is already a member of the Guild."

"Is it a bad thing that he has made the castle the Guild's permanent residence?"

"Yes. Unless you are in the Guild, no one should know where the Capital is. Odin is making it known. If he had been a part of the Guild before, he would know the importance of keeping the Capital a secret; the fact that he got all the members to agree means the Guild does not want to keep with the magical law and will face punishment by the magic system sooner rather than later."

"And no one in the Council pointed that out?"

"I did. Odin got the rest of the Council's full support on it, which tells me they are as greedy for knowledge as he is and don't respect the Guild laws. Sir Carnit isn't able to overrule Odin since he gave him the authority, but he did bring up the rule that a change like this needed a unanimous vote. Odin can't make such a big decision affecting Novvricken on his own."

"Let me guess, you were the only one who didn't vote in favor."

"Yes." His head hangs low, no longer focused on the narrowing path of the trail ahead. Instead, he's looking at his feet and his hooded collar blocks me from seeing his eyes. "With my vote against Odin, his decree was put on hold. My five thousand years as a council member—three thousand of those years as the Lord Chancellor—were put under investigation. Odin said he found evidence proving that I was negligent in my duty and altering historical documents. After trial, if I'm found guilty, I will be forced to resign and be exiled from the island."

A conflicting ball bobs in my throat—to either swallow the information as the truth, of Odin doing everything he can to get Vahildra off the island so he can move forward with his plans, which proves my husband isn't immune to Earthradon's greed, or to cough it out because I'm only getting one side of the story and I should give Odin the chance to explain. Either way, my heart cries for my friend.

"Are these accusations true?"

We come to a fork in the path; both are narrow enough for only one to go at a time. Vahildra takes the lead, but not before looking over his shoulder at me. His eyes are black with red slits, and his complexion is darkening.

"No," A growl of a beast answers—not my considerate friend.

I'm jogging after Vahildra as he walks unnaturally fast.

Tree roots have overtaken the brick path and the few lampposts lighting the trail.

Vahildra moves through with ease while I try not to stumble over my feet.

Shadows from the forest loom over us, making the branches appear more like long claws waiting to snatch anything from below. If I wasn't trying to catch up to my friend, I'd be treading far more carefully down this path.

When the path opens up to a stream with a small dock and canoe, all the eerie shadows pull back, allowing moonlight to cast a charming glow back on the surrounding trees as if we hadn't just run through a cursed forest.

Vahildra is smoothing out some creases in his jacket and pants as I am mildly wheezing. *Cardio isn't my strong suit.*

"If I told you to run, any amount of fear you put out is sensed by the forest, making it come to life." I'm taken aback; Vahildra's voice is back to normal, as are his eyes. "Also, I doubt you wanted to play *Dodge the Wuirrls*. Moving through the forest quickly is the only way to avoid them. I had my eyes out to pick them up if any got too close."

He offers me a clear glass bottle from his trench coat. After taking a couple of sips of the cool water, I cap the bottle and hand it back.

"Wuirrls?"

I'm surprised there isn't an outline of where the bottle is on his person once he tucks it back inside his trench coat with his attire tailored so meticulously to his lean physique.

"They are a divine race from the outer edge of the universe." *Got it —another galaxy race.* "And they are the caretakers of the forest and protect the Father's roots. This path is designed to test those who take it, making them more vulnerable to the imposing allure of a Sacred Eye. My presence as Lord Chancellor made the forest behave, and now your clever wit and sanity are intact for your meeting."

"Is that why you bowed your head before you took off?"

"No. I'm told shifting my eyes is unnerving to witness."

"So, you weren't trying to guard yourself from my response?"

When Vahildra tilts his head to the side and studies me, I wish I had kept my comment to myself.

"No. I only told you about my trial because I plan on putting up a fight, which will no doubt stress your husband. You deserve to know what he's been up to. Then, if he tries to take it out on you, you are not only informed as to what is going on but can put him in his place." He takes a step closer, searching my eyes. "The only emotion I'm tucking away is anger because I'm not going to ask you to comfort me. And why would you react? Do you think of me differently now?"

He's an emotionless void; it's hard for me to judge what he's thinking or how he will react to my honesty.

"I trust what you're telling me is true. It's just hard to digest, and I want to hear Odin's side to understand why, but I would comfort you no matter what."

Vahildra stares blankly at me for a moment, which isn't helping an internal shake I've been experiencing ever since he told me about Odin's involvement with the Council of Scholars.

He takes another step forward and tilts his head the other way. "You thought I was expecting you to choose a side then and were worried about me seeing your reaction?"

"My husband disrespected and insulted you, and I don't understand why he's on a path to get you off the board and this island, which is horrible because you offered to help us have a child, and he's framing you. I want to know not only why he's kept this all from me, but also why he's treating you this way. This behavior doesn't sound like him." *Is Odin's greed becoming ruthless?*

Vahildra's shoulders slump as he looks away and sighs. "I upset you." He closes the distance and presses the gentlest brush of a kiss on my forehead. "If you go up there without a clear head," he brushes another kiss across the same area. "You'll give them more than you should to answer the question you have. Seal it down for now." His third kiss is the most affectionate, lasting longer than the rest, as if he's making a promise to me.

He takes me in, noting my flushed cheeks, but doesn't back away until I nod.

"I'm only expressing my concern for the situation my husband has put you in."

"I hear that, but I also see the emotional tug of war you're putting on yourself. Our relationship is little in comparison to your love for Odin, and I respect that. However, I don't want you to feel forced to choose a side. Your concern for me is unnecessary."

"You can't decide that for me." I close the small distance between us, causing him to crane his neck down. "Just as you can't label our relationship 'little' in comparison since you just kissed me multiple times in a way that—" My heart aches, causing me to choke on my words. *Only Freyr kissed me like that.*

He laces his fingers with mine, a similar pain visible in his eyes, but the misery vanishes the instant I spot it. "We both need to get moving."

My argument dies in my throat when Vahildra raises his other hand to his mouth and pulls off his glove with his teeth. Watching him drag the silky fabric free from his hand, one finger at a time, is oddly tantalizing.

Tendrils of misty shadows and a pair of sparkly-black wisps curl over his hand and weave between the spikes on his forearm, seeping into the metal. The wisps are more curious than the others and they try to reach out to me.

"Touch her, and I'll lock you both back up." Vahildra's dry growl has the wisps pulling back faster than my eyes can process and going into metal spikes like the others.

After pocketing the glove, he leads us to the stone dock.

Vahildra casts his shadow magic out to keep the canoe steady and points it against the current.

The water shimmers like diamonds, and the longer I stare, the more my reflection becomes clear, as if I snagged the water's attention and made it stand still. A presence lurks in the depths and alarms my senses, telling me to step away from the stream.

A hard push against my chest from Skjoldr sends me stumbling backward. If Vahildra wasn't holding my hand, I might have fallen off the other side.

"Rule number one: Do not look into the water for too long."

"That would've been good to know before."

"Telling you not to do something always leads to your curiosity getting the best of you."

"It didn't when I was told about where I needed to go to get the Ethasion stone flower."

He gives me a raised brow. "I remember you trying to fly as high as you could until the magic of your cloak went out, after I told you that there could possibly be a barrier keeping everyone without authorization from leaving the planet."

I pulled my hand out of his grasp. "You followed me?"

When Vahildra told me about the invisible barrier, I couldn't believe it and had to see for myself. After almost falling to my death from the magic of my cloak shorting out, I believe every theory he tells me as truth.

Vahildra shrugs and places his gloved hand in his pocket. "I would've helped you if your cloak hadn't started working when you proved my theory to be correct. Rule number two: Do not go into the Stream of Echoes. And rule number three: You cannot use any magic while on the mountains, or the arches to the top won't let you through; you will have to go back down the mountain and start over again to earn their forgiveness. You don't want to spend three hours going down glass-like stairs and then back up."

"You're telling me I have to paddle upstream? Up the mountain? The stairs sound like the better option."

"Taking the canoe up will get you there in an hour." Vahildra bends down and pulls out two ores. "If the forest found you unworthy of taking the stream, then we would've come to a path leading to the stairs, but a magical donation is required to power the canoe to go against the current." He points to the star siphons on the handles and places his palm over one. "Only a sliver of magic is needed, the rest is given to the island. The magic here is protected from being harvested, making this land the only place leeches can't infiltrate." He removes his hand and places his palm on the other one. "Once you are done with the Scared Eye, you can fly off the mountain."

It now makes sense why I couldn't harvest any magic from the vegetation.

Vahildra hands me the ores and puts his glove back on. "Why did you donate your magic? I'm the one who wants to go up."

"This is my payment as Lord Chancellor for your assistance with the warship."

"I already received a payment, one of which I didn't want. You healed and enhanced my ears. Then you probably made my journey here a lot easier than most people have to endure." With the stream behind him, I close the gap between us so he can't back away from me. "I, Freyja, offer you—"

Vahildras' hand covers my mouth as his other one squeezes the nape of my neck, stopping the flow of my magic ready to come to life and create a brand.

His eyes are almost black and being so close while his aura pushes out an enjoyable wave of cold has me holding back a moan. I'm shocked by my reaction and that I didn't flinch. Every time Odin does this to me, it's not the least bit—

"You are just as bad as—" He stumbles over his words, "Ominous. But I don't have time to teach you a lesson as to why you should never offer to be in debt to someone when they willingly choose to help you. I'll give you this knowledge though. When you are selfless, magic tends to be more helpful." He glances down to where his hand is over my mouth and softens a fraction before meeting my gaze again. "You know where to find me."

Only the lingering cold of Vahildra's presence and the phantom sensation of where his hands were on me are my clues to my friend being in front of me a moment ago. He vanished faster than I can blink. How he was able to disappear without using magic, I don't know.

I step into the canoe and sit down, placing the ores in the holders.

I'm shot upstream with only a single row of ore. The dock is a little speck on the horizon, and behind me is the stream, slowly ascending up and around the mountain in a spiral.

As I row, I run through options for how I'm going to repay Vahildra when I realize he never told me what his other title was.

CHAPTER

SIX

SEVENTH HOUR INTO NIGHTFALL

Water rushes past me, but the canoe stays still as I choose one of seven streams to row towards, each leading to a different mountain peak. There are no differences between them.

"When in doubt, choose number three."

After I steer the canoe to point toward the third stream from the left, I row.

One second, I'm heading down the stream I chose, and the next I'm parallel with a stone dock.

"I'm so flying off this mountain when I'm done."

No rope is in the canoe for me to tie the vessel to the dock.

"Are you going to magically stay?"

When I step out, the canoe remains to the side, motionless and unaffected by the rushing stream.

"Magic is very unusual here."

A stone path lies before me, soaking in the moonlight and stars from above. No longer am I surrounded by forest—just snow-dusted bushes, firs, and boulders with the signature coal texture this island is made of.

Being up so high, I'd expected there to be strong winds. The only normal behavior this mountain has is the drop in temperature, which is ghostly cold.

Shadows follow me as I walk down the path, covering everything behind me in darkness as if a wall is being fortified, preventing me from turning back.

If I allowed Haidion to come, the shadows wouldn't be as intimidating because they would be his. But this journey is something I wanted to do alone. My motivation keeps me moving forward at a steady albeit accelerated pace and keeps me from peeking into the shadows that haunt the periphery of my vision.

The scarce vegetation thins out to a graveyard of boulders, telling me I'm close to the peak.

"At least there was no climbing involved."

A stone arc rises at the end of the path I'm approaching, formed from the stones beneath. Every inch of the archway is engraved with eyeballs. Various colors of gems serve as the irises.

Beyond is a thick darkness, similar to the one following me.

My answer is beyond the arc, and I'm ready to face the truth and accept my fate.

I'm greeted with resistance as I step under the arc. Thick magic passes over my body like a hundred hands sliding over every inch of me. My vision is blurred as I push through.

When the pressure of the magic pulls away, I stumble forward, landing on my hands and knees.

Skjoldr vibrates under my chest. My senses tell me something is looking at me with intensity and makes all the hair on my neck stands up.

I'm frozen to the spot for a moment, gathering my strength before lifting my gaze. Hopefully, my stumble into this position was a sign of respect for the divine organism. *I should've asked how to properly greet a Sacred Eye.*

With a strong push, I rise to my feet, then fall backward onto my ass as I use all my strength to hold down my scream. *What. The. Fuck!*

A massive eye stares at me from above. Four rings of diamond, gold, silver, and bronze surround the gigantic eye with smaller eyes filling every inch of the metal and stone. Each ring is tilted differently; the diamond is the largest one surrounding the eye and is horizontal while the rest are vertical. The color of all the irises matches my own.

My radiant blue-moon hues cut through the thick mass of shadows surrounding us, revealing a hazy galaxy beyond.

Neither Odin, Haidion, Existence, nor Vahildra warned me about what a Sacred Eye looked like. There is no way I can play off my shock.

Instead of pushing myself up with as much confidence as I had before, I sit cross-legged and relax my shoulders as if admiring the stars. No one told me about the proper etiquette for greeting the divine organism either. *I'm just winging it, like I always do.*

"Good evening, divine organism. My name is Freyja. It's an honor to meet you." I press my palm into my chest and extend my arm out in a friendly greeting.

A high-pitched ringing chimes in my ears, telling me someone is trying to reach me telepathically. I shut down my inner thoughts, so they don't get out to the organism.

Zaps of magic spark in my eyes as the pupil of the gigantic eye shifts to become a silhouette of a man.

A voice of musical charm caresses my mind. *Good evening indeed, Freyja. My name is Zachariah, and I am very pleased to finally meet you.*

Green light highlights Zachariah's body and shoots down to the space before me. The silhouette of the man travels in the rays and reforms in front of me, mimicking my pose. Besides his masculine shape, there are no distinct features about him.

I am also thrilled you chose my mountain. He presses his hand into his chest, his greeting matching mine.

Hearing Zachariah speak in my mind while looking at a blank slate of darkness is an entirely new level of unbelievable magic.

If it weren't for the stone beneath me having the color and texture of coal, I'd say I was transported somewhere else, given the slits in the mass of shadows leading into what appears to be the galaxy. *Focus, Freyja.*

It is okay to be intimidated. Zachariah leans back on his hands. *Your honest expression is a welcome change of pace.* He chuckles at my wonderment.

So much for keeping my thoughts locked down. This is going to be harder than I thought.

"I've never seen magic create something like this." I gestured to his orbital eye behind him. "It's astonishing. I'm only intimidated because you said you knew me, even though I had no idea a being such as your-self existed. I thought I was coming here to talk to a saint-like creature."

Understandable. Your husband, mate, and friends must've wanted to have a good laugh when you told them how you reacted to meeting one of my kind for the first time.

"Odin doesn't know I'm here. As for my friends, yeah, that would make sense."

And what about Haidion?

I blink. "I just told you. He's probably going to laugh at me for stumbling in here and then landing on my—" *Wait.* "You know his real name?"

Zachariah tilts his head down, and by the rise and fall of his shoul-ders, it appears that he's sighing. *I am going to let your insult slide since you chose me out of my siblings.* He lifts his head back toward me. *Let's just say I know more about you than you know about yourself. Does that give you a better understanding of the vast knowledge I possess?*

"I'm sorry, I didn't intend to offend you."

When he tilts his head to the side, studying me, I realize the mistake I've made in offering him an apology.

I'm biting my tongue and mentally kicking myself for thinking that this magical being wouldn't be hungry to have someone indebted to them.

First, you were going to offer to be indebted to Vahildra for his generos-ity, and now you willingly offer me a debt for your guilt. Benevolence is rare, you are my new favorite being in all of existence.

If all my thoughts weren't connected to our telepathic communica-tion, I'd curse up a storm and direct all my profanity at him.

"And you don't care if the one you admire wants to impale spikes of ice into every eye staring at us if you indebt me to you with a blood-brand for offering you an apology?"

His musical laugh echoes in my mind as all the eyes behind him snap shut. *I can't pass up the opportunity to leave my mark on your skin for you to remember me by.*

My radiant, blue-moon eye surfaces on his face and the pupil shifts down to focus on my left hand.

A phantom creature wraps itself around my body, teasing my nerve endings with the promised pain that is to come as it waits for Zachariah to command it.

Hold still.

I can't hold my tongue back any longer. "Fuck you, Zachariah."

Thick, invisible, cursed magic seeps under my skin and moves to the back of my left hand.

Skjoldr can't fight off this magic, but the fire in my soul blazes as if it still wants to try.

Zachariah grabs my wrist at the same time I do to steady my trembling. If I wasn't able to see him holding my wrist, I wouldn't have known he was touching me.

My entire hand turns red as an invisible needle inks my skin.

More curses leave my lips as the design of Zachariah's orbital form is drawn with radiant green eyes.

Would you rather the brand not be able to be read by others, or not to be seen by anyone but yourself?

I snarl and grit my teeth. "Not to be seen."

Choosing to hide the brand Nyx gave you, I could understand since you wanted to keep the reason you acquired it a secret, but wanting to hide mine makes me think you do care about your vanity.

Sharing that he saw me and Nyx sealing a bargain tells me I caught his attention some time ago, and I wonder how long he's been watching me.

Once the mark is complete, Zachariah places his other hand over mine, and I almost empty the contents of my stomach from the burning pain coming from the top of my hand as he seals the debt.

What do you think?

Zachariah pulls his hands away and resumes his previous position as if we were going to continue a friendly chat.

I don't care for the design, only what he is going to ask of me. Once I fulfill his request, the brand goes away. Until then, I will have the painful reminder of how infected Earthradon has become and the memory of how I lost my brother staring at me.

Blood-branding resulted from the innocent loss of life during the War over the Frozen Fire Highlands. Under the mountain was raw, never-before-known-or-seen magic.

The mountain pass was in between the Elven and Dwarven territories. Once the frozen fire was discovered, neither wanted to share the land both above ground and underground anymore. The news spread, and the majority of Earthradon was at war to claim the mountains.

Existence and her sisters needed to perform the Trinity Triangle so they could extract the frozen fire out of the mountains and send it somewhere else where no one who was infected with greed could find it. Anyone caught up in the triangles' magic would be killed. An army called the Resistance was formed to push everyone out of the mountains.

Freyr was the leading God who helped form the Resistance alongside the Wolven race. The Resistance kept other races and Gods from joining the Elves and Dwarves or forming their own armies to take the Highlands.

Odin wanted to marry me before I left with my brother so our marital bond would protect me, but I had Freyr to watch my back.

We were making progress after months of fighting until the Dragon race arrived and rained fire down on the mountains. They gave no warning, resulting in the loss of thousands, and my brother's sacrifice to save me.

The Dragons gave us a set date on when they would arrive if the Resistance did not have the war under control, but the lords and ladies commanded them to arrive a month early. The Dragons were tasked by the lords and ladies to hunt down every last Elf and Dwarf until the races were extinct, and they still have them monitor the planet for any survivors.

The vast bloodshed on all sides caused greed to infect and flourish. The innocent blood of thousands who had died became cursed and gave life to an unforgiving, phantom creature that punishes those who express guilt and gratitude, keeping the greed that drove the war alive.

The same thing happens when two beings want to invoke a bargain, pledge, favor, or vow. However, it's up to the one being given the debt to decide if it's to be sealed by only magic or blood. Nyx didn't choose to use blood, and I would have thought Vahildra wouldn't either.

The discovery of blood magic was established and anyone who is caught practicing it outside of creating a bond with their mate or inking a debt is automatically sent to Wardalyn.

With the birth of this phantom creature, no one goes into the mountains for fear of being drained of one's blood to feed the fiend. Along with the pass getting renamed the "Red Cursed Mountains," a forename was given to the demon—Sathan.

When Zachariah placed his hand over mine, his blood was magically transferred under my skin to make the ink rise. With his magic within me, he will be aware of where I am and my state of well-being. He can either tell me what he wants now or summon me to him whenever he wishes. Sadly, the only way I can get this off my hand is to fulfill my debt or kill myself.

"I'll like the sight of my hand better once you tell me how I can pay your debt."

When I decide what I want from you, I will call you back.

The large eye on his face blinks at me, and I shiver.

Before my hand can swell from the pain, shadowy-star magic wraps around my hand as if Haidion were here holding it. My skin is instantly cooled, healing the affected area.

A small smile tilts the corner of my mouth, and if I wasn't connected to Zachariah, I would send a message to Haidion.

Star magic at its finest. Zachariah gets up and stretches out. *Before we get down to business, I'm going to educate you about the history of my kind, what we do, and our purpose. What I am should be commonly known, but apparently, it's not. Your lack of education could also be due to your stubbornness and need to oppose your husband's obsession with knowledge.*

"You still have one eye showing. I suggest you don't irritate me with a lecture."

If I want to talk to you for hours then I will, because you came to see me. And before you make another threat, you should keep that mouth shut to hear what happens to those who threaten me.

"And you should know I do my best work with my mouth open, or do you have the common decency not to spy on the intimacies between my husband and me?"

He takes a step towards me, and I have to crane my neck to see him. *I let your first insult slide, but this time you will pay for that which you accuse me.*

His arm extends to an unnatural length, grabs me by the throat, and lifts me on my toes. There is no pressure on my neck, and I'm a little freaked out as to what kind of magic this is.

But before he can try anything, I place my hand on my chest to activate my spiritual power and press my branded one into his chest, then grab hold of his warm soul.

What the fuck are you doing to me?

Zachariah releases his hold on me as I squeeze. *I don't want to hear shit about your kind. The only time I'll listen to you is when you tell me what I need to do to get this fucking brand off me.* His eye throbs, red veins spider, and the radiant blue light begins to drain as I grip him harder. *Let's move on to business, shall we?*

I keep hold of him until he nods frantically. *How did you do that? We've seen you do something similar to yourself, but we never figured out what.*

I deactivate my spiritual power and cross my arms over my chest. "Is that the knowledge you want to gain in exchange for what I want?"

We stare at each other, unblinking, then he takes a step away. *No. What knowledge do you seek?*

"I want to get in contact with the Deity who can answer my question of what is going to happen to my soul after I die from the asteroid."

I can answer that question for you.

"No, that is not what I want."

Existence insisted that I specify who I wanted to respond to my question, and I trust her judgment to not accept anything less.

What makes you think I can get you in touch with the Primordial Deity?

"If your purpose is to spy on other beings, then you already know the answer to that question."

We don't spy. Our main purpose is to keep watchful eyes on everything from this galaxy to the universe and beyond. Only those who try to steal water from our river or fall in are cursed with an extension of our presence inside them.

Since he offered me knowledge, I will give him a sliver. "Goddess of Existence told me you could."

Zachariahs' eye flinches as he takes another step back. *Fine. As equal payment, I would like to be able to observe everything you do. A magical tether. This is nothing compared to being cursed since you won't be able to sense when I'm looking through your eyes, and only I can see what you do, not my siblings or anyone else of my kind.*

What he's asking is of similar value to what Odin was told he had to pay for what he wanted. My mind is doing a little dance and singing, "fuck you," to my husband for assuming the Sacred Eye Organism wouldn't be interested in gaining anything from me.

"So, you want a front-row, private show of me sucking the life out of my husband?"

His eye narrows. *My kind has rules. Our sight blacks out when anything intimate happens.*

"How is that fair? You can look through my eyes all you want, and I get one meeting with a Primordial Deity."

You have no idea how much star magic it's going to take for me to put a tether on your soul so I can send your spirit out to him and pull you back. Also, Obliteration is eons away, and the amount of starlight I'm going to be using to send your spirit to him is enough to outshine the sun. All of this you would know if you were a good Goddess and listened to my lecture about what my kind can do. Since Goddess of Existence had the patience, I thought you would too.

"If you didn't take the opportunity to blood-brand me, I would've listened, and then maybe we could've become friends."

His shoulders slump, and the eye closes, then opens again. *The butterfly of friendship between us was squashed the moment you chose my path.*

"If you have the magic to see into the future, you could've chosen to change the fate of this meeting."

He shakes his head. *That would've been selfish. This needed to happen.*

"Wait, what?"

I only guessed a Sacred Eye had the possible insight to see events before they happened, but his confirmation has me stunned.

Another thing you would've learned if I had been able to give you the lecture—our time is up.

Green light pulls his body back into the pupil of the orbital eye. All the rings turn until they are horizontal and level with the large pupil. A halo around the iris glows green, and the light explodes, blinding me.

It was an honor to be in your presence and for you to consider me as a possible friend if the Fates were kind enough. Until our next meeting, Freyja. May your spirit forever soar with the light.

CHAPTER

SEVEN

LUNAR NOON ON EARTHRADON

Starlight? That sounds familiar.

Before the first gods of my pantheon were created, my people were given a crystal stone and inside was said to be the power of sound and light. The Father told my people to build a horn tower on one of the cliffs, and whoever guarded it would have direct contact with him. The guard was to use it when the Father needed to summon all beings—immortal and mortal—to him.

The first time I heard the horn blow was when the War of the Frozen Fire Highlands started. A wave of sound and light exploded from the tower, and I understood why my people refer to it as the wail from the legendary Thunderbird and renamed the cliff the Tower of Storms.

Nothing else comes to mind as I sail through the galaxy.

Opening my eyes led to my retinas getting scorched by the blinding green light. It doesn't matter if I'm in my spirit form, I guess, because I'm still reacting as if Zachariah had sent my physical body to the Primordial Deity, Obliteration, who I didn't know existed.

I know who created Earthradon: the Father's three elemental sons, and the Father himself. All four bound their magic to this planet after they created it so all life could flourish.

Who created the galaxy, only one name that rings a bell is Creation, a Deity most everyone has forgotten.

I don't know any of the other Deities. I heard of the Mother a couple of times while I was in the market, but I didn't ask. If I'm meant to know about her, I'll find out. My brother always told me fate has a special way of introducing knowledge to someone when they are meant to learn it.

The Primordial Deity I'm about to meet by his name alone is enough of an indication of what his magic could be capable of, and I need to keep my smart mouth shut.

A jerk forced my eyes to open. The green star light is gone, and I'm floating.

Around my torso is a harness of star light and a translucent green jelly bubble is attached to my face, covering my nose and mouth. *If Zachariah only sent my spirit, then why do I need oxygen?*

Deep, majestic colors of purples, blues, pinks, reds, greens, and yellows reflect off the jelly bubble.

Stars twinkle all around me, some far and some close, but not within my reach.

Cloud-like ribbons of color paint the galaxy, with the starry darkness as the backdrop.

Wherever Obliteration is, he has a beautiful view—

The dimming of stars ahead of me catches my attention.

At first, I blink to make sure I'm not imagining balls of light being blown out, but more and more are consumed by the dark backdrop.

All the cloudy ribbons surrounding me begin to drain of color and are drawn into the growing darkness.

Skjoldr vibrates my chest to waken any of my magic, but either the harness or the approaching darkness prevents it. The fire of my soul tries to hide in the farthest corner of my body as my instincts scream at me to run.

The vortex of nothing absorbs the colors and stars on my sides. Only the star magic around my torso lights up the area; however, it's not comforting since I'm seconds away from being fully submerged in whatever is consuming the galaxy.

All but one spot directly behind me, where my star light tether is coming from, is submerged.

A pop comes from the jelly covering my face. The weird substance floats into the darkness and vanishes as some of the stars on my harness begin to drain of magic.

Every fiber of my soul clenches to stay attached.

Another pop comes from the vortex around me. An orange, luminescent ball drifts down from above. The texture is identical to that of the jelly that left my face a moment ago, although this one has a buzzing glow inside, as if millions of little light bolts strike at once.

Tendrils come out from the sides and reach for my face. If I were able to move, I would. Even unbound, my limbs are paralyzed.

Once the slime attaches itself, I'm forced to breathe, and I consume it. There is no flavor, texture, or sensation of the thing on my face as it moves into my nose and mouth.

What the fuck was that?

A high-pitched ringing chimes in my ears, followed by a devastating presence.

Every ounce of blood, the function of my organs, the tendrils of whatever type of oxygen I'm currently breathing, and the fibers intertwining to make up the threads tethering my soul to my magic and my body all now belong to him.

Without hearing his voice, I know this presence is the Primordial Deity—Obliteration.

An intoxicating, grizzly voice as smooth as honey speaks into my mind. *Deeper breaths help the nerves, Freyja.*

If I had any control over my bodily functions, I would be sobbing as the strongest, most dominating voice in all of existence spoke into my mind.

You're overwhelmed. Here, I'll give you more.

Another orange bubble comes down and attaches itself to my face, as I'm forced to take deep breaths.

The lack of sound is causing some sort of sensory malfunction in your body, dulling your other senses. Your soul is in shock by my presence. You will feel better in a moment, Freyja. My plasma will help you.

Heat blazes harmoniously in my chest, and the comfort helps me focus.

Each orange plasma ball Obliteration sends down helps me become more aware of my body.

When the sensation of my chest expanding and deflating comes back, I uncontrollably laugh for some nonsensical reason.

You have a mesmerizing laugh. Full of fire and life.

"Thank you." The gratitude comes out of me before I can stop myself.

Magic doesn't work the same here as it does on Earthradon. Even if it did, what I would ask for isn't something that can be given. There is a difference between hearing a forced laugh and a genuine one.

"You would ask for me to laugh?"

Hearing you laugh has made it onto my list of the top one hundred enjoyable experiences I've had in my existence. But your voice has made it to the top ten.

"You are too kind, Obliteration. If you don't mind me asking, how am I able to breathe or why am I breathing when I'm only a spirit."

All souls require magic to exist. So, even as a spirit, you need to take in magic.

Since your humanoid body was given life on Earthradon, a planet dependent on an oxygen-rich atmosphere to function, the only way you can consume magic is if it's laced with air. Out here in the galaxy and beyond, there is no air until you get to a planet, but there is magic in the atmosphere.

The races out here have plasma in their lungs to not only consume magic but also help them convert the magic around them into oxygen. Only the Monarchs and Faetriarks don't need oxygen or magic to fuel their souls because, where they are from, they create their own—actually, never mind. This is nothing you need to concern yourself with now. My sincerest apologies for going off-topic.

Anyway, the body you were given life in can't create plasma, so you would need to learn how to create it to be out here as you are. I'm bypassing all that and adjusting your lungs to work with the plasma as if your humanoid form were born with it, so you can speak to me because no one can enter my mind. If you choose to research the topic, know that there are two types of plasma: a liquid and a compressed state of magical matter.

"So, that's why I had a bubble on my face. And when it popped, you sent me another one."

The plasma you had also contained a message from the organism, telling me who you are and why you're here. I would have sensed you if Zachariah hadn't given you plasma, but then you wouldn't be alive.

Since you came to me with a purpose, and paid a heavy fine, I will supply all the plasma you need during your visit.

"You are very considerate."

My magic might be true to my name, but it doesn't define who I am.

"I wish there were more magical beings like you."

Almost all of the Deities are.

"How many are there?"

Your time with me is limited, but I can give you an overview of the Deities.

Creation is the Primal Deity. She created this galaxy and wanted life to flourish, so she made the Mother and the Father to help her. When they created things that got too powerful or wanted to start over again, Creation split herself in half and made me, Obliteration. Over time, the Mother and the Father wanted to see the life they created grow, so Creation split herself again and made Evolution.

The Galexstrials, or as you know them, the galaxy races, were fighting over territory in our universe and bringing their battles into our galaxy. Rather than endure more war, I split myself in half, since Creation couldn't, and made Oblivion. She was able to travel outside of our galaxy and create planes where the Galexstrials could go and claim them as their own without taking up space, like endless pockets. They are similar to the two planes that are attached to Earthradon. The Mother, the Father, Evolution, Oblivion, and I are all Primordial Deities.

Oblivion discovered a powerful being named Constellation. He came here from beyond our galaxy. None of us can sense his whereabouts, but he creates and arranges the stars. Creation allowed him to reside in our galaxy, but not before I made sure he wasn't a threat to what she had created.

The Father needed help creating planets and then life on them; he and the Mother had three sons, Clasp, Tide, and Oxy, all of whom possess one of the magical spirits of a legendary elemental bird. Then there was a scandal between the Father and Oblivion, who had a daughter, Forsaken, who also possessed the spirit of a legendary elemental bird like her half-brothers. Clasp, Tide, Oxy, and Forsaken are all Primeval Deities.

"Thank you for educating me."

I was told that all Gods and Goddesses on Earthradon were educated on who we are.

"My brother didn't want to shove information into my mind. He said I would learn it when I was meant to know. I'm sure he didn't alter my education to offend you."

I understand and respect his logic. What question made you travel all this way, Freyja?

"What will happen to the souls of those who will die when the asteroid hits Earthradon?"

All who are destined to die from the asteroid will be sent to me. Their bodies, magic, and souls will be recycled. The raw magic will be given to the magic system.

There is nothing for Odin and me after death then. We will be brought to Obliteration, and just like I witnessed, the dark vortex will consume us, recycling our bodies to be nothing, our lives only a memory to those who care enough to remember us. Warmth fills my eyes, but I swallow my tears.

"Thank you, Obliteration. For your knowledge and time."

We still have another moment. Is there anything else you wish to ask?

I'm curious about why a race was picked to serve as the magic system, but that topic would only lead to me asking more questions that I don't have time to inquire about.

After taking a deep breath, I ask the question that has plagued me most. "What about Gods and beings who died before the asteroid."

If they were mortals, they either went to the planes of Erresthralla or Orrtiereum, specifically the halls of their faiths if they chose to believe in one, or they were reborn into a different galaxy. Immortal races could either choose to extend their lives in Orrtiereum, be at peace in Erresthralla, go to the Spirit Realm, or choose to be recycled. As for any Gods or Goddesses they have the same choices as immortal races, but they can't go into the planes.

"Wait, a realm exists?"

Yes, there are three, and one more is in the making.

My research is no longer theory, but facts.

My heart beats so fast, I swear it's about to explode from my chest. "My brother's soul could be alive then?" I choke on my words.

Tell me his name.

"Freyr."

I blurted it out with a gasp, then held my breath as I waited for Obliterations' response.

I did not recycle him.

A wail rushes out of me as tears stream down my face.

My brother's soul is alive, and he's at peace. Relief, which I desperately needed, washes over me.

"Thank you so much. You have given me a wonderful gift, and I will forever be grateful to you."

An orange ball of plasma comes down, like they have been doing ever so often, but this one forms into a bird. The orange color becomes darker, changing into a hue of red. A Cardinal spreads its wings and hovers in place in front of me.

I have one favor to ask. Obliteration's voice comes out as soon as the bird's mouth moves.

"Anything you want." If Obliteration wants my soul now, I'll give it to him.

Can you keep a burden safe for me? Once we meet again, you can give the power back.

"Okay." I inhale deeply to calm myself down because I don't want to lose total control in front of what is likely the most powerful deity in existence. "Just define for me what you mean by safe, please."

Of course. Only use it when necessary. Feel free to play with it, but only when you're alone; the power can be learned by anyone who wields the elemental magic of fire. Do not train anyone to create it or allow anyone to study it.

The only exception is if you have a child before you see me again. The power will be tied to your blood as well, so you will need to teach them about it and pass down the rules. Once you give the power back, all who follow in your blood will be stripped of it as well.

If someone outside of your child finds out, they must swear a vow of secrecy on their soul to never speak of it to anyone but you. If they don't take the vow, use the fire to destroy them.

"What do I need to do to accept this power from you?"

Cup your hands so I may nestle between them.

My body trembles as I do as he says.

The Cardinal lands on my palms and relaxes, as if claiming the area to be his nest.

I have the Primordial Deity, who can drain the galaxy of color and reduce a body to raw magic, resting in my palms. This experience is both an honor and tremendously terrifying.

As warmth presses into my palms, Obliteration fluffs out his feathers.

He flaps his wings and goes back to hovering. A sparkly diamond egg with fire roaring inside is in my hands.

Use your spiritual power to place the egg in your chest.

"How do you know I have that power?"

Next time we see each other, I'll tell you, unless you figure it out on your own.

Cryptic, but I'm always up for a challenge.

I bring the egg to my chest, grasping it with one hand and pressing down with the other to activate my power. I don't have to take all the steps I normally have to take to make my power work fully. *Odd.*

The diamond shell of the egg melts into the fire, giving the flames a dusting of stars.

As I bring the fire into my chest, the flames weave together to become a thread, and once my hand is under my skin, the magical thread wraps itself around my soul. My internal fire sings and purrs as the energy blazes through my veins and the power becomes one with my body. The only similar experience I've had is taking a strong dose of starlight crystal.

You are about to be pulled back. I've enjoyed the time we've had together. Look to Constellation for guidance if you have trouble with the burden.

"Thank you for all your help. I'm honored to have met, talked to, and assisted the most powerful deity in existence."

You flatter me. But in all technicalities, no, I'm not the most powerful.

The star magic around my torso glitters brighter as green light begins to illuminate the darkness around us.

"Then who is?"

Evolution, because he cannot be stopped.

An orange ball of plasma attaches itself to my face as a green light blinds me. I'm pulled away and take my first breaths of being at peace.

PART TWO
WHO CAN I TRUST?

EIGHT

NINTH HOUR INTO NIGHTFALL

My deep breaths of peace turned into a power nap.

Gone is the arc I walked under to meet with Zachariah. The stone path is now illuminated, waiting for me to walk back to the canoe. Vahildra said I could fly off the mountain when I'm done, and that is what I'm going to do—after another second of stargazing.

I'm greeted by twinkling stars and the moon's radiance, which reveal the snow-dusted mountaintop. The white glow chases away not only the darkness around me but also the uncertainty in my mind.

Sadness tries to creep in, only because I opened the floodgates not too long ago. However, the resolution of what will happen to me after death has brought on a vast comfort. I might not have accepted my fate back when the Father told me because I wanted to do more with my existence, but now I realize I have done everything I ever wanted.

My heart desires love, which I have with Odin. My soul craves freedom, which is going to come in the next few moments. And I am surrounded by friends whom I'm honored to have known. Obliteration has given me a gift, and I'm going to spend the last of my days being grateful for living for as long as I have.

With a strong push, I'm up on my feet and stretching out.

Odin and I are still going to have a conversation about the secrets we've kept from each other—besides the secret I'm keeping for the

Father—and then I'm going to spend every day showing Odin how much I love him.

I direct soul magic into my cloak; each feather ruffles all at once, absorbing the power.

The edge of the mountain calls my name, and I run to freedom, my soul racing—

A rainbow of light ignites the sky with fire.

The ocean reflects the screaming sky and chases after the blaze, causing massive waves to crash against the island.

The wind rips through, slicing off the tops of trees, pulling shrubs from the ground, throwing the mountain top into darkness from the snow being blown away, and knocking me on my back.

Rough stone claws at my armor as I slide almost to the other side of the mountaintop.

The coal stone beneath me shakes violently until the fire in the sky passes over my head, wreaking havoc on everything in its path.

The mountain calms a moment later, but I'm still panting. *It can't be.*

As I get to my feet once again, a deep, bellowing horn silences all the noise from the island. From frightened voices being carried by the wind from below to the creaks and cries of the vegetation being demolished by thunderous boulders, even the waves mute their assault on the rocky shore, giving way to the call of the Father needing all to come to him.

A memory takes control of my mind, blinding and ravaging all my senses.

"I can see why you like coming in here so often." No matter what mood I'm in, my brother's breezy voice sparks my spirit to awaken and soar beyond what my physical capabilities are.

Freyr holds up an extremely girthy zucchini while waggling his eyebrows at me.

Our laughter fills the garden on a clear, sunny summer day. His hair is a shade away from looking to be on fire in his bun, while his pastel blue eyes sparkle like the ocean on a gentle sunrise.

He tosses the zucchini over to me to put in my woven basket, but I have another idea.

"We can be twins now." Freyr sits back on his heels as I stand and shove

the vegetable down my pants. "Actually, I think I need to chop this in half to look exactly like you."

After flipping me off with his middle fingers, Freyr goes back to picking squash.

"Not all of us can be as well-hung as your Wolven."

My smile drops as I pull the zucchini out and toss it into the basket.

"He's not my Wolven, Freyr. He can never be." I get down on my knees and aggressively pull weeds out. "And stop bringing him up, especially in front of Odin."

"Bralyant was my friend before he became your first love and—"

"He was my first, that's it. We weren't in love."

Freyr pins me with a hard stare, making his sweat-slick muscles tense across his bare vanilla-cream chest.

"And Odin needs to stop being a jealous pissant. At least your past lover isn't living in the same village as you. Odin's second ex-wife's home is within eyesight of your garden for fucks sake, and you work with her all the time. Right now, all he's spewing are insecurities; he's making you feel bad about your past, and I've had it. He needs to pull out his tongue and clean the bull-shit out of his eyes, or I'll do it for him."

I'm on him in a second, pinning him to the ground.

"Say it!"

"Don't marry him. At least not yet. Give your relationship some more time to grow. We are immortal; there is no rush."

"I have insecurities too. I know nothing about being a wife. Just because I can bless couples to have happy marriages and grow families doesn't mean I know how to make a marriage last. But I'm going to figure it out with Odin by my side. I love him, Freyr, and he loves me."

Freyr softens a little. "I think you're jumping into the marriage too fast because there is nothing holding you back since you're both Gods." I push off him, desperate to get away from this heated conversation and the sun. "Tell me, Freyja." I stop in my tracks and turn as he gets up. "If we didn't have the law about intermating, would you be with Odin right now or Bralyant?"

A shutter betrays my body from the strength of his words and focuses my attention on the reality of my heart wanting love but realizing it's with someone else.

Words fall flat as I try to answer him.

"Freyja." His eyes are full of all the love I'll ever need, but my heart has

been wanting more over the past couple of centuries. "This is why you can't marry Odin tomorrow. You and Bralyant might not have been a real couple, but your heart was still in it. Jumping into marriage isn't going to heal it; only time will. If Odin loves you, he will understand why you need to wait."

Warmth fills my eyes as I try to swallow my tears.

Freyr closes the distance between us, cups my face in his hands, and kisses my forehead three times, each more tender than the previous. My brother might not be able to speak the words, but this is his way of telling me he loves me.

I sniffle as my heart swells. "I can't just back out now."

His hands drop to my shoulders, and he pulls me into his embrace. I wrap my arms around his torso, not caring about his sweat-covered body. I crave his hugs more than I desire to wield magic. I'm not only comforted by his touch, but my soul sighs as if she's healing from his love.

"Yes, you can. You can always back out, Freyja." He massages the back of my neck, and I melt into him more. "I'll be there right by your side if you want."

A choked laugh makes me hiccup. "I think not. Anytime the two of you are within proximity of each other, you always find something to argue about."

His deep chuckle helps to chase away my sadness. "I take my chaperone responsibilities very seriously."

I'm met with an amused smirk when I pull back to look at him. "That's why you've been picking fights with him any chance you get, and why you haven't moved into your cabin yet? You've been cockblocking us?"

"You've been fucking a Wolven for centuries; there is nothing Odin can do with his dick that will make you fall more in love with him."

I try to knee him in the groin, but he blocks me with a wink.

His laughter as I try to break free from his hold is drowned out when a horn erupts.

The intensity punches the wind from our lungs and kicks our legs out from underneath us.

My head hits something solid, and my vision blurs.

Freyr leaps over my body just as wood and metal rip from the cabin.

I'm cocooned in his arms while the ground shakes as if the cliff is about to collapse.

We violently roll as colorful fire explodes in the sky, blocking out the sun.

*We fly into the woods. With Freyr keeping me close, he takes the brunt of
the force.*

*Only when the ground settles does Freyr untangle himself from me and
assess the injury to my head.*

*Without being able to hear him, I know what he's saying—the Father
needs us.*

* * *

A high-pitched ringing brings me out of the memory and back to the
view of a calm mountainside and clear skies and ocean.

My rapid breathing and pounding heart have dulled the voice of
whoever is trying to talk to me.

FREYJA!

Heimdall's profound voice hollers in my mind, and I beat my chest
to make my lungs take in more breaths and chase away the hurt of the
memory.

I'm here, Heimdall.

Speaking telepathically is usually only done in short bursts of
messages. Only when two beings are within eyeshot of each other are
they able to maintain a constant connection and communicate mind-
to-mind. Heimdall has an enhanced power that allows him to communicate with anyone for as long as he wants, no matter the distance.

Freyja, I've been trying to reach you for an hour.

*I was asleep after traveling via starlight to the galaxy and back. I went to
Crescent Island.*

*I know you went there, just as I know about you speaking to your friend
before leaving. Odin left shortly after. Is he with you?*

Fuck you, Heimdall, and your power of sight. I hope Haidion used
some type of illusion magic on himself to keep his identity safe.

No, I came here alone. Odin might have followed me.

Maybe Odin heard me leave or was awoken from the chill once I
left.

I don't think so. Have you seen Thor?

No.

Fuck, the explosion of the tower might not have been an accident then.
Heimdall spoke more to himself than to me. *A call came in from the*

Father, and Thor didn't blow the horn. Instead, he left to go to Crescent Island to retrieve a weapon from the Domed Armory. Sigurd entered the tower, blew the horn, and the structure collapsed and fell into the sea. A portion of the horn is still intact, but no one has found Sigurd's body. I sincerely regret not being able to tell you this in person.

The ground below me shakes, emphasizing the trembling coursing through me.

My muscles tense and bulge against the confines of my armor, making it too tight.

Is Saga, okay?

Sigurd was the Jarl of Leifheim's younger brother. He looked after the tower even though Thor told him he didn't need someone to micromanage his responsibilities.

She is out for Thor's head since the explosion looked rigged.

I swallow down my hurt over the loss and replace it with fury.

I would be too. Tell Saga to submit a work order to the Wardalyrians for them to investigate it because she isn't going to take any of our words as the truth, not even yours. And whoever destroyed the tower is out of our jurisdiction to punish. I have signed, empty forms in my desk at home that she can use to speed up the process.

I will pass the information on to her. Athena also sent word to meet at Camp Ariella. Hel and I are on our way.

During the War over the Frozen Fire Highlands, Camp Ariella was founded and served as a neutral location for the injured. No one was turned away. Volunteers from the Atlantean and Nymph races ran the camp while the Lyon and Siren races protected the borders. Gods: Asclepius, Kumugwe, Babalu Aye, Dhanvantari, Apollo, and Goddesses: Sekhmet, Airmed, Aja, and Isis, all swore oaths to provide healing and care to anyone, leaving all animosity and commitments to their pantheons behind when the world was in a time of great tragedy. A memorial was built in the gardens of all who died during the war, no matter if they sought to gain power or to fight in the Resistance.

I'll be there as soon as I can, Heimdall.

I turn my focus to the far edge of the mountain and start to run—

I need you to go to the Domed Armory and see if a specific weapon was taken. Knowing if it's there or not will tell me what Thor's true intentions are.

My steps falter and I nearly fall to the ground.

And what intentions are those?

As I said, the tower looks to have been rigged to explode in an attempt to destroy the horn. Why would Thor break his oath to do something like that?

Heimdall isn't in front of me to witness the demented expression on my face, so the stars and the night sky take the brunt of it, and the moon's radiance appears to have flinched.

Are you implying that Thor is betraying the Father? If he was, why not disable the horn by taking the gem out? Why blow it up and risk someone's life?

Thor might technically be family since I married his father, but he's over a thousand years older than me. I only see him as a fellow God of my pantheon. Unless we are on a mission together, I would never defend his actions. However, if he was doing some irrational shit like betraying the Father, he wouldn't make his plans known.

Freyja, we need to be sure.

I bite my physical and mental tongue before I start screaming about how absurd his thoughts are.

Why don't you just ask him?

I've tried to get a hold of Thor, Odin, and everyone else, but no one is answering me.

Something is wrong with your power.

Freyja, please! I'll willingly let you blood-brand me if you go to the Domed Armory.

Fuck, no! He's really serious about this then. I swallowed down my irritation to help my friend. *What weapon am I looking for?*

The name is Faithless.

Okay, I'm going now. I'll try to contact Odin through our bond. When I hear something, I'll send you a message.

Thank you, Freyja. I hope I'm wrong.

Thick, invisible, cursed magic hangs in the air around me to blood-brand Heimdall, but I shoo it away like a pesky fly. Even though Heimdall willingly offered the debt, I'd never subject anyone to a blood brand.

Up until Obliteration told me my brother's soul was now in the Spirit Realm, I only had my friend Hera's logic to go off of. She discovered all the souls were annihilated, and the creature was brought to life by the innocent blood spilled during the slaughter of the war. I wanted to disprove her theory, and Odin helped me all he could but when we couldn't find anything different, I chose to be oblivious to Hera's findings.

Even though I know my brother's soul is at peace, I still despise most practices of blood magic. Odin wants to renew our vows by performing a blood mating ceremony, to connect us in every possible way. But I told him no when we got married, and I will still tell him no. If I have to write it a thousand times in a journal for him to comprehend my answer, I will. There is no need for us to be blood-mated too.

A quarter turn brings my line of sight to the mountain where the Domed Armory is said to stand proudly—Amormatrlee Ravuletta. Most likely, the armory is hidden from all who aren't making their way up the mountain, because just like I didn't notice an enormous orbital eye when I flew to the island, I didn't spot a building on top of the tallest mountain.

Vahildra's words come back to me about how no magic can be used while climbing up the mountains, meaning I'll have a long trip if there isn't another stream or stairs. And I won't be able to contact either Heimdall or Odin while making my way up. So, before I ready myself to fly, I remove the armor on my left forearm and roll up my sleeve to reveal my marital brand.

Zachariah's branding of my left hand is technically illegal since only a mate or martial brand can directly connect to the soul. He must not be bound by Earthradonrien laws or doesn't care to abide by them.

When Odin and I said our vows, the spirit of our souls weaved together and then inked our skin, forming our marital brand. Part of Odin's soul went onto my arm, as mine did to his, forever binding our spirits through the sacred flesh.

A fiery trail of feathers mixed with a pink mist and coated with a dusting of stars weaves around a scroll of raven feathers, fraying the edges. On the scroll is a line from Odin's vows inked in silver: *"My prayers have been answered, I have found you, and I will never let you go."* I chose to put what my brother said I should do back when I was trying to write my vows. One, because I felt a presence that day as if he were there watching over me. And two for the amusement of Odin's eye-rolling since even in death, my brother still gets under his skin: *"You break your vows, you'll lose an eye."* After Odin and I announced our engagement to all the Gods at the annual summit, my brother whispered those words into Odin's ear as they shook hands.

With a swipe down the raised, inked brand, the colors come to life like a romantic melody.

My mind hesitates as I try to think of what to say to him. Heimdall said he left after me, so he knows I'm out in the middle of the night somewhere. If Odin was angry, he'd track me here through the bond, but if Heimdall has been trying to get ahold of me for the past hour, then maybe Odin wasn't able to access the magic through our bond either.

Odin, did you hear the horn go off?

A deep, rustic voice serenades me, like logs popping in a fireplace, coaxing me to relax.

I did. I just arrived at Camp Ariella. Oh, fuck!

Pain ripples down my arm, alerting me to Odin's well-being. My heart races when the presence of his voice leaves my mind.

Odin!

His presence rushes back a moment later, and I gasp with relief.

Freyja, please tell me you're here and safe.

No, well I'm safe. I'm making my way to the camp now.

The Kraken is trying to pull everyone into the ocean and capsize ships on the horizon.

What the fuck? Hafgura would only attack if he were threatened.

Despite being the largest immortal being both in the ocean and on land, he's a gentle giant and the last of his race.

Odin, who pissed him off?

I don't know. Honestly, we all thought he was dead. No one, not even the races that live in the ocean, had seen him in centuries. When you come, go through the forest. Do not land on the beach.

I will. And also, Heimdall has been trying to call you.

My telepathic messaging isn't working. Everyone I've been running into has been saying the same thing. Can you pass the information on to Heimdall?

I will. And one more thing: the horn tower exploded after Sigurd went inside to blow it. There's speculation that Thor rigged it. They haven't been able to find Sigurd's body.

A moment of silence passes through our bond, but Odin's presence is still in my mind. He's probably trying to figure out what to say to console me, but I'll shelve my feelings for the time being. We have more important things to worry about, like Odin's life being threatened by Hafgura as we speak.

Before I can utter a mental word, I'm consumed by my husband's scent as he taps into the magic of our brand and asks to take control of my mind. With a deep breath, I submit to his control.

The mountaintop's starry night landscape transforms into a warm spring day on the cliff adjacent to my garden. In front of me are the stairs chiseled into the cliffside, which leads to the entrance of the cave Odin made to express his love to me.

A whistle tickles my ears. "Where's my little bird?" Odin's voice sings from below.

I'm overflowing with excitement as I quickly descend the stairs. My bare feet are nipped by the cold stones, but nothing can dampen my growing smile.

My hair flows wildly behind me, and Odin also has me in a white lace, mid-thigh dress with nothing else. If he can focus on creating this oasis for our spirits to go to and chooses to dress me in the skimpy piece of fabric I wore on our wedding night, he must not be in immediate danger.

Each step takes me back to when our relationship first began.

After breaking off my secret relationship with my Wolven friend, Odin came to Freyr's and my home to give me daisies he picked. Rather than leave them at my altar, he wanted to deliver them in person so he could also recite poetry he wrote about me. It was so cringy that I harvested the magic from his offering and used it to launch him off the cliff. To my surprise, he came back a week later to try again. His poetry got better, but I wanted to laugh my ass off, so I threw him off the edge of the cliff once more.

The cycle of him visiting and my throwing him from the cliff went on for months until winter arrived. Odin had stopped coming to my door, and I began to miss him. Anytime we saw each other, he always found somewhere else to be and left before I could apologize. Even though Freyr told me not to, I sent him a letter of apology.

Spring came, and I was preparing the soil in my garden when Odin showed up with a tender smile. He led me to the cliff I had thrown him from and lifted the magic he placed on the mountainside to hide the project he had been working on since he first came to my home.

Another whistle tickles my ears and has me giggling. "Do I hear my little bird coming?"

"Yes, you do!" I project my happiness as I enter the mouth of the cave.

The sun behind me fills the cave with soft, majestic wonder. Hundreds of pink daisies fill the Eden Odin created for me over five hundred centuries ago. His power has preserved it in such a way that I have the perfect year-round oasis.

His poetry is engraved on the ceiling, even the cringy ones he first tried to serenade me with. All the walls show our love story. On my left, the silhouette of Odin coming to my home to give me daisies and recite poetry. My silhouette is shown using magic to throw him off the cliff. On my right are our silhouettes in this cave during solar noon on the Summer Solstice, reciting our vows to each other and then kissing.

"There's my lively, little bird."

My focus is immediately drawn to the center of the garden. Odin only wears a pair of silver briefs. His entire body is covered in tattoos, apart from his face. He is a work of art.

Odin extends his hands out to me as the sun glows against his skin and hair, turning him into a dream I never want to wake up from.

With one leap, I fly over the daisies and into his arms. He pulls me into his chest, drapes his arms around my waist, and kisses the top of my head. His six-foot frame swallows me as I listen to the rhythmic melody of his heart.

"When I find Thor, I will figure out what happened. I promise."

"You didn't need to create all this to tell me that."

One of his hands runs up my spine and comes to a halt at the back of my neck. He massages my nape, relaxing me into him more.

"I wanted to see you, just in case we weren't able to find each other."

I pull back and stare into his berry-blue eyes. "I will find you."

A relieved smile relaxes his shoulders as his fingers dig into the muscles of my neck, melting me against his hold.

"Whatever was used to cause the explosion, I think it mixed with the power of the horn and damaged our capacity to speak telepathical-ly." He presses his forehead against mine. "Let me know when you all are close, okay?"

"I will, but Heimdall and Hel are ahead of me. I won't be able to tell you when they arrive."

Odin pulls away slightly. "You aren't together?" It sounded like he meant to say that more to himself than to me. "So, you and Heimdall's connection wasn't affected?"

"No. We've been able to talk fine." His scrunched-up eyebrows and wrinkled forehead have me taking a step back and placing my hands on his chest. "What's wrong?"

As I search his eyes, he relaxes in a blink, as if I imagined the confusion tightening his face. "That's great. I will keep a lookout for them."

His other hand slides down to cup my ass, then slaps it, drawing a startled laugh from me. "We don't have time for that."

"But we have time for something else. Especially since we might not see each other at dawn, when Ostara's first lights illuminate the sky."

I cupped his face. "It's okay if we have to wait to exchange gifts. Going to the Father is kind of important." I tease, but his somber expression stays.

He pulls my hands down and places them back on his chest. "I want to give you your present now." He leans down and rubs his nose against mine. "Open your present for me, little bird." His soft, pillow-talking voice has me nodding. "Reach down into my briefs."

I raise an eyebrow as he winks at me. "You can't possibly have room for anything else in there."

As I burrow my hands under the hem of his briefs, he gives me a sultry smile. Above his flaccid cock is a folded piece of paper.

"Pull out the paper, not your favorite toy." He nips at my nose, making me giggle.

I do as I'm told as he slides one of his hands back to my nape and rests the other on my hip.

A waxed seal of the Nymphs' crest is on the folded piece of parch-ment. The Great Willow Tree has a magical dusting on its branches, making the tree's season change as I tilt the paper from side to side.

Budding blossoms for spring. An explosion of color for summer. Crisping leaves for fall. And twinkling flurries for winter.

"Open it, little bird," Odin enthusiastically encourages.

Minding not to break the gorgeous seal, I unfold the paper. Green vines are painted gracefully along the edge. In the center is a paragraph written in Nymphfralo.

"It's a poem, and no, I didn't write it." He chuckles, and I lift my focus to him, wanting to see his smile. "I went out and got your gift after I left the house." Odin sighs with frustration and begins to massage my nape again. "You weren't in bed when I woke to sneak out. I guess I didn't tire you out enough."

Guilt begins to drown me, and instead of caving in to tell him why I left, I hold up the piece of paper. "Want me to read it to you?"

He knows I'm diverting, and I can only get away with doing this a handful of times. But whatever is written on the piece of paper must be very important to him, because a smile returns to his face as he nods toward the paper. My aspiration for learning different languages comes in handy in this moment.

"To Odin's Lovely Daisy,

Read the following poem three times when you want to initiate your fertility—"

My gasp is audible as I process what I just said aloud.

I was told by all the other Gods and Goddesses that I had the power to awaken my ability to menstruate, but I would need a spell to do so. I'd planned to seek out my Wiccayen friend to purchase a spell from her after I got the stone flower, but that was before the Father—

"I figured out one part of the puzzle." I keep my attention on the paper, unable to meet his gaze. "There is a special type of flower that I guess you need as well. No one is telling me about it. But don't worry; when there is knowledge I seek, I always find it." My efforts to ignore his gaze have me shaking. "Little bird, what's wrong?" His fingers grip my chin, and he lifts my face to him, and in a second, his happiness switches to firm determination. "What do you know?" *Fuck!*

My left arm tingles from our marital brand, and my soul flinches.

One of the promises Odin had me make to him when we got married was that I'd share whatever knowledge I knew. I thought it was just a vow, not that he would be able to pull information out of me against my will. It's my fault; I should've asked him to explain. He had his two previous wives promise him the same thing, and I didn't give the notion a second to process before I spoke the vow aloud.

Words tumble out of me as the magic of our marital brand tightens around my soul. "I need an Ethasion stone flower from a Celestial. Each petal can be ground into a paste and then spread on my skin over my womb to make me ovulate, guaranteeing pregnancy as long as my partner is fertile."

His eyes narrow. "When did you gain this knowledge?"

The answer is squeezed out of me. "A little under a year ago, when I asked other Gods and Goddess who have fertility magic, they told me what I needed."

He looks down his nose at me. "And did you acquire the flower?"

"Yes. I had to offer Goddess Nyx a debt for her to retrieve it for me."

"And where is it?" His voice is infused with desperation.

"Buried in my garden." He scans my eyes for a moment before pulling away from me completely. "Odin, my love, I wanted it to be a surprise. My intentions were not to break my vow to you. Please, believe me."

I reach for him, but he backs away further. "You can't keep a secret to save your life, so the magic from my prayers and offerings must've granted you leniency." He runs his hand through his hair. "And when were you planning on telling me?" Anger flexes his inked muscles.

Through our bond, his disappointments are transferred to me in bitter waves. "I only acquired the flower recently, and I planned to tell you; I just couldn't figure out when it was a good time." When my voice cracks, he exhales a deep breath like a bull.

"I can't even be fucking happy when all I'm getting from you is guilt!" He slaps the skin over his left forearm, and I jump. "I can't trust what you are telling me, and your actions are making me believe you lied to me when you said you wanted to have a baby."

I don't know how to stop sending my emotions down our marital bond. He's able to do so, but I could never figure it out. When I tried to ask about it, he responded with, "Why wouldn't you want me to have access to how you're feeling all the time?" The discussion turned into a fight, and he didn't come home to sleep for a couple of months.

His hand is over my mouth faster than I can comprehend how he closed the distance between us so quickly. The other pulls at the skin behind my neck, and I become immobilized. With his palm digging in against my mouth and pinching off my nose, I'm unable to breathe, which awakens a throbbing between my thighs.

Odin growls in my face. "You could put Aphrodite to shame for being such a tease with your body and pulling someone's heart around." My arousal doesn't stop pulsating even though I'm being suffocated with humiliation. "I don't want to be fucking played with. You can either be punished for breaking your vow to me, or you can be a good wife and earn my forgiveness."

Skjoldr hums in my chest, trying to find a way to draw magic into my body, but Odin is in control of this oasis—I'm powerless here. My soul blazes violently, trying to break free, but the magic of the marital brand is wrapped around the threads of my existence.

"Do you want to be punished?"

My last punishment made my people suffer more than me. I withheld where the Sprites of Slaughter Sisterhood's Den were. I gave the sisterhood my word, and Odin could've just walked into the woods with an offering, but he didn't want to jump through hoops to speak with the Sprite Mother. Odin was able to disable my power to translate my believers' offerings into the magical wavelength for me to understand what they were praying for, allowing me to answer them. For a year, my believers' prayers went unanswered.

With no other option, I shake my head, causing myself pain by fighting his punishing grip—making me work to answer back to him.

"Lift your dress." I pull the hem of my dress up with trembling hands until he tells me to stop when my ass is bare. "Your pink daisy is begging to be bred." He scoffs, turns me around, and pushes my head to the ground.

He releases his hold on my neck and mouth, allowing me to gasp for breath. I keep my ass in the air and ball soil in my hands.

His hands lazily explore the curve of my ass as blood rushes into my head. "You are going to promise me that when we see each other next, you're going to say the spell three times. Unless you lied to me about wanting to have a child."

I don't hold back my anger. "I didn't fucking lie to you."

He spanks my ass so hard that I almost stumble forward. "There is my lively little bird." He rubs over the pain he caused. "Make the promise, and you will be forgiven."

All the good my husband has done by supporting me and showing me unconditional love isn't enough to make up for all the fucking shit he puts me through at times like this. Every time I thought about wanting to leave him, a little voice came to life in my mind, telling me I'm pathetic; I should be ashamed for giving up so easily. Marriage isn't just a beautiful basket of roses; there are thorns, and they fucking hurt.

The alternative is to fight him, but I can already see where that conversation will go—telling him about what the Father trusted me not to tell a soul. I won't break my word even if it saves my ass. If giving up control is what I need to do, then I will do it. And I'm going to make fucking sure no child will grow in my womb.

"I, Freyja, promise to recite the initiating fertility spell three times to you, Odin, when I see you next. This, I vow to you."

A light sting buzzes where Odin slapped my ass. "Such an obedient little bird." His praise makes my core throb, and I blink away my tears.

His fingers massaged my ass cheek to relieve the pain of the brand. I prefer the sting to his comfort, but I bite my tongue.

Once the buzzing goes away, Odin pulls me up by my hair, and a moan escapes me. Everything spins as blood rushes back to refill my body. I mentally curse for being turned on by his torment.

My back is to Odin's chest. He holds me against him as I fight off the need to hurl my guts up from being punished.

"I forgive you." His lips brush against my ear. "And I love you."

I can't stop myself from repeating them, another vow I promised; to always say them back. "I love you too."

He places a gentle kiss on my cheek, and I shudder at the torment delivered and the sliver of affection. "See you soon, my lovely Daisy."

Odin's presence leaves my mind, and a sigh of relief escapes me when I'm greeted by the gentle night sky, the echoing crash of waves, the armor adorning my body, and the magic potently flowing in my soul.

Tears threaten to stream down my cheeks as my knees wobble.

After being tormented by my husband, I usually have time to myself. And now that I'm faced with the task Heimdall begged me to do, I finally realize how much Odin has hurt me—in almost every possible way a being can be hurt.

Days, weeks, and even months later, I only ever get back up and keep going because of the spirit within me. I pick myself up because I don't want to live my life in a constant state of torment. Not my magic, my strength, my sense of integrity, or my duty as a Goddess—but me —I pick myself up.

My marital brand mocks me, reminding me of the centuries of cruelty I've endured.

Moonlight catches the back of my hand, the blood-brand Zachariah gave me. He said I wouldn't be able to sense him in my mind, like being possessed by a ghost. And I wonder what he would be saying if he were here before me. Though a different face comes to mind as I imagine the scene before my eyes, my brother's face—what would he say?

A cool breeze flares my nostrils, forcing me to gasp for a breath I didn't realize I needed as the wetness coating my eyes shocks the fatigued muscles of my mind like an electrical current reinvigorating a heart to beat once more.

Divorce.

The little voice in my mind stirs—the one that tells me I'm pathetic. Her silver-tongue will be present until all thoughts to end my marriage with Odin are erased.

I wouldn't be able to divorce Odin right now even if I wanted to. Per the laws of a marital brand, I can't slice through it and renounce him as mine until he is present so the magic he gave to make the brand can be returned.

Can all the good that Odin has done to and for me justify the bad? I've asked myself this question a hundred times, and each time I'm met with silence; neither Skjoldr nor my soul respond. I'm alone—and terrified.

With a deep breath, I place everything not about the Father into an emotional box and shelf it. I'll figure out what to do about my husband later. Above my marriage, my pantheon, and my life, answering the Father's call is priority number one. And if Thor is betraying him, I'm going to find out.

As I put my armor back on my forearm, I fire off the message to

Heimdall about what's happening at Camp Ariella, where to land, and everyone's communication being down. I also instructed him not to call me until I called him, so that no magic is used while I ascend Amormatrlee Ravuletta.

I run to the edge.

The soul magic in my cloak comes to life, ruffling the feathers once again.

With a push of my arms, I fly to Amormatrlee Ravuletta.

After circling the mountain for a couple of minutes, I spotted a lightened, stone path leading to an arc made of four trees twisted together.

I let out the magic in my cloak and descended. Once I pass beneath the arc, the use of magic will most likely be monitored; I just hope I don't have to start at the beginning of the trail before heading up.

Before I take a step, I direct soul magic to trigger my telepathic messaging and speak Vahildra's Demonical name aloud, so the magic knows who to send the message to, and then relay the message aloud as well.

"Is there a marked path heading up to the Domed Armory?"

As I wait, I take in the environment around me.

The forest isn't as packed with as many trees, allowing me to see the sky above, and the branches aren't menacing.

Beyond the arc is more of the same, just without the stone path. If there were markers on a trail, they would be carved into the trees. Even though the full moon is radiating like the sun, Skjoldr tries to activate my eye adaptation power.

I growl. "I can't use any type of—"

Something cool brushes the back of my neck, then my forehead.

I whip around, magic at the ready, thanks to my spiritual essence. When I spot nothing around me, I begin to wonder if paranoia is creeping in. Judging by my inpatient shaking, I've either been waiting for a while or my patience is waning to get to Camp Ariella.

I deactivate my magic against Skjoldr's insistence to keep it up. "It's not wise to waste magical energy." I firmly whispered.

Vahildras' smooth and formal presence fills my mind, like taking a sip of the best semi-sweet wine I've ever tasted.

No. The mountain is meant to challenge the being who approaches it.

However, I just gave you clearance for the fastest path to be shown to you. The same rules apply; you can't use any type of magic once you go under the arc, but you can fly away once you're done.

His presence leaves my mind since we don't have a constant connection like what Heimdall can do. *Hold up.* Vahildra and I were able to communicate telepathically, making three of us who were not affected by the horn. If I had more time to figure out the odd phenomenon, I would look into it, but I have a mountain to climb.

Once I take my first step after the arc, a green path of footsteps appears before me. Each step I take makes the ones under me vanish and another pair rises from the forest floor ahead.

Vahildras' presence floods my mind when I'm at the base of a rock wall. Even though there is a gradual path going up and around to my right, apparently this way is faster.

I'm cursing Vahildra's name as I turn around to make my way back to the arc.

By the way, receiving messages won't count against you.

"You could have said that in your first message!" I yelled towards the arc and stone path beyond.

I turn on my heels and climb the rock wall.

CHAPTER
NINE
TWELFTH HOUR INTO NIGHTFALL

After today, I'm going to be adding endurance training to my daily workout regimen. I've been privileged to be able to fly everywhere for the past five hundred years, and now I'm kicking myself in the ass each time I think of how I've neglected the rest of my body's training. If I sit down for a moment, I will not get back up.

These green footprints are a blessing and a curse. I'm climbing the mountain faster than I anticipated, but I'm climbing the mountain, not walking; I'm climbing all the time. The only times I walk are when I need to get to another wall.

My rippling arm, back, chest, abdominal, and leg muscles were pushing me through, but keeping up my pace is painful. Everything hurts as if I tore every fiber connecting my muscles to my bones.

I love having a muscular body, but my shitty endurance makes me wish I was a couple pounds lighter. At one point I was tempted to take off my armor and cloak, but I couldn't use magic to send it to the top.

Every so often, Vahildra sends me words of encouragement, and I waste energy by cursing his name to the stars above.

When it started to rain, he told me to cup my hands to drink some water or open my mouth to the sky because I hadn't thought to bring the supplies needed for an expert-level hike.

Sweat coats my hands, dirt burns under my fingernails, strands of loose hair from my braid are plastered onto my cheeks, the harpy feather annoyingly tickles my neck, and every movement I make as I reach and push up to the top of another rock wall has me wanting to give into gravity's seduction and fall backward.

If it weren't for my armor providing support for my jelly muscles, I would've been reduced to a puddle of bones and flesh.

I grip the ledge of the wall and grunt out my pain as I pull myself up. Judging by the thinning of the air, I'm up high.

Only once did I glance over my shoulder to see what progress I'd made, and the disappointment of there being more mountain ahead than behind me made me not give into the curiosity to keep checking.

After moving away from the edge, I braced my hands on my thighs for a moment to catch my breath before moving forward.

When no green footprints appear, I begin to curse at myself for possibly taking the wrong route, but as I lift my attention to take in the area around me, tears almost rush down my cheeks—I'm at the fucking top.

I empty my lungs as I scream my victory and raise my hands to the sky, thanking the stars above for giving me the strength and patience I needed.

The rain clouds drift away to reveal the clear night sky. With the moon only two-hands lengths away from the horizon, the sun will rise soon.

A quick look down boosts my pride in the achievement I just made —scaling a mountain in three hours. Thanks to Vahildra giving me clearance to be shown the fastest path, this hike could've taken me twice as long.

Amormatrlee Ravuletta might be the tallest mountain on the island, but her intimidating height doesn't take away from the beauty before me. On either side of her, mountains gradually get smaller as the island fills out the curve of the crescent shape, with her proudly marking the thicker middle. She doesn't rule over the mountain range, making the others appear insignificant; instead, it's the other mountains who compliment her, and they are the spellbinding sight, along with the gracefully shaped bay, highlighting the magnificent wonders this island has to offer.

The view of a sunrise must be spectacular with the rays entering the bay since the island faces east, then the sun dropping under the mountains every night for all to appreciate the majesty of witnessing the strength of the mountains blocking out the sun to awaken the night and the rising of the moon.

At the end of my three thousand and two hundred years of existence, I have finally found the most beautiful sight I've ever seen. Instead of Heimdall thanking me for coming up here, I owe him gratitude for convincing my stubborn ass to climb all the way up. If it weren't for Vahildra's support, I would've given up.

With a deep breath, I turn around to face the—

A clink of glass pulls my attention down.

Between my feet is a corked, crystal bottle on its side. The glass is no longer than my middle finger and is in the shape of a crescent with a mint-colored liquid inside.

I almost drop the bottle when Vahildra's voice fills my mind.

I spy, with my deadly cold eyes, a gift from the fountain beneath the mountain as your reward for reaching the top. Don't disrespect the offering from Lady Amora.

"How can you see me; let alone the item I'm holding?"

I don't have time to think about whether or not to drink. The end of my quest is behind me, and the Father needs me. My trust is in my friend.

After uncorking the bottle, I raise it to the sky. "Cheers."

A refreshing liquid quenches my thirst as if I'll never require another drop of water to keep me hydrated. The flavor of milk at the perfect temperature with a hint of vanilla for sweetness silenced my hunger.

Once the liquid hits the back of my throat, magic flutters like a hundred little butterflies.

Drunken giggles escape my lips as the magic works its way to every curve of my body.

All at once, the fluttering stops and wraps around every joint and muscle. Energy is fed into me as my moans and groans are a song carried by the wind.

A phantom hand takes control of my grip. The fragile bottle falls unnaturally fast to the coal stone beneath my feet. Instead of smashing into pieces, the crystal bottle turns into glittering dust and dissolves.

Though I'm filled with enough energy to climb another mountain, my shaking hasn't gone away, and I rub my hands together to chase away the unnerving sensation of something being able to take control.

Light shines into my eyes as I focus my attention on the quest behind me. Standing before me is the Domed Armory, built out of Infinite bricks.

The tent keeper of *"Frost Borne Forge,"* where I found the ingots for my armor, wouldn't shut up about his love and admiration for this structure, a sphere carved out of sparkling ice-like stone. Minerals from comet gemstones make up the base of the bricks, giving the building an invisible appearance if you don't have a clever eye. In either daylight or moonlight, the dome is said to glisten. And no amount of frenzied weather or sweltering heat can break down the minerals, making this building imperishable.

Intricate carvings of all the races are represented on the pillars which mark the entrance. The left one represents all of the races on Earthradon, while the right appears to represent all of the races in the Galaxy, as I am unfamiliar with the majority of them.

My reflection is mirrored back to me as I run my hands over the curved wall, trying to find a doorknob or latch.

After a moment, I locate a circular hole in the middle.

As I stick my hand in, something sharp nicks my finger to the bone.

Fiery red blood runs down my middle finger when I pull it out.

Shadowy-star magic tingles under the wound, but I strictly whisper to my hand to not heal so I won't be penalized for using magic.

When blood continues trailing down my finger, I sigh in relief. I can't see what's within without a sconce of some kind of light.

A red liquid moves under the ice-like stone and fills in groves around the hole—letters making up words are revealed.

"If entrance is what you seek, spill blood to read the riddle."

Well, if one prick was enough blood to fill in the grooves for the sentence, then not much should be required to reveal the riddle.

Even with my logic, I still hesitate to put my hand back inside because blood is more valuable than any currency.

If my blood is given to a researcher like Vahildra, he could figure out what kind of abilities and powers I have, along with weaknesses.

Stealing blood is the best way to figure out how to take down an enemy, control a race, or mutate the blood in someone else to make them more powerful—a Morph—all of which are forms of blood magic.

Only a few races are immune to blood theft. Given the Domed Armory isn't a living being and my blood may be the price to enter, the unknown of what will be done with it after has me hesitating.

"Fuck it."

Each finger is pricked as I slide my left hand back inside. Since I know what to expect, the puncture isn't as alarming.

I'm surprised that my instincts didn't caution me about the dangers of reaching inside, that Haidion's magic didn't come to life to alarm me about the impending threat, or that Skjoldr didn't hum in my chest to caution me that my magic was about to be threatened and taken. Even the fire in my soul has cooled down. Whatever magic makes up this armory is extraordinarily powerful.

My fresh blood spiders out of the hole as my old blood darkens to black.

A jolt of cold energy travels through my hand like lightning.

As I examine my fingers, icy-blue magic bandages the holes, numbing the pain.

Symbols are filled in by my blood around the hole, forcing me to turn my head almost upside down to read the riddle.

I'm curious as to why the instructions were written in Earth-radonic, but the riddle is written in Galex—at least I know why the language is named so. I wonder if all but me knew that the races in the galaxy are called Galexstrials, because if it were common knowledge, at least Freyr would've told me.

Galex is only communicated by hand movements laced with magic. Each symbol is a hand frozen in time, and my blood flows like a stream to make the hand appear to be moving.

I'm thankful to my brother for having the patience to teach me all the languages I wanted to learn.

"You hear me throughout the galaxy. I made it so. I am not acknowledged, and many claim credit for what I have done. I made it so. To see me, you must unlearn what you have been taught. I made it so. I cannot be seen

Just from the second line, I know what the answer is.

I hope it doesn't count against me that I have to direct soul magic to my hand to sign back because the only way to communicate with Galex is through hand movements.

I coat my hands with magic and sign the answer. *"Creation."*

My blood darkens to black, and my reflection becomes clearer.

The ice-like stone turns into dazzling water, but only in the height and size of my silhouette.

Shifting side to side makes the water follow. I guess where I stand before this structure thins out to become a passage through.

With a deep breath, I step forward. A thick liquid squeezes my body as if the material wants to fuse with me to reinforce the structure.

Electrical sparks pulse out of my left hand, forcing the substance to release me. I stumble onto sand, and surprisingly, the pressure doesn't force the air from my lungs.

The shadowy-star magic tingles under my skin before I can tell it to not heal my wounds. Since I'm inside the Domed Armoy, I hope the rule doesn't apply anymore.

Indigo sand, similar to a soft powder, covers the floor of the circular armory. Not a speck sticks to my hands or armor as I stand.

My breath is taken from me as my eyes focus on the panoramic view. Unlike the blurry reflection of myself in the ice-like stone on the outside, inside, the entire armory is pristine glass.

Moon rays come in from the top to illuminate the open space. The temperature is both refreshingly cool and comfortably warm.

A thousand weapons could be stored here, and there would still be space for more. But nothing adorns the walls, and there are no glass cases to protect items that are more valuable than weapons.

In the center, surrounded by black crystals, is a small pond. As I get closer, my reflection is shown back to me as clearly as looking into a mirror.

The water begins to ripple, and the same effect happens in my mind.

Before I can step away, a voice, both masculine and feminine, soft and rough, deep and light, young and old, speaks into my mind.

What weapon do you seek?

Is the Warden of this armory a spirit? "Faithless."

He isn't available. Is there another weapon you seek?

The weapon has a gender—that's odd—but I gave a gender to my spiritual essence by naming her Skjoldr, so I can relate to giving an identity to an important entity, especially since it has a purpose.

"Isn't available, meaning he's not here or he doesn't want to be borrowed?"

He is not here. Is there another weapon you seek?

Fuck. I have my answer, at least. "No."

A thick layer of panic beneath the surface of my beating heart reduces my fascination with the use of magic that makes up the armory and the pond. Skjoldr hums to life, waiting to see how I'm going to react, so she knows what magic to have ready for me. Until I speak to Heimdall, I won't know the purpose of what this weapon can do and why Thor taking it would mark him as a traitor to the Father. I take deep breaths to keep my panic from rising.

Another ripple shifts the water. *The Preserver wants to speak with you.*

"Oh, joy."

The Preserver Guild maintains and guards all the armories, and normally I wouldn't need to talk to anyone unless I was borrowing something.

In a blink, the surface of the pond stills. Black liquid bled from the crystals, covering the top. Once the crystals are drained, the surface hardens.

Moonlight is absorbed and forms a halo around the pond, leaving a gap before me.

"Am I supposed to step in?" My instincts urge me forward while the fire in my soul purrs in agreement.

After I step onto the pond, the halo connects, and the crystals grow to become a palisade wall, with spikes pointing out towards the sand.

The panic that was waiting to surface once I got in contact with Heimdall leaks through now as I wonder what kind of person this

Preserver is, if I need to be guarded so aggressively, and why I need to be guarded.

My soul burns hotter as I flex all my muscles and widen my stance, ready and limber to deliver a strike if I need to defend myself.

The wall of the dome darkens as the moonlight is blocked from entering, leaving the halo as the only source of light. In seconds, the temperature plummets to freezing.

My hands are wrapped in shadowy-star magic, which confirms that whoever is approaching is dangerous.

My exhaled breath is pulled away as a phantom wind blows sand into the air. The fog from my breath mixes with the indigo sand as it spins violently to form a nine-foot tornado.

A silhouette of a being is shaped as the sand and air swirl angrily to maintain form. This isn't a race on Earthradon—it's a galaxy race.

Without knowing if the Nebula can hear me, I sign in Galex. *"You wanted to speak to me, Preserver?"*

Shadowy-star magic curls up to my arms, tendrils poking their heads out to see who stands before me.

The Preserver begins to circle the pond. assessing me while their hands sign furiously. *"Why do you want Faithless?"*

I keep turning with them so they can see my hands moving. *"I was told by my fellow God to see if he was taken before I flew to the Father."*

"Do you plan to harm the Father with him?"

"No. Why would you think such a thing?"

They stop as if hitting a wall. *"Because Faithless has the capability to kill all-powerful beings. A deity would not stand a chance against him."*

What the fuck! I resumed signing. *"Why would a weapon like that exist?"*

"That is classified information." They resume their circling. *"The moment after I allowed Faithless to be borrowed, the horn sounded."*

"Thor would never betray the Father."

A bitter taste fills my mouth since Heimdall planted doubt about Thor's odd behavior and possible intentions in my mind.

"I'm not believing that naïve bullshit, and neither should you. If something happens to the Father, my guilt will rot my soul, as might yours, but much faster due to Thor's deception."

A grim reality weighs down my already stressed-out soul. I want to ignore the stifling sensation, but I won't be negligent given the severity of the situation Thor has placed on the Nebula.

"*Can't you call Faithless back?*"

"*No. I would have to be within eyesight of him to do so. Without the permission of the Governor, I can't leave this island. But even if I had permission, I couldn't survive on your planet without the proper materials to keep me formed.*"

"*I'll drag Thor back here; you have my word.*"

"*Thor gave me his word about his intentions not to use Faithless to kill a Deity. I held out hope that not all of the beings on this planet were corrupt, but I was wrong.*"

The Preserver swirls around the pond too fast for me not to get lightheaded by keeping up. To combat my dizziness, I concentrate on where a face should be on the swirling sand form.

"*Can I take Faithless from Thor?*"

"*Only a Preserver can. If a member of my Guild has honest intentions, they can break the contract with the borrower.*"

A dry, grainy voice comes out of the mass of swirling sand. *They can speak Earthradonic.*

"Oblivion is the only reason why the Intergalaxiate Authority Council hasn't voted in favor of us raining down on your galaxy to fix the problem ourselves. Why Oblivion is certain that we aren't needed, I don't know, but none of them will speak against her if it means the galaxy races will lose the planes she created for us to inhabit."

On my next inhale no air enters my lungs, and suffocation starts to come over me.

Before I can gasp, something pulsates in my chest, taking over the function of my lungs, and I'm able to breathe again. No air rushes down my throat and nostrils, but magic.

"How are you still standing?"

Obliteration's Plasma must still be in my lungs. But more importantly, the Nebula had done something to the air and was planning on choking me.

Tendrils of shadowy-star magic move around me like snakes, my soul magic hums in my chest, and the fire in my soul has her claws out, ready to fight.

I stop signing and speak aloud. "Is your plan to kill me?"

They shrug and run their hands along the halo, making the sand forming the appendages fall to the ground. "Don't be dramatic. You haven't been around any Nebulas, so let me give you some insight: We are known to take out our frustrations on others."

Rather than allow the Nebula to get a rise out of me, I take a deep breath so I can project my assurance. "I want to join the Guild."

The Nebula stops in its tracks, giving my eyes and head a break from moving so much as the bile rises in my throat.

"Joining the Guild isn't something that you should decide on a whim."

I raise my chin. "I will do whatever it takes to protect the Father."

My spiritual power hums and awakens my senses to a comforting strength wrapping around my soul.

I tremble at the familiar embrace of my brother as an external source of heat warms my chest.

I don't know how my power was able to activate on its own or why I'm able to feel my brother as if he is standing behind me. The last time I felt the sibling bond was right before Freyr died, when the magical tether between us snapped, followed by the breaking of his bones.

"Very well."

The swirling sand and air making up the Preservers' body stills and becomes solid. A masculine form is fabricated. His hair is a gentle wave of sand and air, with a pair of black crystal eyes and lips peeking through the sand on his face.

The crystal palisade shrinks back to its original size, dispersing the light from the halo back into the dome as moonlight returns.

The Nebula pats his chest twice and extends his right hand to me. "I'm Locke."

My instincts and Skjoldr are timid about accepting his hand until a gentle push comes from behind me. I may not trust this being, but I trust Freyr. Though I'm not ready to leave his embrace just yet, I know now he is watching over me.

A tender pressure presses into my forehead when I step forward. My heart swells, and when no pain accompanies it, I sigh as the lonely hole in my heart greedily fills with the deeply meaningful passion being showered upon me. If any doubt remained in my mind about this spiritual entity not being Freyr, it's now gone. Our sibling bond bypassed all the stress I've been under just so I could soak up the warmth of my brother's love.

Freyr never said the three words aloud; instead, he always told me by pressing a kiss to my forehead. If he wasn't within reach to perform the physical actions, he'd press three fingers to his lips and press them to his forehead with his signature crooked smile.

Questions run rampant in my mind, wanting to know how our sibling bond reformed when my brother is only a spirit and why I haven't been able to access it—all thoughts get silenced by not one but two more presses of a kiss to my forehead.

A voice similar to my own but distinctively male speaks into my mind, and I can't tell if it's just the memory of my brother's voice or if he's actually speaking to me. *Focus, fierce one. Spread those wings and fly.*

With a deep breath, I walk over to the edge, where the Nebula is patiently waiting for me. When I'm in reach of their hand, the hum of my spiritual power fades, as does the presence of Freyr. *Please don't leave me yet.*

I press my palm into my chest and then grasp his hand. "I'm Freyja."

Locke gently tugs me, and I step out of the pond. The surface becomes liquid once again and gets sucked back into the crystals.

"Remove the armor on your chest."

I use the shadowy-star magic to unfasten the bindings and hold the piece for me.

Locke places his hand in the middle of my chest then his other over my forehead. "Do you, Freyja, wish to join the Preserver Guild?"

"Yes."

Green magic glows from his hands. "You are swearing to not only take on the responsibility of a Preserver but to forsake the duty of your race when called upon, and you are not only taking the oath for yourself but for your bloodline. Every generation of your blood will be held to the oath as well once they reach magical maturity. Do you, Freyja, still wish to join the Preserver Guild?"

No children are in my future, only peace. "Yes."

"Repeat after me."

Once he's done, I take in a deep breath, more for encouragement.

"I, Freyja, forsake all that I am and pledge my allegiance to the Preserver Guild. I vow to the Guild my soul and all who follow in my bloodline. With the Preserver Locke, the stars above, and the shadows around as my witnesses, I, Freyja, swear my oath. Honorable ancestors of the Preserver Guild, will you accept me as your Sister?"

White light replaces the green coming from Locke's hand. He flinches as magic peacefully brands my skin, blood, and soul.

Locke drops his hands once the white light fades. "Welcome to the Preserver Guild, Sister Freyja." He presses his fist against his chest and bows his head to me.

When I go to mimic him, Locke grabs my hand before I can follow suit. "I'm not a Brother. You do not offer that level of respect to me. Only a few ever received the blessing of the Guild's ancestors. All of them hold high stations in the Guild, and soon you will too."

What? "Um, I didn't ask to be one." After my armor is strapped back on, the shadowy-star seeps back into my hands.

"The ancestors deemed you worthy."

"If any harm is done to the Father by Faithless, then I doubt they will still deem me worthy if I can't get to him in time."

"All the Guilds' allegiances are to the magic system, not to any of the Deities. You will receive no punishment if Faithless is used to kill the Father."

"Seriously?"

Locke nods. "The handbook will explain everything and the Governor, Aba Namtar will introduce himself to you in the next couple of days."

"Wait, who?"

"Aba Namtar." He spoke slowly. "If the Aba part is confusing you, it's the title given to all Governors of Guild Races. Until recently, he was also the Governor of the Historian Guild, but all the members elected an outsider who has no respect for the laws and rules by which the Guilds were formed." *I now know what other title Vahildra has.*

If Haidion didn't style my hair beautifully, I'd pull my hair out; instead, the shaking that still hasn't gone away gets worse. No wonder Vahildra didn't express his feelings to me; he's fucking livid.

Locke begins to sign, which allows me to inhale oxygen normally. *"If you have any questions while reading the handbook, tap on your chest twice and then your forehead once, and the brand will connect you to the* Governor. *I appreciate you joining, Freyja."*

Besides being the right thing to do, I won't allow Thor's actions to be the cause of Locke contracting an incurable disease. To die from Soul Rot is not something I'd ever wish upon anyone, even my enemies.

TEN

THIRTEENTH HOUR INTO NIGHTFALL

"Deep breath in, deep breath out. Deep breath in, deep breath out."

No matter how many times I go through the mantra to calm and center myself, my shaking doesn't subside.

All the information I've learned and all I've endured tonight is overwhelming.

I'm a moment away from unleashing all my aggravation on the night sky. If I ever wondered what the opposite of peace was like, I now know.

Flying always clears my head and reduces my stress, but I need to call Heimdall before I do anything else. However, an awareness draws me to my marital brand, and I start ripping the armor off.

When I first walked out of the dome, I wanted to scream Odin's name to the stars. The armory disappeared, just like the arc on Zachariah Mountain, leaving the area wide open with ample space to take my anger out with no casualties.

Odin has not only kept a huge fucking secret from me for the entirety of our marriage, but he has also wreaked his own version of chaos on this island and upon my friend. My husband is the one who deserves to be punished, not me!

I'm about to brush my brand to activate it when the silver-tongued shithead who talks me out of doing anything against my husband gives me a huge headache. My mind is spinning, and I succumb to gravity and land on my knees.

I wrap my arms around myself, trying to recall Freyr's embrace. "Come on, Freyja." My head begins to throb, and I choke out sobs from the pain. "The Father needs you." Redirecting my focus away from Odin is the only way to make the voice go away. "Shelve it for later. You need to get up!" With a growl, I brace the ground and push myself up.

Tears want to fall, but I swallow them and slap my cheeks to replace the need to cry with stinging pain.

"Crying won't make a difference—only action will. Now is not the time to be weak, Freyja."

With one last look at my marital brand, I flip it off before re-securing my armor.

As I direct soul magic to trigger my telepathic connection, my sights are on the horizon.

Camp Ariella is going to take me hours to reach. By the time I arrive, the majority of my soul magic will be depleted. The Great Willow Tree is only a couple of miles from the camp, but if there is a fight to be had, I'm going to be testing the reserves of my magic.

A small thread of hope helps to focus me; I only need to be within eyeshot of Faithless to call him. *I can do this.*

The high-pitched ringing fills my ears, and a fierce, screeching roar severs my connection.

Hurricane-force winds gust around me, kicking up dirt, snow, and loose debris.

Before I can turn away to protect myself from the wave of wind, a shield of shadowy-star magic covers me like a second skin, blinding me from whatever is approaching.

A memory takes control of my mind, blinding me more and ravaging all my senses.

"You tell Freyr," I slice the throat of a mortal soldier and spear an ice spike into the head of another, going through their ears, "that I picked up a weapon, I'll freeze your tits off, Athena."

My friend's powerful dance of spear and shield leaves countless bodies dropping to her feet. "Picking up the short sword saved your neck. Did you think your magic would last from dawn till dusk?" Athena spins and releases her shield to decapitate a soldier coming up behind Hera. "Were you the one who encouraged her to think such nonsense?"

"Are we really having this discussion right now, in the middle of battle?" Hera curses as she throws a slender, ivory dagger at a soldier trying to take Athena's shield.

Dozens of Elven warriors, dressed in pristine silver armor, rush towards us. Before they could lift their elegant, long swords or use their magic, the ground trembles as a monstrous, black stag tramples them. Artemis is on the back of the beast—her servant Aliith. She twists around and rains arrows down on all who try to stand.

Athena's smile spreads wide as she takes in the sight of the cave behind the falling bodies. "Yes." She throws Hera a glare, then meets my eyes again. "The best time to learn any lesson is when you can reinforce the teachings right away."

After Artemis jumps off Aliith, he shifts into a normal-sized wolf and helps to collect her arrows. "Be thankful you have friends who love your stubborn ass."

Hera walks over to Athena and hands her shield back. "I told Freyja about the theory of reserve power we have, but that no one is willing to drain themselves to see if they can tap into it. It's not my fault she didn't listen to me when I advised her not to try it."

She throws me a knowing smirk, and I courtesy flip her off. Everyone knows that if they tell me not to do something, I always do it.

All of them chuckle, brightening the bronze tone of their honey skin and accentuating the gold strands in their warm brown hair.

I walk over to Athena's side as she studies the entrance to the cave at the base of the mountain. She hooks the shield onto her back and leans her weight into her spear. We all might be immortal, but even our bodies have physical limitations, especially after almost six hours of fighting.

Her braid has come out of its bindings and flows with the musky breeze coming from the mouth of the cave. Clouds rush overhead, taking away the sunlight and casting the cave into an unnatural darkness. Athena's gold-plated armor has natural illumination, but not enough to brighten the cave.

The Resistance has been fighting to get this close for five months, and today Athena knew we'd be standing before the mountain. Now we can work on clearing out the mountain passages so the daughters of the Father can form the Trinity Triangle and extract the frozen fire magic.

Hera steps up next to me. "Who's volunteering to go inside first?"

"I'll go." A deadly smooth voice hums from behind us.

Goddess Nyx walks towards us, sheathing a pair of broad-bladed short swords at her hips. A mist of night cloaks her back. Unlike all the others in the Greek Resistance, her ebony armor is molded to her tall, lean frame. The only skin visible is her ruby lips and the snow-white skin of the lower portion of her mouth. Her metal helmet covers her nose and eyes; how she can see, I have no idea.

"I'll join her."

Hera puts her hand on my arm, and her deeply concerned sepia eyes focus on me. "Trust me, you don't want to be near her when she goes into that cave."

Nyx reaches for a long-handled blade protruding from behind her neck with both hands. "Don't deny her the experience of seeing Vile Beauty in action."

I pull away from Hera's motherly hold as Athena clears her throat. "If you want to go, Freyja, watch your—"

Fierce, screeching roars have all of us cupping our ears.

A powerful wave of wind beats against the mountains, triggering an avalanche.

Twenty dragons break through the gray clouds, soaring over the mountaintops and raining fire on the falling snow.

Artemis mounts Aliith, who grows to the full ten-foot size of a mature Wolven. "They shouldn't be here already. We have more time!"

"You didn't see them coming?" Hera screams at Athena.

Athena's eyes roll backward for a second, allowing her to use her power of sight, then roll back to her big brown eyes. Her skin pales as tears rush down her cheeks. Just like her power of wisdom, being told what she sees comes with a cost.

Nyx is in front of her faster than my eyes can process. "I'll pay. Tell us what you saw."

Magic zaps from Nyx to Athena. "Thousands are going to die." Athena's eyes meet mine, and she lets out a sob. "Freyr is going to die."

* * *

A hard blow to the face yanks me out of the memory.

I'm on my side as the mountain shakes beneath me as if something landed on it. Only one race has this powerful presence—a fucking dragon.

The shadowy-star magic works to patch up my face as I sit up, but I curse it away so I can see, not caring if I'm bleeding or bruised. The tendrils pull back but stay in my palms as my soul magic beats like a war drum, ready to be unleashed.

I'm on my feet in an instant and almost stumble backward as I take in the dragon before me.

Even though I don't want to, I have to take a few steps back to get a sense of his height—a quarter of the size of Novvricken's tallest tower with a thick tail and a prominent crown of horns.

His mighty wings are spread wide, measuring more than double his height—abnormal, especially for a not-yet-mature dragon. Since he has four legs, he's not a Wyvern, at least—that breed of dragon is notoriously unpredictable.

A dusting of snow appears to layer his cool black scales, giving him a more graceful appearance. Rays of moonlight make him glow as if the night sky worships his presence.

Before proper introductions can be made, he lowers his head, bringing his mouth only inches away from me—very unusual for a dragon. Either he hasn't been taught how high his race holds itself above anyone else or he doesn't care.

He tilts his head to the side, and I'm greeted with an emerald reptilian eye with a silver slit. Only the royals have gemstone-like eyes and emerald with silver is of the majesty bloodline—he's one of the queen's princelings.

What the fuck is a Princeling doing off the Dragon Island without guards?

An earth-rumbling chuckle vibrates his neck and head as a deep, velvety voice fills my mind, commanding my shaking to settle.

Don't let my looks fool you. I'm not a princeling in the least bit. Too constricting.

He magically formed a channel between us! All races can do this with each other if they grant permission—no magic is required—but for a race to connect with a God has never been done before. Gods can only connect with races when they are in their humanoid forms, never as beasts.

"How did you do that?"

One of the many powers I keep to myself—not even my mother knows. Don't make me regret investing my trust in you.

"Don't worry, I'll forget you ever existed."

A strong huff from his flaring nostrils makes the dirt at my feet blow away.

Against every instinct in my body telling me to get away, Skjoldr screaming at me, and the fire erupting in my soul, begging for a fight, I give the princeling my back—a clear sign of disrespect—and I run towards the edge of the cliff.

The ground trembles, but I keep going since my armor and cloak are flame-resistant.

If I had known the magical properties of my rare armor, Freyr wouldn't have used himself as a shield—it doesn't matter though, I should've fought harder to begin with.

With only my hands and head to worry about, I think of myself as unstoppable when it comes to fighting someone with fire. The day my brother died was the awakening of the inferno blazing in my soul.

Something trips me, and shadowy-star magic softens my landing before my instincts could even tell me an attack was coming. *Skjoldr, you're fucking slacking.*

A screechy huff comes from the princeling. *Who the fuck are you talking to?*

"Don't you dare read my mind again!"

Then figure out how to create another channel so your thoughts aren't sent to me.

The princelings' tail moves in the corner of my eye. He chose to sweep my feet out from under me rather than use his fire or windstorm from his wings.

I was told you would be a feisty one. Makes my job even more entertaining.

As he chuckles in my mind, I'm up on my feet and whirling around to face him. "Unless your job is to kill me, then you have to fucking wait because I've got more important shit to do than be an amusement for you."

He raises his head, allowing me to see both of his eyes, but keeps it low enough that I don't have to strain to look up at him.

I came here to tell you that you won't reach the Father before Solar Noon, and then it will be too late.

"Is one of your powers being a shitty prophet too, or is it an asshole talent?"

Are you done being a smoky bitch and wasting our time, or do you get turned on by insulting someone?

The shadowy-star magic pulsates under my hands as I ball them into fists. The fire in my soul explodes and runs down my arms as if I could throw fire.

"You're the one who stopped me! Keep your pathetic, lizard tail away, and I'll gladly leave."

His laughter booms in my mind. *I'm sure as our friendship matures, so will my impressive body.*

"What makes you think I would consider you anything more than a pile of scales and horns?"

Well, if you and Existence get along then I think we could too.

For a second, I thought I saw smoke rising from the corner of my eye, but it was gone in a blink, as if I had imagined it.

"You know Existence?"

He stretches his wings. *Yes. I can't go into detail regarding our relationship other than to state that she loves me although I irritate the ever-living fuck out of her.*

"So, she sent you with the message?" He nods his boulder-size head. "You could've led with that."

The princeling sits on his hind legs and lowers himself to lie down

Existence said it was time for you to move on from the past, and me telling you outright wouldn't have helped you let go of your grudge against my kind.

"You race killed my brother during the War over the Frozen Fire Highlands! We were making fucking progress, but the Queen, your mother, thought the thousands of innocent lives lost were insignificant and necessary to stop the war. Your kind took the only one in my life I'd ever truly loved!"

Tears threaten to spring free, but halt when the princeling begins to utter the words I thought I'd never hear.

On behalf of my mother and my race, I'm sorry for the loss of your brother.

He must've been taught never to say such a thing, especially since he's a royal, yet he offered me an apology anyway.

Thick, invisible magic floats around me like a pet wanting nothing more than to be loyal. My pain over the loss of my brother makes the allure of using the available magic more appealing. The thick magic embraces me like a hug, coaxing me to punish the dragon for what his kind took from me.

The princeling painfully huffs, then begins to shake, and falls to the ground as the magic whispers to me about taking something from him—a life for a life.

Wetness glazes over his emerald eyes. There is no hate or anger in his gaze but sadness and pain—not for himself but for me. The most powerful beast race in all of Earthradon is at my mercy, and he isn't fighting the magic, as if he's ready for me to ink his innocent soul with a debt he knows he doesn't owe me.

His compassion stops the progress of something trying to play with the trauma in my heart. He did nothing wrong. He isn't at fault. And I won't judge the princeling by the sins of his mother, his queen, or his race.

Heat pushes out from my soul, and shrieks of pain from a creature I can't see fill the air around us. The cursed magic unhooks its claws from my heart and vanishes. At the same time that I gasp for breath, the princeling does too.

Well, that was interesting. The princeling shakes out his wings. *Existence has a fucked-up way of teaching lessons.*

A laugh rushes out of me as I wipe tears away from the corners of my eyes. "You didn't know about what happens when you give an apology or show gratitude?"

I was told about it, and when I asked Existence if it was true, she told me she'd set up a first-hand experience.

Another laugh rushes out of me, but I cough it out instead. "She has good intentions."

When I see Existence next, I will tell her how much her lessons are both helpful and infuriating. Though I know everything she does comes from a good place of unconditional love.

He huffs in annoyance. *I know. I know. At least I wasn't the only one who was being taught a lesson by her.*

I walk over to him and extend my hand out, palm up, hovering above his nose. "I'm Freyja."

The princeling lifts his nose and presses himself into my palm. *I don't want to be known by the name my mother gave me because it carries the expectations of what she and my race expect from me. Instead, I'd like you to call me Starson, after my father.*

Starson's exhaled breath is a wave of warmth as I rub his nose. Dragon scales are supposed to be rough, but his are as smooth as his voice.

He lifts his nose up and to the side, so my hand slides over his mouth and under his chin. I massage the muscles where his neck meets his mouth, and he becomes putty in my hand. Another rule he didn't listen to: Never expose your neck.

Not that I'm not enjoying your warm, nurturing touch, but we need to get going. Climb on.

"Isn't it against the dragon code to let someone ride on your back?"

My words don't stop me as I eagerly climb up and straddle the back of his neck, behind his crown of horns. He also has a much shorter neck than most Dragons.

I don't uphold my title or the rules of my overinflated, mighty race. You can blame my actions on being young or influenced by Existence, but I see what my race is becoming, and if I can't lead them to change, then they will all fall deeper into corruption for power instead of being one of the leadership races that helps to maintain peace like the Wolven.

My first act of rebellion was killing my guards to come here. My second is bringing you to Camp Ariella. Whatever is going on with the Father, the queen has told us not to act or investigate.

"Starson, what you're talking about and doing could get your wings clipped. You know that right?"

He stands up and turns his head toward the last hour of the night sky. A relaxing breath escapes him.

After a moment, he turns his head to the side, allowing me to see his emerald eye. *If we all are destined to die, then I'm going to listen to my soul because it's one of the only good things left in my life.*

His words sing to my soul. "I'd be honored to be called your friend."

Ready to have some fun? His tail wags behind me—a very unusual dragon indeed.

With an enthusiastic nod, he walks to the edge. I grip his smooth horns and clench my thighs.

After a couple of powerful flaps of his wings, he leaps off. A thrilling scream rushes out of me as we drop for an exhilarating moment and soar.

Each beat of his wings pushes us toward the horizon, leaving Crescent Island only a small dot behind us.

The rush I experience when I free fall is nothing compared to this, and the calmness of the ocean makes it appear we are traveling through an endless tunnel of stars.

I bet I can make you scream even louder.

Do it!

Starson tilts his head up, and we climb toward the endless sea of stars in the sky. We level out for a moment, then he tucks in his wings and nosedives down to the ocean.

My soul screams and burns with the power of a tornado, drowning out Skjoldr's nervous cries.

The air begins to scald my lungs and eyes. Shadowy-star magic comes out and covers my face before thinning so I can see.

If it weren't for the tugging of where my cloak is secured to my body, I wouldn't have known if it was still attached.

My armor rattles against my body. The blue-black hue starts to become a lighter shade as the dusting of stars begins to make me blaze like starry-blue light. Magic hums over every inch of my body and Starson's. His scales act in a similar manner as my armor.

Starson's horns pulsate a current of magical energy under my fingertips, numbing my hands. and mixing with the magic already in my reserves.

Blue, starry-fire blazes up my arms—Obliterations' star fire power.

Then a bright light glares in my eyes as we approach the ocean's surface—a blazing ball of light. Our descent towards the water is like a comet soaring through the stars.

At the last possible moment, Starson expands his wings and skims across the surface of the water.

My armor and his scales return to normal, and the fire is extinguished. Only my memory and the fullness of my magical reserves are the only soul-shocking proof of what I just experienced—unparalleled and invincible magic.

Cries, screams, hollers, and laughter rush out of my lungs as the adrenaline high explodes my nerve endings and brings me into a state of blissful peace.

For the first time in five hundred years, all of my resentment and anger have been reconciled, and I am grateful to my brother for saving me as I admire the sunlight rising on the horizon. Instead of being reminded of the lonely pain of what the day will bring, I'm filled with the love my brother was never able to say to me with words but showed through his actions.

CHAPTER

ELEVEN

CRACK OF DAWN (SIX HOURS UNTIL SOLOAR NOON)

Rich hues of reds, oranges, and pinks peak out on the horizon, painting the serene sky bloody—it's a deadly dawn.

Existence's message plays in my mind: What will I be late for?

This trip would've taken me hours; Starson took less than one. He flew faster than I ever thought possible for a Dragon. Maybe it's because he's smaller and has a wider wingspan, but the heavy breaths he's taking make me glad we're not going much further.

We fly towards the lighthouse off the coast of Camp Ariella.

The camp was named after the Atlantean Queen who traded her life to save her stillborn son. King Adom not only commands the most powerful army in our planet's history, but he is also the first ruler to unite some magically imbued races and beast races. His kingdom is the largest in all of the world and is home to not only the Atlanteans but also the Lyons, Harpies, Tauruns, Nymphs, Animal Spirits, and Wiccayens.

When the war broke out, Adom did not hesitate to open his land as a neutral zone for everyone to seek care and healing. He's the leader my brother aspired to become.

We aren't greeted by the sweeping oyster firelight from the lighthouse. *Something is wrong.* These buildings are located all along King

140

Adom's border, either in water or on land, and are always manned to keep track of visitors.

There is also no sign of the Kraken, Hafgura. Ink stains the water as proof of his being here, and only as we approach the beach do I witness the horrors Odin must have witnessed.

The sand is littered with debris from demolished ships and bodies.

Blood stains the water closest to shore, and each wave pushes up more evidence of the assault the Kraken unleashed on all who tried to sail here.

The port is destroyed, as is the stone gate welcoming all to the haven. A raised walkway was built so no one would have to traverse jagged rocks and sinkholes to get to the camp inland, but now the road is gone.

Since Odin said to enter through the forest, I direct Starson to follow the shore until we reach the Iroko tree line.

This forest surrounds the Great Willow Tree for miles and is guarded by the spirits of the Atlanteans' ancestors, which is why only those of the race or Nymph race should enter because their magic can tolerate the influence the spirits whisper.

With the sun rising from beyond the tree line, little rays of light peer through the thick forest and will at least help me navigate through it. I'll have to keep my mind sharp to push off the influence of the spirits.

After pushing the irritation I have towards my husband aside, I try to contact him through our brand as we land on the beach. My brand warms but nothing else. The hope of locating him is lost if the connection between us is disabled.

After strapping my armor back on, I try to call Heimdall, and again, I am met with silence.

I'm not attempting to eavesdrop, but it's difficult since you're trying to contact your mate and friend through our mental channel.

"I thought I was using my telepathic messaging." He shakes his head. "Is being in the channel blocking me from contacting anyone else?"

Normally, yes, because it's a secured channel, but when you tried to contact your mate and friend, the barrier went down to allow someone else to come in against my will. My senses, however, are picking up a disturbance in the magical current and wavelengths here, so that might be the reason why you can't get ahold of them.

"But that doesn't explain why I can't get ahold of my husband."

No matter what mates can get ahold of one another. Starson tilts his head to the side so he can see me. *Do you not sense your connection to him? Because I can.*

"I don't know how you can sense my bond to my husband without touching my marital brand."

Reading a mate's aura is a sixth sense that I have, thanks to my soul's evolution as an adolescent.

"I think there is something wrong with your sense. Whatever you're reading isn't accurate because my husband and I aren't of a race; we are gods. There is no aura."

Are you sure? You're feisty enough to be considered a race.

As I dismount Starson, Skjoldr jerks me forward, wanting to be off him, and I almost stumble. I disguised my unsteadiness by leaning into his neck to pet under his chin again.

"You should probably rest a bit before you fly."

Yeah, I'll make a fire circle. He turns his attention to the horizon and sighs. *And I don't need to rush either, it's not like I have a home to go back to.*

"Go up north to the Norse Lands. We have many mountains and cliffs that a dragon could make a home. I wouldn't mind you as a neighbor."

The muscles around his eyes twitched, the dragon's equivalent of someone blinking to process what was said to them as if they didn't believe it.

He tilts his head back toward me. *Do you mean that? What about your people?*

I wrap my arms as best I can around him. "I do mean it. If my people have an issue, I'll ease their nerves and tell them you're just a playful baby dragon," I tease.

Starson pushes into me. *I'm a two thousand years old. I am no baby.* He shakes out of my hold and then huffs air in my face, eliciting a laugh.

When I fly up there, I'll shift into my humanoid form to not cause any alarm.

"Don't feel pressured to shift if you don't want to. If you run into anyone, tell them you're a friend of Goddess Freyja. It might be a shock to them, but they will trust the words you speak." I walk to the front of his face and press my forehead into his nose. "You have helped me more than you know, Starson. Thank you."

He rubs his nose against me and growls. *That cursed magic is weird.* His scales tint red for a moment, and an invisible creature lets out a shriek. *They are as bad as leeches.*

After another hug, I make my way into the forest as Starson creates a circle of fire for him to regain some of his strength. My eyes must've played a trick on me as his fire appeared to have a coating of stars for a brief moment.

* * *

Second Hour after Sunrise
(Four hours until Solar Noon)

With another swipe over my marital brand, the magic reacts the same as it has been—my skin warms, then nothing happens—aside from knowing that Odin is alive and well, it seems as though none of the other functions of my marital brand are working.

For the fifth time, I fasten my armor.

A voice of doubt tries to whisper into my mind that maybe Odin was one of the dead bodies on the shore. But the brand on my skin tells me that he's still alive.

Another voice of guilt tries to talk me into turning around and pulling all the bodies onto shore and giving them a proper burial.

When a voice of panic tries to enter my mind, I finally figure out that the thoughts and feelings stirring are from the influence of the forest around me.

Stronger rays of the first-morning sunlight peek through the trees. The camp is due east, and I've been hunting to find the direction of the sun.

I accelerate to a run.

Crisp morning air helps to soothe my concern as I pump my arms.

Soul magic fills my body, boosting me to go faster. If the trees weren't so close together, I'd fly through.

Besides my steady breathing and the sound of my boots against the forest floor, the forest is abnormally quiet.

I can't focus on anything other than dodging the blur of the ash-gray and auburn-brown trees.

When I enter a thicker canopy of branches and leaves that blocks my view of the sky and casts thick dark patches on the ground, I swear one of the shadows follows me.

A solid object appears out of nowhere, we collide, magic zaps me, and I land hard on my back.

Something in front of me groans and then laughs. "I think you broke my back, Freyja." His easygoing voice is familiar.

When I roll to my side, an ache comes from my lungs. Each inhale makes my throat as dry as if I had eaten sand. A flutter of magic tickles my neck and chest, instantly reversing the ailment. *Bless you, Lady Amora.*

A man in gold-plated Greek armor lies on his back in front of me as I sit up.

He tilts his head to the side, meeting my eyes. "Perhaps you could carry me in exchange for bringing you to the others?"

"You wouldn't have suffered any injuries if you tried to get my attention rather than use your body as an obstacle, Hermes." With a grunt, I push myself off the ground and walk over to offer him a hand. "I'll carry you if you tell me what the fuck happened here."

Hermes' winged cape is covered in dirt, along with his short blonde hair, but the scratches on one side of his olive-skinned face have my full attention. *Who tried to claw his face off?*

He looks me over for a moment before taking my hand in his. "That sounds like a deal to me." He works the stiffness out of his shoulders after I pull him up. "I've been tasked with keeping watch in the woods and safely guiding everyone to the new rally point."

Many questions tumble over my tongue, fighting to be asked first, but when warmth comes from my marital brand, one question is pushed to the front of all the others.

"Have you seen Odin?" Saying my husband's name out loud leaves me breathless, and only until Hermes answers me will I be able to function.

Hermes pulls a water skin out from under his cloak and offers it to me. "Don't worry, Freyja. You'll be with him soon."

Though I don't need it, I extend my hand to accept Hermes' offering—

Shadowy-star magic attacks the waterskin, knocking it into a smaller tree before I can touch it.

"What was that?" Hermes stares at the tree in disbelief and curses silently.

The magic comes back into my hand as the small tree begins to weep as if it's falling asleep.

My instincts alarm me to get away from Hermes as Skjoldr hums in my chest.

A ghostly cold replaces the heat coming from my marital brand, as if the sensation I felt from it a second ago wasn't truly there to begin with.

"Hermes." Fire blazes in my chest as my soul magic waits for my command. "Why were you trying to drug me?"

His smile has vanished, and in its place is a calculated intensity, as if he had prepared for something like this to happen.

Hermes lunges for me as a massive beast of fur and teeth collides with his body.

Growls and howls come from around us, and in moments, I'm surrounded by Wolven.

Four ten-foot-tall beasts with claws and teeth capable of tearing the scales off a Basilisk and breaking the bones of a Dragon, snarl and begin to circle.

The Wolven who attacked Hermes are out of sight, but the Gods' screams and pleas for his life echo against the trees.

All my knowledge of living with the Wolven comes back to me; if they thought of me as a target, they would've attacked by now.

I take count of what bloodlines are circling me. Since there are five, making up a scouting unit, one of each bloodline should be here.

An Echo, a Delta, a Charlie, a Bravo, and an Alpha. Their eyes are their giveaway. Echo has ember, Delta has black, Charlie has green with a bronze halo around the iris, and the Bravo has royal blue with a silver halo. The Alpha must be the one killing Hermes.

Only the Alpha and Bravo bloodlines have tints of their eye colors in their fur, while the rest have variations of browns, blacks, reds, and grays.

The Bravo's fur color is familiar—blueish-white fur with silver streaks—but I can't recall a name.

I should be severely concerned as to why the Alpha attacked a God and is most likely ripping him into pieces because, unless the Wolven had probable cause, it's against the law.

Gods can only be killed if their believers make a unanimous vote, since they are the ones who wanted them to exist. Dying from illness, a natural disaster, or fighting in a war doesn't count since the likelihood of survival is out of anyone's control.

Only the Wolven and Dragon races, known as Peacekeepers, are legally allowed to kill a God. If the Alpha doesn't have a legitimate reason, they would be sent to Excilum for eternal punishment. However, Hermes hid his true intentions, and I would give my testimony on the Alpha's behalf. Zeus is going to have a field day when he finds out his son was violently murdered.

If the Wolven hadn't shown up, I'd be torturing Hermes for information. I'm sure whatever is going on, the Wolven have as much insight as Hermes did. The race only dispatches units if they are sending patrols out.

Judging by the way their heads move and their noses flare, the Wolven are talking to each other through a channel that no magic can infiltrate.

Not one takes their eyes off me; all are tense. Until their Alpha comes back, all I can do is stay calm, keep my ground, and focus my attention on the Bravo. If the Alpha gives any commands, he will be the first one to act.

They stop circling me, and three take a step back while lowering their heads a fraction. The Bravo is the only one who doesn't follow suit. His attention is most likely on the approaching Alpha, watching and waiting for their signal.

A strong huff of warm air blows on the back of my neck. I'm neither surprised nor startled by the Alphas' sudden appearance.

Those of the Alpha bloodline can move without being heard unless they want to be.

My instincts and Skjoldr tell me to turn and lower myself to the ground as a display of respect. The fire in my soul, on the other hand, begins to pulsate as if she's purring. *Could it be?*

Casually, I turn around and come face-to-face with the Alpha. He stands taller than the rest, with eyes that are a passionate shade of purple with a gold halo.

Alarms blare in my mind as my nerve endings fire off pain from his Alpha aura. My body is telling me to look away, back down, surrender, and plead for my life, while the fire in me rises to the challenge of wanting to test this familiar Wolven.

I slowly raise my hand, keeping it off to the side so he sees it approaching him. As I near his cheek, snarls come from behind me, and the Bravo lets out a gruff growl, silencing them.

A familiar warmth of strength, courage, and trust that I haven't experienced since the death of my brother fills my soul, and I bury my fingers into his black plum fur.

My old friend lowers his head, and I lean forward to press my forehead against his, and we both let out relaxed sighs.

"Hello, Bralyant."

He rubs his head against mine and then presses his nose into the crook of my neck. I wrap my arms around him and allow my stress to be soothed away by the steady beat of his powerful heart.

His form shifts, fur becomes smooth skin, muscular arms wrap around my waist, and a warm face presses into my throat, inhaling my scent.

For a selfish moment longer, I keep my face against his chest and my arms wrapped around his neck to enjoy the natural peace I've always felt around him, one that reminds me of my brother.

"Freyja, I've missed you." Bralyant's rich voice of liquid gold caresses the parts of me where our bodies aren't touching.

Even after centuries, my body still responds to him. A blush fills my cheeks, and I pull away.

Wolven can not only sense emotions but also smell pheromones. I'm not ashamed of being aroused by him; it's a natural reaction, but I can't shake off my nerves about the audience we have. He's going to have to explain why he has a friendly relationship with a Goddess and why she is getting turned on.

Knowing he's naked, I keep my attention up even though the fire in my soul wants me to look to see if he is affected by me as well.

His well-built muscles are defined by his warm, golden skin. Plum highlights shimmering with gold are scattered through his curly black hair, which rests on his shoulders; he grew it out.

Bralyant's lips turn up, and his smile makes my knees wobble.

His hands rest on my hips, and my armor does a horrible job of buffering his warmth from caressing my sensitive skin.

"Did you injure your hands?" Bralyant gently caresses my wrists, sending a sizzle of warmth down my spine from his tender contact.

"No, that happened previously. But I'm fine now."

Something to my right diverts Bralyant's gaze, saving me from having to explain my injuries and I pull them free without drawing his attention back down.

Bralyant grips my chin and turns my head the other way. A silent snarl reveals his fangs. I'm about to ask him what's wrong when the annoying feather brushes against my bruised neck.

He turns my face forward, and his eyes pierce mine with his Alpha stare. I bite back the explanation hovering on the tip of my tongue. I owe him nothing.

Bralyant made himself very clear before I broke up our unofficial relationship. *"You are not a Wolven and sneaking around is all we can do, Freyja."* Decades later, when we ran into each other during the War over the Frozen Fire Highlands, I justified our time together as my farewell to him before I decided to focus on myself, as Freyr suggested I do.

We saw each other again after my brother's funeral. And the night we spent together left me confused. I wrote him a letter about how I needed to be alone to grieve and promised to write him again once I knew what I wanted. Any dreams I had for a future with him were shattered when I unexpectedly received a letter from him. I've tried to bury the memories and feelings I had for Bralyant ever since, but now that he's in front of me, everything is resurfacing with a vengeance.

With a yank, I pull my chin out of his grasp. "Everything was consensual, and don't make my gift a bigger issue than it needs to be."

My old friend relaxes his shoulders to show his unit he's calm, so they can be too. However, his other hand is back on my hip and grips me possessively.

"Did you acquire a new friend?"

Judging from his attention still being on the feather, I know his question is more about the Harpy, but the remark works for this scenario as well.

I tailor my words to answer the question of whether he was referring to the Harpy or Hermes as my newly acquired friend.

"Not in the least. But you got the opportunity to attack Hermes before I could."

I push against him playfully, so I can be at a healthier distance away, keep his hands off me, and hopefully convey we are nothing more than friends to the four pairs of eyes staring at us.

Even though our relationship was never official and is over, if the Wolven King felt like punishing his younger brother, he could still accuse him of intermating, earning Bralyant a chastity harness for a century.

A pleased smile returns to his face as he focuses back on me.

He shrugs while folding his arms across his chest. "The God needed to be taught a lesson about not touching what doesn't belong to him. My teeth left an indelible imprint on his soul."

A part of me wants to ask: And who do I belong to? But I push it away and play with the feather in my hair.

"Are all of your lessons deadly, Alpha?"

For a split second, his attention becomes hungry as his eyes flit down to my lips, but he pushes off my taunt as he rolls his shoulders, puffing out his chest.

"All who've been coming into these woods to get to the camp have been drugged and taken." *Back to business—good boy.* "The races were able to communicate with each other to follow the river inland to avoid being ambushed. The few Gods we were able to save couldn't send out the message because your mind links are compromised. I dispatched units in these woods to find others, but we haven't had any activity in the past couple of hours—until I caught your scent."

The fact he still knows my scent is concerning, though my soul purrs with joy.

I plant my hands on my hips to steady my worry about the possibility of Odin being taken. His being drugged would explain why he isn't responding to me.

I take a deep breath to stop my mind from trying to turn my suspicion into the truth. Even though I'm contemplating wanting to leave Odin, I still care about his well-being.

"Do you know why Hermes was trying to drug me?"

The muscles in his jaw tense. "They are taking all the Gods and Goddesses to a guarded location to either join their side or be put to sleep, so they don't get in the way."

The barrier I was just building to keep my suspicions about Odin away and the one I had already built when Heimdall was questioning Thor's intentions with Faithless are both beginning to crumble.

"Join their side for what?" Low growls come from around us.

Bralyant takes in a sharp breath. "To kill the Father."

My heart beats like a war drum. Each beat punches holes in the barriers, and my suspicions flow out and change into truths.

Fire fills my veins. Flames cover my vision. Smoke comes out of my nose. I can't tell if I'm breathing in oxygen or magic.

Strong hands grip my shoulders. "Freyja, we need to get back to the others. Everyone will listen to your input on how we should go about attacking the traitors, or as we've been calling them, the Unfaithful."

I ignore his words and pull out of his grip. "Where is Thor?"

My voice is not my own anymore. The dangerously powerful fire in my soul is taking over, and Vahildra isn't here to push her back into the cage.

Bralyant doesn't respond right away; his Alpha nature is probably urging him not to answer my question and instead command me to obey his order.

A low growl emanates from the surrounding Wolven at the show of perceived disrespect. He silences them with his own, the alphas call demanding their submission.

He takes a step toward me, lowering his voice. "I just learned that Thor sides with the Unfaithful."

Bralyant knew that wasn't the answer I wanted, so he told me what he was willing to tell me. *Fucking alphahole!*

"Where? Point me in the direction." Keeping the growl out of my fiery voice is difficult.

The gold in his eyes flared, showing me his dominance, but a flicker of concern softens his eyes as he searches mine.

"I haven't been able to infiltrate their wards. What makes you think you can?" *Again, deflecting.*

"I'll figure it out like I always do. Since you won't point me in the direction, I'll find it myself." I bite out.

Bralyant's growl is directed at me this time. Numerous snarls sound off around us.

The tension in the air for a fight ready to break out is thickening. Bralyant isn't giving me what I want, and I'm not going to wait around to be attacked by the Bravo.

"Heimdall told me if we found you, to bring you to him by any means necessary." *Heimdall wasn't taken then.*

Bralyant closes the distance and gets into my personal space. Heat pours off his body as if he's about to shift. He towers over me by half a foot, but his height doesn't intimidate me into backing down.

"And you can either ride on my back or," The corner of his mouth quirks up. "I'll carry your limp body to him."

My soul betrays me as she changes course in an instant and screams for him to bite me, and my eyes betray me as well as they immediately drop to his mouth. Bralyant doesn't miss how my attention shifted to his full lips or the unsteady breaths I'm taking.

He leans down to my ear and whispers. "Ride me for old times' sake?"

His sultry tone tells me all I need to know—he still desires me, but like he stated in his letter: *It's not enough—you will never be enough for me, so why should I waste my time?*

When a sob tries to rise to my throat, the darkness in the back of my mind rushes to the forefront. Smoke devours the memory of Bralyant's letter, granting me strength to fight back tears and relieving me from the claws about to sink into my heart. *Now, Freyja, push him away.*

Bralyant positions himself an inch from my mouth, waiting for my response. Rather than give it to him right away, I take a healthy step back. The heartbreaking sorrow and longing deflate me, but the anger

I've relied on to keep any emotion away from my diseased heart doesn't rush back in. Seeing, touching, and talking to Bralyant only awakens my desire to be loved and makes me forget what he wrote me.

Even though we are a safer distance apart, I can only nod my head.

With a wink, Bralyant's muscles shift and reform with his bones while the silver-tongued voice in my mind suffocates the darkness then shames and scolds me for being an unfaithful wife. I couldn't agree more. I've violated the emotional parameters of my vows, not only in this instance but on countless occasions when comparable scenarios with Haidion occurred, tugging at my emotions to desire someone other than my husband.

My soul pulls back into her cage, I surface, and the temperature around me cools.

Bralyant is once again covered in plum-black fur. Some rays of sunlight come through the canopy, highlighting the gold brushed in.

He lays down for me to mount, and when I'm straddling his wide frame, his muscles flex beneath me, making my core throb. I tightened my grip on his fur, hating how responsive my body is to him.

He barks out a laugh and takes off into the forest, his unit following closely behind.

CHAPTER

TWELVE

THIRD HOUR AFTER SUNRISE (THREE HOURS
TO SOLAR NOON)

If Lady Amora hadn't given me that mint liquid, I'd be asleep by now. Being on the back of Bralyant is a smooth ride. I was tempted to lie on him but decided against it to avoid overheating him anymore than I already am.

As we run alongside a turquoise river, memories of the two of us wrestling to push one another into the water lighten my mood.

Every time Bralyant and I would meet, we always chose a spring, lake, river, or ocean so he could cool down after a long run.

I push the memories away when they remind me of all the passionate sex we had against rocks and trees, in the soft grass above the stars and by a campfire, and in caves hidden by a wall of water.

I curse and mentally kick myself in the ass for allowing my mind to find some sense of happiness. Until I reach the camp, I won't know if Odin has been taken and drugged. The only silver lining I should take comfort in is that the Gods who are not choosing to kill the Father are only being put to sleep, not to death.

Another unit of Wolven emerges from the tree line on our left. As we make our way further down the river, three more units join us. Bralyant leads the pack as everyone else filters in as if they had performed this merging a thousand times.

153

The watchtower, marking the center of the camp, is in the distance, on the other side of the river.

"How are we going to get across?" As the words leave my mouth, a rock path comes into view. "Are we going to cross up there?" Bralyant neither huffs, meaning yes; nor snarls, meaning no.

When we ride past it, he tenses under me. The blueish-white Bravo Wolven gets alongside us, nudges my back, and then lowers his head. I get the hint and lay flat.

A sigh of relief comes from Bralyant as his Bravo keeps pace with him.

A second later, glittering magic rises from Bralyant's fur and comes over me like a blanket. *Is he camouflaging me?* Out of the corner of my eye, I see the same magic emanating from the Bravo and a couple of other Wolven by his side.

Shadowy-star magic grows under my hands, then goes behind my shoulders as a distant whizzing sound alerts my senses to something coming.

Yipes of pain come from the Bravo and a few others from behind us. Arrows stick out of the Bravo's back and sides, but he doesn't slow and keeps his attention on me. When I try to turn to figure out what he's staring at, he barks at me, and I stay down.

Bralyant growls under me and pushes himself to run faster.

More distant whizzing is followed by another wave of arrows coming down on the Wolven. The urge to help is shot down by another growl from the Bravo, as if he knew what I was thinking. The blueish-white Wolven makes me suspect he knows me. I wasn't close with any others besides Bralyant, so no name rings a bell.

The river curves up ahead, going to the left. Hundreds of arrows litter the ground. On the other side is a rock wall that makes up the base of a hill. Given the sharp turn, Bralyant should be slowing the pack down, not speeding it up. To make it across to the other side is too far of a leap, and there is no flat ground to safely land on.

I place my trust in my friend and rub my cheek against him, so he knows I'm okay.

As we approach the curve, the whizzing of hundreds of arrows sing a dreadful melody, promising pain and a slow death. The way my ears are picking up the arrows must be due to Vahildra's hearing enhancement.

We fly through the air after Bralyant leaps right before the edge of the river.

The rocky wall comes up on us fast, and we are greeted by portal magic and darkness.

Bralyant grunts under me as we land, and similar sounds echo from behind us as the rest of the pack makes it into the dark tunnel.

Heavy pants fill the silence and a moment later are replaced by groans and curses from males and females.

Someone scoops me from under my shoulders and pulls me off Bralyant just as the muscles between my legs shift from fur to skin.

After I'm set down, heavy breathing comes from behind me. "I owe you, Watson." *Watson? That name sounds familiar.*

Watson pulls his arms away from me as Bralyant gently grips my shoulders and pushes me forward.

"Five-minute break. Then we are moving on," Bralyant hollers from behind me.

Another set of commands is most likely given by his Bravo. *His voice is familiar too.*

When I pushed my memories of Bralyant away, I must have done the same with anyone else I had known.

Only after the voices behind us are muffled does Bralyant halt us from walking any further into the endless darkness.

His warm breath is next to my ear. "Did any of the arrows get through your armor?"

I didn't realize I hadn't been struck at all. "I'm not in pain."

He sighs with relief. "I'm going to pull them out. Tell me if you feel anything."

After thirty clinks of an arrow landing on the ground, Bralyant turns me, and I'm wrapped in his arms, cocooned by slick, warm muscles. He presses his nose into my neck, breathing me in, checking to see if I'm okay without asking.

I wrap my arms around his torso. "Want me to check your back?"

When he buries his face into the crook of my neck more, I trail my hands up as far as I can to inspect him for arrows or wounds—nothing.

"Why didn't we go to the camp?"

After he takes a deep breath, his nose runs up my neck to my ear. "Camp Ariella is overrun by mortals siding with the Unfaithful. Instead of turning the camp into a slaughterhouse, we moved everyone through the Atlantean tunnels. Since the Unfaithful have ill intentions, they cannot enter."

"Are we going to Atlantis to meet with everyone else?"

Only a fraction of King Adom's kingdom is above land. The majority is underground through tunnels leading to many cities that make up Atlantis, the second-most secured territory in all of Earthradon.

Bralyant's lips grazed my cheek. "We are taking this detour, then going through the Seedling Woodlands to get to the new rally point, the Valley of Souls and Sonnets."

"The Nymphs opened up their lands?" Excitement pumps through me.

I haven't been to the Seedling Woodlands since I was made into existence. The forest is potent with magic and history carved into the hollowed trees.

Then the Valley of Souls and Sonnets is where the Nymphs go to replenish their magic and sing. The water is said to heal the body but also the soul, exactly like my healing power.

Bralyant sighs and presses his forehead against mine. "Did you see the grief sky painted when you came in?" I nod. "The Nymph race was in the Seedling Woodlands during Lunar Noon, performing the ritual to bless the start of the Vernal Equinox for a flourishing spring. Their wards are said to be the most powerful, nearly impossible to break like the ones in Excilum. The traitorous Gods and Goddesses broke through, killed them, drained the spring, and set fire to the woodlands. We didn't find any survivors. They are all gone—extinct."

My shaking can no longer be contained.

Strangled breaths escape me.

Bralyant holds me tighter. "What can I do to help you?"

Footsteps approach us. "We are ready when you are, Alpha."

"Lead the pack, Watson. I'm riding ahead to scout." Bralyant's order left no room for negotiation. "I'll get you out of this darkness, I promise." He whispered against my ear, then kissed my forehead.

After a huff of acknowledgment from Watson, Bralyant pulls me behind him and wraps my arms back around his waist. His muscles and bones shift under me, and soon I'm on his furry back.

A hand squeezes mine. "Don't explode your magic yet, Freyja. Save it for the battle ahead."

Watson's helpful words not only keep me focused on not magically erupting but also remind me of a similar conversation we had in the past. Bralyant was injured during the war, and Watson talked me down from taking my rage out on the Wolven King for not allowing me to visit his brother and redirected my focus on what I could do, which was find the Dwarven who tried to harvest my friends' bones.

More information comes back to me; Watson was also the one who covered for Bralyant when he ran off to be with me and watched over his tent while he healed so we could have time together.

"Thank you, Watson." My words are barely audible, so I squeeze his hand back and hope all my gratitude for what he has done for me is conveyed.

With another squeeze from Watson's hand and the brush of his thumb over my knuckles, I know he heard me.

I find it odd that there wasn't even a hint of the invisible cursed creatures' presence when I muttered the words of gratitude.

I lay on Bralyant's back and tightened my hold on him. After he lets out a howl, we run into the darkness.

A cool, enveloping mist surrounds me, and I'm coaxed to allow the air to drain me of my emotions. I give in, needing to focus my energy on what lies ahead.

* * *

Fourth Hour after Sunrise
(Two hours until Solar Noon)

Bralyant didn't just want to scout ahead; he is giving me time to process. Watson's advice echoes in my mind, and I hold onto it as if it's the only tether keeping me from erupting into a storm of fire and ice.

As we passed through the Seedling Woodlands, the traitorous Gods and Goddesses really tried to see if fire could wipe away their birth sight, but memories can't be erased unless we choose to stop finding value in them.

Thick rain clouds block out the sun and cast a soulless gray on the depleted landscape. The willow trees are nothing more than piles of ashes. There is nothing left that would give any clue that this place was once a bountiful forest created out of magic and love.

The Father didn't want to force the mortal race to believe in him. He listened to their prayers and sowed seeds to create hundreds of willow trees. When the trees reached maturity, the magic system heeded what the Father wanted, and a God or Goddess was carved out of the trunk.

Even though the trees matured, the magical, immortal beings who would serve as the God or Goddess the mortals believed in were only adolescents. The Nymphs raised them all until they reached adulthood.

Freyr told me about his time living in these woods. He thought he was one of the last gods to be created since there were no more Birthing Willows left in the forest. However, the tree he was carved out of didn't hollow like the others. There was enough magic left to create another. The Father told him that if the mortals of the Norse faith wanted another God or Goddess, then he would use Freyr's tree, and in return, Freyr would have a sibling. I was the last god created. Freyr took me home right away, and I was raised by him and our people.

Ever since my birth, children of the gods are born the natural way rather than by the Father transplanting the soul into a Birthing Willow. To create a god took an immense amount of magic, and even a powerful being like the Father has his limitations. If the mortals wanted another god to be brought into existence, the gods would have to give portions of their magic to have the child. Without doing so, the child had a higher chance of coming out mortal.

My mind drifts, wondering if Odin would've given a portion of his magic to our child without hesitation, as I would have done, but I push the thought aside. There are many more important things to be thinking about, like how Earthradon would function without the Nymphs since they cared for the growth of all living things, fertilizing the vegetation with magic along with the air.

We pass by a field of massive piles of ash that still emit smoke and are large enough to have been a village. Given its location in the center of the Seedling Woodlands, this was the Temple of Virbrantrea that Odin told me about, the previous Capital of the Historian Guild Race, and the sanctuary where the Gods and Goddesses were raised and taught about Earthradon's history, the races in the galaxy, and all the Deities.

Freyr told me the thickest trees in the forest surrounded the temple, and each one was carved to represent an immortal race on Earthradon. One for the Fae, Wiccayen, Elven, Dwarven, Mage, Necromancer, Atlantean, Animal Spirit, Vampyre, Dragon, Wolven, Taurun, Lyon, Harpy, Pixie, Nymph, Phantom, Ghoul, Basilisk, Spyden, Scorpion, Siren, Kraken, and all the other Oceanic races I don't know off the top of my head.

The immortal races were brought into creation in a similar way as the Gods, but it was the Father who designed them. One of the largest roots from the Father's tree was in the deepest trench of the ocean. The Father commanded the root to grow into three wombs. Once they matured, a great earthquake snapped them off, and the current carried them to the surface.

One womb ruptured while still submerged, and the immortals that swam out became the oceanic races. The second womb reached land and ruptured once it hit the soil. Those who came out became the land-dwelling immortal' races. The last womb kept floating in the sea, and the outer layer hardened like a shell. The Father sent his sons and Existence to break the immortals free. After a tornado created out of elemental magic was formed, the shell ruptured, and the immortal races that emerged all had wings.

The creation of mortals wasn't thought of by the Father, but by the evolution of organic matter learning how to survive on Earthradon. At first, the magical bacteria only transformed into plants and animals; then, after a couple of decades, mortals came into existence.

Some groups of mortals evolved to wield magic. They eventually formed their own races, and the magic system gifted them with immortality if they continued to respect magic. For a while, the beast races didn't acknowledge the magically imbued ones.

Evolution played a big role in advancing and enhancing all the races, sometimes not for their betterment. The Elven race for instance started as a magically imbued group of mortals and is now extinct because of their greed. Some of the Fae became more humanoid than beast. All the beast races lost respect for them, considered the Fae race as part of the magically imbued, and fought to take their lands. Existence told me there was a war before the Gods were brought into existence. The Wiccayens, Elven, and Atlanteans came to the Fae's aid to help them reclaim their lands, but the Fae fought them as well, not wanting to be associated with the magically imbued races.

Existence and her sisters fought to keep the peace alongside the Wolven. Before the Dragons could be called, the Father's son, Oxy, who holds the elemental power of air killed thousands. The war ended, and the son was punished by eternal sleep. His brothers willingly followed suit, so the races wouldn't fear them too.

Following the war, the immortal races who lived on land were divided into two groups: beast and magical. Races that are magically imbued are not segregated, as the Fae wanted them to be. Even though beast races have humanoid forms, they cannot wield magic in the same way.

Only six magical races remain after the extinction of the Elven, Dwarven, and Nymphs followed by the Mages' departure after learning of the approaching asteroid.

Since Freyr raised me in the Norse Lands, I missed out on exploring the Temple of Virbrantrea and the education the Nymphs provided. I've always wanted to see the place where everyone else grew up, but once a god leaves, they aren't allowed back. Only the words of my friends painted the mental picture for me, and now the image I have is ruined.

"Why would the Gods destroy such a sacred place like this?"

I regret asking the question as my throat begins to swell and a cold heaviness settles over my eyes. Bralyant can't answer me in his beast form without experiencing pain, but I couldn't hold back my thoughts any longer, or I'd lose control of the tether to keep myself magically grounded.

My forehead warms as if something hot was just pressed against it.

Bralyant suddenly winces and turns after sniffing something in the air. He slows and begins to paw at something in the ground. Only when something clinks against his nails does the burning pain subside and his muscles relax.

With his teeth, he grabs the item and turns his head as far back as he can go. I scoot up and pull the amulet out of his mouth. The metal has turned black, but the integrity of the amulet was not affected by the fire. A Willow Tree is carved, but without using some type of magic to restore the amulet, I can't make out anything else.

We only go a little further until we reach a slope. Stone steps zigzag down the side of the hill and to a dried-out spring, with a Colosseum of Weeping Willow trees beyond. The Valley of Souls and Sonnets.

Bralyant lays down, and I hop off. He shifts back into humanoid form and reaches for my hand holding the amulet.

"I need to get this to my father. He will know how to restore the amulet better than I can. If you want, I can ask him if you can have it so you can have a little piece of what the temple was."

His kind, thoughtful offer has me pushing the amulet into his hand as if I'm repulsed by it. I'm already going to have an item that represents death and destruction when I find Thor. Two would be too much for my heart to handle. Accepting his offer also won't help my soul avoid falling back into the grooves I've been trying to smooth out since I moved on from him.

"Everyone is down there?" I point to the Colosseum.

Bralyant nods and does not press me to explain my sudden shift in mood. "All who are still faithful to the Father even after the news broke of his plan to cleanse our world. Earthradon might not require an asteroid to rid our planet of greed, but that doesn't mean the Father is deserving of death. For all we know, killing the Father and harvesting his magic might spread greed even more."

"I agree. Who is on our side?"

"The Allied Army, but they and King Adom are still hours out. I brought four thousand Warrvenors, and my brother and father recruited another thousand volunteers from our race. Five hundred or so Atlanteans that were guarding Camp Ariella. Twenty-five hundred Spartan officers. And a few dozen other Gods and Goddess." His head dips. "One of my units gave their lives to discover the strengths of the Unfaithful."

I place my hand on his shoulder. "Their sacrifice will not be in vain."

He brushes a wisp of hair away from my eyes. "Did I ever tell you how much I love your eyes?" I stop breathing and shudder as his fingers trail down my neck. "You must've been blessed by the ancestors of my race."

When he goes to lean in, I lower my hand to his chest and push against him. "No. I was carved out of a tree to be the Goddess my people believed in. And I will die being the Goddess they believe in. Perhaps when I'm killed by either the upcoming battle or the asteroid, you'll realize that your conspiracy of me being tied to your race in some way will finally disintegrate."

If I had a pebble for how many times Bralyant thought of some way for me to be recognized as a member of the Wolven race, I'd be able to fill the dried-out spring. The only time he hadn't brought it up in conversation was when he wrote me.

His brows pinch together. "Who's to say you aren't going to be saved?" I turn to walk away, but he grips the back of my neck, pulling me back to face him. "And you are so much more than a Goddess. Freyr spoke to my Father, brothers, and me several times about how the Gods could be more than what they were created to become."

I relaxed into his hold, wanting to hear more about what my brother had told him. Then howls come from behind us, and they are answered by more coming from the valley.

Bralyant turns his head in the direction of the pack coming from behind us. I snapped out of the trance I was falling into. Anything about my brother always lowers the shield wall I keep around my heart.

With him being distracted I twist out of his hold and descend the stone stairs. Only when I reach the bottom do I look behind me. Bralyant is still at the top, looking down to where I stand.

My brother never once spoke to me about his theory of the Gods being more, but Bralyant hasn't given me any reason to not trust his word. If we weren't about to head into war, I'd want him to tell me everything my brother told him. His relationship with my brother is one of the main reasons why I can't fully cut him out of my heart. A portion of Freyr is within him, and I'm desperate to have any semblance of my brother back, even if it's just his words.

Wolven close in behind Bralyant. The clearest picture of why we can never be anything more than friends. It was silly for us to think all those centuries ago that we could not only find a legal way to be together but also avoid another scandal like what happened with his oldest brother. I hope this picture is enough for him to finally put an end to his fantasies of trying to keep finding a way. *But why is he still trying even after stating the reality of our situation in the letter he wrote me?*

Since the valley is depleted of magic, it would be wrong to fly across. The Wolven must think the same thing, because when I glanced over my shoulder, they were all shifted into their humanoid forms, had descended the stairs, and were running like I was.

After parting the weeping branches, I enter the moss-covered roots making up the Colosseum. Three-quarters of the levels are filled by naked Wolven; a section is for the bronze-armored Spartans; another is for the elegantly detailed vine armor worn by the Atlanteans; and the few dozen Gods and Goddesses are in the center, along with what must be the Captain of the Atlantean unit, the Wolven King, the Alpha Regent, and the Beta Prince.

Heavy pants come up from behind me. Bralyant stands at my side with the other Wolven at his back. He meets my eyes before taking my hand.

"All rise for Goddess Freyja!" His command is echoed and silences all the chatter.

Before I can hiss at him that now is not the time for proper etiquette, all eyes are on us, and cheers fill the Colosseum.

As all the Wolven applaud me for reasons I don't understand, Bralyant leads me towards the center.

The Wolven behind us are led to join the others by Watson. He gives me a small smile, lighting up his caramel skin and short, midnight-blue hair.

"Freyja!" Hel shrieks as she collides with me, ripping my hand away from Bralyant.

A snarl comes from him as she chokes me with her tits. Her hugs would be motherly if she didn't have such a big rack on her chest.

"I'm so glad you made it here." She releases me, but only enough to allow me to breathe as she addresses Bralyant. "I appreciate you staying out in the forest longer than you were told to."

An irritated male voice silences the Colosseum. "The Goddess is the reason as to why you disobeyed my command, brother?"

A small wince tenses Bralyant's body as he turns his attention to where his brother must be. "Not disobeyed, only delayed." He shrugs off his brother's Alpha command. "I also bring insight into the strength of the Unfaithful."

Someone pries me away from Hel, but only to pull me into their chest. "Did Thor take the weapon?" Heimdall whispers in my ear.

I nod against his shoulder since he isn't giving me a chance to breathe either.

He silently curses and steps away. "You need to share what you found out as well."

Heimdall's rainbow eyes are framed with dark lashes and warm brown skin. His diamond-plated armor doesn't take away from the sternness in his presence, which leaves no room for argument on me trying to convince him to tell everyone about Faithless.

He steps out of the way and raises his arm to stop Hel from crushing me with another embrace. Her protective blue eyes and fair skin remind me so much of my brother. Hel and Freyr were best friends; she stood by his side and helped raise me.

Hel's leather armor leaves nothing to the imagination, and her braided black hair could double as a weapon if she got the right momentum.

As I walk by Hel, she smiles with all the words and affection she wants to express, then nods her encouragement toward the center.

I take in the other Gods and Goddesses first and find three of my friends, but I'm hit with a harsh reality when I'm not greeted by a loving pair of arms.

"Where is Odin?"

Hera approaches me with confusion, her motherly aura enveloping me. Her gold-plated armor has lost its illuminating sheen, along with the bronze hue in her honey skin, and the gold strands in her brown hair. Even her sepia eyes are without their glorious glow. Either her soul magic is depleted, or this is the result of the Nymph race's extinction.

"Didn't he tell you?" She glances at Bralyant, who is just about to come to my side.

"I told you he wouldn't." Isis fixed her gaze on Bralyant, and her cunning voice was tinged with cool bitterness. "Freyja wouldn't have come here if she knew her husband was taken." She meets my eyes. "Artemis' servant dragged me here kicking and screaming after I was separated from my husband during the attack on Camp Ariella. How he was able to magically subdue me is a different story."

Isis throws a hiss over her shoulder before she walks towards Bralyant like a predator who just found her next meal. I pull her in for a hug instead of witnessing my friend start a battle we don't need to be having.

"The important thing is our husbands aren't being harmed. They might be drugged, but I know they are safe." I pull away and undo my armor on my left forearm. "If anything happened to Odin, I would know."

Isis places her hand on my brand as if I held a looking glass for her to see that Osiris is unharmed and safe. Tears threaten to leave her golden eyes as the magic in my brand comes to life, pulsating with the calm heartbeat of my husband.

Allowing Isis to sense my husband is the least I can do since she and her husband didn't choose to create a bond when they married. I don't blame them; the process was complicated, and I honestly don't remember most of it.

I let out a sigh of relief when her attention doesn't linger on the patches on my palms or when she doesn't inch her fingers up any higher. She might not be able to see the brand Zachariah gave me, but if she brushes her fingers over the back of my hand, she will be able to read the debt.

After a deep breath, she straightens herself. "We're going to tear these traitors limb from limb for taking our husbands away." Her golden eyes flitted over to Hera. "I'm warning you now; don't get in my way when I see Zeus."

Hera grins and extends her left, naked forearm. "I only ask that if you see him before I do, you drag me along so I can watch."

The absence of Hera's marital brand is all I need to know; Zeus also betrayed us, and she divorced him. Giving Isis hope is what's keeping

Bralyant from becoming her next meal, so if I need to remain united with her on wanting to save our husbands, I'll keep my thoughts of wanting to leave Odin to myself. An enraged Isis is not the beast we need to be dealing with right now.

Her gold armor dress makes her look both like a queen ready to address her people and a ruthless Goddess who would bloody every inch of her jade-black skin and thick ribbons of dark raspberry hair to protect those she loves.

Bralyant's eyes were on my marital brand, until I caught him looking as he walked past us, towards his impatiently waiting brother.

Every God and Goddess I pass by nods to me, and I return the respectful gesture.

Artemis is leaning against her servant, Aliith. The natural dusting of bronze on her olive skin and gold highlights in her warm auburn hair are dulled. And like Hera, her armor lacks magical luster.

Her crisp autumn eyes meet mine. She gives me a warm smile as she combs her fingers through Aliith's Wolven fur, which is as black as a void. I'm surprised she didn't tell him to shift into one of his other forms to not mock the race that outnumbers us.

Aliith was one of three to receive an Alpha power from the previous Wolven King, Auxiliary, before he was forced to step down.

Auxiliary was Bralyant's eldest brother and took the throne after their father lost his leg. I met him when Freyr first introduced me to Bralyant, and he allowed me to live among the Wolven to learn about their culture.

He had a soft spot for me and Bralyant's friendship and even looked the other way when he caught the two of us together. It made more sense why he didn't punish us when he told his people that the Fates pulled him towards someone who wasn't a Wolven but a member of the galaxy race.

He chose his fated mate over his people, which resulted in his being exiled from the race. Even though he had proof that the Fates blessed their bond, he and his mate were forced into hiding.

When Bralyant's second older brother, Relynt, ascended the throne, he didn't receive all the Alpha powers; three were missing. Auxiliary gave them away believing his brother would become corrupt with power.

All were given the genetic makeup of what a Wolven is. Aliith was given the Alpha power to shift his size from an ant to a mountain, an Animal Spirit was given the Alpha power to open portals to transport thousands of warriors, and the third was the Alpha bite to penetrate any material, but no one has come forward to have it.

I walk by the Atlantean Captain who stands tall in her vine armor, with the crest of the Father on her chest. A cosmic Willow Tree glittering with stars. Her flawless cherry-black skin accentuates the gold stenciling on her hands, neck, and face and brings out the rich hue of her brown eyes. The design mimics her armor and covers every inch of her body. Though she is a foot shorter than me, she stands proudly and has my utmost respect above anyone else for being a part of the Allied Army. Being united is what we need to do today.

Since she has gold stenciling, she's not only a Captain but also of the royal bloodline. I mentally curse at myself for not remembering her name.

The Atlantean Captain nods to me, and I admire how tightly she braided her black hair to her scalp. After giving her a nod back, I turn my attention to a pair of eyes I've felt on me since the moment Bralyant grabbed my hand. Bralyant's Father, Yrradiant, the Alpha Regent of the Wolven.

The Alpha Regent has a softer expression, tanner skin, a lighter pair of purple eyes, and gray strands in his plum-brushed black hair given his older age. Yrradiant may have stepped down after his injury, but he can still run just as fast as anyone else in his race. His position was only created after the uprising Auxiliary caused when he left. Since Relynt held no title other than being the King's son and then the King's brother, the majority voted for the King Senior to be his Regent.

Yrradiant nods at me, and I return the gesture. Next to him is the Beta Prince, Treason, Watson's Father. With little to no age lines on his charismatic face, I would have assumed Watson and him were brothers.

Treason is second in command of the race and the enforcer of all the rules, laws, and punishments, along with protecting the King and his family. Even though he is of the Bravo bloodline, he and his family are respected as if they were Alphas. He's the only white Wolven of the pack and was said to have been blessed by either a Celestial or a powerful Mage when he was a pup. He served for Yrradiant, then Auxiliary, and now Relynt, making him the longest-reigning Beta Prince in Wolven history.

Treasons' thick hair is silvery-blonde and wavy, with longer strands curling against his neck. His frosty-caramel skin accentuates his tough and muscular physique, even though his aura is angelic and compassionate. I am wary of his presence, yet I want to get closer to him.

The Beta Prince has a kinder expression as well when we lock eyes. His are more sapphire-like, giving the silver halo a resemblance to freshly fallen snowflakes on a glimmering lake. Lips the lightest shade of pink curve into a smile that almost sweeps me off my feet. His raised brow tells me that he knows I was a second away from making a not-so-graceful fall as my way of acknowledging him. Heat crawls up my neck as we nod to each other.

Lastly, the Wolven King, whom I purposely chose to acknowledge last, is Relynt.

I'm not of his race, and he shouldn't be staring me down as if he is entitled to my respect and that I should give it to him because of his rank. This is the only time I'm glad to have the title of Goddess because he is a second away from choking on his cock before I kick him so hard in the groin that it will get stuck in his trachea if he doesn't nod to me.

Disdain is written all over Relynt's face, as if he is aware of his brother's and my crime of intermating. He's leaner with a sharper jaw, shorter hair framing his wider forehead, and an attitude that says you should be grateful to be in my presence.

Bralyant being the Wolven King's younger brother doesn't grant him a title; he earned his position as Commander of the Warrvenors, the elite army of the Wolven.

Naturally, by being born into the Alpha bloodline, Bralyant already had respect from most. However, he not only had to prove himself to be seen as the higher-ranking Alpha of his bloodline but also showed exceptional leadership qualities to earn the favor of being selected. He's held the Commander position longer than his brother has been king.

Treason brushes Relynt's arm when he doesn't nod, and he is met with a snarl from the king, without moving his attention away from me.

"Do I need to remind you, my son?" Yrradiant might not have the bark of authority he once had, but his aged voice carries centuries of wisdom that deserves respect. "If it wasn't for Goddess Freyja and her brother, long live Freyr."

All the Wolven repeated the phrase "Long Live Freyr!"

"We would've lost hundreds more Wolven, yourself included, if they hadn't run into the mountain to warn you all about the Dragon's early arrival and then protected your escape when the fire rained down." Yrradiant addresses all who are looking down on us. "It was Freyr who shielded the entrance to the cave with his elemental air magic to redirect the flames as Freyja threw ice spikes at the Dragons and shot three of them down."

Howls fill the arena, followed by chants of my brother's and my name. "Long Live Freyr! Long Live Freyja!"

Yrradiant looks back to Relynt. "You give her and the memory of her brother the respect they deserve, if not as Gods, then at least as selfless beings. It was Freyja who risked her life and it was Freyr who sacrificed his life for our people!" The Alpha Regent's voice might have cracked, but the weight was that of a hundred thunderbolts.

All the Wolven stand and howl. The Atlanteans bellowed their hearts out to chant their creed of love and loyalty to serve the Father. Clanks of swords being slapped against shields followed by stomping of feet come from the Spartans. A chorus of gasps comes from the Gods and Goddess behind me, and a war cry comes from Hel as she chants Freyr's and my names.

I can't stop the tears from falling as I keep my gaze fixed on the king, who refuses to recognize what my brother and I did for his people while he fled with his tail between his legs.

When Relynt snarls at me, my cold tears of grief and pain turn white hot with rage.

"Why should I?" Relynt's Alpha power painfully forces all who are cheering to be silenced. "You might have helped us in the past but look at where we are now! The Gods have gone too far, and all of them deserve to die. If you all weren't created, we wouldn't have to worry about an asteroid coming to wipe us all out. I'm looking to the future, and you," he points his finger at me, "are the reason our blood has to be spilled to cleanse the sins you force us to pay!"

Muffled voices of agreement come from the Wolven, but he doesn't acknowledge them and keeps his eyes on me. "The Father was wrong to trust the Gods and Goddess to keep the secret of the asteroid that's coming. Goddess Athena's servant spilled the news to Zeus. Oh, you didn't notice Athena wasn't here leading the Spartans. That's because these are the ones who remained Faithful while the others attacked Camp Ariella. Athena sides with the Unfaithful alongside her Father Zeus, the most powerful elemental-wielding God on Earthradon, and the second-most powerful, Thor. He betrayed the Father's trust, and if my ears heard right, Thor has some type of weapon now."

"He wields Faithless," Heimdall answers for me.

Growls, grasps, and anxious voices fill the Colosseum. Apparently, all but me knew what Faithless is capable of.

"I went to the Domed Armory to see if Faithless had been taken, so we know what we're up against." My voice felt fragile, but whatever power was in it made all watching from above shush each other to be quiet. "And I joined the Preserver Guild." I don't know many rules, but revealing one's membership in a Guild is common knowledge; however, I'm not concerned right now. "I only need to be within eyesight of Thor, and I can call Faithless back."

Muffled voices were getting excited, until the Wolven King spoke, painfully silencing them all again. "Would you sacrifice yourself, like your brother did, to save the Father to obtain the weapon and prevent it from falling into the hands of the Unfaithful?"

Without hesitation. "Yes."

An evil smile spreads across his lips as if he hoped I'd say that. "Then here is what you are going to do." He begins to approach me slowly. "You are going to willingly allow me to blood-brand you." Angered voices echo, but when Relynt growls, they all fall silent. "The brand will be you giving your life to get Faithless to me. If you die, the magic of your final wish is powerful enough to bring me Faithless. But if you live, you'll get on your knees so I can chop your head off. Then my race will hunt down every last God and Goddess until we bring you to extinction. With your blood spilled to cleanse your sins, the immortal races will be free to live on." He doesn't stop approaching me until he's an arm's length away. "I've always put my race's duty first. I will bring peace, and we can't have that unless you all are gone. My spirit soars for the betterment of Earthradon. Does your soul sing the same or are your words meaningless?"

The bite in his words would make anyone fall, but I stand by some strength I didn't know I had.

Not agreeing would be tarnishing what my brother stood for and what he had taught me. Inking my skin with proof of my word only strengthens my commitment to them. I'm not going to argue with him about blood-branding me because I would proudly wear my devotion to the Father; he can put it on my face if he wants.

My decision, though, affects all the Gods and Goddesses at my back and beyond. I already accepted my death, while they may not have. Out of all the Gods here, only Hel, Heimdall, Artemis, and I were told by the Father about the asteroid. Agreeing to this will shock my friends more than what they've already experienced. But if I allow what they think of me to get in the way, I'm letting down all those who believe in me, including the Father.

Today is also not going to be the day I allow an arrogant king to belittle the sacrifice of my brother. I'd rather scream about how Relynt exaggerated an injury by not coming to Freyr's funeral to pay his respects on behalf of the Wolven race. Bralyant snuck out with Watson while his legs were still healing to be at my back to push my brother's ship into the water.

I won't play into Relynt's taunts, I'm going to be the Goddess I was created to be, one whose words hold the power of her allegiance to not only the Father or her believers but to all life. I'll prove to everyone in attendance that I chose to offer every soul on Earthradon the same opportunity in life that my brother gave me.

The silver tongue in my mind tries to persuade me not to do this, to think of my husband, our marriage, and the possibility of having a family. My voice overpowers her for the first time in centuries.

I only have one question I need Relynt's assurance on. "What of all the mortals who believe in the Gods, what will you do to them?"

Relynt tilts his head to the side and thinks for a moment. I'd rather stand here in silence as he ponders my question. I prefer a well-thought-out response to a hasty decision based on hatred. Just because mortals believed us into existence doesn't mean they should be held accountable for our actions.

"They will not be harmed as long as they keep the peace. And even if they do break the peace, I will not punish them with extinction. I will vow this to you on my soul."

That's all I need to hear. My pride, ego, and stubbornness leave my body as I fall to my knees.

THIRTEEN

Strong hands catch me before I break the connection with Relynt's victorious eyes.

"You are forgetting something, brother," Bralyant growls from behind me.

Relynt's gaze darted away to Bralyant, severing his Alpha power over me, which I willingly submitted to.

"And what is that?" Relynt's voice is laced with hostility, as if he's warning Bralyant not to say what he has planned.

"Any Preserver member can break the contract with a borrower as long as they have honest intentions. That means you and I can both call Faithless."

Relynt's eyes narrow on his brother as his fangs extend past his lips.

Bralyant hands me off to a pair of waiting arms. "I've got you, fierce one" My brother's nickname rolls off Hel's tongue, but I hear Freyr's voice speak to me.

Hel backs us away and supports me until I can stand on my own again. Heimdall comes to our side; his eyes are sparkling, seeing all the possible outcomes of the coming conflict about to unfold before us. When he doesn't usher us away to escape danger, I relax into Hel's embrace and admire my unflinching friend.

"Just because you refuse to acknowledge that we are a part of the Guild doesn't mean I do." Bralyant takes a step closer, making him nose-to-nose with his brother, his king. "I'll take the punishment for revealing our bloodline is bound to the Guild, but I will not have you sacrifice someone else for your cowardice. Oh, you didn't know that Freyja told me about you being the first to run out of the mountain instead of inside with her and her brother to save your race. If my legs weren't broken, I would've been at their side until every last member of our race was out! And if I recall correctly, the Father said some Gods and Goddess are to be saved; who's to say these Gods and Goddess who are here to fight with the Faithfull aren't the ones he is going to choose? You would place the full blame and condemn them all to death. If they are even a fraction as selfless as Freyja was a moment ago in accepting the blood brand, then it is your blood, not hers, that must be spilled to cleanse our world!"

Bralyant's head jerks to the left—blood coats Relynt's claws. "You will bring Freyja back to me and stand down!"

Everyone stops breathing.

The weeping branches above stop swaying.

Thunder rumbles overhead as the air thickens, waiting for the tension to spark and trigger lightning.

Shadows creep in from the corners, joining all who lean forward, eagerly awaiting to see if Bralyant will crumble under the Alphas' command or fight it off.

"No. I challenge you for the Wolven crown!" He spits blood on Relynt's face.

Before my eyes can fully register it, Treason is between them with a firm hand on each of their chests. "On what terms will it be decided upon who loses?" His gruff voice of wild arousal and longing for liberation accelerates my realization of what is about to occur, conjuring images of Bralyant limp and broken at my feet.

Bralyant and Relynt growled their answers at the same time. "Death."

Howls erupt, triggering a shock to my soul.

Watson jumps down from the first level, heading towards Bralyant, as a few other Wolven follow him to escort everyone but the two Alphas and their Bravos out of the arena.

Hel tries to pull me away, but I fight against her hold and cry out my friend's name.

Bralyant whips his head toward me. Four slashes are across his face, thankfully missing his eyes. His enhanced healing is already drying them out, but since it was done by the king's claws, he will have scars.

Heimdall throws me over his shoulder, pins my arms to my back, and carries me away. I can't move to shimmy out of his hold. Hel tries to soothe me, but I can't hear her voice as my heart and soul try to break free of my body to get to him. *What would I even do or say if I did?*

As I struggle, Bralyant flashes me an amused smile. I still in Heimdall's arms when my friend pressed three fingers to his lips and then to his forehead—he loves me.

Hel presses a hand over my mouth as I try to scream the words I thought every time my brother made that gesture to me: *"Say it out loud if you mean it!"* My muffled voice only makes Bralyant wink at me before turning back to Watson.

No. He can't possibly love me. Why would he write that I would never be enough for him and that being with me would only be a waste of his time? Maybe it's because he might die from this fight that he is thinking, *"fuck it."*

I'm not released until Heimdall chooses a spot in front of the Spartan army. Hel sits on my other side, boxing me in. A thought came through of leaping over the railing to get back into the arena. As quickly as the idea came, it vanished when a magical barrier was placed so no one could interfere with the battle.

A cool mist brushes against my leg, calming my erratic, pounding heart as if the air drained the emotion out of me. My enhanced hearing picks up a dog whimper from below. Something moves between my feet, and I blink away what must be my eyes playing tricks on me as I imagine a shadow sliding under my feet.

The last to leave the arena is Yrradiant. He must have spoken some heartfelt words to Bralyant as I watched them embrace. When he approached Relynt, they placed a hand on each other's shoulders, clearly displaying a lack of emotional relationship—*wait, he was walking as if he had two legs.*

Someone leans into me from behind. "When Yrradiant was elected

Alpha Regent, Relynt argued that due to his father's handicap, he wouldn't be an ideal leader for his people to look up to or a good representation as a strong figurehead to other races."

If I could take Bralyant's place in this battle, I would make Relynt suffer a thousand deaths before allowing his soul to ascend.

"Yrradiant was enraged, but instead of reacting like his asshole son wanted him to, he chose to redirect his energy by demonstrating to Relynt that he didn't have to be whole to fulfill the duty. To further prove his point, he had a Mage enchant his prosthetic leg to make it invisible." This stranger's thick, charming voice sends goosebumps up my spine and makes Skjoldr hum in my chest.

A male whom I've never seen before sits behind me. He has black eyes with a darkness that most will turn away from for fear of falling into a void they can't escape. I'm leaning in closer to get a better look at the familiarity in them that my soul recognizes, as if the two shared a similar trauma. What is most intriguing is that this happened back when Haidion first showed me his true identity. I didn't know what it meant then, and I don't know what it means now.

I refocus on his features. His smoky, umber skin defines his long frame. When there is only skin, I avert my eyes from trailing any further and wonder why a Wolven is over here and not with his race.

I'm about to ask who he is when I notice Artemis fussing over the longer lengths of his coily, mineral-black hair. A white halo of thorns surrounds his forehead, and a band of stenciled white roses is around Artemis' right wrist.

"Aliith?"

He gives me a wink before nipping at Artemis's fingers. "I swear I introduced you two before." She flicks his ear and goes back to getting knots out of his unruly hair.

Aliith sits back, crossing his arms across his chest "In my more beautiful forms, never in this revolting one."

When Hel lifted my jaw back up, I realized I was gaping at his absurd opinion of himself.

Artemis finishes with his hair. "He would rather be covered in fur, but I need his arms around me right now. Cuddling before a battle always relaxes me."

With the flick of her left wrist, all her weapons and gold-plated armor sparkle before they are absorbed into her gold cuff, leaving her as naked as Aliith. Her muscles might not be as defined as mine, but her soft curves, succulent breasts, and bubbly ass are a Wolven's wet dream.

I raise my brows as Artemis sits between Aliith's brawny legs and leans back into his chest. "Only cuddling?"

Aliith wraps his arms around her and rests his head on her shoulder. "I might have willingly offered to be her servant, but that doesn't include any sexual assistance."

Artemis happily nods in agreement as she relaxes into him. "Virgin for Life Guild, right here." She gestures to both of them.

He licks her cheek, and she giggles as if she's the happiest woman on the planet. I face forward with a smile. They might not be together in a physical sense, but the chemistry between them is adorable.

Both the Bravos usher their Alphas on opposite sides of the arena. Each of them gives a pep talk as they attach enchanted collars around their necks.

Aliith nudges my back with his knee, and I glance over my shoulder. "Do you know what they are doing?"

I don't, and instead of turning away and possibly missing something, I stand and step up a level to sit next to him.

Hel gives me a knowing look that says, *"Just because you moved away from me doesn't mean I won't still keep an eye on you."* I stick out my tongue, and she returns the gesture. Heimdall's eyes sparkle, and a warm smile spreads across his face before he turns to look forward.

Artemis looks like she is about to fall asleep, and I'm tempted to flick her ear for being able to relax so soundly.

Aliith follows my gaze to his master, then back to me after placing a kiss on her forehead. "If she doesn't relax, she is going to explode. Apollo got taken out of her grasp, and my Goddess won't stop blaming herself."

She has the same guilt as me for not being able to save her brother. I press a kiss to her cheek, making her nuzzle into his chest more.

Aliith nods towards the arena. "The collars strip them of their Alpha powers and bring out the spirit of their beasts."

My body stiffens as my eyes widen. "Wait, they're going to be shifting into their true monster forms?"

He gestures to the group of Spartans with his eyes. "No. There are mortals present."

My internal pout must be written over my face, for Aliith mimics my expression, mocking me.

I roll my eyes, which makes him chuckle. "How do you know all of this?"

Knowledge about the Wolven race is only spoken through word of mouth, like the Dragons so he couldn't possibly have read something about it. Aside from the Father and his daughters, only those in the race know the extent of their magical capabilities.

A glittering aura surrounds his lips. "Auxiliary and I are friends. I'm one of the two beings he trusts."

He has more than just the genetic make-up of a Wolven; he also has the magical powers of a Wolven King, being able to make their voices only be heard by those they choose.

Knowing my voice can be heard, I keep my question vague. "What about the third?"

His eyes meet mine, and I can tell by his smirk he knows what I'm asking—who received the third gift. Unless some new information has been brought to light, Bralyant, his brother, and their father still have no idea. All three of them hounded Aliith and the Animal Spirit to tell them, but neither caved.

"I'll tell you, if you tell me something."

Magic tingles my lips, waiting to see if I will take part in the secrecy of exchanging information. Unless Aliith or I put a condition on when we can speak of the knowledge shared, we take what we learn to our graves and can only talk about it with each other.

He's never offered this to the Wolven royal family, and why he is choosing to share with me silences all the thoughts of whether I should or shouldn't accept this vow of secrecy.

"You are not breaking your word towards your friend, are you?" Aliith shakes his head. "Okay, but only if you also tell me why you are choosing to share this with me."

Magic coats our lips. The words we say will be translated into a language no one understands, but they will sound familiar enough to avoid suspicion about our sharing sensitive information.

"Auxiliary said I could tell a being who I believe will understand the weight of this secret. What you said in front of Relynt is all the assurance I needed. But first, my question." I nod and lean in, even though we don't need to be closer for the magic to work. "Why are you assuming you are destined to die?" His grip on Artemis tightens. "I have no resentment for what you were willing to do, my Goddess would've done the same. Apollo and she agree that all of the Gods should only be spiritual entities and not physical beings, so they aren't influenced by greed. But I have a theory, and I want to know why you think you are fated to die by the asteroid."

"I spoke to Obliteration. Do you know who he is?"

In addition to nodding, he slumps his shoulders in defeat. "He is the one who said you were going to die?"

Technically no, but I nodded because I accepted my fate. "I asked what awaits the souls of those who are destined to die."

He searches my eyes, as if he too sees something familiar. "You're assuming."

"No, I'm not. I was meant to die during the war." My brother not only saved me from being rained on by fire but also from being impaled by a Dragon spike—no armor can withstand that. "Freyr traded his life for mine, and I've been on borrowed time ever since."

"You seriously kept your chill when the Father told you about the asteroid coming?"

"I was angry at first, but only because I thought I had failed my brother and wasted the years he had blessed me with. But then I realized I had everything I wanted, and now I'm just waiting for the Fates to end the ticking of my soul."

"Do you want to hear my theory?" I shake my head and his discouraged sigh has me pulling away from him. "Artemis is right; you are fucking stubborn."

"The spirit of stubbornness inhabits my body. It's your turn to share. Who is the third being Auxiliary trusted?"

Aliith clears his throat. "What is your opinion on an item being considered trustworthy?"

"You're answering my question with a question?"

He arrogantly shrugs. "You didn't specify how I should answer you. And since I wanted to know your opinion, this is the best way to work around your stubbornness."

I crank my middle finger at him, and he tosses his head back with a laugh. "An item has no consciousness, even if it is blessed with magic, meaning it can't make decisions. So, no, an item is not trustworthy."

Did Auxiliary imbue an item with Alpha power? It would explain why no one has come forward claiming to have it and why Aliith and the other friend have remained silent so no one would seek it. They probably have it protected somewhere. And since I only asked "who," he doesn't need to tell me about its location, and technically doesn't need to tell me what the item is since that wasn't my question.

"Your logic is correct. Anyone can use an item unless it is enchanted or blood-forged, in which case anyone who picks it up can make use of whatever power it possesses. But the item isn't considered at fault and is protected by Preserver law from being destroyed."

I nod in agreement. "The wielder is at fault."

He leans back, making himself more comfortable. "The rules don't apply to this item because a soul does live inside."

I flinch and then gasp as an unknown cold energy surrounds me, as if trying to calm my nerves. "You're talking about a soul-forged item?" He simply nods and relaxes, as if this knowledge isn't fucking intimidating. "One exists?"

"Multiple. But we don't have any rules about them since no one plagued with greed has been able to wield them." Aliith lets a moment pass between us as I process this frightening discovery. "Would you still put the wielder at fault, or the item?"

"Well, at that point it's not an item; it's a being since they forged their soul into it." My brain is spinning trying to figure out what the law would be in this scenario. "But since their soul is in the item, they can't use it; their soul and their magic are only the fuel for the enhancement, durability, and revitalization."

Aliith nods. "Their soul is the heart of the item." His casual smile forms into an entertained grin, as if he's enjoying making me squirm. "But since they gave up their bodies to inhabit the item, what makes you think they aren't able to move?"

My blood chills as my soul tucks herself away, and Skjoldr hums, ready to sense a threat. "Like possession? Like what a Phantom can do?" He slowly nods. "In that case, the item is at fault if it moves on its own, but if it is used by someone, then no, but the item also has a consciousness to stop the wielder. That's a fucked-up gray area."

He warmheartedly laughs. "It's only your first day of being a Preserver, and your logic is on point. The Guild has gained a very valuable sister."

"How do you know I'm a sister?"

A symbol I've never seen before flashes over his forehead as a tingling sensation comes over mine, and in a second, they are both gone. "Our Governor sent out a telepathic message about a new sister at dawn. Anything you need help with, I'm at your assistance. And don't fret about revealing you are a part of the Guild but do keep your position a secret."

"Brother Aliith?" Even though he is relaxed and slumped, he proudly nods. "Yrradiant is a brother as well. His sons are on different levels of the seniority ranking system." He nudges my knee, making Skjoldr vibrate more. "So, do you think a soul-forged item is trustworthy?"

I massage the back of my neck to relax my jittery spiritual essence. "Still a no, but they have the consciousness to earn someone's trust." I stretch out my arms to chase away the sensation of some aura still wrapped around me. "But since soul-forged items do exist, there should be laws."

"Our Guild is working on it, but when Auxiliary gave the soul-forged item the Alpha power, the item can no longer be destroyed. Since an Alpha bite can pierce through anything, that means nothing can pierce it."

The weight of this conversation causes me to slump back and my mind to become mush. "If Auxiliary has trust in this soul-forged item, then we can only hope they don't do something stupid."

Aliith's attention goes towards the arena after he chuckles to himself. "I do hope so too."

Magic leaves our lips, signifying the exchange of information has been fulfilled.

A brand of secrecy is woven into our souls, and this magic is more powerful than my vow to Odin to share with him any knowledge I know that he's seeking. As for Aliith's servanthood brand, binding his soul to Artemis's, she has power over his soul, so she could ask him what he talked about, and he would have to answer. Also, depending on when he became a member of the Guild, she was either notified of his joining or knew he was in it.

Watson exits the arena as Treason goes to the center. "A fight for the title of Wolven King has been declared." A wave of howls goes around the Colosseum. "They have chosen to fight to the death." A beat of stomps and claps vibrates the seats and shakes the weeping branches, causing leaves to fall. "Wolven! Howl to our ancestors so the fight may commence!"

Treason runs out of the arena as the Colosseum booms with a sonic howl powerful enough to flatten a forest. The howls, chants, and stomps go straight to the muscles of the Alphas as if they became possessed by a monster to transform against their will.

In the middle of the arena, a ball of purple-gold light appears out of nowhere, silencing everyone. The magical energy hums and pulsates for a moment, then shoots into Relynt.

I clutch my knees. "That can't be good, right?"

Aliith rubs my legs with his. "It means the past Wolven Kings are choosing to watch through Relynt's eyes. I won't bore you with conspiracy theories about what choosing him could mean."

"Keep those to yourself." Aliith's chuckles only make me shake more.

Bralyant and Relynt leap forward on all fours and growl as their bodies shift the rest of the way.

A purple aura is around Relynt, and gold smoke leaks out of his eyes. Relynt shows all his fangs as he straightens to his full height.

Bralyant is a blur of fur and teeth as he lunges for his brother's exposed neck. They go tumbling back, and Relynt smacks into the wall.

All the Wolven gasp in surprise while Aliith's laughter fills the arena. "He didn't waste any time with formalities."

"Is that a bad thing?"

"A display of dominance is the normal thing to do, but since this is a fight to the death, Relynt was naive to think his brother would play by the unofficial rules."

Relynt is able to spin out before Bralyant can get his jaws around his throat. A yelp comes from my friend as the back of his neck is bitten and he's thrown across the arena.

Bralyant rolls as Relynt charges towards him. When my friend doesn't move, I scream his name as loud as I can. He spins and kicks Relynt in the jaw. An audible crack echoes off the trees as Relynt tumbles backward.

Aliith laughs and hollers with excitement, while Artemis sleeps soundly in his arms, unaffected by what is going on. I fight the impulse to pull my hair out and cry as panic thunderously pounds in my chest.

After rolling his shoulders and making them crack, Bralyant circles his brother. When Relynt struggles to get up, Bralyant lunges for his neck, but he stumbles over his brother. Relynt purposely fell back down to sweep Bralyant off his feet.

My friend is on his back with his paws up ready to slash Relynt in the face. But his brother doesn't go for his throat, he bites down on his back leg. A high-pitched yelp comes from Bralyant as he tries to slash at his brother's face. Trying to roll only causes him more pain, and purple blood begins to coat his fur.

My knuckles turn white, and my whole body shakes. I'm no longer spectating. I'm trying to figure out a way to help my friend.

Bralyant keeps trying to go for his brother's face, and I shoot out of my seat when I see a better target.

"His balls! GO. FOR. HIS. BALLS!"

Relynt released his hold, and I started to curse at myself for giving his brother the idea instead. A howl of pain explodes, and I almost cover my eyes to not see Bralyant's junk get ripped off. But it's Relynt's head that is turned up, and his brother is latched somewhere on his underside.

With a kick to Bralyant's face, he releases his hold, and his brother jumps away, allowing Bralyant to get back on his feet.

Shrieks come from a pair of female Wolven across the way. Others are holding them back from entering the arena.

Aliith elbows me as he laughs his ass off. "You just pissed off his mates."

When Relynt's mates can't get to their Alpha, both look to me with the promise of death. I flip them both off, which only angers them more.

Someone magically flicks my nose, and I find Hel staring at me with a pointed look that says, *"Sit down before I break your fingers."*

Heimdall pats her leg, and she stares her daggers at him; he chuckles.

On my own accord, I sit down when the two Alphas start to circle each other. Both are limping a little and leaving purple blood trails.

Aliith leans into me. "Since they are fighting for the title, they bleed their bloodline."

They launch themselves at each other. Relynt aims lower, nailing Bralyant in the gut. He falls back with a grunt as Relynt lunges to bite his balls. Another shriek comes from the arena as Bralyant rolls in time to avoid his brothers' teeth and kicks him in the face again.

I notice a dark-haired female Wolven pacing near Watson, her fiercely concerned gaze fixed on my friend. She encourages him, using terms of endearment as if she were his. *Did Bralyant find a mate?*

A howl of pain pulls me back to the fight. Bralyant is on his belly, and Relynt is on top of him, biting into his scruff. Relynt thrashes from side to side, drawing more whimpers of pain from my friend.

I'm leaping over Heimdall and bracing myself on the railing around the arena. Magic is in front of my face, but it's clear as glass.

Bralyant is yanked away, and I run until I can see his face again. Most move out of my way, and I ignore the few who curse at me for pushing them. I slide and almost stumble to the ground when I'm in Bralyant's sight.

His eyes widen when he notices me. I'm at a loss for how to help my friend. Relynt is going to snap his neck if he doesn't do something. Bralyant's strength is weakening, and he's losing more blood than his brother.

Tactics aren't what's going to help him. I need to say something that will tap into his reserve strength. But not just words of encouragement—a distraction like how he was able to redirect me when I wanted to fly off to find Thor. Maybe I can awaken my friend's soul to give him the push he needs. *Fuck, please let this work.*

I take a deep breath and scream. "You're a coward, Bralyant!" Relynt slows his thrashing, as if he prefers hearing my words to killing his brother "You are a coward for not telling me how you feel!" Bralyant is completely focused on me, as if he has forgotten he is fighting for his life. "If you truly loved me, then you would've said it to my face!" Everyone around me quiets down, and I'm sure I just caused more problems for him than I solved, but I don't know what else to say to set him off. "And maybe!" I've buried this confession for so long because I know we can never be together, but if he's going to die, he deserves to know. "Maybe I would have said it back!"

Bralyant goes limp in his brothers' mouth and cold tears rush down my face. No matter how hard I fought myself, Freyr helped to pull the painful truth out of me. Bralyant was my first love, and I will always treasure the time we have spent together.

He taught me what it means to be a loyal friend, how to convey my feelings without uttering a word, told me to never be ashamed of my body, empowered me to explore my sexuality, and stood next to me, holding my hand, as we watched my brother's ship sail away into the distance.

And what have I done since then? I've avoided him like the plague, attempting to forget about him entirely because he reminds me of the happiest times in my life. I should've written him back and said I understood and accepted whatever relationship he was willing to give.

I might grieve for my brother until the light of my soul dies, but I am done trying to hide my pain and sorrow over losing Bralyant and for what our lives could've been if we were able to be together.

I pray to the Fates that the next generation will be free to love who they want because it's the purest and most beautiful form of magic there is.

I start to mouth the three words to him when light explodes in his eyes, as if his soul was caged and is now finally free. Bralyant pushes off the ground, standing to his full height as Relynt rolls off him. He doesn't waste any time and grabs his brother by the scruff and throws him against the wall, causing the foundation to crack.

Bralyant grabs him by the scruff again and throws him away from the wall, then barrels into him until they are in the middle of the arena. With his front paws on Relynt's chest, he keeps his brother down and clamps his jaw around his neck.

Bralyant's fiercely blazing eyes focus only on me as he bites down.

Relynt's whimpers of pain and struggles to get free stop when the bones in his neck crack, and his body falls limp. I blink as many times as I need to assure myself that Bralyant is whole and alive, so the image of my brother's broken body doesn't replace what I'm seeing.

Screeches come from Relynt's mates as Treason and Watson leap back into the arena, then approach Bralyant with caution.

The Beta Prince is snarled at, unlike his son, who is able to keep approaching. While Treason lowers himself down in respect to the Alpha's threat, Watson comes up to Bralyant's side and rubs his head against his neck. Bralyant deeply growls but moves away from his brother.

Treason moves once Bralyant is far enough away. He drops to his knees and places a hand on the Wolven's neck. Only from my angle do I notice him muttering some words before closing Relynt's eyes.

"My brothers and sisters!" Treason rises to his feet. "When the moon rises tonight, so will the new era of the Wolven, with Bralyant as our king!"

Both of their collars vanish. The aura of energy around Relynt's body darts out along with tendrils of magic and shoots into Bralyant's chest. Light explodes from within him, and he howls with the might of a thousand Wolven, causing the Colosseum to shake and the magical barrier to ripple.

I'm leaping over the railing before anyone can stop me.

Magic passes over my body but doesn't push me back from getting through.

Only I can pick out Hel's voice shouting my name among the thousands of Wolven who are celebrating. *I guess not many favored Relynt as king.*

My name is bellowed out by a voice that causes the glass-like barrier to crack like a spider's web and then shatter a second later. Skjoldr hums her worry in my chest and leads me to believe Aliith was the one who called out my name.

Treason's attention swings to me, a look of worry on his face. His overpowering arms are wrapped around my waist in a flash, preventing me from reaching Bralyant.

"How the fuck did you get through?"

I throw him a question to divert his thoughts away from me. "How the fuck was Aliith able to—"

"Don't," he growls sharply, "Finish that sentence aloud."

My thoughts on Treasons' panicked remark about Aliith are

brushed aside as I fight and fail to break free from his grasp. "Freyja, stop! He's not himself right now."

His authoritative tone drills fear in me that only a father can instill, causing me to become putty in his arms. I let out a needy whimper I didn't want him to hear.

Bralyant's snarl pulls my attention to him. He lowers his head toward his friend while exposing his teeth. Watson stands still as Bralyant sniffs him. With a growl, he sends Watson to the ground, and then his attention jerks to Treason and me.

Treason pulls me behind him as Bralyant approaches us. He does the same thing to Treason, but instead of growling and forcing him to the ground, he nudges him to step aside. When Treason doesn't move, Bralyant exposes more of his fangs.

I direct soul magic into my hands and push Treason out of the way, causing him to stumble to the ground. Though I appreciate his protection more than he can imagine, I don't want him to risk his life for me. No one will ever sacrifice themselves for me again.

With nothing in between us, Bralyant steps closer to me.

Dried blood coats his jaw and stains his fangs; his fur is sticking up, making him appear to be larger than normal; his muscles flex with each breath, and fire blazes behind his eyes, making the gold halo radiant like the sun. The scars his brother gave him only add to his menacing demeanor. My friend is no longer with me—only the beast he's kept locked away.

The only time I've seen his beast was during the war, and he always ran off to calm down before coming back to me. He never wanted me to see this side of him, knowing if he sensed any fear in me, it would break his heart.

My instincts finally came back to me, screaming to run. Even my soul no longer recognizes this as Bralyant. Skjoldr ignites the fire in my heart, and magic fills my body with soul magic, ready to fight. When shadowy-star magic awakens in my hands, I tuck them behind my back, under my cloak.

A snarl comes from my friend and his Alpha power sends waves of pain all over my body. I fall to the ground as he growls above me. Heat explodes in my chest and fights off his Alpha power, but I stay down because I know if I rise, he's going to kill me. It was stupid for me to come in here.

Bralyant goes back to Treason, who is now kneeling. His concerned gaze is focused on me as Bralyant sniffs him again. Only when my friend bites Treason's shoulder, forcing him to shift, does he look away.

Without context, I think I know what just happened. The beast in Bralyant chose who he wanted as his Beta Prince. Even though it's stupid for me to think his beast would choose me, a pang still aches my heart, and I'm once again painting a picture of why we can never be together.

Both of them howl together, and all the Wolven in the Colosseum follow suit.

Once they are done, the two Wolven mates of Relynt jump into the arena and run to his dead body. One shifts as the other pushes his body on her back, then she shifts too and supports the weight of their mate. They snarled at me before walking out of the archway where I came in.

Yrradiant lowers himself down onto the arena and walks over to Bralyant. "Will you be requiring my services as Alpha Regent, My King?"

Bralyant shifts back to his humanoid form and Treason follows suit. "Yes." He places a hand on his Father's shoulder. "But first, go grieve your son and give him the burial he deserves."

A choked cry tries to leave my lips. Even though my friend sounds the same, I don't recognize the new energy in his voice. And I wonder what else will change about him.

Treason's attention is back on me as if he heard my inner distress. His sapphire eyes darken as a cool energy envelops me, attempting to soothe my saddened soul.

Yrradiant nods his thanks to his king, and tears of both love and sadness stream down his cheeks. He shifts and runs to the exit.

"Freyja?" Watson approaches me, his voice delicate with an element of worry.

As he helps me up, I wonder if he is upset that Bralyant's beast didn't choose him to be his Beta Prince. His small smile doesn't give me any hints, but I return the same gesture to him.

Watson's gaze shifts to his father. They must be having a mental conversation because Watson and Treason trade places.

Bralyant's eyes are turned down and closed. Before Watson can get Bralyant's attention, the Wolven King pulls him into his chest. My friend presses his face into Watson's neck and shutters. Watson doesn't hesitate to hold him as close as he can, rest his head on top of his, and run his fingers through his friend's hair. Bralyant's mother was the only one who was able to soothe him like that. I'm glad my friend finally allowed another to be the comfort he needs since his mother passed away before we split up.

Treasons brushes his arm against mine. "I told Bralyant he shouldn't have hidden his beast from you."

His voice catches me off guard, making me gasp. It's finer with the lightness of a romantic melody rather than gruff.

"I enjoy both of yours." The words escaped my lips before I could filter them. "I don't understand why I don't like the tone of his beast." *Why am I stumbling so much around this man?*

"It's because you're feeling deceived by him keeping something so important about himself from you."

The Beat Prince wraps his arms around me as the cool energy from the phantom blanket draped over my body thickens. Both prevent the fire in my soul from blazing. Treasons' embrace fills a portion of the lonely emptiness in my heart, and I relax into him. My inner beast calms from his affection.

"If comfort is what you need or want, howl my name, and I will come for you."

I curl my head against Treason's chest so he doesn't have easy access to my neck. I don't want him to sense my guilt. Not only am I seeking comfort from someone who has a mate, but I'm selfishly enjoying his arms wrapped around me and being pressed up against his chest even though I'm still—

Darkness slashes through my thoughts, silencing the silver-tongue for making me feel horrible about being hugged by someone other than my husband. *Don't feel ashamed. As for Treason's faithfulness, he's a respectful man who wouldn't do anything to hurt his wife.*

Treason nudges his nose on my brow, whimpering softly. "I'm okay." I lift my head and place a soft kiss on his warm cheek. "I appreciate your kindness."

He barely brushes his nose against mine. "You need more of it in your life."

The truth of his words has me pulling away and I'm relieved he gives me the space I need.

As I look away from the Beta Prince, I meet Bralyant's gaze. A hundred words are being said through his eyes, and I don't want to acknowledge a single one.

Before I can offer my condolences for the loss of his brother, he snarls at Treason. *Is he jealous?*

Bralyant takes a step towards me as Heimdall's voice bellows out. "The Unfaithful are on the move. They will reach the Father by Solar Noon."

Existence's message repeats in my mind, and the reality of what led us here takes priority over everything else. With Bralyant as the Wolven King, figuring out a battle plan won't be as difficult. During the war, Freyr and he wanted to unite everyone, but without Relynt's support, no one else agreed, and everyone fought under whatever pantheon or race they were a part of—except me.

Artemis' yawn echoes as she and Aliith jump down into the arena. "You said you have insight into the strength of the Unfaithful; can you share it with us?"

My friend is clothed and armored up, with an intense determination in her eyes, making the fallen debris move out of her way.

The other Gods and Goddesses drop into the arena along with the Atlantean Captain. Everyone forms a circle around us, ready to discuss our strategy. Bralyant doesn't move his attention away from me—not even to acknowledge the fact that he is the center of everyone's attention.

Bralyant takes a step towards me, and I take one back.

"The Father needs us, my King." Treason's voice has reverted to its gruffness from before he consoled me, but with a sharper edge.

"Tell us what we need to know, Alpha." My voice isn't my own, but the strength of my soul growling her command.

"I hope you're ready for a bloody fight." With the lift of his chin, his Alpha presence makes itself known, and my soul shrieks her battle cry, wanting to put him in his place. "And Thor is going to be the least of your worries, Freyja."

Bralyant's dual meaning in his words is only meant for me, saying we aren't done, and he isn't going to be holding back anymore.

CHAPTER

FOURTEEN

FIFTH HOUR AFTER SUNRISE (ONE HOUR TO SOLAR NOON)

I've cracked my knuckles numerous times to find some way to relieve my shakiness. Nothing I do helps, and the shadowy-star magic just goes back under my skin after I caved and asked it to block my nerves. Apparently, Haidion's magic isn't a cure for everything.

If there was water in the spring, the coolness would shock my body enough to give me relief and provide me with a natural portal to call upon the warriors in Valhalla. Since the spring is barren and we don't have a God who has elemental water magic, I'm on the search for a lake or river.

From Bralyant's report, our numbers aren't going to be enough.

The Unfaithful army has not only dozens of Gods and Goddesses but also thirty thousand mortals, a quarter of whom are Spartan. Along with four thousand Vampyres filled with Nymph blood, allowing them to be out during the day and influence the magic in the air. Vampyres can absorb whatever abilities or powers they consume from drinking blood. Most likely, the race will be used as a surprise counterattack. Three thousand Spydens and Scorpions. And three thousand Faeries, which puts us at a disadvantage since King Adom is still over an hour away and we won't have the Harpies to fight the air, leaving us defenseless from aerial attacks.

There have been no other sightings of other races coming to the

Father's aid. The only other support available to fight alongside us was the Valkyrie Guild. Since their job is to help defend the universe, I hoped coming to defend the Father would count. With Heimdall's telepathic power still working, he was able to get ahold of the commanding officer, but all are currently fighting in their own battle outside of our galaxy. Even if they dropped what they were doing, they wouldn't make it to us in time.

Our greatest strength will be in cleverly executing the element of surprise. All were open to my idea of having everyone ride on the backs of Wolven so the combined Alpha stealth power could conceal us until the last possible second. I earned a nod of respect from the Beta Prince, and he offered to let me ride him into battle. Bralyant almost tore Treason's head off for his suggestion.

After our plan was set, Bralyant sent Watson to intercept King Adom and tell him of our battle plan, and Hel went to the Seedling Woodlands to gather what she needed to create transportation for the warriors of Valhalla. Five thousand are at my command as Odin's wife.

"If only I can find water."

My heightened senses are tickled by the melody of flowing water, just as a breeze of fresh, moist air caresses my nostrils.

"Ask and you shall receive, I guess."

I push my way through a thicker part of the Iroko forest. Flying above the overgrown vegetation would make this hunt easier, but just like how Artemis needed cuddles before battle, I needed time alone and a walk to clear my head.

Apart from Heimdall, Hel, and Artemis, no other Gods or Goddesses have spoken to me since my display of willingly being blood-branded to fulfill the late Wolven King's conquest. All of them at least listened to my instructions on pairing up, along with reserving their magic until they were either faced with a Fae or a God, and not to use any magic when around a Vampyre.

All the Gods and Goddesses are armed with Atlantean weapons. The Atlanteans can create weapons out of nature. And now a pair of sickle-shaped, axe-like swords are strapped around my waist, along with a curved dagger. With wooden handles made from the roots of the weeping Willow Trees, the weapons on my sides are artistically detailed, with silver vines and gold leaves in the crystal stone forged by the sand at the bottom of the spring.

Hera and Isis chose to team up together and gave me small smiles after I gave them their blades. Artemis assured me they weren't mad at me. Along with being told that a secret was withheld from them about the Father wiping out a majority of existence, they also experienced the shock of the late Wolven King wanting to take the Gods' and Goddess' extinction into his own hands. I'm just happy they are still choosing to be on our side.

Athena's betrayal stings me more than Thor's. If I face her on the battlefield, my heart will be traumatized, but not as much as Aliith's. He has to face his sister, Moriya, since she is the servant of Athena. I can't imagine what he's going through, fighting your sibling. I'm sure if he has to kill his sister, then he and Bralyant will have something to bond over.

Before I snuck away to find a body of water, Bralyant and Aliith were in the middle of a heated argument about giving the Alpha power back since there is a new Wolven King. I wouldn't have been much help to keep my friend calm since I'm trying to come down from my irritation regarding Nyx.

Hera informed me that after Athena sided with Zeus, she had a vision of Nyx's future. The Greek Goddess of Night would go to any length to ensure that the only darkness that entered her life was caused by her divine might. Nyx paid the price without hesitation and was told that her participation in battle would result in the death of her soul mate. I didn't know such a connection existed, but the vision was all it took for Nyx to believe. She divorced her husband, Erebus, who chose to side against us, and left to go and find her soul mate.

I should be relieved not to be facing my friend, but Nyx ignoring her oath and duty to the Father is only aiding in the downfall of Earthradon. When Athena told me about Freyr's death, I didn't accept it; I fought. I would think Nyx's soul mate would want her to fight. I wouldn't normally criticize someone for acting out of love, but I'm going to since Nyx didn't know before today that she has a soul mate. My friend's heart and mind are being blinded to the bigger picture, and that's what's heightening my irritation.

I push through a shrub and discover a vast blush-blue river with sparkling flurries filled with ivory light fluttering off the surface and into the air.

I sigh with relief. More hope is on the horizon now. With the warriors from Valhalla joining us, we will be able to hold our own until King Adom arrives. Heimdall and Hel will lead them, so I can search for Thor. He will most likely not be leading the Unfaithful army, so I will have a lot of traitorous beings to slice my way through.

All had looked at me during the meeting like I had three heads because I said I didn't need help finding and fighting Thor. I glared at them all until they nodded in agreement—except for Bralyant, who dismissed my comment and moved on. Even though I doubt anyone would have an issue with my spiritual power, I still won't risk telling anyone. Heimdall's eyes sparkled, and whatever he saw assured him, and he held Hel back when she tried to mother-hen me.

An echo of thunder lifts my attention to the gray clouds in the sky. With Zeus and Thor teaming up and both having the elemental magic of thunder and lightning, this approaching storm is their doing.

A thickening pressure weighs down the air and makes me take deeper breaths. The vibrant greens of the forest start to darken as the blossoming flowers of leopard orchids and flame lilies close their petals to protect themselves from the promised weather to come.

Whatever strategy the Unfaithful have devised, I pray to the brightest star in the sky ours is strong enough to withstand their attacks until the other half of our forces arrive.

My shaking hands distract me from the doubtful thoughts being spoken by the silver-tongue in my mind.

I kneel and dip my hands in the water, groaning with relief as my shakiness is soothed by the coolness nipping at my twitching muscles.

With my hands submerged, I become more aware of how hot the rest of my body is. I should get right to work at calling the warriors from Valhalla, but my own selfish need to be comforted before battle grows stronger. The walk did nothing for me, and I need to have a level head. *I have time for a dip.*

Starry-blue light illuminates the veins beneath my skin when I flick my wrist to call out the shadowy-star magic to help undress me.

My reflection in the water catches my attention, and I stumble back onto my ass. The starry-blue light was also under the skin on my face and neck, as well as in my eyes, which were shining like stars.

After a breath to calm myself, I speak to my hand. "Okay, you are not what I wanted. Go away."

When the magic doesn't respond like Haidion's, I pull my hand back in to extinguish—

Starry-blue light shoots out of my hand and across the river to a tree. Everything is ripped off, from the leaves to the tiniest branches and bark, leaving it naked and bare.

My shaking becomes more visible, and I plead for Haidion's magic to come out. The friendly shadowy-star tendrils slither out and harvest the magic I need from a nearby bush to quickly strip me of my weapons, armor, and clothes.

"I'm really glad no one was around to see that." The shadowy-star magic nuzzles my face before going back into my hands.

How are my reserves filled with both shadowy-star magic and starlight? How do I have starlight at all?

Anxiety is already present in my heart and mind. Now the layer is thickening and becoming uncomfortable. Having Haidion's magic to use is one thing because it's similar to mine, but starlight could cause more harm than good, especially in the heat of battle. Wielding magic without the knowledge of how to use it is suicide.

I wrap my arms around myself and squeeze, trying to recall Freyr's embrace. "Come on, Freyja, focus."

A cool breeze coming off the river has me sighing as an electrical current resets my hammering pulse and panicky breathing.

"Just get in the water, Freyja."

As I back up to get a running start, my senses pick up quickened footsteps.

Before I can turn around, warm arms circle my waist and under my legs.

Bralyant is hollering as a shrill scream rushes out of me.

He leaps off the edge of the river, and we dive into the water.

A welcome embrace of cold hugs my body, and my overheated core numbs. The thrill of being taken off guard has me laughing after I breach the surface.

Bralyant appears a moment later, his hair plastered to his face.

Before I can utter a word about needing to be alone, he sprays a mist of water from his mouth, as if he were a Dragon, in my face.

I'm splashing him without thinking about whether I should be playing with him or not.

When Bralyant's head disappears, I stop wading and sink to follow him to the riverbed.

All the marine life darts away from Bralyant, sensing his Alpha aura.

The water's visibility is almost crystal clear. If anything comes, we'll be able to spot it since neither of us is familiar with this body of water.

We always enjoyed exploring the bottom of rivers, springs, lakes, and oceans together. Since water covers half of the Earthradon, both of our interests were piqued to go exploring. After a couple of centuries, we've concluded there are more Oceanic races than there are races on land.

Bralyant's smile widens as my feet are greeted by the silken floor. The emptiness of the space around us, along with the closeness of our bodies, reminds me of what he used to say all the time before we went exploring: *"When we're down here, we are nothing more than two beings who want to be with one another."*

My mind is submerged in happy memories as much as my body is in water, so I don't realize Bralyant is closing the distance between us until my hardened nipples graze his chest.

His arms wrap around my waist and pull me up, so our faces are level.

The muscles of his body form with mine as he presses me into him, forcing some of the air out of my mouth.

Every part we are touching becomes overly sensitive, and if I weren't holding my breath, I would've moaned.

He leans in and brushes his lips over mine before I can grip his shoulders to push him away.

I lose sense of reality, and I'm taken back to the memory of our first kiss. We were in Wolven territory and had been eyeing each other all night. Bralyant nodded toward the woods, and I followed. He led me to a lake; we'd sunk to the bottom, and he initiated our first kiss like this.

When a Wolven kisses someone they go into a frenzy, their

instincts telling them to mate, but the cool water somehow acts as a barrier. All of our kisses were done underwater until I summoned the courage to ask Bralyant to be my first. He asked if I was sure and his hesitancy and willingness to wait only made me fall for him even more.

Bralyant hovers his lips over mine, waiting for permission—a hard thing for a Wolven to do since they are impulsive when it comes to being with someone they desire.

I can't wrap my head around how he can both want me physically and not in his life, but he loves me.

His hard cock pressing against my lower abdomen only upsets and confuses me more. I shouldn't have followed him down here. My selfish desire to want a moment of peace and happiness with my friend has only led him on, which wasn't my intention. *Why can't friendships have a level of intimacy that doesn't translate to wanting anything sexual but is still full of love?*

No matter how hard I tried to convince myself I wasn't falling in love with Bralyant, my heart was always in it. And before we go into battle, I want him to know how important he is to me.

I press a hand to his chest, reading myself to push him away once I'm done signing to him in Galex. *"You'll always be my first love."*

Bralyant shutters, his eyes are full of adoration, and as I anticipated, he leans in to kiss me. As I push him away, my hand goes through him just as his gorgeous lips don't find me. *My spiritual power activated all on its own—again.*

Since I'm already holding my breath and in a relaxed state, I guess no further work is required for me to fully shift, but I didn't activate my power. I didn't consider becoming a spirit as an option to get away from Bralyant because there would be no way I could explain my sudden disappearance. *Fuck. Fuck. Fuck!*

Skjoldr hums in my chest, and before I can stop her, I'm being brought back up. When I breach the surface, my spiritual power deactivates.

Fight or flight kicks in, and I direct soul magic into my arms and legs to swim faster. *Don't freak out. Get to shore and get clothes on.*

A magical push lifts me out of the water, and my clothing floats over to me by smoky shadow magic—*wait, smoky? That's not Haidion's magic.*

Something I can't see mutters, "Fuck."

"You are not doing this to me again." Bralyant's growl silences the insects chirping in the forest.

I'm turned around and pushed against a tree.

Bralyant gets both of my hands in his and pins them above my head.

His hair and body are already dry from his warmer temperature and the obvious fact that my disappearance pissed him off with each angry breath.

"You are not running away after opening your heart to me."

"If I thought you lacked the self-control to not kiss me, maybe I wouldn't have."

"Why didn't you push me away then?"

"I...I—" The words are lost as my mind scrambles.

"You could've punched me in the face or kneed me in the groin. But instead, you used some type of power on me like you did last time!"

After Freyr's funeral, I had Bralyant and Watson stay with me until the next day, when they were rested enough to travel. I couldn't sleep and stayed up chatting with Bralyant. We shared some of the best memories we had with Freyr, and that led to how we'd missed one another.

That evening, I lost my willpower to prevent my heart from opening up. Our conversation turned into him shredding my clothes off and making love to me as if I were his mate. I was not in the right headspace with losing my brother and wanted to be loved so tenderly that I would sob from pleasure.

When morning came, my walls were back up, and I couldn't get Bralyant out of the house fast enough. He kept asking me where we stood, and I admitted that I needed time. My heart was torn even more than it had been after the most passionate night of my life, and his presence would only make the pain worse.

Bralyant understood, and when he hugged me goodbye, he also leaned in to kiss me on the cheek. My spiritual power got activated, and I was able to move far enough away and reappear, making it seem like he misjudged the distance between us.

I don't know how my power got activated without touching my chest; maybe it was from being so emotional about losing my brother, having a memorable night with my friend, or trying to figure out how I was going to break the news to Odin that I didn't want to marry him anymore—

Bralyant's low growl brings me out of my mind and back to the consequences of my actions.

"I replayed that moment in my head for centuries, knowing I wasn't wrong about being a breath away from you. I know how your body feels against mine, and you were where I thought you were, but somehow you moved. Then, when you said during the meeting that you didn't need any help to find and fight Thor, I knew you had some kind of power you never told me about."

His eyes flick down to my chest, not to gawk at my heavy breasts, but as if he can figure out what my power is just by looking at my skin.

"Both times, you didn't wait for me to go ten when you went ninety. You closed the distance completely. Were you attempting to recreate a similar situation to prove your theory?"

His eyes darted back up at me. "No! I wanted to kiss the friend I've been in love with since the moment Auxiliary caught us together."

He takes a few deep breaths before proceeding. "I got a thrill out of sneaking around, but I knew if we were caught, I would have to stop seeing you. When my brother caught you riding me in the woods, I was surprised that I pushed you down to the ground to cover your body with mine like a newly mated male who didn't want anyone to lay an eye on what was his."

My anger rises to come out and play. "You've been in love with me for fourteen hundred years?!"

"Yes. Not running after you when you broke things off was the most painful day of my life. Or so I thought. When we ran into each other during the war and you sought me out, I thought you had finally admitted your feelings to yourself."

With his other hand, he grips a branch off to my left, and the wood starts to pop. "You can't possibly deny that the night we spent together after Freyr's funeral, you weren't ready to profess your love as I made you cum so hard that you cried. The only reason I didn't push you to admit your love for me because you were grieving."

A crack comes from the tree branch. "But then, when I went back a month later to check in on how you were doing, I saw you with Odin and the marital brands on your arms!" The branch explodes in his hand. "If Watson hadn't come with me, I would've shredded Odin to pieces and claimed you for myself."

Fire rushes into my veins. "You said I could never be enough for you! That I was a waste of your time!"

His snarling growl causes all the trees to lose their leaves, the bark to shred, the flowers to wilt their petals, and the grass to flatten.

"When the fuck did I tell you that?! I would never say such nonsense to you."

My eyebrows pinch together. "In the letter you wrote me." *There is no way he could've forgotten.*

He blinks at me, confusion wrinkling his forehead. "I've never written a letter a day in my life. Has grief made you delusional?"

"You wrote me!"

"I. Did. Not!"

His grip on my wrists makes my arms go numb, and my eyes are becoming heavy, ready to release tears.

Raising my voice to him wasn't the best choice of action. Trying to figure out why he either chooses to forget or is in denial about writing to me isn't going to be possible in the mood he's in. Calming him down and de-escalating the situation is my only chance to get answers.

"Bralyant, please let go of me." With my voice suddenly trembling, I know I'm on the verge of breaking.

He leans in until we are nose-to-nose. "It took you until my neck was minutes away from being snapped to admit the slightest hint of your feelings towards me, and I'll lose my shit if I find you dying on the battlefield and you finally tell me that you love me. Your stubborn ass is staying right here until you tell me why you are playing with my heart!"

Odin's similar words play in my mind along with Bralyant's.

A crescendo is reached, like the final war drum before the blade falls on someone's neck—I've been unable to love anyone since Freyr died.

A mask is removed, and the truth is before me. What I feel towards Odin is just a patch to chase away my loneliness—I don't truly love him, but I love the idea of being someone's wife, all because I couldn't be that for Bralyant.

I was emotional when I made love to Bralyant, and I was the same way when Odin tried to reinvigorate my desire to marry him a week after Freyr's funeral. I can't trust anyone with my emotions anymore, not even myself.

And worst of all, I didn't listen to my brother's advice to take time for myself—I let him down.

"I'm done talking to you about this! And you have a mate now, so why does it matter? You should have fought to stay alive for her, not me."

He tilts his head to the side the slightest bit. "Luxury isn't my—" A hint of a grin lifts the corner of his mouth. "Are you jealous?"

I drive my knee up to his groin, but he's able to twist out of the way, relieving the pressure on my wrists as I anticipated.

Shadowy-star magic wraps around my arms while starry-blue light ignites in my veins. Wood had begun to bite into the backs of my hands as I pulled them free, but once the star light surfaced, my skin was no longer being assaulted as if I were wearing armor.

As I move away from Bralyant, I swipe my leg out since his form is unbalanced. He stumbles to the side as I get my hands out, ready to use magic on him if he tries to force me to do anything.

A cold, familiar energy hugs my back.

Out of the corner of my eye, darkness creeps in from the forest, as if Haidion's magic is summoning more shadows—smoky shadows. *What the fuck!*

Bralyant's ears don't twitch when a ghostly growl comes from behind me; the intensity is not directed at me but towards my friend, as if whatever is behind me is on my side.

The cool, smoky energy at my back drifts into my mind. *Hello, Freyja. I'm Haidion's—puppy.*

My bones tremble with fear. Haidion's three-headed monster of a pet is in my shadow. *Does he know you're here? Did he send you to me?*

When Demonicals ascend to become Ancients, they all receive a Cerberus.

No, and no. But, since you spotted me, I'm at your service. The fire in my soul purrs as a ghost of a lick travels up my throat to my cheek.

I compose myself before speaking. "You know better than to force me to do anything."

Bralyant straightens himself as his eyes cautiously glance between my hands and then focus on my face.

"And if you want to remain my friend, you will never pull shit like that on me again!"

He crosses his arms and leans against the tree where he had pinned me. "You do know that wielding shadow magic is illegal unless your race's origin is from Orrtiereum, right?" He tilts his head. "I felt the presence of this magic on your hands, but not the starry-blue light one. What is that?"

"I acquired a new friend, and he owed me a favor." *Well, technically I acquired two.*

Am I one of those two? Haidion's puppy nudges my leg, and since Bralyant doesn't react to something being next to me, this creature must be invisible.

You're able to read my mind? How? Wait, never mind. I can't handle this right now. Okay, rule number one: Unless I ask you, don't respond to my thoughts.

The sensation next to my leg goes away as if I imagined an invisible creature leaning against me.

Bralyant's thumb drumming against his arm draws my attention back to him. "Since I'm keeping this secret now, will you tell me about your other one? Mostly so I can keep a level head about my worry for you during battle."

With Bralyant admitting his feelings, he might be up my ass as much as Freyr was, and I won't risk him doing something stupid like sacrificing himself for me.

"Your emotions are giving me whiplash." What he wrote in the letter compared to how he is acting now makes me think he had a change of heart, but it doesn't matter anymore. "Give me your word that you will never push me to admit anything again, and you won't try to kiss me."

He takes a deep breath, making all his muscles flex and then relax.

"I'm only lashing out because of what I found out after I saw you and Odin together one night."

"And what's that?" Odin's punishments didn't start until after our honeymoon, so he couldn't have witnessed anything of that sort.

"I went to find Auxiliary after I saw you and Odin together. I asked what the bond between him and his fate-blessed mate felt like since she is more of a magical galaxy race than a beast one. What he describes is what I feel towards you, but I don't feel the same spiritual pull as he did." Before his eyes and head completely droop, he adjusts his posture as if to conceal his disappointment. "He found out that if his mate's origin was from Earthradon, then they would've had a better chance of getting their bond legitimized by the lords and ladies, but they wouldn't be allowed to have children." He lets out a heavy breath. "We can be together, Freyja. The only thing stopping us is you."

My fight leaves my body, and my shaking comes back, undoing all the help the water has given me. What he says can't be true. If it were, then the information would be known—Freyr would've told me. *This is not what I need to be dealing with right now.*

Haidion's puppy growls near my ear as if he's on my back, but again, Bralyant doesn't hear him. *Stand down, puppy.*

"You have my word; I won't push you, but if you initiate anything, I won't be able to help myself." When Bralyant winks, I know my friend is back—not the relentless Alpha.

The starry-blue light consumes my attention as I try to figure out how to make it go away without shooting it at another tree.

Haidion's puppy nudges my mind. *Want me to drain the starlight from your hands?*

Um, is that even possible?

A cold mist wafts over me, and a fraction of my energy and emotions drain, followed by the star light evaporating into thin air, leaving Haidion's shadowy-star magic around my hands. *That draining sensation feels familiar.*

Whimpers echo in my mind as Haidion's puppy rubs my leg like he did something wrong. *Have you used that on me before?*

More whimpers answer my question as my mind recalls the times a similar sensation happened to me. First in the cave after Bralyant pulled the arrows out of my back and then while I was nervously waiting for Bralyant's fight for the Wolven crown to start.

Haidion's puppy interrupts my counting. *I've only used my magic on you twice before this time.*

How about when I was about to enter the river before my friend came, or on the mountaintop back on Crescent Island? Something happened during those times as well; I just chose not to think about it too much.

I've only been in your shadow since you entered the Iroko Forest. Whatever you felt wasn't me. I give you my word. But also, you shouldn't be able to sense me using my magic on you.

Swallowing down my irritation, I wave my hand, making my clothing, armor, and weapons float over to me. As I dress, I tell Bralyant about my spiritual power and what scenarios I've used it for.

"You will have a better chance of calling Faithless to you because you can ideally move through the army as undetected as I can with my stealth power, better even."

I unsheathe my curved dagger and walk over to the river. "Are you intimidated by me, Alpha?"

His eyes roved over me as if I were still naked. "I could be persuaded to tell you, but only if you allow me to speak them from between your legs."

Instead of being affected by his flirting, I lightly press the tip of the dagger over my brand, not enough to break the skin, but enough to practice the pattern I need to slice so I can summon the warriors from Valhalla.

Bralyant walks around me and stands on my left side. "Can I see it?" His attention is on my brand.

For a moment, I'm stunned, and I replay his question to make sure I heard him right.

I lift my left arm to him, and he tenderly holds my wrist and elbow as he examines my marital brand.

When he doesn't reveal any hint of emotion, I'm tempted to tell him I plan on leaving Odin, but I keep my mouth shut. And the silver-tongue headache resurfaces.

After another moment, his attention comes back to me as he holds my hand between his. "I need to share something with you, and please understand that this is coming from a good place, not because I'm a stubborn son of a bitch trying to find a way to be with you."

Even though my heart is currently at its breaking point, I nod anyway knowing I've put his heart through a shitload of torment.

"My units and I were in the Seedling Woodlands, investigating what caused the destruction, when smoke started to come from both the camp and the port. By the time I got to the beach, the path to the camp was blocked, and ships were turning around to flee the Kraken. The ships that were being sunk were those that sided with the Unfaithful. The Kraken took out half their mortal army and over a dozen Gods who were trying to fight him."

He takes a breath and brushes his thumb over my knuckles. "There was a reason why I didn't tell you about Odin when I found you."

My marital brand suddenly warms up, as if sensing my need to be comforted.

"I saw Odin pushing the Gods back to the beach and threatening them to stop fighting the Kraken. But I also saw him telling the Gods to enter the forest."

"And then all the Gods were ambushed and drugged," I add.

My brand maintains a steady flow of calm and assurance.

Bralyant's arms tense, but he still holds my hand with a gentle, tender grip.

"My units and I had to go through the forest to get to the camp. All the paths closest to us were blocked, so we had to form a makeshift bridge of rocks over the river—the one we rode past. I dispatched half of my units to the camp, and the others followed me to the port. That was when we saw the Gods being taken. When we heard the shrill of the Kraken, I left on my own to go and investigate. And that is when I first saw Odin."

The growing deception I've been feeling as a result of learning about all the things Odin has withheld from me arouses a scorching sting of doubt that tries to overpower the magic in my brand.

My exhaled breath begins to burn my throat. "What are you trying to say?"

Bralyant kisses my knuckles and takes a step back after releasing my hand.

"You were close to Athena. I felt your emotions when my brother told you about her siding with the Unfaithful. You couldn't believe it. But she was the one who sent the message to all the Gods to go to

Camp Ariella. She was sending you there to be ambushed. Whatever plans the Unfaithful had to take the camp were ruined when the Kraken arrived, but the plan to capture you all wasn't. I only saw one God instructing everyone to go into the forest. You were able to see the truth of Athena's betrayal, and I need you to consider the possibility that Odin isn't captured, he's not drugged. He's siding with the Unfaithful to kill the Father."

My vision is shaky, and I'm not sure if I still have the dagger in my hand because my marital brand's warmth has been replaced by numbing cold magic. The unexpected change silences the alarms as a cold fills my veins and works to extinguish the blazing heat in my core.

The river before me becomes a manifestation of how tirelessly my brand had tried to influence me. From the soft blue water—magical flurries roll off each soothing wave—to the harmonious song the river sings. I'm coaxed into the melody and the assuring embrace, where everything will be better if I only allow the magic of the brand to pull me in.

A tug on my soul catches me before I fall into the loving arms of magic.

I left the fantasy I desired but was unable to attain down there at the bottom of the river. I pulled myself away to go back into reality, but my brand's influence of calm and assurance wants to submerge me back into a fantasy and blind me to reality. My brand isn't just trying to comfort me; the magic is trying to persuade me not to believe or react to what Bralyant has said.

I look down at my brand and mentally scream at it. *Stop!*

This will be the first time in my five hundred years of marriage that I have refused my marital brand's support. Part of the vows Odin made to me was that I'd always receive comfort whenever I needed it because he wasn't good at expressing it. At the beginning of our marriage, his presence in my life and my bed was all the comfort I needed until it stopped being enough and I craved more.

Whimpers echo in my mind. *What am I doing that is upsetting you?*

It's not you, it's—immediately the influence stops, but a mysterious, metallic voice enters my mind. *Are you rejecting the aid?*

It's the silver-tongue voice. I assumed the voice was a figment of my imagination rather than something real and attached to my marital brand.

Are you rejecting the aid, servant?

Haidion's puppy growls furiously. *Who the fuck is calling you a servant?*

I don't know, but something is not right with my marital brand.

When I don't answer the voice, the comfort and persuasion resume.

The word 'servant' repeats in my mind so much that the world around me begins to spin, inducing me to vomit, but my heaves only push the cold up my throat, and I start to suffocate on it.

My brand's magic shifts from comforting me to forcing me into a dissociative state.

Cries of desperation come from my soul as she thrashes and fights the magic of the brand while Skjoldr hums in my chest, warning me that something foreign is within my body.

My name is being shouted by Bralyant, but I have no idea where he is as my vision ices over from my marital brand's magic as it continues to take control over my body.

Make it stop! I beg for Haidion's puppy with every fiber and thread of my existence.

What the fuck!? I can't—

Everything becomes so far away as an unfriendly darkness pulls me into a void as my body ices over from my own magic, aiding in the marital brands' control.

Eye-stinging light peers through the darkness, and a cage made out of silver threads comes into view.

Inside is an avian beast. Ruby-black feathers adorn their body, from the crown above their downcast eyes to the bouquet of their tail and glorious wings, one of which is clipped.

The space is too small for the creature; they are being suffocated. Silver threads tighten around its body as the cage grows. The same magic creates a door and begins to reach for me, and I'm unable to move.

Distressed chirps come from the beast as they lift their head and lock eyes with me. A voice with a wrathful promise of dangerous power fills my mind. *Now you finally see what he's doing to us. But if you enter here too, we won't ever be free.*

Is this my soul? I'm not surprised by the appearance since flying is my first love above all other forms of magic.

A cool mist wraps around me, causing the silver threads reaching for me to hesitate. The mist thickens into smoky shadows and carries a radiant, male voice with the warmth of the sun and the calmness of the moon. *Come on, Freyja! Come back to me.*

Flames of lightning spark from the restrained beast as they begin to thrash, ripping off feathers and breaking some of the bones in their wings.

The radiant male voice pleads as the silver threads break through the mist. *Where's the fearless flame I've been told so much about—the one Haidion loves?*

A dangerously powerful voice layers over my own. *She's right here.*

Thunder cracks, and a humming energy envelops me. An ethereal, winged creature of hazy stars appears out of thin air, protecting me and also attacking the cage. *Skjoldr.*

The threads reaching for me snap back to reinforce the enclosure, but an explosion of fire coats the beast's body. With a triumphant huff, she rages, pushing the storm within her out.

The silver threads explode out and away, lighting up the void of darkness, revealing an even bigger cage, and on the outside is a bridge made out of threads in every color of the rainbow.

My attention is brought back to the beast as she spreads out her wings while the ethereal creature loops a ribbon made out of hazy stars around us until we form a triangle.

An iridescent wave of starry fire in a variety of colors pushes out from the beast, awakening nerve endings I thought I'd never sense again.

The mist surrounding me begins to vaporize, but the radiant voice lingers a moment longer. *There you go! Fight, Freyja! Come back to the surface! Come back to me!*

My beast flaps her wings, and we fly towards the wall of the cage. With a quick turn, I sail through the cracks, and to my surprise, the hazy ribbon is still attached to my now-forming body.

While I fly away, the beast and Skjoldr swirl and create a chaotic storm of fire.

A light is at the far end of the rainbow bridge of threads I'm soaring down. The closer I get, the more ice covers the bridge. As I pass through, the light blinds me. I then jolt forward and fill out a body that is about to become a statue.

Fire thaws my frozen muscles, wakes up my slow-beating heart, and forces air into my lungs.

The smoky voice of Haidion's puppy fills my mind. *You're fucking phenomenal. Now, push the ice off.*

Cracks and breaks come from my hands as I raise them toward the river while the storm inside of me unleashes itself.

Bralyant is suddenly in front of me. Relief floods his face with tears. And before I can mentally scream for Haidion's puppy to move him, black fur collides with his body, and they are out of my line of sight.

A piercing wail of heartbreak and vengeance explodes from my mouth, and the devastating energy of the storm within me is pushed out through my hands.

FIFTEEN

My body is free from the ice, but my soul magic is endless, as I keep pushing out more and more, striking the river as if it were the threads making up Odin's existence.

I can't enjoy the wonderful sight of my wrath erupting because the glow of my magic has blinded me, but I keep pushing.

Skjoldr hums in my chest, warning me to stop before harm can be done to my soul.

Centuries of bottled-up rage that I've never been able to release overwhelms her. She cries out and yanks on any tether of control she can find to stop me. But nothing can stop me because I have held onto this pain for far too long. I'd rip my soul to shreds if it meant I could have some semblance of relief from the heartache I've endured and the abuse I've tolerated—

A gentler tug of a loving caress causes my mind to slow, my heart to skip a beat, my breath to catch in my throat, and my soul to flutter.

Darkness coats my vision, relieving me of the harmful light.

My attention is drawn to my left, towards an aura I wish would surround me for eternity.

A hazy form of starry darkness stands next to me. They are close enough to touch but out of focus. The only part of them I can make out is their eyes—a familiar pair of sparkling amethyst.

Haidion's remarkable voice begs me to put my hands down and to breathe with him.

The first one was excruciatingly painful, but the second is less so, stopping my soul magic from exploding out of my hands. By the third, the violent anger fueling my soul was calmed when a soft kiss is placed on my left palm—the tenderness making me shudder.

Haidion backs away, taking the darkness with him. I beg my friend to come back and stay, but he vanishes on my fourth intake of rejuvenating air.

"No! Don't leave me, please!" I cry out as tears blur my vision.

A second later, his hazy form stands in front of me. I cry out in happiness as tears fall while I take in the pair of purple eyes again, blooming with rapturous passion.

"I'm here, beautiful." My sobbing taints his marvelous voice.

Warm arms warp around me, making my entire body shiver from the drastic contrast between my cold and his heat. Even though I expelled the ice, the phantom caress of the magic still lingers in my veins and on my skin.

"I'm cold." My sniffles are replaced by my teeth chattering as I shiver.

"Would you like me to warm you up?"

"Yes," I breathlessly moan while my soul sings as if an eternity-long prayer has finally been answered.

My friend's soft lips press kisses all over my face, then down to my neck. I hold onto him as tight as physically possible, digging my nails into his warm, smooth skin to convey that if he tries to leave me again, it's going to hurt.

I brush my lips against his chest, and each press chases away the numbing cold. A different type of fire awakens in my soul as I kiss the crook of his neck. Heat throbs in my core and moves down to my thighs as my lips move up, trying to find his.

His tongue laps up and down my neck, then sucks my skin into his hot mouth, pulling needy whimpers out of me and chasing away my centuries of pain and suppressed sadness.

When his sharp teeth graze my bruised flesh, pressure builds down my spine and into my core, begging for release.

I wrap my hands around his neck and yank his head back, wanting the lips I've been dreaming about for centuries, but I pause before slamming my mouth against his, because Haidion isn't in front of me. Bralyant is panting with a wide smile as the stirring heat and pressure awakening in my soul and body pull away, leaving me alone to deal with this mess.

I had never acted on any of my desires for Haidion before this moment. The thoughts to do so have been suppressed, then buried, and finally hidden in the darkness of my mind. I'm overwhelmed with worry by how desperate I was to have his lips, proving to me that my feelings towards Haidion are a lot more than just an attraction. My method for keeping my forbidden thoughts out of sight and out of mind has backfired on me, blinding me to how they never just went away but grew with the intensity of breaking my marital vow the moment I was given the opportunity.

To make matters worse, my infatuation with Haidion made me oblivious to the fact that he wasn't before me. Things could've ended worse if Bralyant and I had kissed, breaking my vows even further.

Shame engulfs my mind, attacking the darkness until nothing is left. The silver-tongue of disappointment and torment fills the void, screaming at me for not pushing him away, cheating on my husband, and being a horrible wife who deserves to be locked in a cage and punished for eternity.

Bralyant lets out a moan, drawing my attention to him. His hungry eyes roved my body as he licked his lips. I push him away when his nostrils flare from smelling something delectable. My cheeks burn with humiliation. *He's smelling my arousal, though it's not for him.*

Something nudges my leg as a smoky voice enters my mind— Haidion's puppy. *Do you want my help?*

I start to mentally sob. *How can you possibly help me?*

A draining sensation halts my erratic mind. In seconds, the throbbing in my core is gone, along with the slickness between my thighs.

I can drain more than just magic, but I guess my power has limitations when it comes to servant brands.

I want to argue and say I don't have a servant brand, but there is no other logical sense as to why the brand's magic called me one. The day Odin and I exchanged our vows has always been blurry for me to remember. However, there was no way I'd agree to be Odin's servant.

A cool energy drapes over my back as if I were being hugged from behind. Instead of allowing myself to mentally sink into a grave from this discovery, I reach for the rage I still have within my soul and bring it to the surface.

Why did Haidion leave?

Haidion? He was never here.

Yes. He calmed me down.

Haidion's puppy is quiet for a moment. *If Haidion was here, he would've sensed me, and I wouldn't be in your shadow.*

But I saw him. Heard him. Felt him.

"What's going on here?" Aliith's stormier tone of voice knocks me out of my internal conversation.

I blink away the last of the haziness clouding my vision.

Aliith is in humanoid form, eyes darting between Bralyant and me as a different kind of darkness looms in the forest behind him, almost as if his presence saps the vitality of the vegetation.

"Freyja's magic got out of control when I opened her eyes to a heartbreaking reality."

I flinch from Bralyant's touch when he tries to wrap his arm around my waist. A muscle ticks in his jaw from my rejection as I pull away.

Aliith's attention stays on Bralyant as he walks towards me, his hands balling into fists, making Skjoldr hum in my chest.

"And you thought taking advantage of her while she was distraught was a kingly thing to do?"

Bralyant's Wolven King aura pushes out, causing hairs to rise on my skin, but it doesn't stop Aliith from getting closer to me.

My friend's fangs elongate as he growls. "I didn't call for you to come here. Run back to your master."

Aliith positions himself in front of me, blocking my view with his wide shoulders and seven-foot frame.

"My master and the others are on their way." Aliith takes a step towards Bralyant. "And my Goddess has a special kind of punishment for those who take advantage of others. Wolven King or not, you'll bear the mark of shame."

I'm in-between them before Bralyant can lunge—not my smartest idea since he's the Wolven King now, but we don't need any more unnecessary bloodshed or fights today.

"He didn't, Aliith. I said yes."

Confusion crinkles Aliith's brow. "Are you saying you wanted his advances even though you're married?"

"Odin sides with the Unfaithful, and he betrayed Freyja's trust. Her infidelity is a miniscule sin compared to what he has done and will do." Bralyant pushes into my hand to get closer to Aliith. "If you speak a word about what you saw or mark her skin—"

He cannot be making threats right now. "Bralyant, stop, please!" Not knowing what else to do, I press my back into my friend, using my body as a shield to protect Aliith. "You saw what you saw." I extend my left arm. "I won't stop you."

Bralyant wraps his arms around me, trying to pull me away, but I force soul magic into my feet, rooting me to the ground. *I deserve this slash—I deserve to be marked for breaking my vows.*

Haidion's puppy growls in my mind. *Believe me when I tell you this, Freyja. Your vows are nullified if your marital brand has been altered to be a servant brand in disguise. You didn't break any vows since you were deceived. Pull your arm back in, or I'll do it for you.*

A light pair of footsteps approach, drawing our attention to the forest. "I'm so out of shape from riding you all the time, Aliith." Artemis leans against a tree while fanning herself. "What's going on?" Her attention freezes on my outstretched arm.

Aliith grabs my wrist, and I automatically tense from the anticipated pain about to come. Skjoldr hums her warning, telling me to pull away while Haidion's puppy roars, causing the light surrounding us to dim. When a radiant energy fills my body, trying to take control, Aliith's other hand doesn't reach for my brand; he places my armor back on and fastens the belt.

His black-void eyes bore into mine with a silent command. "Freyja solved Heimdall's problem. She overexerted herself in the process."

A gasp escapes me and Haidion's puppy when Aliith tightens my armor more than necessary. His message is clear; he isn't going to mark me.

Bralyant relaxes while letting out a silent sigh of relief while the energy wanting to control my body dissipates. I let him pull my arm away because I'm lost in the dark void of Aliith's eyes. They now hold the secret of witnessing my infidelity without marking my skin, as well as the weight of a broken vow of his own, not speaking the truth to Artemis.

Out of the corner of my eye, Artemis walks forward, only to stumble back into the tree. "Holy Aurora. Resting against the tree didn't help one bit."

Aliith holds my gaze for a second longer before walking over to support Artemis.

Bralyant nudges my ear with his nose. "I forget sometimes that you're a powerful Goddess." He gestures with a nod to something over his shoulder.

I follow Bralyant's line of sight after shrugging off his hold on me.

What was once a happy, flowing river is now a crystallized path of fire.

Multiple pairs of feet come from behind us.

A mixture of voices from the races gathered repeat a similar tone of shock, followed by stunned gasps. All of their noises fade away as I step onto the smooth river.

My soul magic must've pushed out the chaotic fire and mixed with the ice covering my body. I not only froze the river but tamed it, making the surface so flat it could serve as a road. As far as my eyes can see, the entire river is frozen over to the falls.

"What have you done to *Mto Ivoire*?" The pained, Atlantean voice pierces my soul.

The Atlantean Captain is on her knees at the river's edge, her hands shaking as she reaches to touch the smooth ice. Gold magic pulsates through the stenciling over her exposed skin as she places her hands on the river.

Heimdall picks up a crystalized, curved dagger of fire and walks over to me. "She created the bridge I needed to allow my power to transport all of us to the Father faster than it would have taken for the Wolven to run there. Good work, Freyja."

Before I can mutter a word of apology to the Atlantean Captain, Heimdall wraps his arms around me. "This was the only way we would've been able to reach the Father by Solar Noon."

His whisper might not have been heard by the Captain, but the intrigued tilt in Bralyant's head tells me he heard Heimdall's comment loud and clear.

"You knew this was going to happen?" I pull away and gesture to the crystalized river of fire we stand on.

"What I saw were two paths and souls of fire. One went towards restoration, and the other towards hope." He offers me the dagger. "But neither can be achieved until you choose to fly."

Being cryptic is the only way anyone with sight can get around the rule of having to pay magic to tell of what's been seen. Heimdall neither confirmed nor denied seeing the events leading up to this point, but his message was clear; nothing can be accomplished until I choose to act.

This bridge will serve our purpose of reaching the Father, but at the expense of eliminating all life in the river and affecting those who rely on it for survival, which is why magic is both beautiful and tragic.

Knowing what I need to do, I take my dagger back from Heimdall.

The blade hums with a mixture of power and the same energy emitting from the river beneath my feet. I don't need to be able to see the future to know this created magic will be fought over. Instead of informing the Daughters of the Father to come and remove it, an offering needs to be made to the lives I cut short.

As I walk back to the side of the river, the Atlantean Captain rises and meets my stare of determination with her own; I stop a respectable distance away.

"As payment for the lives I've ended and impacted, I would like to bless you with the power to learn how to use this magic to protect your race, its creatures, and lands. Will you accept my blessing?"

All those in our immediate area become silent, while murmurs come from the forest of all the other warriors who weren't witnessing the rare gift I offered the Atlantean Captain. Giving a blessing without any magic offered is unheard of.

A God's blessing on a being follows the same rules as when giving wisdom or sight. A payment must be collected, this is why followers leave offerings at the alters of their Gods. But I'm going to pay the cost for this, it's the least I can do.

Of the paths Heimdall spoke about, I'm choosing the one toward restoration because even after the battle is over, we will need to rebuild, and the Atlanteans have always been at the center of healing during times of great tragedy and loss. The Atlanteans are the most generous people in the world, so whatever they can get from the crystallized fire will be used to help others.

A smile with the power of dawn spreads across the Captain's face as grateful tears leak down her cheeks following the design of the gold stenciling.

"On behalf of my race and my cousin, King Adom, I accept your offered blessing, Goddess."

She strides to me and grips my shoulder, and with her other hand, she drags her pointer finger over my forehead and down my nose to my chin, drawing the tree of life on my face—showing me her support.

"Thank you, Freyja."

I'm grateful that the cursed magic doesn't pick up the Atlantean tongue. We don't need the tainted magic here to mix with my blessing, nor do we need the souls rising from the riverbed to be harvested to create a creature more powerful than the one born from the slaughter during the War over the Frozen Fire Highlands.

The dagger will be my focal point for bestowing my gift upon the race since the weapon not only represents the combination of my magic and the Atlanteans but also symbolizes how easily life can be taken away.

After placing the dagger in both of my hands, I instructed the Captain to place hers over it.

In the Atlantean tongue, I enchant the dagger with my blessing and have the Captain prick her finger so all those of royal blood will be able to obtain the knowledge through each generation. This form of blood magic is in the gray area of being illegal, but we have over a thousand pairs of ears and eyes to confirm that I'm not placing a curse on the Atlantean royal bloodline.

Magical powder streams out of my mouth and wraps around our hands, sealing the blessing within the dagger. The crystallized fire forms with the Atlantean metal, but instead of consuming the blade, my magic is wrapped around it from handle to tip.

A portion of my magic leaves my soul; only with time will I rejuvenate what I lost. My power to heal the soul would be able to mend the wound for me, but I can't use any of my magic on myself. But after what happened with my marital-servant brand, apparently Odin can.

The Captain manipulates the metal on her forearm to sheath her new blade. She engraves the blade's name into the handle: *"Bless and Protect."*

I nod my agreement. "A suitable name." Now back to business. "May I borrow your other dagger, Captain?" I made sure to emphasize both my question about obtaining the item and her name.

"Ambar. And yes, you may."

"Nothing ahead will require you to have a dagger, Freyja," Heimdall calls out from where he kneels in the middle of the river.

I call out to him, "Summoning the warriors of Valhalla does." The words die in my throat as I realize I don't have a body of water to summon them now.

Heimdall calls out again, "Leaders, assemble your warriors. Wolven come onto the river first."

I jog over to Heimdall after thanking Ambar in Atlantean for her dagger, which I no longer require. "I can't call the warriors. I fucked up our battle plan," I whisper shout to him.

"Freyja." His profound voice is calmer as he focuses on coating the river with a dusting of rainbows, the unique color of his soul magic. "You don't need a body of water to call the warriors. They arrive as spirits."

"Yeah, on boats."

His head tilts down as he focuses more on his magic, though the wrinkles on his forehead convey that he's confused about something. "If we need them to fight with us in a naval battle, then yes, they come on boats."

"But Odin said..." The sprout of deception grows even more.

A smoky grunt fills my mind. *This husband of yours needs to be hogtied, gagged, and skewered over a blazing fire as punishment for the shit he's put you through.*

I'm going to divorce him. Stop reading my thoughts.

Really?! A warm energy dances around my feet. *If you want me to eat him, just say the word.*

A white, starry light jolts me out of my mental conversation.

Heimdall's rainbow magic combines with the dazzling light rising from the crystal surface and becomes a thin cloud, floating over the river as far as the eye can see.

All in my pantheon had told me of Heimdall's transmutation

magic, but no words could describe the heart-stilling uncertainty of to what extent he could use his power. If he can tap into the magic of the river to serve his will, what's to say he couldn't tap into the magical well of a being's soul?

Heimdall's back arcs as he takes deep breaths. "What did Odin tell you?" His voice has returned to its profound firmness, but it is weaker.

"That I need a body of water and to slice a pattern on my marital brand to summon them."

Heimdall stands and stumbles back. I grab hold of his shoulders to help steady him.

"A pattern carved into your skin?" He shakes his head and grunts in pain. "No, you need to draw runes on a surface with your magic, then shout a war cry." After taking a couple of deeper breaths, he stabilizes himself and turns his full attention to me. "Did he add some sort of rune power to summon the warriors of Valhalla onto your marital brand?"

"Well, no, I asked about it. Odin told me what to do."

When I'm met with his wild stare as if I'm an idiot, I know without a doubt that Odin has lied to me. I hold back my desire to scream, knowing I'll need this energy to summon the warriors.

"Do you know what runes I need to draw?"

Heimdall places his hands on my shoulders as he leans in to reflect his knowledge into my mind.

The symbols flash over my eyes, then I'm pulled to the other side of the river and guided to kneel. I direct soul magic into my left hand and draw runes on the sandy soil.

Only when I'm done does the flashing of the symbols stop. The lines I drew have a layer of magic floating in them.

Even though I don't need Heimdall's assistance, he helps me up. "Heimdall—" He clasps my hand before I move mine to reach for his, probably knowing I want to talk to him. "Um, I just wanted to tell you how grateful I am to have you in my life. After Freyr died, all I wanted was to push everyone who cared about me away." I allow my gratitude to wet my eyes. "You're the elder brother that the Fates knew I needed."

A red undertone warms his brown skin as his smile catches a rouge tear. "If I were to ever be blessed to father a child, I'd want them to be as strong as you." He leans in and presses his forehead to mine. "Stubbornness and all."

After I wrapped my arms around him, Heimdall followed suit.

Concern trickles over my nerves and flutters in my heart when Heimdall doesn't release me after I let go of him.

Heimdall shudders as if he's crying and holds me tighter, lifting me off the ground slightly.

"It's not your fault, Freyja." His broken voice has me pulling away, trying to see his face, but he keeps me pinned to his chest. "Promise me you will never forget."

"Yes, you have my word, Heimdall. Nothing you ever tell me will be forgotten. What's going on? Talk to me?"

When he doesn't answer, I stop fighting him and give my friend the hug he deserves, one I've only ever given to someone I consider family.

A grunt of pain has him tensing. "Once you break your mate bond, never accept another." *What?!*

I haven't told any other soul that isn't in my shadow about wanting to divorce Odin. So, his statement and physical reaction must mean that he saw something and paid the price to tell me about it. *And a mate bond? Odin and I created a marital brand.*

I'm released and turned around before I have a chance to question his prolonged showing of affection, the abrupt change in his mood, and his wisdom that was not ambiguous but direct.

Heimdall has a firm, unyielding grip on my shoulders, so I can't turn around to face him and look into his magical eyes to see proof of what he said.

"I love you, Freyja."

The fight in me has been snapped away.

With all the willpower I possess, I direct the warm energy trying to swell my heart into my lungs.

My complete focus is on the magical runes in front of me, and without needing to take a deep breath, I scream my war cry forward, releasing all the emotions I want gone from my mind, heart, and soul and any guilty thoughts or tugs to turn around and face what's behind me.

CHAPTER

SIXTEEN

Each decibel of my scream shoots a stronger sonic green ray of light and sound out of each rune. The intensity of the magic is the only reason I stop screaming—not because of Skjoldr's humming in my chest, hands trying to shake me, or a concerned voice telling me I've given enough.

From this point on, no soul will be able to influence my stubborn spirit to budge from what I want to do. No one will make me feel anything unless I want to. Never again do I want three words to have such a strong impact on me.

I direct soul magic to construct a shield wall around all facets of my existence that those three words have the potential to affect, while the translucent, green magic creates a portal to Erresthralla in the gray sky.

Warm hands try to pull me, and I rip myself away with a snarl.

"What the fuck did you do to her, Heimdall?" Bralyant growls from my side.

"Something she needed the push to do." Heimdall's words have me tensing as I will my shield wall to build up faster.

A bolt of lightning comes from the green tunnel of sound and magic, silencing Bralyant's argument, and strikes the ground next to the runes I drew.

Bralyant tries to pull me back, but I remain frozen in place like the statue Odin wanted me to become.

"It's a name." *Eirikur did go to Valhalla.*

After the words leave my lips, numerous lightning bolts shoot out, and the sandy soil becomes littered with names. I lost count after fifty, but the light show ends only a moment later, closing the portal, then evaporating the tunnel into thin air.

From the warriors gathering on the river to the wind playing a melody through the forest around us, everything goes quiet.

I hope this next piece of knowledge Odin gave me is true. "Rise warriors."

Lightning shoots up from the names, and in the blink of an eye, thousands of warriors clad in iron plates sewn together on their leathers and furs stand before me, all carrying shields, axes, and single-handed swords.

My old friend approaches me. "We are here to fight alongside you, Goddess Freyja." He presses his fist to his chest twice, then extends his arm to me. "It's wonderful to see you again."

I offer Eirikur the same greeting. "I'm relieved to know that you went to Valhalla." The last time I saw him, he went through a portal fighting a morph demon who was trying to capture me.

"I might not have died on the battlefield, but I did die protecting my goddess and friend."

His massive hand grips my left forearm as mine grips built-up muscle only achieved through centuries of strenuous training. Though he is over a foot taller than me, his height doesn't come with entitled arrogance.

Eirikurs' auburn hair parted into three braids adorns his scalp, coming together into a ponytail over his shoulder. His full beard is a hue lighter than his hair. The ghostly blue eyes behind his thick lashes promise immediate death to all he sets his sights on. And like Odin, all his available skin, save his face, is covered in tattoos but only of the honors achieved during his time in Valhalla.

The warriors behind him part. All nod their heads to the fierce, blonde shield maiden. She's cladded in chainmail fighting leathers, with a pair of short swords on each hip, and a shield on her back. Every muscular curve of her full-figured frame is unashamedly on display. Besides her bulging breasts and physical differences, we could be twins.

"Saga?!" She meets my lunge for a hug with her own. "Wait, you're not dead, are you?" I pull away, and I'm met with a smug grin.

"I've been trained by one of the most stubborn Goddesses in all of existence. It would take a God to kill me, but only if I were to grant them the chance." Gone is the polite, nurturing voice of a Jarl, and in its place is a murderous shield maiden.

I grip her shoulder and pull her close. *"I'm sorry for the loss of Sigurd."*

Her freckled face is all that's holding back the ferocity raging in her almost black eyes.

Saga grabs my shoulder and pulls me in close—face-to-face. *"My brother will be avenged."* She gives the Atlantean accent a wrathful flare.

All Jarls were instructed to learn the fundamentals of every language, and Saga was one of the few who, like me, dedicated themselves to the study.

I press my forehead against hers. "Yes, he will be."

Since Sigurd died only last night, he wouldn't have made it through the system to send him to his chosen eternal resting place.

Saga's eyes dart to my left, and a softness lessens the tension on her stunning face. Before I step out of her way to not block her path to her lover, I meet Heimdall's gaze.

"How is it that Saga is here?"

The muscles in his face tense as if he's either fighting the truth or regretting something.

"I added the rune of summoning all the Jarls to come to our aid since they swore oaths to protect their people and lands."

Heimdall's attention flits to Saga for a brief moment before he turns away and jogs towards the front of the line-up.

Saga blinks in disbelief, as would I if my lover simply assessed me before leaving without another thought.

Before I lose my friend's focus and her heart shatters, I grab her right hand. "Will you take the lead on commanding the Jarls and ride alongside the Spartans?"

After a sharp breath, Saga reverts to the warrior she trained to become. "Yes, Freyja."

Bralyant's Wolven King aura radiates from my left. "I'll see you up at the front." He kisses my cheek and runs off before I can lash out at him.

Saga gives me an inquisitive look, and I level her with a stern stare to compel her to drop whatever she's thinking.

Two hundred Jarls are added to our ranks. All were wearing their corded, metal arm rings, which symbolized not only their oaths but also the magic used to dress them in armor and weapons.

Once I'm done giving orders to Eirikur, I lead Saga and her unit along the riverside to where the Spartans and their king assemble.

Our progress is slowed when we reach a gathered crowd of Wolven standing shoulder to shoulder. Most of them have the common courtesy of looking at who is tapping them on the shoulder and moving out of my way, while others are too preoccupied with whatever is going on further in to acknowledge me.

When a menacing growl emanates from my side, all who block my way step back. "The tension of an unnecessary fight is about to be had again." Treason irritably groans next to me.

"Again?"

As we stride to the center of the commotion, Treason fills me in on how the Wolven have become unruly when told someone would be riding them into battle.

"They are only behaving like this because they don't respectably fear their new Alpha. At this rate Bralyant needs to make an example out of one of them."

Treason's polished voice gives the Atlantean tongue an air of gentility while thoroughly arousing an illicit lust. *Woah, calm down, purple monster.* As for speaking in another language, he most likely did so to keep the other Wolven from hearing what could occur if they don't stop acting like pups throwing tantrums.

An Alpha Wolven is nose-to-nose with Thaddeus, the King of Sparta.

Flawless bronze skin gives Thaddeus's gold-plated armor a natural glow. His feather-tipped helmet, matching cape, and corded muscles remind me of a proud griffin. Sadly, the beasts were already endangered, and the last hundred chose to fight in the war rather than hide away to repopulate. All the officers wear red feathered helmets and capes in memory of their sacrifice.

The muscles on Wolven's tanned skin pulsate, ready to shift.

"Reckell," Treason's gruff and rough voice projects, making all the Wolven flinch and the Spartans cheering for their king quiet down.

Thaddeus doesn't break the stare-down with the Alpha Wolven, wanting the victory of whatever argument the two were having.

Treason is on Reckell's side in a blink, fangs out, growling his authority.

The Alpha Wolven snaps at the Beta Prince only to wince when he realizes who is beside him.

Before Reckell can back down, Treason has him on the ground, shoulders pinned.

The Beta Prince growls like a man possessed until the Alpha whimpers.

"What trouble has sparked such an audience, Thaddeus?" I focus my attention on the other party responsible.

Thaddeus nods to me in respect. "The Wolven said he'd rather be skinned alive than let a wasted piece of mortal flesh like me ride on his back into battle."

Saga chuckles from behind me. "Mortal by life expectancy, but not by strength." She turns her attention to Treason. "Are the Wolven not told of how Hercules blessed the Spartans?"

Treason grabs Reckell by the scruff and pulls his face up. "Answer the Jarl's question."

Reckell whimpers. "I didn't care to learn."

Saga squats before the pinned Alpha. "The Spartans wanted to join the Resistance to fight in the War over the Frozen Fire Highlands, but Zeus told them "no" unless King Vasilis was able to best him in combat. Zeus cheated since the King didn't hesitate to accept his challenge. A Spartan King never backs down from a fight to prove his people's strength. Zeus' son, Hercules, offered his immortality and magic to the entire Spartan race for their king's bravery and the pride of his people. Magic now runs in their blood, armor, and weapons when they are in combat. As Hercules lay dying on the battlefield, he used his last breath to utter his final wish to bless the Spartans so they would keep growing stronger with each generation. You might be a natural killer given your beast, but they are bred and forged to be warriors."

As Saga rises the Spartans holler their war chant. She turns her attention to King Thaddeus; he eyes her in a way that would make his queen jealous.

"I'm honored to fight by your side, King Thaddeus."

She extends her arm towards Thaddeus, and he honors her by crossing his arms to bang his gauntlets together before gripping her forearm.

"As am I, Jarl?" he pauses, asking for her name.

"Saga," I provide. "She will be leading the two-hundred Jarls from the Norse lands and I'm placing her to fight alongside you."

Thaddeus nods to me and leans into Saga. "You are more than welcome to fight in front of me too. I'd never turn down the view of a shield maiden littering the battlefield with corpses."

On that note, I remind the two to meet upfront once their people are organized, and then I leave them to eye-fuck each other.

I weave through lined-up units of Wolven paired with Spartans. Bralyant and his officers make haste to get everyone ready.

When I hear two of my friends, my anxiety lessens.

Isis and Hera are checking over each other's armor to make sure the straps are secured.

"Is there anything I can do?" Their attention turns to me.

Hera drops her signature resting-bitch composure and allows a smile to curve her lips. "I think you should freeze Athena's tits off this time."

My chuckles are painful as the memory of fighting alongside my friends plays before my eyes. "Don't let her decapitate you with her shield."

Hera has the same amused, yet pained expression. She walks over and pulls me in for a motherly hug. After a moment, she backs away, and I focus on Isis.

"You are more dedicated to your duty to the Father than I thought. I respect you for that. No one else would've offered what you were willing to give. But once I find my husband and children, if you or anyone else tries to take them from me again—" A glowing, red hue mixes with her golden eyes, and then blood leaks down her jade-black skin. "I won't hesitate to unleash her on anyone."

"Noted," I squeaked out my response as I caught the sight of her beast.

Isis nods, then swipes her finger to collect the blood and paints her lips with it. She walks over to me, and I lean down to accept her offering. My friend presses her mouth against mine, and after she pulls away, I lick my lips to collect the antidote to her poison.

Isis does the same thing to Hera as magic tingles its way down my throat and into my chest. Isis' beast has a hard time separating friend from foe, providing us with the antidote will at least allow us to escape.

"The Wolven have been squabbling over who gets me in the hopes that I will let them fuck my virgin pussy before we leave. Don't they know I have a beast of my own to ride, and he's bigger!" Artemis grunts with annoyance as she stomps her way towards us.

I notice a certain being's furry absence. "Where's Aliith?"

Artemis softens a fraction and rests her head on my shoulder. "Hopefully ripping the Wolven's manhood off for trying to touch me."

Low growls and snarls come from the Wolven. However, they all cringe when Isis lets another wave of blood come down her face. She paints her lips and comes over to Artemis. My friend turns her head just enough for Isis to kiss her.

Hera walks over and gives Artemis a loving smile. "Do you want to come with us to find the other Gods and Goddesses so Isis can give the antidote to them too?"

"Yeah. It's better than waiting."

Artemis's words weigh on me; we are only waiting on Hel, and then we can get going.

Isis makes her way through the crowd, and Hera loops her arm around Artemis', and they follow.

My shaking becomes visible as I make my way to the back of our army, towards the falls. I weave through units of Wolven and Atlantean pairs and then warriors from Valhalla.

When I get to the end of the line, I exhale a sigh of relief and begin to run.

Being away from the crowds refocuses my mind. Then it occurs to me that I can fly to the Seedling Woodlands.

Joy sparks to life as I direct soul magic into my—

I'm yanked to a stop by someone latching onto my cloak with their teeth. "Bralyant! I'm going to freeze your dick off if you don't let go of me."

My threat has him raising me off the ground like a defenseless pup before I'm let go.

I spin around, colliding with a black-furred Wolven, not my friend. "What the fuck are you doing here, Aliith? Shouldn't you be delivering somebody's balls to Artemis?"

He shifts down and stays in my personal space. "How were you able to fight off Bralyant?"

"Are you being serious right now?" *We don't have time for this.* "Do you not know what the fuck we are in the middle of? We are assembling to go to battle, and you stopped me from figuring out what's taking Hel so long."

He growls. "Answer the question."

I get up in his face as Skjoldr tries to pull me away from him. "I think the more important questions are why did you not mark me, lie to Artemis, and come to the river without her in the first place? Is she that lenient with you, or are you just a bad servant?"

Skjoldr yanks me back, overriding my will. "Answer. The. Question." He grits his teeth.

"Not until you make fucking sense of why it's so important that you know my answer!" He bites the air as he balls his hands into fists and flinches. "Are you going to fight me for the answer?"

"I'd never fight you! I'm being a bad fucking servant right now because I need to know. And if I tell you, then I'm giving forth knowledge that will hurt someone else who didn't want you to know."

I blink and give in to Skjoldr's request to pull me back a little more. "What did Heimdall tell you?" Even though he is tense, his poker face is unwavering and doesn't give me a hint as to what he's feeling or thinking. "A question for a question?"

He shakes his head. "That will still cause them harm."

I throw my hands up in the air, then brace them on my hips. "I directed my soul magic to root myself into the ground so he couldn't move me."

"You can use your soul magic like that?"

"Yeah, just like everyone else."

"Nobody else can do that." He stumbles to the ground and clutches his chest.

"Aliith." As I fall to my knees before him and place my hands over his, I realize what is happening to him. He's ignoring his duties as a servant and being punished for it. "Why are you doing this to yourself?"

Skjoldr screams at me, but I'm able to fight her off as I reach for my power by thinking of happy memories of Freyr and me.

"This pain is nothing compared to the death I was promised." Our eyes meet as a heaviness settles between us.

"You were supposed to die?"

He nods as magic hums, coating my hands in a delicate mistiness of soft blue light. I push it out to alleviate the pain around his soul. Unlike Haidion's puppy, I have no problem overriding the influence of his servant brand.

"Freyja?" He groans in relief, as his body relaxes under my touch. "What is this?"

I chuckle. "Can you live with not knowing?"

He returns my amusement with an appreciative smile. "I think that's why I'm able to fight off my servant brand, because you saved my life."

"That doesn't mean I own it though."

I let the memories fade, and my power pulled back, then I repositioned myself to help him stand.

"I'd offer you it though if my soul wasn't already bound to another." The absolute certainty in his voice makes me speechless, giving Skjoldr rein once again to yank me away from him. "Perhaps Artemis will allow me to be shared—"

An alarming surge of a soul-crushing scream comes from above the falls.

Creatures approach the ledge, increasing the intensity of the war cry, which barrels down on the river below like a tidal wave. The trees closest to the river are pulled out, roots and all, and fly further down the river along with any vegetation and sand. Even the clouds above change course to get away.

The creatures' leader raises its head and lets out a deafening neigh before leaping off the falls and into the river; everyone else follows suit. Instead of water rushing down, thousands upon thousands of ashen-fire horses cascaded down the frozen falls. The river shakes, causing me to fall to my hands and knees.

Heimdall's magic coating the river is unaffected, but the same cannot be said for every thread in my existence telling me to run for my life.

Aliith shifts into his Wolven form and lowers for me to get on, I don't hesitate.

Metal slamming against shields and Valhalla warriors' proud chants come from behind us, answering the war cry hurtling towards them. The clash of spirited voices thins out the thick gray sky, and the sun pushes through with all its might, its rays cutting through the clouds that try to suffocate it. Heimdall's magic is fed by the intensity of the sun, causing the river to glow like a rainbow.

I rub Aliith's tense shoulders. "Stand down, friend, these creatures are on our side." His muscles quiver and then relax.

Surprisingly, Skjoldr isn't humming in my chest to tell me to get off. Why she thinks Aliith is dangerous, I don't know.

I gasp as the creature's leader and the one on his back come into view. Hel rides Sleipnir, an eight-legged silver stallion with fiery white hair, a worshiped creature of our pantheon.

My friend rides up to us with a smile of, *'I know I'm late, but my badass magic makes up for the delay.'*

Sleipnir comes up to our side, he's just as massive as Aliith, but he has a longer neck. They sniff each other and then the creature turns his attention to me. I lean forward and bow my head so he can sniff my neck.

He presses his muzzle against my shoulder, telling me to rise. "You are more majestic than I ever dreamed of, Sleipnir." After he nods in appreciation, he tilts down so I can press my forehead against his.

"I was going to make Ashen Wolven, but Sleipnir showed up and offered his aide." Sleipnir backs up and brings Hel closer to me. "His magic mixed with mine, they are not only transportation, but another five thousand warriors ready to trample and bite the heads off of anyone in their way. Oh, and—" She hands me a cloth bag then grips my shoulder. "One Nymph lives. She offered me the powder from her race's bones to paint our faces to deter the Vampyres from biting us."

"Where is she now?" I urgently inquire.

"Safe, protected, and cared for. That's all she was willing to tell me." Hel looks over my shoulder and lowers her voice. "But she was brought and taken away from me by shadow magic."

"Was there anything different about the shadow magic?"

Hel tilts her head as she thinks. "It was definitely shadow mist like what the Demonical have. Not the smoky shadows of a Shadow Monster."

Haidion's puppy has the same type of shadow magic. Does that mean—*are you a shadow monster? I thought Cerberus's were creatures of blood and flesh, not shadowy.*

I'm greeted by nothing but silence in my mind. *Haidion's puppy?* Nothing. *I just want to know. I trust Haidion, and that extends to you.* Still nothing. *We can be friends if you answer me.* Not a peep, but his absence answers my question. However, another comes to the forefront of my mind. Why didn't Haidion tell me his pet was a Shadow Monster?

The herd of Hel's and Sleipnir's creations ride up. All have coal-burning eyes, eight legs, ashen skin, and fiery white hair. Strapped to their sides are cloth bags.

Hel sits back on Sleipnir. "I had another visitor on my way here. Have you ever heard of a Radiant?" I shake my head. "Me neither. They must be a race from the outer edge of the universe." Hel dismounts Sleipnir and walks to the closest horse. "Anyhow, she and her son offered nourishment to the Faithful army." Hel pulls out two silver apples and walks back over to us. "She said they'd keep us all satiated and strong from dawn till dusk. There are enough for everyone, and the pair were heading to the Allied Army next."

Aliith immediately eats the apple and groans as his body shakes under me. I take his lead and accept the apple. The fruit is crisp and has a hint of honey to counter the tartness. My soul radiates and burns stronger, giving me a visible aura of light.

I'm done with my apple and give the core to Aliith, which he happily takes.

I instruct all the warriors from Valhalla to pair up with a horse since Eirikur is up at the front, waiting with the other leaders to have one more meeting before the battle.

Hel and I distribute bags of apples and ashes to everyone for them to paint their faces.

A whiteish-violet Wolven is the first to shift and accept our offering. "I love my race, but they can be a bunch of pussies sometimes." The growls from the Wolven nearest the Bravo female doesn't affect her as she takes a bite of the apple. "As the eldest child of the Beta Prince, it's my duty to show them what it means to have balls. I'm Reason, by the way."

Before I can introduce myself, she flawlessly shifts and glows like an angel—all were eager for an apple.

News traveled down faster than we could hand out bags, so we didn't have to keep convincing everyone to eat an apple and paint their faces.

With all but one bag of apples and powder, I mount the horse for Eirikur, and Hel, Aliith, and I head to the front of the line.

All the Gods, Ambar, Thaddeus, Saga, Eirikur, Treason, and Bralyant are all assembled in a circle.

Aliith trots over to Artemis and wraps her arms around his neck like a child who missed a parent.

Eirikur and Saga both have the excitement of a child on Yule and an awe-struck expression as they admire Sleipnir.

"This one is for you, Eirikur." I dismount and pat the horse's neck.

Eirikur lets the beast sniff him before he embraces his neck with a hug. "This is the highest honor any warrior of Valhalla could ever receive."

Saga lowly grumbles with jealousy. "Can my unit switch to ride with them?"

"I thought you wanted to ride me?" Thaddeus winks at her.

I met Heimdall's eyes, and he didn't seem the least bit concerned about Thaddeus flirting with his lover.

"Everyone is assembled."

Heimdall nods to me and speaks to the circle. "We ride to the river's end. When we reach the falls, I'll trigger my magic, and the mist at our feet will rise to the chests of the Wolven and Horses. All will leap and be consumed by my clouds, which will transport us. I will get the first wave of warriors into the forest before the Valley of the Father's Arms. Then the second wave of warriors and I will be waiting in the northern woods for the signal."

He turns his attention back to me, and all eyes follow his line of sight. *Speeches are not my thing.*

A magical electrical current calms my hammering pulse as a cool breeze gently pushes me from behind, as if someone were cheering me on. The thought that this is Freyr's spirit trying to communicate with me and that he has been helping me ever since the horn blew soothes my erratically fluttering heart.

"I do not have the same way with words that my brother had."

Everyone chuckles and the weight of giving a speech lessens a fraction.

"The strength of his words was only impactful from the devotion of his actions. He might've been assigned to be the Norse God of Kinship, Fertility, Peace, and Weather, but he didn't let his title define him, his spirit did, and that's why everyone remembers him as the God of his word."

The crowd nods in agreement.

"As I look at every one of you, I don't see a title. Your being here shows me that you are more than what you were told to be and that your souls are fueled by more than magic. Your spirits have the power to influence the world and bring about great change because you are all Gods of your word. That's why the Unfaithful plotted to keep everyone from going to the Father, because they know they're nothing without the magic flowing in the Father's roots, and they're fucking terrified of our spirits. When we ride into battle, our cries will not only emphasize our faithfulness to the Father but will also raise our spirits to sing and soar because we would rather stay true to our word than be corrupted by theirs."

A powerful pinkish-red light shines on my body—no, not on it, but from within it.

The motivated smiles on everyone's faces are replaced by a tear-springing awe, as if they are taking in the most glorious sight they will ever see in their existence.

Aliith and Sleipnir's heads rise to the clearing sky. Treason and

Bralyant follow suit, and all the other Wolven raise their heads as well. The Gods at my back, along with the Atlanteans and Spartans, all join in with their war cries and chants.

I have done what I've always wanted to do; carry on my brother's legacy. From the cool breeze still blowing, lifting the voices to soar, I know he can not only hear them, but in some spectacular, magical way, he is making the galaxy beyond hear them, too.

My spiritual power surfaces as a pair of hands proudly grip my shoulders and lips press against my forehead. "I love you too, Freyr. I won't let you down."

Heimdall approaches me and takes the bag of Nymph bone dust from Hel. "May I?"

I nod, and Heimdall paints my face before Hel uses her blood to draw runes from the top of my forehead down to my chin.

"What runes did you bless me with?"

Hel coats my face with another layer of magic to protect her work of art from being removed. "The ones that forge your soul."

When all have their faces painted, all but Aliith and Sleipnir extend out their right arms for Heimdall to brand us with his power so we can all speak mind-to-mind during battle. He could've made the design simpler, but the Tree of Life with all of the races making up the Faithful army might be the design of my first tattoo once all of this is done.

"King Thaddeus." Bralyant is given a cloak by another Wolven who emerged from the forest. "Please accept this gift on behalf of the Wolven race as our apology for belittling your strength as warriors."

Thaddeus accepts the gift. "Is this Wolven fur?"

"Yes. Reckell was adamant about not allowing anyone to ride him into battle. I was told he'd rather be skinned alive. His pelt is yours and holds all the magical properties of a Wolven."

"Holy Aurora," numerous voices gasped from our circle.

Treason walks over to me. "My family and I are honored to have you lead us into battle, Freyja." He extends his arms out to me, and I embrace him.

"Your leadership is shown through your children. If I were ever to be blessed to be a mother, I would aspire to be as great a parent as you and your mate are."

The Beta Prince lets out a low, raspy whimper of longing. "You are extremely generous for giving me such encouraging words of support. I'm doing whatever I can to be the parent that my pups need in the absence of their mother. I hope wherever my mate's spirit is, she's smiling down on us and rolling her eyes at me every now and then when I mess up." He attempts to chuckle, but it comes across as sniffling. *I can't believe I forgot that his wife died*

It was my first year living with the race when Treason's mate died unexpectedly along with Bralyant's mother. *Shit, I forgot their names too. This is why pushing away the memories I had with the Wolven was a bad idea.*

I reach up and brush my cheek against his.

Treason stills for a second, then lowers his head and nudges me back while embracing me with a hug that has me melting into his warm, broad chest.

I press my nose against his neck and breathe him in. A buttercream aroma wafts into my nostrils, with a trace of vanilla. I groan from the mouth-watering smell and have the urge to taste his skin, but I push that strange impulse aside because this display of affection isn't for me. Even though I can't tell how he's feeling by smelling him, the act of sniffing has him relaxing and letting out little groans that only a beast being soothed can produce.

"*Thank you, Freyja.*" He deliciously growled in Atlantean before planting a searing kiss on my cheek.

A high-pitched gasp that I only ever make in my bedroom escapes me before I can bite my lip to keep it from coming out.

Treason offers me a not-so-innocent smile before he walks over to Isis, who must be paired to ride into battle. The Beta Prince will be leading the second wave of warriors into battle, and if anything happens to our brand's magic to talk to one another, Bralyant will still be able to get in contact with the second wave faster with his channel with Treason.

Aliith approaches Artemis; she lunges into me with a hug. "We'll be cheering you on until you call us out." I hug her back and give a nod to Aliith.

All go to where they are placed in the lineup, clearing out my view of the river we are to run down to the horizon.

When a warm hand tries to intertwine with mine, I pull away.

Bralyant frowns for a moment before replacing his disappointment with a gentle smile.

"Freyr would be so proud of you, Freyja."

I can't help but return his smile at the mention of my brother. "I'm honored to ride with my *friends* into battle." My emphasis on friends registers as he nods more to himself.

"I'm ready when you are, Alpha." *He's only ever called Freyr that.*

Before I can think better of it, I hug him with all my might as my thanks for considering me worthy of being as great a leader as my brother.

Bralyant presses a kiss on my cheek in the same spot Treason kissed me.

I push him away with a snarl, and he takes the hint that he should back away and shift. The Wolven King was undoubtedly trying to replace the Beta Prince's scent on me with his own.

After I climb onto Bralyant's back, he turns his head back to me. His question about my readiness is written all over his face. I nod, and he turns his head up to howl before running down the frozen river.

Howls, neighs, and cheers follow us. Heimdall comes up on my right side, riding on a Bravo Wolven with whitish-violet fur, Reason. On my left, Hel rides on Sleipnir. Even though she will be with the second wave of warriors, she couldn't be talked out of riding at my side.

With the invigorating breeze pushing Bralyant to run faster, Freyr rides with me, and I know in my soul that I won't be going into battle without him.

The river drops off ahead, showcasing miles upon miles of magical forest. Bralyant keeps pace with Reason, knowing if he tries to be ahead, we might free-fall before Heimdall's magic catches us.

A thrill awakens in my soul and floods my veins, but this is a different energy, one I haven't experienced in almost five hundred years. I'm not flying to be free; I'm riding into battle. My mindset isn't focused on wanting adventure but on the fight that lies ahead.

Each rush of air filling my lungs and pumping my heart cements the shift from the Freyja I was when I left my house to the Freyja with over ten thousand warriors relying on her leadership.

Heimdall's profound voice fills my mind as the brand hums on my arm. *With the Solar Noon light.*

All the voices, including mine, chanted the second verse of the Resistance creed when we all rode into the first battle of the War over the Frozen Fire Highlands. *We will ride to fight!*

Heimdall triggers his magic to rise to Bralyant's chest as we near the end of the frozen river.

My friend leaps into the air, and a split second later, white clouds engulf us.

HOW MUCH MORE CAN I ENDURE BEFORE I FAIL?

SEVENTEEN

ALMOST SOLAR NOON

"If the greed of the Unfaithful Army is this vast, I fear what they will do to the rest of Earthradon."

Ambar pushes off the withered tree she had pressed her forehead against to try and get a reading of what lay in the forest, even though all the vegetation was harvested.

The trees surrounding us are still standing, so their strength must be due to their proximity to the Great Willow Tree.

Heimdall's voice enters my mind as the brand on my right arm hums. *The North woods are still lush with vegetation.*

Looks can be deceiving, Thaddeus remarks.

Hera's voice comes through next. *He's right. I can't harvest any magic from the flowers or bushes.*

I'm picking up Fae magic all over, Treason adds.

It's a Fae tactic, Bralyant snarls with revulsion. *They claim vegetation to refill their reserves, preventing themselves from running low.*

Eirikur's voice rushes in. *Avoid the river! Something with fins just pulled a couple of my warriors in when they went down to refill their waterskins.*

Numerous curses nearly drown out Isis as she asks, *Doesn't the Siren Race monitor the river?*

Yes, they do, but neither King Adom nor I have been able to contact them. Ambar's sad aura could make the sky above lose its purpose for wanting to exist.

The ash on her face covers up the gold stenciling as her fading composure as both an Atlantean Captain and a royal shows me that the spirit inside her has cracked and doesn't know how to prevent itself from shattering.

Ambar meets my concerned gaze. "Whatever Oceanic race is allied with the Unfaithful is taking what *Blessiver Soula* represents, and her beauty is in vain. She's the river that swallows rivers, not innocent souls." Her eyes glisten. "These corrupt beings are beyond healing."

The Wolven she paired with nudges her neck and whimpers. Ambar turns and presses her forehead against the Wolven, accepting the offered comfort.

Suppose Blessiver Soula, the river that blesses, becomes magically polluted by the influence of the Unfaithful, King Adom's lands will be impacted to the point of devastation, affecting the lives of millions.

Ambar's voice enters my mind. *Blessiver Soula is a river that connects to the ocean, so it could be any of the Oceanic races. It only flows on the east side of the Great Willow Tree, so we don't have to worry about running into it, but the Allied Army will. I'll try to contact King Adom through our telepathic bond to warn him.*

I'll also contact Watson through our channel to get the message to him as well. Bralyant huffs.

A moment later, the brand stops humming, and the eerie creaks and sways of the trees fill the silence.

Under my boots, the ground is dry, cracked, and sharp. If the Wolven were to run, their paws would get sliced up before we reached the end of the forest.

All the bark is gone, as is the canopy of leaves, and thick branches litter the ground as if they were sliced off. When we first arrived, Bralyant sniffed a branch and told Ambar and me not to touch any of them because they were coated with magic to set off an alarm.

The sun we rode out with couldn't break through the thick, gray clouds looming overhead. A fog hangs in the air, replacing the nakedness of the forest and providing more cover; however, the thickness makes each breath heavy in my lungs.

Ambar mounts her Wolven. "I would have to dig down to the roots to get a reading on the forest and what lies waiting in the valley, but the ground has unnaturally turned to stone. We are going in blind."

Bralyant's voice enters my mind as the brand hums. *I'm sending a unit out to scout the area.*

I would like for Thaddeus to go with them. Bralyant nods to me with a huff, acknowledging my request.

Thaddeus' voice floats in. *I'll gladly go, Commander.*

I think we are all in agreement, Freyja, that you are leading the Faithful Army, Treason states, interrupting my objection to being called by the commander title.

All agree with Treason's statement. Even though it's hard to decipher the voices talking at once, I know none of them was Bralyant. I will not push him to accept the title of authority given to me since his Alpha nature as the Wolven King won't allow him to. I trust that he'll listen to me when the time comes for battle.

Five Wolven, all free of riders except the one Thaddeus is on, trot ahead and gracefully leap and avoid the branches. The fog consumes their bodies after a moment as if they disappeared from existence.

An unsettling presence I've felt since we landed in the forest has me hesitating about getting back on Bralyant. Given the fog and battle ahead, maybe my paranoia is settling in. Not even my senses, the shadowy-star magic, or the Wolven are picking up on any threat of danger. However, my instincts are telling me something is here, and Skjoldr is urging me to go and find it.

My friend sniffs my neck and nudges me with a whimper. "I sense something." His ears perk up as some of the trees halt their ghostly melody of despair and suffering.

I reach for my chest so Bralyant knows what I'm going to do. He huffs in acknowledgment, and I hold my breath to activate my—

A short shadow darts into my peripheral vision, breaking my concentration. The figure scurries to a tree near Bralyant and me, peeks out, and pulls back behind the tree.

Haidion's puppy? When I get no response, I nod toward the shadow and take a wide berth around. Without needing to communicate my tactic, Bralyant remains where he is to be the focal point for the shadow's attention.

My friend stays oblivious as the figure peeks around the tree again. The little shadow is no more than three feet tall and is unaware of me coming up from behind.

The Wolven King is known to have the best instincts in all of Earthradon, so Bralyant not sensing this figure approaching is concerning. The only conclusion that makes sense is that this is a shadow monster. However, I shouldn't be able to feel this being. I didn't pick up on the shadow monster in me back at home or Haidion's puppy unless he was using magic on me.

Also, the shadows on this figure are different. I've seen three distinct types of shadow magic, and this being is covered in an Astroblack, paint-like mist that reminds me of a leech. The glittering powder coating leaves me at a loss of what type of being I'm about to surprise.

I activate only a portion of my spiritual power to grab their soul.

When the shadow being takes another look at Bralyant, I jump over the branch and lunge for where a chest would be on a three-foot figure.

A soul flutters in my hand. As I squeeze, the shadow magic absorbs into the small being.

Black, fuzzy wings come out of the mist as if they were tucked in, and a pair of luminescent, shadow-steel eyes blaze through.

I choke out a startled gasp as I take in the Fae child in my grasp.

He's trembling with worry, but he keeps his chin up. As a child, his skin shows me his mood instead of his eyes. Rather than the flawless glow of raw beauty of whatever skin tone he is, he's pastel gray, meaning he's nervous.

His honey-brown hair is braided back into a bun like all the Fae males do when they go into battle to show off their pointed ears, which he hasn't grown into, along with his wings. The fuzz hasn't even started to shed to evolve into the proud wings of the Fae. He's not even a fledgling yet. This child shouldn't be outside the lands of his court, let alone Faerie territory.

I'm astounded that he has formidable magic at such a young age. No Fae, unless they are a High Lord, can use magic to prevent themselves from being detected as this child did.

The boy's arms are free, but he isn't reaching for weapons or fighting me. Only daggers adorn his body, along with raggedy leather armor. Even though the child isn't a threat to me, he is one to himself.

"I'm just looking for my father." His adorable Fanarzien tongue makes my ovaries hurt, and my womb ache.

Out of the corner of my eye, Bralyant shifts and walks over to us. "Get behind me." I nod toward my backside.

Bralyant's lip turns up on his ashen-painted face. I narrow my eyes to convey that he needs to keep his nose out of the dewy grass and up in the air where it belongs.

As he rounds the tree, I turn my body to block his. The Wolven might not have an issue with nudity, but the Fae boy was not brought up the same way the children of Bralyant's race are. Though Bralyant's cock is tucked inside him and only grows out when he's aroused, his balls are still on display.

Bralyants' sultry playfulness is gone as he focuses on the child. He growls, and the Fae boy surprisingly doesn't cry or scream; instead, the child flicks his luminescent eyes down to his chest and then my arm, inquisitively assessing me.

My friend grips my hips and leans into my ear while keeping eye contact with the child. "Is he what you sensed?"

I take a breath and allow my instincts to tune into the environment. "No. The presence I'm sensing is still here." I'm closer to it as if it's within arm's reach, but it's not the boy.

The tree behind the boy stops swaying and creaking as if it didn't realize how noisy it was.

"I'm just looking for my father." The boy's eyes dart between Bralyant and me.

He can speak some Earthradonic already. Fae children aren't taught other languages until they reach maturity.

"Move on without me. I'll catch up."

I don't know how much of the common tongue this Fae child will be able to comprehend, so speaking in his language will be more effective in helping me figure out why he is here and how to send him home. Bralyant will be no help and get annoyed since he won't understand what we are discussing. Even though the Wolven are Peacekeepers, they know all languages expect Fanarzien for some reason.

Bralyant looks away from the boy to meet my gaze. "We are not moving until we take care of him."

"Take care of him as in..." My friend's eyes darken with murderous intent. "No!" I growl as the Fae boy wraps his arms around himself.

"Compared to what his race has done to mine, I would be doing this boy a kindness."

The dead forest around us must still have some magic left in it because all the noises stop as if they, too, were stunned by what Bralyant was suggesting.

"If my hands were free, they would be around your neck right now. Move. On."

Bralyant tightens his grip on my hips. "Do you know what the Fae did after my race helped them regain their lands during the century-long war over territory?" I shake my head. "They went to our lands, took our children, and placed their mutilated bodies all around their border. Some type of shadow magic was used to harvest the children's bones and blood, and then a barrier was created to hide and protect the Faerie lands. No other race, beast, or magical being can enter. If someone happened to get through, they come back without a memory of who they are or are lost forever."

My shock is hard to contain. "But the Fae race doesn't have shadow magic." *The boy does.*

"They don't, but enough innocent souls were killed to summon the Shadow King and his monsters. Most likely, the Fae offered him the Wolven children's souls in exchange for their barrier being built. Trust me, if we had proof of the Fae wielding shadow magic, we'd notify the Wardalyrians."

The information Bralyant has given me has my mind anxiously swirling. If there is a magical being called the Shadow King, why haven't I heard about him before? Until a second ago, I thought shadow monsters were independent creatures free from being bound by a race like caribou, wolves, and bears. Never had I believed they would have a monarch to rule over them. Now that I think about it, if Haidion's puppy is a shadow monster, they're more like a race because the puppy was able to communicate with me.

My friend also points out that instead of protecting the Fae child, I should be reporting him due to two laws being broken: the first, possible cross-training, and the second, wielding shadow magic when his race's origin isn't from Orrtiereum. Yet panic gets sprinkled on my mental storm of worry for the boy about being found out. What if the child is the product of a couple who illegally intermated and bred, or is a Rarity like me? In both scenarios, I have a soft spot for him, and the child has given me no reason to suspect he's dangerous. I won't jump to conclusions until I know his story, and I'm thankful Bralyant didn't see the shadows covering or going into the boy's body.

"Why is the information about what happened to the Wolven children unknown?"

This heartbreaking piece of history never once came up when I lived with the Wolvens. Freyr had been close with Yrradiant and then his sons, so he should've been told at least about this and would've passed it on to me because we never kept secrets from each other.

"If word got out about the magical power of what our blood and bones can do, we'd be hunted down to extinction. The Fae have kept the secret to themselves, thank the Fates."

"What about the Father, his daughters, or his sons... weren't they told?"

When Existence gave me the history lesson about the war over territories, this would've been an important fact, and she would've trusted me with it.

"One of the Father's sons witnessed the Wolven children being killed. He went on a rampage, massacred thousands, and almost wiped out the entire Necromancer and Vampyre races as well. I guess he never told anyone before he was chained to float in eternal sleep, and the Wolven King at the time, my grandfather, didn't want anyone's pity because nothing could be done. We give anything involving the Fae to the Dragons to take care of."

"I talk and play with them when I can." Our attention darts to the boy. He is still speaking Earthradonic. "Everyone else gets freaked out by things they can't see, but that's why we put pelts in the Skingrove for them. No one goes into Soulwood, so they can have their own space. Well, besides me, because I visit often. As for the barrier, it's cursed, preventing them from going anywhere. They only trick travelers when bored; they do not harm or take anything from them. Something else is making beings disappear." The child trails off, and his gray skin tints darker, indicating his terror.

The Fae boy might've thought what he said was helpful, but based on the heat pouring off Bralyant's body and his tense muscles, he is close to shifting. Behind my friend's intense display of Alpha dominance is the grudge his race has held onto for eons. The information was insightful and reassuring that the children were finding some peace from the trauma they endured, but now I'm questioning the Fae's intentions about caring about them at all.

Bralyant lets out an enraged growl and walks around me to get to the Fae boy.

I pull my hand out of the child's body, deactivate my power, and whirl on my friend, keeping the child at my back.

"You would make this innocent boy pay for the sins of his ancestors? Fuck, no! If you touch him, I'll make certain that your legs remain broken this time." I might have fallen under his Wolven King's influence before, but I won't if he uses it to make me back down.

Growls echo from the fog behind Bralyant and bounce off the trees.

Pieces of wood fall off the tops and rain down. None hits the boy, but my friend isn't spared as one knocks him on the head, only heightening his anger.

I keep a hand on the boy's shoulder to know he is still behind me. To my surprise, the boy wraps his arms around my leg.

Bralyant gets in my personal space. "Do not threaten me again. I'm only going to offer you this leniency one time." In the blink of an eye, my friend is not before me. The spirit of his beast is. "As for what happened in the past, my father lost his siblings. He saw them get taken and was only spared because he was sick." He leans down until we are nose-to-nose. "And you have no room to speak about holding grudges."

"I don't hold any." His brows scrunch up as if I were insane. "I don't hold any," I repeat in a much softer tone.

I'm out of breath as my words soak into my mind, sparking a realization. My hatred and anger are no longer directed at the Dragon race, only at their Queen and the midnight-green dragon who killed Freyr.

Since my brother's death, whenever a dragon flew over, my perception was thrown off as I tried to figure out what color the scales were. Fiery red coated my vision by the time I flew up for a closer look. Something primal within me took over, and I would always blackout as murderous rage took control of me.

Bralyant pulls back slightly as if he can't believe what I've just admitted. "As of when?"

Early this morning and a second ago, so, basically, "Today."

Witnessing a long-term grudge has set the record straight for how I not only need to let go of my hateful views of the Dragons but also want to be cleansed of my sinful way of thinking. I was in Bralyant's position earlier, and even though Starson didn't have the appearance of a child, he was still innocent, along with all those other dragons I attacked and almost killed. I'm ashamed of how I acted and owe my new friend an apology.

"I flew to Camp Ariella on the Dragon Queen's younger Princeling because Existence sent him to come and get me. He willingly offered me an apology on behalf of his race for the loss of my brother, knowing I could've blood-branded him. If I hadn't let go of my grudge, I wouldn't have shown up when I did, and most likely Hermes would've captured me because you were already delaying your orders to go back to Relynt."

A sharp breath and the glisten of wetness over his eyes has me biting my tongue, reprimanding myself for speaking of Bralyant's late brother. I can see the mask he's wearing to protect himself from the emotions he can't fully unleash. The title of being the King of his race must be all that's holding him up.

When Auxiliary was cast out for mating with a non-wolven, Bralyant hadn't dealt with that loss properly, so I can't imagine what he's going through after losing another brother. I worry about how my friend is going to live with himself knowing he killed a family member, even though he had reason to challenge the late Wolven King.

I slide my free hand to the back of Bralyant's neck, massaging his skin to calm him. He slowly relaxes.

"You flew to the camp on the Dragon Queen's Second Son?" His voice drops to a whisper.

"I give you my word." When a pleasurable groan leaves his lips, I stop and rest my hand on the nape of his neck. "Holding onto anger is always easier than experiencing the pain. Trust me."

Bralyant's attention goes to my lips. "What if we do an exchange." The gold halo in his eyes glistens as he takes an enjoyable breath and raises his gaze to mine. "If I can't have that child, would you give me—"

My friend's dream-like gaze shatters as a dozen Wolven peer through the mist behind him. Their low growls make me lose my progress in swaying my friend as he tenses and lets out a sharp breath.

I don't have time to process what he was about to bargain with me because I need him to see reason. "Do you want to be known as the Wolven King who stooped down to the same level of cruelty the Fae delivered upon the children of your race?"

The growling only gets louder, making the Fae boy hold me tighter.

Bralyant snarls, silencing the Wolven. He turns his attention down toward his chest and takes a deep breath. When his eyes meet mine once again, all my hope is gone as murderous intent dominates all of his features.

"If we weren't about to go into battle, I'd let the elder Wolven here, who witnessed the sight of the mutilated Wolven pups' bodies, decide what to do with the Fae child, but we don't have the time. Either you step away and don't interfere with me killing him, or you offer me a debt in exchange for my allowing you to get rid of him yourself."

Bralyant could just walk away and let me deal with this, but my friend is nowhere in sight. I want to be mad and scream because Bralyant can be the example of change and mercy to lead his people to heal, but he can't because he hasn't healed himself. Worse, he's transferring the pain he doesn't want to deal with onto me with the ultimatum, forcing me to pay for saving this child. I would never do something like this to a friend, especially one I loved.

Pain ripples from the shield wall made of soul magic I constructed to protect the tender spots of my existence.

I drop my right hand from Bralyant and find the Fae boy's neck to comfort him instead. He shudders under my touch, and I clench every muscle to prevent myself from breaking Bralyant's legs anyway for traumatizing this boy.

"I, Freyja." Bralyant softens the unyielding mask of the Wolven

King, allowing his surprise to come through. "Offer you, the Wolven King, a debt as payment for allowing me to spare this Fae boy's life." I make the Alpha flinch from my words, which are full of venom.

A gasp of surprise comes from the boy behind me, either because I took on a debt to save him or because he now knows my name.

"My bite will seal the debt that you owe me."

"And what will I be owing you?"

Bralyant doesn't answer or display any indication for me to read as he wraps his arm around my shoulders and places his hand on the right side of my neck. He leans in and brushes his lips over my violently beating pulse before he sinks his fangs into my skin.

My soul blazes and whirls in a chaotic storm, wanting to attack Bralyant, but I remain still and endure the blood-boiling pain.

The veins in my neck thicken as if a substance was injected into me, making itself comfortable. Skjoldr alerts me to something in my body. My soul flares, wanting to push it out, but nothing can be done since it's a magical debt I willingly took.

Bralyant retracts his fangs and then laps up the bite marks to help the wounds heal faster.

The uncomfortable pressure subsides a second later; however, my rage stays, for Bralyant has made a second mark on my neck over the bruises Odin gave me as if he wants my ex-husband to know he's claiming me as his.

The Wolven King peers at the boy. "Don't trust a word he says, and the longer you talk to him, the more his magic will jinx yours."

"This is none of your concern anymore, Alpha," I bit out.

"You are my concern." Bralyant turns and walks away. "Be quick with whatever you decide to do to dispose of him." He says over his shoulder as he and the other Wolven vanish into the mist.

My attention moves to the boy. He peers up at me after I brush my hand over his head. "I almost peed myself."

I bite my tongue and take a deep breath to prevent my laugh from coming out. What the boy said wasn't funny, but his unexpected comment took the edge off of what had just happened between my friend and me.

I kneel before him. *"I want to help relax you. Will you let me?"*

Even though he speaks fluent Earthradonic, I switch to Fanarzien so he knows he can revert to his native tongue.

His ears twitch. *"You're fluent in Fanarzien?"*

"Yes, and I know many other languages as well."

The boy's wings ease down a fraction as he tilts his head. "Helping me to relax won't make me pee myself, will it?"

After I shake my head, he nods, and I place my hand on his chest. "Take deep breaths with me."

On our first intake, I bring forth happy memories of Freyr and me, making my hand hum. My hand emits a delicate mist of soft blue light as we take our second breath. After a couple more breaths, his skin changes from a dark gray to the flawless, glowing hue of the Fae. His coppery complexion dazzles like a diamond despite the gloomy source of light.

"That power is so cool!" The boy's excitement makes his wings flare out and his skin takes on a warmer glow.

"I calmed your soul down." *And dissolved anything lurking in the void around his precious heart.* "Your father brought you here with him?" I stop the reel of memories to turn off my power and brace my hands on my thighs.

His wings droop as his smile leaves his sweet face. "No. I came here alone to prove to my father that I'm not worthless."

An enraged snarl escapes me before I can stop it. "What made you think that you are worthless?"

Tears well up in his eyes as his skin changes to a pastel blue as the glow darkens. And for some reason, the shadows nearby move toward the boy as if they plan to conceal him.

"Because my father said I was." *What the fuck!* The boy sniffles and tries to swallow his tears. "A year ago, I overheard my parents talking about me being selected to be saved. Father said he tried to get someone else to take my place. My gasp was how they discovered me watching them. Mom tried to stop my father from directing his anger at me, but he magically bound her to a chair. She could only watch as he..."

As he wraps his arms around himself, my supply of soul magic thickens as my anger spikes.

"While my father punished me for eavesdropping, he yelled how much of a disgraceful representation I am of his court for my magic being different and a worthless member of his bloodline since I can't throw a blade to save my life. Mom somehow broke free of Father's control, which shocked both of us. She used her magic to get me away from Father, then pulled out a lengthy, slender, curved sword that magically came out of her neck and attacked him. As they fought, Mom begged me to fly to my uncle and stay with him until she came for me. I did, but not before telling my father I'd prove I wasn't worthless."

He takes a breath to steady his choppy voice. "I found out this morning from my uncle that our race was going to battle, and I knew this was my chance to prove myself. After he hugged me and my mom goodbye and left with my father, I snuck out and used a spell to get me..."

He slaps his hands over his mouth and jolts while his eyes frantically look around as if his father were about to come out of the mist to punish him for what he just admitted.

Since the Wiccayens started as a mortal race and became magically imbued, anyone can become one. The fact that this Fae child could use Wiccayen magic means he earned the trust of the magic system and was then taught how to create a transparent siphon within his body, turning him into a channel for magical energy to flow through. The boy can do anything, from casting spells to wielding elements, as long as he knows how and there is enough magic in the air.

Learning the Wiccayen method for wielding magic still counts as cross-training since he's a Fae and not a mortal. I'm thankful none of the Wolven can understand Fanarzien because they would call a Wardalyrian in a second.

I grip his shoulders and give him a gentle squeeze. "I won't tell as long as you don't tell anyone about my power." When he doesn't stop nodding, I grasp his face before he gives himself whiplash. "The fact that you could get here by yourself proves you aren't worthless. You are a strong, brave, young warrior."

All the darkness is pushed away as the boy gleams as if the light of his soul is shining through his skin, altering the hue to a sun-shiny yellow. "You mean that?" His excited screams are muffled by his hands still over his mouth.

I take his hands in mine. "Yes, I do, which is why you need to go home to grow into the warrior the Father of the Great Willow Tree knows you will become." *How am I going to get him home?*

A smoky voice enters my mind. *Haidion's magic can take him home, but since you are sending the magic away, it won't return because you're not its master. You might have some left afterward.*

You're back. Where did you go? My chest flutters abnormally as an unusual chirping sensation tickles the back of my throat.

Did you fucking miss me? I shuddered from the smile I couldn't see but could feel.

No... since you are inhabiting the privacy of my mind, I would like to be told of your departure and arrival, that's all.

An elongated, guttural growl rakes against the traitorous, flushed skin on my neck. *Why do you twist your tasty tongue and part your luscious lips to speak such ugly lies?*

Their flattery flames my cheeks, but their sweet words elude me as I let out my mental growl. *It's probably the same reason you don't reveal yourself.*

Soul-soothing warmth caresses me like a pair of arms had reached out from behind to hug me. *Only because I don't want to terrify this boy even further; it's the only reason I won't allow you to put a face to the voice.*

Rather than shrugging their presence off, I find myself leaning into them. *Is that because you're a shadow monster?*

A low hum from them arouses the chirping sensation in my chest to purr while the vibration strokes my senses, informing me of the mountainous size of their presence. *I will show you what I am if you're still fighting by Sundown.*

I know you're a Cerberus. They tense. *But Haidion never informed me of his pet's name. Can you tell me?* I need to know what name to curse for stimulating me in ways that I didn't know were possible and that I also shamefully kind of—

Admit that you lied, and I'll reward you, sweet vixen.

I mentally roar. *Call me that again, and I'll show you how 'sweet' I can be.*

My threat only has them chuckling with smoky pleasure. *I've been waiting for my turn to play with you for centuries, so I'll take your threat as a promise.*

When the boy starts rambling about magical modes of transportation, the being's hold on me loosens, and their powerful presence backs off. I flex my muscles to shake off the essence of what is unmistakably not just a puppy but possibly a humanoid version of a Cerberus.

"I don't have any of the supplies I used to get here, and the forest is depleted of magic, so I can't harvest any—"

I place my finger over his mouth, and he stops talking. "All I need you to do is give me your word that once I send you home, you will tell your mom how brave you were and listen to everything she tells you to do so you can be saved."

I take my finger away from his mouth. "Are you making me take a brand?"

"No." Branding a child is illegal and highly punishable. "I just need your word."

His ear poked up along with his wings. "You are going to trust my word?" I nod with a tender smile, which makes him smile wider. "You have my word, she-warrior."

I raise an eyebrow. "You heard my—"

He puts his fingers in his ears. "No, I didn't!"

A Fae knowing a being's name means they have the reins over them and their magic. If I knew his name, he wouldn't be able to affect me. Besides magical reign, the Fae's primary source of wielding magic is to harvest it to either use it immediately or fill their reserves. Like the Wiccayens, they can command their magic to do anything they desire.

I advise you to consider the child's ignorance a gift and move on. The shadow puppy firmly urges.

I pull the boy's fingers out of his ears. "I'm a Norse Goddess, but you can call me your friend."

His wings tuck in as his skin shifts to a pastel gray. "My father is here to kill you. Why would he want to kill someone like you? You stood up for me and took on a debt to protect me."

I stroke his cheek. "Anger can make beings do horrible things like hurting precious children."

He wraps his arms around my neck, holding me tightly. A blissful sigh escapes me as an emptiness that I thought would be forever barren begins to fill. While my skin blooms into a smoky hue of rose gold, I'm mindful of his wings and embrace him with all that my power of love can offer him so he can feel nurtured and cherished. Only those who express unadulterated love to me can awaken my power to help them find true love in their life. Answering a prayer to discover love is like gentle guidance, whereas my power directly influences someone to ensure they will find happiness.

Without knowing it, the boy's spiritual essence extracts all the rose gold magic from me and pulls it inside of him. He lets out a sniffling sigh of happiness as his heart beats harder than it did before.

"As my friend, you should know...wait." He pulls back and looks over his shoulders before focusing back on me. "Do you know this language?" Magic covers his hands as he signs, *"Hello."*

I coat my hands in magic and sign back to him. *"I know Galex."*

"Yes, that was the name my uncle told me. My family, except for my father, are the only Fae who know this language and practice Wiccayen magic. As my friend, you should know, I saw my people enter the trees, and some scarier races went into the ground."

The unsettling presence now makes sense. I keep myself calm with a deep breath as my awareness of the trees' proximity is heightened.

"Is that why you are looking for your father in the woods?"

"Yes, I've been going tree by tree, reading all their magical signatures to find either him or my uncle, and then you all showed up. One of the scarier races made this fog, and it affected my senses so much I thought you were my mom."

Scorpion drug fog. He has been wandering the woods for at least an hour if he was becoming delusional, and soon we will be too.

"Why are you telling me this in Galex?"

"I hear their breathing through the cracks, which means they could hear us talking. Oh, by the way, since you said your name out loud, if you meet any of my people in battle and they say your name, immediately correct them and say, "No, it's Eireaf." The Temptational Voice of Coercion will make it so they have to tell you their name."

Who the fuck is that? Do you know who he's talking about? Wait, can you understand Galex?

A smoky huff enters my mind. *Yes, I can. And I knew of him, but this child must be mistaken because the Temptational Voice of Coercion was annihilated. He's been gone longer than Earthradon has been in existence.*

How could this boy, who is probably only three centuries old, know about this being? Something doesn't add up.

I don't know, and I agree. No other magical being exists that can coerce the magic system. The only way we can know if what the child is telling us is true is if the counter-curse works.

Great, now back to my first question. What's a Temptational Voice of Coercion?

The boy signs to me again, pulling me out of my mental conversation to focus on what he's trying to tell me. *"I give you my word that what I tell you is true."*

Curiosity tempts me to ask the boy what he knows about Coercion. Figuring out where this being is could lead the conversation to my gathering more information about the Unfaithful's battle plan. The strong leader I desperately want to be is all for this strategy, but before I can move my hands to form the question, the mother in me that I will never awaken blasts those notions out of my mind, forcing something I hadn't sensed to dislodge from my senses. *Was something trying to manipulate me just now?*

A gasp of surprise fills every corner of my mind as the energy around me crackles. *Oh fuck!*

I take that as a yes. *We need to get out of this fog.*

The shadow puppy growls with alarm. *Focus on the boy before he starts to spiral into a temper tantrum.*

Before the child's frown deepens, I sign. *"I believe you."* I switch back to speaking Fanarzien. "Are you ready to go home, young warrior?"

He nods with a smile. "Since you told me your title, I'll tell you mine. I'm a High Lord's son." His wings flutter out with pride as his skin tone returns to coppery diamonds with a glow of lunar radiance.

The buildup of my soul magic is becoming uncomfortable as my anger turns into crazed fury. I keep my facial expression in check to not let my inner emotions show.

"You're an Heirling." He stands taller as his wings flap.

A realization hits me: If his father dies during the battle, his rank will transfer to the boy, making this child the youngest High Lord in Fae history. Placing such a responsibility on a child makes me want to find his father and send him home too, even though I want to torture the fuck out of him.

"Let's get you home." Holding my palms out, the boy stares at my magically bandaged hands. *Do I need to give Haidion's magic a location?*

No, they will sense what court he belongs to.

"Will you please take this young warrior home?" The shadowy-star magic comes out and wraps around the boy.

"You have shadow energy too?" He bounces with joy. "I thought my uncle, cousin, and I were the only ones! Yours is different than ours." *What's shadow energy?*

We don't have time for me to give you a complete history lesson about the eradicated court. The Fae, whose ancestors originated from the Fallen Mountain of Sothearia, the Court of Empyrean, can influence the energy of spirits, shadows, and all forms of light because they are more in touch with their beasts. Given that he lacks a tail, he must be half-blooded or less.

Even though I don't need to know, I still want to ask. "Do your parents know, or just your uncle?"

"Yes, they know, which is why my father said I'm worthless. My uncle was furious and told me I was not. I'm more in touch with the spirit of my race, but I need to not show off any other special magic to keep the appearance of being a Rarity."

I'll go with the boy to make sure he gets home safely.

Something invisible nuzzles my cheek, and the shadowy-star magic around the boy thickens.

"Hey, can you give me your word that you won't kill my father and uncle if you face them? I know they are here to hurt you, but I still love them, even though my mom says I shouldn't love my High Lord for how he treats me."

I wish I could send this boy home with a smile. "I can't because they chose to fight in this battle as did I, and not all warriors can go home."

Instead of anger or hatred, he gives me a small smile. "Your honesty is refreshing. Goodbye, Norse Goddess."

"Goodbye, young warrior." The Fae boy gets consumed by shadows and vanishes into thin air.

My shaky hands are still covered in black patches, protecting my burns. I will thank Haidion when I see him next for gifting me his magic. I couldn't do what I did for the boy or Crescent Island without his help.

The sight of Bralyant leaning against a tree comes into view as I go through the fog.

I rush over and pull him. "Don't say a word to me, and shift."

Regret slumps his shoulders as he frowns. "I didn't want to do that to you." His eyes land on the bite mark. "I had no other choice."

The tether on my anger snaps. "You always had a choice, and now you will pay for the consequences."

"What does that mean?" He tries to pull me into his arms, but I push him away. "Tell me what I can do to make it up to you." His eyes worriedly search mine.

I direct soul magic into my brand on my right arm. *This is Scorpion drug fog. Soon, we will all be delusional.*

Curses echo in my mind as Heimdall's voice speaks over them. *You guys need to move. Now!*

The anguish on Bralyant's face leaves him in a blink of an eye. "Wait, did he tell you this?" He gestures from where I just came from.

Admitting to it will only lead to an argument, and we don't have time. We need to move. "Either shift or I'll find someone else to ride."

"You will only ever ride me." Bralyant yanks me to him and leans down, intending to kiss me.

I shove him away with a vicious growl I didn't know I could produce. "What the fuck were you thinking?"

Bralyant growls back, matching my intensity, making all the Wolven close to us lower their heads and flatten their ears.

I remain standing tall and allow the fire in my soul to burn through the thick magic trying to influence me. *I will not be manipulated again!*

His eyes shift from side to side when I don't submit. The beast within him whimpers with longing as the fog covers his passionate purple eyes.

"Wolven do stupid things when they want their mates," he breathlessly whispers, and an eager growl turns the corners of his mouth into a sultry smile. "Like skipping over all the protocols to properly coronate you to be mine and instead just howling it as I claim you in front of everyone."

My friend is becoming delusional with his desire for me, and I don't think it's entirely out of his own volition because of the Scorpion drug fog.

His beast knows there is no bond between us; my scent alone would've been the giveaway. The magic of the fog must be feeding into Bralyant's denial. *Maybe the fog influenced him earlier when he started to make a trade for the fae child.*

Bralyant reaches for me again with lustful determination. "I can't be claimed because I'm not just Odin's wife; I'm his servant, too," I rush out in a panic.

He halts. "What?" The fog in his eyes thins a little. "Why the fuck did you agree to that?!"

"I didn't! I thought what we had was only a marital brand, but the magic is acting strangely, and it called me servant earlier."

This could be why I can't remember our wedding; Odin forced me to forget about becoming his servant, but still, I would've had to agree willingly.

Bralyant growls fiercely, and I tense. "If I had my Alpha-bite power, I could sever the bond between you two. But if your marital brand was made under false circumstances, the magic system will be able to detect it and should allow you to renounce him." His attention flits down to my armored left forearm. "Nothing should be in the way of stopping you; if you can't, tell me. I will take pleasure in torturing him until he releases you, then I'll dig you a grave to throw your ex's body in." His eyes snap back up, and he pulls me to him before I can dodge. "Nothing will keep us apart." After licking my nose, the Wolven beast's equivalent of a kiss, he backs away to shift.

I let out a breath of relief for the information Bralyant disclosed about being able to divorce Odin; however, my muscles don't relax.

Skjoldr hums in my chest, my soul flares, and my instincts scream to find another Wolven to ride. In the state Bralyant is in, he would kill anyone I touch if he thought I was choosing them over him. I can't risk that.

As I mount Bralyant, I share through the brand about the Scorpions in the ground, the Fae in the trees, and how they can hear us through the cracks.

Ambar's voice speaks over the others. *I thought I was misreading it, but I swear I felt life in the tree; however, I couldn't read it.*

All the Wolven cautiously trot through the forest, so they don't slice open their paws and can easily avoid the tree branches.

With a deep breath to ease my trembling, I activate the brand. *Thaddeus, report?*

Thaddeus voice enters my mind. *The valley is free from the fog as if there is a forcefield. It does get thicker when you hit the tree line, so hold your—*

Treason's voice rushes in and speaks over Thaddeus. *The Unfaithful are putting up a shield-ward dome!*

EIGHTEEN

SOLAR NOON

If Earthradon were flat, the Great Willow Tree would be visible from anywhere because it is the tallest structure due to the cosmic amount of magic contained within. However, the Father didn't want to make us all feel inferior, so he placed a ward barrier at the tree lines and the hill behind him, so only when someone stepped within the valley's proximity would they be able to see him.

Once we passed through the tree line, all our lungs were relieved of the heaviness. Bralyant asked if I was okay, and after I answered with a "no," he sighed and hadn't tried to speak to me since. Given the twitching of his ears, he must've tuned into the Wolven channel to get his warriors lined up.

Ambar rides by my side as Bralyant organizes everyone. Having her near helps to relieve the awkwardness between Bralyant and me while straddling his back.

Tall grass fills the vast valley as black clouds cover half of the Great Willow Trees monumental size while the rest of the sky darkens. The air around us sparks as if, at any moment, we could be electrocuted. Whatever magic is in the clouds makes the Father's branches weep, creating a canopy.

"The Father only ever lets his vines touch the ground, encasing him, during harsh weather," Ambar remarked next to me.

"Zeus and Thor are probably planning on using their elemental magic to weaken him then."

Ambar shakes her head. "No exterior magical influences can affect him, and no magic can be used within the canopy."

"Hand-to-hand combat only then?"

Ambar nods as she keeps her attention forward. "If the Unfaithful Gods have any strength left after climbing and weaving through the exposed roots to get to the base of the trunk's core, then yes. Weapons and fists can't be controlled, which is why the gods needed Faithless due to the power of the soul that forged inside."

"Wait, Faithless is a soul-forged item?"

She turns her attention to me with a confused expression. "Yes. Were you not told anything about him, even before you became a Preserver?"

"I was only told by the Preserver, who enlisted me, that Faithless has the power to kill a deity. And the information about why he was forged was classified."

"Yes, he can kill unstoppable beings. And the Preserver must not have trusted you enough to share, but I do." She gives me a warm smile, which I return. "It is said that before Earthradon was created, Evolution was trying to gain control and become more powerful than Creation. Two formidable beings of the magic system offered to be sealed into weapons; other deities and mighty beings also gave a portion of their magic. Three Divine Kings of the Cosmos from outside of Creation's Galaxy created the weapons. One king wove the willing souls and offered magic together, while the second used their undying flames to fuel the forge, and the third fused the magical core with biominerals to bring the most powerful axe and sword to life. Just with these weapons in existence, Evolution stopped. The Preserver Guild has been entrusted with the soul-forged items since the three kings disappeared. I'm surprised Freyr didn't tell you."

"My brother had the mindset that knowledge is to be gained when we are supposed to learn it rather than having it shoved down our throats. I guess this is when I'm supposed to learn about Faithless, and what is the other one's name?"

"She hasn't named herself yet, but we will never know because she is no longer in the hands of the Preserver Guild. The Shadow King has her now."

Shit, that can't be good. "Did he take her?"

"No. She went to him. If only Faithless went to him as well, then we wouldn't have to worry about a threat like this."

Bralyant left me with the impression that the Shadow King is a villainous being who should be hated, while Ambar speaks as if we should be grateful that he exits.

"Are you saying the Shadow King isn't wicked or evil, that he wouldn't have done this himself?"

Ambar narrows her eyes at me. "Were you not educated about him either?" When I shake my head, she scowls, not at me but at the absurdity of my cluelessness. "Well, everyone has a different opinion about the Shadow King, but my race doesn't see him as a threat because the shadow beings he controls hunt down and kill leeches and any infectious magic to protect all souls. And not just here on Earthradon or in the planes of Orrtiereum and Erresthralla, but everywhere. The Shadow Realm parallels everything in Creation's Galaxy and beyond."

The action of the shadow monster who attacked the leech back at home was protecting me then, not fighting over who gets to consume my magic and eat my soul.

Obliteration did mention some realms, one of them being the Spirit Realm, where Freyr is. I do not doubt Ambar's word that the Shadow Realm is one of the others because after the Shadow monster consumed the leech, they vanished into thin air and most likely returned to their parallel realm. Knowing that each realm serves a larger purpose makes my role and duty as a goddess seem minor in comparison.

Before I left home last night, I thought only the galaxy races inhabited the rest of the universe and that the galaxy Earthradon is in was the only one in existence. But after hearing that an authority council oversees the galaxies, mortals can be reborn into another galaxy after they die, and that there are monarchs from a place I never heard of before, my mind is spinning. I am left wondering how infinite existence is beyond Creation's galaxy and why Freyr let me learn about it this way.

My soul blazes, wanting to explore all matters of life in existence while a question I've always had but no one has answered for me comes to the forefront of my mind: *Who created the universe?*

I exhale heavily before refocusing my attention on Ambar and my conversation, putting my curiosity aside. "So, you're saying the Shadow King is trustworthy with soul-forged weapons and wouldn't try to use them for personal gain?"

"Yes. My cousin and our people feel the same way. But know this, Freyja: the intention and purpose of the Shadow King are controversial topics that divide and tear apart friends, families, and even allies." Her eyes flick down to Bralyant, then come back to me. "Be very careful about who you talk to about him."

If Bralyant, the Wolven Ambar is riding on, or any of the Wolven we are passing heard her comment, they didn't react or acknowledge it. Bralyant's continued twitching ears tell me he is more focused on talking to the Wolven than listening to our conversation.

"Do you know if Freyr felt the same way as you do?"

Ambar sighs after a moment of silence passes between us. "I don't know. But given the Sageriel method in which Freyr educated you, I'd say he wouldn't have answered your question but rather let you form your own opinion. Knowledge is objective, and depending on who teaches us, what they say will mold our subjective interpretations of it. I am telling you one thing while someone else has told you another. Do you want your thoughts and opinions to be influenced by others or by what you feel is right in here?" She pats her chest.

"Instead of your cousin trying to marry someone to be his queen, you two should co-rule."

She smiles, releasing some of the gloom taking up residence in her eyes. "Adom has thought of it."

"Since he has thought of it and you aren't already the queen, you don't think you're ready for it."

Ambar scrunches her eyes and nose with a playful smirk. "You are Freyr's sister since you can read the soul so easily."

"No, I'm just really good at guessing." My wink causes her to giggle, something she must not have intended, given the surprised widening of her eyes.

Bralyant trots to the front of the lineup while magic hums in the brand on my right arm, and his voice enters my mind. *Everyone is all set up.*

With a look over my shoulder, all the Wolven with Atlantean riders line the front row; the Wolven without riders are in the middle, and the Spartans and Jarls make up the third and fourth rows.

Bralyant did his job of lining everyone up. Ambar and I were supposed to be brainstorm ideas on how to disarm the shield-ward, but we got sidetracked.

How the fuck are we going to get through? This question has not only bounced around in my thoughts but has also been asked by almost everyone connected to our brand.

The unit Bralyant sent out with Thaddeus to scout what is beyond the bubble rides back. Since the Alpha stealth power covered the unit, the Unfaithful Army wasn't alerted to their investigation.

Thaddeus lets out an exhausted breath, even though he isn't the one running. Without asking, he has been overworking his tactical mind to figure out a way to get through, and his grim expression as he comes up to my side tells me he's beating himself up for not figuring out the answer.

"Twenty-foot palisade walls with metal spikes line the dome, going all the way to the river behind the Willow Tree. Only the west side wall, the one we are facing, has over twenty thousand mortal warriors behind them as if they knew we would be approaching from this side of the forest. Behind the mortal army is another palisade wall with the seventy-five hundred Spartans." Thaddeus conveyed this out loud and through the brand to everyone.

Isis chimes in. *The Unfaithful Gods are most likely within the canopy, making their way to the Father's heart.*

Leaving the races waiting in either the surrounding forest or the river to ambush us, I interject. *Artemis, since the Fae will be coming from behind us, focus your attention there.*

Will do, Freyja. I'm honestly surprised they didn't try to take you guys out.

Don't fucking jinx us. Artemis giggles at my comment.

Bralyant's voice enters. *The unit also didn't detect magical traps, trip wires, or sinkholes across the valley, just more Fae magic claiming the grass. It's going to be a smooth run.*

The bond between King Adom and me is working. He just confirmed that the Tauruns can take down the barrier. Should we wait? I contemplate Ambar's suggestion.

War cries come from within the weeping branches, making the curtains of vines rise. Without enhanced sight, I can't tell for sure what is happening.

Treason's voice rushes in. *The inner palisade walls exploded from the war cry and knocked all the Spartans on their asses. The mortals fell, too, but the outer palisade walls are intact.*

The bubble dome ripples like water as magical fires of blue, gold, and purple blaze behind the vines.

Heimdall's pained voice enters my mind. *The daughters have stepped out of the Willow Tree in their flame forms to defend the Father. They are fighting the gods now.* Sharing that piece of information cost him.

Thunder rumbles overhead as lightning strikes the valley. We don't have time to wait since the daughters are going up against Faithless. *Maybe my ice can freeze the dome, and then we can shatter it, but then I will have no magic left to fight.*

Smoky growls waft into my mind. *Save your ice. Use the blue starlight.*

Voices come from the brand, asking what we should do. I tune them out until their voices are a dull whisper. *Will that work? I used it on a tree, but this is a shield-ward.*

Blue starlight disarms when used offensively and arms when used defensively.

What the shadow puppy says rings true. Since I got this magic from Starson's scales, it makes sense. Which also means my armor has the same magic in it.

Heimdall's profound voice pulls me back into the brand's conversation. *Whatever you just figured out, Freyja, it will work.*

Numerous voices ask me what Heimdall is talking about. Explaining to them that my Ancient Demonical friends' Cerberus, who is in my shadow, told me my blue starlight that I got from a princeling would break the dome would not go over well and would start a lengthy discussion.

I talk over everyone. *Bralyant and I will take a five-second lead so no one is immediately around us as I break the dome's magic.*

Everyone tries to ask me how. *I need you all to trust me.* My voice silenced them momentarily, besides a handful of acknowledgments about taking my word.

I lightly tug on Bralyant's ear. "Tell the Wolven not to try to catch up to us and to maintain the five-second distance."

He turns to face me as much as he can. By the glistening of the gold halo around his iris, his Alpha is telling him not to take orders, but he nods to me. I meet the gazes of Ambar and Thaddeus; they don't hesitate to do the same and ride to their assigned stations.

"Face me to everyone." Bralyant turns himself around.

All the warriors' eyes are upon me, and the weight of their stares only increases the chaotic storm in my soul, fueling it to a higher capacity than ever before. My breaths are steady, my heart is strong, and my spirit is ready to die fighting.

"Warriors of Earthradon!" My voice isn't my own, but the dangerously powerful one I now know is the beast my spirit formed into. "Will you let the Father's daughters' cries go unanswered, or will you answer them with your own?!"

Shouts of agreement and growls from the army before me stir the air around us.

"When you unleash your war cry, don't just scream to be heard. Let your spirit soar so the Unfaithful Army knows who is here, who they could not stop, what wrath they have awoken, and whose blood will be painting the sky at sundown!"

A wave of hollers, shouts, snarls, and barks chase away the electrically charged air on a strong gust of wind.

Bralyant's voice enters my mind. *On my howl, they will ride. I'm ready when you are.*

"Ride true." I gripped his fur with shaking hands.

Always for you.

A song my soul used to sing with Bralyant's tries to seduce my heart to swoon for him because he rhymed tender words with what I spoke. I shred the voice I no longer want my soul to soar with.

Bralyant turns around and lunges forward as the army behind us cheers. We pound down the valley, eating up the distance faster than I've ever experienced being on my friend's back.

His strong heartbeat matches mine, and after five seconds, he tips his head up and howls.

War cries of spirits ready to die while fighting carry on the breeze behind us, and the darkening sky above stops spreading its poison.

I tighten my thighs to prevent myself from falling off Bralyant's back. With a deep breath, I do the same with my core to stay upright and wave my hands out, triggering the starry-blue light to glow in my veins.

With all magic, the soul strengthens the magnitude of its execution. Needing to drain my reserves of this starry-blue light, I hold my breath until only my soul is fueling my body.

The starlight pushes out around my hand, creating an aura of blinding light. I don't know from what distance I should shoot. *Everyone is relying on me, and I can't let them down.*

An embrace of strength I sorely missed wraps around my soul, and the tug of a tether pulls taunt, awakening my senses.

My spiritual power activates without my triggering it, and my vision becomes hazy.

A smoky darkness looms over my shoulders out of my peripheral vision, but what catches my full attention makes my soul cry out. A pair of large, smoky-white hands of light press onto the backs of mine, and a familiar presence is sitting behind me.

Before I can weep my brother's name, a sense of Déjà vu brings a memory to the forefront of my mind. The image tries to take over my vision, but the wind hitting my face causes my sight to switch between the two.

I owe Artemis a debt for giving me Aliith to ride to get my brother, even though she told me if I so dared to mumble about the notion, she would put a chastity belt on me for the length of my existence.

The wind whips my face, making my cheeks sting. My eyes burn from the assault of the starlight.

"Freyr!" I scream with all the might in my soul.

"Freyja!" My attention whipped toward my brother's voice.

Freyr's coal-stone armor glitters, emphasizing his location. He isn't by the cave Aliith was bringing me towards; he is further out, helping our warriors to get away. Aliith adjusts course while a Dragon rains fire on the mountain behind us.

Bralyant tries to talk to me through the bond, but I can't hear him or anyone else; all their voices crackle as if they are on a different magical current than I am.

Freyr leaps up onto Aliith with his air elemental magic. "We need to get to the next cave down. Hundreds of Wolven are inside, and none of the runners I sent could make it over."

"Freyr, Athena saw—"

"I don't care what she saw. Even though not every warrior can go home, I will still try my fucking hardest anyway. I know what I'm signing up for; the question is, do you?"

I face forward. "Get us to the cave as close as possible, Aliith."

He howls with the power of thunder and bolts towards the chaos.

Voices are screaming at me as the building light almost blinds my sight.

Fear is potent in the air as the warriors ahead begin to stir with an awareness of a phantom force coming. Their worried screams and shouts go unanswered as to what they should do.

"Not yet, Freyja."

Freyr pulls me back flush against him. I'm nestled between his legs, preventing me from falling off since I have my hands raised to use my soul magic and not gripping Aliith's fur.

"Tighten your core so you remain steady." He pats my stomach, and I clench my abdominals. "Now slow your breathing so you can feed more magic into your ice."

Ice coats my hands and grows up my arms each second we get closer to the mouth of the cave.

A midnight-green Dragon looms over the entrance as if it knows numerous innocent souls are inside. The beast's attention is on the cave, not on us as we approach.

"Almost there." Freyr's hands go over the backs of mine, and I'm surprised that my magic doesn't harm him.

The memory overlaps. The dome changes to the mouth of the cave with the Dragon over it and then back to the dome. Both are too close for comfort as my arms tremble from the powerful intensity of the magic I generate.

The Dragon lifts his attention to us and roars.

"Now, Freyja!" Freyr calls out, and I scream my war cry as I unleash the starlight.

NINETEEN

Starry-blue light shoots from my hands like comets and consumes the entire dome. A spider's web of wards all glow silver before they explode. The bubble stills to glass and implodes. Shards rain down on the mortal warriors and remain intact instead of shattering.

Another burst of starlight pushes out, and the glow leaves my hands. The last of the magic decimates the first palisade wall of spikes and disarms the thousands of warriors behind it.

As we advance towards the front line of the Unfaithful defenses, the rising war cry at my back is drowning out the mortals' rage-filled swearing at the loss of the walls, their weapons, and armor, leaving them utterly defenseless.

My hands are pushed down to grasp Bralyant's fur, and pressure is on my back to keep me down as he leaps and lands on a group of warriors.

A wave of shouts and growls smack against thousands of warriors screaming for the aid of the almighty gods at their backs.

The pressure on my back moves in slow circles, sparking my heart to take a beat. Instead of the circles moving smoothly to help me fall asleep, the pace quickens, which makes the organ thumb harder.

My awareness of my body comes back to me with each strong

pump of oxygenated blood filling my veins instead of magic, chasing away the spiritual haziness.

The magical presence of my brother lifts as air rushes into my lungs, filling them painfully.

I'm brought back to the gruesome battlefield that was drowned out due to spiritual power being activated, and again, it gets deactivated without my say-so.

Below me are massive paws, torn flesh, and slick, red mud. Cool moisture layers my exposed skin as pellets clink against my armor. Steam rises off my friend's fur, a metallic aroma thickens the air, and my instincts warn me of an unstable pressure surrounding me as if the magic in the air is about to strike.

A smoky darkness darts into my armor. Skjoldr begins humming in my chest a second later, alerting me to a phantom-like presence taking up residence. Whatever is inside me has a hold on the threads of my existence, preventing me or my spiritual essence from trying to push the intruder out.

Radiant strength feeds my bones and muscles as lightning sparks from above and thunder follows.

A bolt hits my back, and my attention shoots up at the stormy sky. Something within me howls in agony and then roars with fury.

The world falls for a moment before catching itself.

Bralyant appears unharmed by the strike and unaware of me being hit by lightning. *Did I just survive that, and why didn't I experience the pain?*

Wood at my hips anchors my hands as a cry rushes from behind me. Metal sings its praise as it is freed from leather sheaths. The shaky environment whirls, and silver slices through the air, silencing one voice, then another, and another.

I find my target with every swing, even ones I didn't know were coming up behind me. I'm moving in a way I've never danced in battle before and attacking my opponents with skills I don't recall learning.

A whimper has me whirling and swinging my swords across the back of a naked warrior trying to drive a spear through Bralyant's shoulder. The clean, gaping cuts I made leak blood. The female warrior spins around and slams into my blade, forcing it into her chest.

Blood rises from her mouth and streams down her breasts, gushing like a river as she chokes. Her body sags as the light leaves her eyes. With the tilt of my blade, she slides off and onto the ground.

Bralyant bites the head of another mortal warrior and meets my gaze. His voice comes into my mind a second later while the brand on my arm hums. *Freyja?* He sniffs, then snarls. *Your scent is tainted with something.*

My friend kept asking the same question, and soon, others began questioning him about what was wrong.

Skjoldr finally stops humming as an emptiness echoes in my body for a moment until I refill the space. No longer am I fighting; my arms are at my sides, and I'm standing motionless, unblinking, and frozen in place as if I'm a virgin warrior who's never bloodied her blade or stepped foot onto a battlefield.

A smoky voice drowns out all the voices from the brand. *Your soul, magic, and body are in shock from my possessing you. You need to keep breathing, Freyja. Control will come back in a moment.*

The shadow puppies' command punches against my chest and forces me to let out the breath I didn't know I was holding. Information floods my senses as more air fills my lungs. *You did what to me! What type of puppy are you?*

One that saved your life, and I won't do it again unless you're in imminent danger of dying.

Wait, that bolt was strong enough to kill me?

Metal slices the air to my left as blood sprays my armor. "Freyja, focus!" Saga pulls her swords out of the naked warrior. "Don't join your brother just yet. We need you."

Saga fights with hate in her lungs and anger in her soul as she reduces the mortal warriors' bodies to distorted heaps of vomited flesh. She is no longer the warrior I trained but a spawn of Obliteration; anyone within her proximity is dead even before her sights are set upon them.

Bralyant's growl pulls me out of my awe at my friend's fierce swordplay. He lunges at a warrior poised to throw a spear at me.

Whatever energy I exerted from using the starlight took a toll on me, as if my soul's light was also drained.

Before I can even assess the battlefield, I know I've already let my friends down, as they stay close, protecting me. *Come on, Freyja. Now is not the time to freeze up.*

Your body wasn't made to handle the intensity of the starlight. The fact that you are standing with your senses intact is astonishing. Don't beat yourself up too hard. If you can't physically move, focus on what you can do.

The shadow puppy is right; my body might not be up to speed; however, my mind is sharp and aware. Instead of burying myself in guilt, I push away my disappointment.

Everyone is spread out, tearing and slicing mortal warriors apart, while the Fae and Arachnids wait in the woods to probably flank us. Most likely, these warriors were just a distraction to get us here and to exert our energy.

Unless Athena foresaw me using starlight to break down the barrier, the Unfaithful expected us to work tirelessly to remove the shield-ward. Given the barrier-breaking into sheets of glass, I'm thankful to have ordered a five-second delay for the army to follow Bralyant and me.

"We need to cover our asses."

I send soul magic down to my right arm to trigger the brand. *An attack will come from behind, and we need a barrier from the Scorpions and Spydens. Ambar, can you use your magic to repurpose the materials from their palisade walls and the shattered glass?*

A man's war cry comes from my left. I'm pushed from behind to duck down as he swings his axe where my neck was just a second ago.

Before you ask, yes, that was me. Are you ready to fight, or do you need my help?

Instead of answering, I drive my swords to the hilt into the warrior's groin. With a cry of my own, I rise and pull my blades out, severing his legs from his torso. He flops on the ground like a fish and screams into a bloody puddle. I stomp on the back of his neck and snap his spine.

Does that answer your question?

No. You just proved that you require my assistance. Your bloodlust may be cruel and horrendous, but it does not indicate you're a capable warrior; it only means you're a contender for being crowned Agonizer Incarnate.

I've never met a being who is as bold with their words as I am.

Why don't you come out of my shadow and help me prove how "capable" I am as a warrior.

Was I not being blunt enough, or is your stubbornness so thick that I need to summon the spirit of honesty into my soul for you to realize what I'm saying is true?

From my soul to my skin, strong aggravation and irritable aggression rise. Only Freyr got under my skin like this and triggered my temper, which only made me angrier.

Two warriors slip past my friends and rush to me as Ambar's voice enters my mind. *I can make the material into spikes to funnel the Arachnids where we want them. They wouldn't risk trying to crawl over them.*

Adrenaline pumps into my veins as I block one of the warrior's attacks and drive my sword through the other's neck while cursing out Haidion's puppy under my breath. Surprisingly, given their outspoken nature, the puppy remains silent.

Wouldn't it be better to make a barricade to block their numbing webbing from hitting us? Thaddeus asks.

The warrior's head falls off his shoulders. I drive my free sword down on the other, but my attack gets blocked.

We can do either, but our supply in this area is limited unless we can gather more glass from around, Ambar adds.

I slide my blades down to the warrior's handle guards, and with a quick flick of my wrist, my hilts snag, and I lift them out of his hands. While his swords fly out of his grasp, I drive my knee into his groin and then slice his head off.

He's right; we need protection from the shooting webs, I confirm. *Thaddeus, form a shield wall and keep the warriors back. Bralyant, have the Wolven clear the way for them, kill all the stragglers, and stay on our flanks to funnel the warriors to us. Saga, you and the Jarls help collect the glass with the Atlanteans.*

All acknowledge my directives as I slice through a handful of more warriors before heading to Thaddeus.

After closing the eyes of a fallen Spartan warrior, I sheathed my swords and picked up his shield and spear. "Where do you want me?"

A quick grin lifts Thaddeus's lips. "If Hercules hadn't trained you in the Spartan ways of combat, I'd say in my bed." His flirtation is a pleasant distraction from my shaking, which has gotten worse since I should be dead.

He nods to his side, and I fit into formation like a puzzle piece with my shield up.

Spartans fill the available spaces as the Wolven clear the last of the stragglers and move behind our formed line.

Another wave of mortal warriors who were able to don some armor rushes toward us.

With a deep breath, I direct soul magic into my entire body to strengthen my muscles to withstand the incoming impact.

Behind the oncoming warriors, the inner palisade wall had been built back up. All the Unfaithful Spartans are behind them, rooting for death.

"You all see our brothers and sisters behind those walls of spears?" All the Spartans at my side and behind me hollered their acknowledgment in barbaric anger. "Show them what a true blessed child of Hercules is. Then you can tear into their traitorous sacks of worthless flesh!" My skin crawls as the Spartans chant their bloodthirsty appetite for carnage.

My skin flutters with anticipation as fury ignites my muscles, expecting them to require reinforcement for the amount of shredding they are about to suffer.

Hundreds slam against our shields. The initial impact is nothing compared to the crushing weight of the thousands trying to push the front line forward to break through.

With a grunt and a breath, I tighten my core to stay flush with the shields and shoulders next to me. My muscles burn as I maintain my low stance.

A shield is at my back and is a helpful reminder to stay in formation. The strength of the warrior behind me is only beneficial if I remain steady; I can't be pushed against it, or I will be crushed.

Hercules' wisdom from training replays in my mind.

"Keep breathing through it and remain on task. Echo the commands in your mind if you need to. A warrior's greatest weapon is their will, and as a woman, you have a more determined will because you have an inner strength that the race of men lacks: the stubbornness to never allow someone to tell you what you are capable of."

His words help me stay focused and not falter in my stance and strength. I keep my shield up to protect myself and my fellow warriors on either side.

The Unfaithful warriors are in our bowing circle now. With the Wolven on our flanks, all these mortals are about to be cut down by a maneuver the Spartans call Deaths' Scythe.

"NOW!" Thaddeus' command ripples through the air, causing the mortals' closet to gasp as we all switch from allowing ourselves to be pushed as a unit to holding firm.

We push out our shields and drive our spears into the compact bodies as a unit. The Kings' spear goes through three. *Show off.*

Thaddeus' laugh fills my ears as we pull our shields back into place to block the next line of warriors. Once they compact again, we execute the same strategy.

A male warrior dressed in mirror-like armor with three times my muscle mass slams into my shield. The star on his helmet indicates that he is a General.

His furious green eyes locked with mine. "You will be remembered as history's most despicable Goddess, leading the races to massacre thousands of unarmed mortals. Congratulations, Freyja! You're just as merciless as the Shadow King." The General spits on my face.

Thaddeus orders everyone to attack. Soul magic is directed into my spear as I raise my shield. The blade goes through the General's armor and right into his groin. My rage is reflected in his armor, which is now cracked like a spiderweb.

I pull my spear out with a yank, and the General falls to his knees. He curses my name and holds his groin. I drop my shield, toss his helmet off, and grab a handful of his hair so he's looking up at me. I then drive the spear through his mouth with such force that it gets stuck in his skull.

After I kick the bastard down, I wipe his spit off my face.

There is no more clashing of blades or growling that promises pain, only the grunts and groans of the fallen warriors waiting for death. While I was focused on the General, the Spartans annihilated the rest of the warriors. Nothing stands between us and unstained yards of grass up to the second palisade wall.

What the General said to me haunts my mind. The entire mortal army of the Unfaithful is eliminated, and I can't find any reason to be cheerful for our victory.

The Spartans behind the palisade wall don't move to get into a defensive position or throw anything at us. Instead, they all have wide grins, and an unsettling discomfort twists my insides.

I direct magic to activate the brand. *Thaddeus, halt them. Something is not right.*

Thaddeus barks, and they all stop advancing. "Are you thinking what I'm thinking?"

I pull my spear out with a firm yank and throw it at the feathered-helmet Spartan. She must've been elected to be the leader of the Unfaithful Spartans. The captain doesn't flinch as the arc of my spear is aimed at her.

My spear freezes in midair and remains there. *There is another shield-ward put in place.* I communicated with all.

Thaddeus voice enters my mind. *Do you have any more blue light left in you, Commander?*

With a wave of my hand, my reserves ache and echo with emptiness; not even a tendril of shadowy-star magic comes out. The magic faintly tingling my hands is only keeping the bandages intact.

No, but I can try to—

Heimdall's voice speaks over mine. *Leave it for the Tauruns because the Fae are coming. The daughters can hold the gods off for the time being.*

Thaddeus whips his attention behind him and then meets my gaze. Without telling him to do so, he commands all the Spartans to fall back to the barricade the Atlanteans are building.

I direct magic into my cloak and fly back to the line. *Artemis, remember to aim for the Fae's wings. Gods, get your soul magic stoked and focus your attacks on the Fae as well. Eirikur, stand by for my command on unleashing the cavalry.*

A couple of units of Wolven break from the pack, heading towards the shield-ward dome. They become invisible as they go around the Spartans.

Bralyant sent a couple of units out to check the dome for weaknesses. Why Treason told me this and not Bralyant himself, I don't know.

Thousands of Wolven leap over the barricades, becoming invisible before they touch the ground on the other side.

I land next to Ambar. *Bralyant, where are you all going?*

We are going to meet the Fae head-on.

That is not part of the plan! He snarls in my mind. *Bralyant!*

Within minutes, all of the Wolven are gone. "BRALYANT!"

Ambar catches my arm before I can take off after him. "Unless you have some major sway over the race, they aren't going to listen to you. They hate the Fae more than the traitorous gods. We are going to have to change our plan."

After taking several deep breaths, the magic in my cloak settles.

Ambar releases her hold on me as I growl. "Acting on their grudge is going to get them killed." *I know that better than anyone.*

Whenever I heard or saw a Dragon after I losing my brother, I didn't hesitate to go and attack. I almost died every time and never thought about what the repercussions would've been towards my believers and my pantheon if I were successful. Thankfully, Heimdall always kept an eye on my future and sent Hel to intervene. Once she brought me home, I'd get a lecture from Odin, and by the end of our argument, I was a heap of wretched screams and grieving tears. I see now that holding a grudge is toxic for the mind, body, and soul.

"Agreed. Corruption has many forms." Ambar pulls me out of my mind. "And can easily be mistaken for a justifiable act and become unrecognizable over time, causing the soul to be lost to what is right and wrong." Her eyes met mine. "The gods, lords, and ladies aren't the only ones plagued. I fear for the fate of the Wolven race if they don't uphold their duties as Peacekeepers."

"And what about the Dragons?"

"There is no hope left for them." Saddened anger tightens Ambar's mouth and glazes over her eyes. "Didn't you notice at the meeting the Father called us to about the asteroid he plans on sending that no one from the Dragon race was present?" I shake my head after a moment, realizing what she said is true. *Starson is destined to die then.* "I won't be surprised if they become extinct after today."

"If not by the magic system, then by my own hands." Thaddeus catches his breath from behind us. "They have known power all their lives and lost the purpose of their duty." Ambar offers him a water skin, and he nods his thanks.

"Fucking Wolven." Saga comes up at my side, staring daggers towards the West woods. "What is the plan now?"

Pushing away the grieving ache for my new friend, I direct magic into my brand to speak to everyone mentally and out loud. "The warriors in the dome aren't going to come out and attack us. Thaddeus, mix your warriors with the Jarls and the Atlanteans, provide extra cover for them, and keep an eye on our backs. Artemis, hold off until I give you the go-ahead."

Thaddeus' voice enters my mind and is heard aloud. "We are piling the mortal bodies to cover our backs as we speak. Once that is done, we will file in with you guys." He cut the mental conversation before handing Ambar back her water skin with a wink. "I'll be back for another refreshment."

"Is that your way of informing me that when you're done, I should have more water siphoned and ready for you to drink, Your Majesty?" Ambar rests her hand and weight on one hip, and her aura conveys that she will not be taken advantage of for her kindness.

Thaddeus' gaze is drawn to her posture. Once he meets her eyes, the tilt of her face captures his full attention. His demeanor changes from being playfully flirtatious to a man enthralled by the most impressive sight he's ever seen.

"No." His fingers trail up the water skin and brush against Ambar's. "It's my way of telling you that when I'm done, you're the only refreshment I want if you'll have me." Thaddeus bows to Ambar and returns to help with the bodies.

"I think there might be an annulment in the King of Sparta's future." Saga waggles her brows.

Ambar cocks her head back in laughter, and the intensity of the rain lessens to nothing. "That boy couldn't handle me." She clears her throat as the brand on my arm hums. "We shifted all our swords into bows and crafted more for the Jarls and Spartans, along with hundreds of arrows we made from the roots and leftover glass."

"Without breaking down that barrier, we will be making no forward progress," Saga adds, only speaking out loud and not through the brand.

"Any update on your cousin's arrival?"

Under Ambar's ash-painted face, her gold stenciling pulsates like blood moving through veins. "They are in the South woods. The vegetation is lush, but claimed by Fae magic, and…" She curses. "The soil is fine like powder."

"Scorpions," Saga and I say at the same time.

Lightning strikes the ground in the middle of the valley. Silver wards explode from where the bolt hit while Fanarzien horns blare proudly from the West woods.

Bralyant, if you aren't going to listen to me, keep me fucking updated at least on what you're doing and see! I urgently growl before I can think better of it.

Black blurs crawl out of the valley's gaping opening as Bralyant's voice rushes into my mind. *Spydens are coming out and are heading toward you. We are split up on the far sides of the valley before the tree line. Once the Fae fly out, we will be leaping into the sky. Which is happening now!*

My enhanced hearing picks up feral screeches as a horde of Fae flies out of the tree line. Howls and growls from the Wolven follow shortly after as blurs leap into the sky.

Saga gasps. "They can jump?"

Ambar orders all to be at the ready with their bows as Thaddeus calls from behind for all the Spartans to mix in with our front line.

"Wolven can jump up to eight times their height," I reply as Ambar hands me a bow. "As long as they leap at an angle, they can roll out of a major impact instead of smacking into the ground. But the higher they go, the more likely they are to get injured."

Thaddeus runs up behind me, panting. "And it's not our fault if they get hit in the tail with an arrow."

Ambar hands Thaddeus a bow and a filled water skin. "They won't go that far."

"Under your command, I bet anything will go as long as you desire." He blows her an air kiss and jogs to take his place on the line.

"He might be a boy to you, Ambar, but you should confirm his endurance. Also, he has a nice ass." Saga winks at Ambar and heads in the opposite direction to take her position.

"If you have anything to say on the matter, do so now or forever keep your mouth shut." Ambar gets into her archer stance.

I shrug. "I've seen better asses."

Ambar lets out a relieved breath and turns her focus on the horizon.

A memory of checking out Haidion floats to the forefront of my mind.

He takes off his new jacket to avoid getting blood on it.

My breath catches as I take in the laces that hug his spine. His vest is a corset, and his ass is round and biteable.

I haven't been able to scrub that image from my mind, and I'm glad he always wears jackets with tail feathers. I can't determine which side of him is more distracting.

Haidion looks over his shoulder at me, flashing a mischievous grin. "I'll stop wearing my jacket then."

The memory leaves the forefront of my mind. *What was that?*

You were checking out Haidion's steel drums. They look even better naked, by the way.

Fuck! I jump and nearly fall on my ass. Laughter fills my mind as I blink my blush away. *I thought you could only hear my thoughts.*

While shadowing you, I'm connected to the forefront of your mind. I can hear and see everything there.

What is the likelihood of you telling him about this?

My mind must be playing tricks on me because I don't recall Haidion catching me looking, let alone making a comment like that.

I'll keep this gem of amusement stored away for a rainy day.

When the silver-tongued voice tries to overpower my mind and shame me for thinking of Haidion, I push it away to stop its influence from affecting me.

Allowing myself to divulge into the forbidden darkness in my mind will, I hope, lessen the desperation of desiring my friend. I don't want to have a repeat of what happened with Bralyant after I froze the river.

I clear my throat and assume an archer's stance. "On your command, Captain."

Ambar will be a better judge of when to fire over me because the Atlantean royals are said to have the same eyesight as hawks.

The gold stenciling on Ambar's skin hums, and she nods to me. "Nock!"

Thaddeus echoes the same order and tells his warriors to fire on Ambar's command; Saga does the same.

I send magic down to the brand. *Artemis, if you can, send a volley at the Spydens.*

Are you sure you want to reveal our location so soon? Treason asks.

Fuck. *Hold off, Artemis.* My friend's pouts are audible, and I can picture her adorable face.

As I nock my arrow, Hel's voice enters my mind. *Remember to keep blinking when confronted with an Arachnid, or they will blend in with the environment.*

This piece of wisdom I had not known is passed down the line as the cluster of Spydens closes in.

"Lock!" Ambar calls out.

I draw back my string and steady my breathing as the wind stills.

The Atlanteans repurposed what remained of the palisade wall and spikes, creating crisscross walls. Six pikes are intertwined to form an X, leaving a diamond-shaped opening between each one for us to shoot through. They are double my height, with one spike in the middle going up another couple feet or so. Each X isn't connected to the other to form one solid wall; they are individual shields with—

"Ambar, why are their glass spikes pointing towards us?"

Out of the corner of my eye, Ambar grins. "You'll see." After another breath, I lock onto a target as Ambar shouts, "HAWK!"

Our arrows whiz through the calm air, singing the screeching melody of a predator closing in on its prey. Each one finds a target, though it takes a dozen of them to bring down one Spyden.

Ambar calls for free rain.

"*Come on, shoot at us,*" Ambar mutters under her breath in her native tongue.

If Ambar needs them to react and shoot at us, I know exactly what will help.

Instead of nocking another arrow, I direct magic into my hand and form a spear of ice. With a deep breath, I aim my spear and throw it on my exhale. The weapon cuts through the air silently and is almost invisible to the naked eye.

Only by the cry of a Spyden do I know my spear hit its target. "Do you think I pissed them off?"

The approaching line halts, and Ambar chants inaudibly as if she's repeating a spell to control something.

As one, the Spydens shoot out their silken webbing.

Delight turns Ambar lips up as the threads stick to the walls.

"We retreat to the piles of bodies once they pull the walls down." I nod and bark out Ambar's commands, which Thaddeus and Saga repeat.

A crack comes from the base of the main spear before me as the webbing becomes taut. The walls rip away in a heartbeat, leaving jagged stumps protruding from the ground.

After grabbing a handful of arrows, we all run toward the mounds of piled-up bodies. The Spartans weren't able to make them too high, but we can still crouch behind them and be protected.

The walls fall on their backs, leaving the sharp side up. "You are a genius in building the walls to fulfill both your and Thaddeus' ideas." I rise to shoot an arrow.

Ambar nocks an arrow beside me. *"Please hold your applause until the end of the performance."* She winks and rises to unleash her shot.

A spray noise tickles my ears, followed by a chirping purr as my instincts alert me to something coming.

I pull Ambar and the Spartan next to me down as webbing is shot at us. The silk attaches to the body on top of the pile and is pulled away a second later.

"Fuck! When did you develop enhanced hearing?" Ambar asks with an uneasy laugh as the Spartan besides me nods his thanks and goes back to shooting arrows.

"Please hold all your questions until the end of the presentation." Our eyes meet, and an amused laugh leaves her lips instead of another panicked one.

Together we take a steadying breath to calm ourselves before nocking our arrows and standing to release them.

Screeching comes from the front line of Spydens. Instead of the fallen walls slicing their bulbs as they crawled over them, the entire X is latched onto their undersides, squeezing them together like being caught in a bear trap. When the front line of beasts tries to back up, the tall end gets stuck in the ground, making them form a barricade of kabobbed Spydens.

Dozens of compliments come through the bond. Yet Ambar isn't fazed by any as the gold stenciling on her face pulsates.

My rising amusement over her contraption sinks to the pit of my stomach like lead as Ambar's eyes darken with worry.

Her voice enters my mind a moment later. *The Allied army can't make it through or over the South woods. The ground caved in, and the leaves from the trees are attacking anything that flies above.*

We can hold them—

My voice is cut off by Thaddeus's. *A bed of Scorpions is coming out of the ground from the South woods. It looks like a thousand, maybe more; it's hard to determine.*

My thoughts about how we will set up for the oncoming attack are interrupted by Bralyant's voice. *Another cluster of Spydens is coming out of the crack.*

Ambar curses in Atlantean. *I didn't think to get a read on the valley once we were on it because no one would dare try to dig tunnels around the Father's roots.*

Treason's voice enters next. *You wouldn't have been able to get a reading unless you could remove the Fae magic claiming the grass.* His growl makes me shiver. *Those sent out to do a thorough scout would've had enough time to sense a disturbance.*

Bralyant roars. *Those five I sent out are gone. Fucking traitors!*

Could the Arachnids chew the roots as an attack to weaken the Father?

Saga's question is answered by Ambar. *No. Two races from the outer edge of the universe guard the Father's roots.*

Saga and I are apparently the only ones who don't know that, as all the others agree with Ambar's input.

The reprieve offers no comfort since we are about to be overrun by thousands of Unfaithful warriors we hadn't accounted for.

I may have expected a rapid fire of questions bouncing around in my mind about what we should do; however, there is only silence. Only the beat of my heart and the respirations of my breath fill the void.

Heimdall's voice enters my mind after a long period of silence. *What's your call, Commander?*

Another brick of lead stacks onto the other and begins to painfully stretch me. *Everyone is solely waiting on me.*

Being the Norse Goddess of War and Death doesn't mean I'm a

natural-born leader with a killer instinct for knowing what needs to be done. *I'm not my brother.*

The stench of rotting flesh and murky earth wafts in the air, delivering the message of our impending demise. The Fate of Death is here, and he's waiting to collect more souls since we will be boxed in.

Instead of figuring out a plan or calming the worries of my warriors so I can reignite their courage, I collapse against the wall of bodies and lean my head back to rest against them.

The weight of every soul presses down on my shoulders and causes the threads forming my existence to weaken.

Only intrusive thoughts of my inevitable failure as the Commander and a Goddess invade my mind. *The second wave of reinforcements having to change course can't be a coincidence.*

I bring my knees up to my chest, dragging my boots through a muddy puddle that is soiled with more than just blood.

If the Unfaithful have more Arachnids waiting to be called upon, they could have more Fae, or worse, races we didn't know sided with them.

My shaking intensifies as the fire in my soul slows its whirling, causing my veins to fill with an icy cold.

We haven't seen the Vampyres yet, and the forces of the Unfaithful are already overwhelming ours.

Nausea boils up from the lead weighing down my stomach. Thinking in the forefront of my mind isn't helping me.

I close my eyes to fight off the bile rising in my throat and brace my hands on the backs of my thighs to prevent my shaking from becoming noticeable.

I've only ever felt agony like this after an argument with Odin, and these moments are the only occasions when I experience being cold. I know eventually, I'll recover from these miserable ailments, but I normally have time to do so. I'm in the midst of a battle; I don't have time to endure this.

The smoky voice of the shadow puppy fills my mind. *Why aren't you sharing your thoughts with the others?*

Voicing my speculations will only spread fear, and my not having a plan will make them all lose hope.

Since the shadow puppy saved my life, I won't reprimand them for reading my mind.

It sounds to me more like you're projecting your insecurities.

I'm not my brother! A strangled sob tries to rise in my throat. *He was always quick to come up with a clever plan. He's the Commander they'd need to lead them to victory, and instead, they are stuck with me, someone who wasn't even supposed to be here. Freyr saved my life, and then you. What if all my decisions from this point on will only lead to their deaths since that's where my soul is destined to go?*

My eyes water, and I squeeze them tighter to prevent any from flowing out.

Like you said to that little boy, not every warrior can go home. These warriors fighting alongside you knew what they signed up for when they entered the Colosseum.

Pressure rests on my chest, over my heart, as if something is sitting between my legs and leaning into me.

And leaders aren't considered great or inspiring only by the battles they win but by their determination to never give up.

Strangely, the shadow puppy exerts heat, and their warmth helps chase away the numbing cold that is turning me to stone.

Strip away the pressure of disappointing everyone and push away the high expectations you're holding yourself to by comparing your actions to your brother. The most important concern you must address is: will you give up, Freyja?

"Freyja?" Ambar's soft, pleading voice makes me snap open my eyes. "I swear the warm tone of your skin was shifting to a frosted sheen a second ago. It must've been a trick of my eyes."

The weight of the shadow puppy lifts off my chest, and I'm nudged in multiple spots. *Um, are you sniffing me?* Not even a second later, the presence between my legs vanishes.

Yes, I was checking on your magical well-being.

Ambar reaches for my hand. "It's okay to be overwhelmed. If you need help, all you have to do is ask. No one here will think any less of you for it."

Before Ambar can touch my skin and possibly use her empath power, I slide my hands onto my lap and tighten my armor. Even though a silent sigh sags her shoulders a fraction, she offers me a small smile. Other's magic has affected my body without my permission too much already today.

I'm not going to give up.

I look at the battlefield I cowardly couldn't face a moment ago.

Remember, Freyja, that asking for help is not a sign of weakness.

My face is licked multiple times, and I'm surprised to find a coating of slobber on my cheek.

A surge comes from my brand as someone's panting voice fills my mind. *More Fae are coming. Their strength is more than we anticipated... almost double.*

Before Bralyant's voice fades, a high-pitched yelp of pain floats through. His cry is a shock to my system and cracks the shield wall around the tender spots of my existence.

Alpha, move your forces into the North woods and call when you are clear, then join our second wave. Artemis, rain fire once word comes from the Wolven King. All leaders in the first wave: have your warriors stay in their current positions so we can draw the Unfaithful in, and once they are too close for comfort, I will call our second wave.

I meet Ambar's eyes; she is beaming with determination; her soul is reignited. "When you hear the howl, you and Artemis will rain fire on the Fae." I place a hand on her shoulder. "From this moment on, take point with leading the first wave. I will be more helpful being in the sky."

Ambar claps her hand on my shoulder. "I won't let you down, Freyja. Try not to get hit by our arrows."

"Don't worry about me. Until the Fae recognize where our second wave is hidden, I will focus on the Arachnids." Ambar squeezes my shoulder and orders everyone to nock their arrows.

A cool breeze kisses my skin. No longer is the wind still; instead, it's whirling. The feathers of my cloak are ruffled as if the air is extending its aid to help me.

My cloak is tugged from behind as I try to stand, keeping me kneeling.

Before you fly off and do something stupid and reckless, are you sure this is the best course of action toward victory, or are you trying to prove something to yourself? Going into battle on your own should only be determined by one's ability and not by how stubborn they are.

My temples burn, and my jaw tightens to bite back the furious words that want to erupt. When I let my tongue loose on them previously, it did nothing, but my willpower to put them in their place is too strong.

I don't owe you an explanation, and I won't remain on my knees while a being I don't know well judges my actions. Either keep what I should and shouldn't do to yourself and let me go or leave.

A long moment passes, and when I start to think the shadow puppy won't listen, the tension on my cloak eases.

I flex my fingers and roll my shoulders as I prepare to take off.

I would stand by your side even if the probability of coming out alive wasn't in my favor, but only if the courage to stare the Fate of Death in the face was formed by selflessness to serve others and not selfishness to serve oneself.

Don't allow my actions to pressure you to do something you're uncomfortable with.

After directing magic into my cloak, I push off from the ground and soar into the sky.

Chuckles of seductive charm cause the cool air around me to become euphorically warmer.

I'm perfectly comfortable with biting your ass for deflecting from the fact that I'm right about what's motivating you. Only because we haven't officially met yet will I tolerate your stubbornness.

My sarcastic comeback is forgotten when a calloused thumb runs over my cheek. Before I can stop myself, I press against the contact, causing the tender spots of my existence to sigh with want.

Try not to get yourself killed. You don't want your last memory of being on your knees to be in front of a pile of corpses, do you?

Fuck you!

An attractive, guttural laugh echoes in my mind. Without a doubt, their voice is identifiably masculine.

What happened to your smoky tone?

Unlike the last time, when I couldn't tell when the shadow puppy left, he made his absence clear. The radiant warmth my heart and soul became dependent on vanished, leaving me empty, vulnerable, and lonely.

The piercing agony I've been trying to shield myself from creeps in, attempting to drain the vitality from my soul. How the being was able to keep the illness I've been fighting for centuries away, I don't know. I might be living on borrowed time, but I'm not accepting that today is the day that I'm fated to die.

CHAPTER

TWENTY

SEVENTH HOUR AFTER SUNRISE

With a twist, I avoid a spray of webbing shot at me. My enhanced hearing is helps me get closer to the Spydens. Only by dumb luck have I ever gotten the chance to fight one up close. Thanks to a dare gone wrong, Haidion and I found ourselves in a nest and had to figure out quickly how to dance with one.

The left flank of warriors focuses on the oncoming cluster of Spydens instead of trying to aim at the approaching Fae.

I pass the last mound of bodies my warriors are using to shield themselves when a blast of webbing is shot at an Atlantean right as she stands to unleash an arrow. The Atlantean's cry is one of fear. Not just of dying a slow, painful death but of letting the warriors she fought next to down for being captured.

I use my soul magic to create an ice dagger in my palm. I aim for the threads that pull her toward the approaching line. Once I find my mark, I lock my wrist and throw the dagger, which quickly vanishes from my sight. The connection severs, telling me I hit my mark.

As I land next to her, I form a shield of ice in my right arm. After stabbing it into the ground, I frost my hands to protect myself while I remove the webbing. Once I pull the last thread, the silver lines over her face and exposed skin glow once again as if her magic is taking a reviving breath.

"Thank you, Commander."

Tree roots slither out of the ground and onto her body like blind snakes. They wrap themselves around her torso and pull her back towards the mound of bodies she was taken from.

To be an Atlantean is to be respectful towards nature and the balance of all life, and in return, they are allowed to harness the environment for what they need because the magic system knows what has been borrowed will return. The Father chose wisely when he selected their race to care for the Willow Tree. All the roots the gods are working their way through are thanks to the Atlanteans. And if Thor can crack open the bark, he has layers upon layers of woven, thorny vines to get through.

Silk webbing hits my shield but is unable to stick. After sliding my arm back in the shield's braces, I pull it out of the ground and take off towards the approaching line.

My shield collides with a Spyden, knocking them on their back. I spin around and come back down, driving the shield's edge into its head.

All the Spydens stop and face me, as if they are all greedy for my magical innards over the dozens of warriors a few yards away.

Since they are in their beast forms, all are at least ten feet tall. Each has eight legs, three pairs of black eyes, a bulbous abdomen, a pair of stingers in the front, and a brittle fuzz layering their camouflaged skin. I remind myself to keep blinking.

I dodge a pair of legs and roll under a Spyden. I form spears in my hands and thrust them into their underside. Another pair of legs tries to grab me, but none are lunging forward with their fangs or webbing to subdue me. I get underneath another and execute the same fatal blow.

I don't know why my presence is thoroughly distracting them from the others and why they aren't trying to kill me; I'm just going to take advantage of it.

Numerous legs try to sweep me off my feet. I keep myself moving, never staying in one spot. There are so many that evading and striking becomes overwhelming.

One leg knocks me on my ass, but before the Spyden can pull me towards them, another one attacks the one trying to bring me closer.

The pair forgets about me and starts to fight each other. Using the distraction, I thrust my spears into both of them.

A howl echoes from the distance as my brand hums. *We are clear.*

Artemis' voice rushes in before I can ask Bralyant if he's hurt. *Shield yourself, Freyja!*

After rolling out from underneath another Spyden, I bring my forearms together and form a dome of ice around my body like a coffin.

The Spydens try to break through it with their fangs, but a force from above plummets into them, splattering their blood all over my dome of ice. The tips of arrowheads broke through; however, the integrity of my coffin remained intact.

You were supposed to be aiming at the Fae, Artemis.

It was only a hundred or so, and Aliith was getting worried about you taking on the Spydens single-handedly.

We were all a little worried, Hel chimes in. Another howl sounds in the distance, this one more enraged than the first.

Once the volley is done, I break my forearms apart. The ice dome explodes, sending shards in every direction. All the Spydens who were standing are now down. Those further away turn their attention everywhere, trying to determine where the attack originated.

Arrows zing through the sky from the North woods and from our first wave. The Fae littering the sky drop to the ground by the hundreds. They break apart into groupings of three. Their left and right flanks go higher into the sky as the one in the middle lowers. Within seconds, they will be able to determine where the arrows are coming from.

Thaddeus's slightly panicked voice enters my mind. *These Scorpions are getting too close for comfort.*

I'm on my way. Eirikur, it's time to cleanse the field of Arachnids. I push magic into my cloak and fly towards our right flank.

As I soar over the mounds of corpses, the first wave is ordered to remain where they are so no one is trampled over.

Nordic horns blare causing the puddles below me to ripple.

A strong gust of wind from behind me carries our warriors' menacing cries and the horses' soul-crushing neighs.

The crack of bark and Spyden's shrill scream make me glance over my shoulder.

An endless band of ashen-fire horses ride out of the tree line. Their forceful presence sends out a surge of white fire that pushes aside trees, tears up the grass, sloshes bloody pools of water, and makes the ground unstable, per the Spydens' attempts to remain upright.

I don't know if the Fae and the Arachnids took part in the slaughter of the Nymph race, even though they are just as guilty for siding with the Unfaithful, but I hope the realization hits them that these horses aren't the monsters here, it's them for wanting to kill the Father.

As if the Fae heard my thoughts, the three units halt their approach. Something besides the wind is ruffles their wings as sickening dread thickens the air. I bet they think the horses are creatures from the unknown depths of Orrtiereum that we summoned to fight with us. A laugh tickles my throat. *Looks can be deceiving.*

Calling for aid from either plane is illegal because they are considered different worlds that happen to be attached by the Fathers' roots. I think the planes should be helping us, but the Father granted them their independence, and his daughters only oversee the dynamics of how the operations affect Earthradon. I couldn't even call Haidion for help, or he'd face a heavy penalty. Beyond the Allied Army, there is no one else to call.

Artemis sends another volley of arrows that simmer like moonbeams and fall upon the Fae violently like a hailstorm. The ones who get hit are stripped of their armor and weapons as they plummet.

Bralyant's voice enters my mind. *Hel and I established a healing den for all warriors who cannot keep fighting. Once we Wolven reenter the field, anyone who is too severely injured will be taken out; just call out "Ariella."* After most acknowledge his statement, he speaks again in a low voice too sensual for an audience. *Freyja, where are you?*

I want to snap at him and curse his name for the Fae to learn since he broke off from our unified front to execute his plan to satisfy his race's grudge and broke my trust.

I am about to dance with the Scorpions.

Wait until I—

My war cry drowns out the rest of Bralyant's comment as I send shards of ice toward the Scorpions.

I land, and just like with the Spydens, the Scorpions' attention latches onto me and not my warriors. They, too, are in their full beast forms. Polished, black, metal-like scales make up their four-foot-tall bodies. They have six legs with massive pincer claws and a curved stinger tail that rises five feet above them. Even though they have six pairs of eyes clustered together, they have poor eyesight, especially during the daytime.

All crawl towards me with haste, fighting one another to be the first one I face. With their almost impenetrable scales, focusing my energy on killing one while surrounded will take too long.

In my left hand, I grow an ice blade tall enough to reach their stingers, while my right arm is coated in a log of ice.

Haidion and I also faced a couple of Scorpions during our dare gone wrong, and we learned a standard shield is useless. Their claws can snap anything if it isn't both dense and thick. After Haidion commented, *"I have the perfect weapon for the task in my pants, but I'd need to pump it up first,"* I thought of this version of a shield so the Scorpions would struggle to try and clamp onto it, distracting them as I went for their stingers.

A smile plays on my lips as I launch myself forward.

With my core tight and my knees bent, I make it rain stingers and blood. Scorpions shriek at losing their most prized bodily characteristic as their meaty claws are dulled in their attempts to clutch the ice around my arm.

Every part of my body begins to burn as I force more air into my lungs and keep up my lethal pace.

My balance falters when the ground beneath my boot starts to tremble. I miss a stinger when I swing, and a crack comes from my arm coated in ice. The Scorpion I'm facing manages to clamp down and keep me still. Their other claw breaks my sword and slices the back of my left hand.

The pain radiating from the gash goes numb from the Scorpion's venomous shrill of joy.

My attention focuses on the tail. The stinger is glistening with poison.

With my left hand free, I reach for my chest while expelling all the air out of my lungs, but their stinger is already shooting toward me before I have the chance to activate my—

A green light explodes from my chest, blinding me. All the Scorpions shriek as I'm yanked away from the claws gripping my arm by a phantom force. My ice is shattered in the process.

My right shoulder pops from being overextended. Screams rush out of me as I'm thrown into a puddle.

The green light dims, allowing me to have my sight back. A nasty gash is on the back of my left hand, cutting through the brand and going all the way to my bones. I must be in shock because neither the pain in my hand nor my shoulder is registering.

Threads of green, starry magic emerge from the gash, pulling the skin together. The brand hums before the light vanishes completely.

I blink at the absence of the injury; not even a scar is visible. Never before had I heard about brands healing themselves or protecting a being. Maybe because this is a blood brand?

Shouts of fearless warriors and neighs of horses come from behind me as Eirikur's voice rushes into my mind. *Freyja, move!*

Skjoldr hums in my chest and pushes my magic into my cloak. I'm lifted off the ground just as the cavalry of our second wave gallops through the bloody puddle I was lying in.

Only one being I know can help reset my shoulder. *Isis, where are you?*

In the middle of the field, helping Heimdall, Treason, and Hera defend our wounded.

I try to spot them in the mass, but it's useless. *My right shoulder got pulled out of its socket. How do I put it back in?*

An angry howl-like cry sounds in the distance as Treason's voice enters my mind. *Where are you?*

Determining my precise location is impossible, and the only way I know how causes heat to crawl up my neck. I never howled unless I was drunk on alcohol or lust, yet doing so would give my exact position to Treason...and Bralyant. *The Beta Prince better get here first.*

I take in as much air as my lungs can and howl. My wail causes the cloudy sky to shudder.

Treason's determined voice speaks over Bralyant's. *I'm coming, Freyja.*

The second wave collides with the scrambling Scorpions, who are still disoriented after being blinded.

Shrills shouts, curses, clanks, grunts, and growls become the chaos of the battle before my eyes.

Lightning strikes the ground before the tree line of the South woods. All my muscles seize up as a burning heat is shot down from the base of my neck to my toes. Even though I didn't get struck, my body reacts as if I'm reliving the trauma.

The moisture from my mouth and throat evaporates, making each breath sharp and raspy. Three meaty stinger tails rise out of the crack in the ground.

A humanoid scorpion male climbs out; his impressive frame is covered in glossy black scales from head to toe. If it weren't for his multiple stinger tails, I would've thought he was just a regular warrior choosing to fight in his other form, but no, it's Drafasa, the Autarch of the Scorpion race. If he's here, then so is the entire Arachnid Army.

Drafasa raises his arms to the side while tilting his head to the sky, unleashing a deafening shriek that has me cupping my ears. Thousands upon thousands of Scorpions and Spydens start crawling out from behind him.

My instincts tingle as if I'm being watched. I can barely make out the features on Drafasa's face as he brings his head down. He tilts his head to the side as his stingers wave at me slowly, causing my lungs to twist into knots and squeezing every last ounce of oxygen out of me.

Heimdall's pained voice enters my mind as Drafasa lowers his arms. *Freyja, fly away!*

Drafasa pushes the two outermost fingers down on one hand, then brings the three still up to his face, where his mouth would be if he wasn't armored up. He raises his hand towards his forehead and presses his fingers to his skin.

His message stings the tender spots of my existence. "No! You don't love me anymore." Even if he can't hear the words, I need to scream them out loud. "And I have stopped loving you!"

The soul magic I built up to protect myself cracks, leaving an opening large enough for the memory of when I last saw Drafasa to assault my mind and heart.

"It would mean a lot to me if you were there to help push his boat into the water."

Besides Drafasa's silky, shoulder-length, tawny hair that flows with the wind, he remains still as a stone on his knees in front of my brother's altar. The large boar he brought as an offering lies before him, leaking blood from its freshly slit throat on the bone-stone dais. Only the summer night's cool wind, the sorrowful breaths we take, and the drips of blood hitting the steps fill the loneliness in our ears and hearts.

"All in attendance won't utter a word about seeing you there. You have my word."

I can barely speak above a whisper because my voice sounds almost identical to my brother's, and hearing myself causes me to explode into screams and tears.

Drafasa's stinger tails curl in on themselves and start shaking. The muscles on his back begin to tense, causing his flawless, brass-brown skin to become taunt as if his scales are about to rip free from him.

I slowly descend the dais backward since my presence is upsetting him more than helping.

He produces an eerie shriek while taking a breath. The sound crawls under my skin and has me twitching to fill my hands with ice. Drafasa has never given me a reason to fear him, but my spiritual essence tells me I must get farther away and be on guard.

"It doesn't matter. If I stay away any longer than a day. Ladiya will tell everyone about us being mates, and she will hunt me down with her entire army... she's outrageously possessive of me." The abrupt sharpness in his gruff voice is like claws against metal. "I've spent centuries keeping that insufferable, obsessive bitch in the dark and away from the only good thing in my existence. Even in his death, I won't allow her anywhere near Freyr."

I remain still. Instead of keeping my mouth shut on the topic, I take a deep breath and ignore the memory of my brother sternly telling me not to bother trying because the words wouldn't altar Drafasa's soul. Why Freyr felt so strongly about that assumption, I don't know. The fact that he didn't speak up about Drafasa's position has me thinking that love makes people not only emotionally blind but also morally blind.

"Then you should be rejecting Ladiya as your mate instead of agreeing to marry her. If I had to choose between being able to love who I wanted and having to accept a mate that goes against my sexuality to rule, I'd choose my happiness, and Freyr would want you to do the same."

His stinger tails uncurl as he rises to his feet, and I respectfully keep my gaze above his waist.

"Since my happiness is gone, no thanks to you, the decision has already been made for me." He turns towards me, and the cluster grouping of his black eyes makes him appear to only have two on his smooth, angular face. "Whatever happiness you have in your existence, I suggest you make as many memories with them as you can because the next time I see you, I'm going to kill the one you love." He brings three fingers to his lips, kisses them, and drags the digits across his throat. "You have my word, Freyja."

My soul whirls with a fire so fierce my vision is coated with red haze. Scorching heat pushes into my fingertips and toes. Pain ripples along my spine, making my muscles quiver.

My brother loved Drafasa so much he took whatever relationship he could to be with him, but gone is the shameless prankster I once knew, and in his place is a ruthless king who holds a vengeful grudge against me.

Even though it's taking me a while to come to terms with it, I'm not to blame for my brother's death, and I won't stand by and watch the man I used to consider a second brother vindictively kill my warriors as if he's giving me a preview of what will be in store for the one I care about.

Another lightning strike comes from behind me, but I'm locked on Drafasa, who is beckoning me to go to him with a curl of his fingers.

Soul magic has thickened in my veins since I stopped breathing. The immense heat coursing through me mixes with my magic, making my feather cloak glow and smoke like embers.

The pain in my shoulder is forgotten as I form ice blades in my hands.

CHAPTER
TWENTY-ONE

My friends' voices bounce around in my mind, trying to get my attention. They think what they are doing will make me listen; little do they know that hearing them only fuels my motivation to obliterate the Autarch until no piece of him is left. I might not hold anyone as close to my heart as I did Freyr, but witnessing my friends die at the hands of Drafasa will break me.

A cataclysmic howl tears through the air behind me as I fly like a shooting star.

All the Scorpions part for me as Drafasa begins to extend his arms as if he's welcoming me in for a hug.

"I'm going to fucking kill you!" I scream, tears flying away from my eyes.

The howl encircles me as if I'm the one producing the melodic energy. Fluorescent silver-blue waves of light ripple over and around me. *What the—*

Drafasa vanishes and a mound of corpses takes his place. The pulsing energy drops me as I plow into the pile of dead.

My blades slice through the rotting corpses, coating me with foul blood. They break into pieces as I collide with the ground and roll; I must've not made them durable enough.

Only when I land in yet another puddle do I stop. I was sent only a short distance away from the main congestion of the battle. *At least this one has no blood and guts in it.*

White furry paws stand before me as I try to push myself onto my hands and knees. Treason's snout is inches away from my face. He blows the wet hair out of my eyes with a huff, then leans down and nudges his nose against my injured shoulder. I wince, causing him to snarl and whine, both furious and concerned that I am hurt. His teeth clamp on the back of my cloak, and he heaves off the ground and onto his back.

Arms pull me flush against their chest as my legs automatically straddle Treason. "Do you have a death wish, Freyja?" Isis scolds me from behind.

Treason rolls his shoulders to adjust Isis and me further away from his blades.

"I'll answer your question if you answer mine. Who moved me away?"

"*A portal did.*" Per the gruff tone, Treason's beast just spoke aloud. In their beast form, Wolven can only communicate in brief phrases. That must've caused him discomfort.

"I'm aware a portal moved me, but I want to know who it was." Treason tiptoeing around admitting who exactly used portal magic and Isis's lack of a response has me snarling before I answer the question asked of me. "Centuries ago, the Autarch threatened to kill ... one who brings me happiness. So yes, I do."

I always wondered why Drafasa hadn't sought to kill Odin since he made our marriage known to all. Before we said our vows, I shared with Odin what Drafasa said he promised me because I wouldn't marry him if I was going to lose him. He assured me that no one would get within arm's reach to hurt him. After our honeymoon, he ensured that no one from the Arachnid race could enter the Norse lands.

Treason snuffs while tipping his snout down in acknowledgment and leaps forward, veering left and running toward the North woods.

"I don't need to go to the healing den. Just reset my shoulder."

"We're not going there. With the Fae upon us, Hera established a haven in the middle. I'll push your shoulder back into place there." Isis' beast purrs, and I stiffen. "If you try to go after the Autarch again without talking to Heimdall, I promise you that I'll shift into my beast form, pin you down, and lick your hands until your nerve endings go numb so you're temporarily incapable of using magic."

Isis's power of metallic sunshine slithers onto my shoulder and wraps around my neck. The essence becomes a phantom reptilian with bloody eyes formed out of little specks of fluttering light as if tiny bugs made up its not-entirely-solid body.

The snake-like ghost remains motionless like a statue and patiently waits for its master's command. My only relief is that Isis hasn't ordered the snake to burrow under my skin.

Her power can only be used if a threat is in the best interest of her target. It cannot be employed for selfish reasons. A portion of her magic leaves her body, lies in wait, and informs Isis if she needs to deliver or retract her promise. If punishment is what needs to be done, then she takes a portion of the being's soul, leaving her poison so the soul can't heal from the loss.

Whatever Isis' secondary source for wielding magic is, it makes her a Rarity, and it is freaking terrifying. Like Nyx and Artemis, her power is unknown to Earthradon. Most Rarities have elemental magic or harvesting magic.

A growl of courage I didn't know I had the guts to produce rumbles from my chest and heatedly leaves my lips. "You think that threatening me is a wise choice?"

Strong gusts of heat pound against my chest. I'm not surprised by the feral behavior of my magic in response to Isis' threat. She is one of the few beings who intimidate me. After a spell I helped her find went wrong, she can transform into a monstrous creature. The spirit of my soul always prepares herself for a fight when her beast begins to surface.

"You are no match against the Autarch without a well-thought-out plan. I admire your fearlessness, but your stubborn mindset needs to allow some worry in so you can think instead of acting instinctively on emotions alone."

I only react when I hit an emotional spike because that's when I experience an immense amount of unstoppable and invincible energy. The situation that triggered me always calls for a high level of strength.

Freyr and Hel took a cautious approach when training me. They said I shouldn't push myself to reach the extreme of my magical potential because the high would trigger a lust and result in an addiction to always wanting to be in the "almighty" euphoric state. However, I think their timidity in encouraging me to keep pushing was because they had difficulty knocking me down and gaining high ground when I was in my "frenzy."

The phantom snake rattles at me and hisses. I bare my teeth as a screeching growl rushes out of me from the deepest part of my existence. I would flinch and panic any other day, but not today. I'm standing my ground.

Isis lets out a sigh. "I'm not trying to invalidate your reasoning for wanting to attack the Autarch or talk you out of it due to the repercussions you'll face if you end up killing him, but you need to remember the reason you are fighting isn't to end him but to put a stop to the traitorous gods before they can kill the Father."

She's right; in my rage, I only saw Drafasa. He knew what my seeing him would do, and I fell for his baiting. *You need to be better, Freyja.*

With the absence of my shadow companion, the disappointing ache in my heart echoes and reminds me of how lonely I am. I squeeze Isis' hand, and she holds onto mine as we ride. Something deep within me sighs with relief when the serpent slithers back towards Isis.

Treason dodges another mound of bodies as I scan the battlefield, trying to figure out what threat had come out of the other crack I had heard. Only waves upon waves of our warriors register as far as my eyes can see.

With a deep breath, I direct magic into the brand. *Who came out of the crack?*

Bralyants' voice silences everyone else's. *Nothing came out, but a portion of the cavalry got pulled down.*

Eirikur's voice enters my mind. *Around a thousand warriors fell. I don't know if any survived.*

We are rejoining the fight now. A howl echoes in the distance as the Wolven race out of the forest.

Fae begins to swarm above. Their silhouettes cast shadows on the stained grass. Isis trembles from behind me and squeezes my hand tighter.

"You okay?" I asked over my shoulder.

She presses her face against my back. "I will be once we get inside Hera's haven."

A black blur runs out of the forest; their rider is covered in moonlight.

Artemis, you will draw all the Fae's attention to yourself if you don't dampen your soul magic.

Just like how my magic takes the form of anything relating to ice, Artemis' magic takes the form of variations of light.

Her confident, cheery voice fills my mind. *That's what I'm hoping for.*

Arrows of white light shoot through the sky, exploding when they near the Fae and blinding them. My vision becomes spotty from staring at the light.

Skjoldr hums in my chest while my instincts urge me to escape something I can't see. A thick webbings of magic passes over me, like claws raking over every nerve and thread in my body and soul. My blood boils. *What did we just ride into?*

I clap my hands together, and a ball of whirling frost forms when I pull them slowly apart. With my vision still spotty, I rely on my instincts to direct the frost around the three of us, molding exoskeletons of ice around our bodies.

After the War of the Frozen Fire Highlands, Odin pondered whether utilizing my ice in this manner could shield me from the cursed magic. He never got around to helping me test if his theory was correct. I made some headway on forming the frost; I just haven't been able to control it unless I'm in dire need to protect myself.

Treason skids to a halt, yipping like he got stung in the ass. *"What are you doing?"*

Hands try to pull my arms down. "We are safe. Hera made a dome using her magic to protect the haven." Isis hisses her discomfort as she tries to stop me.

The spots in my vision begin to fade, allowing me to take in the translucence threads of weaved light that make up the dome we are inside.

Hera stands in the middle, her sandy-bronze magic gleaming off her hands and armor. Skjoldr calms down when the pressure of Hera's magic lessens, but my instincts remain alert.

My frost coats Treason's fur in a glittering blue powder, waiting for my command to form the armor. Isis winces from behind as she tries to console me to put my hands down; her jade-black skin has a paler complexion due to my frost. *Was I the only one who sensed the abnormality in Hera's magic?*

I pull my magic back in between my hands, allowing Treason to flex his muscles so he can lower himself to the ground.

The moans and groans of our hurt and dying warriors have Isis releasing her grip on me.

"Go. I can wait." I nod for her to attend to the others whose conditions are worse than mine.

Isis slides off Treason and levels me with a knowing stare. "No, you'll try to do it yourself and cause further harm to your shoulder."

"I can't since I have to extinguish this first." I hold up my hands to show her the whirling blizzard between them.

Isis caves when Treason huffs at her.

I slide off and focus on pulling warm memories to the forefront of my mind. Usually, my body heat is enough, but not this time. For some reason, my magic isn't listening to either Skjoldr or me.

Something tingles on my left arm, causing a recent memory to surface.

Odin moves his hands around my neck and squeezes my throat more than he has ever done before. While I'm clawing at him, he lifts my legs against his chest so he can go deeper. He's thrusting into me at a intense pace and cracking my back in half. Sooner than I wanted, my entire body starts to shake, and my climax rips through me. The noises escaping me are a combination of pleasure and my struggle to not die. Odin follows me into euphoria, spilling himself inside me while moaning loudly like a triumphant king winning a war.

His panting face meets my eyes in the mirror on the ceiling above our bed. "I love that your pussy becomes so needy for my seed while I choke you." He starts to thrust into me again. "Can I be rougher?"

Odin doesn't release his hold on my throat, so I have a hard time making out the words, but it only makes me wetter. "Yes!" I dig my nails into his ass, making him snarl. "Fuck. Me. Harder."

More memories of the two of us having mediocre sex pass by until I reach a non-sex memory. The one of me throwing Odin off the cliff. However, the amusement I usually experience isn't there, and my magic is only being fueled to strengthen. *Why am I thinking of Odin?!*

The humming on my arm answers my question. Odin is pushing the memory to me, probably sensing my worry about trying to put my magic out. Odin trying to help me only causes the blizzard in my hands to strengthen to an intensity that has me sweating and my arms shaking.

In my growing fit of rage, I can activate my marital brand by directing soul magic into it. Odin's voice comes through, but I scream over his. *You can't control me anymore!*

Fire erupts under the skin of my left arm. The humming of the brand turns into sizzling pain as if I'm being burned, but no further pain follows, only the pleasure of silencing my ex-husband.

The darkness in the depths of my mind reaches out and swallows the memories that keep playing and keep others like them away.

With Odin's influence out of the way, the blizzard in my hands is on the verge of exploding if I don't use it soon or think of something to calm it down. Maybe the shadowy-star bandages on my hands will protect my skin enough for me to suffocate it.

As I close my hands, the magic whirls faster and begins to burn me. The shadowy-star bandages tingle, losing their integrity.

A memory peaks through the darkness in my mind, making me pause. Haidion and me on the beach.

Tendrils of sparkly-shadows stroke a tender spot of my existence, asking permission for the memory to be played in the forefront of my mind. *Fuck it.*

Haidion brings my hands to his lips and kisses them.

With each soft kiss, the pressure of my magic wanting to unleash its wrath calms. The whirling of my soul slows, the lonely crater in my heart begins to fill up, and the illness I've had no luck healing from stops its progression. I shouldn't indulge in this memory any more than I need to, but I stay for a selfish moment longer.

Haidion glances down at my lips after using his magic to braid my hair into a tiara. As heat burns in his eyes, he clenches his fists.

When I expect him to look away, he's in front of me faster than my eyes can process.

He dips his head down as his arms wrap around my body. Rather than capture my lips, he stops himself. His gaze flicks from my mouth to my eyes, conveying his intentions, but he doesn't close the distance. Having power over him makes my core tremble and throb.

Shame forms in the shape of misty hands, and they claw into my friend's shoulders as a silver-tongued voice lectures me about how I'm being unfaithful and a horrible wife.

Haidion ignores the force attempting to pull him away and remains focused on me, waiting for my response as if the claws digging into him were a minor annoyance he could simply dismiss.

Every time we've ever gotten this close in my thoughts and dreams, it's only when I tell him "no" that my guilt shreds him into a million pieces and burns the pile until it becomes ash, leaving me in the dark to think about what I've done.

But... this voice is not my subconscious; it is a voice coming from my brand. The brand my husband hid a servant binding in without my knowledge or consent. *I'm not Odin's anymore.*

Threads of fire wrap around the misty hands and the overwhelming heat forces the claws to unhook from Haidion and disintegrate.

All is quiet except for the calm push and pull of the star-freckled waves as they reflect the night sky and the tranquil melody of the leaves from the forest dancing with wisps of wind, all while illuminating the full moon's glow.

I never want to leave this wonderful dream and wish a heavenly haven like this existed outside of my mind so Haidion and I could have a hidden place to be together where our yearning for each other isn't forbidden.

For the first time in almost five centuries, my thoughts and feelings towards Haidion no longer have to be shackled down. This is only a daydream. I can do whatever I want and finally live out the fantasy of being desired and cherished.

Haidion's brows scrunch together in confusion. "What do you mean when you say you're no longer Odin's?"

"I'm divorcing him." My eyes well up with happy tears as I say the words aloud. "I can allow myself to be fully embraced by your darkness now."

I gasp in relief as I finally slide my hands up Haidion's chest and into his thick, ebony curls. My heart swells as a loving smile of sensual grace spreads across his handsome face.

"I would wait another ten thousand years for you, my darling Freyja." His remarkable voice sounds so real.

"The wait is over. I want to be wanted by you." I don't recognize the confidence in my tone, but it causes a growl of longing to rumble from Haidion's chest.

He raises a brow as wicked amusement flickers across his eyes, causing them to sparkle. "Can you repeat that?"

I brush the tip of my nose against his and whisper. "I'm ready to be yours if you're ready to be mine."

Haidion lets out a sighing moan as I tangle my fingers in his silky hair. "I've been ready."

I gasp in surprise. "Really? For how—"

I snap my mouth shut and push the thought aside. This isn't real. It's only a daydream. Of course, I'm would make him speak like he's been pining for me for centuries.

"Freyja, I've been—" I lean in and silence him by brushing my lips faintly across his like a feather.

Before he can close the distance between us, I dig my fingers into his scalp and jerk him away before his mouth can touch mine. I chuckle with wicked amusement, satisfied by his shock, as a sinister smile spreads across my face.

My edging draws an exasperated groan of lustful impatience out of him. Carnal hunger scorches in his eyes, turning them from sparkling amethyst to a blistering golden haze of burgundy.

"I'm no longer capable of restraining myself from having your mouth on mine." His voice drops to a lower, more lethal octave than I've ever heard from him. "If you wish for me to stop, simply speak the word "red.""

Haidion's thick, cushiony lips devour mine in a kiss that has me moaning and producing sounds I've only ever sung during sex. Tears stream down my cheeks as I whimper into his soft mouth. Never before have I felt such happiness from a kiss that it made me cry.

As I wrap my arms around his strong neck, his hand slides from my waist to the back of my head, deepening the kiss.

Every movement of his mouth is an act of worship. He kisses feverishly as if his desire for me has been bound for ages and he only has one chance to express his love. I'd rather suffocate than have any space between our mouths. I want to be fused together, body to body, mind to mind, and soul to soul.

Haidion is voracious as he licks my lips and sucks them into his mouth as if the taste of me is insatiable. He unleashes himself on me, pouring out every *ounce of his desire to prove how ecstatic he is that I want him to be mine. This is more than kissing; this is ravenous lovemaking. I've never been loved so passionately or had someone utterly obsessed with making me feel wanted.*

I suck his bottom lip into my mouth and bite on it lightly before I let it go.

An intoxicating, guttural moan leaves his lips and causes his body to shudder. "Fuck, Freyja. I'm addicted to that mouth of yours." Haidion rests his forehead on mine. "This can be our reality if you so desire." He cups my face in his hands and gently kisses my puffy lips. "You need only tell me this is what you want."

"I do want you." Another stream of tears trickles down my cheeks; they are cold and hold a truth I don't want to shed into this fantasy. "But it will only ever be a dream because we are forbidden from being together."

I didn't want to speak the words aloud and drag heartbreak into this escapism I conjured; still, this version of Haidion is one I don't want to withhold my pain from.

"No, Freyja. The only barrier preventing us from being together is our willingness to do whatever it takes to be each other's melody so we can sing and soar for eternity."

My soul swoons, allowing his seductive rhymes to make my beast sing. Heat explodes in my chest and spreads throughout my entire body as something within rises to the surface. The threads making up my existence reflect in his eyes. My soul reaches for his, wanting to entangle and bind us together.

"Oh, Freyja." His lips tremble as bloody tears start streaming down his face.

"Haidion, what's wrong?" He had never cried in front of me before. My primary concern is that an unusual shade of blood flows from his tear ducts.

If I needed proof that this was all a dream, I have it in the form of the crimson-gold dripping on his immaculate attire. My friend would be having a fit because his jacket has a stain that no cleaning remedy can remove, but he acts as if he doesn't care that his suit is being ruined. But why am I conjuring up a vision of him shedding tears of blood?

Haidion gives me a kiss unlike any other I've ever had. This isn't just a heated joining of mouths but the forging of souls sealing an unbreakable vow. I only need to press my lips against his with as much vigor, and then the lonely, empty void in my heart and soul will be filled.

He breaks the kiss but doesn't move away; he stays close, waiting to see what I will do.

When I don't lean in, he touches my cheeks as an essence brimming with compassion and understanding rubs against my soul like the delicate sweep of his hands that stroke my face. "No matter what you decide, I'll kill anyone who tries to forbid us from being together as friends or as—" He begins to choke.

Blood drains out of his mouth as his bronzy-brown skin pales. Haidion's eyes darken as he falls to his knees. His throat is ripped open by three gashes, causing him to drown in his blood. The glittering enchantment that brought my fantasy to life is reduced to ash and blows away, deteriorating the landscape into a ghostly husk of what it once was.

My screams are my only company until an arm is draped over my shoulders, consoling me. "We can be miserable together now." Drafasa leans in affectionately as if he hadn't just killed the one I—

Sharp thorns drain the warmth from my body, filling the void in my heart with a poisonous promise of everlasting suffering.

A cage, void of color and light, builds around us while silver threads wrap my body as a metallic voice whispers of how I'm going to be tormented for eternity.

Drafasa is thrown out, the cage locking behind him. He whirls and grips the bars while his stingers try to reach for me. He screams my name as if he cares while I'm consumed by a darkness that isn't my friend.

CHAPTER

TWENTY-TWO

Warmth caresses my face, then travels down the length of my body, licking the ice until it melts and frees me from the cage. A voice of frost and fire cuts through the darkness, pulling me out of the void that's trying to lock me away from the light of reality.

"Freyja, whatever method you used a moment ago isn't working anymore."

Treason's tone is cool, collected, and determined, yet heat radiates from his body. This warmth isn't from him about to shift; this is a reassuring embrace filled with promises of protection from whatever elements are thrown its way.

Was Odin trying to control me again just now? No, he couldn't have been. I didn't go into an Oasis of his creation. But then why did I kill Haidion and then lock myself in a cage? Perhaps I was bringing up my fears so I could show myself that there is no chance in my reality that I can be happy with Haidion.

The blizzard ball is still in my hands, spinning so fast that it is nauseating to look at.

He drops his hands from my cheeks to my shoulders. "The aura of your magic is affecting the integrity of Hera's."

The dome of woven light was thinner. The gruesome battle of warriors against Fae and Arachnids still rages beyond the haven. One

312

of our foes ventures too close, and something shoots out, but whatever invisible force Hera unleashes can't keep up.

A Scorpion uses its stinger and creates an opening. Before they crawl inside, diamond axes slice its meaty tail from behind.

Heimdall's attention locks on me. His rainbow eyes sparkle, lessening the tension in his body. As he resumes chopping the beast into pieces as if its existence insults him, I try to call out, but only wheezes leave me. *I need him to tell me what I must know before facing Drafasa.*

When I try again, bile rises from my throat as tears threaten to spring free.

Haidion's dying face makes me incapable of directing magic into my brand to call Heimdall. If I can't even muster up the energy to send a message, I won't be able to contact Haidion. *He's not dead. He's not dead. He. Is. Not. Dead.*

My attention darts away from the barrier that is slowly being woven back together to my left forearm. I don't know why setting my eyes on the spot could reassure me of Haidion's well-being. We don't have a brand that would share that type of information, but at this moment, I wish I had something, anything, to tell me he's okay.

The dream felt so real. I wanted it to be real, too. I wish every word, touch, smile, tear, and kiss happened in reality, not in a conjured fantasy. Leaving the ecstasy of being wanted and adored only brings forth pain as the daydream replays in my mind, not peace or happiness as I hoped it would.

No matter what I try, my desire will always be forbidden. And until I get this marital-servant brand off me, I will keep getting punished for it. I don't think I'm strong enough to endure this vicious cycle of tormented suffering and starved longing much more. It would be easier to not give in to Haidion and keep things as they are. *I'm happy with the way things are, right?*

"Freyja, look at me!" Treason's fatherly tone makes me obey his command. "Let me help you."

His sapphire eyes search mine as the halo of silver glistens. I can only manage to give him the faintest of nods.

Treason's hands came over mine, and to my surprise, he didn't wince or show any signs of pain from touching my magic. He brings my hands to his mouth and blows warm air on them. Little by little, they begin to defrost, and the blizzard slows.

My thoughts drift back to the memory as Treason warms up my hands. Like the other memory I had of Haidion, the conclusion of this memory changed because I desperately wanted to kiss him last night. I guess the previous one of me checking out his ass was altered because I secretly wished he caught me looking.

Even though it was only a daydream, I can't deny the underlying worry that the tender spots of my existence must have been trying to make me realize. Haidion's life is in danger, and until I can ensure that Drafasa won't harm him, I need to keep him safe both physically and emotionally. *Haidion will not die because of me.*

"Freyja, you need to try to calm down." Treason switches to Waregen, the native tongue of the Wolven, catching me off guard. "Your magic is tied to your emotions, believe it or not. Take a breath with me, but before you blow out, take another one so your lungs are filled, then let it out."

Treason leads me through the breathing exercise. With each repetition, I push my exhale onto my hands, just like he does. When we take our sixth breath, my hands are sweaty, my magic is gone, and my mind is refocused on my task.

I direct soul magic around the tender spots of my existence to reinforce the damage that has been done. I then push all thoughts of Haidion out of my mind. Lastly, I flex my muscles and shift my limbs to get ready to fly.

"Ow," I whimper. *I forgot I still have a dislocated shoulder.*

"You remind me of my youngest pup." Treason gives me a small smile. "I can reset it for you."

"Yes, please," I beg, desperate to be healed and find Heimdall.

Treason removes the armor on my chest and right arm before helping me to the ground. As I lay down on the surprisingly dry grass, I take another breath and push the nauseating pain bubbling in my stomach aside as best I can.

"Is your youngest your favorite?" I switched to speaking Waregen; talking in a different language is a helpful distraction.

Treason kneels on my right side; his smile turns into a full grin, warming his frosty-caramel skin. "My seven other pups seem to think so." A small flash of pain diverts his eyes for a second. "Marcson had the least amount of time with his mom. As a method of coping, he trained harder than necessary and then denied being in pain or injured. He pushed all of my and his siblings' concerns away because the only one he wanted to comfort him was his mother. When he told us that the Fates pulled him towards his mate on the rise of the moon last Autumnal Equinox, our happiness knew no boundaries. I'm eternally grateful to whichever Fate blessed my son."

It may have been the Fate of Love, Growth, Death, or Time. Only his son and his fated mate would know which of the fates had blessed them.

All the races, aside from the mortals, believe in the Fates. Even some gods choose to place their faith in them, but it's not widely accepted, so those who believe in them must remain silent. We all know that the Father created the world and everyone on it, yet he cannot answer prayers like gods or the Fates can. Since he embedded himself into the planet, he can't use his magic like everyone else can; instead, he allows his soul to fuel our world and everything on it. *The Father is the definition of being selfless, and what does he get for it? To be taken advantage of.*

"The Autumnal Equinox was only six full moons ago. Have they come out of their den yet?"

Treason answers with laughter, "Lakonna isn't letting Marcson leave until she's pregnant."

I chuckle. "I'm sure your son doesn't mind a bit."

"No, he most certainly does not." He clears his throat. "Keep taking those deep breaths."

I do so as he holds my right arm and gently goes through some maneuvers to help move my shoulder back into place. The pain is uncomfortable and would probably hurt more if I hadn't followed his instructions.

"Can I give you some advice?"

On my exhale, I answer him, "I'd be honored to receive advice from the Beta Prince."

Treason helps me sit up, places my hand on his broad chest, and begins to knead the muscles in my arm and shoulder. "You shouldn't underestimate the strength of the races just because most can't exert magic. Our magic is within the beast of our souls, and one trait we all have in common is heightened senses that are lethal. I mean no offense, but all Gods and Goddesses have the instincts of mortals." I can't help but chuckle because he's right. "But our primary strength isn't within ourselves but in the unity of our race. You might have a pantheon, but is the loyalty there such that thousands will respond to one being's cry?"

A blunt dagger of truth plunges into my chest. "No, it's not." My voice is only a whisper.

I don't regret the words coming out of my mouth or care if anyone around me heard them; I just hate how vulnerable I sound.

There have been many instances when I needed assistance while fulfilling my duty as a goddess, but we were trained to work independently. After Freyr died, the thought of contacting Hel, Heimdall, or Odin always made me feel like a nuisance, a burden, and weak because they never had to call for aid. After I met Haidion, he had the luck to visit me when I was in over my head with shit or was about to go into it.

A couple of range-of-motion tests set my shoulder in working order. "So, that portal you opened… is that a Beta Prince power or one that was gifted to you when you were blessed as a pup?"

Treason raises an eyebrow as he helps me stand up. "I can't tell if Watson didn't understand what transformation I went through or if he wasn't sure if he should tell." He picks up my armor for me. "How I was "blessed" wasn't by a powerful being but by my soul evolving. So no, it's not because of my rank as the Beta Prince. Hold."

It takes me a second to register that he's waiting for me to hold my armor to myself so he can help. He moves to stand by my side once I do as he says, and his clever hands strap me in as if he's done this a thousand times, even though, as a Wolven, he only wears the skin he was born in.

"Are you a Rarity then?"

Treason tightens my armor more than I usually do. "No. If we weren't in the midst of battle, I'd heatedly immerse your mind in my judgment on the matter to the point you'd beg me to stop."

"I give you permission to turn me into putty." The comment stumbled out before I had the chance to catch it. "I mean my mind." *Oh, Fates, have mercy.*

"Don't pull your hair out about it. I'm not some young pup who would hump anything that hinted towards sex. An ailment from losing the love of my life is an almost nonexistent libido." A chuckle escapes him. "Frees up my time."

"You never considered getting another mate?"

"No," he says immediately, leaving no room for uncertainty. "Blessed by the Fates or not, my heart and soul belong to my wife, Churania. The memories of our love and the pups she allowed me to father are all I need to be happy."

Treason's gaze becomes empty as if he's detached from reality. After a brief second, a snarl leaves his lips, followed by a cough, and then he refocuses on his task.

He continues before I can ask what upset him. "Anyway, to make a long story short, I don't agree with the Rarity title since only the Gods are privileged to be labeled as one, not the races."

The air I was inhaling began to burn my throat as if I were swallowing poison. "Are you serious?"

"I take it that you didn't know." I can only nod my head.

Freyr was the one who told me I was a Rarity and how the label would protect me. Either I didn't comprehend who the title protected or assumed the label was given to all.

Treason moves to my arm. "You should be wearing a helmet and palm-less gauntlets or gloves."

"I'm more in tune with my surroundings without a helmet on... and I also like to feel the wind in my hair. As for the hand protection, I didn't know palm-less armor was a thing." I clear my throat. "After all this is done, would you like to come over for dinner and drinks so we can resume the conversation about Rarities?"

I needy my knowledge of Rarities to be corrected. I want to hear his opinion on the matter and then figure out why the label only benefits the gods, but not right now. We don't have the time for that discussion or one about what makes his portal magic different from what the Gods can do to enter the plane of Orrtiereum or Erresthralla.

"Take alcohol out of the equation for me so there is no risk of an inappropriate uprising, and you've got yourself a date." *An uprising...?*

My cheeks heat up. *Oh, that type of rising!* "Do you mind if I check on your other straps?" He gestures toward my lower half.

"Go ahead." I widen my stance, and he drops to his knees.

My stomach flutters as heat sparks in my chest. He's just helping to secure my armor, yet the action of someone other than myself attending to my well-being causes the loneliness inside to whine for more.

"The Mages forge palm-less armor, but since the arrogant cowards left thinking they could avoid their fate, you will have to go to Crescent Island. There is a smithy called Frost Borne Forge, and they can make you a pair." Treason's hands pause on the straps on my upper thigh. "When was the last time you got armor maintenance?"

"The Orckrainien I won the armor from had it repaired and resized for me after our fight about six hundred years ago."

His gaze snaps up to mine. "You're joking?"

Confused, I shake my head. "Magically forged metals last much longer than basic metals. But I know about the shop you're talking about from my recent visit to Crescent Island."

Since I wasn't interested in learning about metal, Freyr didn't teach me. Part of my brother's teaching method was to not push knowledge onto an unwilling learner so they would not become resentful. Hel and Heimdall disagreed and called me ignorant. I would only have myself to blame when and if fate decided I needed to be taught. In all likelihood, I would learn the hard way.

Instead of protecting myself with metal, I used my ice to construct armor and weapons, which made maintaining their strength and integrity simpler. When an Orckrainien encased in a ball of fiery light crashed onto the shores of Leifheim, I fought him for not taking responsibility for the damages he caused. I was in awe of his armor and had to have it.

I had worn the armor for combat during the war over the Frozen Fire Highlands, and I haven't gone more than a day without wearing it because the magic within has given me a sense of comfort I lost when my brother died.

Treason got back to his feet, staring me down as if he were about to interrogate me. "What scumbag told you that and manipulated you into believing it?"

My first instinct is to shove him away and defend myself, but the fight in me leaves as shadows emerge from the depths of his eyes, and his muscular body grows tense. He subtly shakes like he is about to shift, keeping his temper in check with the flex of his fingers and the regulated pace of his breaths. His assertive tone was not intended as a challenge or an insult but to make me comprehend my naiveté. *He's not mad at me; he's worried about me. It's as if he cares.*

I'm frozen in place. We are strangers with no relationship other than a brother and sister-in-arms fighting together against a common enemy. He has no reason to care or even allow himself to expand the capacity of his worry towards me. His children are out on the field fighting right now, and instead of being with them, he's before me with a glassiness forming over his eyes.

My dignity as the leader is about to shatter if I don't move or say something to stop this moment from affecting me.

He reaches up and caresses my cheek. "Who?" His whisper encourages and reassures me that he will catch me if I fall.

Something within me gives, and I close my eyes as if not being able to see will help me protect myself. Maybe all the events of today and the battle are finally crashing down on me since I'm in a safe place with someone giving me their undivided attention, or maybe my determination to not allow anyone to see me vulnerable has finally reached a breaking point.

"Odin." My husband's name leaves a sickening taste in my mouth.

Treason's fingers trail down to the back of my neck and massage my nape. I let myself rest my head against his chest because I physically can't hold it up. The Beta Prince allows me to lean against him until my heart stops trying to come up through my throat and my lungs stop constricting air. *Now is not the time for an internal physical attack and mental assault, Freyja.*

My breath catches as he rests his head on the top of mine. "Ever since I was a young pup, I have been interested in all things relating to metal. As a Wolven, I never need to concern myself with armor, but I found working with the stubborn material and forming it into something to accentuate its beauty enjoyable and satisfying."

There is a softness to his features when I raise my head and open my eyes. He's looking at me with such kindness and empathy that it feels wrong and uncomfortable because I don't deserve his compassion. I never experienced this level of intimacy from anyone but my brother. I'm not his family. I mean nothing to him. *Why is he treating me like this?*

I'm having difficulty forming words to tell him that his affection makes me uncomfortable, so I raise my hand to stop him, but before I can touch him, he lowers his arm.

"I'm intuitively observant and instinctually sharp due to my race, but only a master blacksmith can detect when magical armor has been neglected because they know where to look. All armor with magical enchantments has a concealment spell, so others don't know the armor's durability is waning or where any damage is."

He takes a step back from me. "If the wearer has an active lifestyle, they should see to the care of the armor's repair every year and the siphons every decade, but if they only wear the armor on occasion, then every decade for repair and a recharge of the siphons. Without a living entity to tie magic to it, it will dilute over time. Once you get more acclimated with the Preserver Guild, I'm sure you will learn how to attend to the upkeep of magical items."

Treason kneels before me once again, and before he lifts his hands to my upper thigh, he pauses, waiting for my permission even though I had given it to him earlier.

"Go ahead." My voice was just above a whisper.

Making my voice sound small, I hoped, would cover up how weak I was feeling, but his paternal gaze was locked onto my soul, measuring every breath and noting the tremor in my hands from suppressing my shaking.

After an intense moment of not knowing if he would point out my obvious distress, he lowers his attention to the straps of my armor. "If I were to remove the concealment spell, you'd be horrified with your armor's appearance. Fortunately, the maintenance of the siphon crystals forged into the metal is stellar. The magic alone has been keeping your armor intact and taking the brunt of the damage inflicted."

With a tsk, he pulls my straps tighter as if to fuse my armor with my skin. I take a deeper breath to try to level out my voice and thank the stars that he doesn't glance up and stays focused on his task rather than note my wobbly mental state.

"Until recently, I didn't know that my armor held any magical properties like my cloak, so I don't know how the siphons have been attended to or refilled since I wasn't made aware."

Since Odin was the one who told me I didn't have to attend to my armor for a while, I doubt he would've refilled the siphons. None of my friends studied the craft of blacksmithing, so they wouldn't have known. And what happened on Starson was a one-time occurrence and wouldn't explain all the centuries prior.

Treason rises to his feet and begins to inspect my cloak. "Even the magical integrity of the dusted crystals on the feathers is spectacular. Judging by the immaculate magical upkeep of your attire, I would've thought you'd tended to the siphons monthly with star magic."

"Wait, my cloak needs to be attended to as well?" Treason gives an affirmative huff.

Odin must've known since he had the cloak made for me. He must've been refilling the siphons because I love flying more than anything. Surely, he's also been attending to the magical upkeep, but why not the physical? *Wait, star magic?* That does not make sense. Neither Odin nor I have...

The brand on the back of my left-hand hums, and Zachariah's musical voice plays in my mind. *Star magic at its finest.* His presence and the humming vanish as soon as the dots connect.

"My friend has star magic," I blurt out, without considering whether I should speak the words aloud.

Treason attention isn't on me but rather on something further away, as if he's trying to piece something together in his mind.

"It's not my place to conclude why your friend has been attending to your armor without your knowledge, but I will interject that all enchanted items are either recharged by solar or lunar energy or by the wielder's magic." He blinks and comes out of his thoughts, refocusing back on me. "Star magic isn't on the market, so they have been gifting you theirs."

My gaze drops to my hands. Haidion had left his magic in me and said, *"I could leave it elsewhere."* At that moment, I only considered that he was implying something sexual given how he chuckled and bit his lip. Now, I see his reaction in a whole new light. On the surface, he was teasing me while the truth of his statement lay underneath. Instead of asking *"Where?"* aloud, I kept it to myself.

Haidion tending to the magical care of my armor makes sense, but why didn't he tell me, and why has he been giving me so much of his magic?

"Whoever this friend of yours is, they must care about you." Something sparks in Treason's eyes. An answer to a question he was pondering perhaps?

"My friend…" The memory of Haidion saying three words has my heart swelling to the point I need to scream, but I painfully hold it in. "Cares for me strongly."

Treason looks at the armor on my left forearm and barely restrains a growl. "I will conclude one thing for you, Freyja. You deserve better."

"Odin is not my husband anymore." Saying the words aloud is the only strength I'm able to grab onto so I don't collapse and become a screaming mess.

"Good. He would fucking know about your armor needing maintenance." A world-shattering growl that he physically tries to swallow grumbles out of him. "Your armor might not last through this battle. You'll need to be careful."

Treason paints a clear picture for me: Odin hadn't cared the way a husband should. I mentally curse myself for how blind and stupid I've been. Note to self: Don't trust anyone's comfort when dealing with grief. I will not be fucking manipulated ever again.

"If my armor fails, I have my ice to protect me."

When Treason's ears twitch, he casts a brief look behind him before returning his attention to me. *Either one of his pups is calling him or his king is.*

"I have one last piece of advice to give you." Treason exhales. "If this battle doesn't end in our favor, you won't be safe." He takes a step toward me and brushes his fingers against the Harpy feather I forgot about. "Seek out Namtar, he's the Ancient Demonical of Disease. My friend can strip you of your Godship and then align you with a race of your choosing."

"That can't be possible. There is only one way that I can have my title stripped." *Wait, Treason is friends with Vahildra too?*

"He has a special power that can alter a being. I give you my word that it is true." Treason's fingers graze my cheek. "My pups would be more than happy to have you as a part of our pack, and I'd make sure you wouldn't go a day without being cared for."

If my chest wasn't uncomfortably swelling and my mind wasn't being ripped apart, I might've been able to school my features and conceal the pain coming from a lonely place in my heart that has been empty for almost five centuries. When my brother died, I lost the only family I'd ever be able to have.

Although Treason's suggestion is sweet and endearing, no family could handle someone like me. All my broken edges are too sharp, and I'd hurt them more than they would be able to help me. Keeping everyone at arm's length is safer.

My mouth wobbles. "I don't know how to express my gratitude for all you have done for me."

His hand slides down to my neck. "The only thing I will ask of you, Freyja, is to choose happiness and make sure it's your own."

Treason pulls me in for a hug when a muffled cry escapes me, and I don't resist. I allow him to hold me as if I were one of his pups, pressing me into his chest and resting his head upon mine. On reflex, my arms wrap around his toned torso. His body pushes off tranquil heat, and I selfishly melt into him, wishing I could never let go.

CHAPTER

TWENTY-THREE

NINTH HOUR AFTER SUNRISE

Can anyone hear me? No response. *Bralyant has an average-sized cock!* Still nothing. *Fuck me!*

Ever since I left Hera's dome, I haven't been able to speak to anyone through the brand, but I can hear all of them. I guess all my curses and insults are only for me, the forefront of my mind, and the spiritual void to hear.

Not being able to speak to anyone isn't the worst thing since my commanding duties are delegated. It gives me a valid reason for why I'm unable to respond to the irritated growls of the Wolven King, who wants me to fight next to him so he can keep me safe. *Blah!* Regardless, being unable to talk through the brand impedes me from Heimdall's lecture and my goal to confront Drafasa.

I cut a Fae's leathery wing in half with a slice of my ice blade. *"Get fucked!"* The warrior violently screams in Fanarzien as he uncontrollably tumbles towards the ground.

"If you're offering, then no, it looks like you're having trouble with performance!" He flips me off, signaling that he heard my taunt in his native tongue.

My laughter is short-lived as Skjoldr hums in my chest. I drop just as three Fae warriors collide with each other, exactly where I was a second ago. Skjoldr has been doing her job as my second pair of eyes as

324

my instincts alert me to magical danger. The valuable seconds allow me to reinforce the frost layer on my armor and cloak so the Fae's magic can't affect my siphons or harvest my magic.

"I never had a foursome, but I'm intrigued."

After immersing them in my thick, blinding frost mist, I fly up and circle the squawking warriors. Not knowing who to play with first, I count. "Wing. Wing. Wing. HAND!"

The male screams in agony as his chopped-off hand plummets. Disabling a Fae from wielding magic makes it easier to kill them. The Fae still has another hand, but he won't take any risks; he'll have to rely on his inner beast and skill with hand-to-hand combat. Rather than fight me, the warrior fly's down, chasing after his hand.

I keep up my taunting as I circle around them to maintain the mist while avoiding the thrusts of their swords. "I hear palm-less gauntlets are a thing. Oh darn, you pulled your hand away. Wing it is."

Another Fae uncontrollably tumbles down to the battle below. Cutting off his wing was an asshole move; but he'll grow it back once he removes the joint connecting to his shoulder. In the meantime, he will be grounded.

"I went into this new experience with such high hopes, but it's obvious that you're just basic bitches when it comes to having fun."

I pull the magic from my swords up my arms to form an extra layer of armor. As the warrior swings aimlessly, I punch his swords out of his hands, shattering the metal, and then get into his face.

He jolts back as I wrap my hands around his neck. "Since you lasted the longest, you get the pleasure of my kiss."

He pauses and blinks at the unexpected statement. His jaw drops. I don't need their mouths to be open, so I'm curious if he'll die quicker.

I take a deep breath and draw the mist into my body. I lean in, press my lips to his, and expel the freezing air from my lungs. When I pull back, all his sharp, flawless Fae features turn ice blue as the aerial battle around us comes back into view. Before the weight of his crystalized body becomes too heavy, I let go. Normally, my victims would just die instantly, not turn into statues. *Interesting.*

Haidion refers to my innovative tactic of killing my opponent as the "Kiss of Kindness" since those I frost to death die without pain, or so he interrupted in the minds of my victims before they perished.

Skjoldr pulls me up to avoid yet another Fae trying to grab me. I might not be as fast as them, but I have better maneuverability and can shift on a whim.

I direct frost into my hands, fashion a whip, and cast it out to latch around the warrior's ankle. Instead of stopping, he continues to fly away, tugging me with him.

With the wind stinging my eyes, I can't see and don't have enough strength to make him stop. Letting go is my only option, but I turn the mist rope into solid ice before I do. He drops due to the added weight, taking out a few others on his way down.

Alarms sound in my mind as a sharp twinge comes from my chest. I skid to a stop and roll over a couple of times before I'm upright and floating. Skjoldr hums, alerting me that I'm running low on magic while my instincts tune my senses to take in what's around me. The Fae pulled me almost three-quarters of the way toward the West woods. No one is in my immediate area except the bodies of fallen Wolven and Fae. I'm alone, and I need to get back.

Fire blazes under my skin as an armored forearm wraps around my neck from behind, putting me in a chokehold.

The aroma of vanilla and berries makes my mouth salivate against my will. Angular, leathery, and perfectly symmetrical wings flap in the periphery of my vision. Only one type of Fae has such a strong presence and is clever enough to sneak up undetected—a High Lord.

"I'll play with you, Red Dove." I shiver as his breathless voice of enchanting hunger strokes the back of my neck.

The fragrant warmth of silken nectar fills my mouth and nostrils, blocking the air and forcing me to only breathe in his magic. *Fuck, I should've frosted my face!*

"You just have to swallow the potent load of my magic first."

The High Lord's purple-tinted armor digs into my throat, pinching my skin as his large frame drapes over me. His wings flap steadily, keeping us hovering in one spot.

If he wanted to kill me, he could've done so. What he intends to use his magic for could range from putting me to sleep, shredding me from the inside out, or controlling my body, but I have to willingly breathe it in first.

Trying to attack him is suicide, and given my weakening magical state and the advantage his position has, I'm limited in what I can do. Without the ability to contact anyone, I'm on my own. Using my spiritual power would be a last-ditch option. I would need to kill him. No ifs, ands, or buts about it. The Fae are known for capturing beings who can tap into their spirit, and the ones taken are never seen again. Defending myself is my only option. Once I'm free from his grasp, I can attack.

The High Lord's presence continues to make me salivate. Not wanting to choke on my saliva or risk swallowing the liquid, I push my dignity aside and drool.

I grip his forearm, one hand close to his inner elbow and the other closer to my throat. Since he's keeping us up, I pull my magic out of my cloak to force him to support my weight and conserve my magic.

We drop a fraction, and the momentum is enough for me to unbalance him and use the downward energy to pull—

He wraps his free arm around my waist, pulling my backside flush to his front. "Predictable. What a shame." He sighs with boredom. "My magic will only make you a more willing participant in what the other Lords and I have in store once we win this battle."

If all of the High Lords are here, so is the entire Faerie Myriad. Since no one can enter their borders, I have no idea how large their force is.

His hand slides down the middle of my body. "Trust me when I say I need to keep you in this position because once you see my face, you'll want me to put my heir in you."

That hand of his flattens above the apex of my thighs, pushing my ass into him more. *Killing the arrogant Fae would be too kind.*

All I was able to accomplish was relieve some pressure on my neck. I might not be breathing, but the panic of being suffocated is still causing my pulse to hammer, and the tiniest shift helps me to calm myself.

He brushes his nose against the shell of my ear, and I tense to hold back my hiss. "If you insist on wanting to fool around with me, then let me be of service."

Leaning into me more, the High Lord pulls in his wings, and we drop. Since he's pushing his weight onto me, we naturally start to tumble as we plummet.

The pace of our spinning causes the pressure of his forearm around my neck to tighten, then loosen, and repeat with each rotation. I might not be using my throat to help me breathe, but my vision starts to become spotty from the lack of blood flowing.

"Come on, Red Dove. Give in. I'll make sure you enjoy both our time together and the gift we High Lords have in store for you: liberation from your husband. He only married you to ensure it's his seed that will father your child and not your mate's. If anything, we are doing you a favor."

My body tenses from the soul-shocking information, and a squeal of pain escapes my lips. No, that can't be true. I'm a goddess, not one of a race. I can't have a mate. Only by the Fates could I have one, but I haven't felt the pull of my spiritual essence guiding me towards someone.

The brand on the back of my left-hand hums. Zachariah's voice plays in my mind.

Your husband, mate, and friends must've wanted to have a good laugh when you told them how you reacted to meeting one of my kind for the first time.

Starson's and my voice enter my mind.

Do you not sense your connection to him? Because I can.

"*I don't know how you can sense my bond to my husband without touching my marital brand.*"

Reading a mate's aura is a sixth sense that I have, thanks to my soul's evolution as an adolescent.

Heimdall's voice entering my mind has me almost sighing in relief, but it's only a memory, not a current conversation via our brand.

"*Once you break your mate bond, never accept another.*"

The humming of the brand on the back of my hand vanishes a second later.

I force the hopeful thoughts that promise to fill the loneliness in my heart out of my mind. If I do have a mate, I can't be theirs. I have a duty to fulfill, and I plan to do whatever it takes, even if it means giving up my life. The only voice I'm going to listen to is Heimdall's. I vow to myself that once I figure out who I'm bound to, I will break the bond. No one will hold me back from saving the Father. *Skjoldr.*

I bite my tongue and internally wince from the burning sensation of my spiritual essence branding the skin over my sternum and sealing my magical vow into my flesh for all to read and see.

I focus on my current task. If I could talk and the High Lord and I weren't somersaulting through the air, I'd use this opportunity to interrogate him for information.

Why is Odin so determined to have a child with me? Maybe that's the reason why he wanted me to be his servant. What makes me so special in his eyes that he'd go to such great lengths to get me pregnant? I didn't tell him about my spiritual power, so that can't be it. Does he plan on divorcing me or killing me once I give him a child? That last question doesn't matter because it won't happen, but I'm curious why the High Lords are trying to help me. Should I accept their help? No! For all I know, this is his way of attempting to manipulate me. Until I beat the truth out of Odin, I'm not taking anyone's word about liberating me.

With a grunt, the Fae flares out his wings and stops our spiraling descent.

My chest clenches, screaming to gasp for air from the sudden jolt. Not wanting to use any more excess energy, I allow my body to go limp.

Blurs of light and darkness dance in my vision as the spinning sensation continues. I close my eyes to try to calm myself down. I'm at a loss for how to get out of this. Using my spiritual power is my only option.

"Red Dove? Goddess?!" Panic flushes the arrogance out of his voice.

A soft thud and the steady flow of wind from his wings ceases.

I peek through my lids. We are on the ground, and my feet are dangling only inches from the grass. Using this as my chance to distract him, I release my grip on his arms and become a dead weight.

"Fuck! Are you dying?" He presses his finger into my neck, and my pulse is almost nonexistent, causing him to urgently curse. "No, you can't die!"

The warmth of his magic starts to pull out of my nose and mouth.

Tall grass brushes against my legs, and the toes of my booted feet touch the ground. I fight off my desire to act before all of his magic is out. Not reacting and waiting for the opportune moment is a skill I normally have no patience for but have managed to acquire, thankfully.

He removes his forearm from around my neck as the last of his magic leaves me. I let my head slump forward, so I'll have more space to—

His fingers grip my chin, and he turns my face to the left. "This will be our little secret." he whispers against my cheek.

Tingly lips crush against mine, and a forceful tongue pries my mouth open. A rescue breath of star magic is pushed down my throat and into my lungs, and I am powerless to fight it off. All High Lords were gifted with three siphons of star magic to help them run and protect their courts and perform miracles if they felt gracious.

I instantly gasp for breath, but not before biting his lip. "You ungrateful—"

I slam my head back as hard as I can, eliciting a loud cracking sound and infuriated screech.

While I direct frost-mist to cover the lower half of my face to protect myself from breathing in his magic again, I twist and drive my elbow into his throat.

He releases his hold on me as gagging gurgles heave out of him.

I withdraw my Atlantean swords and whirl around. My blades just miss his throat as he vanishes in a cloud of powdered starlight.

With my magic running low, if I use any of it to fly, it will heavily cost me, and I don't want to be at a disadvantage while in the air again.

On my exhale, I create a barely visible layer of mist over my body so my instincts can be heightened to sense the High Lord.

Tingles of awareness arise from my left. I tighten my hold on my swords and add another layer to the mist covering my face. Skjoldr hums in my chest, wanting to fly me away. I internally growl to warn her not to act on my behalf.

Only my tired breaths, the swaying grass, the whistling wind, and the distant boom of either fighting or thunder fill the void of space around me.

"I wonder..." The low rumble of the High Lord's voice floats by my left ear. "is the shade of your hair braided upon your head the same as the hair snuggled between your thighs?"

"I'll claw out your eyes and shove them up your ass before you get the chance to find out." He scoffs as if I'm incapable of fulfilling the threat.

Something sharp grazes my throat as I direct all the frost to latch onto the invisible Fae. My magic bonds to him like snowflakes on glass, exposing his silhouette and a thin dagger.

Needing him to believe that I can't sense or see him, I straighten, hesitate to swallow, and flit my eyes without moving my neck as if I'm searching for the source of the pressure against my flesh. When I lightly coat someone with my magic, the being can't sense it unless they have an above-normal body temperature, like a Wolven.

"If I were to bloody your lips and this cute little mound resting above it..." His blade glides over my mouth and up onto my nose. "will your second pair of supple lips and the knoll of pert flesh weep just as profusely?"

"You are a sick, perverted fuck."

He chuckles with delight as I clench my thighs. The mental picture of him violating me assaults my mind. *Come on, Freyja. Think of a way out of this and instill fear in him.*

Given my exhausted magical state, physical fatigue, and average experience in swordplay, my options on how to fight him are limited, even more so if this High Lord is the little faerie boy's father. With only physical characteristics to go off of, I can only assume that I can't kill him if I don't want to force the boy to take his father's title. Rather than make this arrogant being bleed out of every orifice he has, I need to think of a way to send him home traumatized to the point he'd fear leaving the borders of his court.

The abyss of darkness lounging in the depths of my mind decimates the image of myself being tortured with a ferocity that gives me chills. With my mind clear, an idea is pushed forward of how I can protect myself from the Fae's dagger and create a distraction so I can strike the pointy tips of his ears. I don't know why such a thought came to me since I'm not sure why maiming would not only be the cruelest punishment but also horrifying. No other ideas I fire off give me as much confidence as the first one.

"Tell me your name, Red Dove, and I'll leave whichever face I find most pleasurable unscathed." I'm so glad I listened to my gut and didn't trust his words from earlier about him wanting to help me. "It's only fair since you wounded one of my mantels of masterpiece."

Laughter explodes from my lungs and booms in my mind.

The Fae's snarl turns into a seething screech. "You won't be laughing when each of the High Lords has their fun with you, whore."

"And you wanted me to trust your word about 'liberating me' from my husband. All the while, you perverted lords selfishly wanted me for yourselves." My laughter turns into wicked amusement. "I'm going to castrate all of you, then I'll make you swallow each other's sacks of heirs and sew your mouths shut." His gagging only makes me smile wider. "That way, each of your mantels of masterpiece will be evenly fucked up." The darkness in my mind purrs with eagerness.

Overwhelming energy presses down on my shoulders, heightens my nerves, and tingles what I had thought were depleted reserves. An illuminating magic glows in my veins, ready to use. Skjoldr couldn't have obtained it for me because the Fae had claimed all the vegetation. I'm at a loss because I exhausted all the starry-blue light and gifted magic Haidion lavished upon me.

Skjoldr tugs me one way while my instincts alert me to danger approaching from another. *Well, duh, I'm in danger. Tell me something I don't—*

A chirping purr and a spraying hiss come from behind me. "Fuck!"

Webbing cocoons the High Lord. Because of the magic coating him, the silken threads do not entirely adhere to his frame, allowing his invisibility to remain.

His wings flap in panic as he tries to use his dagger to slice through the webbing, but it gets stuck. "I'm on your... shit!"

Skjoldr hums in my chest and pushes magic into my cloak, pulling me toward safety.

I dart into the sky as another spray tickles my ears. Webbing is roped around my legs, and I'm pulled back down, slamming against the firm ground.

Grunts leave me while the numbing magic makes my skin shiver from its attempt to influence me. Whatever material makes up my armor has a natural resistance; however, I wonder how long it will last, given what Treason told me about its integrity.

My magic gets redirected into my hands, frosting them. I drop my blades and begin to unwrap myself.

The High Lord curses as another spray of webbing coats his body, and he, too, is pulled onto the ground.

A fabulous laugh, full of vengeful hatred, comes from the forest. *"Nothing personal, High Lord."* An Arganile tongue grates against my nerves, hindering me from getting free.

I'm swiftly pulled towards the tree line, which has thinned from the Scorpion drug fog. My focus on trying to get the webbing removed is a lost cause because I'm being pulled over the bodies of fallen warriors. With weapons lying around, I tuck my head into my chest as close as I can and wrap my arms around the back of my neck.

"I have been waiting for this day for centuries!" The Spyden unleashes the full capacity of her lungs, bellowing out an ear-piercing screech of victory.

The webbing around my legs is pulled so hard that I'm lifted off the ground and sail through the air. My bare back smacks into something that recoils from the impact and then bounces forward without letting me go.

Threads of woven silk are secured between two trees, forming a magnificent web. Above me is my cloak. Only the string around my neck is left attached. Being dragged must've ripped the others off. My armor might be able to resist the magical influence, but it isn't repellent against the adhesive. I dangle a couple of feet off the ground and am right smack in the middle.

"We finally meet, mate-wrecker." She switched to speaking Earthradonic. *How considerate.*

I raise my head. "I can speak your—"

My words become jumbled as I take in who is in front of me. The Autarcha of the Spyden race, Ladiya. Drafasa's wife and mate.

TWENTY-FOUR

An hourglass of round curves is highlighted by unblemished, milky skin that is only achieved when one doesn't get sun exposure. Ladiya is soft and succulent in places where I am toned and muscular. Her pin-straight, silky hair drapes over her shoulders, covering her glossy breasts and falling all the way down to her wide hips. Like all the other beast races, there is not a scrap of fabric on her. As the Autarcha, only she can shift into her humanoid form whenever she wants. All of her race have to ask her permission.

Three pairs of normal Spyden legs come out of her back as she walks towards me on two humanoid ones. Curved fang tusks protrude from the sides of her cheekbones. They slope past her chin and curl up so the tips are level with her lips. Her three pairs of black eyes create an arc from the sides of her nose to her forehead.

Ladiya takes her time to look me over. "This…" She gestures to all of me as a snarl of disgust curls her lips. "Is this what my mate is so obsessed with? Put a cock on you, and I would've thought you were male. The only thing going for you are those eyes." She gags as though she is sickened by giving me a compliment.

"If I had a cock, I would rather bite it off myself than ever think about getting aroused to fuck you with it."

Her opinion on my physical appearance didn't provoke me to spew the insulting remarks. My pent-up hatred for her did. Now that my wrath has been reawakened and she's within my reach, her death will be delivered by my hands.

A month after my brother died, news spread of Drafasa leaving Ladiya at the altar. I was surprised he listened to my advice, but then she publicly shared that they were mates and Drafasa was forced to marry her. I have hungered to kill Ladiya ever since.

During my dare gone wrong, I told Haidion about my desire to kill the Autarcha of the Spyden race. He offered to take the blame even without my informing him why I wanted her dead. We got close to her burrow, but the fear of running into Drafasa with Haidion by my side made my hunger lessen for the time being. *Now I'm starving.*

Ladiya angrily chitters as she plants her legs down and pushes herself up to be at eye level with me. "You are the reason why my mate hasn't touched me besides being forced to consummate the night we married. I'm looked at as an unfit ruler who can't interest her mate to have him fill her womb with infalings, and I'm disrespected by all females who think they can try and seduce him to have me replaced!"

"And you think that killing me will make your situation any better?"

A confident smile widens her lips. "Yes. My mate would sneak away during the hours of the sun while we were all asleep. When I woke, he was always in a foul mood and remained in solitude for hours, muttering your name constantly, lovingly. It turned him into a pile of screams and tears about how much he missed you. Once you die, he can finally be free from the torment you are putting him through."

My brother's and my names almost sound identical; she must be mistaken. Drafasa's tears aren't for me; they are for my brother. He's been grieving just as long and hard as I have and is probably going to my brother's grave. I can't think another reason of why he would endure going out during the day.

If Drafasa wasn't so dead set on taking away my happiness, we would have each other to lean on. He was the only one I considered family without being blood, and he took what we had and tore it to shreds then made me out to be the villain.

I don't like hating him. It fucking hurts. And if I were to come close to killing him, I don't know if I could do it. My affection for him is still in my heart and hasn't gone away; it's only turned into the opposite emotion since he threatened me.

"My death won't free him from the torment he is in. Only yours will."

Drafasa might have put himself in his current situation, but I won't allow the man my brother loved to spend the rest of his existence in misery.

Ladiya has no royal immunity that protects her because she came to the battlefield. Her death would lead to some legal headaches, but those are minor details I don't give a fuck about.

She laughs pompously. "That would make Drafasa more miserable since I'm his mate."

"Fuck that logic. Drafasa doesn't want anything to do with you. You would put his happiness first if your truly cared about him!"

"But the magic system determined we were compatible."

"What makes them think they can determine if two beings will love each other or not? Guess what? They fucking don't. They can only determine if a pair within the same race is capable of producing powerful offspring. Love has to be built, and he doesn't want to build it with you."

She anxiously lowers herself to the ground as pain flashes across her brow, making her flinch.

"Given that he was forced to fuck you, some of the threads making up your bond might not have connected, but you don't need a magical tether to someone's heart to know how they are feeling. You are being ignorant due to his lack of attention, which is causing all in your race to see you as worthless. You are using the bond as an excuse to not see it. You are the one causing him more harm than me."

Having a mate can be beautiful. It is a unique love language thread only they can understand. The magical connection is only the base and can grow into whatever the mates want their bond to evolve into. Only once had I seen an example of how special a mate bond can be. It was one that was blessed by the Fates, not the magic system.

The primary purpose behind a mating bond created by the magic system is to bring evolved offspring that are better suited for change to life. But because greed is so rampant on the planet, most beings see it as a way to advance in rank. They believe themselves to be the strongest members of their race for having one. To reject a mate nowadays, compared to when Freyr was growing up, usually ends with one being forced.

As for the fated mate bond, I'm not entirely sure if it's any different. I don't understand why both connections exist, aside from one being a result of the magic system and the other being a result of the Fates. Given what happened to Bralyant's brother, Auxiliary, it's ludicrous that the laws of the lords and ladies take precedence over what the races believe in. He shouldn't have been exiled because the Fates had blessed him with a mate from a different race.

Ladiya's attention darts to my sides. With my peripheral vision, I saw the shadows of the trees nearest me are thicken and block out the natural light, decreasing visibility and shifting energy as if the forest was about to change.

"You are wrong." Her arrogant tone denying all I had said, makes my soul whirl in a storm of fire, promising carnage. "Once you are gone, he will love me, you mate-wrecker!"

A molten heat rises from my core, filling every muscle until they shred from the capacity of energy fueling them. Pops come from the metal of my armor as the straps begin to tear. The chaotic storm in my chest ramps up, wanting to be unleashed.

The cooling effects of my armor can't keep up. My body heat is not only putting stress on my armor but is also causing the webbing to sag. I've never been able to use my body heat to influence magic before.

As I try to tug my arms free, I finally realize I can't move them or my hands. They are attached to the webbing, allowing the numbing magic to drug all my nerve endings before I even realize the silk was adhering to my skin.

All my magic should be tranquilized, but the storm in my chest is still brewing. Spyden's numbing magic can go as deep as compressing a mate bond, so why my soul is still fueling my body with energy, I don't know.

Ladiya shrills, making the silken threads vibrate. Venom glistens on the tips of her fangs. Waiting for my body heat to dismiss the integrity of the webbing will take too long. My only option is to use my spiritual power to fight her, but I need to break free first.

"I'm only going to inject you with my liquefying poison." Ladiya runs a hand over my armor. "I want you to feel your insides melt and me sucking them out of you."

I bare my teeth while jerking my body to get myself free. No one can see us due to the shadows thickening, and I can't direct soul magic into the brand to call for aid.

Bile rises in the back of my throat as my stomach twists. My heart pounds in my ears as she drags her hands over the straps on my hips. Sweat runs down my back as she undoes one buckle, then another. I'm breathing so heavily that I'm going to pass out.

"I'll make you scream louder than my mate ever could." She smiles sweetly as she removes my armor.

A tendril of nerve-enhancing magic floats near my ear. The crisp, feather-lite touch massages my lobe. *Offer me her name.*

The influence of the whispering voice tempts my mind to obey, but it isn't trying to take control of my will. I don't know what this voice is, but Skjoldr faintly hums in my chest, encouraging me to answer. *Wait.* If she is waking up from the numbing, does that mean my heat is breaking down the webbing's magic?

Ladiya leans in, her fangs inches from my body, glistening, ready to inject me with the liquefying poison. I'm out of time to free myself. I mentally shout as she pulls down my pants. *Ladiya! Her name is Ladiya!*

The fragrant sweetness of citrus and a woodsy musk wafts by my nose as a tendril of familiar shadow magic slithers in front of my vision. The tendril rushes down my body and enters the Autarcha's parting mouth.

"Oh, Ladiya." An unholy, melodious voice that promises punishing pleasure calls out from the shadows.

She straightens unnaturally as fear warms her complexion. Tendrils of moonlight come out from the darkness behind her, wrapping around her body, forcing the legs on her back to go limp, and arching her torso until she is bent over backward in a painful stretch. Her body shakes, wanting to break free, but she can't move; she can only scream in terror.

"Just because you two are both women doesn't mean you're exempt from touching her without permission."

Ladiya's neck is bent back until she faces where the magic is coming from. Two more tendrils of moonlight slither out. Instead of going to her, they fly to me. The tendrils lift my armor into place and strap it back together.

A choked cry of relief escapes me, causing the moonlight magic to slither up my body. They brush over my pulse and soothingly stroke my neck until the rapid fluttering calms to a steadier rhythm.

Don't react. Skjoldr faintly hums in my chest, acknowledging the whisper's request for me.

As the tendrils slither back to whoever is concealed within the darkness, a light of realization goes off in my mind as to what is happening. Ladiya is being reigned, meaning I just offered her name to a—

"I'll give you her name if you let me go, Fae!" Ladiya squeals in desperation.

Sarcastic laughter causes the shadowy depths to ripple and part. "Giving up another name won't save you. You see, we can only learn names by hearing them spoken or offered with no strings attached. We can't be gifted a name. We can't buy it. We can't make or accept a bargain. And we can't take it by compulsion."

The shadows are thinned, revealing the form of a Fae with a tall physique, apex predator wings, and...*is that a tail?*

"Then I'm taking her down with me!" Ladiya shrieks with rage. "Her name is Freyja!"

No part of my body or threads of existence acknowledges anything besides being enamored with Ladiya's body twisting. I wonder how much more pressure it would take for her spine to snap.

The Fae in the shadows obnoxiously tsks. "That doesn't seem to be her name. I guess I'll only play with you while she watches, Ladiya."

Her mouth slams shut with an audible smack. She screams the name over and over as her body tremors.

With a flap, the last of the shadows parted. The Fae spreads his black, elegant wings to their full width as he steps out of the darkness. The edges aren't angular like all the other Fae I've seen; they are pointed like feathered daggers. They are still perfectly symmetrical but have a powdery texture instead of a leathery one, and there is a tremendous difference in size. His wings rise another two feet above his already towering stature.

Given all the Fae's differences, including his black, snake-like, fuzzy tail, it is apparent that he is more in touch with his inner beast than the everyday Fae. Perhaps he's from the Fallen Mountain Court the shadow puppy told me about.

Ebony-rose petals with an icy-matte sheen adhere to his leather like scales. His intimidating frame is adorned with numerous weapons. A pair of broad-bladed short swords are sheathed on his hips. A lengthy handle of something I can't determine is protruding out from behind his neck. Lastly, curved daggers poke out from his leather boots, inner thighs, and forearms.

His flawless, fair skin glows so bright that he becomes the main light source in this cloud of shadows. Pointed ears poke out of his amber-golden hair, which caresses his sculpted, scruffy face. The longer ends rub against his neck, and the shorter strands attempt to conceal his eyes. *Why isn't his hair braided like the rest of them?*

His mouth widens in a striking yet forbidding smile as he rakes his fingers through his hair to comb it back. He has fangs.

His spicy brown eyes are drawn to me rather than the shrieking Spyden in the middle of us. The protective aura in his stare gives me a false sense of security. He's my enemy, fighting on the opposite side of this battle to kill the Father, and I'm in a defenseless position.

I shouldn't be overthinking why he's helping. Instead, I should use his compassion and stab him in the back as soon as I'm free since that's what anyone from his race would do. However, he saved my life from Ladiya, so I'll give him the chance to change my mind about how I perceive him. *But if this Fae is the boy's father, he's at the mercy of my motherly wrath.*

Tendrils of magical light that range from warm to cool to dark twist around his arms. They are overlapping, maintaining harmony, and not overconsuming each other. A familiar tendril of Astro-black mist catches my attention. It's the same paint-like texture that I'd seen on the Fae child, and come to think of it, the darkness surrounding us is made out of the same kind of magic, too. I was too absorbed in watching Ladiya's every movement to take a good look at the thick mist. *The boy mentioned that he and his uncle both have shadow energy, so could this be his uncle?*

He tucks in his wings and unsheathes the daggers on his inner thighs. I squint from the near-blinding light of the blades made out of Solar-Steel-Stone and Lunivium. The soul-scarring metals glisten as if he were holding rays of sun and moonlight in his hands. I only know of these metals because Odin has been obsessed with looking for them; he'd be willing to give his body weight tenfold in gold for the Fae's blades.

"Would you like for me to entertain you?"

His Fanarzien tongue is exotic and causes Ladiya to whine with need, even though she's in immense amounts of pain. If I were in a weaker state, I, too, would find the sound of his voice stimulating. *He must've guessed that I would know his language.*

Ladiya's mumbling is mostly unrecognizable, but after she repeats her comment a couple of times, I determine she's asking him to speak in a language she knows.

The Fae's attention goes to her for a moment, and he shakes his head, causing the helpless Autarcha to whimper and cry.

His attention comes back to me. "Or do you have an input on how Ladiya should suffer?" He twirls the daggers in his cunning fingers, the handles now pointing towards me, while he holds the soul-altering blades in his bare palms. "I'm open to either, *Bah Sundrae.*"

He knows Norliska, my believer's language, and he even has a broody-rough accent as if he studied the tone of how my people speak. I'd rather be addressed as Bah Sundrae than Red Dove, but he shouldn't call me "My Precious." To be called that name extends the intimateness to someone claimed by another.

"I'm not your *Sundrae.*" His eyes twitch with awareness, but he doesn't nod in agreement. *"And I want to kill her with my own hands."* If I kill my tormentor, then the memory of her won't traumatize me as much.

"Most would say that your Fanarzien accent needs work, but I like the wild tone in how you speak my native tongue. Is that how your voice naturally sounds?" He chuckles when I don't answer him. "'I'll find out soon enough."

Ladiya's skin starts to lose its natural glow. Not being able to understand a language would make me anxious, too, so I made sure to learn every single one.

He twirls the blades and assesses me like he has all the time in the world to contemplate what to say and how to act. "Given that no blades are strapped to your body and your magic is numbed, how do you plan on killing her?"

"I said how. With. My. Hands." Since my soul is still whirling, I have confidence activating my spiritual power.

"Considering your hands as weapons is sexy but also reckless, given any injury could prevent you from wielding magic."

"I'm reckless? You are twirling two of the most harmful blades on Earthradon in your bare hands."

He shrugs as if what he's doing isn't a big concern. "So, you're going to show off how skilled you are at wrapping your hands around a thick ligament of flesh and squeezing?"

"Once I'm finished with her, I'll gladly use my hands to get personal with you since you're so interested in what I'm capable of doing with them."

The bite in my tone makes him stop showing off his irresponsible tricks with his blades. "If you get personal with me, I'll return the favor."

For a flicker of a moment, his lips curl up into an intrigued smile, altering his demeanor from that of a being who should be approached with caution to one who is inviting me to challenge him.

A thought occurs to me: Unless I can convince him to leave, he will witness me using my spiritual power. *Fuck.* Before I can move forward, I need assurance that he won't say a word about what he sees.

"That's fair, but what you're going to see me do, you must take to your grave. Deal?"

His brow lifts in surprise. "You want to make a bargain with me." It's a statement, but when I nod, he taps his blades against his sturdy neck. "Will getting personal with me lead to my dying?"

My pulse quickens, and I realize I've been staring at his neck for far too long. I lick my lips to moisten my parched mouth as my stomach churns with nervous energy due to my failure to answer him immediately.

"Only if you try to kill me."

His wings flap as if shaking off some knotted tension, then relax as the magic around his arms dulls to a more bearable brightness.

"I won't. If you don't believe me, you can read the magical vow I have tattooed on my chest, promising I will never kill you."

"Wait, what?"

He sheathes his daggers. "We will do our exchange. And until I'm asked about who killed the Autarcha, you can't kill me. When I'm asked about her death, I can only admit who it was, not how she died."

I will circle back to his statement. He tilts his head and gives me a knowing look; he knows that conversation is not done.

"We will do our exchange. I will not kill you. Once we are done here, you can only admit my physical characteristics and my title when asked who killed the Autarcha. You can't speak about anything else aloud, telepathically, or through any other form of communication with your hands. You take what you know to your grave." I lift my chin. "Do we have a deal, Fae?"

Wind plays with his hair, obscuring his vision. However, the intensity of his stare remains as if nothing in creation could break his concentration from me.

A pink halo forms around his irises, and the veins in his wings glow, telling me he's... actually, I don't know what pink means. I'd never seen a Fae's wings glow before. *He's an unusual Fae.*

"You know how to word what you want when dealing with a Fae." He pushes the unruly strands of his hair back behind his ear, then flattens his palm over his chest and nods. "You have yourself a deal, *Sundrae.*"

Magic zaps the base of my neck and races down to the middle of my back. The pain from the needle tattooing my spine causes me to flinch and wince while the Fae curses and snarls. Since we made no distinction about whether they could be visible or not, everyone will be able to see or interpret them. I'm also glad and surprised that he didn't choose to blood-brand me.

"Be sure not to stab yourself when you play with it." I snap my attention to the Fae as he rolls his shoulders and flexes his arms. "The brand is removable, and can only be used by you. Just stroke a portion of it, and the weapon will come out. Place it over the same spot, and it will go back in. If you forget to put it back, it will do it automatically when you get too far away from it."

The pain from the needle subsides and I exhale a sigh of relief. "You tattooed a removable blade in my back as a brand?! I didn't know that was possible."

With a hand on the back of his head and one cupping his jaw, he rotates his head, stretching his bitable neck. "The manipulation of magical energy is a skill that can be taught. It's forbidden to use like blood magic. Depending on how personal you want to get with me, you'll see that every tattoo on my body is not just for show."

My concern on the matter gets cut off when his neck cracks with a loud, horrifying pop, eliciting a relieved groan from him. I'm painfully snapped out of my trance and recoil involuntarily. *No! No!*

After frantically roving my eyes over his frame, I allow myself to breathe. *He's in one piece. Not broken.* A choked gasp escapes me when the most terrifying image I've ever witnessed flickers in my mind. *He's alive. Not dead. Alive and whole.*

"Sundrae? Are you...?" The earnestness of his tone makes me instantly lower my attention to my body and tune out everything besides my breathing. *Come on, Freyja, not now. Get ahold of yourself.*

Tendrils of sunray magic slither around my body, lowering me to the ground. "What are you doing?"

His race isn't known for being considerate, charitable, or doing things for others unless it benefits them. Using magic to help others is a give-and-take unless they willingly want to.

When Hera and I found out we could harvest, no one from the race would teach us; we had to learn on our own since we couldn't find any documentation about how the race wields its magic. Also, we are fighting on two different sides of this battle; how is he justifying helping his enemy?

He shrugs, leans against a tree, and crosses his arms over his chest. "I don't want to get personal with you while you're suspended. I'm not into that."

"The hue of the veins in your wings says differently." I take a jab at what the shade could mean to distract myself so I can calm down.

Because the forest floor is only inches away, I do my best to control my erratic breathing. The last thing I want is to pass out from hyper-ventilating.

Once my feet land on the ground, the webbing releases me. I fall to my hands and knees, not caring about my dignity, and claw my fingers into the hardened soil. If I hadn't already made a deal not to kill him, I would've made it at this moment.

He warmly chuckles. "That is not what pink means. I'm... eager for you to live because when a redhead dies, a man is destined to never orgasm again. Since I witnessed you being taken, my gut instinct told me that if you died, then I'd be the one affected."

"That sounds like superstition." *And a partial truth to cover up his true intentions.* I push off the ground and dust off my hands.

"Maybe, maybe not. I wasn't going to risk it." He nods to the muffled, sobbing Spyden. "I'm ready to be entertained by your hands, *Sundrae.*"

Taking the few steps required to close the distance between Ladiya and me is much more difficult than anticipated. Not being able to breathe was okay because I needed my spiritual power to work. But each inch I take causes me to clench my thighs tighter, and my shaking makes each step unstable. *Come on, Freyja. Focus.*

"You're safe." His voice was a delicate whisper. "I won't let go of her unless you tell me to."

The promise in his words reaches out and soothes me. A caressing energy wraps around my heart so it won't break, while another shields my mind so no further torment can enter.

I keep my chin up as I approach Ladiya's twisting form. Her upper body is turned up, so she faces me now. All of her eyes are glossy, and her now sickly-toned skin has tear stains running over her cheeks and up to her forehead. If she had any teeth, they would shatter from the force of her trembling lips.

"If I die, so does he." I paused before lifting my hand to her chest. "You have some sway over the Fae. Have him release me and I'll renounce the Autarch as my mate. You will never see me again."

I lift my gaze and find the Fae solely focused on me. His eyes and the veins in his wings are no longer glowing pink. Every muscle on his body is tense, and I can't tell if the tightening in his jaw is due to pain or if he's on the verge of lashing out. Either way, he needs to release his hold on her.

I raise my hands and sign to him. *"When I nod, release her."*

Without being able to direct magic into my hands since they are numbed, I have to sign each letter instead of letting the magic form the words I want. Signing in Galex also allows me to determine if this Fae is who I think he is. The little boy said only his family except his father knew Galex. Without having to directly ask, his response will answer for him.

From the faintest breeze swaying the trees to the dull hum of life beyond the mist of unease, all goes deadly silent when the Fae's tail calms like the morning sea.

The drastic shift in energy zeros in on me, raising the hairs on my body. If I hadn't known that he was in control of the shadows, I would've thought a monster was about to pounce.

His breaths are strong yet muted, making Ladiya's heavy pants of restlessness abrasive against the abnormal cloud of quiet. The Fae unfolds his arms and firmly wraps his hands around the hilts of the blades at his hips, his knuckles whitening.

If him telling me I was safe wasn't enough to make me relax, it's the determination to be ready in a flicker of a moment was. Even though I'm no longer attached to the webbing, the influence of the poison will remain in my system for a while longer. Using my soul magic is out of the question, which means I have no backup plan if my spiritual power doesn't work. I might have learned how to get out of someone trying to restrain me into submission, but not how to fight or to kill.

"I will release her on your signal, Norse Goddess." He understood me, which means... *wait, how does he know I'm a Norse Goddess?*

"What will it be?" Ladiya's question pulls me away from him and back to her.

My heart takes its last beat, and the whirling storm in my soul expands. The moisture in her eyes reduces as I place a hand on my chest. I nod, and the anxiously horrified expression on Ladiya's face switches to that of a cunning manipulator in the blink of an eye.

She lunges for me with all her regained strength. The tips of her fang tusks are inches from my face as her hands reach for my waist. Her eyes go wide when her efforts to kill me are shattered as I push my hand into her chest.

A strong heart beats against my palm, and I flex my fingers, enjoying the texture of her silken organ and warm soul. She's at a loss for words as her eyes swell again, but no tears leak out. With her soul in my grasp, her body goes into shock. I don't bother to hold her up and allow her to fall to her knees.

Slowly, I squeeze the fluttering organ, sinking my fingers in to grasp her soul. Dozens of threads are woven together, and I slide them between my fingers. The twine-like threads are velvety, weigh nearly nothing, and are as breakable as glass. I only know I'm holding them because the pulsating strands give off wonderfully warm energy.

Only a few times have I had the experience to comb through someone's soul, and from the Sprites who willingly allowed me to practice on them, the experience is a state of forced surrender. All hope is gone, and the being is left on a threshold of going wherever my hand tells them to.

Fortunately, one of the times I was able to practice was with a Sprite who had a fated mate. I can only assume that those who are just mated must have a similar bond. I don't find a muscular thread of passionate heat in the center of the cluster in my hand, making up Ladiya's soul. Drafasa might have been forced to take her as his wife, but he didn't allow the bond to form.

Petrified shock freezes Ladiya's face as I rip her soul out of her body. She falls face-first into the ground with a heavy thump from the strength of my pull. Freyr would've wanted me to untie each strand, but I didn't have the patience, and she didn't deserve her passing to be anything less than excruciating. Nothing is in my palm, much to my disappointment. Maybe if I had activated my full power, I would've witnessed her soul flying away.

Wisps of my hair brush against my ear. "Are you ready to get personal with me, Freyja?"

My hand collides with his armored abdomen when I pivot towards the Fae. The startling proximity of how intimately close he is makes me take a step back. He's far taller than I expected, a little over seven feet.

"Just because I'm given a name, doesn't mean I have to do anything with it. If I wanted to reign you, I would've done so already, *Sundrae*."

True, but he can always change his mind. I never met a Fae who wasn't thirsty for more power because reigning allows them to develop and expand their reserves, permitting them to hold more magic. It's immoral and twisted that they are rewarded for manipulating someone against their will.

Skjoldr faintly hums in my chest, encouraging me to breathe. "Why did you tell me not to react to my name?" My voice has a harmonious tone to it, as does his.

"When a Fae learns someone's name, a pesky voice tries to co-inhabit our minds. Tuning her out when I don't want to reign is manageable, but if I'm using my power, then she has a handle on my self-control."

"Is she there right now?"

He nods, takes a deeper breath, and lets it out slowly. "If your muscles had flinched or you even twitched with awareness, displaying that you acknowledged your name being said, she'd force me to control you too."

"That's horrible." This Fae saved my life from Ladiya and the greed and corruption of his magic. "Can you…" I bit my tongue to stop myself from asking the outrageously inappropriate and offensive question.

"Get rid of it?" He chuckles as a little noise slips from my lips, betraying me. "No. It's not something we can get rid of. I've tried. But thanks to my lineage, I have a stronger will to fight against her."

His wings flap with pride as if they have a mind of their own. "From witnessing what happens to others who control more than one being, it seems they too are being reigned to satisfy the voice's desire to dominate. Some even forget what they did but wouldn't allow the memory loss to frighten them into never doing it again since their reserves were enhanced because of it."

"This isn't known knowledge. Why did you tell me?"

"Maybe if others understood us, we wouldn't be seen as completely vile. How my race's magic works and all the others should be known or at least available for all to learn. I disagree with the race code of secrecy, especially since only the beast races are the ones enforcing it."

"That might be due to the century-long war over territories." He nods in agreement.

What he's saying rings true. During my time with the Wolven, I was only ever taught about the morals they live by and witnessed their way of life; nothing about what it means to be a beast of their race.

If I ever were in a discussion about their race, all would be shocked by the knowledge I had gathered about how they are a devoted pack that looks after one another and doesn't hold back from expressing themselves. They are a liberating race who are proud of who they are and I'm honored that I was given the change to live among them.

A window of realization opens in my mind and allows in a light I didn't know I was supposed to be searching for. Freyr had wanted me to figure out from my time with the Wolven that not only was their race misunderstood, but all of them were. I wasn't meant to learn about them specifically but to see past everyone's judgment so I could take that knowledge and apply it to others.

My shoulders slump with disappointment, and I drop my head in shame. It has taken me most of my immortal life to finally grasp what my brother wanted me to learn. He could've told me until he was blue in the face, but only when the concept was applied to another race, like the Fae, has the lesson truly begun. I was meant to learn this in my own time when the lesson would better help me when I most needed its knowledge and guidance.

A brawny, calloused hand extends out from the window, and I place mine in it and allow myself to be drawn into the light. I'm pulled out of my thoughts and into a hazy reverie of peace.

I had forgotten where my hand was placed against the Fae's body and hadn't noticed I had balled it into a tight fist. His hand covers mine, and his touch comforts and relaxes me, helping me to flatten my palm against him.

He tightens his hold and slides my hand over his armor. The material appears as a dragon's hide, yet the scale-like petals are soft, like if I ran my hand through a field of flowers.

Once our conjoined hands reach the middle of his chest, he stops. My attention is drawn to his wings behind his broad shoulders. The veins are glowing pink once again, along with his eyes.

His gaze ensnares mine when flames of light flourish to life in the depths of his spicy brown irises, as if his soul is reaching out, eager to meet mine.

"Beauty before the beast." His sultry tone serenades me and tickles my back muscles as if he stroked my spine with his tail.

I'm at a loss as to what he's implying for me to do. *Wait*, I'm supposed to be getting personal with him, and he's probably expecting me to use my power on him as I did with Ladiya.

The environment becomes sharper and darker when I yank my hand away, bringing me out of an unusual trance and back to reality.

I gasp for air and start to question if my spiritual power has been activated the entire time, but the thought is thrown away because I can't speak in my spirit form.

"I have no need, want, or reason to reach in and grasp your soul. Just because I can do it doesn't mean I will."

I place my hands on my hips to reinforce my choice. I'm happy my voice lost the pleasant tone and returned to my wild one.

The pink in his veins and eyes starts to pulsate. "Then get personal with me another way because only after we do so does the secrecy portion of our bargain activate."

"And what exactly is classified as personal? A kiss?"

A vein on the side of his forehead pulsates strongly as if he's about to have a migraine. "Getting personal means you open up by sharing a part of yourself. What I told you about my race I don't consider an exchange of personal information because I would tell anyone if they were willing to listen. And yes." He crosses his arms over his chest. "Performing an intimate act counts as being personal."

I have to open my heart up to him; that's what he's implying. *Fuck.* And whatever I share with him, he doesn't have to keep it a secret since it's not part of our bargain.

"Okay. But I won't kiss you without your consent."

He flinches as if I smacked him across the face. "Are you serious? You have put your trust in me multiple times. Why should now be any different?" *Have I put my trust in him?* "Yes, you have." He holds up his hand and extends his thumb. "First, when I told you not to react." His pointer finger comes out. "Second, when I told you that you were safe and I wouldn't let go of Ladiya unless you told me to." The middle finger joins the other two. "And third, when I spoke your name, you didn't keep holding your breath." He drops his hands to his hips. "Do you think you'd permit me to stand this close to you if you hadn't trusted me any of those times?"

My thoughts stagger as the three instances he brought up play in my mind, overlapping one another. Skjoldr had been the one I trusted in two out of the three situations since she always has a better reading of magic and instincts, but she hadn't reassured me when the Fae told me I was safe. I had chosen to trust him all on my own.

"Just accept my kiss. I'm not giving anything else that could be used against me."

His eyebrows pinch together as he leans in slightly. "I could've asked you for secrecy too, but I didn't. Nothing is stopping you from telling any Fae or anyone else about what I've done here."

My heart skips a beat, and I gasp, realizing he's right. He has left himself at my mercy. But why would he trust me? I'd given him no reason to. It is his fault he did not ask me to take a vow of secrecy.

He takes a step away, our proximity upsetting him. "You would rather break fidelity than open up to me." The pink hue in the veins of his wings and eyes fades. "If a kiss is what you want, then apparently, I misjudged you. You are no better than the majority of the entitled males of my race."

Red covers my vision, and I ball my hands into fists. "I don't have a husband anymore!"

A satisfied grin sweeps across his face as he relaxes his posture. "Oh? Tell me more."

Talk about Odin? Yeah, I can do that. I only have anger for him, and that emotion is strong enough to keep the illness at bay. I'm not sure why or how, but I'm relieved to be free of the pain while I'm angry.

"Okay."

The energy around us shifts as if the world has slowed and would patiently wait for us to be ready to re-enter.

The powdery texture on his wings twinkles and flutters. Thousands of fireflies take the place of his tremendous wings. They dance around him before tucking themselves under the petals that make up his armor. After a moment, the rhythmic flickering lights settle as if the fireflies have drifted off into a peaceful slumber.

He sits and motions for me to join him. "Use as many colorful and vulgar words as you wish to describe him. Don't hold back any details involving his shortcomings in the bedroom."

I can't stop the laugh from leaving me as I sit across from him. "Well, he couldn't keep up with my appetite, and I was always left wanting more."

"Ah, he's that special type of asshole."

"That's not the worst of what led to me wanting to leave him."

My chuckle, I hope, sounds genuine. I need to keep this conversation light to prevent myself from experiencing any strong emotions. I pull my knees to my chest and interlock my hands in front of them. Holding myself like this will hide my shaking and help me focus on how much I divulge about my marriage with Odin.

"He can't hurt you anymore."

I'm rendered speechless. There is no way he could have known. How could a stranger see through the mask I've been wearing for centuries? Even my friends, with whom I'm closest, hadn't picked up on or suspected anything was going on with my marriage.

He extends his hands, offering me to hold them. "I can help you through this if you let me."

His voice reaches out and embraces me in a cozy hug. The comforting sensation of utter peace pulls a memory from the darkness and into the forefront of my mind. It was the year after Haidion told me his name and showed me what he truly looked like.

All I wanted for a winter solstice gift was for Haidion to stargaze with me all night, and all he desired was to stay with me until morning. Our wishes came true since Odin had forgotten where my gift was stored and couldn't recall what it was. So now, I'm lying next to Haidion on a snowy mountaintop with Odin's promise branded on my skin that he will leave me alone until morning so I can enjoy the night in solitude.

I lean over to Haidion, not taking my eyes off the sky. "I've never seen the Aura Borealis paint the entire night sky before. Only a few strands every couple centuries or so." I rub my shoulder against his. "I'm so happy that you're here with me to witness this."

Sensing Haidion's attention, I look over and see his affectionate smile. His lips part as if he's about to say something, but he quickly closes them. He turns his attention back to the sky and raises his arms. He moves them as if he's constructing the tendrils of color to the harmony with which he's waving his hands. With a side glance, he nods for me to join him. The notion of doing so seems silly, but I lift my arms and move them in a way that complements the silent song.

Haidion's laughter joins mine as we keep swaying our arms and rolling the air in our fingers. I'm not laughing because what we're doing is amusing. I'm laughing because my souls is at peace for the first time in a while.

My laughter is silenced. "Holy Aurora!" I blink numerous times and even rub my eyes. "What's happening to the sky?" I look over at him. "Did we do this?"

Haidion leans into me, his shoulder pressing against mine. "The Fate of Light only dances when a song is sung to her. No sounds left our lips, but we moved our hands to the melody our souls sang."

I gaze back at the sky and watch in awe and wonder. The tendrils of light wrap around one another, creating a silhouette of a woman wearing a lavish gown. She sways and twirls, holding onto the tendrils of light as if they were ribbons and moving them in harmony with her dance.

"I've never seen a Fate before. Because of you, my belief in them is stronger now than it was."

I brush my hand against him to convey my thanks, but I can't find it in me to pull away. If I do, will this peace he has brought me to go with him?

When I hesitate to move, the nagging voice in my head reminds me that I shouldn't desire to hold another man's hand and that I need to leave and admit to my husband how unfaithful I've been. Odin told me he doesn't want me to be friends with an Ancient Demonical, but not having Haidion in my life is like trying to stop me from remembering my brother.

Just as the voice in my head starts to win, Haidion's fingers rub against mine. My breath hitches as it trails up the back of my wrist and draws circles against my skin. His touch grounds me like a tether and helps me realize that accepting his friendly affection isn't wrong. I know for certain that I'm not cheating on Odin by being with Haidion. I don't desire my friend the same way as my husband. If that ever changes, I will address the issue.

I turn my hand, and he slides his hand into mine. We interlace our fingers and hold each other's hands all night until the sun rises.

The darkness lounging in the back of my mind begins to push forward, wanting to join in on the memory, but something brushes my hands and pulls me out.

"*Sundrae.*" I jerk my attention up.

The Fae is closer to me than before. His folded legs are next to my feet, and he is softly running the tips of his fingers along the backs of my hands.

"Even if I were blind, I could still recognize the energy of a soul who's been abused."

My chest tightens, and pain stabs into my heart as my eyes start to get puffy. A sob-like scream rushes out of my mouth as I press my forehead against my knees. Trying to prevent myself from experiencing the energy of my emotions is becoming difficult, especially with the presence of an unforgiving illness.

"You are safe, Freyja."

The sense of helplessness that comes with being unable to stop the rot from killing me and knowing that someone I thought I could trust was more than happy to torture me are no longer present. We are still in the mist, seated in the lifeless forest, but the environment's energy has changed as if I were taken to a reality where neither Odin nor my illness exists.

The Fae's concern shines from the depths of his eyes, his soul ready to take on my burden if I let it. Skjoldr doesn't hum in my chest, encouraging me to place my trust in him.

Unconsciously, my heart armors up as my mind connects with my tongue, ready to fire out a comment that would push the Fae away and deter him from trying again. I'd rather make him angry with me so his desire to help me is forgotten, but his soul is locked on mine. To remove him would lead to this part of the bargain not being fulfilled. I could just give him the cold shoulder on the topic and move on to talk about something else...

"The longer you remain silent the more power you give him. He's currently suppressing your voice. He's making you unable to communicate how you feel because you are unable to feel safe enough to talk about it, and it seems impossible to trust that I won't emotionally abuse you as he did."

His demeanor embodies empathy, and his eyes glisten with gentleness. Before me isn't a ruthless Fae, but someone who cares about me.

A memory obscures my reality.

It's nighttime, and I'm sitting in front of my brother's grave as snow falls. Small hands covered in scars reach down to me. My friend's injuries are the hazards of being a fearless Goddess and a consequence of being the most stubborn soul the Father ever brought to life.

"If you're going to cry, then do it standing up. When you physically

make yourself smaller, you are allowing your mind to convince you that you are weaker than you are. And you, Freyja, are anything but weak."

Existence's passionate voice is both gentle and thunderous. She usually sparks a light in me, and together, our energies would be fed and rumble in an uplifting harmony of unpredictable chaos and fierce majesty. That was before... when I was full of explosive life. Now, I'm slowly decaying from the inside out.

"You're wrong. I wasn't strong in the first place. I let my brother die. My ability to produce tears is gone; all I have now is blood to shed."

One of her hands leaves my peripheral vision. "Then let's shed some blood together."

She offers me her favorite battle axe made from celestial cyanic crystal.

I glance up at her. "When Thor asked to just touch it, you nearly chopped off his head. Why would you allow me to hold it, let alone use it to fight you?"

A never-ending wonder of artic-blue eyes glisten like snow diamonds, shining a refreshing light into my sorrow-filled soul. Her butterscotch-blonde hair is braided back into a ponytail, showing off her warm ivory skin and sassy lips of fire. Metallic-feathered armor hugs her like a second skin, revealing her muscular magnificence and captivating curves.

"I might allow Thor to enjoy the pleasures of my body, but that doesn't involve letting him into my heart. Only the Father and my siblings were allowed in there. Then I met this bluntly honest beauty who didn't tremble in my presence and looked me dead in the eyes and said, 'I heard from the asses you fucked with your axes that you were thick, but they sadly didn't mention that you were also fun size.'

A sound I thought I was never capable of producing again tickles the back of my throat.

She tosses her axe at my feet. "Accept my help, Freyja. Not because I make you laugh or because you are my friend and I love you, but because if you don't, you'll fall victim to Soul Rot. Imagine hundreds of thorns around your heart, stabbing into you and draining more than just your magic. Don't allow your grief to control or deteriorate you because once the Soul Rot begins, it can't be reversed."

Too late. Those thorns prick into my swelling heart. To prevent Existence from getting suspicious, I pick up the axe.

The pleading Fae before me comes back into focus. All I want to do is tell him the truth about why I can't open up, but I won't be selfish.

If I tell the Fae I have Soul Rot, he will have to fight the instinctive urge to check if he is free from the rot. Since I'm carrying the disease, it will be able to sense that he was checking and could enter him once he was done, knowing he wouldn't check again for a while.

The illness sounds more like a phantom parasite since the rot can be transmitted from one being to another. Most assume that's a method of ridding themselves of rot, but the illness won't leave its main host until they die.

Soul Rot takes a couple of centuries to consume the vitality of its host. I've not only kept my illness a secret, but I like to think I outlived the life expectancy rate.

From the grief of losing my brother and Drafasa threatening to kill the one who brings me happiness to pushing Bralyant away, I let myself fall too deeply into a mental grave. It wasn't until Odin and I exchanged our vows that I sensed I was infected. I have no one to blame but myself because it's not my brother's, Drafasa's, or Bralyant's fault.

Anytime I experience an overwhelming emotion, the thorns grow to absorb the energy and try to pierce my heart. It's only by my strong will to not waste the second chance at life my brother gifted me that I am able to push the rot back. Love and sadness are the only two emotions I find challenging to suppress.

There are only two options to stop the progression of the rot. One way is by making a shield wall of magic around my heart. Doing so will protect the void where the rot is so it can't sense the energy of my body and experience emotions. And two, by redirecting the emotional energy to fuel my soul magic. As long as I'm not blindsided, like what happened with Haidion, the second method is an option. If I could use my spiritual healing power on myself, I would, but I can't. There isn't anything that can be done. I can only endure.

Getting the Fae angry would just be easier, so we can move on to another topic. But I've been desperately wanting to talk to someone about all the shit Odin has put me through. A stranger is honestly my best choice, given we don't have an emotional connection that would drive him to take matters into his own hands. I don't want anything to be fixed. I only want to be heard.

I take a deep breath and gather every ounce of strength as I grasp the Fae's sturdy hands. "I just wanted to be a good wife."

CHAPTER

TWENTY-FIVE

Venting has turned my mind to putty and judging by the flex of the Fae's jaw, he's about to unravel me further. He's been quiet the entire time, nodding assuringly. He's actively listening, and now it's his turn to talk.

"What you had with your husband wasn't love, Freyja. It was ownership." The truth punches me in the chest, and a painful sob escapes me. "Take another deep breath."

The overwhelming emotional energy leaves my body when I breathe and follow the Fae's instructions. My heart and soul have been safeguarded, just as the Fae promised.

Never in the past five centuries have I dreamed that I could vent about Odin without feeding the rot. Not all the tears I'm holding back are ones of sadness for having to open up about my past, but ones of relief for finally being heard.

Getting the words out was all I wanted to accomplish. He respected my desire to not want to cry. Whenever my voice cracked, or I let out a sob, he would lead me through a couple of breaths to center myself before continuing.

He squeezes my hands to the point of pain, then slowly relaxes his hold. These compressions have been a comfort and have grounded me to stay strong.

"I don't know how your marital brand works since you created it, but I agree with your Wolven friend. You should be able to renounce your husband." He rubs his thumbs over my inner wrists. "Do you have anyone else you can talk to about this?"

"My Ancient Demonical friend would probably be as attentive as you are if I gave him the chance." A laugh tickles the back of my throat. "He'd go hunt him down afterward. Then torture him for eternity since he sees death as too kind a punishment."

To my surprise, the Fae doesn't curl his lip in disgust or freeze with horror at my being friends with Haidion.

"He sounds like a devoted friend, but is that what you want? For him to take care of your husband for you?"

"I want to kill my husband myself." *If I'm able, that to is another story altogether.*

"You could start by telling your friend you don't want him to do anything on your behalf, only to listen and hold your hands. Or do you suspect he wouldn't listen to your wishes?"

"I'd like to think he would, but I don't think I could open up to him because..." *My heart and soul cannot take letting someone in only to lose them.* I clear my throat. "Because..."

The whole truth is on my tongue, not the vague version. Speaking the words aloud will force me to face the truth about how my affection for Haidion has always been greater than I ever admit to myself.

With how close we are, I could easily picture us being together. But I won't. Haidion once admitted that there is more to him than I know. I can't be with someone who keeps me at arm's length. I'm not innocent of withholding parts of myself either; I haven't told Haidion about the extent of my trauma or anything about Freyr. I would think he would feel the same way as I do.

From how I see it, there is a level of trust we haven't reached yet, and with my time coming to an end sooner than his, it wouldn't be fair to him to be anything more than what we already are. An attraction to Haidion is all I will allow my thoughts to divulge.

The Fae chews on his bottom lip. "Would it help if you were to talk to someone who has gone through what you did? I'll be there as you talk to her if you want, so you're comfortable."

I'm not the only one who's been abused by their spouse. "Who is she?"

An adoring smile warms his lips. "Now it's my turn to get personal with you." The tendrils of light flowing around his arms brighten. "I have a mate, but she was betrothed to my elder half-brother. I'm a bastard in more ways than one, making me unable to fight for her. I was ready to offer her an escape with me after I told her about being mated. She wanted nothing to do with our bond or my brother because she was in love with her childhood girlfriend. I wouldn't force her to be with me because her happiness is what I wanted." He nods towards something behind me. "Everything you said to Ladiya, I agree with."

"You are probably the only Fae in existence who would ever do that."

He chuckles. "My mother raised me with the values and morals of where she came from. Anyway, my mate couldn't escape her marriage, and I couldn't bear to see her unhappy, so I went to her girlfriend and asked her to marry me. After sorting out all the details of how our marriage would be one of convenience, she agreed. She could be with her love as often as they wanted without suspicion since they would be in-laws. Over the centuries, we have all become good friends."

"Forget your race. I don't think anyone in all existence would ever be that selfless."

"She may have rejected the bond between us, but not my offer to help her be happy."

The pink halo around his irises fades completely. Before I can ask him about his happiness, he clears his throat and continues.

"My brother started to beat her after decades of infertility. A woman of a beast race needs to climax to get pregnant, along with ovulating. My brother was going to resort to giving my mate drugs to make her more...compliant, and if that didn't work, she was going to be sentenced as a slave to his court for being barren, and my brother would marry another."

Liquified fire fills the corners of my eyes. "Having laws about only giving a woman value because of the miracles her body is capable of performing is fucking sickening!"

"I agree." He drums his thumbs without touching me. "The law should've been repealed after a couple of centuries following the War Over Territories." I nod my agreement.

Per Noble Law, only when a female, mortal or immortal, gives birth to a baby will their rights be given to them, and they will be seen as equals. Until then, they belong to their fathers, and the responsibility moves to the husband once a marriage is arranged. Goddesses and those with royal birthrights are the only ones excluded.

I've fought until there was no oxygen left in the courtroom for the lords and ladies to breathe, stating that the ideology of women needing to prove their faithfulness to their race is more harmful than beneficial. The ability to reproduce is not the defining characteristic of a woman, just as it isn't for a man.

Only with the authority of Existence and her sisters were Isis, Hera, and I able to speak to the lords and ladies about women's rights. Each of us serves as one of their sources to provide testimony to their arguments. With only six of us able to represent those who can't be heard, we exhaust ourselves, especially since every century a new set of lords and ladies are sworn in and we have to have the same arguments all over again.

Odin, along with all the other gods and goddesses, repeatedly reminded Isis, Hera, and me that it is not our role to influence Earth-radon's governance, as that was not the purpose of our creation. Our assistance should not go beyond listening to our believers' prayers about society's pressure and then blessing them if we choose to. We were also warned that if the leaders of the races wanted to, as long as they had a majority vote, they could accuse my friends and me of trying to force the ideologies of our faith upon not only them but their governing rulers. But the Fate of Chance must be on our side because the only obstacle we faced was insomnia.

I finally stopped listening to others about what my role as a goddess should be after a century of mourning the loss of my brother. I pulled myself out of the vicious cycle of what I could've done to prevent Freyr from dying and directed my energy to those whom I could help, since sulking wasn't going to bring him back. I feel guilty for taking so long to utilize my privilege to advocate for those who lack voice. My biggest regret was not listening to my gut to act on what I thought was right, which is why I won't limit myself to who I can help. If I could, I would change my title from being a Norse Goddess to a Goddess of Life who can benefit all, like the Fates.

My hands are squeezed, but it does little to pull me out of my mind.

"Would you be interested in spilling some political blood with me? I could use another pair of skilled hands."

His question and comment are lost on me as my heart rate increases. An infuriated rumble deep in my soul makes my chest uncomfortably tighten. Fire fills my veins as the pain travels to muscles I didn't know I had in my back, but they are just as sore as the rest of my body.

"I've heard thousands of prayers. Women cry and scream their souls out for me to sway their fathers' minds to find them someone who will love them and then beg for me to bless them with a child as soon as possible. All plead for me to get the laws changed. But the voices of those who ask why I am not answering their prayers, the one that assume I don't care about them, and sob their souls dry, asking if ending their lives would bring them more happiness... Those prayers make me feel like a failure."

I close my eyes to prevent my enraged tears from falling. "I listen to every single prayer! I try my fucking hardest to help them all, but I'm limited! There is a balance that must be maintained. No matter how hard I fight, I can't sway the minds of the..." I choke on my words.

The oath I took wraps around my soul and squeezes it. To utter the words would result in the memory of the Fae before me being altered, and punishment would also be given to me. Breaking my oath to become mortal, which I'd contemplated doing once in my youth, would result in stripping me of my magic and title. If I do so, my job will be entirely handed over to a group of beings that my people don't believe in. The Norse people prayed to the Father for me to be created, and I can't live with the guilt of letting them down.

Something fuzzy brushes under my chin, startling me. A silent question flickers across the Fae's concerned face after I open my eyes.

I clear my throat and redirect the conversation back to him, knowing I can't and won't complete what I want to say. "So, is your mate a High Lady now?"

He studied me for several seconds before relieving the tightness in his shoulders by rolling them. "The laws the lords and ladies put in place only inspired the High Lords to create more rules. There will never be a High Lady unless they all change their minds. My mate is the lady of my brother's court, given that she's married to a High Lord, but she wanted to become a warrior. Since there was no Noble Law regarding what females are limited to do once acquiring rights, the High Lords elected not to allow them to be in an occupation where they can harm their bodies, like enlisting in the army."

"The High Lords need to be castrated."

He nods. "All goes back to the same issue of the lords and ladies controlling how our planet evolves. I guess telling the immortal races they couldn't intermate or interbreed wasn't enough. I think the mortals are upset over the fact that immortals don't desire them. In return, the mortals want nothing more than to see us unhappy for eternity." His sneer tells me all I need to know: he hates the mortal race.

"I don't know for sure why they have rules put in place about who we are not allowed to be with, but I believe the rulers of Earthradon shouldn't be all mortals. I'm glad that not all mortals are like the lords and ladies."

When his revulsion doesn't wane, I take a deep breath and expel my frustration. Now is not the time to argue with him. "I derailed us. Continue."

"I think you can put two and two together about what happened for my mate to have a child."

I rock from side to side. "I told you about my sex life." A bashful shade of pink tints his cheeks. "If you don't want to discuss it, it's okay. Don't make yourself uncomfortable."

"It's just...unorthodox."

I lean forward as if I'm about to tell him a secret. "I lived among the Wolven for centuries; trust me, I've seen a lot of variations of sex, especially in a group setting."

He lifts an eyebrow in...*is that astonishment or intrigue?* "Okay... well..." His ears start to tinge the same shade as his cheeks. "My wife was...in the middle of the two of us. She...warmed us up, and when my mate and I were both ready to..."

His eyes shift, searching for the word. I want to say it for him, but I keep my mouth shut.

"Ready to...reach a pinnacle, my wife moved, and I...switched to my mate. We performed the same method for my wife." His sigh of relief allows the color to drain from his face and alleviates the tension of this difficult conversation.

"Did all of you want to have children?"

"Absofuckinglutely." His joyful smile could outshine a child opening their Yule presents. "They were both pregnant together. Tending to them are some of my fondest memories, aside from my son and daughter being born and raising them."

The happiness he's radiating is contagious, and I can't help but smile as well. "If you don't mind my asking, why do you still call her your mate?"

"I know she isn't my mate, just as my wife isn't my wife. I'm only calling them by those labels because it's not my right to disclose their names."

"She rejected you then?" The questions came out before I could stop myself. "I didn't...I'm not trying to—"

His chuckling silences me. "As tempted as I am to see your cheeks flame a darker shade of crimson, we didn't choose the more...playful route in getting personal with one another." He clears his throat, darkening the amusement in his spicy eyes. "Yes, she rejected me."

"Are you okay?"

The Fae's brow quivers, making me realize the type of question I'd asked him, one of consideration as if we were friends.

"Fighting the predatory urge to breed was...uncomfortable, but being knotted by the Fates to mate wasn't a maze with only one way out. The more I tried to be free of it, the weaker the bond became. Once my mate agreed to allow me to help her become pregnant, the knot finally released me from my duty."

"Wait, I'm confused. She rejected you, so you shouldn't have experienced the effects of the mate bond, but you're speaking as if you two were bound."

"Because I was knotted to her by the Fates." He slowly repeats, as if I didn't comprehend what he said the first time. "I guess you've never heard of it before. Well... my type of Fae is becoming extinct, so we feel a carnal lust to reproduce. It remains until it's satiated, but I'm given the strength to resist if it's not something I want. I'm fortunate that I have a choice in the matter; a prehistoric beast race from the cosmos that was hunted to extinction didn't have that as an option. Their blood forced them to comply, while I only had a magical tether to untie."

My mind is spinning as my knowledge of mate bonds and fated mates collides. The magic system matched him and his mate because they could produce powerful offspring and were somehow compatible enough to make one another happy. Since she rejected him, like Drafasa did to Ladiya, nothing formed. On top of, they also have another bond that was connected by the Fates for the sole purpose of helping to save his species of Fae, not because they were fated. I didn't know having both types of connections was even possible and that the fates linked beings together for any other purpose. I'm glad that he had a choice to remove the knotted connection and that it is now gone due to fulfilling his so-called duty, but seriously, why do these bonds even have to exist?

"Freyja?" His tone softened with an added hint of doting sweetness. Is he speaking to me in his daddy voice? "What is it that you are not getting, so I can help you understand?"

I'm more pissed off than anything, and since my anger is rising, it's not the best time for me to be taught a lesson.

I clear my throat. "So, your brother never found out that you two were mates?"

"I don't mind explaining it to you." Even though he only leans in slightly, his nurturing aura wraps about me, his kind words smothering me.

"Stop talking to me like that." I squeezed his hands to give emphasis. "I got it. Let's move on with you getting personal with me."

He levels me with a stare, intensifying the energy encompassing me and almost influencing me to give in and obey him. I return his glare, causing a silent snarl to flare his nostrils.

"Do you know what I do to my kids when they are being stubborn, *Sundrae*?" His growl curves my lips into a taunting smile.

I lean forward, leaving only a couple of inches of space between us. "Does it involve reddening a different pair of my cheeks, Ginger?" *Where did that come from, and why do I want him to spank me?*

His throaty laugh has me sweltering. "I think for the sake of all who are beyond the mist, you best not taunt me." He reveals his fangs with a challenging grin. "Unless *Bah Sundrae* wants to be...played with."

I would've thought after all the centuries of being punished by my husband that the notion of the Fae reddening my ass would trigger me, but it doesn't. For the first time since I was with Bralyant, I'm aroused by the thought of being spanked, as long as it's not Odin doing it.

Awareness of my being quiet has heat crawling up my neck. The breath I take to retort about him calling me 'Bah Sundrae' again gets sucked out of me. Quicker than I could process, his eyes shift into slits, and I get a glimpse of the beast lying in wait under his skin, a Rizaver, a monster that even the Dragons fear.

I clench every muscle in my body to prevent a cataclysmic surge of power from escaping me. The primal, dark side of me that I only ever unleash around Haidion wants to come out and play. There is no doubt the Fae before me won't be a worthy opponent; however, now is not the time for the whirling storm within me to be let out.

I lower my knees, cross my legs, and scoot forward so we are flush against one another. He's taken off guard by my getting closer and making myself more comfortable. The pink halo forms around his irises again, making me second-guess my choice to get closer since I don't know what the color means.

"How about we finish this first, and then we can talk about playing with one another?"

"Yes. Of course." He clears his throat. "Um, you allowed me to ask questions about your life, so is there anything you want to ask me?"

His tail goes around my back and under my cloak, escaping my peripheral vision while the length rests next to me. I want to swat the ligament away; however, this might be a display of goodwill among the Fae, like the Wolven sniffing a being's neck to check to see if they are okay.

"So, your brother never found out that you two were mates?" I asked again.

He gives my hands a tender squeeze. "My brother suspected his wife had cheated due to my son's enhanced magic, but my wife and I were able to convince him otherwise..." His eyes flicked down to something on me. "You met my son, by the way."

"I have?" Warm energy floods my chest as I wait for him to confirm what I already suspected.

A glassiness covers his eyes when they lift back up to meet mine. "I wasn't strong enough to break free from the tree to protect him, which is insane because I'm also his Guardian. Do you know what that is?"

I nod. "It's another Guild Race."

The magic system selects beings to be Guardians and charges them with defending a newborn immortal from infancy through maturity. These children require more guidance since the magic system detects they are going to be very powerful magical beings.

"We are given an incredible amount of magic to assist in mentoring and protecting the one we have been charged with. I could obliterate the asteroid from hitting Earthradon if my son was in danger of being killed by it."

"Would you live?"

"No. If my soul doesn't get disintegrated from using that mass amount of magic, I'd still be able to watch over him as a spirit." I shiver when a gentle breeze brushes across my forehead. "My job as his Guardian is to give my life for his; however, I could only manage to manipulate the tree I was in and the ones around me. Why my Guardian magic didn't activate for me to use, I don't know." He brings our conjoined hands toward his face. "When my son said, "Why would I want to kill someone like you since you protected me and took a brand to save my life?" I made a magical vow that I wouldn't kill you."

The Fae observes me before bringing my hands to his mouth, waiting for me to reject his offered affection. I nod, expressing my consent, and he delicately kisses my inner wrists.

"I'm honored to have made the acquaintance of one of the most altruistic beings in existence."

I bring our conjoined hands to my face and wait for him to tell me no or pull away. His eyebrows pinch together with skepticism, but he slowly nods. I slip my hands out of our embrace and kiss each of his palms.

A tender sigh escapes his lips while the tip of his tail brushes an exposed part of my lower back. The velvety fuzz has me squirming and screeching. *Well, that's a noise I didn't know I was capable of producing.*

"Whoops, my bad." The Fae feigns innocence as he holds back his laughter and pulls his tail back to be behind him. "Anyways, my mate is who I would introduce you to if you wanted to talk about your trauma with someone who has gone through it as well. I'm sure my son is going on and on about you, so convincing her won't be an issue."

I involuntarily flinch when a soft breeze tickles the now-sensitive skin on my lower back. "If we make it through today, I will think about it."

His smile widens as the pink hue in his eyes brightens. "If you don't mind my asking. Were you and the Autarch lovers? Did you seek comfort in him from the abuse?"

"Oh, stars, no! We are neither of those things. He was...with someone I was close to, so he's family." Was family.

"Speaking of family." He squeezes my hands before pulling away and resting his elbows on his knees. "The Fae who attacked you in the sky and got webbed by Ladiya first was my elder half-brother, Constantine, the High Lord of the Court of Tenebrous."

My mouth drops. "You just gave me his name."

"You have been overpowered by one man too many." The pink in his eyes fades while he clears his throat. "I was battling a goddess and her wolf servant when my High Lord summoned me. A red-headed goddess was kicking our asses and his, and I was permitted to unleash my beast if it meant I could capture her."

He was fighting my friends! The reality of our situation hits me like a frenzied Harpy.

"I broke away and saw Constantine was in a losing battle, and instead of assisting him, I watched because I was hoping that the goddess would kill him. Then he got webbed up. I couldn't have asked for a more perfect situation to end my brother's life. But in my excitement, I made a rookie mistake. He reigned and commanded me to go after the bounty—"

"Wait, why did he refer to me as a bounty?"

He tilts his head to the side, confused. "Because your husband, my bad, ex-husband offered one to have you returned to our rally point alive."

"That's why I'm been being fought over?"

He gives a nod. "I found the sob story of a god worrying about his wife not making the right decision by fighting on the opposite side and him refusing to face her on the battlefield hilarious. It sounded more like he was terrified of being killed by her."

My soul magic tingles in my fingertips. *Thank the stars it's coming back!*

"By the time I got to the forest, my brother's hold on me had lessened enough that I was able to fight it off. I planned to admit that I wasn't strong enough, even in my beast form, to obtain the bounty. In return, the High Lords wouldn't try to go after her unless they were all together, which wasn't going to happen since they'd have to give power to someone else to command their courts during battle. I wasn't going to let any more of our warriors die because of a husband's cowardly way of wrangling his wife. But then I heard a fierce voice, the one that saved my son, and I allowed my spiritual essence to guide me through the hazy forest."

I'm caught off guard by the red halo of light forming around his irises. Anger. "My promise to not kill you doesn't extend to protecting you, but I couldn't let the Autarcha torture you to death. If you are going to die, it's going to be on the battlefield, not at the hands of a delirious bitch."

A question that I should've asked a while ago has me safeguarding my heart with the little magic I have. "Why are you fighting in the Unfaithful Army?"

The Fae's aura shifts from relaxed to alert. "With the gods being able to harvest the Father's magic, we can protect our planet from the asteroid, cleanse our world from greed, and he can rejoin with his true love. There is evidence that if the Father were to leave, Earthradon would remain intact. He has been bound here long enough and deserves to be rejoined with his love." The red halo begins to pulsate. "Why are you fighting in the Callous Army?"

"The gods aren't going to just take the Father's magic, they are going to kill him! Did you ever stop to think that maybe the Father is infected by greed as well, and harvesting his magic will only make matters worse?"

He's up on his feet faster than I can process. "That's not true! The Father isn't going to die."

My cloak awakens by exhilarating magic, and I fly to my feet in a strong breeze. "Thor is in possession of Faithless."

His eyes widen with realization, and he blinks away something I can't read fast enough. "Thor gave the races his word. He made a magical vow that the Father wouldn't be killed and that his magic would be used to cleanse Earthradon." He takes a step closer making our chests almost touch. "Are you telling me you accepted your fate of dying?" he asks with genuine curiosity.

"If I couldn't convince the Father to find another way to cleanse our world without an asteroid, then yes. I was going to live out the rest of my days in peace until all of this started."

"You mean you were going to spend the rest of your existence being abused?"

He scans my eyes for the answer as if he can see into my soul. *It was stupid of me to tell him about my past trauma.*

I take a step back from him. "Don't talk to me as if we are friends!"

He spread his arms out, his muscles straining his armor. "We can't kill each other. We might as well be friends."

I laugh mockingly and place my hands on my hips. "What we have is a truce, and once we go back out there, we are enemies. And, also, if you thought of me as your friend, you would've told me your name, Ginger!"

The red halo around his irises vanishes. He schools his features while pressing a hand to his chest, tucks his other arm behind his back, and bows at the waist to me.

"Illyrical Sirius Caelum, my lady. It's an honor to be in the presence of such a radiant soul." Before me is not a warrior with absurdity laced in his voice but a refined gentleman.

Hands grip my shoulders before my knees give out. I was taken off guard by him telling me his full name, and the respectful way he addressed me was a punch to my pride and wit. The air gets knocked out of my lungs, erasing the energy fueling my rising anger. I would have fallen to the ground if it weren't for... *wait.* His hands are nowhere near me. *Who is holding me up?*

A strong wind takes away the phantom sensation of something gripping me and ruffles my cloak, bringing my attention to the absence of my magic in the fabric. How was I able to be lifted off the ground?

"If I wanted just a truce, Freyja." Illyrical straightens, appearing taller. "Then I wouldn't have opened up to you." His voice, promises punishing pleasure as it drops an octave. "I would've wrapped my tail around your slender throat and fucked your mouth with my beast tongue while we leveled this forest to be nothing but ash."

Don't imagine it. Don't imagine it. Fuck! I'm imagining it.

"But then you didn't choose to use your spiritual power on me, just as I didn't decide to reign you. I wanted to get to know you so I could understand why the fierce goddess who put herself between my son and the Wolven King was fighting against me." A pink halo illuminates his eyes and glows proudly. "No matter what, once we step out of these woods, you are my friend, Freyja."

His words wrap around the core thread of my soul as if the Fates themselves sealed his statement as a vow.

"Illyrical." I don't know why I took the time to pronounce each syllable or suddenly became breathless. "Illyrical, I don't think being friends is a good—"

"Please." I'm taken aback by the vulnerability in his voice. "Can you at least give yourself time to think about it?"

I ponder. *If a battle didn't divide us, could we be friends?* "I...I guess... maybe we—"

A painful growl rushes out of me as thorns press into my swelling, hopeful heart. *No. No!* I can't be friends with him. He's, my enemy. He attacked my friends. He's going to kill the Father. Illyrical. Is. My. Enemy.

Anger fills my chest and lessens my pain, giving me the strength to snarl aggressively. Regret creeps in for lashing out at one of the two beings who could not only keep the rot away but also take on the burden of my past, relieving a portion of my misery. Having my life dictated by soul rot changes me into a different version of myself so I can survive. *I fucking hate this disease!*

"I will never be your friend!" The pink in his gaze quickly shifts to blue or gray. I don't care to determine the shade while the natural glow of his skin sickly and his eyes shimmer like sharpened blades. "And while I've been in here selfishly talking about my issues, the battle is still going on! You may be opposed to claiming me as a bounty and turning me in, but was this also your strategy to save your fellow warriors by keeping me away?"

Illyrical's attention dips to something on me, and before I can follow his gaze, he tips his head back and laughs.

"If I didn't know you were a goddess, I'd say you were part Fae, Harpy, Taurun, and Siren." He sticks out his thumb. "It is hard for you to trust." His pointer finger comes out. "You have no filter when it comes to speaking your mind." He makes a show of displaying his middle finger. "You are incredibly stubborn." His ring finger joins the ranks of the others. "And you have such dark, sexual fantasies." *I really shouldn't have been so detailed about what kind of sex Odin said no to.*

I stick up my pinky finger. "I might also have part Dragon in me since all I want to do is make you scream by blowing you—"

"Oh? You want to blow me?" Illyrical crosses his arms over his chest with a smile full of venom.

"Don't cut me off when I'm talking! I haven't done that to you!"

Illyrical leans in as if he's about to tell me a secret. "You can try to get a rise out of me all you want, but it won't work. I see through your bullshit mask, and I will always call you out when you wear it, *Sundrae.*"

A startled gasp escapes me instead of the rage-inducing words I am ready to fire at him. The fireflies come out from under the petals of his armor and form back into his tremendous wings.

He takes a couple of steps back and stretches out his powerful extremities. "Are you ready to go back into battle? Can you feel your magic at all?"

Skjoldr hums in my chest as magic tingles in my hands. *Why did you respond to him? Whose side are you on?*

"There better be a battle to return to." I bite out. "If not, then I'm glad that our bargain doesn't include me being unable to harm you. Because if I see you, I'm going to permanently alter your body, so you will be able to suck your cock and choke on your balls."

His tail comes up between his legs, and he flicks off some barely noticeable flecks of dirt. "Our absence has only been a few minutes since we've been in my magic field. Time is slower. Is that a yes on your magic working?" *He did not just dismiss my threat!*

"How is that possible?" *Fuck! My curious mouth is betraying me too.*

Illyrical glances up at me stoically, conveying that he won't answer until I answer his question. When I don't respond, he goes back to his task. An awkward moment passes before his tail lowers, but he goes on to pick the dirt out from under his nails.

I growl. "Yes, my magic is working."

"Good." He doesn't bother to look up at me until he's done. "When you decide to embrace me as your friend, I will tell you all about my magic. And if you see my brother again, feel free to kill him. If not, I will before this battle is over."

"Won't the magic system see that as brother fighting brother to be High Lord? Shit like that could curse you and your family."

A sexy-as-fuck smile warms his complexion to the same hue as his spicy brown eyes. He looks different with a darker skin tone; it's more natural for him. I gasp. He just shifted his skin tone. And his eyes aren't brown anymore, but the same luminescent, shadow-steel shade as his son's. The only part of him that stayed the same was his amber-golden hair. Is he hiding his true form from me, or does he always conceal his appearance?

"You better be careful, *Freyja*." He purrs my name in Norliska; the gruffness strokes my spine, and I forget how to breathe. "For a second, it almost sounded like you cared about me. Are you already tired of wearing that mask, or did it slip at the thought of wanting to watch me get myself off with how you plan on contorting my body?"

I dig my nails into my palms as I ball my fists to trigger pain so the throbbing goes away, but the small hurt only makes the sensation intensify. Before I speak, I take several deep breaths to ensure my voice is level and not breathless.

"I care about your children," I grit out through clenched teeth.

"Which also means you must care about their daddy." *Fuck him and his arrogantly attractive smile!*

"Please, Illyrical. Just think about it."

The heat from his smile changes into one of egregious anger. "I have more than two reasons as to why I need to kill my brother. You wouldn't understand. You can be who you are and don't have to hide."

My assumption about him concealing his true self from me was correct, and Illyrical is also right. I don't know what hiding my identity is like. "Your son will take the throne then. He's too young."

"He won't!" Illyrical exclaimed with absolute certainty. "After I remove my camouflage in front of the court, my mate and I are going to reveal the scandal. With my brother dead, no one will prosecute us. We will be shamed and forced out, but we planned to leave anyway to the Fallen Mountain of Sothearia and be free anyway."

A second later, his anger dissipates, softening his features. *"I'm sorry for snapping at you. You didn't know. I immensely appreciate you being concerned for my son."* He knows Atlantean as well. "You'll make an amazing mother someday." He switched back to Fanarzien.

I tense up as a longing ache comes from my womb, wanting to be filled with a child. Sometimes, I can hear a distant giggle, but in this moment, I only pick up an echo of a distressed infant's cry.

An awkward silence passes between us. Balling my hands into fists isn't helping my confidence to move on from this topic. I can't even look Illyrical in the eyes without breaking down. Even though I accepted my fate, I regret not having had the chance to become a mother.

The clinking of glass pulls my gaze from the mist to Illyrical. I gasp. A crescent-shaped vile containing mint-colored liquid is in his grasp. It's the same one I was given when I reached the top of Lady Amora's Mountain. He knocks it back, letting out a pleasurable groan, but he doesn't drop the bottle; instead, it vanishes into thin air.

My plan of questioning how he acquired the potion was drowned out by him clearing his throat. "If you find yourself in need of my assistance or company once more, simply call upon the magic I gave you."

My reserves hum with incredible energy. The veins in my hands are illuminated by the radiance of the sun, moon, and shadow as they flow together in harmony.

"You gave me your magic? When!?"

He throws me a wink and turns towards the mist.

"I know nothing about how your magic works!"

With a strong flap of his wings, he takes off. All the shadows chase after him, causing the forest to brighten from the few rays of sun poking through the gray clouds from above.

Since Illyrical is a Fae, his magic should function similarly to harvesting, meaning that once I use it, it disappears.

Given my weakened state, I should appreciate any form of protection that will help me defend myself, but my frustration makes it difficult to do so. It was one thing to allow his magic to influence me, but giving me his magic makes me want to cleanse myself until I'm sunburned red. The act is too personal. The gift of Haidion's magic to me was the result of centuries of friendship. Illyrical is... him, and I aren't...

"Your gift doesn't make us friends, Ginger!" My scream pursues him as he vanishes from sight.

TWENTY-SIX

TENTH HOUR AFTER SUNRISE

A long, echoey howl comes from behind me as I turn on my heel to head out of the forest. A mighty roar follows, silencing the wind streaming through the depleted woods and the shouts and cries from the valley beyond.

My ears are practically bleeding from the deafening strength. The reverberation ceases only when I cup my hands over them.

A sonic blast of pastel magic tears through the Scorpion Drug fog, obliterating the haze. The ground rumbles beneath my feet. In the distance, a towering wave of dirt and debris surges towards me. Trees beyond my capability to see in the distance explode and get consumed by the tilled earth while the section of the forest closest to me gets ripped out of the ground and is launched skyward—me along with them.

Skjoldr hums in my chest, and the strings of my cloak reattach to my body. After a hard yank, I stop flying uncontrollably and hover in the air while my eyes spin for a moment longer.

Potent magic flexes my muscles with each breath I take. My irritation with getting personal with Illyrical has lessened since I restored a portion of my magic while chatting with him. However, this second wave of energy won't be able to provide me with the same amount of strength I had before I headed into battle.

The sickening unsteadiness of my spinning vision subsides, but my shock prevents me from following my instinctual warning to fly back down to the grass.

"Burning souls."

Acres of the decimated West woods assault my eyes, and tears threaten to break free as the desiccation processes of the North and South woods start to lose their lusciousness.

With the Fae claiming all the vegetation encircling the Great Willow Tree, I fear they plan to eradicate the entirety of this land. I doubt the one Nymph who remains will be able to return this sacred place to its former serenity. What was once a valley of spiritual peace and unconditional love is going to become a barren wasteland.

The wave reached the middle of the valley, partially filling the crack from where the first wave of Spydens came out with not only the forest's remnants but also fallen warriors.

I'm pulled away from the grim sight as rays of blinding sunlight penetrate my soul and slice through the thick, gray sky, pushing back the dulling darkness.

Renewed hope reinvigorates my strained soul and battered body as I take in the Allied Army coming to our aid.

Thousands upon thousands of Lyons run towards the valley with Atlanteans and Wiccayens on their backs. A dust storm is behind them, the tell-tale signal of a herd of Tauruns stampeding. And beyond where the sun is the brightest, Harpies cry out from the distance. Though I can't see them, the air around me becomes frenetic, making each breath I take sharp—the warning energy of an incoming swarm.

Skjoldr hums more violently in my chest, warning me of her intention to get out of harm's way. Before she can, I descend towards a blueish-white Wolven at the head of the pride.

"Hello, Watson." A rumble vibrates his back when I straddle him as if he's trying to greet me back.

He releases a relieved whimper when I bury my fingers into his fur. I lean forward and rub the side of my face against the back of his neck to soothe him and convey that I'm okay.

As I lean back, a familiar Lyon approaches Watson's left flank—Rawldur, the Falmenir Makuba of the Lyon race. His blistering blonde mane is full and draws attention to his imposing, beastly body, corded with bulging muscles. The couple of feet the Lyons lacks in height, compared to the Wolvens, they make up for in strength.

Rawldur emits a gurgling growl. His purr triggers my core to hum as if I could respond to him in a beastly kind of way. A flush blooms over every inch of my body. I don't know if I simply get aroused by animalistic sounds or if I secretly wish I were a beast myself. His greeting was not sexual in nature, given Rawldur's six or so lyonesses to warm his den. His part in the war is what he's been bred and trained to do. Nothing will distract him from fulfilling his purpose, especially if the outcome threatens his pride.

"He sees you, Freyja. As do I." My attention is captured by the smooth, baritone voice that could convince me to believe the most absurd things.

Adom Leeater, King of the Atlanteans and the Commander in Chief of the Allied Army, rides on Rawldur's back. The gold stenciling on Adom's black-olive skin highlights the contour of the muscles that compose his chiseled figure, making him a fine work of art. He has the same warm brown eyes and black braided hair as his cousin, but his braids have gold bands.

A skirt woven from the finest cotton drapes loosely around Adom's waist. The red, black, and green fibers form a diamond-fence pattern with a pair of ram horns colliding in the center. Slits just below his hips highlight his muscular quadriceps. Besides a royal piece of jewelry, nothing else garnishes his solid frame.

His long neck is adorned with a thick vine necklace of mahogany wood beads. Each one is engraved with the story of how his courage, resilience, humility, integrity, influence, accountability, and spiritual connection to his faith earned him his title. Aquazanite feather crystals are placed between each bead; they, too, have markings and represent one of the many elements readily accessible for the Atlantean King to wield.

"I see you." I flick my gaze to Rawldur to extend the greeting to him.

"A little breathless, are we, Soulfire?" A smile blooms on Adom's silken face, widening his lips.

His teasing uplifts a portion of the tension on my shoulders but doesn't bring a smile to my face. I should be thrilled and bellowing my war cry with the same strength Rawldur did when he unleashed a tsunami of magic on the West woods. But after taking in how this battle affects the valley, I can't reach for my hope until the shield-ward dome is down.

The angelic spirit behind Adom's exquisite eyes darkens with worry. His gaze sweeps across my body. It takes me a second to realize my error. I didn't respond to him with a witty remark.

I grasp my shoulder and nod. "You honor me, even though I don't deserve it. Given that your arrival wasn't greeted by the spiked heads of all the traitorous Gods in the Unfaithful Army, I'm not worthy of being called by such a name."

There is no hiding the emotion written across my face. If I were to try sparring with him now, he would see my mask and be determined to peel it off. Letting him know one of the truths about how I'm feeling is better than him seeing what I wasn't quick enough to cover up.

"*Freyja.*" Adom's Atlantean tongue gives off an imposing yet consoling energy. "By your logic, I don't deserve any of my titles."

He presses a finger against his mouth just as I part my lips to argue. I snap my mouth shut from his request for him to speak and for me to listen.

"For what you did for my people and the injured after the war when I failed to protect them, I should've renounced myself as King. You were distraught from the loss of Freyr, wanting to go home and grieve, yet you answered my cry for aid."

The memory comes to the forefront of my mind.

My brother's company of warriors and I finish loading our fallen Freyr onto our ship. As I call out for all to make sail, the wind wafts in my face and carries the roar of King Adom.

A moment later, an Atlantean horn blares in a pattern from the Iroko forest beyond Camp Ariella, calling for aid. With all the beings at the camp either hurt, dead or having seen enough battle, no one moves to go.

I turn to my warriors, who pause on their task to get the boat ready to set sail. "I won't think of you any less if you want to stay with the ship." My gaze meets the captain's. "If any trouble comes this way and I'm not aboard, leave me behind."

Eirikur, a beast of a man whom my brother would've approved of courting me over Odin, steps towards me. "The next boat I want to sail on will be the one that will bring me to Valhalla." He turns to the others. "What say you, Norse warriors?"

Blades smack against shields, which turns the heads of all at the camp. Our war cries shift the wind's direction; rather than work against us, it soars with us. With the wind pushing at our backs, we run through the forest as if we are flying, our cries echoing off the trees.

We reach a clearing, and the wind knocks all those who are standing on their asses. I quickly assess the field. A Demonical binds Adom like a pig about to put on a rotisserie while morph demons take the injured Atlanteans through a portal and try to wrangle the other warriors. Though the Demonical was cloaked in a mist of shadows, I knew from their presence that they were an Ancient. We're outnumbered, but with the determined looks on my warriors' faces, that won't going to stop us.

On my cry, we run together as one and become a unit of swords and shields. Together, we fight the morphs like savage beasts. When our line doesn't break, the demons move to our flanks to attack us from behind.

A stillness in the air and the shift of something powerful upon us have me realizing that a Fate is here, and they are ready to claim all our souls. I met Adom's eyes and read the same knowing truth in his pained, defeated face.

The air electrifies as hope ignites from the depths of the forest. Screams and screeches, howls, and growls come from the woods. The warriors who can still fight rush onto the battlefield. Even though we are now evenly matched, the morphs are insanely stronger, and when one falls, the demon begins to piece itself back together and rises once again to fight.

My ice shield breaks, and I'm pulled away from my warriors by a monster who has the build of a bear but the skin of a snake and is covered in a thin mist of shadows. They haul me up and roar in my face like a Lyon. My magic becomes numb like I've been trapped by a Spyden's webbing, and with no weapons adorning my body, I have nothing to attack this demon with. If all the morphs are as powerful as this one, then no victory will be won here. I led them all to their deaths.

The monster raises his head in a roar as a sword is thrust into his throat. I'm released and scramble back. Eirikur pulls his sword out and stands in front of me.

My friend looks over his shoulder at me and flashes me a confident smile that decimates my fear of dying. "We will win this battle." He tosses me his shield and sword. "I will make sure of it."

"What are you doing?!"

Eirikur pulls out a necklace, puts the pendant in his mouth, and charges the morph. I scream my friend's name as he vanishes into the void with the demon.

I didn't realize how close we were to the portal. I was seconds away from being brought into it if Eirikur hadn't saved me.

An eerie horn sounds, making the temperature plummet. I don't know who raised an alarm, but it didn't sound like a call for aid, more like a warning.

A herd of shadow monsters comes out of thin air, and to my shock, the morph demons retreat into the portal like cowards, dropping the Atlanteans they were trying to capture. Only the Ancient Demonical is left, and they aren't letting Adom go.

I pick up Eirikur's sword and shield and call off the warriors from attacking the Demonical. If anyone is going to face this Ancient, it's going to be me. I'm done having others risk their lives to help me.

Before I can get within a foot of the Ancient Demonical, they use magic that seizes my body as if they control my blood. My vision fades to black, but a fire erupts from within me and pushes his control over my body out. I'm quick and slam the shield into their face, shattering it, and thrust the sword into their heart. Like the others, he flees into the portal, closing it behind them.

I try to blink away the memory, but it's difficult. The darkness in my mind comes to the forefront and consumes it. With my thoughts free from the traumatizing past, I remind myself that Eirikur got the glorious death he wanted and that I shouldn't feel guilty about him dying.

"You told me, Freyja, "When everyone looks back, they will not remember that their king failed them, but that he did everything he could to protect his people." Adom grasps one of the wooden beads in his hand. "On that day, I earned this token, just as you earned the legendary name." I'm still puzzled about why Soulfire is legendary to his people.

Adom glides his fingertips over to the feather crystals in the middle of his necklace. "In your time of uncertainty, here is my wisdom to give to you; the day you fail as a leader is the day you no longer care to protect those you love." He gestures to the valley beyond with a nod. "And today is not that day."

The stenciling on Adom's face pulsates as he brings the feather-crystal to his lips, triggering all of them to glow.

With a wink, he beats on his chest while calling out a battle chant. Thunder answers him and keeps the rhythm of his pounding going as the air echoes his voice to fill the valley.

Fae horns blare. The thousands of eyes in the sky turn towards us.

A secondary horn call from the Fae sounds, this time in a rhythmic pattern. Without needing to ask Adom, the humming in my chest from Skjoldr answers my concern for me—the Fae are coming.

Illyrical's face flashes in my eyes. I cut down on my concern for his well-being before any kind of feeling could grow for him. *It's a good thing I can still harm him.*

Adom bellows another chant, and the thunderous drumming intensifies.

My heartbeat gets drowned out along with my intake of air. If I thought I was tuned out of the conversations through the brand while talking to Illyrical, then I must be tuned out of my own body because I can't even sense myself.

Adom's shrieks to the sky above in Harcaniel, the cawing tongue of the harpies.

An overwhelming number of squawking screams answer as the friction in the air stings my skin and the pressure of something closing in makes my body want to explode.

Thousands of harpies fly overhead in blurs, blocking the sun's rays. The swarm is formed in a pattern that reminds me of fanged teeth. Multiple sharp points with a deep V of space in between them, while the Fae are assembled in three triangles that form together to make a bigger one, leaving an open space in the middle.

I find myself praying to the omnipotent beings the races believe in. "Fates, please have mercy on the souls trapped in the Fae's trinity triangle."

Bone-breaking smacks of flesh collide together.

A concussive eruption of static-like magic bolts out of thin air and blankets the valley, going all the way to the forest and silencing Adom's thunderous chant.

Watson's red-stained fur pulls me out of the discombobulated haze of not being able to sense my body and prevents the tortuous image of my brother being impaled from surfacing.

I frantically comb through the hair on his neck, trying to find the wound so I can put pressure on it. With him running as fast as he is, the injury will bleed that much quicker.

"Pull off, Watson! Don't keep running with this kind of injury." How could he have sustained such an injury without my noticing?

As a large, thick drop of warm rain hits my cheek, Watson growls and shakes off my hands. The fragrance of copper floats into my nostrils, and the pungent smell only thickens. My hands have droplets of blood on them, as do my arms and thighs. Watson isn't injured. It's raining blood, which can only mean—

"Adom, why the flying fuck did you think having the Harpies go into their frenzy state was a good idea?"

Anyone in the air and not a Harpy is now a target. *No more flying for me.*

"Only a hundred are in the frenzy state. The rest have their claw guards on, allowing them to still fight the way they know how without activating the neurological-frenzy mindset of their beast."

A neurotoxin in the Harpies' claws gets activated when they cut into someone, triggering them to go into a frenzy. They don't stop attacking until they reduce the being to bloody pieces. Only the Sovrinarch, the dominant leader of the Harpy race, can command them to stop.

"As for why, it was to distract the Fae. The energy the harpies give off when their plan of attack is to go into a frenzy state makes them more of a threat than me. I needed to be in the valley to unleash a concussive surge to shock the vegetation so it could no longer be harvested."

Adom doesn't bother to wipe away the blood from his mouth or eyes. Atlanteans are immune to any blood-borne illness and can't get sick from a disease or bacteria that spreads from contact with blood.

Cutting off the Fae from being able to replenish their magic will tip the scales in our favor. The race will have to limit their use and resort to hand-to-hand combat. Against a Harpy in their frenzy state, the Fae must bring out their inner beast to have a fighting chance. The thought of seeing a Rizaver in action has me gawking at the sky in anticipation, not caring if droplets of blood hit my face.

"Freyja, is your brand to communicate with the others not working? Ambar is asking me. I told her you're with me."

I lower my gaze back to Adom. "I'm unable to talk to anyone."

As I refocus on the battle we are running towards, I tune back into the people talking through the brand. Ambar and Bralyant are conveying that they are moving all of our warriors, wounded or not, away from the center to get clear of the approaching stampede.

Adom calls out, "After I part the mass, the army will split to form a barrier so nothing can get in the way of the Tauruns. I'm going to be heading on through until I reach the dome. Are you two riding with us?"

Watson snuffs out his answer, and I give Adom a firm nod.

"Get behind me and enjoy the show."

With a wink, he raises his long arms and spreads his fingers. The gold stenciling on his body pulsates like a heartbeat, while the beaded necklace levitates off his shoulders but remains around his neck. He closes his eyes as he takes a deep breath that tightens all his glorious muscles. When I think he is going to let it out, he doesn't. He's holding it in.

I grip Watson tighter when I almost bounce off him as we run over the filled-in split in the valley's center. Adom is only holding onto Rawldur with his thighs. I would've fallen off, but he remains upright and immovable.

After Watson gets into position behind Rawldur, the ground splits alongside us, and a pair of translucent roots shoot out. As they eagerly wrap around Adom's fingers, he balls his hands into fists.

A defensive line of Spydens forms. Without needing to judge distance, I know we are within. A spray noise tickles my ears.

"Adom!" my lungs and spirit wail.

The muscles on his back tense as he slams his arms down. Thick, veiny roots erupt from the cracks alongside us. Adom shoots his arms forward with a bellowing shout, and the roots lunge toward the awaiting line of Spydens. With the wave of Adom's arms, the roots mimic his movements as if they were extensions of his extremities.

The webbing gets dissolved on impact, and the Spydens fly off to the sides as he sweeps them off their feet. More roots erupt from the ground, replacing the others when we get too far away from their cracks.

Adom parts the battlefield, pushing the warriors still up and fighting and the fallen. With a glance behind me, the Allied Army is maintaining the width of the path their Commander has created. As we reach the shield-ward dome, the last of the warriors move aside, revealing the herd of Tauruns stampeding.

Rawldur and Watson turn us to the left side of the dome. Adom's necklace stops levitating just as he slouches forward. He pants heavily for a moment as the translucent roots sliver back into the ground, the cracked earth closing once they are out of sight.

I jump off Watson and grab Adom's leg and Rawldur's shoulder. Adom doesn't notice my arrival until I'm in front of him. He blinks at me as I place my hand on his chest.

"What...are you...doing, Freyja?" He asks weakly, telling me without saying that wielding the elemental magic took a lot out of him.

"Groping your sternum since it's the sexiest part of your body."

A pained laugh escapes his lips as his chest spasms beneath my palm, causing him to wince. I pull forth happy memories of Freyr with one breath, and as I take in another, my hand gets coated in the delicate mist of soft blue light, my healing power.

Tears stream down his cheeks as he takes deeper breaths. "*Freyja?*" His soft mutter in Atlantean is so endearing that I can't help but give him an appreciative smile, ignoring the question I knew he wanted answered.

Thorns prick my hand in an attempt to stop me from healing Adom. He has soul rot.

A dozen questions pop into my mind. Rather than ask one, I pull forth the memories of Freyr that make me tear up. I've only healed a couple of beings who had soul rot, and memories that cause me to get emotional strengthen my power tenfold.

Adom places his hand over mine. "Freyja—"

With my other hand, I place a finger over my lips. His attention flicks down. Instead of gripping my hand to remove it, he keeps it there.

"You are an intelligent being, Adom. I know you can piece together what I'm doing and figure out why I can't tell you anything. Rather than us being anxious about the questions we want to ask each other, do you think you can let go with me so we can focus on what is more important?"

Adom's soul surfaces in the depths of his eyes, and instinctively, I tense, knowing he could be reading my inner emotions.

"If I were a good friend, I would pull you aside once this battle is over and ask for you to confide in me why you have such a strong mask on. But I'd be anything but good since I know how fucking stubborn you are."

A laugh escapes me as I suppress the need to cry, causing me to hiccup.

"I would buy you as many drinks as you desired. When you couldn't stand on your own, I'd fly you home and whisper endearing words into your ear until I had you sobbing and cracking that mask of yours. Once you're utterly exhausted from venting, I'll tuck you into bed and kiss you goodnight without feeling an ounce of guilt or regret for the events that led you to open up to me."

Adom glides the hand he has over mine to grip my shoulder while his other one reaches out to caress my cheek.

"All the emotions you have bottled up, Freyja, will kill you."

His tone transforms from charming to serious as his eyes fall to my chest as if he can see the rot draining the vitality from my heart and soul.

Fortunately, being inebriated affects the rot since it's feeding off my body to survive. When I almost reach a breaking point, I drink until I pass out. Odin was always gone to not witness me being cocked off my ass or severely hung over since he was always the reason why I'd reach my emotional capacity of trying to ignore my feelings.

After opening up to Illyrical, venting doesn't scare me as much as it used to. However, I don't want to tell my sob story again until I divorce my husband and possibly maim him. After that, I'll gladly drink and vent because the story's ending will be happy and not about me being a prisoner of misery.

"Tag team with me to convince Ambar to become your queen, and I'll drink you dry of all your palm wine."

He leans in close, leaving hardly an inch of space between our faces. "It's a deal."

Adom presses a kiss on my forehead, causing the veins on my face to tingle. My heart flutters as if something has ruffled my spirit's feathers. I'm too consumed with the sensual gratitude he expressed toward me to consider the strange sensation.

With one final stab, the thorns attempt to make me fear that they will latch onto me before my power disintegrates the last of the rot. The threat doesn't make me budge, for I know if this rot were to enter my body, Skjoldr would sense the intruder immediately since the parasite carries traces of Adom's spiritual blood. Since my friend's magical makeup isn't entering me with the purpose of reproduction, its presence is a red flag to my spiritual essence.

Adom exhales a sigh of relief and presses his forehead against mine. Without needing to ask, I know the rot is gone from how his muscles relax under my palm. Any damage the rot caused to his heart will take time to heal or might remain, depending on how long he's been suffering. If he had pushed the strength of his soul too far, he would never be as powerful as he once was, which could lead to the stripping of his immortality.

I force my dread into the darkness of my mind before it rises.

Adom moves his hand from my shoulder to my cheek, encircling my face between his palms. "How can I repay you?"

I place both my hands over his chest as the soft blue light of my power dims. "You don't owe me anything, but if I die, I only ask that you please don't go near my body."

Rot can live in the body for a day before it has to find a new host, and I would be devastated if Adom got infected with it again.

Rawldur and Watson growl, drawing Adom's attention away from me before he can respond.

Adom slides off and extends his hands to me. Even though I don't need his help, I allow him to wrap his arms around me and pull me down. His touch awakened a part of me that craves affection, but as Adom's expression shifts to that of the courageous commander he strives to be, I lock down my selfish desires.

Rumbles vibrate the earth as the Tauruns approach. The ground force of the Allied Army keeps the path clear as the Harpies assault the sky, sending their victims down in pieces.

While on all fours, the Tauruns are half their ten-foot height. Like the Harpies, they have more of a creature-like humanoid form. When they change into their beast forms, their hands shift into hooves, their faces harden to stone, and their noses and mouths elongate like a bull. The intimidating amount of muscle mass always stays.

Judging by the two pairs of engraved gold horns sticking out amongst the silver ones from the sun's gleam, the Emperior, Coalston, and the Emperiest, Maytower, are leading the herd. With the birth of their first child not even a couple of moons ago, I'm surprised that they are both here. After muttering a quick prayer to the Fates for the boy's safety, I force myself to push my opinions aside and focus on the shield-ward dome.

Even though the traitorous Spartans are further away from the palisade walls, I can sense their smug grins. I will enjoy their faces switching to sheer horror when the Tauruns break through the dome.

As the herd approaches, the ground shakes violently. Insects that hadn't already retreated from the unscathed grass buzz, hop, and fly away.

I hold my breath, readying myself to activate my spiritual power. Once an opening is made, I'm ending this battle.

Gold tendrils of glamorous magic wrap around the horns of the Emperior and Emperiest. A surge of power has the tendrils shooting out to connect with the other horns. As quick as a flame-licking oil, the entire herd lights up in a graceful wave of ghostly silver light, with two gold beacons at the front.

If I hadn't been trying not to breathe, my breath would have gotten stuck in my throat. The allure of magic is both mysteriously beautiful and terrifyingly lethal.

My soul vibrates in my chest with anxious anticipation. My shakiness has surprisingly gone away ever since I got personal with Illyrical, so I don't understand why my instincts make me uneasy.

The Emperior and Emperiest unleash a powerful snort. A puff of silver smoke rushes out and collides with the dome, highlighting its size. Together, they scream with a skin-shredding moo, triggering the entire herd to echo their cry and pulsate the magic around their horns.

Countless short bursts of bright light ignite when the Tauruns hit the dome. The flashes cause Adom, Watson, and Rawldur to shield their faces. Everyone in the dome's proximity cannot handle the light except me. My spiritual power got activated without my doing so. I can make out the herd running into the dome at a faster rate than those who can get through on the other side. *Maybe the barrier is thicker.*

I direct magic to push me forward and fly over to the dome. I don't need a big opening. Being in my spirit form allows me to travel through anything as long as it isn't warded. How was I able to get into the arena after Bralyant's fight? The glass-like ward wall must have had a weak spot...

Oxygen rushes into my lungs as I drop to the ground. Screams of horror and anger explode out of me as I dig my nails into my scalp while taking in the carnage.

The Tauruns are making it through, but in mutilated pieces, as if they were being sent through a meat grinder. Piles of ground-up beings are blocked from view due to the flashing light. They aren't even breaking the dome; they are just opening a tunnel big enough to allow them through. How they are being killed isn't what's terrifying me most—it's that the herd isn't stopping!

TWENTY-SEVEN

I direct magic into my cloak and fly back. If I hadn't gone up, we wouldn't have known what was happening until it was too late.

Watson, Adom, and Rawldur are turned away, shielding themselves from being blinded by the light. Adom is kneeling, forming something in his hands from elemental magic.

"We must stop the Tauruns. Rather than breaking the dome, they are being slaughtered by running into it!"

Rawldur growls, and Watson lets out a huff. "There is only one way we can get the Tauruns to stop." Tendrils of fire and metal swirl around Adoms' left palm, while tendrils of water and shadow curl around his right. "The magical command the leaders cast out was for them to charge into the dome. With them dead, the authority over controlling the herd goes to whoever is next in line."

A huff of irritation comes from Rawldur and Watson.

"Even if their son was here, he couldn't command them. He's a newborn infant!"

Adom nods, pinching his brows together even more as he concentrates on the item taking shape in his hands.

"I know. The rules of monarchy for the race aren't ideal for this situation. Our only option is to threaten the herd to divert their attention, but then they will go after us until we are neutralized, and then they will return to attack the dome."

"Is there no other way to pull them out of the command?"

Rawldur whines as Watson lets out a whimper.

Adom exhales a sigh of relief as the elemental magic is drawn back into his necklace, leaving behind a pair of spectacles.

"We would have to remove their horns."

Not only is Adom's proposal nearly impossible, but a Taurun would rather die than have their horns removed. A dehorned Taurun is a mark of dishonor and curses those who follow in their bloodline.

"We can lead them away from the valley and set up a trap. Caging them is the best option we've got."

Adom hooks the dark metal frame over his ears and rests it on the bridge of his nose. Through the hazy glass lenses, his eyes are obscured. The fact that he's no longer tense and can face me indicates that the spectacles he created must be able to shield him from the light at my back.

"They know what they signed up for, Freyja. Every one of those Tauruns knows the potential cost they would have to pay to break the dome."

"The dome isn't breaking though! Their magic seems to only be allowing them to get through. We are going to cage them."

Watson snuffs in agreement as Rawldur lets out a low, guttural groan to Adom. "I might be the Commander in Chief of the Allied Army, but we joined up with the Faithful Army, led by Goddess Freyja. Her word is the law."

Rawldur nods and growls at us while gesturing behind him.

Watson nudges me with his head, pushing me towards Adom. "Context would be great."

"Rawldur will divert their attention." Adom grabs me by the waist and lifts me onto Watson's back before I can put up a fight about being able to do it myself.

I reach down to help pull Adom up, but he shakes his head. "I'm going to direct them towards the North woods. The Atlanteans are setting up the cage as we speak." His attention shifts to Watson. "Get our Commander a safe distance away. We can't lose her."

Adom smacks Watson's ass, and to my surprise, he doesn't growl or bare his teeth at Adom. He becomes flushed with heat as a shudder of shock ripples through his body, pushing him to take off running.

"You do know that I can fly off you, right?"

Watson grumbles as he veers to the far side of the dome, closer to the river. Not a soul is over here. And if there wasn't a battle in the distance, this patch of valley would be peaceful.

While Watson tilts his head away to avoid the light, I slow my breathing and press my fingers on the sides of my eyes. My spiritual power activates, but, only my eyes shift. A silver blaze makes up the dome with star-like webbing, keeping the shape of the dome and disbursing the magic.

This angle allows me to witness the slaughter of the Tauruns entering the dome. There is a thickness to the shield-ward, almost the exact length of their stature. Once their horns make it through, there is a flash of bright light, and they are pulled off. The rest of the body is ground into a paste. The horns are piled up behind the palisade wall by a liquid magical substance. *Why are the horns not being damaged? Why keep them?*

A deafening, mighty roar ripples the dome, freezes the blaze, and stops the flashing light.

As I deactivate my spiritual power, the herd of Tauruns goes flying toward the far side of the dome, and the tunnel seals instantly.

Watson and I recoil as an outburst of mooing screams disturbs the battle in the valley. Judging by Watson's shaking, I'm not the only one terrified. Facing a stubborn Taurun is comparable to fighting a frenzied Harpy.

A ring of fire erupts out of thin air around the dome's base. They grow like pesty weeds, causing the visibility to shift from being clear to a smoky haze. I can only make out blurs of figures moving.

The skull-splitting bellows of the Tauruns fade, telling me that Adom and Rawldur must be using themselves as bait to lead the herd away. Without asking if my assumptions are valid, voices come through the brand, confirming what is happening.

"We need to gather the Wiccayens to—"

Watson lifts his nose in a huff, drawing my attention to who is approaching. Lyons ride forth with Wiccayens on their backs. *Adom is a step ahead of me.*

"Goddess *Freyja*." A mystical, feather-light voice of enchanting wonder purrs my name. "I see you still haven't considered adorning the battle dress I crafted for you."

Watson and I swivel our heads around, searching for the source of the disembodied voice.

"Tell me." A claw-like nail tugs at my bottom lip while a strand of my golden-copper hair is twirled out of the corner of my eye. "Have those bulky adhesions of metal served you well while wielding magic?"

The muscles in Watson's back tighten. He turns his head as far back as he can go. A snarl curls his lips, revealing fangs. With a huff, glittering magic rises from his blueish-white fur.

Watson's magic outlines a petite and curvaceous silhouette that I've had the pleasure of exploring.

I lean forward. "Are you disappointed that you couldn't sneak up on me in a more devious way, Vianre?"

Cackles of malicious lust and delight toss the silhouette of my friend's head up in the air.

The invisibility spell she must've cast flutters off her body with a snap of her fingers, as if a hundred butterflies with reflective bodies chose her as their perch.

Brown leather palm-less gloves cover her arms. An irresistible shade of red leather covers her shoulders. The thicker material is layered, like petals overlapping one another, with the top section curving up at the ends. Her trench coat is the same shade of red, with gold shimmering throughout, as if the article of clothing had been painted with a mist of fresh blood mixed with the sun's strongest rays. The high-collar corset has a slit in the middle that shows off ample breasts and a sliver of her moon-touched skin. Sun-shaped gold buttons run the length of her leather skirt, matching the color of her gloves and heeled lace-up boots.

The Wiccayen race comprises Witches, Warlocks, and Wizards, and all have similar tastes in fashion. Only one is allowed to wear red, their Nexurous Supreme, the Crowned Mistress of Morgannaelmore.

Flawlessly straight, sun-worshipped hair rests on her shoulders. Velvety crimson lips smile at me as her long lashes innocently flutter, emphasizing her shadowy black eyes. A red leather tricorn hat with peacock feathers on one side completes her outfit.

Watson drops down quickly, causing Vianre to bounce off his back. She lands on her feet as gracefully as a cat. If I hadn't been holding onto him, I would've been tossed off too.

She whirls with a devious grin, curving her lips and showcasing her pearly white teeth. "Oh, Watson! It's wonderful to see you. How is your big sister faring? Getting divorced is a bitch."

I leap down when Watson tenses. He faces Vianre, lowering himself down to get face-to-face with the five-and-a-half-foot Crown Mistress as if he's seriously planning to pounce on her.

"Watson! What the fuck are you doing?"

He knows better than to attack the leader of the Wiccayen race, especially since she isn't actively harming him. Being sent to Wardalyn would be a mercy compared to what Vianre could do as a form of punishment. She loves to add more statues to the collection in her garden.

Vianre doesn't take her attention off Watson as she shushes me like a baby who is crying for no good reason.

"You know, just the other day, I thought about how I might be able to help Reason through this difficult time, and I came up with an idea. Hear me out!" She takes a confident step toward him. "I am positive that rubbing my sparkly bundle against hers will bring a smile back to her face. What are your thoughts?"

Watson lunges before I can direct soul magic into my limbs so I can have the strength to hold him back from Vianre's taunt.

She narrowly avoids his teeth as a mist of some kind of glimmering blue potion explodes in his face. Watson yips as all of it goes into his nostrils. Every muscle on him bulges as if he were given a performance enhancer. Like Haidion, Vianre has an invisible magical pocket where she holds her potions and supplies.

"Simmer down your boiling cauldron. I jest, of course." Watson lets out an annoyed huff at Vianre as she walks up to his side and rises on her tiptoes to reach his ear. "Let the big, bad boy out. You already keep one part of yourself hidden. Don't suffocate the beast's needs as well." To my utter shock, Watson relaxes and licks her cheek, making Vianre bounce joyfully. "Go fuck them up!" With a hard slap on Watson's ass, he takes off with a howl.

"Uh…" I raise a finger in the direction where Watson ran off, too. "What did you do?"

She rests one hand on her hip and twirls a strand of her hair with the other. "I killed two birds with one stone. Watson's beast wanted to come out and play, and I know that you would've flipped your shit if you knew he was only here to babysit you."

My soul whirls as fire not only courses through my veins but also burns the back of my throat. "Babysit me?!"

Vianre skips over and takes my hands in hers. "Please don't blame my friend. He was only following orders, which was why I used a potion on him so Bralyant would blame me and not my snuggle bunny."

I direct magic into my brand and scream, even though I know it's pointless. *Fuck you, Bralyant!*

After taking a deep breath, I squeeze her hands. "I won't."

Vianre squeals and throws her arms around my neck. She lifts herself off the ground to kick her little feet, expressing her gratitude. The scents of lavender and coconut drift into my nostrils, calming my growing fear of how to demolish the shield-ward dome.

I wrap my arms around her, keeping the strain off my neck. "Since you refer to Watson as your snuggle bunny, I take it you care about him a great deal?"

She nods against my neck. "I would say I love him like a brother, but siblings don't cuddle with one another unless…" She gives me a knowing look when she pulls away. "…there is a terrible snowstorm." I burst out laughing as heat flushes my cheeks.

A pang strikes my heart as a memory tries to surface. I turn into my shoulder as I choke on my breath. Before the rot attempts to feed on me, I push aside the cherished memories of the best winter solstice celebration I've ever experienced and reach for the fire burning in my veins. The anger Bralyant awoke is enough to keep the rot away from my heart and soul.

"I'll know if Bralyant tries to send Watson back over here or if he's coming." She plays with a wisp caressing my cheek. "I used a spell to keep in touch with my friend during battle, and… it kind of connected with his one to Bralyant." Given there is not a single red blemish on her skin, it's obvious she does not feel an ounce of regret.

As I set Vianre down, she places quick kisses on my cheeks and forehead before releasing her hold on me.

"Why was Watson setting himself up to attack you if you're friends?"

"We have a rule about not messing around with each other's siblings." She spins on her heels and heads toward the dome, throwing me a smile over her shoulder. "I'm glad Freyr and I didn't enter into the same agreement."

Vianre vanishes faster than I can blink, with no trace of magic left behind. I'm at a loss for how she could disappear without the use of any spell or potion.

The Wiccayens dismount and form a circle around the front and sides of the dome. While they clasp one another's hands, the Lyons remain close, ready to roar or attack anyone who threatens to disrupt the Wiccayens as they spell cast.

A red figure appears more towards the front in the last free space. When Vianre joins the others, an incredible flash of silver light illuminates the siphons within their bodies. The shimmery light grows outward like roots and wraps around their linked arms, connecting their magical channels so they can become one.

The flames before them brighten to a shade of yellow that could put the sun to shame and rise until they connect at the top, forming a cage around the dome.

Spirited chants intensify the tendrils of light after the Wiccayens complete the first séance of a spell. The light pulsates when they finish the second, and after the third is completed, the cage around the dome begins to spin and then compresses.

Rumbles ignite the black clouds above in a pattern of flashes. When the lightning doesn't strike, I glance around. Paranoia creeps into my senses and has me second-guessing my instincts. The signal couldn't have meant anything. Something is coming, and I can't alert anyone.

Water sloshing and a murky smell of disease and death are carried on a bone-chilling breeze.

I whirl toward the Blessiver Soula. The river is rising.

With a thrust of magic, I fly to where the last Wiccayen, a wizard given his hooded cloak, stands. He pulls in hazy-pastel magical energy with his free hand, muttering a low chant with the others nearby. All are oblivious to the water creeping up the hill.

Even if I were to drain myself dry, I wouldn't be able to freeze the river. I have only minutes to decide to alert the Wiccayens, breaking their chant, or fly to the front of the dome where the Lyons are so they can alert Adom.

Skjoldr hums in my chest, reminding me of how little magic I have left and proving that I can't face what's coming.

Magic fills my cloak, and I fly back to the front of the dome. After informing one of the Lyons what's happening, a few dozen return with me. To save my magic, I ride on a Lyons' back.

TWENTY-EIGHT

The water has risen to the hill's peak, yards away from the Wiccayens. Per the voices speaking through the brand, the water is doing the same on the other side of the dome.

Ambar's voice speaks over the others. *I'm on my way to you, Freyja. Whatever you do, do not disturb the water!*

As she says the words, the Lyon I rode on widens his stance and inhales deeply. Stepping in front of him would tear me to pieces; all I could do was scream for him to stop, but it was too late. His mighty roar pushes the water back.

The wave travels down the hill, over the river, and onto the other side. An unnatural force pulls the wave back, growing twice as tall as before as it hurtles towards us.

I form my hands into fists, raise my arms above my head, pull down, and crash my forearms together. A shield wall of ice, twice my height, forms. I slam it into the ground in front of the line of Wiccayens and brace myself for impact.

The wave crashes on the bank and barrels up the hill with a vengeance. As water pummels against my ice wall, the waves consume the Lyons.

Sweat pours down my face as my arms shake from the force pushing against me.

I remind myself to keep breathing and reinforce the wall. Given the saltwater pounding against me, my ice isn't going to melt as fast. Since the water isn't going through the dome, my ice wall pushes the wave away, preventing the warriors behind me from getting consumed, unlike the Lyons.

When the water begins to pull back, I break my arms apart and gather the ice to wrap around my upper body. The current is strongest in the middle, not allowing the Lyons a chance to gain their footing. I can only watch in sympathetic misery as they barely hold their heads above water as they float down the hill. They disappear once the wave rejoins the river.

Before the water settles, it creeps back up the hill, this time faster. Skjoldr hums in my chest, alerting me of incoming danger as my instincts pick up someone approaching me from behind.

"Freyja!" Ambar calls out as she launches off the Lyon she rode on.

As her chest rises and falls rapidly, tears well in her brown eyes, diluting the richness. "When none of us could get ahold of you, we thought you—" Ambar lets out a terrified gasp.

Gone is the concern for my well-being as her attention shifts to the river. Her nose wrinkles in disgust as her eyes widen in disbelief. Fear drains the gold stenciling from her exposed skin as she walks down the hill, towards the rising water.

I rush to her side as she lets out an agonizing scream and falls to her knees. Tears stream down her face as she cups her hands to collect a pool of murky, foul-smelling water in her palms.

"Why does the *Blessiver Soula* reek of death?!"

"Because my men were hungry, Captain." An unbelievably beautiful voice of danger and charm lures my focus to the river.

Teal onyx eyes gleam as they catch the faint rays of the sun seeping through the cloudy sky above me. The Siren's metallic mauve scales shimmer and emphasize his formidable frame. Scars on his abdomen, limbs, and neck, as well as a bite mark on his right hip, show the viciousness this Siren has endured, proving he's a fearsome predator of the ocean.

The scales on his face shift as he pulls himself out of the river, revealing the breathtaking satin-opal skin of his humanoid form, which begins to sparkle in the dim light. The fins on his eight-foot body, from the back of his neck to his hands and feet, fuse to his scales as if they were merely tattoos.

Straight, long, ombre hair in sea-inspired colors sticks to his sculpted chest. On either side of his head, pointed, finned ears grow. And, for some reason, he's exposing the bulge of his cock and balls rather than concealing them beneath his scales, which are thicker than most armor.

Having a large package is great if he knows how to use it, but more importantly, there is no need to put it on display for battle. It would be the first spot anyone would strike. *Actually, I think that's just me.*

Ambar is on her feet in an instant. "Eterna, your mother, the *Cheriefi* of the Oceanic races, and the Mighty Kiani of the Sirens made a treaty with the Atlantean King to not hunt in the *Blessiver Soula*." The gold stenciling pulsates back to life, accentuating the intensity of her anger. "I do not doubt that you were educated. Why have you done this, Murrdirel?"

Each step Murrdirel takes causes the water to push further inland. I glance over my shoulder; the water has reached the Wiccayens' feet.

"She did make that promise to Adom, as well as allying with his army and pledging our race to serve as enforcers to the lords and ladies, ensuring their rules are followed." He scoffs. "Sheriff of the Sea. Knowing that title would become mine filled me with honor and pride, but no longer." When the gills on the sides of his neck and torso try to take in air, his body shutters, forcing him to breathe through his nose. "My mother's talk of peace with the land dwellers earned her many enemies. I would have remained by her side if it hadn't been for this."

With a flick of his wrist, a clam shell skitters across the water and stops before my shin, hovering in place. The polished white bone with the trident emblem on top indicates that the shell carries a message from the Mighty Kiani. Only the middle prong is filled with coral magic, while the other two are empty.

I rub the spine, causing the shell to slowly open. An iridescent bubble bust of Eterna takes shape. She smiles with the tenderness only a mother would greet a child she loved dearly with.

"Kailani." I fight off the hypnotic effect of Eterna's Mermerrayl tongue. *"We all thought that the Fate of Freedom named you so because you*

would be the next Mighty Kiani of our race to lead us towards a future beyond our imagination. But Freedom has destined you to be more. The depths of the ocean will never liberate your soul. They will only ever be the walls of a cage, keeping you from growing into the powerful being you were meant to become. Please accept this gift. Toss the medallion into a body of water, and a portal to your freedom will open. Farewell, fate-blessed child.”

The bubble pops, revealing an empty shell with a foamy cushion of blackened moss.

Ambar lifts her gaze back to Murrdirel. “What has this got to do with you tainting the river with the death of innocent souls?”

Coral mist explodes in my hands. As the crumbling shell falls into the water, something shiny catches my eye.

“My mother tried to convince me that allowing Kailani to leave would provide her with the sense of freedom she desired so she could be happier here.”

“You are still not making any sense,” Ambar remarks.

I squat in the water and comb through the grass and shell debris. Even though I can’t see due to the murkiness, I keep my eyes peeled in case I spot a shimmer of a shiny object.

“Kailani is my fated mate!” Murrdirel wails with the strength of a raging sea, causing the water to shift the smooth object away from my fingertips. “My mother knew and gave her what she needed to leave me before I could tell her.” It sounds like he’s crying, but I’m too concentrated on my task to look up. “I realized how foolish I’d been in putting my trust in my mother and how ignorant I’d been in blindly following her without questioning her actions.” His tone evens out as the tip of my middle finger brushes a metal object. “No longer will she brainwash another soul.”

“What have you done?” Ambar’s voice shakes as I clutch a thin, circular object.

My soul whirls with excitement, and my heart beats faster as I pull my hands out of the water and take in the silver medallion.

“I heard the tail end of my mother’s message to Kailani when I went to her grotto to ask her to take a night swim with me. I sent one of my scale minions to retrieve the shell while we were out and listened to it after I left her.” His voice cracks as he stumbles over his words. "My heart... shattered because... I knew she was going to... leave me." He takes a deep breath, trying to smooth out his voice. "I confronted my mother. She tried to convince me that what she'd done was for the best. All I saw was red. My vision only cleared after I shredded every scale from her body."

I rise to my feet and examine the coin. The side facing me is etched in a dialect I don't recognize. The letters bend and transform into a language I can read, Earthradonic. *"Toss the coin into the sea, and Freedom will deliver you to me."* A ghostly aura is layered over the coin. Little specks glitter when the light hits as if microscopic, winged insects are orbiting the medallion.

My soul twirls with selfish delight, urging me to toss the coin into the water, but the reality of what Murrdirel said hits me. The medallion to Kailani's freedom is in my grasp, and she doesn't have it.

"You admit to killing your mother?" Ambar asks with intense authority.

"Yes..." His grief chills the water as it rises to my knees.

Ambar exhales a long, disappointed sigh as silver light fills her hands. "I hereby arrest you, Murrdirel, for the murder of your mother under the law of the lords and ladies, the governing monarchs of the United Races of Earthradon."

Murrdirel sags his head and shoulders as Ambar approaches. When a wheezing sob escapes him, I trail my gaze down his body. His breaths are familiar to me. They are painfully sharp when he tries to take deeper breaths. I recognize the despair dimming the light of his soul and the darkness gradually devouring energy from his dazzling aura.

As I take a step towards him, some type of magic I'm unfamiliar with ripples over his face. If I hadn't been looking at his reflection in the water, I wouldn't have seen the translucent mask cover his face before his scales shifted back into place over his humanoid skin.

He lifts his head. "Oh, Ambar." His sorrowful visage and grieving eyes vanish instantly, replaced by a vengeful smile. "You're such a wild little thing, aren't you."

Ambar comes to a halt when he begins to sarcastically chuckle; the magical mask he donned concealed his shattered soul and only displayed the clever predator luring us in with his stunning eyes.

"Do tell me how you intend to restrain me, given how much water you're standing in."

"Freyja." Ambar's bizarre, silver magic dissipates as she clutches the handles of the swords at her hips.

A pained wince leaves Murrdirel's lips while my brand hums. Ambar's voice enters my mind. *Get out of the water and as far away from it as you can.*

Don't! Murrdirel abruptly implores, then drops his voice to be unbelievably gentle. *You can't run, Freyja.*

Only when my friend's cursing voices enters my mind do I realize Murrdirel didn't speak aloud. He spoke through the brand.

"How did you—?"

Murrdirel cuts me off. "I'm on a tight schedule and have an offer to make, Captain." His attention shifts to me. "But first, let me clear up any confusion. The skin-melting moss is only neutralized after hearing the message three times. Now that the medallion is out of my mate's grasp, I intend to keep it out of her possession so she doesn't have the chance to escape." The intensity of his stare has his lower lip wobbling.

"And you don't think I won't give it to—"

He cuts me off again as he turns his gaze back to Ambar. "King Adom," Murrdirel's commanding voice drowns out all the other voices in my mind. "You are to disband the Atlanteans from the Allied Army and renounce the lords and ladies as your governing rulers. Then—"

"Adom doesn't have access to communicate through the brand," I interject.

"I know. I want all who ally with him to hear this as well." He gives me a shallow nod as his eyes drift further down my body before he picks up where he left off.

"Then you must pledge your allegiance to the Oceanic races. As the Mighty Kiani of the Sirens, I will testify to your loyalty to the newly established Sea Lords Alliance. You will become a Lord of the Sea. All in the alliance will protect the underground portion of your kingdom instead of just the Siren race."

The pulsation of the gold stenciling on Ambar's face tells me she is conveying everything Murrdirel is saying to her cousin.

"Once you agree, we will pull back our armies and let the land dwellers continue this battle. But if you don't agree to anything that I've said..."

Scales shift on his chest, revealing a star siphon shaped like a starfish. The coral-tinted magic glows fiercely, indicating the full capacity of raw power at his disposal.

"I will flood all the tunnels leading to Atlantis. The Oceanic races will consider you prey along with all the races that live on land and fly in the skies."

Ambar curses at him in Atlantean while numerous shouts and snarls come through the brand. "You should've returned the siphon when you decided to disband your race from the URE. That's what an honest leader would've done!"

Coral light pulsates from the siphon. It's larger than the five that the Gatekeepers have combined. After a second, it clicked how he obtained such a powerful item. The lords and ladies had a trident made to help the Cheriefi bring order to the Oceanic races. Murrdirel didn't just keep the weapon. He removed the siphon and attached it to his body.

"My King is on his way here to give you his answer." Ambar side-steps, placing herself between Murrdirel and me.

Murrdirel chuckles with eerie excitement. "I don't mind waiting for his answer, but..." He rubs the bridge of his nose, "...as I said earlier, my men are hungry, Captain."

From the river, a chorus of devastatingly seductive wails arises. Each thrust of the petrifying harmony makes the water lap at my thighs, further numbing my legs.

Startled roars quickly escalated into desperate cries as the group of Lyons that came with Ambar were pulled underwater. One of them was only a couple of feet behind me.

Pools of blood rise to the surface, discoloring the water and perfuming the air.

Ambar attempts to suppress a sob, but it transforms into a painful moan. "Why did you bring only men to fight? Where are the women?"

That should be the least of Ambar's concerns right now, but I can tell she is stalling. If there is one thing that Sirens love more than feeling superior to others, it's hearing themselves talk.

Ambar and I cannot fight Murrdirel and the many Sirens in the water around us all on our own. We need help. Until either more Atlanteans or Adom come, all we can do is keep his attention off killing the Wiccayens who are still in their trance to break down the dome.

Skjoldr's hum in my chest weakens, as does the lower half of my body, as I am numbed to the bone. If I were at my peak of magical strength, I could fly above and throw ice daggers at the shadowy blobs moving in the water, but I must use my magic sparingly.

"The females were…" Murrdirel rubs his temple.

I hope he takes all the time he needs to answer Ambar's question since no one else is being killed. Fates forbid that something else goes on while he's talking that could divert our attention from him.

"Let's just say they were not happy at the sudden shift in leadership since my mate was supposed to be the next ruler. Even though I told them she was planning on leaving us, they didn't believe me. So, I sent them away to where my mate is to give them a chance to think about their choices before angering both their Mighty Kiani and the High Lord of the Sea."

"You're a High Lord?" Ambar asks as calmly as she can.

The Atlantean Captain might be trying to prevent our situation from escalating further by asking him questions that will only fluff his ego, but a tether in me just snapped.

"You locked them up!" Murrdirel's proud grin falls as I interrupt his grand tale of how he rose to become High Lord of the Sea.

Ambar might have been able to overlook the detail he disguised about how he dealt with those who spoke out against him, but I can't.

Before guilt can weigh on his mind, heart, and soul, the emotion is replaced by one I know too well, anger. "Keep talking and you'll be sent there as well!" He blurted out in warning.

His threat is lost on me, as is my interest in the bit of metal in my grasp. "If you truly cherished your mate, you would want her to be happy. Controlling her will not make her want you, and threatening the female warriors will not make them fear you. Both your people's respect and your mate's love must be earned. If you continue to force your will upon them, you are going to find yourself in a lonely and miserable eternity."

A wince causes his eyelids to squint slightly, as if I've caused pain to the vulnerable parts of his existence. Rather than following Ambar's lead, I will take a different approach. Now that I've gotten past his arrogance and the shield of anger, I know how to reel out the other emotions he's trying to suppress. Perhaps this mask he put on earlier was to help protect his state of mind, just like the one I wear to prevent soul rot from draining my vitality.

"Fly. Away." I ignored Ambar's mumbled warning.

Each step I take is like walking on glass due to how numb my feet are becoming. I round Ambar, giving her a wide berth so she can't reach out and try to stop me.

Murrdirel's gaze is fixed on the space between us as if he can't believe I'm approaching him.

"You're on the path to imprisonment!" His heartbreaking tone feeds my determination.

The water lapping at my hips scratches against my armor like serrated claws. Each wave is more excruciating than the one before it. My fight or flight instincts are screaming at me, and the erratic dulled humming in my chest from Skjoldr is urging me to fly out of Murrdirel's sight.

Though the being I'm approaching may be dangerous, but he's also suffering. Soul Rot normally doesn't make itself known to its host for weeks, but that's not the case for those infected by someone else. I don't know if my theory is correct until I can feel inside him.

If his actions are influenced by his mate bond, I have a way of finding out. I slip the coin inside my forearm armor so I can use both hands.

Honestly, having a magical tether connect two souls against their will is terrifying since most couples are strangers. The magic system and the Fates linking the beings together aren't romantic in the least bit since they aren't taking into consideration the souls they are condemning to be with one another. I'm severely thankful I'm spared from this.

The closer I get to Murrdirel, the more I hear an echoey, haunting noise, as if something is crying for help. My blood chills and it's not from the cold water. How I'm able to pick up on Murrdirel's soul must be due to my enhanced hearing.

"Please," Murrdirel mumbles too softly for anybody but me to hear him as he hardly moves his lips while redness creeps into the corners of his eyes.

The last thread of common sense to possibly sway me to listen to any of the warnings to get away from the Siren snaps. Everything he's said to me has been a clear message to get away, but laced in his arrogance was a silent cry for help, and I'd be damned if I ignored it.

Ambar's gaze penetrates the back of my skull. I know how stupid and reckless I'm being. The majority wouldn't dare admit this, but all races on land are doomed if they find themselves faced with an Oceanic race. Over the centuries, most have forgotten that over seventy percent of Earthradon's population is in the water. Not only are we outnumbered by them, but their living conditions are far more perilous than those on land will ever have to experience. The water is our only means of protection against them, but only if we aren't in it.

With only feet separating us, I must crane my neck back to maintain eye contact. Since Oceanic races can detect phantoms, I need to be within arm's length of him before I activate my spiritual power.

The water shifts around me, triggering a sense of claustrophobia.

Something moves out of the corner of my eye followed by a forceful push of water, causing me to almost stumble into Murrdirel.

Ambar utters a distressed cry, and Murrdirel's eyes are drawn to something above me. "*Stand down, Aireie,*" he firmly orders in his Mermerrayl tongue.

I glance over my shoulder to check on Ambar, but my view of her is blocked by... oh, fuck me. Her gasp was not because something had breached the water to attack her. Instead, it was a reaction to the solid mass of midnight lavender scaly muscle standing mere inches behind me.

"*The longer you delay, the more suspicious they'll become.*" The Siren at my back whispered his urgent warning in a low tone. "*I'll get her out, but you need to act—*"

"Murrdirel!" The Atlanteans' King's voice booms from behind me and is accompanied by a chorus of chants matching the strength of a tsunami.

"*Now, brother!*" Aireie's command causes the wailing of Murrdirel's soul to change from hopelessness to agony.

Murrdirel lifts his hands just as the siphon on his chest starts to glow. The water surges forward, pushing me back against Aireie's painfully solid chest.

Impatient Sirens, all ready to slaughter, fill the air and vibrate the water with horrifying wails. Most would consider it a battle cry and prepare themselves for an attack, but those who have fought against the Oceanic race know better. The Siren's game of who can litter the surface with more floating bodies has begun.

A tall wave containing darkish blurs wipe out the line of Wiccayens from the corner of my eye. One by one, the flames surrounding the dome thin to nothing, stopping the progress of breaking down the shield-ward magic.

"I'll see you on the other side, you foolish guppy." Murrdirel's voice wavers as he murmurs in Mermerrayl, his eyes glazed and fixed on the Siren standing behind me.

"I'll beat you there, you unruly urchin." Aireie's cockiness wanes, his chuckle sounding more like a gloomy groan.

When sturdy hands grip my shoulders, I'm snapped out of their tender moment and become a dead weight. The sudden jerk down is enough for me to twist out of Aireie's hold. I turn towards him and thrust my hand towards his face. The momentum of my icy blast has him flying out of the water.

Murrdirel surges towards me. Feral fury has taken the place of his grief. The sudden shift is one that only an elder sibling is capable of when they believe they have failed to protect their younger sibling. With a wince, I push away the haunting memory of my brother reacting the same way and direct the remaining ice on my body onto my palm.

My palm freezes on Murrdirel's abdominal muscles as his chest collides with my outstretched hand. With a twist, we dive into the murky, freezing water. I wrap my other arm around his neck and my legs around his hips right before he starts to spin us underwater.

When I don't let go, his large hands come over mine, trying to pry me off him. Fearful concern creeps on his face ever so slowly as the seconds pass, and he fails to break my frozen grip off him.

"Let go and escape! This might be your only chance," Murrdirel viciously gurgled.

When I shake my head, a pained wail leaves him. He stops us from twirling. My nausea is relieved, but my head keeps spinning for a while longer. Being submerged in water has helped me expel the last of the air out of my lungs faster than I would've done above the surface.

"I'll do it for you then." Murrdirel digs his fingers into my hair. "May the Infinite Sea have mercy on you, Freyja." He gives my scalp a hard yank.

Water fills my lungs and assaults my eyes as we shoot to the surface. Darkness fills my vision as I cough so hard that the muscles in my legs and arms lose their strength, and I slide off him. If it weren't for my hand still being frozen to him, I would've been submerged in water once again.

As I steady myself to remain standing, Adom calls out to me, just as Aireie wails to Murrdirel. Their voices clash, and I can't determine what either of them said.

Murrdirel gives my scalp another yank. The searing pitch of my scream sharpens the air, causing all who are nearby to shriek in terror as if their eyes had been gouged out of their sockets.

"Call off the Allied Army, Adom! Or I'll send your commander to a place where no one will hear her screams." I blink the darkness away as Murrdirel's free hand slides down to the armor on my forearm.

I press my free hand over his heart, but the pain he's caused makes it impossible to push the last of the air out of my lungs. Even if I could, the war chants of the Atlanteans overpower my senses. I can't tell if my heart is beating or not.

"Call out my name, Freyja!" I'm unable to identify the frantic voice, but their desperation tunes me into the energy of a threatening force about to be upon Murrdirel and me.

I don't have time to help him. The realization hits me so hard that tears leak out of the corners of my eyes. I'm powerless, just like I am when I am unable to fulfill all of my believers' prayers.

With no other options, I turn upward to the sky and scream. "Time!" I bawl my soul out, hoping the all-powerful Fate will be drawn to my plea. "I need more time!"

Tears stream down my cheeks as the thorns of the rot push into the tender spots of my existence. Darkness once again tries to coat my vision, but I push it back and fight the desire to collapse from exhaustion.

"Please! Anything! I, Freyja, will give you—"

Energy shifts in my magical reserves. Astro-black mist explodes from my hands, creating a web-like dome around the two of us. A paint-like texture fills in the gaps, blocking out the world and light around us. Only the faint glittering of delicate light buzzing around provides us with enough illumination to see one another.

A familiar intimacy embraces me, soothing my soul and drying my tears, reassuring me with gentle strokes down my nape that whatever exists beyond the dome will wait for me.

It takes me a second to realize that this magic isn't from being blessed by the Fate. This is the magic that Illyrical gifted me. The mist is identical to the kind that he had hidden us in back in the woods.

"Do you have any clue as to the type of magic you're wielding?"

The drastic change in Murrdirel's voice from harsh to soft makes me flinch and triggers the energy around me to charge as if ready to strike him.

Murrdirel's hand loosens from my hair as he takes in the dome surrounding us. His fingers release my scalp, and something cool strokes the tender area. I shudder from the soothing relief and almost take in air to let out a moan.

From the back of my head, the coolness travels down my body. My muscles are caressed, a silent plea for me to allow whatever is embracing me to take on the burden of standing if I only lean back. I don't know if the spiritual tranquility offered to me is an effect of Illyrical's magic, just like how Haidion's shadowy-star magic would protect me without being asked. I don't have time to ponder or to divulge in the comfort.

Concern creeps to the forefront of my mind, followed by an intrusive thought that has me second-guessing myself. *What if the gifted magic won't stay up long enough?*

Hmm, odd. Normally I hear my brother's voice in my subconscious to talk some sense into me, but this time, I heard Haidion's.

Murrdirel whips his head around. "What the fuck?" A thousand terrors flash through his eyes, dulling them to gray. *What's spooking the shit out of him?*

With Murrdirel distracted, I activate my spiritual power and sink my hand into his chest.

His head jolts upward as I grasp his beating heart in my palm. The Siren's face contorts in shock, then disbelief, and finally horror, petrifying his body, all while his attention is locked onto something beyond me, preventing him from looking away.

An idea that only Haidion would have come up with has me conjuring his voice. *I wonder how many tugs it would take for him to bleed and which orifice it would leak out of first.*

The corner of my mouth twitches while a chuckle tickles the back of my throat. It always fascinates me how a being reacts to my probing inside their soul.

Since Murrdirel caused me pain, I'm tempted to let the darkness I keep buried out just for a second to play, but I'm already providing him with enough nightmares to last him for eternity.

I swear I hear Haidion teasingly whimper the dome I made, begging me to reconsider before I drive the darkness back. I blink the absurd thought away.

One of my theories about his odd behavior is disproved when I encounter no thorns. With a gentle push, I sink my fingers in deeper. Dozens of delicate, velvety strands of twine part for me as I reach further in for his mate bond.

Murrdirel jolts when the back of my finger brushes against the muscular thread. Passionate heat pulsates frantically from the bond as I run my fingers up to where it's knotted. I let go of my control, allowing my power to activate fully.

A haze greets me, confirming that I am a spirit. My attention is caught on the web dome, and I hesitate to reach forward with my other hand. Around us isn't just a blanket of unique magic but a living entity, given how the shape fluctuates like muscles, flexing and relaxing, and the warmth pulsating like blood moving through veins. The delicate lights buzzing around have more of a shape, one of a flying insect. This magic is beyond anything I've ever seen, and I wonder if Illyrical is more than just in touch with his inner beast, but a Rarity.

When the webbing of the dome starts to thin and the size starts to cave in, I push my other hand into Murrdirel's chest. With considerable slowness, I ease in, making my way to the center. My fingertips brush against the strong cord. As I trace the thread, I note a pattern of ridges. That's odd. After a couple more strokes, I realize what's different about it and freeze. Something is wrapped around it.

The texture of the second thread is silky. As I tug on the strand to get a better feel of it, the thread tightens around the muscular bond, causing the heat radiating to violently pulsate. When I don't remove my fingers right away, something nips them, and a malicious energy sizzles throughout my hand. I don't know what the tendril is, but my instincts tell me it harms Murrdirel's mate bond.

After grasping the bundle again, I slid my fingers to the top and located where the silken thread had knotted itself. To my surprise, the tendril is not connected to the soul like the others but rather has a strangling grip on his mate bond.

With meticulous concentration and painstakingly slow movements, I untie the knot and work to unwind it. Once I reach the bottom, I find one more knot. To keep myself focused, I don't pay any attention to the decreasing size of the web dome and take comfort in the steady beating of Murrdirel's heart.

The muscular thread flexes when I unwind the last of the tendril. Murrdirel's mate bond blazes with vigor as I pull my hands out of his chest. He lets out a shuddering sigh as tears run over his smiling face.

A gasp of relief escapes me, pulling air back into my lungs. My spiritual power deactivates, causing Murrdirel to blink at my sudden appearance. Recognition smooths out his furrowing brows and awakens his soul to shine in the depths of his eyes with gratitude as if he knew what type of magic I used on him.

"Freyja..." His esteemed voice cracks as his lips tremble. "How did you know—?" A terrifying gasp rushes out of him as his gaze darts away from me. "What the fuck is that thing?!"

To my utter shock, my other theory about Murrdirel's odd behavior proves to be correct. Something was influencing him, but I have no idea what the fuck is in my grasp.

Since I'm not in my spiritual state, I shouldn't be able to see what I pulled out, let alone Murrdirel being able to. But as clear as day, a worm-like creature of black, luminous light is trying to squeeze itself out of my hand. Besides the silky worm being able to stretch itself out, there are no other distinctive features.

"Is that a leech?" I shake my head, unable to look away from the wiggling creature. "What in Tide's tomb did they infect me with?"

"Are you saying someone put this inside you?" I meet Murrdirel's eyes, and he defeatedly nods his head.

Before I can ask who, he clears his throat. "Freyja…" His eyes start to swell with tears, and the grieving sadness from earlier surfaces. "I'm in no position to ask you for anything, but I hope you won't mind fulfilling this one request for me, especially after what I did to you." He takes a breath to try to steady his trembling voice. "I need you to kill me. Once I'm gone, the title and magic will shift over to my mate. Kailani will have the power to free herself and our female warriors and liberate the Sirens and all Oceanic races from the corruption that plagues our waters."

"You're free now. You can make things right yourself."

He shakes his head. "No, Freyja. This is my fate, and I have accepted it." A gentle smile brightens his eyes and warms his skin. "I planned to get myself killed by Adom today, but you were able to detect that something was off about me and were willing to risk your life to help, even though you barely know me. Having this moment of being free from that creature and feeling my mate's happiness through our bond is more than what I could've asked to experience in my last minutes alive." The Mighty Kiani of the Siren Race and the High Lord of the Sea fell to his knees before me. "For what you have done, I, Murrdirel, offer you, Freyja, the magic of my last—"

I slap my hand over his mouth. "Don't you dare finish that vow."

An immortal's last breath is when the most powerful form of magic is generated from their soul. A dying wish is so sacred that nothing, not even the magic system, can influence or stop it. The only time I'd seen that wisp of fluttering light, similar to a butterfly, was when Hercules gave his last breath to bless the Spartans. Because of it, they are on the path to becoming their own immortal race one day. I had always wondered what Freyr's last breath was and if it came true. The magic was designed to be the immortals' last wish so they don't die with any regrets or fear of abandoning their loved ones without the reassurance that they would be alright.

"Offering your dying wish to me for something I selfishly desire is a grave disrespect to the sacred magic." I bring my other hand closer to him, and his eyes dart between the worm and back to me. "I'll put this creature back inside you if you don't nod, agreeing that you won't finish uttering that vow."

When he nods desperately, I remove my hand and pull back. "What about your fated mate? You're just going to leave Kailani?"

He lifts his chin high. "She deserves someone better than me." His eyes dart around the dome. The mist is thinning. "Please, Freyja…" When our gazes meet, specks of light flutter away from the corners of his eyes like leaves falling from a tree. *Is his soul crying?* "Help me free the ones I love."

The waning of the shadows surrounding us allows light to enter. As if a pocket were opened, I'm given a peek at what awaits us. Even though the spirit of chaos is wreaking havoc, everyone seems to be moving at a fraction of their speed. Sirens are dragging Lyons into the river. The Wiccayens are in waist-deep water, trying to form a barrier of silver light to prevent a wave from crashing down on them, and the Atlanteans are fighting the Sirens underwater.

If we can't get the water to recede, the Unfaithful Army will easily win the battle. Only four races… well, three now since the Nymphs have been wiped out, can fight against the Sirens on their turf. If taking Murrdirel out of the picture will tip the scale back in favor of saving the Father, then I must do it.

Murrdirel's lips tremble to form a thankful smile as I nod in agreement. A squeezing in my chest causes wetness to glaze over my eyes, and each breath I take has me shuddering. Rather than be racked with guilt about being unable to find another way to save Murrdirel from the fate I will be delivering him to, I bury it down with all the other chaotic emotions I've experienced since I left my home last night. *But first, how am I going to get rid of this creature?*

Fingers of gentle grace travel up my arm. The barrier of my armor does little to protect me from the intimate sensation. Goosebumps rise as the fingers glide, stopping at the back of my wrist. Slow, sensual strokes circle my weary joint, then swiftly travel to my clenched fist and seep between my knuckles. My hand is being held as if by a faithful friend, and when the cool energy lightly squeezes my sore palm, I know what the magic is asking of me. Since I put my trust in Illyrical before, my doubts about his magic helping me are nonexistent.

With the slightest relaxation of my hand, the creature darts out and back towards Murrdirel. He falls back into the water, the worm a mere inch away from his chest. The creature whips around violently, straining to close the distance, but the energy surrounding my hand is now humming in front of me. It's no longer soothing but irrevocably lethal as it holds back the worm.

The tip of the creature's head turns towards me. Dread coils in my stomach right before a scream rips through me. The same malicious energy from before slithers up my ear canal.

Murrdirel's panicked voice gets cut off. My hearing has become impaired.

Not knowing what else to do, I claw at my ears, wanting to get whatever is digging into my head out. Teeth of sizzling energy sink into my mind and start to manipulate my thoughts.

Help. I need help. Someone, anyone, please! I try to scream, but I can only feel my lips moving and air being expelled. My pleas I can only hear in my mind.

I hear you, Freyja.

The darkness in my mind expels the energy as a fire of smoke and shadows explodes out of thin air before me, consuming the worm and the dome.

A wisp of coolness soothes the hurt the creature caused my ears and strokes the parts of my mind that were assaulted.

I'm utterly grateful that Illyrical's magic acted to protect me just like Haidion's did.

My body shakes from the violation, and I nearly collapse. Fatigue cries out from every joint and muscle, wanting to rest from not only the trauma of what I just endured but also the hours I spent fighting with no sleep.

"Freyja." Multiple voices call out my name to get my attention.

Murrdirel is before me. "You're blessed by the Fates." It's more of a statement than a question.

"No, I'm not. Why would you think such a thing?" I pant breathlessly.

He blinks at me. "You have to be. How else could you have wielded Fate magic?"

"Freyja!" My name is called out again by a familiar, deep voice.

Adom runs towards me, parting the water as he does with the intensity of a nurturer determined to save their offspring. The memory of my brother overlaps, causing my lungs to cease and my heart to pound in my ears.

"Fuck! We are out of time. You must act now, Freyja."

The booming of my blood pumping harder muffles Murrdirel's voice, but there is no mistaking the urgency in his tone. I pull my attention away from the heartbreaking image and ignore Adom's cries for me to run to him.

My legs give out as I rush to close the gap between Murrdirel and myself.

Murrdirel lunges forward and wraps his arms around my waist. "I got you. I'll hold you the entire time if that's what you need, *brave sea filly.*"

He sits back on his heels, and I take advantage of his study frame to get my footing. "I'm no baby."

His gritty chuckle stills the rushing of my blood. "You're a *rambunctious calf* in my eyes."

I brace my hands on his shoulders and pull myself away slightly to gaze down at him. "And yet you have faith in me to help you?"

"You are Freyja, goddess of your word." He stops himself from reaching up to tuck a strand of my hair behind my ear and instead sends a stream of water to do it for him. "Freyr would be so proud of you."

I close my eyes to prevent tears from falling, but I can't stop my lips from trembling. "I always keep my word." I lean forward and press my forehead to his. *"Thank you, Murrdirel."*

"It is I who owe you a thanks, Freyja." Murrdirel expresses his gratitude in Atlantean.

He draws me in for a hug that only an older brother or sister would give a younger sibling. His scaly touch makes me shudder as his hands press into the small of my back, where my skin is exposed. It's been centuries since I've received such an overwhelming and loving embrace. Steadying my breathing to prepare myself to uphold my word has never been easier, but still, I mutter a prayer. *Brightest star in the sky, give me strength.*

Adom's Atlantean tongue curses from behind me. I snap open my eyes and drive my knee up into Murrdirel's groin.

He releases his hold on me and topples over in pain. Once I get a safe distance away from him, I pull the medallion from under my armor and toss it into the water beside him.

A portal is spun open by celestial light, and the gossamer threads do nothing to stop the water from rushing into the void of darkness.

"No!" Murrdirel lunges towards me, but before his hand can graze mine, muscular arms wrap around me from behind and pull me out of his reach.

Ice rushes to my fingers, and with a punch in the air, mist shoots out of my palm and pushes Murrdirel backward. He thrashes to escape the suction of the water pulling him towards the portal, but it's useless.

"Freedom! The coin wasn't meant for me." His voice begs for the Fate to hear his plea. The passionate worry in his eyes pierces my battered heart. "It was to free—"

Murrdirel's voice fades as he gets pulled into the void of darkness, but the portal doesn't close.

My feet are swept out from under me as a grunt of pain comes from Adom. I slip out of his grasp and get sucked into the current.

Skjoldr hums frantically in my chest and directs my magic to my feet. Ice coats my shoes, and before I can get my footing to cement myself to the ground, a stronger tug from the portal jerks me closer.

My magic gets redirected into my cloak so I can fly away, but an ache in my chest from the thorns stops the flow.

Blood pumps hard in my veins, feeding my tired muscles. With every ounce of strength I have left, I fight against the pull of the water.

Ahead of me, Aireie fights with Adom as I thrash. Without a backward glance, I know I'm only moments away from being taken into the void of darkness.

Adom's eyes lock with mine before Aireie drives his fist into his jaw. The Atlantean King escapes my view as he flops into the water, and my last shred of hope goes with him.

My friend's name echoes in my mind and makes its way to the tip of my tongue. I don't know why the thought of calling him would help.

A force from underneath pushes me out of the water. I fly into the air, scrambling like a baby bird as Adom's head breaches the surface from where I was before.

My cloak jerks me to a halt, stopping my ascension into the sky. Relief soothes the concern on his beautiful, pained face as my gliders deploy. I might not be able to remain in the sky, but at least I can get safely down to the ground without the help of magic.

My grateful smile mirrors Adom's, but it quickly alters to project my soul-crushing screams as he gets pulled into the void of darkness.

I slam my hand on my chest plate to pull in my gliders so I can dive down and reach Adom faster, but the mechanism doesn't do anything. Skjoldr hums in my chest when I try to direct magic to deactivate them. *Why are you doing this to me!?*

Only my screams reach my friend. Adom presses his fingers to his lips and raises his arm to the sky. Since his gaze is fixed on me, I feel the warm brush of his lips against my forehead as he bids goodbye.

Numerous screams and shouts emerge from the battle below, but it is Ambar's heartbreaking wails overtake the others as the portal closes.

I'm no longer in control of my tears. The drops rain freely on the calming water below. I only wanted Murrdirel to be taken. He didn't deserve to die, and there was no other way for me to help him besides sending him away. But I didn't think it would've led to the risk of Adom being taken as well!

Pain that I only experienced once in my life surfaces. Adom might not have been my brother, but again, I wasn't strong enough to protect myself, and I failed yet another person who had such high hopes for me to be a beacon of hope and strength.

Skjoldr takes control of my gliding descent since I'm a sobbing mess. I focus on pulling anger into my heart to stop the thorns from draining what little magic and energy I have left.

When the Fate of Freedom extends her help, those who take it are stripped of what responsibilities and titles they held, freeing them from who they were and severing anything that. tethers them to the galaxy from which they came. It gives their existence a clean slate. The portal leads to the Infinite Sea beyond Creation's Galaxy.

For Murrdirel, I saw using the medallion was the better option since he wouldn't have to die for his mate to receive the title and power to free and lead her race. Maybe they can be reunited since they are fated, but that's solely my wishful thinking. I didn't consider that Murrdirel would be happier if he died so Kailani could find love with another. I chose to not believe him when he said his mate deserved someone better than him. Murrdirel deserves happing after all he suffered and what he was willing to sacrifice to help those he loved.

This way of thinking goes against my opposing opinion that connecting two beings against their will isn't romantic and couldn't lead to love. The fact that the mate bond was in his soul tells me that the two willingly chose one another, and from the passionate heat coming off of it, their love wasn't fabricated for them. They formed it themselves. *Ladiya was right, I am a mate-wrecker.*

CHAPTER
TWENTY-NINE
ELEVENTH HOUR AFTER SUNRISE

The anger I built to reinforce the shield wall around my heart strengthens and sickens me. My aggression is making me both resent and hate myself. Allowing these corrosive emotions to protect me will only last if I keep reminding myself of my failures. I might not be in danger of the soul rot sucking away my vitality and magic, but I am assaulting my mind with harmful words to keep my anger fueled, which will cause detrimental harm to my mental state. If I had any hope that I would survive this battle and live on to have a happily ever after, I might be more concerned, but I am destined to die, and this is how I'm choosing to go out, saving the Father and all of the beings who inhabit Earthradon.

My feet land on the damp grass at the top of the hill, and I nearly slip due to the slick surface.

As I steady myself, Atlanteans try to grab hold of anyone they can with roots, either pulling them back up the hill or holding onto them while others dive into the water and swim to their rescue. Atlanteans can breathe underwater for extended periods and swim faster than any land race, allowing them to have a fighting chance at surviving in any body of water.

Strong hands grip my shoulders, and I'm spun around. Ambar

grips the nape of my neck, pulling me down to be at eye level with her. Even though her hold is tight, she's shaking.

"Adom..." She chokes out her cousin's name as if it is painful to say. "Where did...he...go?"

I know Ambar knows from her reaction, but the desperation in her voice shows she doesn't want it to be true.

I gently place one hand on her neck and the other on her shoulder. "He's free from our galaxy."

The gold stenciling on her skin loses its rich hue and depletes to the same shade as the ash painted on her face. A glowing soul frantically flickers like a flame in the depths of her eyes, trying to grab onto any amount of oxygen to stay lit while suffocating.

Angry sobs break free from her as she presses her forehead into my chest. She doesn't muffle her wails or swallow her tears, not caring about drawing anyone's attention. I was the same way when I lost Freyr. Adom might not be dead, but he's gone forever.

All who are in our proximity halt what they are doing as they gaze upon their shattering captain. Dozens of Atlanteans who aren't reeling people out of the water drop to their knees and press their hands and foreheads to the ground, uttering a prayer.

A red-dressed figure weaves between the Atlanteans, minding not to touch or disturb them. Vianre meets my eyes as she briskly walks over to us. Even though her features are soft with empathy, her aura emits determination and strength, both attributes the leader pressed up against me needs to have right now.

"There will be time to grieve. Your people and the Allied Army need you." Vianre's feather-light voice causes Ambar to stiffen against me.

Before Vianre can lay a comforting hand on Ambar, I'm pushed away, and the Atlantean Captain strides away from my friend, causing her to stumble back.

"I know what is expected of me. I know who I need to be." Ambar stops when she reaches the tip of the hill before it descends to the river. "I'm just not ready!"

Atlanteans fight Sirens while warriors of the Allied Army get either pulled out or dragged out of the river. I'm not sure how many more people are down there who need to be rescued, but the water is rising again from the combined efforts of the Sirens wanting to reach the top of the hill again.

At our backs, the Allied Army and those Faithful to the Father build a defensive barricade to keep the Unfaithful away from our closer proximity to the dome, both on the ground and in the air. But each second we are unable to break through the barrier separating us from the Great Willow Tree, the closer the Father's death is approaching. Judging by the shaking in Ambar's clenched fists, she is thinking the same thing too.

Vianre takes a step towards Ambar. "I wasn't ready either. I lost my husband when I won the trials to determine who was the most powerful to duel the Nexurous Supreme for the crown. As the Wiccayens' first female ruler, I didn't have any Elder Madams to ask for advice, nor was I given guidance by any of the Elder Sirs, even my father, because they wanted me to fail. No one was there for me when I needed support the most, but I'm here for you."

Ambar turns to look back at me. "I should've listened to Adom and stepped into the position sooner."

"There is no shame in taking your time. Don't judge yourself so harshly. By doing so, you're only disempowering and undermining yourself."

"Freyja is right, Ambar. You can't dwell on what you could have done. You need to focus on what you must do." There is not a trace of offense in Vianre's tone from her previous statement being disregarded.

More tears run down Ambar's cheeks. "This is not how I imagined displaying my power as a ruler." She turns to look back towards the river. "I wanted my first act to be as memorable as all my family members who came before me. Like my grandfather, who carved out a river to bring water to the driest parts of the continent. Like my aunt, who built Atlantis, a utopia for all who live in insufferable climates to settle down in and thrive. Or like my cousin, who allied races that had been at each other's throats ever since the century-long war over territories."

Vianre takes another step towards Ambar. "Leading the Allied Army to protect the Father will be one of the most memorable acts any leader could achieve—"

Whispering voices pull my attention to shimmering tendrils of silver light coming from behind us.

The silver strands are floating out of the dozens of Atlanteans who...I jump back and almost fall from slipping on the wet grass again.

I take in the warriors. They're nothing more than a soupy pile of gooey flesh, bloody organs, mushy muscles, and soggy bones. While tree roots start to consume them, the tendrils fly over to Ambar.

"Ending a battle is just as impressive as preventing one—" I step forward and pull Vianre back to me, cutting her off from the motivating speech she was giving Ambar.

When she begins to protest, I grip the sides of her face and turn her to the tendrils. She tenses, noticing the magic floating toward Ambar. I release my hold on her and she turns her head to follow them back to the decomposing corpses.

Vianre leaps onto my shoulders like a scared cat who has gotten wet and is seeking higher ground.

Ambar shudders when the tendrils begin to wrap around her fists. A pained sob leaves her as they work their way up her arms. The whispering voices become a chanting hum, causing the silver light to pulsate like a heartbeat.

One tendril goes to her ear, and she lets out another sob. *"Your sacrifices will not be in vain."* The broken tone of Ambar's Atlantean tongue has Vianre sniffling above me.

Pairs of grotesque arms shoot out of the ground, causing Vianre to shriek and fall off my back. I catch her legs before she falls.

Ambar's attention is drawn to the disturbance. She turns hesitantly as if she doesn't want her last ounce of hope to be drained.

A delicate gasp of shock and relief escapes her as disbelief flushes her face. She looks down at her arms, covered in silver light. Tears fall as she murmurs how grateful and unworthy she is to receive such help.

She is neither terrified nor bothered by the sight like Vianre, which makes me think she and perhaps her race are familiar with whatever creatures are surfacing from the ground. None of the Atlanteans who are witnessing what's coming from soil are concerned, saddened, or horrified. Instead, they look upon the graves with wide eyes and anticipation, as if a blessing is about to be bestowed upon them.

The hands quickly dig themselves out of the sticky, foul-smelling soil. Seven bodies made out of a liquefied concoction of the soupy remains and tree roots spiral together and weave to take form as they pull themselves out of their graves and rise. All are double my height, almost twelve feet tall. Their humanoid bodies have no distinguishing features besides their biological gender.

Vianre tries to right herself to sit back on my shoulder, all the while mumbling as if she is trying to talk but can't.

I pull her down and turn her to face me. "What is it?"

Her eyes are almost bugging out of her head. "Why are you not freaking out? Do you not know what they are?!" Before I answer her, she cuts me off. "Those are Wuirrls! You know, one of the divine races from the Kingdoms of the Cosmos that are on the outer edge of the universe."

Wuirrls. Those were the creatures Vahildra told me about after we ran through the forest back on Crescent Island. I thought he said they were a galaxy race, or maybe that's how I interpreted them. The only races that I know exist beyond Earthradon are the galaxy races, but after being told from both Ambar and now Vianre that there are kingdoms out wherever the Cosmos is with more races I don't know about, it's making my head spin and scream. *Why didn't Freyr tell me about them?*

"Do you not know what they are?" I shake my head, unable to form words. "Wow, okay, well, they can only take shape when they consume remains and magical minerals. I knew they guarded the Father's roots, but I didn't know they willingly worked with the Atlanteans."

There is no way I would've turned down learning about other beings since I wanted to know how to write and communicate in every language. If Vianre knew about them, then there is no reason why Freyr wouldn't have known since they were close friends. I'm about to curse out my brother's name if this is another moment of his method of me learning when I'm supposed to be taught about it rather than overwhelming me as an adolescent and shoving it down my throat. *I fucking hate feeling like an idiot.*

I swallow down a painful grunt to not unleash my frustration and anger but rather harness it to fuel myself. "I don't think they offered their help willingly. More like the Atlanteans called upon them, offering up their bodies in return for their aide." *All to help their grief-stricken captain.*

Near and far, Atlanteans bow their heads. Regardless of whether the Wuirrls are aware of their presence or give them their gaze, every single member of the race bows.

The Wuirrls walk up to Ambar as one. One of the males stops before her. The other two males stand on her left side while the four females stand on her right. The lead male reaches out to lift her chin to him while his other hand wraps around her left arm. Before Ambar can strain her neck, the Wuirrl's body contorts to bend its upper portion so they are face-to-face. From my point of view, I can't determine how close they are.

Ambar speaks to him. Her voice is muffled as if something is pressed against it. She gags slightly as if something is...

Vianre covers her mouth and gags as the Wuirrl steps away from Ambar. A pair of tendrils from his body slither out of her mouth and left ear.

Bile would be rising in the back of my throat, too, if I hadn't had centuries of experience witnessing the heinous things Haidion performs on the targets he is told to kill.

Ambar nods to the Wuirrl and turns around to face the river. The male straightens to his full height and moves to her side, but not before wrapping his arm around hers, leaving her hand free. He strokes her inner wrist as she magically signs in Galex.

"You four, find Kailani and free her. Kill those who want her to not become the Mighty Kiani of the Siren race. You three find Murrdirel's brother, Aerie, and keep him out of Kailani's way. Once she takes the throne, if she doesn't want him around, then do with him as you wish. Questions?"

They shake their heads in unison.

The Wuirrl breaks the arm that was around Ambar's. As his arm regrows, the spiral of minerals and remains consumes the metal on her left arm and the magic from the deceased Atlanteans. Ambar's armor and the silver light combined with the spiral. All four move harmoniously and remain around her arm like a loyal pet.

The Wuirrl, who must be their leader by how all look to him, nods to Ambar as his body hardens. All the others follow suit, and as one, they leap forward, each growing fins before diving into the river.

"Stop all rescue attempts!"

On Ambar's command, the Atlanteans release their hold on the roots leading to the water as those in the river scramble to get out. Some are able to bring the ones they rescued with them, but the majority have to leave them behind.

Sirens tear into those left in the water while others remain at the river's edge, sending us menacing looks and waiting for the water to rise up the hill we are upon.

"By my authority as the Atlantean Queen, I deem the *Blessiver Soula* a threat to the Father." All the tendrils of silver light finished wrapping around Ambar's arms. "All who are in the water, this is the only warning I give. If you do not wish your fate to be tied to the *Blessiver Soula*, make haste to the ocean." The gold stenciling on her skin pulsates back to life.

Sirens wail from the river.

Ambar takes a deep breath and runs down the hill. With each step she takes, her pained cries turn into chants.

Thunderous bangs vibrate the ground beneath my feet and increase in intensity the closer she gets to the water.

The beat reaches a peak and suddenly cuts off right as Ambar leaps in the air.

Everything becomes silent as if the noises around us were sucked away, from the wind bristling from the storm above to the Sirens gleefully echoing their thirst for carnage.

Vianre and I hold our breaths as Ambar descends into the water.

Sirens gather below her, forming a circle where she will dive into the river.

Once her feet touch the surface, she is consumed by both water and Sirens.

A beat more deafening than a crack of thunder shakes the ground and assaults my ears as silver light explodes, parting the river.

All of us on the hill are hit by a sonic wave, knocking us on our asses. Once the wave subsides, I scramble back to the top on my hands and knees.

Ambar stands in the middle of the riverbed, whole. Her arms are extended at her sides as silver light beams out of her hands.

The water shoots up, forming enormous waves on either side of her. She empties her lungs in a scream. An eruption of star magic mixes with the silver light. Before the waves break on the surface, they turn to crystalized stone, along with the entire river.

Ambar's screams turn into wails of pain as she sways and collapses. All the noises of the battle and storm above come back in force, muffling the distressed cries of the Atlantean Queen as the magic continues to be expelled from her.

I scream her name as I get to my...

Hands grip my shoulders, preventing me from standing up.

A blur of furry darkness leaps over me. Aliith hits the ground and runs down to the riverbed.

"No, Freyja! You will be turned to stone." Artemis pleads, grasping my shoulders from behind. "Aliith can stop it and save her."

When I nod with a huff, she lets go of me so I can stand.

Before I can walk over to offer Vianre a hand, Artemis pulls me in a bone-breaking hug and doesn't let go. She clings to me. It's almost as if she is holding on for dear life, fearing that I'll slip away from her.

I wrap my arms around her waist and cave into her affectionate embrace.

When Vianre clears her throat, I lift my attention towards her. She brushes dirt off her backside while eyeing Artemis with suspicion.

"Aliith offered himself to be your servant as a mortal. Besides being bound to live as long as you, by what magic, other than shifting into any creature you desire, is he able to help her?"

Artemis stiffens in my arms and turns her attention towards Vianre, not breaking from our embrace. "Uh, he has access to my magic, of course. That's how he can shift." *She's a horrible liar.*

I speak before Vianre can. "Crowned Mistress, you need to round up the Wiccayens again. The rest of the dome needs to be taken down."

Vianre is skeptical of Artemis' claim, but now is not the time for them to engage in a debate over the legitimacy of what magic a servant is or isn't allowed to use or for Vianre to question what magic Artemis possesses to help Ambar. We can't afford to lose anyone else, so the why and how aren't as crucial for her or myself to know right now.

The use of my friend's title has her attention turning to me, and as I hoped, she nods and turns on her heels.

When she is out of sight, I lean toward Artemis's ear and whisper,

"Under other circumstances, I wouldn't have redirected her because I, too, want to know how Aliith was able to help Ambar. I suggest you become a believer in the Fates and pray to Memory if you don't want either of us to hound you for an explanation once the battle is over."

I kiss her on the forehead and let her go. The last I heard of her was when Illyrical told me he had fought against her. I'm glad to see neither she nor Aliith are harmed.

"In due time, you will know." No denial or deflection; Artemis' statement is firm, leaving no room for doubt. "When the moment comes for him to tell you, please be patient with him. He's moody." She pulls me in for another hug, a different one than before, one she'd give someone she... "I love you, Freyja. Stubborn ass and all."

Since I anticipated her comment, I was able to deflect the emotion from affecting me, which only heightened my anger.

A boisterous laugh captures my attention. "I did love my ass, but after sitting on it for hours while drugged, I'm starting to hate it."

Artemis pushes out of our hold, shrieking, "Po Po!"

Her attention lands on her brother, and she bolts for him.

Apollo's short, golden hair is gleaming from the sun at his back. Some of the longer strands obstruct his view and snag on his scruff, but they can't contain the joy in his baby blue eyes. The bronze sheen on Artemis's olive skin glows, matching her brothers. Even the magical luster in her gold-plated armor matches his.

"I go to sleep, and you two let the world fall into chaos." Artemis jumps into Apollo's waiting arms, causing him to grunt and laugh some more. "You see, this is why I can't ever take a break." He holds her close and buries his face into her shoulder.

Seeing them together makes me think that maybe it wasn't because the Nymphs went extinct that their appearances dulled. Perhaps it was because they were separated from each other. *Could love be powerful enough to affect a being's magic?*

I dismiss the thought and turn my attention away from them for a moment before their display of sibling love stirs up my grief.

"Freyja." Apollo's endearing voice pulls my attention back to him. "I heard your voice in my drugged state. The wind carried the words you spoke to where we were being kept. I swear on my magic that's what helped us to awaken." He pulls an arm off Artemis and extends it to me, welcoming me to join them for a hug. "Freyr would be so proud of you."

When I nod my thanks and don't move towards him, he shakes his head and mouths, "So stubborn," and wraps his arm around Artemis.

"How many of you got drugged?" I ask.

Apollo presses a kiss to his sister's forehead when she buries her face into him more. "A couple hundred, but only about fifty of us came here. The rest chose to sit this battle out and remain neutral."

Anger boils in the back of my throat over the actions of my fellow pantheons. The Father gave them all life, and this is how they repay him: by turning their backs on him when he called for our aid. Does loyalty mean nothing to them?

The actions of the gods and goddesses who are deserting the Father by becoming neutral speak of how naive they are. No brain cell in their minds must be working because if I were in their position and woke up to a battle going on to take the Father's magic and kill him, I'd be concerned about what that would mean for my magic and existence.

The theory that Illyrical mentioned, which speculated that Earth-radon could still exist without the Father's presence, could be true. But since the Father gave us all life, does that mean no magic would exist here if he were to leave? An argument can be made that the magic system keeps magical vitality flowing through our planet and veins, but who's to say they won't turn their back on us for what we've done by killing a Primordial Deity? These are the thoughts that every person possessing magic should be think about rather than wanting to avoid choosing sides because it's the 'safer' option.

After muttering a mental prayer to the Fate of Chance to be on our side, I clear my throat to soothe my building irritation so my voice is even before I address Apollo again. "Do you know how many traitorous gods and goddesses could be inside the dome?"

Apollo's eyebrows pinch together as he stares off into oblivion for a moment while he thinks. "There were a hundred or so who were going to storm the tree. The rest who sided with them were given other tasks. I blacked out before I could hear what they were planning."

"Did you see Odin?" The mention of my ex's name doesn't awaken my marital brand as it did in the past.

My blood chills as Apollo nods. "I saw him when I arrived at Camp Ariella. He told us all to go into the woods. I woke up from my drugged state to see them drag me into an underground tomb. I saw him enter after I was chained up, but I blacked out shortly after. I was one of the first to wake up, and he wasn't there."

Artemis pulls back and takes his hands in hers; red burns from chains encircle his wrist. "How did you get free?"

He hesitates to answer. "A shadow monster freed us. When I woke, it was breaking the chains with its teeth. I tried to free myself even though the monster wasn't killing the others, but I didn't hope it wouldn't change its mind. When the creature got to me, I swear it had multiple heads because two sets of teeth worked on breaking the chain on my wrists while the third one rested its head on my chest and awoke my spiritual essence. I hadn't realized I couldn't access my magic until the creature pressed itself into me. Once all were freed, the monster left."

Could that have been Haidion's puppy? "By how you described the creature, it sounds more like an Ancient Demonical's Cerberus."

Apollo shakes his head. "I thought so too at first, but this monster wasn't made of fur, only smoky shadows." He chuckles in disbelief. "I can't believe a shadow monster freed us."

"I told you they weren't all bad." Artemis directs a chipper smile at her brother. "Perhaps the Shadow King sent him as his way of helping since he can't intervene directly." Apollo nods towards me, making Artemis turn in my direction, noting my confusion. "My bad. Of course, you don't know much about him since Freyr taught you differently and told us not to share anything with you. Okay, so—"

She rambles about the Shadow King and what he does, but all I can hear is my internal screaming as I curse my brother's name. I have no problem filling myself with anger now. Besides my brother keeping things from me, he told our friends to do so as well!

Thunder cracks overhead, bringing us back to what we need to be focus on. There will be time later for me to ask them why Freyr told them not to teach me important things like there being a Shadow King.

As I turn and run towards the dome, Apollo calls out to me, "Oh, and Freyja!" I look at him over my shoulder. "Isis is gone."

I stop in my tracks, skidding to a halt. "Gone, as in she's dead?"

He shakes his head as he runs up to my side with Artemis in tow. "Her family was in the tombs with me. They chose to come along to fight in the battle, but when Isis was reunited with them, she opened a portal, and they vanished."

"Since when does Isis have portal magic?" Apollo shrugs in response to his sister's question.

I was going to ask the same question myself if she didn't. Gods who deal with the afterlife have ways of entering the planes through portals, but Isis's area of expertise is healing, influential promises, and restoring the souls of the deceased to wholeness. Only her husband, Osiris, can open a portal for her to enter Orrtiereum when he wants her to visit him in their pantheon's portion of Wardalyn.

A memory hits me so hard that my chest tightens and pounds like a war drum. Freyr was long dead, but I still brought him to Camp Ariella for Isis to mend him. Isis was able to bring her husband back, and he was in pieces compared to my brother. I'll never be able to forget her face as she looked up at me after kneeling over my brother for hours, trying to mend his body and call his soul back. The redness in her eyes was from the tears she was attempting to hold back as she uttered the words that made me scream so loudly that Bralyant heard me on the wind back in the war camp that was thousands of miles away.

Before a similar scream can escape me, the darkness in the back of my mind rushes to the forefront. Rather than shredding the memory to pieces, it wraps it up in shadows, severing the connection between my mind and body and preventing me from reacting to it as if the experience had never happened to me. I'm thankful that I found a way to calm down from the episode, and I am amazed at how I did it so quickly.

I can't believe that my stress level is so high that just the thought of Isis's magical capabilities was enough to trigger an internal physical attack and a mental assault from one of the most traumatic memories I have. In the past, when an episode like this occurred, I'd move myself to a calmer environment where I felt safe, but I can't do that now. I can only take deep breaths and do my best to numb myself. *I have a task to do, and I can't fail.*

"I'm shocked she left." Artemis leans into her brother's ear and whispers, "She was determined to kill Dad."

The reality of who is before me and what God I could face once I'm inside has me wondering if my friends will hate me if I'm the one who has to face their father.

"He doesn't deserve to die." Apollo places his hands on her shoulders. "You and I both know this greed plaguing our world isn't natural."

"Are you saying something is influencing him?"

"Yes, but not something. Someone. And I think I know what type of being it is." He takes a breath and turns to fully face me. "Zeus needs to be freed from the whispering voice of greed that has infected his body. Do I have your support, Commander?"

Artemis's face pales. "Fates almighty! That's who you think is influencing him?"

I massage my temple, trying to soothe the headache that's been building from my lack of sleep and is only worsening because I don't know who or what they are talking about. "No matter what, Zeus is to be held responsible for his actions. He is commanding the Unfaithful Army; all these deaths are held accountable on his head as they are on mine."

"But that doesn't mean he needs to die. Nor you if—"

A glittering blood-gold haze passes over Apollo's eyes. If I had blinked, I wouldn't have noticed he was shown either a prediction or a prophecy. He has the power to see the outcomes when the Fate of Chance tosses his coin for an immediate answer to something about to happen or sees the roll of the Fate's dice for something that could happen in the future if certain stakes are put in place. Unlike Athena and Heimdall's power, he can't share what he saw, or it won't happen.

He clears his throat and advances toward me. "Give me the chance to see if my theory is right."

"I'm not going to risk the fate of the Father and Earthradon if Zeus is only seconds away from ripping the his heart out."

Apollo's features strengthen with determination, causing his aura to radiate uncompromising devotion. "Please don't make me tie you up."

I cross my arms over my chest. "Like you have anything that could restrain me."

My confidence from a second ago lessens to half as Apollo pulls out chains with cuffs from his back. "I took an extra pair that wasn't damaged. I planned to use them on my father, but if you stand in my way, they are going on you."

"Apollo Leto!" Artemis uses his full name, the one Hera gave them, so they always remember who their birth mother was. But the name doesn't faze him one bit.

"I'm not backing down, Emi." He keeps his gaze on me as he tilts his head slightly toward his sister. "I want your word that you won't seek out his death, Commander."

When it comes to setting the mind to something, Apollo is one of the few who can challenge my strong will since he, too, possesses the spirit of stubbornness. If I'm an immovable mountain, then he's a persistent bull who doesn't know when it's best to rethink his decision to go head-to-head with me. Odin's abuse might've been his method for trying to control my mind, but no matter how hard he hit, my spirit never broke. Freyr was the only one able to get through my stubbornness and convince me that my way of thinking wasn't in my best interests.

"Apollo, I can't promise you—" A bolt of lightning strikes somewhere behind me, lighting up his eyes, followed by a thunderclap a second later, which mutes my voice.

My instincts, senses, and Skjoldr warn me I should run, but I won't until I know Apollo won't use those chains on me.

Not only does the storm get stronger with each second that I hesitate to answer him, but so does the strength of his determination. It doesn't help that the clouds above us are darkening and trying to cast shadows over his sculpted body and face, but the light of his soul shines through. His beauty transforms from angelic to menacingly magnificent. Before me isn't only my friend but the Greek God of Sun and Light, Healing and Order, Prophecy and Weather, and most importantly, a son who'd do anything to protect and save his father.

Artemis steps forward. "I might not want to believe that our father is being influenced, but I trust you, brother." He looks away from me and turns to his sister, smiling warmly at her in appreciation. "I'm with you, now and forever."

My blood runs cold, exposing the enormous hole in my lonely heart. Their uniting against me should be enough to fuel my relentless determination, but it isn't. If I don't want tears to spring from my eyes or wonderful memories of my brother and me to surface, I have to reach for something deeper. A harsher emotion to protect myself from the rot, but I can't. I could never feel hatred towards them.

I plead under my breath to the Fate of Memory not to let my past affect me, then bite my lip to hold back a wince as the rot crawls closer to my vital organ.

Before Artemis can lace her fingers with his, Apollo wraps his arm around her waist, pulls her in, and presses his lips against hers.

Most would consider this taboo, but action is the next best thing when words aren't enough to express how much you care for someone. Apollo and Artemis' relationship isn't romantic, but everyone chooses to judge them for it. They don't find it weird to kiss one another on occasion, just as Freyr and I didn't mind cuddling, even if there wasn't a storm.

Rumors about the Greek pantheon secretly encouraging inter-family mating and breeding, resulting in incestual blood magic, have been circulating for centuries due to their being more powerful than the other pantheons. All arguments aren't made out of facts, only hate, since the Father created the majority of their pantheon from the Birthing Willows, proving that all who throw accusations at them are resentful zealots. Just because they were brought into existence at the same time doesn't mean they are siblings.

Apollo and Artemis, however, weren't born from the Father but from a Nymph. Because Zeus is one of the most powerful beings on Earthradon, the lords and ladies didn't punish him for breaking the law, but they did condemn Leto to Wardalyn and the twins to be sterilized. Unfortunately, because the operation was done when they were babies, their nymph forms were unable to develop alongside the magic of their mother's race. Being robbed of a part of themselves has only brought them closer together.

After Artemis kisses him back with equal tenderness, she rubs her nose against his. They part and turn toward me. "Please, Freyja." They softly pray in unison.

My decision isn't based on the fact that it's my responsibility as Commander to see to the Unfaithful Army being stopped, but on the fear of being a failure if Earthradon doesn't stay whole if the Father's heart is taken out, resulting in endless deaths.

I have come to terms with the fact that I'm going to die; however, the beings on this planet haven't. Hundreds of thousands of voices are in my head, screaming, crying, and begging me to save them. After centuries of being unable to answer all the prayers I acquire, I won't let anyone stand in my way of doing what needs to be done, no matter the cost. However, my decision will result in two powerful gods turning against me, and above everything else, we need to work together.

My final decision gets stuck in my throat as my breathing becomes sharp.

Pain blossoms in my body, like petals unfurling from a bud. The sensation spreads, causing all my muscles to tighten.

A wave of scorching heat rains down from the back of my head, following my spine, and continuing to my feet. *What the—*

Metal hits the ground as Apollo shoves Artemis down with one hand and yanks me to the ground beside his sister.

White light explodes, blinding me. Thunder booms, deafening me. If the weight of Artemis's body wasn't pressed beside me, I would've thought I was dead because of how suddenly and painlessly most of my senses were taken from me.

Grunts and panting breaths come from Apollo. The contrast of the spidering blueish-white bolts of sparking light in front of him has darkened his frame to become a shadowy silhouette.

I let out a sigh of relief, seeing that he was whole. His body is solid like stone, his arms spread out wide, and his hands clutch a sphere of glassy, golden light sphere.

Despite Artemis' pleas, I sit up more, not believing what I see. In the sphere, Apollo holds a lightning bolt that goes all the way up to the sky, preventing it from striking and vanishing.

An inspiring cry of strength and courage bursts from him as he moves his arms in a circular motion, sucking the bolt into the sphere.

The ground beneath his feet trembles as he gains control of the mighty magic in his grasp. Apollo lunges forward, thrusting his arms out in a shout of aggressive passion. The lightning rod glows gold as the magic blasts out of his hands. He doesn't send it back into the sky, but the obstacle we've been attempting to break through for hours.

Light explodes, but no thunder cracks. The attack is soundless, like an assassin. Hope courses through my veins, chasing away the pain, and a smile spreads across my face when I spot the crack in the middle of the dome. When the gash doesn't reform, a laugh rushes out of me.

The Spartans within the safety of the dome move with haste, getting behind the palisade walls. One runs into the weeping branches, a runner most likely informing the others we are finally breaking through.

Apollo turns to us and offers a hand to Artemis. "Want to attract some lightning for me?"

Artemis jumps to her feet when he pulls her up. "I knew the game of Anger, Catch, and Fire we played as kids would come in handy one day." With a flick of her wrist, her bow appears in her hand, and a quiver of arrows on her back.

"Get Father's lightning to start chasing you." He switches his gaze to me but tilts his head to the side to continue speaking to his sister. "I'll be right behind you once I finish up here."

Artemis whispers, "Please," addressing her concern to both of us. When neither of us breaks our stare, she groans, "Stubborn bulls," before taking off toward the dome.

A memory rushes into my mind when Apollo picks up the chains and walks over to me.

Odin walks towards me. In one of his hands are belts, while the other is balled into a fist. He pins me to the living room floor and restrains my arms and thighs. With him cutting off the circulation in my hands, trying to wield magic is impossible. He pulls me up so my ass is in the air, then jerks my pants and underwear down while keeping my face pressed against the cold wood floor.

"I told you not to go near shadows void of light!" Odin's roar causes my blood to cool.

"I didn't realize that the darkness was unnatural."

I hadn't seen Ominous in months, and when I spotted him lurking in the shadows along the edge of our Winter Solstice celebration, I couldn't stop myself from going to him. Ominous carried me, bridal style, the majority of the way to my cabin. That was all he wanted as a gift, to have me near and talk about everything and anything. I was happy to oblige since it was a long hike.

I rolled my eyes when he said he had two gifts for me. Ominous is an overachiever, but revealing what he truly looks like and his name was something I had never expected him to share with me. I was so shocked at being in the arms of the most handsome being in all of existence that I forgot that Odin left early to retire to the cabin because he was tired.

Ominous created an illusion to make it look like I was walking alone, but I was so used to his shadows that I didn't think they'd look any different from the natural ones in the forest. Odin had spotted me coming out of the woods, sprinted to me, slung my body over his shoulder, and rushed us inside.

Despair and desire were written all over Haidion's fac, while the sparkle in his eyes dulled. He followed in Odin's shadow, only revealing himself to me. His lips had parted to speak multiple times, but no words ever left him. The aura of his presence lingered for a moment after the door was slammed shut, and then he was gone as if he never existed.

"How could you not?! You know what nightmares plague me! You know how fearful I become when I'm triggered by a darkness I can't see through." Odin spanks me four times. "I. Won't. Lose. You!"

My husband is more than scared of the dark. A Rizaver cloaked in a shadowy void of fire assaults his dreams. Odin is tortured ever so slowly, and my being near him causes more pain. He wakes up every time in a panic, holding me and screaming that he will never let me go and that he'll endure the worst torment because me being his is worth it.

Tears burn my eyes from him punishing me harder than usual. "How can I earn your forgiveness?"

Odin pants heavily. "By learning what it is that I want from you without my telling you."

"That's impossible." He spanks my ass with such force that the wood digs into my cheek.

Odin would leave me strapped for what felt like hours. After a century, I learned he didn't want me begging him to let me go or crying out promises of doing better at being a good wife. Those were empty words. He just wanted me to kneel there in silence, like an obedient little bird. My time of waiting might've dropped over the years, but the recovery time never shortened.

With Illyrical's help, the memory is shown to me in a different light. I wasn't a failure as a wife. I was a victim of marital abuse.

Odin removes the restraints and rolls me onto my back. I'm so fatigued that I am unable to prevent him from pushing me over. My ass hits the floor, heightening the burning pain and making me aware of the welts he'll be tending to. No matter if I got battered outside or in the house, Odin always tended to his lovely daisy. That's the only time I'd receive a gentle kiss from him.

Odin kneels next to me, a belt in each of his hands. "Are you with me, or will you fight me, Commander?"

Reality filters back. Apollo is at my side, holding the chains in his hands.

I roll away from him, swing my legs around, and kick him in the chest with all of my strength. Apollo flies back and lands on the ground with a hard thump.

My friend rises with anger in his breath. The spirit of his stubbornness turns Apollo's features into stone, ready to attack me with his horns.

Apollo stops suddenly when our eyes lock. Something deep in his soul flinches. In a blink, the unbending will of his determination vanishes. He blinks again and stumbles, looking down at himself as if he can't believe what he was about to do. His face contorts into an ashamed frown as the light he generates dulls, allowing the shadows from the clouds above to consume him.

"Fuck!" Apollo drags his free hand through his hair, tugging it. "Freyja, I wasn't thinking clearly a second ago. I wanted to help my father so badly that something took over, and I became oblivious to how my behavior and actions affected you. Please, Freyja, you got to believe me." He attaches the chains to his belt and holds his hands up in surrender. "I give you my word that—"

"You threatened our commander!" A familiar voice growled, "Giving her your goddam word means nothing!"

My chest is tight from hyperventilating, and my blood is rushing through me so fast that I'm about to pass out. But as I take in the

Wolven above me, my body relaxes, and my fight or flight instincts quiet.

The Beta Prince towers over me. His sapphire eyes darken to obsidian. The silver halo around his irises spider towards his pupils like webs being formed, ready to capture and consume all light. *I didn't even hear anyone come up behind me.*

Treason keeps his gaze fixed on Apollo as he kneels and hauls me to my feet. A snarl leaves him after his nose brushes up against my neck. He knows I'm not okay without having to ask, but he still does in a whispering tone.

If I say it aloud, I'll break down, and if I admit it to myself, I'll become a husk of who I am because I'll exhaust every ounce of energy I have left in crying from the centuries of abuse I put up with and did nothing to stop. Instead of uttering the word, I nuzzle into his neck.

He doesn't react to my non-verbal answer; he's still like a statue. *Maybe I didn't convey my feelings correctly.*

Treason wraps his powerful arms around me and presses me against his chest. I take in his sweet scent and relish in the safety of the Beta Prince's arms.

At the sound of Apollo's approaching feet, Treason growls and turns us so he's closer to him, not me. "If you want to keep your feet attached to your legs, you will back away. I don't care if you're a God; you intended to bring harm to my commander, and I will tear you limb from limb if you as so much breathe on her."

Something in Treason shifts. His aura emits another signature of the type of being he is. This instinct is how all beings on Earthradon, magical or not, can identify what each other's race is without having to ask.

I don't have the strength to pull myself away to look up into his eyes for my instincts to comprehend what's changed about him. Treason is the only reason I'm standing.

Apollo's voice is muffled, but Treason's is clear. "If you truly think of her as your friend, you will respect her choice of not wanting to talk to you and go do your duty to the Faithful Army. Only your actions can prove the words you speak are truthful. Our commander will deal with your betrayal once she is ready. Now. Leave!" His growl intimidates Apollo into listening to him.

Treason being protective reminds me of my...I freeze in his arms. He reminds me of my brother. Not even at this moment, but ever since I entered the Colosseum, he has been as attentive to my well-being as Freyr would've been.

Fear shocks my senses. Treason found his way behind my shield wall and into the tender spot of my existence. I'm so comfortable being in his embrace that I'm seconds away from crying and relying on him to take care of me. Just the thought of the possibility of someone emotionally supporting me scares me. *What if he's taken from me as well?*

"Freyja, can you wrap your legs around me, or do I need to scoop you up in my arms?" Skjoldr hums and directs my soul's magic to fill my legs. "I'll keep an eye on Apollo after I drop you off at the healing den."

"I'm not going there!" I push out of his hold and then utter a mental thanks to Skjoldr since I would've fallen on my ass from how weak I am.

"You ran into my arms like a scared pup, which is why I'm concerned." He takes a step towards me. "Please allow me to bring you to the healing den. It doesn't have to be for long. Even a few minutes away from the battle can help. No one will think any less of you."

Many thoughts occur at once. First, it's not Apollo's fault as to why I was triggered. He didn't know and didn't deserve Treason's wrath. Apollo snapped out of his stubbornness and realized what he did was wrong, which is a lot of work for someone who is determined. Yes, my trust in him thinned, but I can see why he didn't back down; he'd do anything for someone he loves, as would I. Secondly, I almost broke down in Treason's arms, and now he's seen a part of me I didn't want anyone to see.

I nod towards the battle at our back. "You may return to your Alpha. I am no longer in need of your assistance." *Why did he show up in the first place?* "Wait, did Bralyant send you to babysit me?" My breath hitches when his eyes shift to their normal hues.

"I sent myself to protect my son since he was ordered to guard you. I sensed he wasn't with you, and he was reluctant to tell me why he wasn't. So, after transporting Hera and all the wounded to the healing den, I ran here, fighting along the way."

"I ordered Watson away." I snapped. "Your king's command got overruled by the commander of the Faithful Army."

His presence begins to overwhelm me as he takes another step forward; I almost take one back. "If that were true, Watson would've just told me that rather than tune himself out of our family channel to avoid answering me." He mouths the word "liar."

"If you give me your word that you will run back to your Alpha, I will stick to that story so that Watson will not face reprimand."

Confusion lifts his brow as his gaze flits all over my body, inspecting me like he did with my armor. When his eyes reach mine once again, a smirk emerges in the corner of his mouth.

"You have my word. I will get to my Alpha with haste." All the air gets sucked out of my lungs when he closes the gap between us. "Where do you want me?"

"Not in my bed!" I'm taken aback by the comment I blurted out. *Fuck, why did my mind think his question was something sexual?*

His chuckle shows off his fangs. "Good choice." He leans down to my ear as if he's sharing a secret. "Because I tend to break them." *Oh, Fates, save me.*

I take a healthy step back. "I'm not your Alpha. I'm just your commander. Run back to your king."

"No," Treasons declares with stern authority. "I'm fighting alongside my Queen."

"What the fuck did you just call me?! Never mind, because it doesn't fucking matter. You're just making sure I stay alive so I can retrieve Faithless and die fighting to protect the Father. Otherwise, I mean nothing to you." Treason recoils and stumbles back as if I slapped him. *This is for the best.* "And. You. Mean. Nothing. To—"

Lightning strikes multiple spots closer to the dome, muting my voice from delivering the final blow to get Treason off my ass and out of my heart. Thunder follows, but the intensity of all of them cracking at once has me pressing my hands over my ears.

Even though I'm a distance away, I can spot a circle of Wiccayens formed along the base of the dome. One by one, each of them is hit by a thunderbolt. Their bodies burst into flames and melt before they can cry out their pain or beg the Fates for mercy.

I'm struck motionless by the sight before my eyes. The image of

Freyr being impaled by a dragon spike overlaps with all the Wiccayens being hit. Each strike of lightning flashes the most terrifying image in the forefront of my mind to the point where I don't know how to stop it. How to stop seeing my brother being killed.

I scramble to my feet, fighting the windstorm my brother is hurling at me while he should be concentrating on the flames pounding at his air shield. I had the midnight-green dragon in my sights, and I wouldn't fail at hitting him this time, but my ice spike went off course when Freyr yanked me behind him. He pushed me further into the cave with his elemental magic.

We should both be moving since the last of the Wolven are out, but we're pinned. Aliith ran away with them and used some of Artemis' magic to blind the dragons so they could get away. I was able to take down three dragons while Freyr made it almost impossible for the others to remain airborne. Right after the third dragon fell, the green dragon came with a vengeance.

"Stay the fuck down, Freyja!"

With another backward thrash of his hand, he pushes more air my way. My feet are swept out from under me, and I land face-first into mud.

A growl vibrates my body as I wipe my face clean with Freyr's discarded tunic. "The dragon would be dead by now if you hadn't pulled me away, asshole!"

I clap my hands together to form a ball of frost mist, allowing it to coat my body. Freyr's elemental magic is only an angry breeze compared to a whirling tornado. Wanting to be certain that I won't wind up back down with a face full of mud, I direct soul magic into my legs and stay low as I make my way to Freyr's side. I curse at myself for not following through on my workout regimen to become naturally stronger so I wouldn't have to waste my magic like this.

My chest aches much more than my muscles since I'm tapping into the last of my magic. I'm confident the reserve magic Hera told me about will give me enough to make one more ice spear. If only Freyr would stop working against me, then our chances of killing the green dragon would be in our favor.

Freyr finally stops directing his elemental magic at me and reinforces his air shield as flames burst through. He's also running low.

"For once in your life, can you please tell stubbornness to fuck off?!" Freyr bellows over his shoulder.

With the intensity of the fire, my brother is in his naked glory. If he hadn't magically removed his coal-stone armor and clothes, it would've melted to his skin by now. Only his air magic protects him from getting burned, but he's sweating profusely.

"Maybe for once in your life, you should have faith in me rather than come to my rescue before I call!"

I direct some of my frost mist over to him. He groans in relief as my magic soothes his hot skin.

"I expect a big thanks from Drafasa since I saved his favorite parts from getting burned."

Out of the corner of his mouth, a smile forms. Even though we are both trying to stay cool from the powerful heat of dragon fire and battling the forceful pressure trying to drown us like a waterfall, my brother still manages to humor me, trying lighten the mood.

I don't think of it as a distraction, more like grounding oneself. I was taught to have a tether to tug on when in the mist of battle. A lifeline to help pull me out of a situation if I'm being overwhelmed so I can take a moment to collect myself before returning to my task.

The warmth of our sibling bond pulsating at a rhythmically calm pace tells me he's focused and thankful for my help. I'm Freyr's tether, as he is mine. Now, if only he would have as much faith in me as I have faith in him.

With a deep breath, I send three pulsations down our bond and then blow him a kiss.

His features harden into fearful panic as I activate my spiritual power and become invisible. I duck out of the air shield while my brother shouts my name. My brother's voice is drowned out, but I still feel the vibration of his roars through our bond.

The green dragon landed on the ground, crushing warriors with his body, swinging his tail, and flapping his wings to prevent anyone else from getting close to him. Our only saving grace is that the dragon isn't advancing forward. He's remaining still, an easy target.

I clap my hands together and pull them apart. A ball of my magic whirls in my hands. After compressing it and turning the misty mass into a solid, I pull my hands apart and form the—

A pain strikes my heart as if I got speared. I cry out and clutch my chest as I fall to my knees. My spiritual power deactivates as I gasp for air, causing me to become visible. Each beat from my heart makes my screams turn into ear-piercing screeches.

Something inside me begins to shed like I'm being skinned from the inside out. My spiritual essence's irritating humming from trying to warn me off from attacking the dragon finally dulls, but their presence starts to slip away. Strength, which I didn't even know I could lose, starts to strip from me.

What is happening? This doesn't feel like I'm tapping into a magical reserve. Did Hera lie to me?

Flutters like wings rise from somewhere deep inside of me. The sensation comes to the surface, right underneath my skin, filling the emptiness. A fire that is hotter than a dragon breath ignites from my core and crawls up my throat, causing me to choke. My muscles stretch and rip like something is trying to break—

A startled growl stops the firestorm as the green dragon's attention shifts my way. Dragons can't form facial features, but I can tell through his emerald eyes that he's smiling. Now I know why he's stopping at nothing to try and kill me; he's one of the dragon queen's princelings, given the eyes of the majesty bloodline, and since I dared to cause him harm, he now must kill me or suffer shame from his race.

He rises to his full height and lets out a roar that has me tumbling into the rocky cave. The physical injuries are nothing compared to whatever is happening inside my body.

Whimpers escape me as I cry from how broken I am, but I still try to roll onto my side and rise.

"Freyja!" Freyr is at my side, helping me to sit up. "This wasn't meant to happen. Not now."

He places his hand on my chest, and my pain is soothed by his touch, as if he's healing me, pushing back whatever is trying to claim my body, and giving me the strength I was losing. Freyr doesn't have any healing magic or powers, but I think he must have an ability since a brand becomes visible on his forehead every time. Wait, what was on his face just now? Was it important? Even my thoughts have no clue what I was thinking about, not even a moment ago. Another wave of pain-relieving energy rushes into me. My sigh of relief sends my concern away, never to return.

"If you're talking about the war, that isn't something that can be scheduled. But if you're talking about the dragon trying to kill me, we wouldn't be in this situation if you didn't pull me away."

I try to stand, but Freyr keeps me down. "You would've died!"

"You don't know that!" His features are tight with determination as if he

has proof, but his complexion softens suddenly. "Freyja." This is a first; my brother never backs down from fighting my stubbornness with his own. "I need you to stay here and wait for Drafasa." He takes my hands in his, and the healing aura surrounds me in a comforting embrace like his hugs. "I'll be back, okay?"

His eyes redden, and tears stream down his cheeks. Never have I heard my brother plead or cry in front of me. My stubbornness is disarmed, and the fight leaves my body.

"Okay," I whisper.

Freyr gasps in surprise and relief as a smile spreads across his magnificent face. "I give you my word. I'm not leaving you." He presses our hands to my chest, "I'm with you." With the proudest smile I've ever seen, he leans forward and presses three loving kisses on my forehead.

I shudder at the meaning behind them; it's his way of expressing his love to me. Warmth fills like a river of wonderous energy through our bond as he rises to his feet and goes to the mouth of the cave.

A brownish-black dragon has joined the green one. He's about ready to expel his breath since the green dragon is probably out of gas to create more fire.

Freyr creates his air shield, moving his arms in a precise way—a technique only elemental wielders understand. From my lower vantage point, I catch the green dragon whipping his body around, and a spike from his tail comes off and flies right toward Freyr.

Fire erupts from the brownish-black dragon; I don't think Freyr noticed the green one sending a spike his way. I'm up and running towards my brother, shouting his name. I know he can hear me from the pulsation of the sibling bond, but he doesn't move.

My brother's air shield falters, his magic and strength waning as I feel how weak he is through our bond. Just a few more feet—

My spiritual essence yanks me down as an ice shield forms. I didn't know I had enough magic to make a shield and prevent it from melting from the fire. She saved me. Never has a spiritual essence done something like this for their immortal host—it's unheard of.

"No! NO! FREYR!" I scream at the sight of flames engulfing my brother's body.

Freyr's thunderous roar of pain and wrath is silenced by bone-breaking cracks. My brother's half-charred face is looks back at me. There is no light in his eyes, and his body is limp with a dragon spike in his abdomen, almost severing him in two. He's a god; there's no way he can die. My brother is not dead. My brother is not dead.

I reach for the warmth of our sibling bond, and...it's not warm, it's not even there. It's gone. He's gone!

The darkness in my mind can't keep up with the internal physical attack that keeps assaulting my mind and body as the memory keeps playing repeatedly.

My gasps of panic turn into screams as I fall to my knees. Numerous sharp pains pierce my heart. With each rapid beat of the organ, the soul rot is draining me of my magic and vitality. The magical shield walls I had around my heart have shattered, and now there is nothing in the parasite's way.

A familiar voice bellows out my name. He begs me to allow him to help. Considering the fast rate at which the rot is working, the words I would call out might be my last.

Treason's worried voice speaks both closely and far away, but I can't figure out what he's saying. The Beta Prince shouldn't be focusing on me anyway. I'm not the one getting struck by lightning. While he is fussing over me, others are dying. The thought of Vianre being one of those has wetness coating my eyes and stinging my tear ducts.

"Hand her over. I can help her."

Not wanting to leave this existence with regrets, I muster the last of my strength to call out and say goodbye, but plump lips press mine and take my last ounce of energy.

THIRTY

There's no pain. No thorns. Nothing is draining me of my vitality and magic. I don't remember the last time I felt such relief. Death is peaceful, but an uncomfortable pressure pulls me away from this tranquility of light I find myself in.

I'm jolted out of the serene darkness and into a haziness of dreary colors when fangs retract from my neck.

A silhouette of something darker than night is above me, while a blob of light comes into my view from my right.

"Freyja?" Treason whispers soothingly. "If you can hear me, I'm going to heal you."

A glide of warmth tingles my nerves from head to toe. Something deep inside me purrs, enjoying the mind-blowing sensation. I become more aware of my body with each pass of something slick and hot with soft ridges that would feel pleasurable on my...it clicks as to what Treason is using to heal me with—his tongue.

Someone taps on my right hip. "She's injured here too." At the sound of Aliith's voice, Skjoldr hums back to life.

A pair of faces come into view. "Since that cut isn't serious, I'm not licking Freyja there until she is coherent enough to give me her consent." Treason gives Aliith a deadly glare, reinforcing his statement.

I shoot up from Aliith's arms. My sudden movement sends Treason on his ass. A smile widens his face, relieving the stress lines that formed above his brow.

"I wouldn't move too much if I were—" Skjoldr jerks me out of Aliith's lap and onto the ground with a hard thump. "Or don't listen to me." Aliith drops his arms from a cradling position as if he were holding me against his chest.

"What did you do to me, Aliith?" I press my hand over the spot on my neck and search for a scab or a scar but find nothing. "And you didn't have to heal my wound completely, Treason."

The action of healing takes away from Treason's ability to heal himself when he gets injured. I can understand Bralyant healing my wounds fully because he cares deeply about me, but Treason has children out here fighting who have priority over me. He shouldn't be wasting his magic on tending to my wounds.

"Instead of complaining about us helping you..." Aliith's determined aura dares me to fight him on this. "...maybe you should accept that it has been done, and there isn't anything you can do about it." His mouth tilts up in an arrogant smile. "Or I'll give you something else to waste your breath on." My mouth starts to drop in shock, but I snap it back shut, causing him to chuckle.

Treason hides his snort by clearing his throat. "You're our commander." He spoke proudly. "And I can only speak for myself, but most importantly, you are my friend." The Beta Prince offers me his hands. "I'd do anything to encourage and support you." Something laces his words as if he's declaring a vow to me, yet there's no magic upon his lips.

Him calling me his friend makes my heart swell. It's not enough to cause me any pain, surprisingly. I take a deep breath and enjoy the warmth of his words, erasing all the hurtful words I was going to say, and place my hands in his. I might not be admitting that a friendship is blooming between us out loud, but Treason's eyes glimmer with happiness, hearing the words that are not being said but being shown.

"By the way, a-hole..." Treason's gaze shifts to Aliith, "...if you tell Freyja to do something, she will do the opposite. And..." A sly grin dominates his sinuous lips. "...you don't have much for her to waste her breath on."

Aliith's laughter absorbs the thunder rumbling above us. "I knew she was stubborn, just not ridiculously so."

Treason laughs along with him; they act like best friends who enjoy roasting one another. The tension lessens as the two continue being friendly.

I don't fight Treason as he pulls me into his chest. "Oh fuck!" I moan. "You're so soft."

Aliith can't stop laughing. "That sounds like a personal problem, Tea Tree."

Treason's hand leaves my back, and judging by Aliith's coughing, Treason most likely flipped him a rude gesture from his remark.

"You are on a high right now with the pain I took away, both physically and mentally." As I rub my cheek against Treason's chest, Aliith enters my peripheral vision. "You'll feel invincible for an hour, then all the aches you have will return as if they need to make up for the time they were gone. Everything will feel amazing as well." Aliith leans closer and smiles amusedly. "I guess if I say now is not the time for you to explore any sexual fantasies, you'll be humping my friend and me?"

"No!" I pull back from Treason completely as I realize I'm burrowing myself in between his pectorals. "How does biting me translate into healing, and what exactly did you heal?" I cross my arms over my chest, determined to not move until he tells me.

Aliith's eyes narrow as the humor in his face vanishes and is replaced by intense dissatisfaction. "If you had asked nicely and without attitude, I would've said, 'Let's wait until after when I'll have more time to explain.'" He closes the gap between us. "But your stubborn ass knows no bounds and needs a good adjustment before I'd ever open myself up to you."

Treason grips Aliith by the shoulder, turning him away from me and towards him, but Aliith doesn't break our stare. "Shift." Aliith forcefully wrenches himself out of Treason's grip. "You are never yourself after you use your magic."

Aliith whips his head in Treason's direction and unleashes an outrageous snarl.

Treason neither backs down nor compels Aliith to submit. "Shift. Now!" Treason's features may be fixed with anger, yet his voice is full of care.

With a snarl, Aliith backs away and shifts into his Wolven form.

"Hey." Treason's voice is barely above a whisper, and I have to lean in closer to hear him. "Don't let him get a rise out of you. He gets moody after using his magic." Before I can lie about getting worked up, he brushes his thumb across my lips. "Now is not the time." With his touch, he disarms me.

I mentally curse at myself. I can't believe I confessed to myself that I was ready to lie. This man has a way of making me stumble in more ways than I thought were possible.

Lightning strikes as thunder booms. I'm shocked I didn't sense it coming like the other times, and I'm happy not to be triggered by them.

Aliith whines, to which Treason responds with a huff and a nod. "We need to get to the dome."

After placing a warm, lingering kiss on my forehead, he shifts. Treason lowers himself so I can get on, and the pair run side by side, heading towards the dome.

Numerous cracks are visible even from our greater distance, meaning once we get closer, I can get through.

I lean down to get closer to Treason's ear. "Can you send word to Rawldur to get his people ready to attack and have Thaddeus assemble the Spartans to ride on their backs?" He snuffs in acknowledgment.

The brand on my arms hums a moment later, Treason's voice filling my mind.

When Heimdall speaks, I jump up and move away from rubbing my face into Treason's back, snapping me out of my reverie for wanting to be enveloped in fur.

More than the walls will be falling once the dome is gone. A moment of silence passes, with no one speaking before Heimdall continues. *On behalf of our commander, she is proud of everyone on this battlefield, the ones still standing and the ones who have fallen. All have fought bravely here today, and because of that that, I offer this insight. We don't have to storm the tree to bring the traitorous gods to their knees. Our commander doesn't expect anyone to follow her in, and she won't think of you any less. Listen to what your soul is telling you about where to soar, whether it be back home with your loved ones or to remain here with your brothers and sisters in arms. Whatever you all decide, may the Fates be in your favor.*

As the Fates in yours, all reply to Heimdall.

His words were exactly what I would've said. I'm not mad at him for speaking for me; only that he has cut me out of speaking in the bond.

A pair of illuminating red arrows rain down from the sky ahead of us, freezing me in place before I can lean down to ask Treason to pass a message onto Heimdall. I'd recognize the polished crystal from any distance. Cardinal blaze comes from Primalcore, a type of stone that, when polished, can be used in weapons. In crystal form, the wielder can whisper their magic into the stone, and the arrow will find its target from whatever distance.

Treason growls, "Fuck" at the same time I utter it.

Aliith lets out a murderously painful howl as if injured, yet he lurches ahead too fast for Treason to catch up with him.

Dread ways on me as Aliiths drops to his knees in the distance, letting out a wail of anger and sadness, causing the storm above to stop thundering.

I jump off Treason and stumble over. A sharp cry rushes out of me as I fall to my knees.

Apollo and Artemis are lying on the ground. Arrows are protruding out of their chests. Both are shaking while blood streams from the corners of their mouths. Their gasps turn into gurgles, and when they cough, they expel blood.

"Freyja?" Apollo coughed out.

I sniffle to try and hold back my tears and crawl over to him. "I'm here."

As he blinks up at me in surprise and gratitude, a faint smile grows with the realization that I'm above him. "I don't deserve to ask...this of you..." All the words I want to say to him, that it wasn't his fault for triggering me because he didn't know, that he's still my friend, are on the tip of my tongue, but I bite it back. "Can you bring me...to—"

Before Apollo can finish his question, Aliith carefully picks him up and brings him over to Artemis, depositing him so they are right next to one another.

"Turn them towards each other a little." Treason drops down next to Apollo as Aliith goes back to Artemis. "It will allow the blood to come out. Yes, just like that. Keep her resting against your leg." Treason uses the side of his thigh to help keep him up, and Aliith is mimics his stance.

I crawl over, not having the strength to stand.

Artemis chuckles, but it's agonizing. "I told you to duck, you stubborn bull."

Apollo's laugh is hoarse. "I'll trust you from now on."

Both exchange smiles that lead to grimaces of pain. Aliith shushes them in comfort as he pushes the hair out of their faces.

Treason breaks the ends of the arrows off. Then he carefully removes their chest armor and rips their padded vests open in the middle, along with their white silken tunics.

Apollo looks to Treason. "Tell me...what you see."

"Your wounds were clean-cut; the arrowheads weren't jagged or serrated. Judging by where they entered, the metal pierced your lungs and possibly the bottom of your hearts."

Artemis nods. "That's where it feels like they are. It's terribly uncomfortable."

"Freyja, can't you heal them?" Aliith begs me with watery eyes.

He saw me use my power on him, but it only works on souls. "I can try." I glance back from where we came. "Treason, call for a Wiccayen. I can keep their souls tethered to their—"

Before I can reach for their chests, Treasons snatches my hands. "No! If the poison touches your skin, you will be infected too."

"Poison?!" Aliith and I say at the same time.

Treason points to the sides of where the arrows are sticking out. Bubbles of foam are in the cuts, and the skin around the area is starting to separate from the muscle.

Aliith's mouth wobbles. "What is that?"

"Sorbane. The arrowhead must've been laced with poison." Treason heaves a heavy breath. "It causes severe pain in the soul, and when the infected fights, it begins to torment them. The toxin is known to cause immense suffering before the being either dies or their soul evades their bodies. If they fight it off, then they will be able to pass on, but if they leave their bodies before that, they will become leeches...We won't know which fate will befall upon them."

"That's what Churania died from?" Aliith asks in a quieter voice.

Heavy droplets of tears fall from the Beta Princes' reddening eyes. "Yes, as did Bralyant's mother. She tried to help her but got infected as well."

Without him saying it, I read the words he couldn't speak on his face. He doesn't know if his wife passed on or became a leech. The realization of what is going to happen to my friends weighs heavily on me.

"Don't you... dare touch us, Freyja. Give me...your word." Apollo did his best to come across as stern and assertive, like the bull he is, but his voice is weakening.

My hands itch to grasp theirs, but I keep them balled on my thighs. "You have my word. I won't touch either of you."

"Freyja." Shifting my attention to Artemis, tears fall from my eyes. "Don't...be the one....to kill my father or...you'll get...infected...by the Temp—" She coughs hard and gasps for breath, which makes her whimper.

Apollo reaches for Artemis's hand, but she smacks it away. "Don't you dare heal me."

"Emi, please. Let me save you."

Tears stream down Artemis's cheeks as she locks eyes with her brother. "Wherever you go, Po Po, I will follow."

Only when he nods does Artemis let Apollo take hold of her hands. "Don't you worry, Aliith. We are going to fly." His baby-blue eyes brighten like the sun.

"Aliith." Artemis shifts her attention and gives him a smile that has her eyes illuminating like the moon. "I free you from servanthood."

The white halo of stenciled thorns on his forehead vanishes, as does the band of white roses on Artemis' right wrist.

No words leave Aliith's lips. Only tears fall from his eyes as he brushes Artemis's hair.

"I love you." Artemis puckers her lips.

He dips down and gives her a kiss. "I love you too."

"You remember what I promised you when you became my servant?"

"Yes, but no, please don't keep your word!" Aliith frantically spoke. "I don't want to live for eternity without you two."

"I also promised you something as well," Apollo chuckles. "You are going to need it for how much trouble you get into," he says with a heavy heart of admiration, then turned his gaze back to Artemis. "Are you ready to fly, Emi?"

She gives Aliith one last smile, then flits her attention to Apollo. "I'm with you, Po Po."

"For forever." Apollo grasps Artemis' arrow with his right hand.

Artemis does the same but uses her left. "And always."

Together, they pull out each other's arrows.

No gasps of pain leave them, just spurts of blood from their chests and mouths. Both of their smiles drop as their pupils blow out, and the radiance of their souls drains from their eyes and skin.

"No!" Aliith's stormy roar causes the grass around us to drain of color and wilt until there is nothing left but dirt. Only a small patch where we are remains unaffected.

Their final wish comes out of their mouths as white light and petals. They twirl and take on the shape of butterflies, then fly over to Aliith.

He jumps back, trying to escape the sacred magic, but can't. They land over his heart and burrow under his skin. An aura of light expands from him, then pulls into his eyes. The gifts that Apollo and Artemis gave him are sealed into his soul. Judging by what Aliith said to them, I have an idea of one of the gifts—he's a true immortal now.

A glint of gold armor catches my eye. Aliith shifts his gaze with me as if he also saw it.

Athena stands on the other side of the dome with a bow at her feet, her shield and spear nowhere in sight, and her owl servant on her shoulder. A heartbroken expression is written all over her face as she takes in her fallen siblings. Moriya rubs her beak against her cheek, trying to comfort her as lightning explodes all over the dome, striking the ground with vengeance.

Aliith seethes with rage. "That. Fucking. Traitor!" His roar has Athena retreating into the weeping branches. Moriya hovers in the air, her attention locked on Aliith for a second before she follows her master.

An explosion of magic darker than night and thicker than water shreds Aliith into pieces as he hastily shifts into his Wolven form. He runs towards the dome and jumps through an open slit with a growl full of wild wrath. The kinds of fearful screams I'd only ever heard Haidion cause in his victims' nightmares break loose.

Treason is on his feet, a curse leaving his lips. "Wait for Rawldur. I'm going after Aliith." He waits for me to comprehend, but I can't acknowledge his words.

Screams tear out of me as I grip the ground, digging my nails into the soil.

More curses leave Treason. He shifts and runs as I'm engulfed in a blizzard.

A whirling tornado of white encircles my fallen friends and me.

"Athena will pay for this." I close their eyelids so it looks like they are peacefully sleeping. "And as for Zeus, I won't kill him. Faithless will."

I fill my lungs, turn my face up to the dark sky, and unleash the wrath of my soul—expelling all the pain causing me to spiral into a mental grave of hopelessness.

My blizzard explodes into the sky when I push off the ground and lift my arms. Rather than have the ice strike the darkness, I move my arms in a way I've seen my brother do thousands of times to control his elemental magic. Hope ignites in me as my ice storm follows my instructions and attacks the dome.

The spiral of whirling chaos slashes through the dome, then veers out and around, then attacks from another angle, much like an avian predator. Controlling my magic like this has me feeling all the damage it's causing and how fast it's soaring. This is the high of almighty power that my Freyr and Hel didn't want me to experience. I ignore all their words of worry ingrained into my mind. This beast will no longer be contained.

Once there is no shield-ward left, I pull my arms to my sides, and what's left of my magic comes back to me like a loyal pet. I reinforce my armor with ice and form daggers on my forearms, a shield on my back, and an axe on my hip.

I'm amazed by the amount of magic I have; it must be due to my adrenaline rush. The rot is almost forgotten, and each breath I take is deeper and fills my lungs to a capacity I haven't been able to in centuries. Whatever Aliith did to heal me replenished some of my soul magic. Skjoldr hums, telling me I'm low again, but it doesn't matter; I'm armored up, and the dome is down.

My instincts alert me to something at my back just as a purring groan rumbles behind me. Rawldur is at eye level with me as I turn around. What's left of the Spartans are on the Lyons' backs. It's difficult to count the amount of each race before me, but I know in my heart that our numbers have halved, and I feel deep in my soul for every one of those deaths.

Rawldur nudges his nose against my cheek, and I press my forehead to his.

"*I'm sorry for your loss, Freyja,*" Thaddeus utters softly in Atlantean. "I never knew you could wield your ice like those with elemental magic can."

"My brother was very creative with how soul magic can be contained and controlled."

I'm nudged by another Lyon until I'm pressed against Rawldur's mane. "I appreciate your kindness, but I need to get Faithless in my grasp."

Rawldur nudges me with his shoulder into the Lyon at my back. A gasp rushes out of me as I take in the unusual Lyon. He's rosy-white with streaks of silver in his mane, making the hair look like snowy fire. He's not as built or tall as his Falmenir Makuba, he is still mighty, with strong muscle filling out his leaner frame.

Thaddeus gestures to the Lyon with a bow. "Freyja, meet Roareeien, Rawldur's firstborn."

Roareeien nods to me, then lowers himself so I can mount him. "*I'm honored to ride you into battle, young Makuba.*" I switched to Whemida, the language of the Lyon race.

Rawldur nips his son in the ear when he deeply purrs beneath me. An irritated snarl leaves Roareeien, but he doesn't show his teeth, conveying his submission.

"Now is not the time for flirting." Rawldur snuffs in agreement with my statement.

"It's just casual flirting to alleviate the tension." Thaddeus winks at me, and I snarl at him.

With a great roar from the Falmenir Makuba, a ripple effect of roars rises from all the other Lyons. The Spartans cry out their appetite for blood and carnage, causing their gold armor to spark.

Roareeien must be as impatient as me; he takes off just as I squeeze my thighs tighter.

I lean down to get to his ear. "I'll save your ass from your father. Just tell him I commanded you to go." He purrs underneath me, and I flick his ear, making him chuckle.

A ray of sunlight comes from behind us, causing the armor of the Spartans at my back to brighten like a raging wave of gold, but the radiance that's blinding the warriors ahead isn't them, but Roareeien. He's glowing like a beacon of fire and hope.

Whatever defense the traitorous Spartans have falters as the soldiers ahead cry out in agony from the blazing light. Roareeien plows into each barrier of their shield wall. All we pass appear weakened by his radiance as if the magic in their souls is being drained.

A clash of black fur upon gold armor pulls my attention up near the weeping branches. "Up ahead. Can you bring me to the Wolven?"

With a huff, Roareeien veers to the right, where there is less blockage, so he can sprint.

Aliith and Treason fight off a hundred or so warriors who have formed a circle around them. Roareeien leaps over the barrier of Spartans and lands in the opening with Aliith and Treason. With a deep breath, he unleashes his roar, causing a quarter of the assembled to fly back. With them being so close, they are most likely dead before they hit the ground.

As I slide off, I throw my shield toward the Spartans and latch onto the energy of my magic, moving my hands in a sweeping motion. My shield follows and spins quickly, decapitating the line of Spartans closest to us.

I laugh as my ice erupts without my command, exploding one warrior's head. "I wonder what more damage I can cause with this." With a broad smile, I pull out my axe and reach down to grab a Spartan shield.

The four of us fight together. Blood sprays on me from every angle as bodies topple.

Whimpers come from my right. Treason has fallen to the ground and is bleeding heavily. Protruding from his left hip is a spear. Apollos' and Artemis' soulless eyes flash in the forefront of my mind. Anger swells as I throw my shield into the neck of one Spartan and my axe into the face of another.

I clap my hands together and form a ball of whirling frost. Skjoldr hums in my chest, alerting me to my lowering level of soul magic, but I ignore her. *I won't lose another friend.*

"Aliith and Roareeien, duck!"

When they drop down, I separate my hands, and mist explodes and flows into the gasping mouths of the Spartans. They turn blueish purple. With a twist of my wrists, as I ball my fists, all of them suffocate. Within seconds, the Spartans near us become statues and appear to be choking.

The frozen warriors make a natural barrier to protect us from the others, but no one turns our way or even glances in our direction.

I run to my friend's side. "Treason!" My chest tightens as my voice wobbles in panic. "It's going to be okay. You are going to be okay." I coat my hands in mist and part his fur to assess his injury.

Treasons' whimpers turn into groans of relief. "*Cold feels good.*" His beast happily moans.

Out of the corner of my eye, Aliith snaps at Roareeien when he takes an arrow out of his tail with his teeth. "Play nice, children," I shout over my shoulder.

Either Roareeien got offended or wanted to rejoin the fight because he leaps over the barrier of statues. Aliith doesn't hide his snuff of arrogance, delighted that he left.

He shifts down and comes to my side just as I finish parting Treason's fur. The spear is horizontal in his hip, and half of the tip is lodged into his body.

"The blade is in his joint and possibly close to the base of his spine." I turn to Aliith. "Did...Apollo give you his—?"

"Healing power, no. Even if he did, I don't have love in my life anymore to be able to activate it." Aliith blinks as if he's shocked. *I don't think he meant to reveal that to me.* "Treason told me..." He looks down at his friend. "...that he was running low on magic while we fought, so he couldn't blanket himself to protect his body from fatal attacks. I'm not a full Wolven, so licking him won't help." He sadly chuckles. "That would only excite the old man."

Treason lets out a growling rumble, then swishes his tail at Aliith, which makes him genuinely laugh.

"Once I get him to the healing den, I can pack his wound. However, he will keep bleeding." Aliith's eyes glisten with realization and sorrow. "This is beyond any of our skills to heal, Freyja. He needs either a god to heal him, or he'll have to find a body of water and wait until the full moon rises to heal." A small smile appears as Aliith sniffles. "I thought I was supposed to be the irresponsible one." Tears stream down his face. "Why did you chase after me if you knew you wouldn't have lasted much longer?"

I reach over to where Aliith has his hand on Treason and place mine on top of his. "Instead of asking yourself these questions that will go unanswered for the time being, how about you ask the ones that will help Treason get better, like what can be done right now to help him?"

Aliith gives me a grateful smile as he turns his hand in mine and gives it a squeeze. "I need to bring him to the healing den."

Only when Aliith releases my hand and stands do I realize Skjoldr didn't hum and try to get away from him. Perhaps she is finally warming up to Aliith.

He slaps Treason's ass, making him yelp. "Shift, Beta bore. I'm not hauling you there in your big ass beast form."

Treason snaps his teeth in his friend's direction. Aliith's kind-hearted smile and laughter are contagious, and I try to clear my throat before Treason fully shifts, but from the knowing look he gives me over his shoulder, he knows I laughed.

"Are you smiling because you also like seeing me in pain?"

My cheeks redden. "No." I gasp.

Aliith rounds Treason, so he's out of eyesight and magically signs in Galex. "*Distract him for me.*"

"Oh, really?" Treason pushes himself up to get on his hands and knees. "Your rosy cheeks say otherwise." His teasing tone only makes his perfectly sculpted body more appetizing.

"I only became flushed because you caught me checking out your sexy back." Admitting what I would typically keep in the darkness of my mind only makes me blush harder. "And the reason I laughed was because I liked the sound of Aliith's laugh. He says he has no love in his life, yet his laughter says otherwise." Even though I want to see Aliith's reaction, I don't look his way, so Treason's attention isn't drawn to him.

Heat flushes Treason's entire body as he tries to figure out how to respond to my comment.

Aliith takes advantage of his distraction and snaps the spear off, leaving the blade in Treason's firm butt.

A growl rumbles out of Treason as he whips his head around to Aliith. "I would've let you break it off if you would've asked me, a-hole."

"Yeah, but did it hurt as badly?" Aliiths gives Treason a knowing grin. "Anticipation makes the pain hurt worse than the shock of getting it done and over with without their knowing," he mockingly stated, as if the statement had been lectured to him dozens of times.

Treason rolls his eyes and returns his gaze to me. A little smile arises, then transforms into a lopsided grin, making him appear younger as his pupils dilate.

"Are you high?" The Beta Prince doesn't break eye contact with me as Aliith hauls him up and puts his arm over his shoulder.

"Only on the sight of you." Treason attempts to sound sexy, but his giggles make it hard.

"Oh yeah, he is." Aliith chuckles. "In their beast forms, Wolven burn off the sedating chemical that floods their blood when they heal because their body temperature is much warmer than in their humanoid forms. He'll be in happy land for a little bit. Say bye-bye to Freyja, Tea Tree."

"If the star glow of your eyes is as magnificent as the globes of your ass, then they are a sight worth waiting to experience."

Warmth crawls up my neck as Aliith chuckles. "Don't you mean to see, you ancient coon?"

Treason's head sways in Aliith's direction, and it makes him laugh for some reason. "I want to do more than just stare at her ass."

Heat flushes my entire body as a whistle of surprise leaves Aliith.

"You're so lucky that you're already injured, or Freyja would've punched you in the mouth."

I'm able to cover up a response that wants to tumble out of me with a cough.

Aliith looks towards the Willow Tree and back to me. "If you find Athena, leave her somewhat alive for me. I have a special talent that her wisdom won't know how to fight. As for my Moriya, she's mine." His growl punctuates his claim to solely deal with his sister.

An idea rushes into my mind. "Wait, maybe I can replenish his magic."

Aliith brows scrunch. "How?"

Rather than explain, I place my hands on Treason's chest and bring forth the happy memories of Freyr and me. My hands are coated in a delicate mist of soft blue light, but I can't push my power into his chest. His soul isn't hurt or doesn't need to be calmed down since he's already high. I'm surprised he, at least, doesn't have soul rot since he lost his wife.

Treason closes his eyes and hums as he enjoys the warmth coming from my memories.

"Nothing is happening," Aliith points out what I already know.

"Please," I desperately whisper under my breath. "Please replenish his magic." Tears fall down my cheeks. "I can't lose another friend."

Cool energy shifts in my magical reserves and expels lunar light from my palms. I empty all the gifted magic Illyrical had given me into Treason's soul.

The radiant blue light illuminates his heart and veins as the magic replenishes his body. Tears of happiness gush out of my eyes as the gash in Treason's hip begins to heal.

Aliith reaches down and pulls the spear out. Blood gushes for a second, then stops its flow as his muscles and skin are weaved back together, leaving only a faint pink line.

"Freyja?" Gone is the drunken state in Treason's voice. "By the Fates, how are you wielding such powerful magic?"

"Because not even the Fate of Death will take you away from me. I won't allow it."

Those were the words I wanted to say to my brother after I brought him to Isis so she could heal him. Saying them to Treasons makes my heart swell—a sensation I wanted to feel then, but I'm overjoyed to experience it now.

I grab Treason by the nape of his neck and pull him down so only a breath and space are between us. "Don't you dare run yourself that low on soul magic ever again."

I project the words my brother spoke to me a hundred times over with the same intensity and concern he had always expressed to me.

Treason's eyes glaze over with tears that catch on his soft smile when they trickle down. Rather than answer me, he leans forward and rubs his cheek against mine, and I immediately burrow my face into his neck.

A voice clears when Treason starts to wrap his arms around me. "Unless you want me to do something reckless without you, you should probably stop groping Freyja."

"Can we finish this later?" Treason whispered against my ear. "I want to properly show you my appreciation."

Before I can answer, Aliith growls impatiently. "Come on, senior pain-in-my-ass, we got some gods to chew since you're no longer incapable of fighting."

Treason chuckles as my entire body burns. "You see why I call him 'a-hole?'"

I direct mist under my armor and sigh internally. "His nickname was easy to comprehend, but why does he call you 'Tea Tree?'"

"That dinner we agreed upon, I'll tell you then."

Treason's smile reaches his eyes just as he is dragged away by an irritated Aliith. I catch myself perusing his defined back muscles and notice that his veins are still glowing. The frosty sheen of his caramel skin is more prominent, along with the silver in his hair and the halo in his eyes.

Energy hums in my reserves, alerting me to what magic I still have left. I direct soul magic into my reserves to investigate how much more magic Illyrical gave me. A powerful source of warmth wraps around the tendril I sent in while my spiritual power flickers, attempting to activate without having to empty my lungs.

I catch up with Aliith and Treason as they weave through the statues. "You better keep your word about that date, Lunar Prince."

Treason whips his head around, displaying a grin like I just stroked his ego the way he likes it.

A statue crashes in front of Treason, startling him and making him yelp in surprise.

"Keep focus, you sack of beans and cream, or I might just chaperone this date of yours." Aliith's laughter echoes off the statues as we reach the Great Willow Tree.

Treason is right; he is an a-hole.

THIRTY-ONE

With the Lyons and Spartans keeping the traitors busy, nothing is in our path from entering the weeping branches.

"Are you ready to find out if your husband is a traitor, Mrs. Invincible?"

I level Aliith with a withering stare, which earns me a smile of approval from Treason. "It's Ms. Invincible, and yes." I pick up a pair of swords and a shield. "Let's get this slaughter fest started, Mr. Moody."

Deep chuckles rumble out of Treason as Aliith releases a snarl. "I told you, she divorced him."

Aliith gets in my face, startling me enough to take a step back. "Repeat what you just said."

A crack of wood being forced into the ground has me stumbling backward. Aliith catches me before I fall. Skjoldr hums in my chest, not liking his touch, and I mentally curse at her to decide whether she likes him or not.

"Almighty ones, please save us from this fate."

Aliith and I follow Treason's gaze. To our right, a group of Spartans are operates a contraption that drives a wooden spike into the ground. Once the spike is three-quarters of the way in, they quickly drag a flat, damp log across the top, creating a vibration.

I scream. "You're all stupid to think they would side with you!"

Aliith growls. "The traitorous gods have doomed themselves. To think they would escape here alive by calling upon them for aid."

Treasons snuffs in agreement with Aliith's statement. "We need to get out of here."

"Take her first and then come back for—"

"Not a chance!" the Beta Prince barked, grabbing Aliith's and my hands.

Treason's eyes shift to obsidian as the silver halo spiders to his pupils, creating a web. His skin radiates as if his soul is surfacing while a cataclysmic howl of melodic energy tears through the air. Fluorescent silver-blue waves of light twist and twirl, creating a portal leading to a void of darkness.

"I thought you could only take one with you at a time?" Aliith yelled over the howling.

"Thanks to Freyja, I'm strong enough to carry two and then portal all whom I love to safety. Even if I couldn't, I don't trust either of you to not get into trouble while I'm gone, so the three of us are leaving together." Treason grips my hand tighter as I push the last bit of air out of my lungs.

The ground violently shakes as the soil beneath our feet starts to cave in. "I call being the prince's stern guard!" Aliith hollered as he jumped onto Treason's backside. "You can be the bitch guard."

I'm happily astounded that Aliith can find some amusement in such simple things as calling out vital guards for the Wolven Prince, even with all the terror arising.

Treason let out a huff as he adjusted Aliith's legs around his hips. "It's bow guard," he growls at Aliith, then looks at me. "You can be wherever you want, just as long as we're touching."

My friend brings our hands to his lips and gently kisses my worn knuckles. With a wink, he steps into the portal just as I reach up to my chest and activate my spiritual power.

The void of darkness embraces Treason and Aliith as I drift backward. As the portal closes, I hear someone shouting my name in a phantom howl on a nerve-awakening breeze, causing my soul to shudder.

I take a stabilizing breath of reassurance, reminding myself I did the right thing. I've come so close that I won't retreat because of some unruly Basilisks.

Air erupts out of the ground, sending me flying backward. I hit the solid earth hard and slid over the slick grass; the pain would've been worse if I hadn't had the shield strapped to my back.

Shrieks and hisses emerge from the broken ground before the weeping branches. As their head rise, I coat my hands and my entire head with my mist. Since I have battled with a Basilisk before, I know their lethal poison can affect every sense and can seek out prey even before a being can see their fearsome eyes.

Ten Basilisks extend to their full height, towering over all like dragons. They shimmer in a variety of greens, blues, and browns. Judging by all of their monstrous size, they are well past maturity. Rattling tails with spikes add to their daunting deadliness, lengthy, curved fangs the same length as my sword, and slicked-back spiked scales make up their skin.

Their gold-flaming eyes of solar light emit alluring rays, trying to draw in prey. By the dozens, warriors fall, frozen in fear. Some scream for mercy as their eyeballs melt from staring into the light for too long.

What's left of the forest surrounding the valley to the stained grass and bodies, turns a lifeless shade of gray. No wonder the Father didn't choose to save any of them either. Their race has become the most corrupt of all. Magic isn't what they want; they want the power to claim whatever territory they desire.

I can't believe the Unfaithful called upon them for aid. Do they not know that the Basilisks won't partake in being a part of a side? They only fight for themselves, and being the last of their race, they have chosen to go out in murderous glory.

The Basilisks scan the battlefield. My instincts and Skjoldr alert me to the stare of the tallest one, the Serrultan, the father of the Basilisk I killed centuries ago.

Arighness's son, Barighness, knew the rules about trying to claim territory. I gave him the chance to leave the lands he was attempting to claim alone, and no harm would've come to him. Haidion offered to take care of the young Basilisk for me, but if the race wanted to expand their territory, an example needed to be made.

At the time, I was so drunk on my darkness that I made Barighness suffer when he didn't back down from trying to kill me. He was a legal adult and knew the consequences of his actions. Being a son of the Serrultan wasn't going to give him immunity from being killed. He learned that lesson the hard way. I have no regrets about performing my job, only taking a child away from a parent.

"*Goddess Freyja.*" The Serrultan hissed with venomous hatred.

All let their jaws drop, and a sucking vortex builds up liquid in their mouths as they prepare to unleash their venom.

Numerous voices shout in my mind, asking where I am or to simply call out for help. But it's Hel's soul-shaking, reality-altering, motherly scream silences them all.

A sonic wave of the Basilisk's shriek releases their poison. Spirits rain down as a body of glittering light appears out of nowhere and drapes over me.

We hit the ground hard as shouts of blood-curdling pain come from whomever is cursing above me.

Eyes of every color of the rainbow stare down at me with loving concern. "I got you, Fierce one."

Heimdall falls to his side, his muscles spasming as he gasps for air.

Screams rush out of me as I scramble to my knees and assess his injuries. Tears rush down my face as screeches of pain shatter and tear me from the inside out. His entire back is melting down to the bone, even though he's wearing armor.

I redirect the mist from my face and layer it over—

"No!" Heimdall snatches my hands and forces me to look into his sparkling eyes. "Keep your mist on and focus on me." His pained, weak voice sends more streams of tears down my cheeks.

Heimdall reaches down, grimacing, trying to hold back how much agony he's in. "Take this."

He taps the diamond axes at his sides. I make haste and remove them before the poison melts them as well.

"I will keep them safe for you." I quickly replace my leather belt for his diamond-plated one holding his axes. "What can I do to save you?"

Heimdall shakes his head. "This is my fate...yours is safe now." His eyes sparkle again as he takes my hand in his. "To love and forget...will hurt you. To forgive and continue to love...will cost you." His brown skin starts is turning a sickening shade of dark gray as he squeezes my hands. "He's worth...loving. But it's...your choice."

"What are you trying to say? Who is he that you are referring to? And why are you telling me this over what I can do to save you?!"

The pressure of his hands holding mine wanes as the light from his soul dims in his eyes. "He loves you...just as much as...I do, Freyja," he whispers, and a second later, his sacred light leaves his lips and flutters off into the distance.

My cry insults the hissing from the Basilisks as they shriek from someone trying to scream louder than them. I empty out my lungs as the faces of my fallen friends flash before my eyes. *No, not friends. My family.*

Skjoldr stops the flow of the soul magic that I want to unleash. I can't expel the same amount of magic as I did when I lost Apollo and Artemis onto the Basilisks, so I finish emptying my lungs and activate my spiritual power. *Fuck being seen. This ends now.*

I will my soul magic to make me sprint forward, over the fallen, through the bloodied grass, past the Basilisk, and into the weeping branches. I'm getting to Existence and her sisters; once I see Faithless, I'm calling him to my gasp, and I'm going to save the Father!

My spiritual power gets deactivated once I'm through the weeping branches.

Soft light illuminates the Great Willow Tree. With how peaceful the branches sway and the light dances over the bark, I wouldn't have thought there was a battle going on beyond the weeping leaves. Only the sounds within the enclosed space reach my ears.

Clashes of metal against metal and cries of my friends fighting with the strengths of their souls echo all around, followed by the grunts and groans of the Unfaithful Gods battling against them.

Bodies of fallen gods and goddesses lay lifeless, some in pieces, as I climb up the thick, windy routes towards the commotion. From the sounds of it, a fight is being had on the platform above that serves as the base where the Father comes out of the bark to speak to those who come with questions or concerns.

The thunderous voice of a passionate soul who'd die fighting rather than giving up, even if the odds were against her, roars from above as she unleashes her cry of fierce majesty. Blue flames ignite from the platform, spreading out like wings and sweeping gods by the dozens.

As they tumble down, roots twist and stick up, impaling some of the traitors while others keep rolling. If Existence is fighting with her wings out, she's alone while her sisters are further in, holding back the ones trying to reach the Father's heart.

Sparks ignite in my blood, making me climb faster. "Existence!" I cry out.

"Our time is up." A voice that I thought I was prepared to hear spoke with an arrogant chuckle full of entitlement. *Seriously, what did Existence see in that drunken, red-headed ogre of a man.*

"Well, feel free to drop to your knees for me one last time, and your misery will be over." Even though Existence is out of breath, she still portrays sheer dominance in her voice, as if there is no other option but what she wills.

Faithless might not be in my sight, but with Thor being so close, maybe I can—

A smack of flesh hitting flesh has a pair of artic-blue eyes staring down at me from above. Existence's left cheek is swollen and red from being slapped by her ex-lover. *Like father like son.*

"Freyja," Existence gasps out with a smile that melts my heart.

Her braided, butterscotch-blonde hair falls and is closer to me than she is, and I almost reach for it rather than the next tree limb. Blood coats every inch of her skin and armor; only her feathered wings of blue flames matching her eyes aren't stained.

"I'm going to personally make him pay for laying a hand on you!"

"Make it hurt." A rogue tear falls from the corner of her eyes, making me hesitate to climb. *She never cries. Why is she—*

An almost silent blade slices through the air.

Blood splatters over my face as my friend's severed head rolls towards me.

Like a novice warrior who has never experienced gore in their entire life, I shriek in terror while releasing my hold on the tree limbs. I tumble down the steep hill and land flat on my back, Existence's head rolling down to my side a second later, and then her body.

As the fire of her wings extinguishes, the warmness in her ivory skin pales to a ghostly white, and blood begins to pool around her body.

A burning sensation crawls up my throat, wanting to escape along with my screams, but the two collide with one another, and only choked gasps and whimpers of pain escape me. Existence face adds to those of whom I lost. *My friend is dead. I distracted her. She is dead because of me!*

No tears leave my dry ducts, for I have run out of sadness to spill. No magic builds inside me. No power surfaces. The aches and pain Aliith took away are coming back in force, leaving me with little to no strength to even stand. I'm powerless. I couldn't save my friends from being killed, so what chance do I have to save the Father and Earthradon?

I'm hauled into a tug of war as I solely focus on Existence's lifeless body. Only when my feet leave the ground do I snap out of the hopeless trance.

Multiple gods try to reach for me, all arguing about who deserves the bounty. Somehow, I hadn't noticed being brought outside the weeping branches.

"She's mine!" Ra's blistering breath makes all who had hands on me let go.

The leader of the Egyptian Pantheon knocks off my shield and wraps me in his hot arms, restraining me to his feathered chest. He flaps his golden wings, and we fly up into the thundering sky.

Like some other gods, Ra sought out an Ancient Demonical who could transform beings into creatures of their choice. The alteration is permanent, but Ra wanted to appease his believers since they all wanted him to be a humanoid hawk.

"Odin has placed a high value on you being returned to him." Ra tilts his beak face down to the side as if tuning into hearing something. "But what those idiots don't know is that you are the more valuable reward than anything else in all of existence. Best we keep that between us."

We are submerged in gray darkness as we leave the battle and the Great Willow Tree behind. Lightning tries to strike us, but Ra maneuvers effortlessly to avoid the bolts, and soon, we are in the clear sky with only tiny, puffy white clouds and a blazing sun ready to set in the west.

"So, what's your plan then? Keep me as your servant or pet and breed me to have your child."

"Fates, no!" Ra squawked. "Once you give back the feathers your brother swindled, I'm taking you to the Fate of Freedom. I might not agree with the Father's plan, but I draw the line at Odin wanting to keep you locked in a cage."

"What the fuck are you talking about? Odin bought me this cloak. And why has everyone been wanting to free me from this galaxy?"

"You'll find out. And as for your cloak, maybe you should rethink everything your oh-so-honest husband has told you." He slaps his hand over my face. "If you don't want to become someone's caged pet, you best stay quiet. Horus won't dare fight me if he thinks I claimed you for myself." When I don't nod in agreement, he keeps his hand clamped over my mouth.

A shriek comes from the distance as a dark blur jets towards us.

Isis's son, Horus, circles a couple of times to slow himself down. His yellow-ember eyes narrow as his black falcon feathers ruffle, as if anticipating a fight. Just like Ra, Horus also sought out the Ancient Demonical to transform his body.

"Hello, friend." Ra greets Horus with a bow of his wings. "As I remove the cloak for you, why don't you tell my pet how you lost your feathers? It seems her husband has filled her head with lies."

Horus pays him the same respect and bows, then flaps his wings to hover in place. "Freyr paired up with an Ancient Demonical in a card game and cheated, so I would owe them both debts. The Ancient asked for my furcula bone to be delivered to him when I die, and your brother asked for my feathers so he could make a cloak for you as a wedding present. If she doesn't believe that, then she is perfectly conditioned to be another's plaything, Ra." *That can't be true.*

With the loss of Freyr, I hadn't wanted to marry Odin, let alone be in a relationship with him. Even though I rejected him, he gave me my wedding present anyway. The notion of having freedom and not being tied down made me fall back in love with him and uplifted my spirits after losing my brother.

Both of them may be lying to me, but why make up a story to just get a cloak back?

I might not understand why everyone wants to free me, but they must know something I don't. The fact that a bounty is placed on me to be returned tells me that Odin will stop at nothing to have me back. What truths I know are that Odin has lied to me and has hidden a servant binding in our marital brand. He has done everything in his power to ensure I stayed with him. So, that means what Ra and Horus are saying is the truth and that Odin has been manipulating me for the past five centuries.

Fire fills my veins from Odin's betrayal. The nagging, silver-tongued voice in my mind tries to put me in my place, but I tear it apart until nothing is left.

"The Ancient Demonical of Transmogrify might have been able to help me grow my feathers back, but they are just not the same." Horus crosses his arms and huffs as Ra's hand moves down my body to untie the strings. "At the time, my all-powerful mother said you had been through enough, but now that you're Ra's pet, you won't need to fly anymore."

"Why won't these things come untied?" Ra yanks and pulls at the strings while Skjoldr hums in my chest, supplying magic to keep the cloak attached to me.

If Skjoldr hasn't given up on me, then I won't give up on myself. And the fact she is fighting for me means breaking free from the galaxy isn't what I need to grow into a stronger immortal. I'm needed here, and I'm not done fighting.

I break away from Ra's clutches with an upward thrust of my hand into his jaw and a backward jab in the ribs. With no one holding onto me and no magic activating my cloak, I free-fall for a moment until I can deploy my gliders.

Silky leather flaps fan out from under my arms, down to my ankles, and between my legs. I glide away faster than my cloak is able to allow me to fly.

A second ago, the calmer white clouds and gentler rays of sunlight before dusk blanketed the sky were peaceful, but now I'm holding back my screams. I might not be falling to my death, but being so high up without any ability to fully control my flight with my cloak is nerve-racking.

Only after Vahildra put the notion in my mind to see if there was a barrier keeping us all here did I get gliders installed into my armor. After almost falling to my death when the cloak was not working for an intense moment, I knew I needed a backup plan.

It was not my smartest choice to escape the clutches of Ra, but my other option was to be freed from this galaxy. He can't know where to find Freedom; it's just another ploy to use me as he wants, just like the High Lords of the Fae.

Odin has been manipulating me for the entire time we've been married, so my friends are the only people whose words I trust. Come to think of it, Odin and I have never really been friends. I don't think we ever were to begin with. *Focus, Freyja.*

Besides an intense warning from my instincts telling me that something is coming, I have no idea from what angle I will be captured or how I will get back to the Great Willow Tree. *Maybe I can take control of their wings and—*

The air begins to strongly pulsate, like a monster closing in on its victim, desperate and impatiently wanting to feast. A lethal aura chases away the rich hues of dusk light and brings forth darkness as if night were racing to cover the sky, sick of waiting for its turn to shine. In the distance, a bluish star glistens and shines brightly as it gets closer. The light is near blinding; the wide span of wings is all I can register. *It's a dragon.*

With a twirl, the beast dives into the thundering black clouds, leaving my sight. The darkness that surrounding the black dragon is consumed by their scales and the blue light. *Did the dragon queen send someone to scope out the battle?*

Squawks and shrieks come from above as Ra and Horus fly down towards me.

My muscles are ready to expel the last of my strength in order to commandeer one of them to fly me back to the battle. Horus won't stop until he gets his cloak, and Ra is determined to free me. I don't believe Freyr cheated to get Horus's feathers; even if he did, my brother made me this cloak, and I'm not letting it go, which means I need to take out both of them. Only because Horus is Isis's son will I not kill him.

I steady my breathing and empty my lungs. Using my spiritual power will be more effective than trying to fight them with Heimdall's axes.

I'm about to tilt to the side to face Ra and Horus, but a pair of green globes in the darkness below catch my attention.

A black dragon flies up and out of the thundering clouds with their jaws open.

Skjoldr directs soul magic into my cloak and yanks me away from the dragon's teeth, which barely miss me, but not the two Egyptian gods that were on my ass. In a second, Ra and Horus are crunched into pieces and expelled out of the dragon's mouth with a puff of fire.

With the dragon being in the light, I can take a better look at—

I scream both verbally and mentally, "Starson!"

Freyja! I shudder with relief as Starson's deep, velvety voice warms my mind.

With another swoop around, Starson flies towards me, his claws open. I collide hard with his scaly palm. All the air gets pushed out of my lungs, but he has hold of me—that's all that matters; no more freefalling.

I didn't know you were up here. I heard your voice on our channel but I didn't know you were this close. Fuck! I almost killed you.

Skjoldr directs magic into my armor and reels in my gliders. *How about we just call our apologies to each other even.* Starson raises his hand towards his crown of thorns, and I nestle back into my spot on his neck. *Not that I'm complaining, but why are you here? I thought you were going up to my lands.*

Existence is dead. I felt our bond snap. I might not have been able to feel her through it, but her presence in my mind, heart, and soul is now gone. He roars and flies down to the dark clouds below. *I can sense where she is, and once I get there, I'm killing everyone in my sight.*

The shadowy-star magic doesn't come out to block my face, forcing me to close my eyes.

Starson, if you do that, there is no going back. Dragons can only attack battles unless ordered to. I will cover for him if anyone asks who killed Ra and Horus. Isis is going to kill me, though.

I'm going to die either way, and I'd rather go out avenging someone I loved.

Trust me when I say this. All those down there don't deserve to die because I know who killed her. An idea pops into my head. *Give me a chance to pull back the ones who are innocent, and then you can rain fire.*

Who killed her?

Thor. He sided with the Unfaithful, who are also here to kill the Father. My warriors have been fighting since Solar Noon to stop them. Allow me to get them to safety first, please!

I flatten myself as much as I can so the wind doesn't whip against me as aggressively.

We keep descending, getting closer to the thunder from the sounds of the harsh storm brewing below.

Ideas roll around in my head about how I'll be able to convince him, but my thoughts get jumbled when we jerk to a stop.

When I open my eyes, I find that we are hovering above the dark clouds. Starry-blue light radiates off his scales along with my armor. Since I'm holding onto his horns, some of the energy gets absorbed into my reserves, making my veins glow blue for a second before the magic settles in.

After a moment of silence, Starson lets out a huff. *Fine. I'll fly ahead and come in from the west since diving down in the storm wasn't ideal for my wings. You have until you see me on the horizon to get everyone out, and then I'm going to unleash all the fire making up my soul, even if it shreds me to ribbons.*

Sadness creeps into my heart, but if this is how he wants to die, then it would be wrong of me to take that from him.

Understood.

CHAPTER

THIRTY-TWO

The memory of Haidion's puppy telling me how blue starlight works comes back to me. After repeating the knowledge out loud to myself, I take a confident breath. *Brightest star in the sky, please give me strength.*

I slide off Starson and enter the dark, thundering clouds. Since I can't reach anyone through the brand, I need to get down to the battlefield as quickly as possible and warn everyone.

This is going down as my worst idea in the history of ideas. Lightning triggers me. I can't see, and my gliders could fail. All of these factors would indicate that my chance of not dying isn't in my favor. However, I should've died multiple times today, but I didn't.

I felt the Fate of Death skittering around me earlier. At the time, I thought it was taunting me as a reminder of where I should be, dead. The meaning of his presence wasn't that at all. He was showing me that now is not my time to die. Each time I kept moving forward, he fated it so that I couldn't die by throwing in variables, allowing me to be saved. This whole time, a Fate has been alongside me, and that's all the encouragement I need to do something as risky as diving down to the battlefield in a storm.

Rather than deploy my gliders right away, I free fall, shooting down like a star.

With a quick pull of my arms, blue starlight glows in my veins and radiates from my palms. Instead of bringing my arms out to unleash it, I press my palms to my chest. When nothing happens, I tap my armor, and the starlight coats my body from head to toe, draining my reserves of all that I got from Starson.

"Please, Fate of Death, let this last for as long as I'm in the sky."

Even though the intensity of falling isn't pressing against my face or flaring my nostrils and eardrums, I still close my eyes to avoid the sight of lightning flashing.

My instincts alert me to something coming as Skjoldr hums in my chest. A tingle of awareness flutters over my skin like wings, followed by a blast of white light. I have no idea if that means that I got struck or that I was near a bolt, but it doesn't matter because I'm okay. I'm alive.

Muttering the mantra to reassure myself falters when another sensation flutters over my skin.

When panic begins to make me hyperventilate, the darkness in my mind comes to the forefront and nudges my thoughts, recalling a memory.

I bounce on my feet, ready to take the leap. "This is not a silly idea, Haidion."

Haidion places his hands in his pockets as he looks over the cliff. "You want me to catch you before you collide with the rocks?"

"Yes!" I smile with giddiness, excited for the adrenaline rush I'm about to experience.

He turns to me, arching a brow. "If you want me to flex how amazingly powerful my shadow magic is, all you have to do is ask."

I stop bouncing on my feet and take a deep breath. "You trusted me with telling me your name and revealing your identity." I gesture to the rocks below. "This is my way to express how much I trust you."

The bored amusement Haidion was expressing, shifts into a warm softness that has my heart melting. "Really?" He looks down to the rocks below and back to me, a broad smile widening his cushiony lips. "You trust me to catch you?" The reality of why I had him bring us to a snowy mountain out in the middle of nowhere, where it was almost pitch dark, is finally sinking in.

No feelings of doubt stops me from giving him an exaggerated gentleman's bow. "I do."

After I give him a wink, I go over to the edge and back up until my heels are almost off the ledge. "Keep a wisp close so you can hear me. If not, I will just scream your name when I'm ready for you to come."

When I look back up to Haidion he's biting his lower lip as he assesses me. "Alright, Freyja. I'm ready to prove that I'll always come for you when you scream my name."

"That's the spirit! Not only am I trusting you to save me, but to hear my cry when I need you."

Haidion chuckles and mumbles to himself, "Right over your head." He must not register my confused expression as he walks over to me because he keeps speaking as if I don't have my brows scrunched in a silent question. "Do you want me to initiate?"

I shake my head, replacing my confusion with excitement. "No, I got this." I remove my cloak, handing it to him. "Keep this safe for me."

Haidion takes my cloak, holding it as if it's a priceless gem. "Anything you want me to hold onto, I will always keep safe." In a blink, my cloak vanishes in thin air, going into his magical pocket. "You are trusting me with a lot. It seems like I will owe you something in return."

"There is one thing that you can give me."

He leans in until our chests are almost touching, his breath warming my cold skin. "And what is that, my darling Freyja?" The endearment has me internally shuddering from how remarkable his voice is.

I swallow down an emotional lump. "Your word that I can rely on you."

Haidion brushes a strand of hair behind my ear. "I will prove to you how much you can rely on me." I find myself leaning into his touch, even though I shouldn't. "How my people show their devotion is to take a life that they weren't fated to end." I gasp when he cups my cheek and immediately wrap my hand around his wrist, but I don't pull him away. "One day, Freyja, I will kill for you, and then you will know how much you can put your trust in me."

No magic tingles his lips, but it's not the magical seal of his word that I want, but the emotion he conveys. My stubbornness recognizes the same strength of willpower in others. The determination with which he spoke shows that he will be true to his word.

I walk my fingers down his arm and over to the gold buttons on his burgundy jacket. "Be sure to kill them with that impressive sword of yours."

My friend flirts with me, and I can't acknowledge it. However, teasing him is a gray area that we both wander into often. Nothing happens because

I make sure it doesn't get taken too far, so I find it okay to be playful with him.

A wicked grin curves his lips. "Fortunately, I am equipped with two swords for your enjoyment."

Before Haidion can see the heat crawling up my neck, I push off him and fall backward toward my death.

My instincts alert me to something coming as Skjoldr urgently vibrates in my chest. I push the darkness away, ending the memory before I want it to be over, and then open my eyes.

I'm greeted by a grayish, misty darkness that I still can't see through. My eye adaptation power doesn't work in dense clouds, mist, or smoke.

Rather than rely on my sight, I tune into my instincts like I have done hundreds of times. After that day of me proving my trust in Haidion, I've become addicted to the rush of falling off a cliff. I learned how to not only trust him to catch me but also to trust myself when I decided to keep my cloak on and knew when to pull away before I collided with the rocks. *Never would I have guessed that my centuries of performing that stunt would prove useful. I smile to myself.*

Crisp vegetation floats into my nostrils along with a dewiness, like how the natural scents of the forest arise when it rains.

I deploy my gliders as green leaves come into view. With a twist to the side, I bank over the top of the Great Willow Tree, hollering out the rush of the thrill while a smile stretches across my face so wide that it hurts.

The gray mist thins even more a moment later, and I'm soon out of the clouds.

I'm quickly reminded that I'm not alone in the sky as colorful feathers come into my peripheral vision. *"Goddess!"* An alarmed male voice squawks in Harcaniel.

A pair of feathery arms wrap around my torso, bringing me face-to-face with the Harpy. Judging by the woven golden vines of leaves around his strong arms, he's the Sovrinarch.

"A pleasure, Malvik, but I wish it was under different circumstances." I switch to his native tongue. *It always surprises me how well I can match his tone as if I were of his race.*

Malvik is no more than five feet tall, the average size of a male Harpy with feathers reminiscent of a bloody dawn. "All of us leaders have tasked our warriors to keep an eye out for you. With no one being able to find you and the Atlantean King gone, leadership to determine what we should do has been fought over."

"Everyone needs to evacuate to the North Woods. I have a friend coming that will take out the Unfaithful."

The Sovrinarch's feathers fluff out, this time with agitation. "What type of ally of yours will we be dealing with?"

"No one will be dealing with him besides me. When I say evacuate, I mean fall back. My friend and I will take it from here. Pass on the word to others and bring everyone alive on the battlefield to safety." When he tries to argue, I raise my voice to a higher pitch and squawk, "That's an order!"

Determination sharpens his feathery features, but they flatten a second later as my soul burns in my eyes. "Yes, Commander. I will do so and pass the word on to the other leaders."

"Tell all to alert the gods and goddesses who sided with us as well. The Wolven King will know who. I can't reach anyone through the brand we made to talk to one another."

Pain aches my chest as I realize that the brand on my right forearm hasn't hummed once since I reentered the battlefield, nor have I heard any chatter. With Heimdall dead, his magic binding all of us together has gone as well.

Malvik screeches and releases me right as a Fae is about to collide with us. The Fae makes a grab for me, but the Harpy thrusts his beak into his eye socket, causing the male to cry out in agony and horror.

I spread my arms out wide and glide through the air, dodging warriors engaged in aerial combat. Knowing that there could be frenzied Harpies still in the sky, I need to get to the ground.

A face flashes before my eyes—Illyrical's.

Though we are on opposite sides, he doesn't deserve to die, but if I alert him, he'll most likely tell all the Fae and those who side with the Unfaithful.

My moral compass spins as I avoid Fae trying to grab me. The image of Illyrical's son stops the needle and points me in the right direction.

Skjoldr hums in my chest, tugging me in the opposite direction I'm traveling. I listen to her and head to where she thinks Illyrical is.

A sense of safety relaxes my body, even though I'm in the midst of an aerial battle as I continue to search for Illyrical.

My instincts alert me to something coming, but the high-pitched screeching of a Harpy tells me all I need to know. Skjoldr pulls in my gliders, and I freefall just as a frenzied Harpy passes over me.

Fuck! I should've told Malvik to command all of them to stop. I would think it would be common sense, but maybe he hasn't ordered them yet since I left him while he was fighting off a Fae.

The frenzied Harpy follows me down. Judging by the smaller frame and the duller feathers, it's a women, which means she's faster and can maneuver in the sky more easily than a man.

I pull out the diamond axes and flip onto my back. With each swipe, the Harpy quickly counters and slices her talons in the air, barely missing me.

In frustration, the Harpy whips around, her wing colliding with my side and causing me to roll in the sky. She slashes me across the face. I spin, and she continues to attack wherever her talons can reach.

Terrified panic has me screaming as I swing my axes violently, trying to get her off me. Although her assault isn't breaking through the blue starlight, her claws digging into my skin are the equivalent of getting pinched. I don't know how much damage this magic can take before its durability decreases.

She's being driven by the neurotoxin to reduce me to bloody pieces. The only way I can stop her is if I kill her. And if her claws break through and she slices me, I'm doomed. Even if I manage to break away, the neurotoxin will be in my body, and I will have the frenzied desire not to tear others into ribbons but myself. Fighting it off is possible; however, the urge to claw myself will be provoked if I get sliced, and as soon as my blood spills, I will want it to keep spilling.

I sheath my axes, direct soul magic into my legs, and deploy my gliders. The Harpy doubles over as I drive my legs into her abdomen, but it's not enough. I fly away, but she's still able to chase me right into a familiar darkness of Astro-black mist.

A web-like dome made of a paint-like texture smacks me in the face. Instead of falling backward into a spin or freefall, I land on a firm block of shadows that make up the bottom of the structure.

A delicate buzz of insects coated in faint, glittering light illuminates the dome along with my starlight.

Before the webbing cracks seal me away from the outside world, the Harpies fighting the Fae only inches away slow down.

Screeches pull my attention from the magic back to the Harpy.

I flip around just as she starts to take a swipe at me. She, too, is standing in shadows, her taloned feet barely visible. Oddly, the darkness is solid yet still puffs and floats around like clouds.

The Harpy spreads out her wings, ready to launch herself at me, when a whistle has her whirling her head around.

"Do you happen to know her name?"

Illyrical's exotic Fanarzien tongue stimulates me with the desire to be punished by whatever pleasure he's willing to give me.

"No." I bite my tongue when I almost moan back to him in the same unholy melodious tone in which he speaks, wanting to please him.

The dome ripples like water and parts for an apex predator with flawlessly fair skin. Before the shadows reform to seal him in, they stroke his tall frame as if they can't resist touching him.

The buzzing insects pull into him and go under his ebony-rose petal armor, leaving him to be one of the main sources of light.

Fierce determination dominates his face as he tucks in his wings and unsheathes the blades at his hips. A pair of broad-bladed short swords made out of a lightning-silver metal with black veins are in both of his large hands.

"Is this how we are always going to meet, *Bah Sundrae?*" His spicy brown eyes flit between the Harpy and me, assessing how to attack.

"No" is the only word I can manage to give him, but this time, it comes off as a breathless moan even though he switched to speaking Earthradonic.

The corner of his mouth quirks up as he moves his blades fluidly around him. "Do you like what you see, you beautiful bee?" Even though the Harpy's feathers are a pastel yellow, the insult of being called a 'bee' has her turning to face him fully, screeching her lungs out. "I'm only here for my hummingbird, but that doesn't mean you and I can't play first." He slices his blades through the air, making them sing. "Come warm me up for her."

Faster than I can process, the Harpy bolts towards Illyrical.

He flawlessly sides-steps her, whirls around, and slices her wings off with his blades. Lightning erupts from the black veins of metal, causing the Harpy to shake like she just got struck by a bolt.

The Harpy falls to the shadow floor, but instead of landing with a hard thump, she and her severed wings fall through.

All the desire I am experiencing turns ice cold. Even though I know Illyrical is on the opposing side, seeing him kill one of my warriors has anger boiling inside of me.

I'm up on my feet and unsheathing Heimdall's axes before I can remember why I sought him out in the first place.

Illyrical chuckles as he sheathes his blades. "Did you not like the nickname? I found it fitting because of the warm welcome I received when I entered my shadow void." He eyes me with a knowing look.

My anger simmers down as my curiosity gets the best of me. "What's a shadow void?"

I can't help but question or ask about anything dealing with the topic of shadow magic, as if my soul is dying to know more, not allowing me to resist the lure and mysteriousness of the type of magic it secretly wants.

"You switch moods just as fast as my daughter switches outfits." He clears his throat and gestures to the dome around us. "This is a void of my shadows, some of what my shadow energy can do. Once I'm inside, I can either transport myself around, similar to flying, or I can let them expand and seek out an access point to the shadow realm. But for the most part, I use it as my own plane to conduct business I don't want others to see."

His gaze flits over me, assessing my body. "But I find it odd that you can influence my shadows. They normally don't... purr for me or worship my body when I enter."

Illyrical's calmer tone soothes me into a sense of safety, and I find myself sheathing my axes. "Won't the warriors notice the mist?" His previous comment is lost to me as I take in the shadows as if seeing them for the first time.

Out of the corner of my eye, he shakes his head and walks over to me. "If they don't blink, perhaps they will notice it, but since time slows down in here, from the outside, we are only gone for a second." He grips me by the chin and pulls me to face him, a serious yet concerned expression blanketing his face. "Why are you in the sky, Freyja?"

"To find you." I shake myself out of his grasp, realizing how lost in the moment I was when his eyes locked on mine. "I mean, I came to warn you." I take a healthy step back from him. "A friend of mine is coming, and he is going to lay waste to the battlefield. I didn't want you to be among the masses that get killed."

He drops his hand and places it on his hip. "You do know what that means, right?"

I roll my eyes. "I'm only here because I didn't want your children to be without their father."

Illyrical dramatically stumbles back and places a hand on his chest. "Denying that we are friends hurts, you know." His teasing grin almost makes me smile. "How long until your friend gets here?" Back to business. *Good boy.*

He arches a brow. "What did you just call me?"

I blink at him, confused. "I didn't say anything. And as for my friend's arrival, I don't know. He's coming from the west, though."

Illyrical straightens. "You have a dragon as a friend?"

"I didn't say that," I blurt out, which didn't help convince him otherwise.

"It's not hard to piece together. Dragons fly in the light, so they can't be seen until the last second." He lets out a hard laugh and rubs his hand over his scruffy face. "Is it because of the beast that lays dormant inside me the reason why you don't want to be my friend?"

Needing him to agree to flee has me speaking the truth. "Trust. More trust needs to be developed between us for me to consider you my friend," I pant, out of breath. "Can we drop this conversation and move on to you agreeing to retreat?"

A warm smile spreads across his roguishly handsome face. "Yes, *Bah Sundrae.* But first, I have a brother I need to tie up." His grin turns mischievous. "I'm sure he would want a front-row seat to the entertainment coming."

I don't bother to argue with him on the topic of killing his brother, but at the mention of family, Drafasa's face flits across the forefront of my mind. "Are you going to tell the others, the ones you sided with?"

Illyrical's eyes pinch together. "If we all leave, the Basilisks will know something is up. I planned on only telling my friends." He strokes the side of his neck as if to soothe himself. "It's going to be a tragedy, but the Basilisk's must be stopped."

I nod in agreement.

"Us races weren't told about their participation, by the way. At first, we were excited about having such monstrous beasts on our side, then they released their acid rain." Illyrical's jaw tightens. "I was fighting the leader of the Basilisks, demanding him to tell me why he betrayed us when I saw you gliding with a frenzied Harpy on your tail. He told me before I chased after you that he doesn't care about saving the Father or freeing him. He only wants to reign over Earthradon." He squared his shoulders. "Both sides share a common enemy now."

That changes things. The Unfaithful deserve the chance to escape as much as my warriors do. Just because they are on the opposite side doesn't make them evil. They are fighting for a cause, just like I am. The Basilisks are the only ones who aren't innocent in this, for they seek to kill anyone who stands in their way to rule.

"Tell anyone who will listen to flee the battlefield." He blinks at me in surprise. "And seek cover in the South Woods, for all my forces are moving north."

The shadows of the dome begin to thin, allowing in light and the sight of the fight happening outside. "Unfortunately, the Arachnids aren't going to pull back. The Autarch is determined to kill the Basilisks. He fights like a man possessed to avenge the one he loves, which is odd since he didn't give a fuck about his mate."

"You need to convince him." When Illyrical's shoulders slump as if he's about to tell me something I might find devastating, I reach for his hand and grip him tight like a life preserver. "Please!" I beg.

He gives my hand a tender squeeze. "Oh, Freyja." Illyrical's eyes soften as if he can see into my soul, the pain I won't admit to myself if Drafasa dies. "I wish I could, but I'm not a High Lord. He won't listen to me."

"Drafasa," I say. "His name is Drafasa." His eyes widen in surprise. "If you can't reign him to make all the others retreat, then just worry about getting him out and to safety." I press my forehead into his chest, not able to take his soul seeing through mine. "Please, Illyrical. Please get him to safety." My voice shatters into whines of desperation.

I have seen too many people I care about die today. Drafasa and I might not be close anymore, but I can't deny that he holds a place in my heart, and to lose him, too, will kill me.

Illyrical's hands cup my face, and I close my eyes when he lifts me to face him. "Yes, Freyja. I will save him for you." He brushes his fingers over my brows, smoothing my concerned wrinkles "You're giving me the chance to prove to you that you can not only trust me to get this done but with someone you clearly care about." For some reason, I open my eyes, meeting a soul that is blazing like fire. "And I will not disappoint you."

Illyrical's tail wraps around my waist and pulls me into him while his wings cradle me to his body. I'm embraced by a hug that has me melting into his grasp. I want to fuse myself to him so I can be wrapped up in his protective aura. Here in his arms, I feel safe and comforted, like I have never experienced before. The relief has me sighing and moaning into his chest.

Illyrical strokes the skin at the nape of my neck, soothing me. "You're so strong, *Bah Sundrae*," he whispers into my ear. "Keep being strong."

Strong? No, I'm not being strong, I'm being weak and vulnerable.

I push myself out of his embrace, causing me to stumble a little. "Your comfort is no longer needed." I don't regret his touch or kindness, only guilt for wanting him to take me away and keep soothing me. "And I'm not your *Sundrae*, so you better get it through that thick head of yours before I pound the realization in for you." I snarl and allow my stubbornness to rise so he knows how serious I am.

Illyrical brushes some hair out of his eyes, unfazed by my abrupt withdrawal. "The mask looks hideous on your beautiful face." He crosses his arms over his chest and leans towards me as if sharing a secret. "After this is all over, I'm going to take pleasure in beating that stubbornness out of you."

I lift my chin. "Unless you are all talk, how about you get me out of this void so there can be a battle in the future."

He straightens and flexes his brawny torso as if restraining himself from pouncing as a smug grin widens his lips. "As the hummingbird desires, it shall be."

Screams replace my retort to being called that nickname as I fall through the floor of shadows and into the last sun rays of light, coloring the setting sky as it turns to dusk.

THIRTY-THREE

DUSK

No soft pastels of reds, oranges, pinks, and purples fill out the blanket of clouds or the setting sky. No, it's painted a bloody crimson. And the storm above the Great Willow Tree only makes the shade look uglier, a perfect reflection of the battlefield below.

It took me only a moment to deploy my gliders after Illyrical dropped me. As I descend to the ground, I take stock of who remains on the battlefield. Sadness creeps into my heart as I see the Arachnids fighting the Basilisks beside the Fae. Being so far away, I have to place my trust in Illyrical to get Drafasa to safety. As for my warriors, all who can still fight are searching for wounded and bringing them to the North Woods.

Starson's voice enters my mind as my feet hit the ground. *The tree of the Father is in my sights. You have minutes.*

My heart beats so loud that I hear it in my ears, ticking like a clock. There isn't going to be enough time to get everyone off the field, let alone the injured.

"Fuck. Fuck! FUCK. FUCK!"

A heavy brick of realization weighs in my stomach and makes me want to vomit. *Can you connect me to the Wolven King?*

One moment.

Snarling growls fill my mind as if a Wolven just got nipped in the ass. *Who the fuck are you?!*

Bralyant, It's me, Freyja.

There is a moment of silence before he speaks again. *Freyja! What? How? Never mind. Where are you?*

I'm right smack in the middle of the field. But that doesn't matter. The pressure to dry heave crawls up my throat, and I try to swallow it down. *You need to call everyone to get off the field. We don't have much time until my friend gets here.*

You have another newly acquired friend?

I admit the truth, needing him to grasp what's coming. *A dragon is coming, Bralyant! The one that I told you I rode to Camp Ariella on. He's coming to torch the battlefield in a matter of minutes!*

Bralyant curses. *That's a hard call to make, Freyja. But I'll command all to listen. Those who disobey you need to accept that what they do with their life is their choice.* I nod, even though he can't see me.

There is silence for a moment; Bralyant is probably sending word out. Now I know how Ambar felt when she had to pull back her people from saving the others.

A dry heave retches out of me to the point that I'm bent over, bracing myself on my knees. Thankfully, everyone remains distracted by the Basilisks, and no one pays attention to me.

Bralyant's voice comes back into my mind, his tone soothing. *Breathe, Freyja.*

He knows me so well. He knows I'm getting sick over this call, and that only makes me desire his comfort. I take in steadying breaths, needing their strength to fill my lungs so Bralyant doesn't disarm me further.

Please tell me you are in the North Woods or on your way there, Bralyant.

I'm not. I'm on my way to you. I might not be able to save everyone else, but I will save you.

Turn around! I plead.

No! His beast responds with a harsh bark, utilizing his alpha dominance to coerce me to listen to him.

Fire fills my veins, and I blaze through his influence. *Bralyant! Go back now!* I order.

Bralyant's voice cracks in pain, losing the strength he had a second ago. *You don't know what it was like to hear that you and Freyr were battling a dragon alone and had no one to help you escape him.* He conveys what sounds like centuries of pent-up guilt. *If I had been smarter and hadn't wandered off into a cave alone to scout, my legs wouldn't have been broken.* He tries to cover up some sniffles by clearing his throat. *He wouldn't have died if I had been able to help.*

Don't you dare take the blame! It's not your fault. You are not responsible, nor am I.

A thought occurs to me. I've been assessing the field and getting sick while I should be running to safety because I'm right in the line of fire. Unless the Fate of Death has something up his sleeve to save... I take a sharp breath, realizing something I should've picked up on sooner.

I mentally scream as my hands begin to tremble. *Turn around, Bralyant. Please!*

This can't be happening. I can't have Bralyant become the variable who risks their life to save me. No! I won't allow it.

And you are acting exactly as I was—all guts and glory. No! I'm coming to save you. I can't live without you. You are the sun that pulls my moon. You are the water to my tide. And you are the magic in my soul.

My instincts alert me to something massive approaching just as Skjoldr tugs me in the opposite direction. Coming from the North Woods is a dark speck of a furry beast.

Bralyant's voice takes on a tender tone that has my heart swelling. *I love you, Freyja.*

All my old feelings for him start to surface and sway me to run towards him, but my feet and thoughts stop when I realize that is probably what the Fate wants me to do.

No matter what I say to Bralyant, he won't listen. He's going to get to me, no matter what. If this is the Fate of Death's doing, then what strength do I have to overwrite his will?

Starson's voice enters my mind. *I'm closing in.*

I whirl to the West Woods. A sliver of darkness cuts through the dawning sky—a beacon of shadowy light with mighty wings.

My name is called from behind me, returning my attention to

Bralyant. He will reach me in time, but we are in Starson's line of fire, and he would shield me just like Heimdall did.

What can I do? Starson isn't going to hold back from firing, just as isn't Bralyant going to turn around and flee.

My heart beats stronger in my ears. The ticking pounds into my skull and causes bile to rise in my throat. The anticipation of knowing what's coming is making me sicker than I was before, knowing that the first person I loved besides my brother is going to die to save me.

"What can I do," I mutter to myself. "How can I save him?"

One rogue tear manages to fall. I thought I had spent them all. This one is cold and unsettling, as if it holds the truth and is squeezed out of my soul. There is nothing that I can do but watch it fall into a puddle of blood. Pain burns my eyes from not being able to continue to cry and from the sun hitting my face.

Warm energy comes to life in my reserves. The light inside me awakens from the rays now shining upon me by the dozens. Solar light fills my hands like glowing orbs as if I hold the sun in my palms.

This light is more than warmth and fire but of perseverance and hope. Just like on a stormy day, the sun doesn't give up on shining through, emitting its rejuvenating rays of light to all, even if they are in the darkest shadows.

I cry, "Please protect him and those who desire safety."

I thrust my hands out towards Bralyant and scream my soul out, unleashing the fire in my veins, and the light awakens in the threads of my existence.

Solar light blazes out of my palms like pulsating rays and shoots towards the North and South Woods. One tendril breaks off and punches Bralyant in the chest, then wraps around him and pulls him to the North Woods. His screams and pleas to save me only have my voice crying out louder, pushing the magic out as fast as I can.

Dry sobs rush out of me as tendrils rapidly pull wounded warriors off the battlefield and bring them into the woods; only those who chose to stay and fight remain.

Starson yells into my mind. *Freyja, you need to move!*

I'm not leaving until the last of the magic is expelled, I call back to him.

Starson huffs in my mind instead of saying the words aloud. He respects my choice to not move as I have respected his choice to shred his soul in order to avenge Existence.

The solar light leaves my hands and I fall to my knees. Barriers of blazing sunlight cover the North and South Woods. Without having to ask, I know deep down in my soul that they will protect the warriors behind them from the chaos about to erupt.

Starson's nervous voice enters my mind. *I can't fire knowing you're in my path. I need you to command me.*

On my signal. I push up to my feet, using the last of my soul magic to strengthen my legs. *Roar.*

A screeching roar vibrates the air and pierces my ears as a heavy set of mighty wings flap from behind me.

The storm stops, and the rays of light brighten, casting his shadow across the battlefield.

All who remain to fight turn my way as I raise my arms as if I had wings of my own. *Fire.*

Raging sweeps of blazing warmth push from behind me in waves, building to an intensity that has me falling onto my hands and knees. One more blast of scorching air has my cloak flying up over my back, covering my head and hands as a force pushes me down to the ground.

* * *

I'm jolted awake by a roar that vibrates the ground I'm lying on. I blink in confusion as I take in hot air in my lungs. *Did I pass out?*

My body is covered in layers of sweat as if I had been baking in the sun all day, but nothing stings, and I can still feel the air brushing over my skin, so my nerve endings haven't been burned. I know my armor and cloak can tolerate intense heat, but I never imagined they could stand up against dragon fire.

As I push up onto my hands and knees, blue starlight still covers my armor, but just faintly, and something glides off my back. A heap of charred feathers turns into ash. It takes me a second to realize it was my cloak that slipped off me and is now a pile of fine powder. Embers sizzle, and the wind lifts an unpleasant scent from the heap that was once my reliable cloak.

Devastating shrieks come from me as I clutch the pile; the heat is not burning my skin but is still warm. The desire to heal rushes out of my soul through my veins as my eyes burn, wanting to spill tears, but I can't. I can't bring anyone or anything back to life.

Another realization has me screeching to the point of causing my throat pain. I can't believe for the past five centuries, I was wearing a gift my brother had made for me. And just when I found out a part of him had been with me this entire time, and he granted me the freedom to fly, it's gone, turned to ash just like my brother. It's like losing him all over again.

Terrified screams and agonizing cries lift my attention to the burning field. I can't even see the Great Willow Tree anymore because of how much smoke there is.

Pushing off the ground, I stand with strength I didn't know I had left in me and run in the direction that I hope will lead me to the tree. There is no time to hold onto something that will never have life in it again. Later, I will grieve, but for right now, I must run.

Grunts rumble out of me as I pump my arms and pant with each step I take as I sprint and dodge pyres of fire.

I can only see a couple yards in front of me due to the smoke, and every inhalation of air burns my raw throat from how much I screamed. Any ailments that affect my ability to breathe influence my ability to activate my spiritual power.

A rattling stops me in my tracks, and I unsheathe the axes at my hips. They didn't melt, but the diamond-stone belt and blades now glow red and are as hot as fire.

"*Goddess Freyja,*" a Basilisk hissed from the flames to my left.

My hairs raises on my spine as I turn in their direction. Since they need time to refill their glands to shoot poison, I'm in the clear from being rained on, but their fangs and blood are still toxic. That is why killing one is difficult because the one fighting them rarely lives. It was only because of my harvesting magic that I could control Barighness' body and kill him.

A fluttering sensation trickles over my face from the starlight. I can't see the beast, but its influence is still trying to affect me. With the protection lessening, I don't know how long the barrier will last.

"*Killer of my son.*" A different Basilisk emerges from the fire; its scales are sleeker and brighter, and its skin glossier. It's a female, Barighness's mother, the Serrultana.

"Barighness knew the price he had to pay for trying to gain territory that wasn't his to take, Braxshi. From a mother who desires a child but is barren to one who lost one, my heart goes out to you." I hissed so she could understand me better since the race doesn't have its own language, just a certain way of rolling the tongue.

Braxshi shows her fangs as she slithers around, circling me with her enormously long body. *"You know nothing of the pain I feel nor the wrath I have to kill you."* I force myself to look away every second so I don't maintain eye contact with her, but the starlight's fluttering sensation constantly tingles my face. *"But I know what will be worse than your death."* She rises to her full height and opens her jaws wide, allowing her tongue to slither out. *"Losing someone as precious to you as my son was to me."*

"I have experienced such a loss. And not just from the past, but from today." I grip the axes tighter. *"I've been ready for your wrath."*

I knew this day would come, but this time, I didn't have Haidion shadow talking into my mind with pointers that helped me win the fight with Barighness. I don't have time to fight her. I need to get to the Father.

Braxshi hisses with offense. *"My wrath will kill you in seconds, and I don't want you dead. I want you to suffer!"*

She lunges for me just as the smoke parts above for a massive set of jaws.

Starson digs his teeth into her neck and severs her head as he soars. It happened so fast that I didn't register Braxshi's body falling towards me.

The axes find their way into the sheaths without my doing so as I run. I'm tripped by a fallen Fae engulfed in flames, with faint tendrils of black light emerging out of him.

Braxshi's headless body lands just feet away, but her blood spurts out and hits my left shoulder. Pain like I never experienced before claws into my collarbone and walks its way down to my left breast.

Soundless screams rush out of me as I arch off the ground from the poison dissolving my armor, boiling my skin and blood. I swear I hear Braxshi's voice hiss in my ear, cursing me to suffer.

The blue starlight absorbs into my armor and stops the metal from melting. However, my skin is still burning from the poison. Fire erupts from the innermost part of my soul, races into my veins, and flushes my skin. An internal battle of pain has me rocking from side to side while each force fights the other.

An axe is in my hand before I can figure out how I possibly unsheathed it, and a force I can't see pushes the metal over the affected area. The glowing red light from the metal emits heat as intense as the fire burning around me, sizzling my skin, cauterizing the wound, and burning off the venom.

Memories of my life flash in the forefront of my mind as a ghostly figure of a starry night kneels over me. I relax from their friendly aura, causing the pain to lessen and my breathing to slow down as if I'm ready to fall asleep and escape to my dreams. Every fiber making up the threads of my existence stills, waiting to see what will be stripped of me as I take my last breaths before darkness takes me. But in a blink, my sight is replaced by smoke rising to a sky I can't see, and flames grow wilder out of the corner of my eyes. Instead of taking my last breath, I'm gasping for air and coughing from the smoke I inhaled.

A Fate was over me—there is no doubt in my mind, and they... saved me. "Death?"

"Freyja." A disembodied voice of love and sacrifice floats around me like a welcoming spirit.

"Father!" I gasp and scramble to my feet, causing pain to radiate from my left shoulder and chest.

"Freyja, I need you to listen to me very carefully."

"I'm coming for you." I heave myself over the Basilisk's massive body and start running.

"Freyja, please, stop." Skjoldr halts me even though I want to keep running.

I'm surrounded by the Father's voice as if he's holding me to his chest. "I'm going to stop them." I cried out. "I can get Faithless from Thor and—"

"It's too late. I was wrong with my plan on how to cleanse the world, and because of my actions, greed has spread even more. I don't have much time left." My face is cupped by hands I can't see. "I need you to remember what I tell you. Can you do that for me?"

Before I can nod or answer him, his touch leaves me with a breeze, followed by a raspy curse.

"Father!" I scream and reach forward, even though I know it's worthless since he's a spirit.

"I'm here, Freyja. But I won't be for long." A pained voice circles me as the Father grasps my hands. "You need to alert the Shadow King and tell him to assemble the Playmakers." He cuts me off before I can ask who they are. "And pass this message on to him. The heirs must be protected, no matter the cost."

"I give you my word that I will. Are they killing you, or are they setting you free?" Even though there are more pressing questions I should ask instead, I want to know if what Illyrical told me was possible.

"I don't know, Freyja, but whatever they are doing is hurting my soul and magic. I severed my connection to my soul mate so she wouldn't be affected too." He cups my face once again. "There are only a few shreds of hope left in our universe, and restoration needs to be activated or, all you know, love will be taken." The Father deeply groans in pain, which has me shaking uncontrollably.

"I give you my word that I will bring restoration to Earthradon."

"You are not needed—" He gasps in pain as his hands drop to my waist and pressure presses against my thighs as if he had fallen. "Here. You need to be freed."

"I took an oath as a goddess of Earthradon." I drop to my knees, and the pressure of the Father moves to my face as if he's pressing his forehead against mine. "I'm not leaving when my planet needs me the most."

"Freyja, I can't stay much longer." The pressure of his touch lessens, but his voice lingers and is barely audible. "I don't know if I'm dying, but soon they will find my heart, and I want my last words to be spoken to my soul mate." A pair of lips press against my forehead. "Please listen to me. Seek out the Shadow King, pass along my message, and have him bring you to the Fate of Freedom. Goodbye."

I fight off Skjoldr's influence, push off the ground, and bolt into a sprint. Even though Skjoldr warns me against it, I direct soul magic to frost my body and run through flames instead of dodging them. I'm covering ground faster than before, and the added coolness relieves my sore muscles, allowing me to run with little pain.

The weeping branches of The Great Willow Tree are in my sights, fueling me to run faster.

A concussive energy blows out from the branches, lifting them towards the sky.

I'm knocked on my ass by a wave of sound I thought I would never hear in my lifetime while painful roars come from the sky, followed by Starson crashing somewhere beyond the tree.

The vivid hues from the willow tree drain as the limbs fall back down and weep more profusely than before. What's left of the grass and forests surrounding the valley are drained while the storm above finally thins and reveals a bloody sky.

No screams leave me as I fall onto my back. My shaking stops as my skin becomes numb and my heart rate slows. The tethers holding the strings making up my existence loosen as darkness creeps into the corners of my vision. All the strength I had before is gone. No pain surfaces from my depleted body, nor does magic hum in my soul. The only thing I have left is my breath, Skjoldr, and a deadly silence.

PART FOUR
WHY DOES EVERYONE WANT MY FEATHERS?

THIRTY-FOUR

"Why, hello there." I mentally curse at the sound of the familiar sing-song voice of alluring arrogance.

Loki, Hel's father, the Norse God of Mischief, Trickery, Deception, and Shapeshifting stands over me with a smile that makes me wish I had a hammer to smash his perfect, white teeth in and crack his skull to bloody his porcelain face of elegant exquisiteness. He dresses as immaculately as Haidion, except his suit doesn't have tail-feathers, and he doesn't wear a top hat. Instead, he carries a red-jeweled cane with feathers carved into oak. His "staff of surprises."

In the last rays of light, his short galaxy-green hair reveals highlights of blues and yellows. Not a speck of blood stains his black suit. Gold buttons go from his leather belt all the way up to his throat and to his black gloves. His attire is simple and formal, with pointy leather shoes and thigh-length gold-stenciled black capes attached to his shoulders. He breathes luxury, sparing no expense, especially on the teardrop ruby cuff links.

Loki nudges me with the end of his staff. "Are you dead?" He chuckles as I bare my teeth at him. "I do enjoy how feisty you get when you're nudged." He squats down next to me, tapping my joints with his staff. "Do these still work?" He sighs when they don't spasm. "You look like a dried-up fish, especially with that makeup on."

If I had any strength left, I'd tackle him to the ground, right into a bloody puddle. "Whose side are you on?"

"Come on, Freyja. Do you even know who you are talking to?" He stands up and waves his arms, making the capes flutter like wings as he spins on his heels. "I'm Loki. Whose side do you think I'm on?"

A growl rumbles out of me. "Your own."

"Precisely." Smiling broadly, he spins his cane. "I'm glad to see that your mind is still sharp. You're going to need it."

I'm about to ask why when a hissing starts from behind me. Straining to look, I see a reptilian humanoid with blueish-black spiked scales approaching. If I had even an ounce of strength, I would take advantage of the Basilisk's exposed manhood. Only males from races with scales can conceal both portions of their reproductive anatomy within themselves. I don't have a clue why he's exposing himself, but I'd make him regret not tucking it in if I could move.

Loki nods to the Basilisk. "Greetings, Serrultan. How's the missus?"

My cauterized skin begins to burn once again, remembering the pain of the venom. Perhaps that's the reason I can't move. The wound might've been sealed, but the poison could still have made its way into my bloodstream.

I tense at the sight of Arighness swaggering over as if he's about to claim a prize. Never before had I seen what he looked like in humanoid form. His beast form is so massive that I never paid attention to the color of his scales.

"*Dead.*" I take glances at him instead of locking my eyes with his. "*Freyja summoned a dragon and commanded him to kill her.*"

Loki stops twirling his cane. "Oh dear, well, this is awkward." He sweeps his gaze over me before looking at Arighness with a cunning smile. "Odin would be more than happy to compensate you for your loss if you bring Freyja back to him."

Arighness releases an enraged hiss. "*No amount of riches will bring back my wife and son.*"

"I fully understand why you want to kill her." Loki places his hand over his heart, then gestures to me. "But I just can't see all that money go to waste."

Before Loki can lean down to grab me, Arighness grips him on the shoulder. "*You touch her, and I will deliver the same torment upon you.*"

The Norse God looks to the fist gripping him and sighs. "You know, this is my favorite suit." He tilts his head to the side, giving the Serrultan a malicious glare. "And you're wrinkling it."

With a swing of his staff between Arighness's legs, Loki brings the Basilisk to his knees. "Nighty night, snake." Loki nails him on the back of the head before he can hiss his offense.

"That isn't going to keep him out for long."

Loki shrugs and snaps his fingers, making his cane vanish into thin air. "Long enough for me to claim my riches." He kneels and gives me an excited smile. "Let's go join the party."

My muscles burn with anger, and when I can't move an inch to fight, I know the venom is the cause of why I can't move.

He hauls me over his shoulder like a sack of potatoes and enters the weeping branches. I mentally curse at myself for almost complimenting him on how strong he is to scale the tree roots and climb them with me over his shoulder.

Hoots and hollers of celebration quiet as Loki pulls himself onto the platform. "I believe I have something of yours," Loki announces in a smug tone, no doubt giving all a shit-eating grin.

Instead of throwing me down, Loki lays me gently on the ground. Dozens of gods and goddesses from all the pantheons are staring at me, but it's one set of berry-blue eyes that has some strength returning to my paralyzed muscles.

"I see you found my little bird." Odin shifts his attention from me to Loki. "I will see to it that you are greatly compensated."

"I'll take my payment now." Loki flicks his wrist, and a playing card with a silver crescent moon pops out of his glove. "If you would be so kind." He holds out the card to Odin.

My soon-to-be ex-husband touches it, and the moon glows in every color of the rainbow for a second before dimming. "It's a pleasure doing business with you." Loki throws me a wink as he places the card in his pocket and saunters over to his wife.

Angrboda, Hel's mother and the Norse Goddess of Chaos and Destruction gives Loki a pleased grin. When she meets my gaze, she returns my glare. The goddess's silk almond skin, pine-green eyes, and wild brown hair, tangled with leaves and branches like precious gems, make her look like a tree nymph. Beneath her fur armor is a frosty beast that I have yet to meet to understand why she is known as the Mother of Monsters.

At Angrboda's booted feet lay the bodies of the Father's other two daughters, Evasion and Eternity, both beheaded like Existence. An angry shriek releases from me, making my tear ducts burn. All but Odin take a step back.

"I believe you have something to say to me, little bird." The brand on my ass cheek stings, forcing my attention back to Odin.

The sight of him dressed in armor used to make my "purple monster" come to life. Odin's domineering aura accentuates his bear fur-covered, strong shoulders. His cloak falls all the way down to his leather-bound feet, which I spent more times than I liked sucking for his pleasure. The impressive muscular stature of Odin's long legs, corded arms, and chiseled torso are adorned with silver-plated armor lined with white fur. The gray hairs in his braided beard and hair made the beast within me purr. Hera said I have "daddy issues" because I am so much more aroused by Odin's more mature appearance.

Odin leans down, whispering something into Frigg's ear while handing her a folded piece of paper. She giggles and smiles with a too-friendly nod and flutter of her lashes. Odin never gave me a reason to not trust him when he and Frigg would hang out, so I didn't see the harm in their remaining friends. Now I see a pent-up attraction that is on the verge of exploding when Frigg bites her lower lip, and Odin's eyes flick down to them.

Jealousy doesn't cause the fire to be stoked in my chest, but the anticipation of Odin's unfaithfulness does. If he kept himself in the gray area and didn't let anything get too far, like I did with Haidion, then that's okay. But by the way they look at each other, I think more than words have been shared between them following their divorce.

A crown of antlers with a rare blue diamond in the center adorns Frigg's head. Sunflower-blonde locks cascade down her slender frame all the way to her waist. Her skin is light and flawless, making her shine amongst all the others. The darkest of brown eyes smile up at Odin like a flower drawn to the sun before locking them with mine, and a prideful aura twists her lips into a conniving smile. I don't know how she made it through the war without getting a drop of blood on her floor-length white armored dress and cloak, but it's just as pristine as she appears.

Frigg unfolds the paper Odin had gotten from the Nymphs and holds it out for me to read. Given that he sides with the Unfaithful, he must've left last night to slaughter the entire Nymph race after getting the spell.

The burning sensation on my ass intensifies as I delay in reading the poem aloud. With my voice as my only weapon, I curse out my soon-to-be ex-husband. "I will never bear you a child. You have my word."

As expected, his face tightens with anger as gasps come from the onlookers. Everyone present knows what I vow will come true. My brother proved how much power was in his word, and I follow in his footsteps. There might be no magic in it, but there is a strength that hasn't been broken, and Odin knows it.

Kneeling, Frigg grips my hair and pulls, forcing my head to tilt back further than what's comfortable. "Read the poem to your master, servant."

No tears leak down my eyes, but a shiver of sadness travels down to my soul. Frigg calling me a servant makes the truth more real. And if she knows that my marital brand has a hidden servanthood in it, then I've been made a fool of. And by the full smile she is trying to hold back, she knows it. Of course, Odin would've told her. They talk about everything and anything, just as Haidion and I do. I should've been suspicious of their relationship sooner.

With another tug on my hair, I focus on the poem and grit my teeth as I repeat the rhyme three times.

To Odin's Lovely Daisy,

Read the following poem three times when you want to initiate your fertility:

"Rays of the moon, come fill my womb. Awaken the flood, bring your blood. Permit me to nourish, so eggs will flourish. End my suffer, bless me, Mother."

The pain on my butt vanishes, and though I don't see it, so does the brand Odin tattooed on my ass cheek.

Another pain awakens in my lower abdomen. It's subtle at first, but it builds at a rate I'm not prepared for. Screams rip through me, burning my throat. By some miracle, I'm able to clutch my stomach and shift into a fetal position.

"What the fuck have you done?" Angrboda calls out outrageously. "Why would you awaken her menstruation when you don't have the proper medicine or an ample supply of moon blood to nourish her body?"

"What type of husband are you?" Loki sneers at Odin with disgust.

Odin looks at me then at the letter and back, not believing what he's seeing. "She made a vow to me..."

Loki gets in his face. "She could die from this!"

"I didn't know." Odin staggers back, gripping his hair.

I've never seen him in distress before; he is normally always so strong and stoic when it comes to his emotions and expressing them.

Angrboda shoves Frigg aside, kneels by my head, and presses her palm over my temple. "She's burning up already." The goddess looks at Odin with so much anger that I could almost consider her an ally if she hadn't had the Father's daughters at her feet. "Freyja needs to be tended to immediately."

A roar comes from my soon-to-be ex-husband. "I will decide if my wife needs to be tended to."

Commotion stirs from the other gods and goddesses watching. All condemn Odin for being so careless. His true colors are being revealed. Their verbal recognition about his behavior has shame burning inside me for not realizing sooner that I shouldn't have put up with him for as long as I have.

"Well, technically, she's your consort." Frigg flips her hair over her shoulder. "We never truly got divorced, Freyja. We only separated so he could breed you." She leans over my body. "You ever wonder why Odin murmurs in his sleep? He visits me in my dreams and makes sweet love to me. And all those times when he's gone for so long, he's sleeping in my bed cuddled up with me. No real sex, but soon that will change."

With what little strength I have, I undo the straps holding my armor on my left forearm. I only feel one pair of eyes on me while shouting and curses rise around me. Whoever is watching isn't raising the hairs on my back as if they are going to raise an alarm, but I still make my movements minimal.

When Odin shouts to make all quiet down, I slice my forearm against the glowing metal of Heimdall's axe. A different cry parts my lips as Odin turns to me, along with all the eyes on the platform.

I meet Odin's betraying blue eyes. "I, Freyja, renounce you Odin as my husband."

Doubt creases his brows as he slightly shakes his head. "You can't divorce me."

With a glance at my arm, not only is the wound being cauterized, but the marital brand vanishes.

Relief has me laughing happily. *Bralyant was right.* "It seems like the magic system is making sure that I can."

Soul magic returns to me, making me moan as a strength that was depleted is filled. Not fully, but enough for me to function and fight off the venom. The pain in my lower abdomen, however, persists.

"You're still mine, little bird." Odin pulls out a pair of chains with cuffs from his back. "I won't allow anyone else to have you."

"Don't worry, my love, you will still have her." Frigg turns to Odin and leans towards his cheek, but he turns his face and gives her a smoldering kiss.

Frigg bounces on her feet and wraps her arms around him. "That's right, show your pet who you truly love." She turns her attention towards me while Odin kisses her neck as if he's unable to resist. "I can't believe you waited this entire time to divorce him. You could've done it at any point in time but chose to make a big spectacle of it."

That can't be true. Hera was the one who told me that I needed to be face-to-face with Odin to divorce him. Did she lie to me? No, she couldn't have. She sought out the answer herself when she first wanted to divorce Zeus when she found out that his so-called "blessing woman to have children" was him cheating on her. Just like when she told me about the theory of having reserve power within us that everyone is afraid to tap into, I found out that her theory wasn't correct. I can't blame her for not knowing the truth, but I'm annoyed that I have to figure it out this way.

Odin wraps his arm around Frigg's waist. "Chain her up and bring her home." He tosses the chains to Angrboda. "Frigg and I have to meet up with Thor to ensure Zeus and Athena are doing as we all agreed upon with the Father's heart."

If Thor isn't here, that means neither is Faithless. My last resort to defeat the unfaithful gods is gone. Hopelessness creeps into my heart, causing it to ice over.

"I'm not taking part in this." Angrboda stands up and kicks the chains back to Odin. "I'll take her home, but that's it."

Odin becomes a stoic void. "You will pay for disobeying me." With his emotions locked down, his face doesn't give anything away, which makes Loki snarl.

I quickly strap my armor and unsheathe one of Heimdall's axes, but when Odin picks up the chains, the weapon falls from my grasp as a memory assaults my mind.

The images are covered up by my darkness, but it's too late. My episode was long enough for Odin to flip me onto my front and chain my hands to my lower back. The soul magic I regained a moment ago goes numb, as does Skjoldr, and makes the darkness in my mind vanish, leaving me utterly alone and powerless.

Odin picks up the axe and sheathes it into his belt, but before he can take the other one, he flies off my body with a grunt.

I'm flipped onto my back and dragged to the edge of the platform by Hel. "If you want her, then you are going to have to kill me first." Her protective voice promises death.

Hel puts herself between Odin and me, forming bone blades in her hands.

"How are you using magic?" everyone gasps.

My friend gestures to the fallen bodies of the daughters with one sword as the other waves in the air above us. "Wherever there is death, I'm able to collect. Especially since they offered up their bodies. I will ensure that my use of the magic left in their bones will be used to right what has been wronged."

"Monster," Frigg spits out in disgust as she moves to stand in front of Odin, unsheathing her axes.

"The only monsters I see are the ones in front of me." Hel's attention moves to her parents and then back to Odin and Frigg.

When my courageous friend swings her blades and leans into a lunging position, I'm pulled off the cliff.

The clang of weapons echoes as I tumble down. The pain of hitting the rocks is welcome compared to the feeling of my insides shredding apart. To my surprise, I roll through the weeping branches, all the way outside. Pain makes me curl in on myself and gasp for breath.

Groans come from my right and I turn to see Hera pushing to her feet.

"How did you get through the barrier?" Another wave of agony makes me curse. "Actually, never mind. Do you think you can remove these chains?"

"Are they causing you pain?"

I shake my head as she tries her best to get the chains off, and I tell her what happened.

"I did not know the truth about divorcing Zeus until he told me after I renounced him. As for starting your menstruation, why did you vow it to Odin?"

Opening up to her about Odin's abuse is not a conversation I want to be having right now. "Get me drunk first, and then I will tell you."

Hera faintly laughs. "I have a feeling that's what got you into this mess to begin with." She curses under her breath. "I would have to use my magic, and I only have a short supply of it left."

I look at her over my shoulder and see the strain of indecision on her face. "I'll offer you a debt if you use your magic." I don't want my friend to run herself dry, but I want the cuffs off.

"A debt from Freyja," she says more to herself than me. "Yes. I will take that."

"I, Freyja, owe you, Hera, a debt for removing the chains."

After Hera tells me to look away, her sandy-brown magic comes to life. What feels like talons of fire dig into the skin of my lower back as she brands me. The chains vanish and I rub at my freed wrists.

"Can you stand?"

A sudden pain in my abdomen makes me shriek in pain, answering her question.

"Okay, okay." Hera starts to shake as she looks from the weeping branches to the North woods. "I'm going to open the barrier again. I have enough magic to try that. Hel and I were able to get out, but no one else was able to. Treason couldn't even portal. Um, try to crawl or something. I'll be right back."

Hera takes off, and I try to move. With my soul magic numb and the absence of Skjoldr, I only have my physical strength to rely on, and it's not much.

As the sun sets in the sky, the woods surrounding the valley darken, forming a shadowy barrier around the battlefield. With only a few clouds above, the moon and stars will lighten the field of soulless bodies tonight. The anticipation of the light leaving the valley has me trembling. When night comes, so will the Ghouls. The fallen warriors deserve to be buried, not eaten.

"Freyja," Hel's voice sings to me as a butterfly of sacred light lands on my hand. *"I give my power to you. Let it be the hope when all other options have failed you."*

Tears are squeezed out of my soul as the butterfly flies into my chest. The Fate of Death has claimed another one of my friends.

Nothing can comfort me. Skjoldr doesn't hum in my chest, nor does the darkness in my mind push forward memories to help soothe me. I've never been alone before. I always had someone or something to help me stay focused.

My attention is drawn down to my patched-up hands. I only need to call Haidion, and he will be here. He always shows up in situations like this, but never once have I called him. Even if I did, Demonicals are only permitted to come out during the night hours because of a rule the lords and ladies put in place. I have to hold Odin back from taking me until nightfall. *I can do this.*

"I know I still have magic in my reserves, and I know you are listening, too." My hands hum, and I let out a sob of relief. "Leave me and get your master. Tell Haidion where I am, and that Freyja needs help," I plead.

To my surprise, the dusting of stars over the black patches vanishes.

Doubt creeps into my mind, and I silence it with Haidion's voice, repeating his comforting words repeatedly.

Without knowing how to activate my magic, I only have Heimdall's axe to protect myself until Haidion gets here. Dozens of gods and goddesses will be upon me at any moment, and I need to prepare myself.

The possibility of what Odin will do with me if I cannot escape his grasp has me shaking with nervousness as I try to push myself up. I fail, landing hard on the ground. Going with my ex-husband could give me answers, but I couldn't even escape the metal cuffs without help and offering a debt. He might not know how I got free but knowing that I did will only make him try harder to restrain me. The risk of being unable to escape his clutches isn't worth any new information.

With another push, I manage to get on my hands and knees for a second before my insides heat to the point of boiling. I clutch my abdomen and burn my lungs with screams that nearly drown out the sound of my name being hollered by Odin and the others as they pass through the weeping branches.

Another wave of pain has me falling face first into the ground when I try to grip my axe. Questions bombard me about how I got free and where Hera is, but only screams and coughs leave me. My body hurts, and my armor is too tight. I am on the verge of removing everything when Odin seizes me by the hair and lifts me to face him.

"Take back your word," he angerly whispers, trying not to be heard.

I cause myself more pain as I shake my head, speaking in a fiercely determined voice I didn't know I had the strength to summon. "Never."

Odin pushes me to the ground, and my face smacks against the blood-splattered soil. My vision becomes speckled with dark spots for a moment, then refocuses.

Frigg tries to console her love, but it's no use. Odin's anger is so intense that he's pacing, and the undertone of his skin is turning red. Knowing how unpredictable Odin can become when he's enraged makes fear run through my veins.

My ex-husband suddenly stops his pacing. Something in the distance draws his attention, and the longer he stares at it, the more color drains from his skin and eyes. *What the—?*

A familiar voice of smoke and fire speaks into my mind as the last rays of light escape the horizon. *I'm here.*

All the voices behind me go quiet when darkness explodes out of thin air, blocking the dusk. The sky shifts to night before my eyes as Haidion steps out of the misty shadows and immediately locks eyes with me. He's not in his suit and hat, but in starry-black armor that mirrors the lights winking in the heavens above. A glittering aura surrounds him, making everyone else see a merciless monster while I see my loyal friend.

Emotional sobs rush out of my lips as soul-wrenching tears drench my skin.

With the roar of a beast being unleashed, wings grow from Haidion's back, and shadows spread like wildfire as a pair of obsidian blades extend from his hands.

Three pairs of eyes, all sets of different colors, glow with power as the misty metallic form of his Cerberus towers behind him.

Darkness consumes everything Haidion and his Cerberus pass. Only the eyes and the purplish glow of his blades and wings illuminate him and his forward momentum.

"I see you didn't obey me when I told you to not befriend a Demonical," Odin growls. "All of you, go deal with the demon and his dog. They have no reason to be here."

His level of authority has all the gods and goddesses running forward. Only Loki, Angrboda, and Frigg are missing.

"He isn't a demon. The only demon here is you!"

Haidion's attention is still locked on me when I swing my gaze back to him. His blades slice through all the gods and goddesses despite their magical defenses, weapons, and armor. His attacks always hit their mark, and his opponents drop without spilled blood. His pet, on the other hand, causes carnage as he rips apart those who dare try to fight him. They are a fierce pair, having each other's back. I know deep in my soul that the fate of the fight was decided when Haidion stepped foot on the battlefield.

"Oh, my little bird, haven't you learned by now?" I turn back to Odin and manage to flip onto my back. "All who prevent me from gaining knowledge are demons to me."

"I'm not your little bird anymore!" I roared.

Haidion's voice enters my mind. *I'll gladly finalize your divorce for you.*

Terror has me shaking uncontrollably as a webbed portal made of blood and feathers opens behind Odin. *I didn't know he had portal magic.*

"You are safest with me, Freyja," Odin utters sweetly in a tone he's only ever used after he's done punishing me. "You have my word that you will be well-cared for and protected from all who want you for themselves.”

“No!”

Another wave of agony hits, and I can’t do anything but clutch my abdomen as he approaches me.

I cry out before I can stop myself. “Haidion!”

Odin’s left hand reaches for my shoulder and keeps falling until it hits the ground. A fountain of blood just misses my armor and splatters over his severed appendage as a bellow of pain erupts from my ex-husband.

“Do you not know what the word ‘no,’ means?” Haidion’s remarkable voice is deep and ruthless, like fire consuming a forest as smoke suffocates all.

My friend stands behind me, and with all the strength I have, I dive for his legs. I hold onto him like a terrified child; there is no masking my shaking or tears.

Pressing his severed arm into his side, Odin lunges for his hand with a grunt. But before he can reach it, Haidion stabs it and flings it back towards the middle head of his Cerberus. The three heads fight over their snack before it’s broken into three pieces and swallowed.

“My little bird said your name.” Odin smiled smugly. “Your magic can’t work on me now, Haidion.”

After noting the absence of my friend’s glittering aura, I whimper and mentally punish myself for revealing his name. A moan quickly replaces my apologetic whine when Haidion cups the side of my face and strokes my cheek in soothing circles.

The harsh words with which I was mentally punishing myself are replaced by Haidion’s voice. *I’ve been wanting to step out of the shadows for centuries.* The darkness in my mind returns, stroking my nerves and lessening my pain. *But I’ve been waiting for you to be ready for me to reveal myself. I can’t imagine a more perfect time.*

“I don’t need magic to kill you, Odin.” Haidion’s voice frightens the night sky, preventing the stars from shining and the moon from rising. “And I’m not going to be the one to do it.” He looks down at me with pride gleaming in his amethyst eyes. “She is. I’m just going to torture you until she is ready to end your existence.”

Odin’s remark is cut off by the growling of the Cerberus’s three heads. He looks from the beast, to Haidion, and then to me. "I will be back for you, Freyja. For you are mine."

Odin runs for his exit and Haidion's pet gives chase. "No!" The Cerberus stops, sliding on his ass before it reaches the closing portal. "Good boy," I murmur, sliding off Haidion and hitting the ground.

Exhaustion and fatigue rake over my body. The pain isn't the worst part anymore; it's the draining sensation leaking between my thighs.

The Cerberus licks my face as Haidion drops to his knees beside me. "You came."

A small smile curves his lips, but what catches my attention are the tears leaking down his cheeks. "I'll always come for you when you call out my name."

"I won't make it a habit. I give you my word." My vision doubles as Skjoldr hums to life in my chest.

My friend shushes me and cups my face. "We can discuss the benefits I'd willingly provide for you later. But first, what's ailing you? I've never seen you so pale."

When I try to take my next inhalation to tell him, I'm unable to fill my lungs.

"Freyja?" His hand moves over my pulse, and even I can feel how weak it is. "Freyja!"

Darkness takes me. But before I can fall into an endless void, stars surround my body and bring me back up. I don't wake. However, I'm aware of pressure against my lips and a tingly sensation being pushed down my throat and into my lungs. Haidion is giving me a rescue breath of star magic, but it's not enough to keep me awake.

CHAPTER

THIRTY-FIVE

Tendrils of cool darkness tug me in the direction of a sacred light. With each step I take, the darkness follows like a loyal pet, embracing the light with me.

Colors of red, orange, and pink come out of the brilliant illumination and weave together before attaching to me like a tether. My veins are filled with strength, my heart beats with passion, and my lungs fill with rejuvenating air.

Pulsations come through the tether. Home waits for me on the other side.

Before I run towards the light, I reach out to one of the tendrils before it escapes into the darkness. The pulsation of the strand shudders, unsure how to beat. When I bring the cold towards the other strands, it doesn't weave together. It remains on the outside, as if afraid to consume the light and hesitating to be joined.

I extend my hand to the darkness, and he wraps his hand around mine; the action fuses the tendril in with the others. All the colors move in harmony as the darkness and I run towards the light.

* * *

"I'm not leaving her."

Haidion. I'd recognize his voice anywhere. He has two powerful tones, both similar in strength, rivals like fire and water that work in

515

harmony. There is an arrogant challenge in his voice that is always present like fire and water mocking one another when they dance.

My eyes flutter open to see a ceiling of black mirrors, just like the one I have back at home. I lay upon a large four-post bed with a button-tufted headboard covered in lunar blue satin sheets. The circular room is illuminated by a glittering aura and orbs of warm light in living trees with leaves and flourishing mint-green roses. The stone walls are a lovely rosy pearl with golden violet trim and star quartz floors. Two grayish-black wooden doors are opposite me, and a pair of double doors are to my left. Floor-to-ceiling curtains of icy gray drape across three arched windows. An armoire, a writing desk, and a button-tufted couch sit to my right, facing the windows. A spiral stair-case takes up the far-right corner, leading to a nest with a balcony. The room's grayish-black furniture is luxurious and covered with vines as if the wood were alive and growing right out of the floor.

"Freyja?" Haidion leans forward in a cushioned chair to my left.

Shadows clear away from his eyes, revealing dull amethyst hues. His tired eyes were baggy and bloodshot. His loose white tunic shows off the top of his chest, and a pair of black trousers hug his body, but he looks like shit. His chest rises faster than normal, and exhaustion slumps his shoulders, which is odd for him since he yells at me for needing to have good posture. Either he is terribly sick, or he stared death in the face and lost. Something is haunting him.

My throat hurts when I go to speak. "If you look like that, then I don't want to see what I look like."

Haidion leaps to his bare feet, throwing the chair out behind him. His thick, ebony curls fall out of a lazy bun as he drops to his knees by the side of the bed. His hand inches towards mine. When I close the remaining distance, my friend shudders with relief as he takes deep breaths to calm himself.

"You lost so much blood. I didn't think we were going to have enough moon blood to give you. And then the medicine caused your heart rate to drop too low and…"

Tears run unrestrained down his face. This isn't the strong, flirta-tiously charming Haidion that I know; this is a new side I've never seen before. He's expressing deeper, more vulnerable emotions that even I don't feel comfortable enough to share with him. I did back on the battlefield, but that was life or death for me. Maybe I was in such a state while I was out that it seemed like life or death for him.

He brings my hand to his mouth and presses kisses to my fingers. Now it's my turn to shudder at his soft lips against my skin.

"I thought I lost you." The crack in his voice pierces my heart and slices through my soul.

Without first assessing my body to see how injured I am, I slide off the bed and fall into him. A dull pain awakes, but I'd endure anything to reassure Haidion that I'm alive.

Haidion gathers me in his arms, pulling the blanket away from my legs and positioning me so I straddle his hips. As he buries his face into the crook of my neck, breathing me in, my skin blooms into a smoky hue of rose gold. Groans leave him as he absorbs my power. Seconds pass as his breathing evens out, and his heart rate becomes strong and steady.

"You shouldn't be wasting your energy on me. My darkness is too vast, and I don't want to consume all of your light." His voice is small and almost too quiet to hear.

My retort gets cut off when his fingers slide up and down my spine in soothing strokes. He's never touched me like this before, and with the silk rubbing up against my skin, little noises that I only make when I'm in bed escape me. *Wait, why am I wearing silk?*

Pushing off of Haidion a little, I take in the deep purple nightgown. Dirt and blood still coat my skin, so no one bathed me, but where did my armor go, and who changed me?

"Valrir undressed you, and she tended to your menstrual bleeding." Judging by the thick cotton underwear I have on, she got really personal with me. "She and Iraijah are also seeing to it that your armor is repaired." He answers my unasked question. "They are my left and right hands. I trust them with my life."

I nod and play with the strings of his shirt, almost tempted to keep untying them. "How long was I out for?"

Haidion's fingers keep trailing my spine as his other hand remains on my hip. "Twenty-six hours, thirty-eight minutes, and one second." I gape at him, and he chuckles. "You needed time to heal. Valrir told me she needed almost three days."

A realization hits me. "I'm not on Earthradon, am I?"

He gives me a wide smile. "You are in my home. I call it *Memoreea Fevaira,* or in the common tongue, The House of Memories. This is my guest bedroom."

I'm in Orrtiereum. The only times I'd ever come to the plane was with Hel, tagging along as she saw to the upkeep of the afterlife for our believers. Afterwards, she would accompany me to Wardalyn to ensure that the beings of our faith who were sent there were punished accordingly for the crimes they committed. Just the thought of Hel has tears blurring my vision. I don't want to cry in front of Haidion or in general, but I can't help it. I can't hold them back, and it angers me.

When I hide my face in Haidion's neck, he pulls our bodies together again. "What's upsetting you? Is the room not to your liking?"

Shaking my head is the only answer I can provide him, as memories of Hel and me flash in the forefront of my mind. The reel ends with the butterfly flying into my chest.

I'm here for you, Freyja. All you need to do is extend your hand out to me, and I'll be there for you. As Haidion spoke into my mind, the darkness collected the memories and brought forth coolness and comfort.

I hold him tighter, as if I can shield my heart with his strength so he can fight off the painful memories, just like how he parted the battlefield and left bodies in his wake.

I don't know how long he holds me, but I gradually become aware of my sticky face and the inability to breathe out of my nose. "I need a bath."

"I got something better than a tub."

I pull away from him in surprise. "What do you have?"

He only answers with a wink before his hands drop to my bare thighs to hoist me up higher so he can stand. Without my armor, I'm able to wrap my legs around his waist and lock them together. But as I squeeze my thighs, an uncomfortable pain awakens in my core, and I lean into him, hissing.

"You are due for more medicine and moon blood. Once you are done cleaning up, I'll nourish you."

He walks to the left door opposite the bed as a tendril of his magic reaches out and opens it for him. We step into a large bathroom. A bouquet of white roses with black leaves, stems, and thorns blooms to life, lighting up the area. Their roots delve deep into the ground and rise to support the glowing glass bowl sink with a rose-shaped spigot and a galaxy countertop. A toilet and a massive step-down soaker tub made of pristine black stone take up the far-right corner of the room. In the opposite corner is a spiral staircase and a circular glass enclosure with a wooden floor.

Haidion places me on the counter. The warm surface on my butt makes me yearn for his coolness as he lets go and steps away. Rather than pouting, I scrub the desire away.

"The spiral staircase leads to an indoor spring that my bathroom and this one are connected to." He pointed to the enclosure. "And this is the shower. Think of it as a bath you stand up in. Rather than soaking your body, the water constantly pours over you."

I look at the shower with skepticism. "How does it stay warm if no fire or enchanted stone can heat the water?"

"Hot and cold water comes in through pipes in the walls. They are pressurized from tanks that store the cold water and heat it up. If you are interested, when I give you the tour, I can show you them. I know you like to see things work."

As Haidion walks over to the shower, I jump off the counter and undress. My reflection shows that my body is covered in bruises and sticky with dry sweat. Dried blood coats my hands, face and neck.

With a twist of my hips, I check out my ass; the brand on my cheek is gone. I sigh with relief and peruse the rest of my muscular body. A set of glass chains twisted into an infinity symbol is tattooed on the small of my back. A sheathed blade is on my spine; the long handle has a carved intricate design of shadows and sacred light entwined with the sun and moon. Out of all the brands, only one coils anger in my heart. Bold line-work outlines Bralyant's bite on my neck, signaling that I belong to his pack and to him. My last newly acquired brand, the promise I made to myself, takes the form of a blazing green thread strung around a double-bladed axe between my breasts. Out of all my brands, my favorite is the white willow tree on my lower abdomen.

The sound of rushing water fills the room, and I untie the feather from my hair and undo the tiara braid. My inner thighs are stained with blood, and dried salve covers the area where the poison burned my skin. The paint on my face is patchy, licked off by Haidion's Cerberus. I'm quick to wipe a tear away and turn from the mirror. My heart hurts knowing that I would never see the runes Hel painted on my face, the runes she said my soul is forged by.

"If you turn the nob to the right, the water will get warmer, and if you turn the nob to the left, it will get cooler. If you need anything, I'll be..." Haidion's face flushes red when he turns around. "I'll be outside."

I blink at him, confused, as he walks to the door. "Why are you so skittish?"

He braces against the doorframe. "I'm not. I'm giving you privacy."

"You know I don't have a problem with showing my skin, and you told me you don't either."

Haidion has had his fair share of being around people who chose to be naked. He once told me some Demonicals wear just enough to hide their precious parts, while others choose to wear cloaks to hide who they are entirely. Only a few dress fully like he does.

Butterflies come to life in my belly, not out of shame or embarrassment, but because of how he will react to seeing all of me. We've been friends for centuries, and I always had to hide a part of myself from him. Like the Wolven, I wouldn't mind being naked all of the time, but society calls for me to wear clothes. I want him to not see nakedness as a sign of anything other than me being comfortable with who I am.

"I know. It's just..." He trailed off.

A sharp pain of hurt starts to dig into my heart. "Why won't you look at me? Is it because I'm covered in bruises and scars?"

Wood cracks under Haidion's grasp and falls to the floor.

I grip the vanity and clench my thighs together as wetness starts to make them slick. My core throbs with desire, begging to be touched. After every battle, I yearn to be reminded that I'm alive. At the sight of his strength, I want nothing more than to have those hands on my body and wrapped around my neck.

I mentally curse myself for not thinking this through, and now my forbidden thoughts are running free.

Haidion turns and strides over to me with purpose in his every step. Steam tries to consume him, but it parts, not daring to touch his skin.

He braces his hands on the counter, caging me in as his eyes scan over the entire length of my body. He is so close; my heavy breasts almost touch his tunic. His gaze lingers on the scar on my left side before meeting my eyes.

He leans in, leaving only a breath of space between our faces. "When I look at you, I see strength. Not because you almost have as many muscles as me, but because of the fierce light of your soul. It's a flame that can't ever be put out."

Something inside me purrs, wanting nothing more than to melt into him.

"But I also see the blank face of a being I need to hunt down for hurting you." Haidion's eyes darken, becoming the predator I've always admired. "I want to torment them." He tilts his face to the side, so his cheek brushes mine. "I want to torture them." His whisper goes straight to my needy clit. "And then when I'm done with them..." The soft lips I constantly force myself not to stare at graze my ear as his voice drops to a deeper octave. "I want to watch you kill them." *Is it possible to cum without being touched?*

I bite my lower lip to hold back a moan. "She is already dead."

His chuckle caresses my overly sensitive skin. "No one is beyond my reach, even those who have already departed."

"You're speaking as if you're the Fate of Death." My teasing tone turns into a breathy whisper.

Haidion pushes off the vanity with a wickedly satisfied grin. "Enjoy your shower. I'm going to go take one myself." He walks to the door but pauses to look back at me. "The vents in here will take the steam away, but sounds will travel since they are all connected." He bites his cushiony bottom lip. "Don't worry about being quiet if you choose to soothe any special kinds of aches."

Realization sparks in my mind at what he's implying when he winks. He knows exactly how my body was reacting. Being caught basically begging for his touch catches me off guard, and doses me with embarrassment for being so responsive to him. Without having a proper response to his comment, I act instead.

Ice forms in my hand, and I throw it at his head.

He dodges at the last second and bolts out of the room as the ice shatters into flakes of snow.

Laughter erupts from the other side of the door. "Oh, how much I enjoy playing with you, my darling Freyja."

The retort I had planned falters in my throat as I recall what he said about the vents and sound. How does he know the sound travels? A realization hits me as to what type of guests stayed in this room. Rather than ponder that thought, I step into the shower and turn the nob to cold.

* * *

Two outfits were laid out for me when I got out of the shower; a green tunic with tan leggings and fuzzy, leather slippers or a red, silk night-gown with matching undergarments. I toss the nightgown on my pillows and dress.

When I step out of the guest bedroom, I find Haidion leaning against the opposite wall. He's in another pair of tight-fitted black pants with a midnight purple tunic. His hair is braided into a tight bun, and I hold back my pout because I want his hair out and free like mine.

He pushes off the wall, brushes my hair away from my eyes before offering his arm. "Have I ever told you how gorgeous you look with your hair down?"

Heat crawls up my neck as I shake my head. "You've rarely seen me with my hair down."

"True." He brushes a strand behind my ear, sliding his fingers over my chin. "They are like regal waves of passionate fire."

By the way he smiles warmly at me, I know he sees the tinge of red on my skin. Thankfully, my stomach rumbles, pulling me out of a trance.

"One time I almost lit my hair on fire." He blinks at me in surprise, breaking the reverie he was in. "That's why I braid it all the time, even though it sucks because I like it long. Maybe I should just cut it short to make my life easier."

The thought of cutting my hair causes my soul to screech, but my tirade successfully returns us to the friend zone.

Haidion clears his throat and starts to give me the tour. His room is right across from mine. Down the hall is a door that leads to the under-ground spring and the stairs to the tower. The walls are the same star quartz as the floor in the bedroom, and vines branch out in all direc-tions beneath the crystal-clear floor. With each step we take, petals bloom. Every couple of feet, vines pop out of the floor and create bouquets of luminous spring-colored flowers. Black mirrors cover the ceiling, and the walls are textured. Unique places, animals, and people I don't recognize are carved in stone.

"This is why I call my home the House of Memories." He gestures to the images as we approach a grand staircase with a railing made of thicker vines. "Whenever someone walks the halls, the house shows them their memories."

The same design flows throughout the house. In the main foyer, we pass three double black doors with gold trim that lead into various areas of his study, library, and by extension, the gardens. On our left are floor-to-ceiling windows covered in gold curtains. At the end of the hall are massive stone double doors that lead to the lower part of the house where his housemates stay.

Vines twisted into several chairs surround a long table in the middle of the dining hall. The table is a terrarium of succulent plant life held up by even more vines. Lining the back wall are more covered, floor-to-ceiling windows. Mouth-watering aromas waft from the door at the back of the room, making it clear it's the kitchen.

Surprisingly, the vines have enough give in length to allow Haidion to pull out a seat for me. "My home is magical because of the Rose Oak Tree that I planted... wow... forever ago. Once the tree took root, my friends and I built this house and allowed room in the floor for it to grow. The base and lower branches are in the spring underneath, and the canopy is in the tower. The magic detects all movement in solid form, spiritual form, and shadows. I like to know when someone is in my house." I nod, my amazement making me speechless.

He sits at the opposite end of the table, a nervous chuckle leaving him. "I know my home is kind of overwhelming, which is why I have all the curtains closed." Concern pinches his brow and his natural smile falters. "Where I live is much different than where you do." He leans in, placing his elbows on the table and folding his hands together. "The last thing I want is to scare you away."

I manage to sputter out, "Your home is lovely." A stemless, black crystal glass with gold leaves appears in front of me out of thin air. I take a sip of refreshing water to soothe my dry throat before continuing, "I agree with not seeing all of your home just yet. After everything I went through, I just need to feel safe."

"You will always be safe here." My heart melts as he speaks with confidence and certainty. "For as long as you are in my presence or under my roof, no harm will ever come to you. You have my word."

Tears spring from my eyes, and before I can wipe them away, shadowy-star tendrils do. They wrap around my body in a hug before settling into my hands, giving the patches a glimmering glow once again.

Haidion gives me a tender smile before he whistles. A black plate of food piled high with biscuits and two slices of a crusted pie appears in front of me, along with a vial of sparkling, purple tonic and a black rose petal teacup filled with blue-tinted milk.

"The tonic is for the pain, and the moon blood, or, as Valrir calls it, "moon milk," is for magical and physical nourishment. I had it flavored, so it's not as bland." His eyes shadowed over for a second. "You are going to need the tonic for one more day and you should drink the moon milk every day until you know your cycle has ended."

"Did you just ask her or something?"

Haidion cuts into his pie and takes a bite, a little moan of delight escaping him. "No. That was her telling me she wouldn't be able to join us for breakfast. It seems that my puppy can't be trusted to not barge in here. So, she is staying with him."

A chuckle tickles the back of my throat. "I would love to meet him."

He smiles with amusement, curving the corners of his mouth. "He's kind of a handful and likes to speak his mind."

"Oh, I know. I met him before the battle." The words tumble out of me right before I recall that Haidion didn't know he was with me.

I quickly tell him about when I first noticed that his puppy was with me, the Fae child in the woods, how he helped me with use star magic, and that he possessed my body before I got struck by lightning.

"He was very helpful. Please don't punish him."

A muscle ticks in Haidion's jaw before he smooths it out with a smile that doesn't reach his eyes. "He won't be." He gestures to my food. "If you would like anymore, just ask." Rather than poke and prod him to tell me what's bothering him, I eat.

The pie is flaky and filled with a mixture of eggs, breakfast meats, onions, peppers, and mouth-tingling spices that have me moaning like Haidion was. I normally don't eat anything spicy because Odin liked everything simple, but I find myself shoveling the pies into my mouth. Before I ask for more, I move onto the biscuits. Each bite has little pieces of apple that melt on my tongue, and the creamy glaze has my tastebuds singing their relief from the spicy food I had a moment ago. After finishing those, I take my tonic and sip my tea. The milky taste of lavender, chamomile, cinnamon, and honey has more moans leaving my lips. I sit back in my chair and place my hand over my belly. *I'm glad I didn't ask for seconds.*

There is comfort in my belly, but none in my mind or heart. I might've slept for a while, but that doesn't chase away the pain that is starting to surface. Nor does it protect me from the reality that I'll face once I get back home.

"Since you're comfortable enough to be around me naked." Haidion places his knife and fork down after finishing his last bite of biscuit. "Can I ask about the multitude of brands you have on your body?"

"Four of them are debts, one is a bargain, and another is a vow I made to myself."

Something shifts over his features that's too quick for me to determine. "I'd be more than happy to help you to clear those debts."

My brother told me that getting the magic system to remove a debt without fulfilling it always comes at a higher cost, which makes me wonder why Haidion would think that he can help me.

"I don't need your help to clear them, but I appreciate the offer. Do you have any brands?"

Haidion brings his glass to his mouth. "You'd be surprised at what my magic can do." With a wink, he takes a long sip, letting out a sigh before wiping the corner of his mouth with a black napkin. "I don't have any brands. Tattoos, yes." He sets down his glass with a soft click. "Most frown against beings inking their skin just because they want to."

"I don't. Never feel like you have to hide parts of yourself from me." I would reach for his hand if he weren't so far away.

A grateful smile lifts his lips. "In due time, my darling Freyja, you will know everything about me. Especially if you wish to stay."

My jaw drops. "If I wish to stay," I repeat. "You'd let me move in with you?"

"Yes." His certainty has my heart skipping a beat. "With everything that's going on back on Earthradon, if you don't feel safe or you just need time away, my guest room is yours for however long you like."

"That is the most thoughtful offer anyone has ever given me." Tears want to spring free, but I hold them back. "Thank you." It's a relief to not have to worry about expressing gratitude or apologizing here, but I know deep in the strands making up my soul that Haidion would never take advantage of me. "But I don't know how I can. I was born on Earthradon, and I have a duty as a goddess."

"The paperwork I'd take care of, and as for the details of you still being able to work, we would figure it out."

I can't help but smile. "I'll think about it. I need to go back as soon as possible." The faces of my fallen friends flit over my vision. "I want to bury the fallen."

Haidion nods. "Of course." He stands and walks over to me, offering a hand. "You should get more rest then."

I give him a bemused look. "I just woke up..." A yawn has me slouching. "Why am I so sleepy?"

I'm pulled out of my chair with delicate gentleness. "It's the tonic. The only way to combat this is by sleeping it off rather than staying awake and facing the pain." When my steps falter, Haidion picks me up and cradles me to his chest.

I sleepily try to get out of his arms. "I need to go." Haidion chuckles at my weak attempt to break free. "The Ghouls will eat them."

When Haidion brushes his lips across my temple, I stop my efforts to escape. "The Preserver Guild has been protecting the valley. Come morning, the Dragons will oversee the burials. The land will be neutral, but I doubt no conflict will arise."

He walks with purpose up the stairs, and it almost seems like we are flying. "Why wasn't I called then? I joined the Preserver Guild on the day of the battle."

"Have you met the Governor yet?"

Technically yes, but not about the guild. "My good friend, Vahildra, hasn't graced me with his presence since the day I went to Crescent

Island." I rest my head on his shoulder, giving into the cooling comfort of his aura.

The doors to the guest bedroom open, but Haidion doesn't walk through. "Your good friend?"

"Yes, we are friends." I tap the skin scrunched between his brows. "Is someone jealous that I have more than one Ancient Demonical friend?"

The odd look he was giving me was gone in a second. In my sleepy state, I couldn't tell if it was curiosity or irritation, perhaps a mixture of both. "It makes sense now why Vahildra offered to come and tend to you rather than entrusting the duty to Valrir. He's the one who gave me the supply of moon blood, made the tonic, and salve."

"How was I able to drink the moon milk and tonic while I was asleep?"

"You don't remember?" His eyes narrow when I shake my head. He appears to be both concerned and angered by my memory loss. "You woke up every couple hours when the pain was getting severe. After Valrir helped you change out of your padded undergarment, I nourished you, and then you asked for me to rub your back until you fell asleep."

My heart starts to fill with an emotion it hasn't felt in forever. "I don't deserve your friendship."

"You're right." My breath hitches when he leans in. We are so close that I can feel his cool breath on my warm lips. "You deserve much more."

A whimper of longing threatens to escape me, and it takes all of my self-control not to drop my gaze to his tempting mouth.

I quickly divert my thoughts. "Is it really blood?" Haidion only answers me with a wink as he walks into the room.

My body starts to go limp as Haidion places me on the bed. "Want me to change you into this?" He holds up the skimpy red nightgown.

If I had any strength left in me, I would make a snarky comment. Instead, I kick my slippers off, remove all my clothing, and snuggle into bed. "Don't let me sleep in, please. I want to be back to Earthradon by dawn."

Haidion takes all the clothes to the second door next to the bathroom and sets out another folded bundle on a chair before settling on the couch.

"Are you staying in here?"

Haidion tucks his hands behind his head. "The last time I left you alone while you slept, your heart rate dropped." Silence fills the room for a moment before he speaks again. "The reviving breath of star magic can only do so much... I thought I was too late to bring you back." Sadness is potent in my chest, as if my senses have become empathic and are picking up Haidion's emotions. "I would like to stay close so I can sense your heartbeat better, just in case it happens again."

Longing to keep him close tightens my chest and dampens my eyes. "Yes, you can stay."

A barely audible sigh comes from Haidion as he relaxes on the couch, propping his perfectly symmetrical feet up on a pillow. "Thank you." He whistles, and all the illuminated roses close, casting the room into darkness.

I didn't think I could actually die from starting my menstruation. No one told me it was a possibility or what I would need to nourish myself. It was almost as if they wanted me to die. *Or free me.* I dismiss the unwanted thought and snuggle up with a pillow.

"Thank you for everything you have done for me, Haidion." I swallow down the desire to ask him to lie with me. "I would've been lost without you."

"That's what friends are for. Goodnight, my darling," he calls out sleepily.

A tender sensation strokes my mind, soothing me into a comfortable slumber. Peaceful moans leave me as a whisper of smoldering warmth sings three words that make my heart swell, and surprisingly, they bring me no pain.

CHAPTER

THIRTY-SIX

Each step I take towards the Great Willow Tree, one of my friends falls.

A ghostly figure of starry night pulls their essence out of their bodies before I can attempt to activate my power to hold onto their souls long enough for someone to heal them.

In the distance, someone shouts for me as the ghostly figure grips my shoulders. Have they come to claim me? No, I can't let them! I must get to the Father.

With all my strength, I fight, screaming for them to let me go. No matter what I do or how loud I shout, they remain anchored to the spot.

An explosion of light and sound comes from the now-wilting willow tree. Wails and sobs break free from me as I fall to my knees. Fire engulfs the field as the Father screams, calling out for me to bring restoration. How can I? Why would he trust me with such a task? I failed him. I'm a failure. I don't deserve to keep on existing.

* * *

A lethal darkness of cold wrath takes the memories away, pulling me out of my nightmare and into the light.

Haidion is above me, panting. His tunic is shredded, and he's

529

holding onto my shoulders. "You're out." My chest heaves with rapid breaths, making me aware of how tight and sore the back of my throat is. "Are you alright?" I can only shake my head.

Haidion gets off and helps me sit up. Being upright allows more air to come into my lungs, but the action of breathing is agonizing. Wheezes and whines come out of me as I grip my throat with one hand and ball the bedsheet in the other.

A moment later, a glass of water is pressed against my lips. "Sip slowly." I do as he says.

The liquid is soothing and cools down my feverish body. As I sip, I watch my exhaled breath ripple the water. The motions help to calm my racing heart.

Wonderful coolness embraces my hand. Slowly, I loosen my grip on the sheets and turn my wrist to clasp the silken softness. It takes my mind a moment to process that I'm holding Haidion's hand. Rather than push him away, I keep holding him, allowing his touch to ground me as he keeps the glass pressed to my lips.

Once I finish the water, I lean back against the headboard. "Did I hurt you?" My voice comes out raspy.

Haidion gives me a wicked grin. "If you wanted to see me shirtless, all you had to do was ask."

My chuckle turns into a hard cough. "That doesn't answer my question."

"No, but it made you smile." I can't stop the tears running down my face as my heart swells.

Haidion puts down the glass and leans against the headboard with me. "I'm here for you." He gives my hand a squeeze.

Rather than allow him to keep seeing me broken and weak, I ask, "Will taking more tonic help to keep the nightmares away?"

"No. The tonic is just for the pain." When he reaches over to wipe a tear away, I lean away from him. Without needing to look, I feel his sadness at my rejection, and it only makes me want to cry more. "But I can get something to help." With another squeeze of my hand, he gets up. "I'll be right back."

Once he is out of the room, I bolt to the bathroom and shut the door.

Tears burst out of me as I slide to the floor and bring my knees to my chest.

All of those I lost crash into me like a devastating wave, submerging me in anguish. Their faces flit over my vision, reminding me how I could do nothing to save them.

I don't know how long I sit there, but when knocks interrupt my breakdown, I wipe my tears and stand.

After splashing water on my face, I open the door to see Haidion is back on the couch, lying down with his eyes closed. He's wearing a new tunic, black this time, and there is a vial on my bedside.

"I have a hard time falling asleep. My mind races, and I can never calm myself down without exerting myself to the point of passing out. I grabbed you some tonic from my medicine cabinet that helps me on nights when I'm restless." Haidion says softly.

After swallowing the bitter liquid, I wash it down with some more water and snuggle back into bed. "Thank you again," I murmured into the darkness.

"I'll do anything to help you, Freyja." He turns onto his side, towards the curtains. "You need only ask."

* * *

Haidion was gone when I woke up. Maybe he heard me stirring and left to give me privacy, but not seeing him on the couch has an ache squeezing my heart.

After adorning my undergarments, I dress in a lilac tunic that fits me more snuggly than the one I wore yesterday. Black leggings, brown knee-high leather boots, and a vest to match complete my outfit. With an appraising look in the mirror as I braid my hair, I am certain that I appear ready to spend the day digging graves.

When I open my door, Haidion is there, leaning against a wall. His eyes are shadowed over as he offers me his arm. "Morning, Freyja." A chuckle leaves him. "My friends say hi to you as well."

Nervousness has butterflies fluttering in my stomach. "Am I meeting any of them today?"

The shadows vanish from his eyes as he gives me a boyish grin.

"Only one." The smile has him looking younger; whoever we are meeting must be a very good friend of his. "The garments you are wearing enhance your already breathtaking beauty, by the way."

I shrug off his compliment before my blush can show. "By the end of the day, these nice clothes will be covered in dirt, as will I." I take in his outfit, a burgundy suit with gold stenciling and buttons. "You look ready to attend a ball."

Haidion shakes his head and lets out a heavy breath. "Like I have told you numerous times, this is my casual attire. What I wore yesterday was what I wear when I'm not feeling one hundred percent." As we reach the stairs, he leans down to my ear and whispers, "I normally don't let anyone see me wearing such clothing or see me when I'm in a distressing state, so I would appreciate it if you kept that between us." I shuddered when his lips faintly brushed the shell of my ear as he pulled away.

An elegant voice of determined strength calls out with a groan, "Stop flirting and get your ass down here, you raspberry rabbit. I'm hungry." If Haidion wasn't holding me, I would've stumbled down the stairs at the sight of the beautiful being leaning against the bottom railing. "I'll warn you now. If you even eye-flirt, Freyja and I will eat alone in peace while you go dine with the other buffoons."

Her short, curly red rose hair, partially shaved on her right side, glitters like stars and makes mine look like dirt in comparison. A deep rosy blush is brushed over her warm beige skin, and her lips are like decadent cherries. Sharp blue-green eyes take me in from head to toe as Haidion and I descend. She wears form-fitting, full-body, frosty silver armor line with gold, giving her the illusion of being made of metal. The intensity of her beauty matches her strength and towering height; she's at least a foot taller than me. I'm both empowered and intimidated by her presence.

Haidion chuckles at her comment. "If you banish me away, then the others will plow down that stone door, jealous that you get to have alone time with my darling Freyja." His claim of me as his darling sounds different than how he normally says the endearment.

She gives him a challenging smile. "I'd like to see them try." Her gaze flicks to me as we reach the bottom step. "No one gets past my defenses."

Haidion gestures to her and bows his head slightly. "Freyja, I'd like you to meet Valrir, my right hand." She extends her hand out as he gestures to me. "Valrir, this is—"

"Your obsession," Valrir finishes for Haidion and gives me a reserved smile. "I've heard much about you to the point of wanting to put daggers in my ears."

I brace her forearm, and she immediately grasps mine with a bruising grip that almost makes me wince. She's testing me, and instead of displaying my dominance in strength, I use my clever mouth.

"I'm sure you want to put those daggers in your eyes for having to clean my bloody thighs. Thanks, by the way, for tending to me."

Haidion laughs so hard that he coughs as Valrir takes a second look at me, either sizing me up for a kill or truly seeing me for who I am and not what Haidion has told her.

She lets go of my arm and gives him a pat on the shoulder. "She is going to fit right in. Now, let's eat."

Floor-shaking bangs come from the stone doors at the end of the hallway, making Valrir groan. "Why did you tell him?"

Haidion clears his throat. "It was funny."

Valrir walks back over and flicks his ear, making him hiss. "And now your puppy is off his leash, wanting to come and say hi."

She pulls me away from my friend, making him growl possessively. I can't help but chuckle when she flips him off. Haidion pulls out my chair before I can do it myself. Valrir rolls her eyes as she takes a seat on my left.

I squeal as I take in my favorite breakfast. A cup of hot apple cider is next to my moon milk and a small vial of tonic. My plate is full of buttery baked potatoes cut in half with smoked ham, sunny side-up fried eggs, a side of beans, and roasted tomatoes. On a smaller plate are black raspberry muffins with extra berries on the side. It was forever ago that I told Haidion what my favorite foods were, and I'm both surprised and touched he remembered.

After I down my tonic and my moon milk, I dig into my food.

Haidion's eyes sparkle as he picks up his fork and knife and cuts into his—

"What type of bread is that?" Instead of muffins, they both have loafs on their smaller plates.

Valrir pulls off a slice, not bothering with silverware. "Rosemary garlic bread," she moans after devouring the entire section and pulling off another piece.

Haidion chuckles. "Valrir and I both have an addiction to garlic bread."

"And as your right hand." Valrir licks her fingers and looks at his loaf. "I should inspect your bread to make sure it's not poisoned."

He points his knife at her. "Touch my garlic bread, and you will lose a finger."

She picks up her knife. "Wouldn't be the first time. And in the end, I was victorious."

This might be normal for them, but I've seen enough fighting. Uncertain if I'm about to watch a duel over bread, I ask, "So, Valrir, is there a difference between the duties of the left and right hands?"

Valrir sticks her tongue out at Haidion before lowering her knife and turning to me. "The left hand helps with the emotional well-being of their ruler. He sorts out Haidion's private affairs and looks at how they affect his rule and reign and has more ideas on how to better himself and his station."

"I don't intend this to be a judgment on your choice, Haidion, or for you to take offense, Valrir, but shouldn't I have met your left hand first?"

"No," they both say in unison.

"The right hand overrules the left when it comes to personal affairs that might mix with professional ones," Haidion states. "My left hand, Iraijah, is as excited to meet you as I am to have you here, so it would be a mixture of his personal interests getting in the way of his duty."

Valrir eats a spoonful of yogurt. "Iraijah's judgment is clouded along with his." She points her spoon at Haidion. "So, it's my job as his right hand to be the voice of reason, logic, and when to bring the hammer down. I also see to the diplomatic side of his professional affairs, maintain allies, keep track of enemies, and basically babysit his ass."

Haidion runs his fingers over the edge of his glass. "I always have either Valrir or Iraijah in my shadow every time I leave here." He takes a deep breath. "They were respectful of our time together but were still there."

Realization hits me so hard I sit back in my chair with a thump. "For five centuries?" Both of them nod. "Why have you waited so long to tell me?" I don't wait around for his answer, leaving my half-eaten plate of food and them behind as heat burns in my chest.

Haidion calls for me, but it's not his hand that grips my shoulder and whirls me around. "He is of a high station," Valrir declares with a level of authority that has me almost taking a step back. "He's one of the most powerful beings I know, but he needs someone to watch over his back. And with one of us being in his shadow, we can feel when leeches try to attack him, and it's fucking often because they sense how lethal his magic is."

"Valrir." My blood runs cold at the sound of Haidion's demanding tone. My attention snaps to him like prey latching onto the sight of the predator about to devour them. Valrir tries to ignore the command in his voice as she clenches her hands. "While I appreciate your words, I was mistaken in adding you to this conversation. It is clear to me that this discussion is intended solely for Freyja and myself.

She doesn't move to look at him until a moment later. "I'll be in your shadow when you leave." Rather than go back and finish her breakfast, she is swallowed up in white shadows and flies down the hall towards the double stone doors, the petals chasing after her movements.

A lethal cold I hadn't noticed before pulls away as Haidion's features soften. "I'm sorry I didn't tell you." He places his hands in his pockets. "The only reason I didn't is because there was a barrier on me being able to open up to you fully, and now there isn't."

Only one thing comes to mind. "Odin." Saying my ex-husband's name leaves a nasty taste in my mouth and stops my stomach from demanding more food. "Me being married was the barrier." When Haidion nods, I take a step until I'm in his personal space. "Why was my marriage what kept you away from me? I mean, stopped you from telling me?"

A fraction of warmth fills his eyes, but it is gone in a second. "To protect my friends. You told me Odin seeks out knowledge to the extent that you have to tell him if you learned anything."

During one of my lower moments after Odin punished me, Haidion was insistent on wanting to hang out shortly after. Holding back my tears wasn't a problem because it was an unusually cold summer night, but I couldn't silence my tongue. I told Haidion of my vow to Odin: that if he seeks out knowledge about something and I know it, I was to share it with him. Somehow, I had the strength to fight the marital brand's influence when I was asked what I knew about shadow magic.

"If you were worried about that, then why did you tell me your true name and reveal your identity to me?" After the day I told him about my vow to my husband, I didn't see Haidion for months until Winter Solstice.

Haidion cups my face. "Because not being with you was killing me!" He lowers his hands quickly and takes a healthy step back. "At the time, you were happy with Odin, and I accepted that I could only give you a portion of who I am so I could protect my friends. To reveal more about myself was to take an even bigger risk, but to have you in my life was worth it." His breathing comes out heavy and strained.

My anger is extinguished. I close the distance and pull Haidion in for a hug. His arms immediately wrap around me, and our bodies are fused together, his cold with my warmth.

"I understand. Just please..." I trail off, knowing that if I ask him not to hold back parts of himself, I must not either, otherwise, I will be a hypocrite. "Tell me when someone is in your shadow."

Due to the sensual and intimate nature of our embrace, all I can think about is the daydream where we passionately kissed as if the world were about to be devoured. When I pull back, I see his soul shining in the depths of his eyes.

"We are alone right now. We've been alone ever since you first woke up here." His hand trails up my side to the nape of my neck. "And if you choose to stay with me..." Slowly, he massages my skin in soothing circles, and I melt into him. "...no one will enter this portion of my home without your permission. I promise." He kisses my flushed cheek lightly, like a feather brushing against my skin.

My body shakes with need, not just for physical pleasure but to be cherished and loved further. "I'm ready for you..." I blink and rush out,

"...and me to go. That's if you're done here. I mean, good to travel." I step out of our embrace, relieved that he lets me go.

"I actually do need another moment with you before we leave." Gone is the sensual affection his soul was caressing mine with, and in its place is perseverance to protect. "I'm worried about you going back to Earthradon. Even though the land is neutral territory, there might still be conflict for you from each side. If a leader is still alive, that means there is still hope. The opposing side might go after you, or the warriors you led into battle and the families with lost loved ones might try to unleash their anger on you."

"Are you trying to convince me not to go?"

"That was not my first thought. I merely wish for you to know that I may exhibit a tendency to be a bit protective. While we're digging graves and burying bodies, I will certainly honor your privacy if you so wish, but I will remain vigilant for any possible dangers." Before I can ask anything, Haidion lifts his hand, and a piece of paper with a wax seal appears out of thin air. "I got myself a bereavement pass so I could go to Earthradon during the hours of the sun." He slides the paper into his front jacket pocket. "You do intend to still head north, correct?"

"Yes, but I have a concern as well." As fast as my happiness came, it left, and my frown returned.

Haidion grips my hand and gives it a squeeze. "Whatever it is, you can share it with me. I'm here for you."

I bite my lip as nervousness flutters in my belly. "During the battle, Odin put a bounty on my head to have me brought to him. Loki did, so that won't be an issue." Anger furrows his brow. "But some were trying to capture me with the intention of freeing me from this galaxy." That lethal cold wave wafts out of him again. "I don't know why. The only thing I can think of is that they just wanted me out of the way, or they didn't want Odin and me to have a child."

I wish I could take the last part back, but I couldn't help it. A part of me wants Haidion to know my worries, even though being emotionally vulnerable scares me because I don't want to be taken advantage of.

"I will find out for you," Haidion stated as if he was pledging his soul to me, fortifying his word on getting the task completed. "And if you allow me, I want Iraijah to watch your back. He will only make himself known if you are being taken or bound. He'll remain in the shadows, but not in yours."

"That's fine with me."

The past couple of times I was captured, I only escaped because someone intervened. I want someone to watch my ass since I obviously needed the protection, but I can't constantly have that support. I will have to figure out how to avoid being taken all on my own.

I pull Haidion in for another hug. "You're such a good friend." This embrace isn't like the others; he isn't putting his full strength into it. He's holding himself back. "Um, are you ready to go?" I ask, pulling away to look up at his face.

Haidion's attention is on something distant. In a snap, his natural smile returns, but his eyes remain dark.

A ring of shadow fire appears in front of us, and I'm lifted into Haidion's arms.

Before the void of darkness consumes us, I bury my face in Haidion's neck and hold on tight as he moves through the portal. I will never get over the sensation of floating with no way to move while being pulled in a multitude of directions, as if at any moment my soul and Skjoldr could be ripped from my body. Haidion can navigate the portal while keeping me close to him, even though it feels like we're weightless. By the rush of wind hitting the side of my face, I know he has his wings out, and we are flying faster than ever before.

A moment later, a grieving morning sky with flying dragons above and a shimmering barrier preventing entry into the valley greets us.

After Haidion sets me down, I walk over to get a closer look at the blue, translucent magic. "How are we supposed to—"

As a mass of black fur darts towards me, I stumble into Haidion.

"It's alright, Freyja. It's just a Preserver." *One that I know.*

Before the Wolven fully shifts out of his massive form, I lunge at him, and wrap my arms around his neck. "I'm so glad to see that you're okay."

"What the fuck, Freyja?" Aliith pushes me off him, his chest heaving. "Do you have any idea how worried Treason and I have been?!" I'm at a loss for words. "Do you have any idea how hard it was to watch fire rain down on you while we had to remain behind that barrier?" He doesn't let me answer. "We thought you were dead!"

Only our breathing fills the silence until Haidion casually steps up to my side. "We wish to pay our respects." He takes out the piece of paper from his pocket and holds it out for inspection. "My pass." When Aliith doesn't make a move to look at it, a lethal cold emits from my friend. "Preserver." The commanding voice has me shaking, and I flinch at first when Haidion reaches for my hand.

Aliith's eyes burrow into me, seemingly unbothered by Haidion's magic. He radiates so much anger that my senses warm me to prepare for an attack as Skjoldr urgently hums in my chest.

"I believe you." Aliith bangs his fist on the barrier, causing it to open.

Haidion nods to him as he walks us through. "Friend of yours?"

"I don't know." He intertwines our hands and gives me a squeeze, but I don't look at him.

I understand why Aliith is upset, but the question of whether he's my friend or not leaves me at a loss. I can't worry about that right now; there are more pressing matters that need my attention, like burying bodies and figuring out my next move. If the traitorous gods and goddesses think I'm going to accept defeat, they are wrong. I will get the Father's heart back and bring restoration to Earthradon. And while I'm doing that, I have to find out how to contact the Shadow King and give him the Father's message.

"Shall we?" Haidion tugs on my hand, and I follow.

In silence, we walk toward a group of beings assembled in front of the wilting branches of the Great Willow Tree. As shovels and water skins are being handed out to newcomers, someone calls out that there is no assigned section to bury bodies, no matter what side they fought on.

When Haidion and I approach, my name is uttered in hushed whispers. Some call me commander and nod in respect or greet me as a goddess and bow. But most look upon me like the deaths are all my fault until they realize who is standing next to me.

A glittering aura surrounds Haidion, letting me know the crowd sees the monster. Fear takes hold of everyone, or maybe it's my friend who has taken control over them.

I squeeze Haidion's hand, and his voice enters my mind. *Yes, my darling?*

Don't "darling me." Stop tormenting them.

As you desire. But those who desire your death will be added to my torture list. Haidion doesn't bother to lie about taking control of their minds. To ask him not to harm them is like telling him to stop breathing.

All at once, the crowd slumps like they are suddenly overtaken by exhaustion, but it's a sign that Haidion is no longer in their minds. *The might of his magic amazes me.*

A growl comes from behind us, but quickly turns into a gasp. "Freyja?"

I whirl around to find Treason. A dozen emotions pass over his face, but he lands on concern as he focuses on Haidion.

"Ominous is my friend. He came with me for emotional support." I understand Treason's concern. Most of the time, when a being is seen with a Demonical, they are either their current prisoner or plaything.

Treason nods his head in respect. "Ancient."

Even though Haidion isn't bound by our rules, he still honors Treason's title by bowing. "Your Highness."

When Treason goes to do the same, I snap, "No friend of mine bows to me."

One moment, Haidion's hand is in mine, and the next, I'm in Treason's strong arms. "I thought you were dead." Even though he sounds upset, he doesn't let go or ease the tight hold he has on me, as if I were one of his pups.

Treason rubs his cheek against mine, and I whimper, enjoying his affection. He presses his face into my neck and breathes me in. After finding my well-being satisfactory, he drags his lips to my forehead, and places a kiss on my skin. Heat creeps up my neck, and goosebumps rise all over as I tremble in his arms.

I'm shocked that he performed such an intimate act, especially with a crowd watching us. Such a kiss is normally used between lovers, but we are only friends. I push the thoughts of what this means away and bury my face in his chest. With all the death we experienced and the pain we endured, our embrace is more than just comfort, it is to reassure one another that we are alive. In this moment, I don't feel anyone else's eyes; it's only Treason and me, as if the world has been whisked away and we are in our own realm of existence.

Treason whines in relief as I rub the side of my face over his heart. "It will take more than fire to kill me." My words repeat in my mind as I realize the weight they carry for my friend at my back.

As I suspected, when I turn out of Treason's grasp, Haidion has deflated a little and looks like he doesn't know if he will ever see me again.

When I reach for him, he pulls me to his side and rests his forehead against mine. All the onlookers have moved on to bury bodies and don't dare look our way to judge the affection being given to me by an Ancient Demonical.

"Can I have a word, Freyja?" Treason asks, keeping a respectful distance away.

"Do you mind getting us a pair of shovels?" Haidion hesitates as he releases his hold on me, but not before placing a kiss on the back of my hand.

He walks over to Treason's side and leans in. "In my absence, should any freckle on her flawless skin be harmed, your fur shall be affixed upon my mantel."

"I expect nothing less. And perhaps if I fail, you might reconsider that my pelt ought to be used as a rug in your bathroom. That way, I would consistently have to take your shit."

To my surprise, Haidion chuckles, and Treason cracks a grin.

Treason takes my hand and leads me up the field a ways away until no one is in our immediate area. "What is it?"

"Firstly, Bralyant is here. Ominous was doing a great job at masking your scent, as am I, so you don't need to be bothered by him. But knowing how obsessed he is with you, be prepared for his presence throughout the day." I nod in understanding, but I wish Haidion had told me he was masking my scent. "Secondly, the Father's daughters are nowhere to be found. We think the tree absorbed them."

Pain aches my chest at the thought of Existence. "That makes sense. The daughters were born from the Great Willow Tree."

"And thirdly, the lords and ladies made a decree that all gods and goddesses are to be taken back to their pantheons. The Preservers already took care of that. All the rest have to stay here and be buried here."

I already knew that the bodies would have to be buried here, but for the lords and ladies to make it an order for all the fallen warriors of the races to remain is unfair. "Why would they do that?"

My question was more for myself, but Treason answers anyway. "I don't agree either, but there is nothing we can do." His cracking voice stops me in my tracks.

An internal pain makes his soul tremble. "No." I shake my head. "No," I repeat as my sight becomes blurry.

Tears stream down his cheeks. "My portals found my children, but four of them were dead. The same arrows that killed Apollo and Artemis were in their chests." He erupts into sobs as he falls to his knees. "I can't bring them home to be buried with their mother."

I kneel next to him and pull his face into my chest, wrapping my arms around him as tight as I can. There are no words; I can only hold my friend as he cries his soul out. Praying to any of the Fates won't be of any use now. Their paths were already decided, and without their souls tied to this planet, I can't bless them.

I can help. I look up to find Haidion standing behind Treason. In the Beta Prince's distress, he must not have sensed him approaching. *I can create an illusion of Treason's children being buried and then portal them to his home.*

It's his choice. But if he agrees, whatever the cost, I will pay for it.

If Treason is a friend of yours, then there will be no cost unless he insists. However, I will have to leave you to go and help him.

I'll be okay. Thank you, Haidion.

Treason pulls away but stays in my arms. "I needed that. Mr. Moody, as you call him, made me cry, but I wasn't ready." His eyes widen as he whirls around, pulling me behind his back. He relaxes once he sees Haidion, then tenses.

I'm telling him what I just told you.

To my surprise, Treason doesn't growl at the intrusion of Haidion speaking into his mind. The Beta Prince relaxes a moment later, and both nod to each other. Some look passes between them, leaving me feeling left out.

Haidion sticks the shovels in the ground and offers us both a hand. "I'll be right back." Before handing me a shovel, he kisses my palm.

Do you mind if I leave some of my magic in your mind? That way if you need me, you just have to think and speak to me.

Yes, that's fine. How do you plan on not getting your clothes dirty?

Haidion flashes me a wicked grin as he pulls a shovel out of the ground.

Who says I'll be wearing them as I dig?

With a wink, he and Treason walk off to where his pups are.

Rather than indulge in that sight, I push the thought into the darkness of my mind and start to dig.

CHAPTER
THIRTY-SEVEN
THIRD HOUR AFTER SUNRISE

More volunteers show up as the sun rises. I stay towards the West Woods, burying Fae and Wolven, while the majority start from the willow tree.

My tears land on the soil as I pat it down, burying another Fae. Thoughts roll around in my mind about how I'm going to get the Father's heart back. All my ideas go back to needing Faithless. Having him will assure me that I can face Zeus, but I need to get him from Thor.

I'm halfway done digging another grave for a Wolven when my senses pick up someone approaching.

"Freyja!" Bralyant leaps into the grave and pulls me into him. "I thought you were dead."

Knowing I caused him heartache, I allowed him to hold me for a moment longer.

But as he pulls away, his attention goes to my naked left forearm. "You're divorced."

I rolled up my sleeves after the first dug grave and contemplated taking all my clothing off except my boots; however, I figured this would happen, and I don't trust Bralyant to be around me when I'm naked anymore.

When his lips broaden in a smile, I start to dig again. "Since you don't have a shovel, I guess you are here to annoy me?"

"No, I picked up your scent and had to see you." A moment of awkward silence passes before he speaks again, "After we are done, can we go to your home and talk?"

I snap, "No, I don't want to go back there."

Realization hits me in the chest when I think about going to a place where Haidion isn't. The cabin was my home, but the thought of Odin being there has me unwilling to return. Perhaps Haidion is right; I need time away.

"Come home with me then. No one will talk against me about you staying for a little while."

"I'm not going anywhere. I just want to bury these bodies in peace."

"I didn't mean now. I'm talking about after."

I whirl and face him, spearing my shovel into the ground. "I'm not going home with you! And I don't have anything I want to say to you or talk about."

He grips my shoulders and pushes me against the wall of the grave. "If you don't vent, you're going to fucking explode." When I try to shrug out of his grip, he growls.

I growl right back. "I don't need to vent to you. Not right now, not later, not tomorrow, and not ever." I need him to understand, so I say the truthful words that will shatter his soul. "You might want me, but I don't want you!"

Sadness creeps into his eyes as fury increases his rapid breathing. "You don't mean that. I love you, and you love me."

"I loved you. Past tense, not present."

With a twist, I escape his hold, but he lunges for my arm as I try to climb out of the grave. "Don't touch me!"

A lethally cold wind wafts from above me, and when I look up, I find Haidion staring at Bralyant as if he's about to kill him with his gaze. "Unless you want to lose your hand, I suggest you don't touch her again." His presence relaxes my hammering soul.

Bralyant growls, "And who are you?"

Haidion offers me a hand, and I cling to it like a lifeline as he pulls me up. Bralyant jumps out and stands on my other side. Both men glare at one another intensely, and I realize that the glittering aura around Haidion is gone, meaning that he has revealed his true form.

"Isn't it obvious?" Haidion keeps his tone calm, and his intimidating demeanor controlled. "I'm Freyja's newly acquired friend. Although the term 'new' might be outdated since our friendship is five centuries strong." He extends a gloved hand towards Bralyant. "I'm Ominous."

Bralyant stares at his hand and doesn't reach out to shake it. He chuckles while meeting my eyes, but he isn't the least bit amused. "You not only married a god to ignore your love for me, but you also became friends with an Ancient Demonical, a monstrously dangerous being, to fulfill the thrill you want in life."

"That's not an original compliment, but I'll take it." Haidion pulls off his gloves and shakes the dirt off them before putting them in his inner jacket pocket.

Bralyant ignores Haidion's comment with a snuff of dismissal. "I'm not mad, Freyja. It just shows me how thick your stubbornness is to fight your love for me."

A crunching sound comes from Haidion. "It actually sounds like." He's eating an apple. *Where the fuck did he get an apple?* "Freyja has moved on, and you are in denial." He takes another bite.

Bralyant turns his gaze to my friend with a snarl. "Why do you think that you are part of this conversation?"

Haidion grins like a cat who just caught a mouse. "You made me a part of this conversation when Freyja told you to not touch her, and you tried anyway."

Bralyant puffs out his chest. "And you're here to fight her battles for her? Do you not think she is strong enough, demon?" My blood runs cold.

"Bralyant!"

Devious mirth lurks in Haidion's eyes. "I'm only here to pull Freyja away from you. The last thing she needs is the death of the wolf king on her hands."

Haidion! Calling Bralyant a wolf is just as bad as a Demonical being called a demon.

Bralyant's muscles flex as a growl rumbles out of him. Haidion doesn't meet his eyes; instead, he moves his attention down the length of the Wolven King's body. He smirks and takes another bite of his apple before meeting Bralyant's violent gaze.

"I'm a Wolven. And you can snicker at my groin all you want, because my cock has been fucking Freyja for longer than you two have been friends." *Fuck, this has gone too far.*

Before I can get a word out, Haidion laughs. "Given her lack of desire for you, it is clear that the quality was inadequate."

I direct soul magic into my hands and press my palms on both of their chests. "That's enough!"

Haidion frowns at me like I just took his favorite toy away. "What did I do?" He dramatically fakes innocence with a hand over his chest, cupping mine. "I simply intended to get acquainted with your average-sized friend."

"If she lets you between her legs, just know I taught her everything, and she will always remember I was her first."

Fire burns in my chest, and the last thread I had that cared about Bralyant's well-being turns to ash.

The lethal cold coming from Haidion turns so sharp that each breath I take begins to claw at my insides, but a radiant warmth embraces me, protecting me from the invisible talons and soothing the aches in my lungs.

I'm so sorry about that, Freyja.

It's okay. I'm okay. If I had your power, I would've done the same thing.

Please, let me play with him one more time?

Bralyant is dead to me. I lower my hands from their chests. *Have at him.*

Rather than take control of Bralyant's mind or cause him pain with sharp talons, Haidion brings the apple to his lips. He laps up the juices with his girthy tongue before twirling the tip in circles.

The fire in my chest travels down my core and pools in between my thighs. *What the fuck?*

Treason yanks me from between them and takes my place before Bralyant lunges for Haidion; I didn't even realize that he was watching the entire time. "Alpha, we have more important matters that need your attention. And as for you, Ancient, you might have a pass, but disturbing the peace will earn you a trip home with a Wardalyrian."

Haidion raises his hands in surrender and takes a healthy step back, but not before offering me his hand. I allow him to pull me to his side and wrap a protective arm around my waist. He offers me the half-eaten apple, and I don't hesitate to finish the rest of it.

Bralyant rolls his shoulders and locks eyes with me. "I will find you afterward, Freyja." His attention drops to where Haidion has a hold of me. He growls, then shifts into his beast form.

Treason gives me a sympathetic look before he shifts too and takes off after his Alpha.

Once I'm done with the apple, Haidion makes it vanish with a twist of his wrist.

My attention is drawn to the shadowy gold stenciling on Haidion's jacket, and I can't help but reach out to trace it. "I thought you were going to play with him a different way."

When I look up at him, he gives me a wicked grin. "Do tell me, my daring *larvaelet*," he purrs as he leans in, our faces only inches apart. "How would you have wanted me to torment him?"

Before I can bite my lower lip, black starlight covers his amethyst hues. All the playfulness drops dead as his features harden with irritation.

The light vanishes a moment later. *Haidion?*

I'm being summoned by the Sons of Judgment. They need to see me. He brushes dirt off my face as he tightens his hold on my waist. *I'm sorry. I can't stay here with you.*

Don't be. My hand trails up his neck, wanting to touch his skin, but I step out of his hold. "Be safe."

Haidion's mouth widens in his signature smile of wickedness. "Never. It's no fun." He catches my left hand before I can turn away from him to go back into the grave. "If you need me, my darling Freyja, you need only call, and I will be here."

"I know you will be," I breathlessly whisper as warmth fills my chest, knowing how true his words are.

His eyes stay locked on mine as he kisses my palm, pressing his full, soft mouth into my skin.

Before I can contemplate doing something reckless, he vanishes into thin air.

The feeling of his lips lingers on my palm, as if he's still kissing me. My heart swells a little, and I'm greeted with no pain. Perhaps coming to the point of death made the soul rot weaken. Either way, I find myself smiling a little. Even with everything that's going on, Haidion manages to put a little happiness in my mind, heart, and soul.

* * *

Solar Noon

With the sun beating down, the vibrant colors of dried blood and lifeless bodies glow like flowers trying to soak up the sun.

Every time I lift my shovel, I see the faces of all the beings I killed during that first hour of battle. When my shovel hits a rock, the vibration and sharp noise of stone against metal make me flinch, as I remember being struck by lightning. The only way I'm working through it is by pushing the images into the darkness of my mind and counting. Keeping my mind on being more efficient with digging is the only way that I can remain mentally strong to bury the fallen warriors.

After rolling a Wolven into the hole, it only takes me a fraction of the time to cover them up before I move onto the next. I've made my way to the South Woods, but I still have another dozen bodies or so until I'm done with this corner section.

A lead brick drops in my stomach when I spot a pair of feathered wings like daggers in the distance. I'm running so fast that I'm surprised I don't trip over bodies.

The Fae is lying on his front, making me unable to see his face. I drop to my knees and turn him toward me as my hands shake. A shudder of relief rakes through me as I take in a Fae I don't know. I blink a few more times to make sure, but it's clear as I wipe my eyes that this isn't Illyrical. With his side half-burnt, I'm surprised his weapons didn't—*wait*, his weapons are gone, not melted.

"When a Fae dies, all their weapons go to their next of kin." I whirl to find Illyrical standing behind me, alive and whole. He takes a step closer as I stand, curiosity in his spicy brown eyes. "Why were you inspecting his body?

"I was checking to see if he...was you."

He drops his shovel from his shoulder and starts to dig. "Hoping I was dead?"

"No."

Illyrical's attention shifts to me. We are locked on each other for an intense moment before he smiles. "You do know what that means, right?"

I pick up my shovel and start to help him. "Well, since you're alive, I hope that means so is Drafasa."

He laughs and starts to dig again. "Pissed off, but alive." I nod my thanks and keep digging. "Wait. You are going to take my word for it?"

"You have given me no reason to not trust your word." In the depths of his eyes, his soul brightens.

We fall into silence as we bury his friend. I catch Illyrical looking at me out of the corner of my eye multiple times. If his gaze was on my ass, then that would give me a clue as to why his attention is drawn to me. But he isn't checking me out, it's more like he's deep in thought.

I pat the soil down, and before I can move onto another body, Illyrical offers me a glass bottle of water.

"Much appreciated." Seeing that he has his own, I down half the bottle.

After Haidion left, I returned his shovel and grabbed a few water-skins, but I run out of water an hour ago. I've been forming ice and rolling it around in my mouth to hydrate with a mist layer over my body to keep cool.

With a flick of my wrist, mist forms, and I hold my hand out to Illyrical. He eyes me for a second, before taking it. The mist covers every inch of his body, and he lets out a sigh as his wings and the petals of his armor flap out; the frosty sheen brightening as it absorbs my magic.

A wave of emotion passes over Illyrical's face, and I push the desire to read him aside. "Is your brother gone?"

"Yup. Turned to ash. His court is in chaos without a leader being selected, but that's not my family's problem."

"Does that mean you can stop hiding who you are?"

He nods with a smile of happiness. "After I'm done burying my friends."

Rather than move onto another Wolven, I put my shovel over my shoulder. "Let's go find them so you can go home to your family and be free."

Illyrical eyes glisten. "Why would you do that?"

The full truth is on the tip of my tongue, but I swallow a portion of it. "Your family has suffered enough. You all deserve happiness, and the sooner you get home, the quicker it will become a reality."

I'm ready for Illyrical to call me out, but he just slings the shovel on his shoulder. "This way."

* * *

8th hour after Sunrise

My hands can't stop shaking. It's not from fatigue or exhaustion, it's worry. Haidion has been gone for five hours, meaning he's been in Orrtiereum for twenty. I wouldn't be anxious if I had heard from him, but I've received nothing. *What could be taking him so long?* I send him a message and get back to patting the soil flat.

"Freyja?"

Sensing Illyrical's attention on me, I quickly glance over so he doesn't see my unease.

"Prepare yourself." He's tense, his attention on something far in the distance. "We have company."

At first, I'm hopeful that maybe he spotted Haidion, but when I turn my gaze to look, I spot a large pack of Wolven running our way.

Illyrical throws his shovel into the ground and stands by my side. "The Wolven King is coming."

Realization hits me: Bralyant is coming with a pack, and Illyrical is at my side. "You need to go. This might be neutral territory, but I don't trust him to not do anything."

"If I run every time my race clashes with theirs, then it only proves that my race was guilty of crimes we didn't commit." Before I can ask, he continues, "I also don't trust the new king. I'm not leaving you alone with him." He takes my hand and gives it a quick squeeze.

"There is something that I need to tell you about the Wolven King."

His body tenses even more as they get closer. "What's that?"

I swallow a lump in my throat. "That Wolven I told you about, well, that's him."

551

"You are friends with the Wolven King?" At least there is no judgment in his tone.

"We were until recently, and..." I continue in a whisper, "...we used to be lovers, and he wants back in my pants."

He's quiet for a moment, then mutters under his breath, "Well, depending on how this plays out, it will tell me where we stand." His features shift into something more stern and ruthless; the uncaring facade his race is known for.

Bralyant and Treason shift into their humanoid forms, while the rest remain as beasts and circle us.

Illyrical nods his head to the Wolven King and Beta Prince, but only Treason acknowledges his respect. Bralyant stares at the Fae like he wants to rip him to shreds.

It's clear that there is a commotion going on, yet the dragons flying above don't even look over.

"I thought you had more important tasks that needed your attention, Alpha?" I don't bother to withhold the venom from my voice.

The Wolven King doesn't break his stare off with Illyrical. "You being near a Fae who isn't dead is on the top of my priority list."

Treason steps between them. "As you can see, Alpha, she is not harmed nor being reigned."

Bralyant snarls, "She's still near one of them."

To stop any further conflict, I step forward.

Betrayal stings Illyrical's soul, making him flinch. His cruel mask shatters, revealing his hurt and sadness.

As Bralyant reaches for me, I clap my hands together and pull them apart. My mist explodes and surrounds Illyrical and me.

"Ask your Beta Prince what my mist can do once inhaled, Alpha." I flick my attention over to Treason, whose eyes are wide with worry.

"I know what you're capable of, and I also know that you won't hurt me," Bralyant says as he and Treason come closer. "Why are you acting like this? I told you what his kind has done to mine."

A screeching snarl rolls out of Illyrical. "We didn't kill those children!" He turns to me, and from the depths of his soul, he pleads, "I give you my word, *Sundrae*." By the way he said the word, it sounds like a term of endearment.

"What the fuck did you call her?!" Bralyant roared.

All the Wolven growl, eager to be let loose to attack. Treason de-escalates the pack's aggression with a snarl. They all lower their heads, not just in fear but in a show of respect that can only come from a leader who has served for centuries and proved his strength and grit.

"Your emotions are affecting the pack," he whisper-yells. "If you don't lock it down, they will lash out without you commanding them." Bralyant bares his teeth, but the Beta Prince doesn't back down. "Is this how a leader is supposed to act? Would your father act this way?" To all others, Treason is overstepping by not listening to his Alpha, but I see a compassionate friend.

Mid-shift, Bralyant takes Treason to the ground and clamps his jaw onto his shoulder. To my surprise, Treason doesn't make a sound and allows his Alpha to assert his dominance.

Illyrical grips my shoulders when my mist turns to shards of ice. "Don't you dare attack. His beta spoke out of turn." Tears threaten to stream down my face as I take in the scene. Treason, covered in dirt and bleeding, bares his teeth at the Alpha. "I know it's a hard sight, but if you care about the prince, you need to not act on his behalf."

Only when I nod and send my ice to the ground does Illyrical let me go.

An empowering voice of peace and strength enters my mind. *Oh, stars almighty. What type of trouble have you gotten yourself into?* Although the voice sounds harmonious, it's clearly irritated.

Valrir, are you in my shadow?

Yes, I came to get you. Haidion got put in a holding cell. I wouldn't be worried if I could talk to him, but our communication cut out, and I can't get into his cell.

Blazing warmth from deep in my soul is unleashed and fills my veins. *Take me to him.*

A portal of radiant light intertwined with metallic shadows opens from the South Woods. A deadly mist with a soul-draining aura claws its way over the grass, coming our way.

"Shadow monster!" Illyrical bellows.

All the Wolven snap their attention to their backs. Their growls and whines make Bralyant stop his efforts to make Treason submit. Orders are barked out, and the pack retreats.

Bralyant turns his gaze to me, and I snap, "If you dare leave your beta in the dirt, I will kill you!"

My words impact my old friend's soul, and he flinches. With no other Wolven around, he doesn't assert his dominance, nor does the stubbornness of his alpha make him bare his teeth at me for commanding him. Instead, he lays down and allows Treason to climb onto his back.

Illyrical pulls me behind him and takes out the curved blades at his hips. "Go with them. I'll hold it off."

Before I can utter a word to tell him to fly away, a void of darkness coats my vision, and I become weightless.

I automatically close my eyes as my body and soul are tugged multiple ways as Skjoldr hums in my chest, directing all the air out of my lungs.

All you need to do is go through the stone wall and don't stop until you see Haidion. Whatever you do, remain in your spiritual form. Once you see the state of his condition, come back out. And yes, Haidion told me about what type of magic you wield; it sounds impressive.

My spiritual power activates as I'm dropped in a dimly lit hallway lined by torch-like sconces with black starlight emitting from them.

Where exactly am I? What level in Orrtiereum are we on?

We are currently in Castle Ceaxia, the heart of operations for the Ancients, on level five.

Just as I'm about to go through the stone wall before me, a Wardalyrian in his gargoyle form walks down the hallway. His stone wings fill the corridor, and his head is only a couple inches from the ceiling, making him well over eight feet tall.

I back out of the way as the Wardalyrian approaches the wall. He scratches his nails across the stone in a pattern, revealing a hidden metal door.

Of course. Valrir lets out an irritated huff. *As soon as you get down here, our luck of getting to Haidion has changed.*

I can't help but grin. *The Fate of Chance must like me to roll in my favor.*

Doubt it.

With a heavy pull, the door slides to the right. I follow the Wardalyrian inside and almost gasp when I see Haidion dangling off the ground with his arms and legs outstretched by chains, like he got caught in a web.

Haidion lifts his head. "Normally, when an Ancient is summoned, it doesn't involve them getting detained and chained."

"It's a new protocol when the Sons of Judgment aren't ready to see you right away," the Wardalyrian grumbles in a voice like rocks grinding together.

Haidion huffs in annoyance. "Then why didn't they call me when they were ready?"

The Wardalyrian shrugs. "You can ask when you see them."

Haidion is lowered to the ground, but the chains aren't removed.

As I trail after Haidion and the Wardalyrian down the hall, Valrir's voice enters my mind. *The chains are why I couldn't reach him. All his magic, abilities, and powers are blocked. Even soul connections are severed, basically turning him mortal.*

They could be the same chains the traitorous gods used on those who didn't side with them in battle.

If that's true, Freyja, then that means the gods were given the chains, and the Sons of Judgment might've chosen to side with them. Fury burns in my chest, warming my soul to the point I start to see my shadow. *You need to calm down.*

I reach Haidion's side and fold my hand over his. Even though I can't really touch him, the sight of our hands together helps me ground myself.

"The Sons are ready for you." The Wardalyrian unhooks the chains from Haidion and gestures for him to walk through a pair of behemoth-sized double doors.

There are black starlight wards all over the entryway. I won't be able to enter, and Haidion's magic isn't going to work for a bit. The choice is up to you. Either stay out here with me or follow him.

With a powerful push, Haidion opens the doors just enough for him to enter.

I'm not leaving him alone. I follow close behind him.

Torches of fire illuminate the vast, circular room. The space is large with multiple levels that extend upward towards an opening at the top, reminding me of a colosseum.

Ahead of us is a row of six thrones made of gold and silver bones.

They sit on a raised dais, with one that sits behind the others, taller than the rest. If the rumor that the Fate of Judgment helps the sons from time to time is correct, the larger throne must be theirs. From what Haidion has told me about the sons, there is no relation between them and the Fate. The Sons of Judgment are named after their late father, Victrielle Judgment.

Six beings sit on the thrones wearing bloody ash velvet cloaks and white metal masks. I cannot make out their eyes behind the shadows, but I can see their stout frames and pale hands.

Haidion pantomimes, taking off an imaginary hat and putting it back on as he bows. "You guys could've at least bought me dinner first before chaining me up."

A deep, voracious voice comes from the group, but I can't tell who speaks. "If we thought wining and dining would make it easier to gather intelligence, we would've done so. And before your smart ass asks, no, we wouldn't try seducing you either."

"Normally, we are put into a waiting area when summoned, not our own personal cell. I was afraid someone was going to come in and suck my cock. That would not have gone over well." I have never heard Haidion sound so arrogant before.

A head on the far-left tilts. "Oh? And why wouldn't it have gone over well if I were to have gotten you off while you waited? Is there a lucky lad or lady? Are they a slave or your whore?"

Haidion chuckles. "If you wanted me to spill my guts out about who is hardening my cock nowadays, then you should've gotten me drunk first."

"You do admit to having someone in your life, though?"

Haidion puts his hands in his pockets. "Is that why I was summoned here? You want to know if I have someone special in my life so you can go grab them and use them as leverage to get me to talk." He leans in as if telling them a secret. "I hate to break it to you, but I know how interrogations work."

The brother on the far right waves his hand. "Enough! You were brought here because the gods on Earthradon threw a fit about what you did on the night of what they are calling the 'Bloody Equinox.'"

"How fitting. And they have no reason to be pissy. They deserved to be tortured for killing the Father. Don't you all agree?"

"We don't care. We're only annoyed that we have to deal with the privileged brats all on Earthradon call gods."

Haidion's upper body flexes, putting strain on the fabric. "They killed the Father. You all should care."

A brother on the right shrugs. "Our plane is still standing, as is Earthradon. Clearly the deity's presence wasn't holding them together as all thought. With him gone, there will be no threats to our existence."

"The Father being gone isn't going to stop the asteroid." Haidion's raised voice echoes. "Earthradon and Orrtiereum are still bound to be culled. Only Erresthralla is safe because no greed has plagued them."

"We aren't worried."

Haidion attempts to ask why but gets cut off. "You were in your right to go up to Earthradon, but you did injure dozens of gods."

Haidion waves his hands. "But did they die? No, I only injured their souls."

"But your Cerberus did kill some of them, which we must address. Since the beast was under your command, you are held responsible. So, we have two options for you. One, we execute Nightnir. Or two, we take away your title, and you are hereby banned from ever going to Earthradon unless you are invited by the lords and ladies, a ruler of a race, or a leader of a pantheon."

"Take my title," Haidion stated without hesitation. "You are not killing my pet. Nightnir did nothing wrong. Those gods betrayed the deity who gave them life. They deserved to die."

I couldn't agree more, but my heart sinks at the decision he had to make. His choice now affects my own. I won't go without seeing Haidion. Home was where the happiest memories I had were made, and now my happiness won't be able to come and see me. I lost too much already. I won't lose him either.

"Very well. After we are done with you, you are to report to Namtar so he can strip you of the privileges the title granted you. He will also perform an evaluation to determine if you deserve to keep your office, remain working, and have access to Wardalyn and Excilum."

Black starlight wraps around Haidion's neck. His entire body stiffens as he is painfully forced down to his knees.

"Now our interrogation will begin." All the brothers laugh while one walks down the dais and circles Haidion. "Throughout your questioning, if you wish for your pain to cease, all you have to do is tell us who this special someone is." With a wave of his hand, the band glows brighter.

Haidion lets out a growl that turns into a screeching scream of pain. Never have I heard him in such agony, and I plan on never hearing it again.

I stand in front of the brother and reach for his soul. But before I grip the threads making up his existence, energy tingles in my reserves. A tendril of sacred light wraps around my hand as if someone has taken control over my arms. My hand moves further inside his chest with utter gentleness. I'm shocked that my interference doesn't make the brother aware of something happening.

My fingers wrap around a strand of black starlight, and my other hand reached inside.

The brother starts to hyperventilate and clutch his chest, releasing Haidion from whatever force was causing him pain. "Something is inside me."

"That's impossible. Your black starlight keeps all the leeches, shadow monsters, and phantoms away."

Once both of my hands grasp the thread, I work quickly to remove it. A second later, the collar around Haidion vanishes. The tendril of sacred light goes back into my veins, refilling my reserves.

As my friend gasps in relief, the brother who was controlling him roars, "My power, I can't access it!" He grabs the back of Haidion's head and lifts him up to face him. "What did you do?"

Haidion spits in his face. "I did nothing but dirty your mask." He gets slapped across the face and falls to the ground.

"Without your power, brother, we need to secure our planes with wards, or all types of creatures will be able to enter," another brother urgently states as the rest nod in agreement.

All of them grow bone wings, but only five fly out of the tower. The powerless one stays for a moment longer. "We know the Shadow King is walking among us and that there is an Ancient helping to cover his tracks. He has an entire realm. He doesn't need to be on our plane."

Haidion leans against the first step of the dais. "What makes you think it's a guy running the show?" He tries to stand but can't. "And what's so important that they can't come and look around? Are you all hiding something?'

The brother walks so close, Haidion has to strain his neck to look up at him. "I am going to ask you this one time, are you helping the Shadow King? It would make sense since you chose his name as your Demonical one."

Haidion chuckles. "Perhaps I'm just playing with him, mocking his name. Or maybe I am him and just down here to fuck around like I'm on holiday. I am the Demonical of Illusion after all."

I cover my mouth to hold in a scream as Haidion gets punched. "You are no king."

Blood drips from Haidion's mouth. "That we can agree on."

The brother spreads out his wings. "You are dismissed." He takes off in a gust of wind.

Once he is out of sight, the tendril wraps around my fingers like a snake and doesn't move to get free, as if it plans on staying.

What am I going to do with you now?

When I look at Haidion, the answer hits me. I can't think of anyone else who could be more perfect for this power.

As I approach him, the tendril wraps around my wrist, making its way up my arm as something with a fluttering heartbeat behind me shrieks in protest.

A glittering darkness explodes before I can turn around, and Haidion is before me. His eyes mist over in shadow fire as he bares his teeth like a predator about to consume its prey. A deadly cold wind assaults my lungs as sharp talons dig into my soul and squeeze, causing my existence to suffocate.

When I gasp for breath, Haidion's eyes widen in horror. "Freyja?!" He releases his icy hold as he gathers my limp body into his arms. "Oh, no. Freyja, I'm so sorry. I didn't know it was your magical signature I sensed." Only wheezes and pained groans leave me as the talons retract ever so slowly. "You're going to be okay. I'm going to make sure you are alright. I'll take you home, and you will be okay."

Haidion carries me out as a strength I didn't realize I needed to function weakens. Deep in my soul, I know that if those talons were to merely brush over the threads of my existence, they would snap. I'd be nothing more than a body of blood and a soul of ash.

THIRTY-EIGHT

Slick warmth passes over my face in multiple spots. I awake from whatever was trying to smother me, and I'm greeted by three pairs of red eyes. Tiny black heads yip with excitement, and it takes me a second to realize that a creature is next to me, a Cerberus. They stand on one of the steps leading to the black soaker tub I'm in, and I realize I'm in the guest bathroom.

Warm water sloshes over my face as I try to sit up. My body is weighed down by glass-like eggs filled with radiant light. With a strong push, my upper half breaches the water, encouraging the puppy to wag their three tails so fast that my eyes can't keep up.

Warm laughter comes from the doorway as Valrir walks over. "You're such a good girl. Did you wake up Freyja for us?" The puppy runs around her feet in excitement. "You better go tell Daddy."

With a unison bark, the Cerberus takes off. A moment later, someone grunts.

Valrir smiles broadly, and the expression makes her aura more friendly. "That's Nightnir."

"I didn't expect Nightnir to be an actual puppy."

"Oh, she isn't. A Cerberus can shift their size from adorable puppy to a behemoth of a beast." Valrir picks up a green fleece-lined wicker basket from the vanity and holds it out to me. "Place the eggs in here gently. Trust me, you don't want them to crack."

"Why do I have eggs on me?" As suspected, the eggs are extremely heavy. No wonder I wasn't floating on the water's surface.

"Rather than having you wake up to someone you don't know healing your soul, Haidion thought it would be better for Iraijah to place his eggs on your body. And before you ask, no, he doesn't lay eggs. Iraijah harvests soul light and places it in glass siphons."

I place the last egg in the basket and sit up fully. "Why does he harvest soul light? Doesn't that mean—"

"That the soul dies?" Valrir finishes for me as she places the lid on the basket. "It depends on how much he takes out of them." She stands and lifts the basket back onto the vanity. "Don't go judging him. The souls he harvests from do not deserve life." Her gaze drops to my body. "How are you feeling?"

Not caring about my nakedness, I stand with strength I never had before. "Amazing." The darkness in my mind pushes the memory of Haidion looking like he was going to kill me to the forefront. I swallow. "Where is he?"

Valrir nods her head to the door. "He didn't want his face to be the first you see in case you—"

I don't bother with a towel as I walk out of the bathroom. Haidion sits on the couch, facing away from me, with Nightnir on his lap.

Valrir whistles, and all the puppy's heads shoot up. "Come on, girl. Let's get some dinner."

With a final lick of Haidion's face, Nightnir jumps off the back of the couch and runs after Valrir. The doors shut on their own, leaving Haidion and me alone.

His breaths are steady and strong as he keeps his attention on the closed curtains.

I softly call out, "Haidion."

He chuckles. "I don't deserve to hear my name on your lips. It's rhythmic and ignites my soul with the sweetest fire I want to be devoured by. I think the more fitting name you should call me is 'vile demon.'"

"I would never call you that." My heart cracks at his self-deprecating use of the derogatory term. "If you call yourself that name again, I'll freeze your dick off." Haidion takes in a deep breath as if he's about to speak, and I tackle him to the floor, pressing my hand over his mouth. "Don't you dare!"

His eyes pinch in confusion as his voice enters my mind. *I was only going to start my apology to you.*

"Oh." My cheeks heat up as I remove my hand from his mouth. "I thought you were going to be an asshole and try to say it again to see if I would keep my word."

"I know the power behind your words." A small smile spreads across his lips. "And if I was going to act foolish with you, it wouldn't involve me losing my cock. I'm kind of fond of it."

Speaking of his cock, I'm straddling him on the floor, naked, and he doesn't seem to care that I'm getting his suit all wet. My attention doesn't linger on the closeness of our bodies as I take in the bruises on his handsome face. His left cheek is slightly puffy with discoloration, making his bronzy brown complexion a little darker, and there are streaks of red from where the son's knuckle broke skin. Fury fires in my soul, hungry to sever the hand that hurt my friend.

Haidion's smile turns sad. "We've got to stop meeting like this." When tears slide down his cheeks, I pull him into a hug as tight as I can.

After a second, he wraps his arms around me and sobs into my shoulder. "I'm so sorry, Freyja."

Tears leak from my eyes at how vulnerable he's being, showing me a side of him I've never known. The act of trusting me with his heart has my own swelling. My soul warms and sings, wanting nothing more than to be in his arms.

My mind wanders back to how I responded to the lightning strike. Will I feel the same soul-tearing pain if I see Haidion go beast mode again?

Haidion pulls back. "You tensed." He pulls a handkerchief out of his front jacket pocket, wipes his face, and blows his nose. "What's going on in that pretty head of yours?" I climb off him and wrap myself in a blanket. "It must've been serious since you're shielding yourself from me."

"I'm wet and getting cold."

He joins me on the couch. "That's bullshit. You're rarely cold." Without invading my personal space, he faces me. "You can tell me, Freyja."

No, I really can't. I wish I could say.

In the past, Haidion always fought disguised in an illusion, and the most I'd ever seen of his inner beast was the transition of his eyes. He'd never once shown me his beast form. Whatever he is turning into, I could possibly be triggered by it. I don't want to fear my friend. That would crush his soul, which is why I can't tell him.

"No matter how painful it might feel, I want to know the truth, Freyja. Protecting me from it hurts you." Haidion turns away. "You are already hurting enough."

"I'm healed."

"That's not the hurt I'm talking about." His suit starts to rip from his deep exhales. "I hurt you right after I told you that as long as you're in my presence, you won't be harmed. I gave you my word, and I broke it. I took your trust in me and ripped it to shreds."

"My trust in you isn't broken. You didn't know it was me."

Haidion stands up, rips his jacket off him, and pulls apart his corset and tunic, revealing his bronzy brown skin. His muscles are softly toned and ripple along his torso and his back. But what shocks me are his tattoos; fiery-black feathers cover his entire backside, from his neck and past the hem of his pants that hug his hips.

He kneels before me and places his hands on either side of my legs. "I want you to mark me. I broke my word, and I want to earn your trust back. This is only a fraction of what I need to do since there is no undoing assaulting you." I wince. "You can't call it anything else, Freyja. I hurt you."

My eyes become watery as I think of Odin and how he hurt me. "But you didn't mean to." I cup his face in my hands. "If you knew it was me, you wouldn't have, right?" He goes to argue, and I lean forward. His breath catches. "I forgive you," I softly mutter.

"You can forgive me that easily?"

"Yes, because I know deep down in your soul you didn't intend to hurt me."

"I still want you to brand me." Haidion's voice is shaky, but his arms remain firm as his chest flexes with each breath. "Please."

I shake my head. "My trust in you hasn't lessened. And besides, the power in the words you speak can only be shown through action." He stares into my eyes for a long moment before he nods. "Also…" I lean back and push him away with my foot. "…if you wanted to show off your remarkable body and tantalizing tattoos, you didn't need to shred your suit." I playfully frown. "It was one of my favorites."

"I'll be sure to have another made." He catches my foot before I can pull it away. "Care for a massage?"

I've never been offered that before, not from Odin or Bralyant. The only attention I ever received from them was sex. Even a simple back massage led to something sexual. Would this be something more for Haidion? I desire to be worshipped tenderly, and my throbbing core isn't helping me think coherently. But just because it's only a foot massage doesn't mean it's going to lead anywhere. Would I want it to? Would I want his hands to slide further up and massage my legs? Since he's already on his knees, would I want him to lower himself a little bit further and—

I jump when there is a knock on the bedroom door. "Vahildra is here," Valrir calls out.

Haidion growls out an annoyed breath. "I know. I sensed him." He places my foot down, severing the contact that had brought my forbidden desires to the forefront of my mind. "I'll be down in a minute."

"Better be only a minute, or I'm pulling you out by your ear."

At the sound of Valrir's motherly voice, my arousal diminishes. "My offer is still available whenever you want it." Haidion stands and picks up his clothes.

I leap off the couch. "Wait, can I come?"

A smile spreads across his sensual lips. "Yes, Freyja, you can come. It's time for dinner anyway." After laying out an outfit for me, Haidion says, "You never have to ask for permission unless you enjoy requesting it." With a wink, he leaves the room.

Heat crawls up my neck at his words, and I'm back in a forbidden place I shouldn't be. He has no idea what that phrase does to me, and the thought of touching myself before I dress has me stumbling.

Realization dawns on me; I imagined my friend almost going down on me. Just a simple phrase has me wanting to fuck my fingers until I scream.

I grip the back of the couch as my thoughts spiral. Just thinking about Haidion has me breathless and sensitive to the point where just a little friction would make me cum. I'm attracted to him, but acting on my desire could complicate things for us, especially since I want to live with him. Also, I'm scared to step over that line and leave the gray area we've been stuck in. Staying in the friend zone is the safest option. And with everything that I need to accomplish, there is no time to be selfish.

After a quick cold-water shower, I dry off, and leave my hair loose. I don the clothing Haidion left out for me; an off-the-shoulder white blouse, green leggings, and slippers. I roll my eyes at a pair of black lacey undergarments, but I still put them on.

Haidion walks out of his room just as I leave mine. He wears a star-speckled black vest with purple buttons. Without a jacket, his muscular ass sticks out.

"I thought you'd be waiting for me." I take Haidion's arm and walk with him.

He leans over. "I needed a couple of extra minutes to...compose myself." *Compose?* "But you never need to wait on me. You're free to head down without me. I know I take a while getting ready."

"I like you courting me." The words tumble out of my mouth before I could filter them. "I mean, I like walking with you."

Haidion halts. "Freyja?" When I bite my lip, he turns to me. "Is there something on your mind? The walls are blank with indecision." I look around and see for myself that the walls are flat. "You can tell me anything," he says in a tone of such tenderness and concern that my eyes warm with tears.

"I heard what punishment you took from the Sons of Judgment, and the thought of not being able to see you would break something in me." Admitting this little bit of truth from my heart has my throat clogging with emotions that I don't want to let out. "You are also one of the most important relationships in my life." A smile of happiness that I never thought I'd feel again stretches my lips. "I would like to live with you." Haidion doesn't blink or move a muscle; I'm not sure he's even breathing. "I know it's going to be a change being room-mates, and I still have my duty as a goddess, meaning I need to go up every so often—"

I'm lifted off the ground and spun in circles. Giddy, shrill laughter leaves me as I'm twirled in Haidion's arms. The walls change to memories of us.

"We'll figure everything out." He wraps me up in a tight hug so we are as close as we can get. "I'll make sure you can still work and travel back and forth."

I sigh in his embrace, enjoying his body wrapped around mine. I savor the press of his muscles against my own, and relish in how his cold tames my warmth.

We breathe as one as I wrap my arms around his neck and whisper into his ear, "That's the best gift you could ever give me."

"Challenge accepted." Little things, like the dedication in Haidion's voice, bring me such happiness that I almost cry tears of joy and utter the three words that are starting to fill with truth.

"Pray tell, what exactly are you two celebrating?" asks a smooth voice of cordial formality with a bit of emotion in his tone.

I turn to find Vahildra at the bottom of the stairs with Valrir. His face has the smallest of smiles as he takes in Haidion and me. His attire is all black, from his glove and his boots, except for a dark green, knee length trench coat.

Vahildra's warm brown eyes reflect happiness. "It's wonderful to see you again, Goddess Freyja."

"Lord Asphyxiator." A single chuckle leaves Vahildra, making Valrir blink in surprise.

Recalling what he told me about guessing his age, I think of a number. "Are you eight thousand years old?"

Vahildra shakes his head with a tsk. "That's still too young for me."

"If you're guessing his age, then you are not even close," Valrir offers.

"Don't you dare aid her." The Ancient Demonical of Disease gives her a sharp look at, but by the roll of her eyes, she is unaffected.

"Lord Asphyxiator," Haidion rolls the name with his tongue. "That name is fitting for the cold suit of bricks." My mouth drops.

Vahildra focuses on Haidion for an intense moment before shifting to me. "I overheard your declaration that you want to live under the same roof as this imperfection of a man. But do you truly know what kind of being you will be sleeping across the hall from?"

"I might not know everything about Haidion, but he doesn't know everything about me, either. In due time, we will reveal more to each other as trust is earned, and I think living together will strengthen that bond."

Pride shines in Haidion's eyes. He loops my arm with his, and we descend the steps.

Once we reach the bottom, I wrap my arms around Vahildra, needing to lessen the tension. "Hello, friend."

Vahildra embraces me with a hug before linking my arm with his. "Has Haidion shown you the gardens?" He glances over his shoulder, and a look of disdain passes between the two men. "I know how much you enjoyed our stroll on Crescent Island. Would you like to accompany me?"

Haidion comes to my other side. "We have important matters to discuss."

"And dinner is getting cold." Valrir takes my arm and leads me into the dining room.

I look back to see Haidion and Vahildra in an intense stare down as shadows coat their eyes. Haidion must've felt my attention on him because his expression shifts into a smile as he moves to pull out my chair. As he takes his seat, I turn my attention away from his ass.

Dinner is a grilled fish covered in a spicy, tomato-based sauce on a bed of greens and limes. I also have moon milk and a glass of white wine. Everyone else got the same meal except Valrir, who has a hearty bowl of vegetable stew and a loaf of garlic bread. Of course, Haidion has a loaf as well, and I'm tempted to ask for a piece.

"I'm sure you have something to say about me losing my ancient title that you worked so hard for me to obtain. I'm ready for the lecture," Haidion grumbles to Vahildra.

"I'm here for professional matters only, and not just for you. Welcome to the Preserver Guild, Freyja." He pulls out a thick leather book and a red letter from his jacket. "I stopped by your home, and when you weren't there, I decided to come here to see if Haidion knew where you were. I found a piece of mail for you on your doorstep."

He hands both to me and when the leather touches my skin, something on my forehead warms. Vines etched into the book glow green and shift into the sigil of a weeping willow tree with thorns for vines. The light dims as the book's metal clasp unlocks. My name and rank are engraved on the inner lining.

"That sigil is what you felt on your forehead. Only when you complete the reading and recite the creed to me will you be inducted into the guild. You will receive no assignments until then." Vahildra's soft expression hardens when he looks at Haidion. "They interrogated you as well?"

Haidion nods and takes a long sip of liquid that doesn't look like wine. "The only thing they learned was that I'm an arrogant asshole."

Valrir doesn't hide her chuckle. "That's an understatement."

They flip each other off before Haidion glances back at Vahildra. "What did you tell them about the Shadow King?"

"They suspect me, but to harm me would've caused a deadly illness or disease to be unleashed."

My interest in the book is gone. "Are either of you helping the Shadow King?" Vahildra doesn't look at me right away, but when he does, I'm greeted by the most serious expression I've ever seen before. "I'm only asking because I have a message I need to give to him."

Haidion's brows rise. "Oh? What is it?"

Uncertainty has me hesitating. "The Father spoke to me before he died. And the last time he told me something important, it was to be kept confidential. I would like to tell you, but I won't." I glance between the two of them. "So, can either of you point me in the direction of how I can contact the Shadow King?"

Valrir pulls the spoon out of her mouth and points it at Haidion. "He can help you." His eyes widen with worry, and he curses in a language I don't know. Valrir simply shrugs and goes back to her soup. "She was going to find out anyway."

Vahildra swirls his wine under his nose before taking a sip. "You knew this was going to happen sooner or later."

Haidion throws him a look of anger before he addresses me. "Freyja." He gets out of his chair and kneels at my side. "I wanted to tell you in a different way."

When he mumbles about how sorry he is, I cup his face in my

hands. "It's okay." Relief floods his face. "You didn't trust me enough to tell me that you're working with the Shadow King." Tears fill my eyes. "I'm just worried about what the Sons of Judgment will do to you if they find out."

Haidion pulls me into his arms, knocking the book and letter off the table. "They aren't going to find out. Nothing is going to happen to me."

I hold onto him as tight as I can. "I can't lose you." As I utter the words, tears fall. "I lost so many already. I can't lose somebody I... somebody I..." I take a deep breath, allowing his musky scent of smoke and spice to ground me. "Somebody who makes me so happy."

Haidion whispers. "You won't ever lose me, and I appreciate you opening up to me." His nose nudges the shell of my ear, making me shudder. "You make me so happy, too."

I pull back, but not before wiping my tears away. "Well, it's only fair since Valrir revealed something about you that you clearly weren't ready to tell me. I respect that. But now you can help me get a message to the Shadow King." I look up at him. "You have my word that I won't tell a soul about it, and if I need to take an oath, I will."

Haidion beams down at me. "The strength in your word is more powerful than any magic in existence." He bends to pick up the book and letter but hesitates before handing them to me.

"What is it?" I inquire.

"You got a letter from the Dragon Queen."

With shaky hands, I take the red letter. "Why would she write to me?"

All are quiet as I remove the wax seal of a mighty pair of dragon wings, unfold the paper, and read the letter aloud,

"*Goddess Freyja,*

You are hereby invited to Elbtearid for the execution of my youngest princeling, Varnus, on the 2nd day following the Vernal Equinox at Sundown.

My son made you his last request, and I'd be terribly disappointed if you denied his invitation.

You may bring another with you as moral support. Have them sign their name below and enter the portal using the crystal.

-The Dragonnira, Queen of the Dragon Race

House of Prestige and Honor."

"Prestige and honor. Why did she align herself with her maiden house and not the one she was married into?" Haidion muttered.

My blood runs cold. *Starson must've been taken after he fell.* "What time is it back on Earthradon?"

Vahildra takes out a star-silver pocket watch. "It's the Tenth hour after Sunrise."

I hold out the letter to Haidion. "Will you go to Dragon Island with me?"

Valrir clears her throat. "I'm not trying to be rude, Freyja, but Haidion has responsibilities he needs to attend to." She eyes the back of his head as if she's trying to burn her words into his skull, so they sink in.

"I have to agree. A couple hours away on Earthradon might not seem like a lot, but it is here." Vahildra sips his wine as he stares meaningfully at Haidion. "Now more than ever, you need to attend to your duty, or you will cause suspicion."

"Well, it's a good thing I'm the Demonical of Illusion. Valrir, you know what to do. Use the magic I lent you and make everyone think that you are me. Nothing is more important than me going with Freyja." The others seem ready to argue, but Haidion raises his voice as shadows cover his eyes. "My decision has been made, and I'll hear no more. Is that clear?"

Valrir rises from her chair, her gaze hazy with shadows as well. "Crystal." She hits his shoulder as she vanishes in white shadows.

"Freyja." Vahildra stands and buttons his jacket. "Considering how much you care for Haidion, I understand why you want him to go with you. But if you truly worry about him being found out, he needs to not go."

I know what he's doing; he's making me change my mind rather than trying to convince Haidion to change his. "Tell me the truth." I look into Haidion's eyes as I pull my hand away from his. "Will your absence cause the Sons of Judgment to suspect you?"

"Yes, but I need you to trust me when I say I have a plan."

I cross my arms and take a step back. "Why would you take that risk?"

A warm smile spreads across his lips. "Because nothing is more important than helping the ones you love."

His words sing true as my heart swells. There is no pain, and nothing drains me of my vitality or magic. I sob, trying to cover it with a cough, but that only makes it worse.

"I need to use the bathroom," I manage to get out clearly as I rush out of the room.

Haidion's voice enters my mind. *Can I go with you, please?*

Yes.

I run to my bathroom with tears in my eyes. Not even a moment later, claws scratch against the wood on the other side, and whimpers follow.

Nightnir pops her heads in when I open the door. The moment she sees me, she bolts inside and licks my face, taking away all my tears. I can't help but laugh, and my heart melts when she cuddles against my chest.

Holding her helps ground me and stop my hammering heart over the realization of how true Haidion's words are. Through his actions, I know Haidion loves me; I just don't know what to do with the emotions that follow. Do I want to say the words back? Yes, but they aren't completely filled yet. *What's holding me back, then?*

With Nightnir curled up on my lap, the absence of her warmth on my chest answers my question. The soul rot is preventing me from filling them. If I allow in any emotions that make my heart swell, I will die. Building a shield wall to prevent myself from being affected is the only way I've lived so long. Yet, my heart has swollen when I'm around Haidion, and I experienced no pain.

After emptying the air out of my lungs, I press my hand to my chest and feel around. I'm greeted by nothing. My soul is radiant and strong. Tears fall from my eyes again. *How am I cured?*

My face gets licked again after a drop falls on Nightnir's fur, and I lift my head. My gaze falls on the basket. Valrir said the eggs hold soul light that helps heal the soul. If it's like my power, then I'm healed.

A sense of relief washes over me as a weight comes off my shoulders. Tears gush down my face and happy sobs leave me. When I'm introduced to Iraijah, I will need to thank him for not only healing me but also saving my life. The question is now: do I take down my shield wall?

I look down at Nightnir instead of answering the question. "Not talkative today?" She yips and barks while wagging her tail. "I meant actual words."

When she tips her heads to the side, I tilt mine, too. A wave of realization dawns on me as someone knocks at my bedroom door.

"Freyja," Haidion calls out. "A crystal appeared as I signed my name."

Nightnir jumps out of my arms and happily yips for her daddy to enter.

I stand and open the door. "Do you have another pet?"

Before my eyes, Nightnir shifts into a full-size beast so Haidion doesn't have to bend over to scratch the back of her heads. "No, just her."

I'm about to ask him about the being that was with me during battle when I see the crystal in his hand; it's shaped like a small wand. "It's a portal maker, and since runes are engraved on it, it will bring us to a certain location." His eyes trail down my body. "I should probably pull out something more fitting." With a whistle, tendrils of his magic come out of a pocket next to me, holding up my armor. "I'd give you the axe and the belt, but if we show up with weapons, we will be killed on the spot."

I can't hold back my excitement as I lunge forward and hug Haidion, almost knocking off his hat. "Thank you. Thank you. Thank you!"

He wraps an arm around me. Nightnir nuzzles her way in, wanting to be a part of the hug, but just ends up splitting us apart. Someone whistles from down the hall, and she takes off. A curse echoes from Vahildra, followed by a groan as if he got ran over.

"Vahildra takes care of Nightnir while I'm gone since she and his Cerberus, Valgorlas, are mates."

"Are they sentient?"

"No." *Then who was it that spoke in my mind?* With a wave of his hand, clothing from the closet flies out and lands on my bed. The armor opens up, ready for me to step in. "Since the deadline is Sundown, we should probably get going."

I nod and start to strip. "Were you the one putting magic into my armor?” I ask, recalling Treason’s comment about my siphons being attended to. “I’m not mad. I just wish you would’ve told me.”

Confusion clouds his eyes as I dress. “I didn’t tend to your armor. I don’t know how.” He leans against the doorframe. “Knowing my luck, I’d make the siphons shatter from how powerful my magic is.”

Vahildra calls Haidion’s name, and he snarls. “I’ll meet you by the stairs.”

If Haidion wasn’t the one who tended to my armor, who did?

THIRTY-NINE

ELEVENTH HOUR AFTER SUNRISE

When I hold the crystal, it starts to glow yellow, and a portal opens.

Haidion and I pass through, whisked away to a stone dock in the middle of a foreboding fjord.

Since Haidion has pockets, I hand the crystal back to him for safe-keeping. "Do you have any idea where we are?"

There is nothing else around us except for a dark and smoky forest at our backs. The air is thick and sticky, leaving an unpleasant taste in my mouth. Everything in the forest is still, as if the branches are trying not to draw attention to themselves. The waves crash on the shore like souls are trapped within, trying to claw their way out. Similar sounds of cries for help come from beyond the tree line, and they are as creepy as the ones from the water.

Haidion takes my hand as his voice enters my mind. *We are in the south-east part of Earthradon. Ghoul territory.*

Hairs raise on my spine, and I can't disguise my tense trembling. My senses are tuned into everything so much that every little noise puts me on edge. With dusk approaching, the sun setting on the horizon is our only protection from the race that lurks in the trees behind us, for they only come out during the hours of the night.

We should probably not speak, so we don't draw attention. I nod in acknowledgement. *I'm also masking our presence.*

I squeeze his hand, noting the glittering aura that surrounds us. *Have you ever dealt with a Ghoul before?*

Many times. But they are nothing compared to the demonic monsters that live in the last two levels of Orrtiereum.

When a moment of silence passes, and my paranoia starts to make me see things that aren't there, I squeeze Haidion's hand tighter. *Talk to me about anything or everything. I'm starting to see things out of the corner of my eyes.*

Haidion leans into me. *It's not your imagination. I see them, too.*

My blood goes cold. *Are we safe?*

For as long as the sun is up, we are. If our ride doesn't come by then, I get to show off my impressive swords to you again. And maybe... He leans in more, as if he's going to speak into my ear. *...I'll let you touch them.*

Thankfully, Haidion pulls back before he can detect my shiver. *Why didn't she portal us to the island?*

She wouldn't give up the chance for us to see how impressive her island is. He leads me down the dock to sit. *I personally know the Dragon Queen, by the way.*

Personally? As in, you slept with her or something?

Haidion grins at me. *You are a good guesser.* A vicious heat stirs in my soul and climbs up my throat.

He brings my hand up and starts to draw imaginary circles on my outer wrist, but his touch does little to calm me down.

We got as far as undressing one another, but then she wanted to have full control and tie me up. I didn't trust her, so I stepped away and allowed my illusion to be used by her. I wanted to find out why she wanted to strap me down since she wasn't the dominant type. It turns out she wanted me to impregnate her.

So, she planned on raping you? Hot rage radiates from my body to the point the veins in my hands start to glow.

Haidion's cold wafts around me as his eyes lock on mine. *Believe me when I tell you this, Freyja. I'm okay.*

He brings my hand up to his lips and kisses my scorching skin. Each press of his soft, luscious mouth simmers down my heat. After a couple moments, I'm calmed down physically, but not mentally.

How I see it, I was in control the entire time. I could've stopped it but chose not to. Haidion lowers our hands to rest on my thigh. *The only suffering I experienced was how much my anger was trying to rip me to shreds for not acting. I want to do unforgivable things to her. Then, she would become a permanent prisoner in my dungeon, where not even the Fates could hear her screams.*

Haidion might be keeping his lethal cold under control, but his soul is furious, wanting to be unleashed.

Just like he did for me, I bring his hand to my mouth and kiss the back of his wrist, going up to his knuckles. After each press, I lightly drag my lips from one knuckle to the other. Never have I given him such intimate affection; it's always been holding his hand or a hug. This action feels like it could mean more or lead to more, but every time Haidion has done it to me, it was only to show me he cares or to calm me down. I feel safe giving him the same type of affection back and trust that he won't misinterpret this act as being anything more than a friend showing how much they care.

Judging by the delicious coolness of his soul and how blown out his eyes are, Haidion is relaxed from my touch. I find myself relaxing, too. Perhaps this is why Haidion likes to touch me; it grounds him.

Did she find out?

Haidion blinks out of a trance and silently laughs. *I clapped from the corner of the room when she begged me to cum. She kicked me off the island and told me if I were ever to return, she'd have me killed. But this...* He holds up the letter. *...protects you and me from harm. And if any of the Sons of Judgment are notified of my presence on Earthradon, I have this to show them I was invited here. Not directly, but it still counts.*

I lower our hands back to my thigh. *So, we are going to a place where we are both wanted dead.* Haidion might not know why I hated dragons, but I did tell him my stories of when I faced them during the war and my reckless attempts to attack them.

At least you aren't alone. Haidion gives my hand a squeeze. *We will face them together.*

To soothe my nervousness, I lean over and rest my head on his shoulder, an action I've never done before but feel comfortable doing. *Just don't leave my side.*

My mind is caressed by the same tenderness his lips embrace me with. *Nothing will come between us.*

* * *

Dusk

The last rays of sun dust the sky, and I hold Haidion's hand a little tighter. We sit on the ledge of the stone dock, talking mind-to-mind.

To pass the time, I told him how my visit to Crescent Island was, the events leading up to the battle, and what I experienced. Besides my personal time with Odin and Illyrical, and the daydream I had while trying to calm myself down with Treason, Haidion now knows everything as if he were there by my side. I don't think I'll ever tell him about Odin's abuse. I want to keep it in the past and forget that it ever happened. As for us kissing, well, I'm not entirely sure I want that to stay in the past.

Haidion squeezes my hand. *Thank you for opening up to me. I'm sure all of that wasn't easy to recall.*

The feelings of his fingers drawing circles on the back of my wrist helped ground me so I could speak of everything without expressing too much emotion. Since we are going to Elbtearid, I can't allow myself to get emotional there. I need to be on guard. Even though the letter ensures I won't be harmed, showing the dragons any kind of weakness will have me mentally broken within the hour.

Although resting on Haidion's shoulder has been soothing, it has caused a kink in my neck, so I sit up and stretch. *You think we should've waited to enter the portal until Sundown?*

Judging by the small size of the crystal, there's only enough magic inside to keep the portal open for a short period of time.

So, if I would've touched it when I first got the letter, I'd be sitting here waiting?

Yup. It would probably please the Dragon Queen to know we've been waiting here for as long as we have. But the letter did say Sundown, so I wouldn't have touched the crystal until then.

I turn to face him. *Then why did you let me touch it?*

He gives me a wicked smile. *I kind of guessed we would be transported here since it's the closest port to the island. Since this land is littered with tortured souls, I wouldn't need to have anyone in my shadow since the leeches would rather go after them than me. The reason I let you touch it is because I knew we would be alone. What better place to spend time together unchaperoned than a spine-chilling forest with a fjord that sounds like it's going to reach up and pull us down?*

My laughter is hard to contain, and placing my hand over my mouth doesn't help. With us being in one of the creepiest places I've ever been to and waiting to go to a place I'm dreading, I find myself smiling and happy. Only Haidion can pull such emotions out of me while making me feel safe.

Those three words he spoke to me two nights ago replay in my mind. Although I'm not anywhere close to saying them, I'm starting to fall for my friend. What scares me is the love I would have for him, which I don't think would be just out of friendship as his is to me. Just because he likes to show me affection, tease, and flirt doesn't mean he likes me; that could be his love language. Bringing the topic up to him is something I'm not brave enough to do. Perhaps once I get the Father's heart back from Zeus, I will be.

You're so beautiful when you laugh. My breath catches in my throat. *Your smile makes this place feel like a wonderland of fulfilled dreams and desires.* He tilts my chin up and then drags his fingers down to my neck. *And for as long as I look into your eyes, I'm at peace.*

Warmth swells in my chest as it pools between my thighs. *You shouldn't say such things.* The words come out before I have a chance to filter them.

His brows scrunch; he's either intrigued or worried, but I can't tell because my own emotions are distracting me. *Why can't I say lovely things to you?*

Because I don't know what to do with them. Though I like the endearing words, how am I supposed to act without scaring myself or regretting my actions? Also, following my forbidden desires could jeopardize our friendship if he doesn't feel the same way. I could be mistaking what his actions mean since I never experienced such tenderness, even from Bralyant. The bottom line is that I can't lose Haidion, so whatever I decide, I must be sure because I can't fuck it up.

When I don't respond, Haidion removes his hand from my face. *Am I making you uncomfortable?*

"No!" I rush out. *Sorry, no, you are not. I'm just—*Water ripples out of the corner of my eye. *It's just that we have company.*

As we stand, a Leviathan breaches the water. Judging by the multiple pastel colors of its scales, the serpent-like dragon is female.

Leviathans can only swim in the water, and they are the Peace-keepers for the Oceanic Races. Even though they reach the same size as a mature dragon, they are considered lesser since they can't fly like Drakes. I'm honestly surprised that the Dragon Queen has been able to keep them under her rule.

I'm revealing us.

Once the Leviathan's lavender-pink slit eyes land on us, she raises her enormous head to the stone dock and opens her mouth, revealing fangs as long as my body.

Freyja, I possess a deep affection for my right hand. Therefore, I advise against breaking it unless you are prepared to substitute the extracurricular activities in which it is frequently engaged.

Sorry, I didn't realize how hard I was holding your hand.

After I let go, I assess the gaping mouth in front of us, noting that there is no gas building up to make fire nor does she seem ready to eat us.

A yawning roar leaves the Leviathan as she sticks out her tongue.

I know what she wants. Can you please hand over the crystal?

I know the meaning of the cue as well. Though I'll take the risk, my darling. Before I can argue, Haidion steps forward and places the crystal on her tongue, seeming to not care about the fangs that could close on his arm.

After he steps away, barely noticeable waves of gas build in her mouth as she takes a deep breath through her nostrils. When some-thing by her uvula starts to spark, Haidion pulls me behind him and wraps us in shadowy-star magic.

Heat pours out of the Leviathan's mouth, and when flames ignite, she turns her head to expel yellow fire that transforms into a portal of yellow light.

A guttural huffing and the slight shake of the Leviathan's head tells me she's laughing.

I'm about to laugh as well, but it dies in my throat when Haidion lets out a deep growl. His muscles flex under his suit, molding the fabric to his skin. With each inhale, the material strains, and with every exhale, the rumbles coming from him only grow stronger, as if the beast within is starting to break free.

The Leviathan's eyes narrow, and she snarls.

Haidion returns her warning glare with his own. He lowers his gaze ever so slightly in a menacing manner while his lethal cold permeates the air. Even though the talons aren't directed at me, I sense their presence and sharpness. Rather than going into her mind to pull some strings to control or scare her, he's going to attack.

Before I can think better of it, I snatch his hat off and step away from him.

His attention immediately moves to me, severing his eye contact with the Leviathan.

Another laugh leaves the beast as she lowers herself until her neck is level with the dock.

Haidion's shadowy-star magic is absorbed back into him, but his body remains tense. *My darling, you know what happens when someone takes my hat. And even you aren't immune to being punished.*

To my surprise, his words about punishment don't cause me to tense as they would if Odin had said them.

With a deep breath, I take a brave step backward, getting closer to the woods. *Then punish me.*

If you insist. Haidion's eyes rove over my body as he prowls forward. My plan to switch his mind from beast mode into play mode works as a wicked smile forms on his face. *I typically allow my prey to suggest methods of torture. If I deem it suitable, I carry them out. Therefore, please specify what you would like me to do to you.*

I'll let you decide if you do what I want first.

He ponders for a moment, then his smile widens. *It's a deal. Do I have your word that you will honor this, or do I need to brand you?*

"You have my word." *But I am interested in what you would brand on my skin.*

Another time. He continues moving in a low stroll, which only makes my heart beat quicker and harder.

I want you to stop getting closer to me and close your eyes.

Immediately, he obeys, shocking me. I have never held such power before. Now it's my turn to prowl around him as he stays still. The darkness in my mind comes to the forefront, thinking of all the things I want to do to him, but I push it back and place the hat on his head the way he likes.

I lean close and whisper, "Even though I'd love to see that lethal beast of yours come out and play, I'd rather it be when we are faced with the Dragon Queen. She fills my body with rage for what she did to you." He shudders as a deep groan leaves him. "Tell your beast to pull back his talons, and I'll reward him."

If the Leviathan is going to transport us, Haidion causing the beast soul-shredding pain won't end well. We won't be able to get to the island, and I'll disappoint Starson. I won't be able to be there for him as he takes his last breath.

When Haidion pulls his lethal cold back into him, I press my lips against his swollen left cheek. "Good boy." A warmth I never felt from him before radiates with each beat of his heart. I back away towards the Leviathan. "You can open your eyes now."

He whirls toward me. Determination tightens his features and flexes his body. His eyes are blown out as shadow fire roars from his soul. Each controlled step he takes towards me only fuels whatever desire he's trying to restrain.

What are you going to do to me?

He gives a husky chuckle. *That wasn't part of our agreement. You're going to have to wait and find out.*

A whimpering moan tries to escape my throat. Rather than push the issue and figure out why Haidion looks ready to eat me alive, I mount the Leviathan's neck.

The last shimmer of sun is on the horizon, darkening the woods at Haidion's back. *At least this Leviathan isn't trying to kill us like the other one we faced centuries ago.* I try to keep my tone steady, but it's as shaky as my body.

My friend keeps his eyes locked on me as he approaches the end of the stone dock. *Ah, yes. Our first adventure together.*

More like the first time you showed up at the precise moment that I was about to be in a shitstorm of trouble.

The memory comes out of the darkness of my mind, but before it can play, Haidion slides behind me. I'm very much aware of how close his body is to mine, especially when his arm wraps around my waist, pulling me between his thick thighs.

Haidion leans forward, his nose brushing against me as his cold mixes with my heat. *Would you rather I sit in front of you?*

"No!" *I'm okay where I am.*

A pleased growl leaves him as his hands settle on my lower abdomen and pull me flush against his front. *Good. Now, hold onto her horns. Yes, just like that.*

Once I grasp the Leviathan's horns, she heads out to the end of the fjord. *I hope it doesn't take us long to get there.*

Haidion chuckles. *I hope it doesn't take us long, either.*

His elongation of the word 'us' has me questioning his statement, sensing there is a hidden double meaning, but the ring of fire we are approaching consumes my full attention.

Not a single flame touches our skin as we are whisked away to the calm ocean, Udiein. The sun sets, and the moon is being pulled up by the twinkling sky, officially making it Sundown.

Haidion leans into me, his lips brushing my ear. "Welcome to Elbtearid."

The island before us is massive; some peaks reach so high that I can't tell what's sky or mountain top. Rays of light from the moon and stars make the water crystal clear. Everywhere the waves hit against the rocky shore, the water illuminates the island and moss.

Monumental statues of every dragon breed surround the island: Dragon, Wyvern, Drake, and Leviathan. Smoke billows from their mouths and their eyes glow gold. The Dragon and Wyvern breeds have their wings extended, ready for flight. The Drakes are poised to pounce, and the Leviathans are raised out of the water at their full, imposing height. All look so life-like.

Haidion leans into me. *The fjord we are approaching is the visitors' entrance, and it also happens to be the only body of water leading to the center of the island. It is said that this land was a star that crashed while the Father was building Earthradon. This body of water is called the Stream of Starlight because the water filters out the brightness, revealing the beauty within and how alive the magic is as it interacts with the environment. Some believe the island is alive, but if the race were to acknowledge it as truth, everyone would want this land.*

We don't need another war on our hands because the dragons will wipe everyone out.

His nod of agreement makes the tip of his nose run up and down my ear, and I find myself leaning back into him more, almost resting my head on his shoulder.

Horns with a strong base stir up the wind as we enter a narrow fjord. The steady beat of drums echoes off the stone walls around us.

The preserved dragons of the Majesty bloodline line the stream until the space opens into an area large enough to be a lake.

Fire erupts from the dragons' mouths, igniting the top of the water in starry-red flames that reach the entrance.

Horns blare again, and the drums increase their tempo.

Mountains upon mountains encircle the valley of water, sealing the lake in like a cage.

Pain claws into my back as the beating of the drums intensifies, making me aware of how tall the island is; it's almost never-ending, and that fact has me shifting to hold onto Haidion.

Don't move. I stop myself just before I lift my hands from the Leviathan's horns. *Even though you see nothing, the Queen is watching. Any movement to pull in on yourself will show her your fear.*

How am I supposed to dampen down my fear of wanting to flee? This feels like a cage.

It's intentional. She wants visitors to experience a sense of hopelessness and a weakening of confidence. Straighten yourself from me, yes, just like that. Remember your rage for her. Feed off that because I know your anger is endless, just as mine is.

My rage; I let my soul feed on it and use my self-control to keep the forbidden darkness in the depths where it needs to stay for the time being. Haidion's words fuel the energy in my soul. It spreads out like wildfire, making the Leviathan under me flinch. My brother's face, and the midnight-green dragon that killed him are all I see.

Straight ahead is a castle built into the rock of the tallest mountain. The surrounding mountains on either side have smaller, less magnificent castles.

Their kingdom is built in the mountains, so their structure are easily repairable. The minerals here are used in construction, and in the process to preserve dragons. I nod in understanding, in awe of the kingdom's resourcefulness.

We stop in front of a stone dock connected to a thin strip of sand,

and a network of caves that are only big enough for humanoid dragons to fit through.

Once we dismount, the Leviathan vanishes under water.

Haidion keeps ahold of my hand after helping me onto the dock, squeezing reassuringly. *I would like to shield your mind. They have an ability that is unparalleled to that of any other race. No one knows what it is, but there is a reason they were chosen as Peacekeepers. I'm still trying to figure it out. Will you let me?*

Of course.

Something brushes my mind, and I allow it in. Haidion's presence fills my mind as a thick strand of glowing shadows appears in the darkness of my consciousness.

Anything you think or imagine, I can pick up. Like us talking, if you speak to yourself, or if you recall a memory. I'll be able to see all of it, and it's not one-sided; you will see and hear things from me if I let them pass through. If you don't want to see or hear anything, just push me out. It won't sever the connection; it will only mute it for a moment. Talk aloud. We don't want to give away that we can mind speak; it's disrespectful if the pair aren't mates. Unless you want to claim that, keep mind-to-mind talking to a minimum.

The word "mates" has the brand on my chest warming, reminding me of the vow I made. My body straightens even more, and my blood runs cold. I don't think I'm even breathing. All the pressing matters I've been concerned with, from needing to get here to see Starson, and figuring out how to get the Father's heart back, are pushed aside as thoughts of who my mate is come to the forefront of my thoughts. My brand's reaction to Haidion's comment can't be because he is mine; it's just a reminder of what I promised. No matter who my mate is, we are forbidden to be together because it would be intermating.

A realization hits me so hard in the chest, I almost stumble. Sadness creeps into the tender spots of my existence, making me want to curl in on myself and sob. Even if I wanted to be with Haidion, I couldn't; we would be intermating. The only way we could be together would be in secret. Is that something I want to do again?

The drums reach a crescendo, followed by the rhythmic sound of horns blaring to match the melody. My heart beats hard in my chest as my body tenses again, bringing me back to reality.

"Should we move...?" My question gets lost when I note Haidion doesn't have a glittering aura surrounding him. "Aren't you going to illusion yourself?"

"We can only move once the Queen welcomes us, and to wear any mask here is of the highest disrespect."

If we have time, I want to introduce you to an old friend of mine.

A screeching roar comes from a huge dragon as it lands on the rocky cliff above a cave in front of us.

I let go of Haidion's hand. It's the dragon who killed my brother; his midnight-green scales shine proudly as if a layer of fire coats his body, and there's an intensity that heats his emerald eyes. The silver slits narrow as he solely focuses on me.

The drums pound passionately, and the horns blare proudly as the green dragon opens his mouth and expels fire on the sand before the stone dock. It takes every fiber in my body to not flinch. The memory of him pounding into my brother's air shield begins to play, but the thick strand of glowing shadow expels it, pushing the memory back to where it belongs.

Don't shy away from the flames. Allow them to heat your rage, fuel your energy, and keep the memories away.

With each breath I take, the heat spreads from my head to my toes, and from my mind to my soul.

The fire whirls like a tornado and gets gradually absorbed into a silhouette as it walks out of the flames. Once the winged being is completely visible, the fire vanishes, and the instruments stop.

A curvaceous woman in a lavish, see-through, white silk gown with a long train of red hydrangeas steps onto the stone path. Her jade-gold metallic scales are visible through the thin fabric, and flowers adorn her tail and slender wings. A silver crown of emerald rests atop her head, and a ring of a single red diamond with a gold slit that matches her eyes sits on her ring finger. The Dragon Queen might not be of the current royal bloodline, but her lineage was once royal.

She touches her round belly as she walks closer and images of her riding Haidion flash before my eyes.

She found someone to cum in her cunt; that child sure as fuck isn't mine. The thoughts and images leave as quickly as they came. *Sorry, Freyja.*

Don't apologize. I'll take on the burden of your pain. Doing so will help keep mine under control so nothing slips.

A voice of disdainful courteousness has my mental nails sharpening like I could grow claws. "Goddess Freyja." She bows her head just a fraction, enough for me to recognize, but to anyone else, she just tilted her head.

"Dragonnira."

Her attention shifts to Haidion, and there is malice in her eyes as she tightens her hold on her belly.

"Ominous..." I take a step towards Haidion. "...is my dearest friend and whom I chose to accompany me." Just with a brush of my hand, he intertwines his with mine.

He doesn't bow; he only tightens his lips into a thin line. "Emerial."

A snarl leaves the Dragon Queen. "You lost the right to call me by my name."

"And you lost my respect when you tied me to your bed."

The green dragon climbs down and shifts mid-movement. A voice of sin and satin angerly hisses, "You are a guest here!" The massive, broad humanoid dragon with mighty wings and muscles powerful enough to take down mountains walks to Emerial's side. "You might be immune to harm, but if you dare disrespect my queen, you will be escorted out. I implore you to keep your personal dislikes to yourself." His silver-slitted, emerald eyes move to Haidion and my conjoined hands and growls. "I doubt you want my company in his place, Goddess."

"You are the spitting image of your father, Rhax. Long may he soar the eternal skies in peace." Haidion gives my hand a squeeze. *Keep fueling the fire, Freyja.* "Long live his bloodline. May forever the House of Eloquence and Dignity reign." *And sincerely, fuck you, Emerial.*

Emerial narrows her eyes at my companion as I lift my chin. "Your escort, your Highness, would lead to the ruin of your kingdom, would it not?"

Rhax crosses his arms over his chest. "If I have to be in close proximity to you, I'd restrain myself."

If you want to get under his skin and have him repulsed by your presence, flirt with him.

Trusting Haidion's word, I spread my lips into a sweet smile. "I can't say the same." My eyes rove over his insanely well-built, tall stature while biting my lip.

Rhax flinches with a startled snarl, like I slapped him, breaking his threatening composure.

Warmth caresses my mind as if Haidion's lips brush against my skin. *Well done, my daring larvaelet.*

Emerial holds out her arm right as the male dragon takes a determined step toward me. "That's enough. Freyja, you have an hour with Varnus before his execution." Her voice become aggravated as she growls to Rhax, "Lead them to his cell and behave yourself."

Rhax nods, tucking in his wings. "Follow me." The dragons turn and enter different caves.

Haidion brings my hand to his mouth and places a kiss on my knuckles as we walk. *Are you doing okay?*

I'm managing. You?

Rather than Haidion placing my hand on his arm, he keeps holding it. *For as long as I have you by my side, I can endure anything that causes me pain.*

I could not agree more. If it weren't for Haidion, the memories of my brother's death would be playing in my mind, reducing me to a pile of screams and tears.

FORTY

SUNDOWN

Pebbles rain down from a commotion happening above. If it weren't for my eye adaptation power, Haidion would be covered in dirt.

Rhax chuckles as he looks at me over his shoulder. "Are you doing okay back there? Do you need me to hold your hand instead, Freyja?" A teasing grin curves his lips and shows off his sculpted jaw.

"It's 'Goddess' to you," Haidion snarls, his grip tightening on my hand.

Rhax whirls around to face him. "I'll call her whatever I want." Dirt falls on his wings, and he doesn't even seem bothered by it.

Neither back down nor lower their eyes. Even though Rhax is half a foot taller, Haidion doesn't break the Princeling's stare.

"Well, I'm going to go visit my friend while you two keep this contest going." I give Haidion's hand a squeeze before I let it go. "In what direction am I heading to, your Highness?" *Are you going to be okay if I leave you alone?*

Go see your friend, Freyja. My shadows will guide me to you.

Rhax doesn't look my way as he lifts his arm and points to a left-hand turn up ahead. "Varnus is being held down that way."

It's a good thing I can see in the dark, or I wouldn't know where he was gesturing.

As I walk by, his wings flex, and my fingers accidentally brush against them. Rhax stiffens as something within me jolts at the contact. He growls low in my direction, and I do the same, my anger heightening.

Without having Haidion's hand to hold, I stay to the side of the cave, dragging my fingers over the smooth stone as I walk through the darkness.

My steps falter when I come to a circular cavern, but there aren't any caves to continue down. Some light filters from above, as if there are holes in the ceiling. The minimal light helps me make the metal bars in the floor.

A familiar, deep, velvety voice echoes from below me, but the tone is angry. "I asked to be left in peace until either my request shows up, or it's time for me to join in on the festivities."

"Starson?" I gasp.

"Freyja?!" Scaly hands grip the bars by my feet. "Fuck, I forgot how beautiful your eyes are. They are as bright as the sun in total darkness, cool like the moon, and twinkle like stars."

With a blink, I make out the frosty-black scales and the emerald, silver-slitted eyes of my friend. "Starson!" I sing happily as I drop to my knees and grip his hands. "How do I get to you?"

"In the middle of the bars, there is a handle. You can pull the hatch up. But you don't have to. It's actually against the—"

Before he can finish, I'm on my feet, using all my strength to lift the square door up. As I position myself to slide down, Starson's scaly hands grip my thighs and help lower me. After I close the door, I put my arms around his strong neck and wrap my legs around his waist, so he doesn't have to strain to look at me.

He sighs in relief, enfolding me in his arms. "I didn't know if you made it, so when I made my last request and my mother said you were still alive, I had everything I wanted." He pulls away to stare at my face. "To have you here is something I only dreamed about."

I press my forehead to his. "Now that I'm here, what is it that I can do?"

His large eyes close as he rubs his nose against mine. "Stay in my arms. I want to feel your heartbeat and the rise and fall of your chest. I want to be reassured that you are alive."

With slow strokes, I massage the nape of his neck. "I can strip down if you like."

He chuckles. "I don't want to upset your mate. I'm already getting my scent all over you."

"I divorced my husband. Odin worked alongside the traitorous gods to kill the father." I swallow down the lump of emotion that tries to spring free.

Starson narrows his eyes. "The bond I sensed before is still there, though."

"Like I said, I'm not a race. I can't have a—" The brand on my chest hums, reminding me of why I made it in the first place. "I do have a mate," I murmur. "Can you sense who it is?"

He sighs. "I could point you in the right direction since I can sense the tether, but that goes against the unofficial rules. Since you aren't a race, you can't tell where the bond is tugging you to. It's their responsibility to tell you."

Rather than use our last moments together to figure out something that can greatly impact my life, I push my selfish desire away to focus on my friend.

"What happened to you? I heard you fall from the sky."

He holds me tighter. "The shockwave made me unable to fly and breathe, as if the air were taken away for a moment. The hard land forced me to shift into my humanoid form. I knocked out and woke up to my brother flying with me in his arms. I did not know where he was taking me, but before I could ask, the Wyvern Guard showed up and escorted us back home. I was put in this cage, told what laws I had broken, and sentenced to the dishonorable death penalty." Tears fall from his eyes when he opens them. "It's going to fucking hurt, but these are the last of the tears I'm going to shed. I won't give everyone the satisfaction of seeing me in pain."

After I brush his tears away, I hold his face in my hands. "Where do you want me?"

He takes a minute to gather himself. "I know it's a lot to ask, but I want you in front so I can see you. That way, I have something to focus on while they are dishonor me."

"You have my word." Starson might not know what power my words hold, but he can taste the strength behind them.

My lips find his, but I don't press mine fully against him yet; I wait for him to close the gap. He is hesitant at first, but groans when his full lips form to mine. They are as velvety as his voice, and I allow him to dominate the kiss since it will be his last. He isn't feverish to devour me; he is slow and tender, as if he has hours to enjoy my lips.

"Wow," he mumbles, out of breath. "I've never had such a sensual kiss before." To me, it was a nothing special, but I keep that comment to myself. "Do you kiss all your friends or only those you make promises to?"

"Do you kiss everyone with such gentleness, or are you falling in love with me?"

Starson chuckles and rests his forehead against mine. "In the short time that we've known each other, you've touched my soul in ways only one other person has. Existence was special to me since she was my Guardian. I know if we had more time, you'd be special to me, too." He pulls back and stares into my eyes. I can see the hues of my irises reflecting in his. "I've never felt freer than I do when I'm in your arms."

Tears fall down my cheeks, and it is his turn to wipe them away. "You mean something special to me, too." My words are barely audible and hardly comprehensible as I swallow down more tears.

"Freyja?" Rhax's voice echoes from above. I can't see him, but I can sense where he is by the heavy sound of his feet.

"Perhaps..." Haidion's remarkable voice causes the darkness to thicken. "...she went down the wrong corridor. You didn't give her a directions; you merely pointed. It's kind of dark, and she can't traverse through it as well as you and I can." *That is a lie. Haidion knows I can see in the dark.*

"No. I sensed her come this way."

Someone walks over us and stops. *You are not supposed to be in his cage. I have nothing against saying goodbye to a friend properly, but you are breaking a rule. Even though you weren't told about it, that isn't going to save you.*

When someone walks over to the door, Starson groans. "Brother. Leave me in peace."

Rhax drops to his knees and takes a deep breath. "Why am I smelling Freyja's scent on the door?"

Impossible. I have your scent masked.

Now it's my turn to groan. "Can you please give us some privacy? I'm not done fulfilling his last request."

The door is yanked open. "You need to get out of the cage, Freyja. A Wyvern Guard is coming." The urgency in Rhax's tone makes me pause. *Is he concerned for me?*

Yes, and I am as well. Tendrils of shadow brush against the back of my hand. *I'm sorry to ask this of you, Freyja, but you need to get out. I am going to have to cast this cavern in darkness pretty soon if you don't. If the guard finds you down there, both of you will be punished.*

My pulse quickens as panic rises in my throat. "Starson, I do not wish for more harm to come upon you."

"I understand. I don't want them to punish you for being in here, either."

We hold onto one another, but by the rattling of the chains, I know he's bringing me to the door. Rhax opens the hatch quietly as possible. The tendril leaves, brushing at the shell of my ear right before a soft touch of fingers takes their place. Without needing to ask, I know it's Haidion.

I pull back to hold Starson's face. "I shall be your sun tonight."

"And the moon and the stars." His mouth turns up in a smile. "I'll tell Existence you said hi."

Tears fall from my face as I'm pulled out of his arms. Starson pushes me up by my hips, and Haidion gets me to my feet.

When Rhax closes the hatch, I start to fall to my knees, wanting to touch Starson one more time, but Haidion catches me.

"Freyja," Rhax mutters softly and respectfully. "You need to go."

He stays behind while Haidion and I walk back down the corridor, enveloped in shadows.

Don't make a sound.

I nod against his chest just as the echo of stomping feet and low grumbles fill the cave. Haidion pushes us against the wall right before a Wyvern Guard unknowingly passes by.

After a moment, Haidion continues to lead us down multiple caves.

"Do you know why a guard is going to Starson?"

"The execution is happening now." Pain squeezes my chest and I start to hyperventilate. "We are heading to the area above us where the guests are. Rhax told me where to go after I won our staring contest."

"Guests? Who else was invited to this?"

Haidion maneuvers us through more caves, and the commotion from above gradually grows louder. "Besides the race, those who lost a loved one because of Varnus, and the rulers of Earthradon, the Queen's closets friends are also here to provide her with emotional support."

Before we ascend the steps that lead outside, Haidion pulls me further into the shadows. My back is pressed against the wall, and he covers me with his body, protecting me with his darkness.

Haidion cups my face in his hands. "What can I do to help you face what we are about to walk into? Now that his last request is done, they aren't going to wait." Drums in the distance start to play lightly, but they still have me shaking.

Take deep breaths with me.

After copying his breaths, I'm in more control over the shaking, but not the chest pain. "I need to be his focal point. I will have to be in a spot where he can see me."

"Done. Anything else?" Determination brightens the hues of his amethyst eyes.

"Make my heart skip a beat."

My heart skips several beats as Haidion leans in and kisses my tears away. His soft, plump lips worship my skin as they remove any trace of me crying. He has never been so tender with me before. I find myself gripping onto his jacket to pull him closer until his chest presses against mine. I thought he was going to scare me with an illusion, not bring his lips only a hair's width away from my mouth.

Haidion pulls his face away, a little out of breath. "Anything else, my darling?"

I am out of breath, too, as I take in his handsome face. "Don't leave my side."

With a wink, he leads us up the steps and into the light.

A Colosseum of coal stone surrounds us. I'm surprised the ceiling isn't open to allow in natural light, but with it closed, the sound of people and drums is so loud that I almost have to cover my ears. Torches line each level, giving the walls a glossy texture.

Haidion weaves us through the crowd as everyone heads up to find their seats. Tables, chairs, and a feast of food were set out, as if they were having a celebration before the drums started to play.

"Freyja?" I look up and find Isis staring down at me with concern while her husband leads them to their seats.

Fury burns in my chest. "You left!" I yell as Haidion keeps tugging me along.

Pain-filled anger tightens her face, and tears fall down her cheeks. "I wanted to protect my family. I failed!"

Realization hits me. Isis and her husband are here because their son died. I don't know how they know, but they do. It makes me wonder if they blame me as well. There is no judgment in their eyes, but I don't fight Haidion's protective hold as he pulls me closer.

Isis's voice becomes distant as we get to the center of the Colosseum, where cushioned chairs are placed in a circle.

Haidion growls low at the sight of all twelve lords and ladies adorned with silver masks and gaudy, gold crowns. They are dressed in their best gowns and suits as if this were a grand ball. One of them halts before she sits down. Her head tilts to the side as she looks our way. A lord hands her a gold letter, and she walks over to us.

Haidion holds my hand tight as he takes off his hat and bows to her. "Lady of Earthradon."

Through her silver mask, I can see her green eyes blink in shock at his gentlemanly greeting. "You honor me even though you don't have to. I wonder, is it because you are not supposed to be here? Technicalities or not by being Goddess Freyja's moral support, you weren't directly invited." Her voice is honeyed, but full of venom.

"Goddess Freyja." She switches her attention to me, dismissing Haidion as she bows her head. "We were told of your possible attendance to this execution and thought to bring you this."

Judging by how her eyes cut into me, she wants me to open the letter now. After I take it from her grasp, I slide my hand under Haidion's jacket and tuck the letter into his inner pocket.

Her eyes narrow as the muscles in her slim neck tense. She holds her hands together in front of her like she's about to give a speech, but falters as a cold presence washes over us. It isn't lethal, but it is still alarming. My senses tune into the presence, classifying the aura as an unknown being while Skjoldr hums in my chest, urging me to run.

"Ominous." A sleek voice of finery and poise caresses my senses, like it's about to take control over them. "I didn't expect you to be here. What a treat for me."

The shadowy bond between Haidion and me glows in the depths of my mind and pushes the influence carried in the Ancient's voice away.

Haidion gives my hand a squeeze before he lets it go and lowers himself to one knee, bowing his head. "Ancient Demonical of Trans-mogrify, it's an honor to be in your presence."

An arrogant chuckle comes from the red-cloaked Ancient, and the lady has the audacity to chuckle at my friend, too. I wish I knew her name. The lords and ladies wear masks to protect themselves from magic and hide their identities. For the same reason, the Sons of Judgment wear them as well. The masks are one of the finest pieces of Elven-infused magic armor the Dwarves made.

Drums increase in bass, making the lady gasp. "Well, it's getting rather exciting in here, so I better go find my seat." She looks down at Haidion before sauntering off. "I'll see you at Lunar Noon, Goddess."

"Ah, you must be the reason why this cockroach was allowed to come out of the shadows." The Ancient holds out his ghostly white hand to me. "I'm Nigel."

I lift my chin. "If you want to exchange pleasantries, then remove your cloak and tell my friend to rise."

Laughter rumbles out of him. "So demanding. I can see why Odin had to reprimand you so often."

My blood stops moving as my pulse ceases to beat. "You know Odin?" I could hardly get the words out due to a force tightening around my throat.

"Odin and I are great friends." Odin told me to never befriend an Ancient Demonical and yet he did. *He's a fucking, controlling hypocrite.*

Fire attempts to erupt in my veins, but my body is as cold as stone.

Nigel leans in. "He's going to be so jealous when I tell him I saw you here with this demoted Demonical." His attention goes back to Haidion. "First of all, how dare you cut off my friend's hand. Secondly, I appreciate you doing so because now I can perform some experiments on him. And thirdly, I really can't believe Namtar let you keep your office and work. What did you have to do, hm, suck your mentor's cock?"

"Are you giving me permission to rise and speak in your presence, Ancient?" Haidion's voice is pained as if he's clenching his teeth, doing his best to hold back his anger.

"Actually, no." He takes a step closer to me, getting into my personal space. "The Sons of Judgment know that you have been staying with him. Before you think about asking for dual citizenship, are you ready to get on your knees like Ominous?" Only a choked gasp and wheeze leaves me as he gets closer. "Your title up here will mean nothing. You will be at the bottom of the poll like him." I can't even flinch when he brushes a strand of hair behind my ear. Whatever power he has is making me not only remain still, but unable to control my bodily functions. "I don't speak for Odin, but it would be in your best interest to remain on Earthradon and smash that cockroach's heart to pieces."

Nigel pulls back and walks in the direction of Emerial and Rhax.

Haidion rises, catching me before I fall to my knees. *I'm so sorry, Freyja.* "I know it's going to hurt, but you need to breathe."

Each inhalation burns as my blood starts to pump. *What kind of magic is this?*

Blood magic. There was nothing I could do to stop him. He had control over me, too.

I'm a gasping sack of flesh as Haidion basically drags me over to a pair of chairs.

Aren't you in pain as well?

My pain is not as severe as yours because I've been developing immunity.

How?

"Freyja!" Rhax calls out my name as he runs over to my other side. "Who did this to you?" My friend growls at him when he tries to help support me.

Haidion sits me down and holds me up, even though I want to curl in on myself and scream at how painful it is to have oxygen in my body.

"She had a visit from the Ancient Demonical that is talking to your mother."

Rhax's eyes burn with rage as translucent fire coats his body. "If he brought harm to Freyja, then my mother's boy toy is no longer welcome here." *Boy toy?*

Haidion surrounds me with his cold as Rhax marches off with purpose.

I moan at the soothing relief. Each breath I take is easier, and soon the pain vanishes. *Perhaps he is the father of her baby.*

If you are right, then I know exactly how I'm going to get my title back. "How are you feeling?" His words are laced with worry.

"Better," I assure him.

Haidion's eyes shadow over for a brief second. "Good because the Wardalyrian just showed up. He's the executioner."

Blood magic is illegal. I won't let Nigel get away with this.

If you want to press charges against him, we would have to leave right now and get you checked out by Vahildra.

I growl, knowing that I can't leave. Nigel has earned a place on my kill list, right under Rhax.

Again, I'm sorry. You were hurt in my presence, and there was nothing I could do to stop it.

I tsk gently. *Don't apologize. You were under control, too.* I retake his hand in mine, and a smile lifts the corner of his mouth.

It will be the last. I'll find a way to send my immunity to you through our bond.

A roar comes from Rhax as he towers over Nigel. The Ancient bows his head and kisses Emerial's hand before he's escorted out of the Colosseum by Wyverns. Even in their humanoid forms, their arms are wings. They double as swords and shields, making them the protectors and enforcers of Elbtearid.

How did Rhax confront Nigel about hurting me without proof?

I had Valrir go into his shadow. Whatever ability his possesses allowed him to figure out that Nigel used magic on you and what his intensions were.

My eyes widen. *That's one mighty strong ability.*

Agreed. During our staring contest, I discovered he possessed some sort of mental ability, but now I know roughly what it is and can defend us against it.

Rhax escorts his mother over to us, seating her on my right while he sits on her other side. "Here." Emerial holds out a flask made of dragon scales. "It's dragon fire. In liquid form, it has healing properties. You only need a sip per use. Since you were harmed on my island, it's yours."

She levels me with an angry stare as I take the flask from her. "You cost me so much in one day. I have to hand over something we'd never give to an outsider, you sent away my moral support, and you are the reason why my baby boy is being sentenced to be tortured before he's killed." Tears fall down her cheeks. "Pray to the Fates that you remain barren. Hold no love in your life and have no secret you would risk your life to protect because I will take every single one away from you. You have my word, Freyja."

Her wrath matches the intensity of Braxshi's. The reminiscent pain of the venom comes back and stings my chest as if Emerial engraved her promise into my skin.

"You can't blame Freyja for all the hardships you have endured." Haidion's voice is lethal, yet calm as he locks eyes with the Dragonnira. "You, your lover, and your son all acted of your own volitions." He brings my hand to his mouth. "If you act on your threats, I will personally see to it that you aren't true to your word." His eyes flit to mine. "This I promise you, my darling Freyja. I will protect everything you hold dear and anyone you love."

Haidion's kiss soothes the burn, but awakens a blush. He's showing me affection while thousands of eyes look upon us. Without needing any context, Emerial knows what he means to me. She flashes a cruel smile before she looks towards the Wardalyrian approaching us. Keeping Haidion and my friendship in the dark protected him. Now, the whole world has seen him, and he's even showing everyone his true identity.

Removing my hand from Haidion's, I lay the flask in his palm. He secures it in his jacket, and keeps his hand on the armrest, in easy reach if I need to hold onto him. I won't need it, anger at the Dragon Queen and Rhax is all I need to push forward.

"You are going to wish you didn't make those threats to me, Emerial." I look over at her, but she keeps her attention forward. "For the sake of your child." I place my hand on her belly, making her jump. "You wouldn't want her to grow up motherless."

Her rage and the fire she was about to spew vanish as she blinks in surprise. "Her? I'm having a girl."

"Yes." My power tingles in my palm as I rub her belly. "A strong baby girl." I remove my hand, and the Wyvern guards I hadn't seen before relax, as does Rhax.

Emerial holds her belly, a smile spreading across her face.

"My sister will not grow up motherless." I meet Rhax's eyes. The concern he had for me has vanished, and an unforgiving anger has taken its place.

"Dragonnira." The Wardalyrian lowers his head and wings before bowing on one knee.

The Dragon Queen straightens. "Have you brought the requested weapon, Major Aux?"

"Yes, your Majesty." His gruff tone isn't as gritty, which is a relief to my ears.

The humanoid gargoyle stands, and an executioner's sword appears out of thin air above his outstretched hands. The handle and guard are made from scales, and the black blade glows internally with fire. Light moves under the metal as if dozens of souls are trapped inside. The notion becomes a heavy brick of truth as I note the numerous names engraved on the blade.

Bile rises in the back of my throat as I meet Major Aux's eyes. One eye is alight with luminous fire, while the other is a piercing iceberg. I don't recall if the gargoyle that escorted Haidion to the Sons of Judgment had such an eye color. Perhaps these are the eyes of the being inside?

Emerial holds her belly a little tighter, and Rhax leans in close to her, silently growling at the blade. "Betrayer," they mutter in unison.

Major Aux nods. "The blade that can cut through the bones of a dragon and trap their soul and power."

"Why is it called Betrayer?" I find myself asking before I can think better of it.

Emerial clears her throat, her attention not wavering from the blade. "The weapon was forged by King Maurdr, my greatest grandfather. A dragon betrayed our race, so he crushed the traitor's bones, made it into a weapon, and placed his soul in the blade. Before he died, he used his last breath to make sure any dragon who betrays our race must be killed by his blade." Tears run down her cheeks. "Anyone who is killed by it will suffer for eternity." She audibly sobs. "Instead of my son resting in peace, he will be trapped in that blade." She cries so hard that she almost falls over, but Rhax catches her before.

"That's not his name," Major Aux states with authority, making Emerial jump. "He prefers 'Soul Collector.'"

Haidion stands abruptly. "I think it's best if we move along." My eyes widen in shock as he matches the Wardalyrian's tone of voice.

I reach for my friend's hand to pull him back, but Major Aux yanks him, pulling him forward so they are face-to-face. "If you dare speak up to me again, it will be your neck that I chop off next."

Major Aux's daunting voice and eight-foot-tall frame would make me curl in on myself, but Haidion lifts his chin. "Understood."

He gets smacked so hard across the face that he falls to the ground. I catch him before he lands, using my body to cushion his. A glittering aura surrounds us. I don't know why Haidion is trying to illusion us, but that's the least of my concerns as I take in his swollen, cut, and bruised face. One cut barely missed his eye.

An arrogant huff comes from Major Aux. "Now both sides of your face are cut up, pretty boy."

The glare I give the Wardalyrian has him narrowing his eyes at me. I ingrain the color of his irises into my memory. I will make his body bleed before I freeze his wounds, ensuring the pain will sting for eternity.

A familiar, radiant male voice with the warmth of the sun and the calmness of the moon speaks into my mind. *Back down, Freyja.* It takes me by surprise, and I break eye contact with Major Aux.

With a grunt, the Wardalyrian officer sheaths Soul Collector to his hip before he turns to Emerial. "Shall we begin?"

Rhax tries to hold her, but she pushes his comfort away. "Yes, Major Aux. Proceed with the execution." The wrathful voice of a grieving mother is gone, and in its place is a mighty ruler.

Haidion rolls to his feet faster than I thought he'd be able to. Rather than me helping him, he helps me to stand and assesses my body for injuries.

"I'm fine, Haidion, but you aren't."

He shrugs off my concern as his glittering aura vanishes, and we sit. "My *pretty* face has been hit harder." The word definitely got under his skin.

Out of all the insults he could've called me, he went with that, Haidion curses in my mind, and I have the odd notion that I wasn't meant to hear that comment.

Eager to put a smile back on Haidion's face, I grasp his chin lightly to make him face me. "You are one of the most handsome beings in the entire existence of the universe." I don't know where this bravery has come from, but it's gone in an instant.

Haidion gives me a smile that has my toes curling in my boots, my heart skipping beats, and heat crawling up my neck and down to my thighs. The world falls away, and I'm trapped in a trance of uncertainty and anxiousness when his eyes dip to my mouth. His pupils dilate when I lick my suddenly parched lips.

His glittering aura starts to radiate out of him as he leans in closer to me. *Is he about to—*

He pulls away, taking his magic with him when Emerial holds up her hand, and all quiet down.

She keeps her hand raised as a circular slab of stone lowers feet away from us, splits in half, and disappears into the void of darkness below. The deadly silence makes the sound of metal scraping against stone louder, filling the enclosed Colosseum.

The ground shakes as a familiar head rises from the darkness. Starson's eyes relax when they find mine, and a small smile flashes across his face. It falls when he looks at who I'm sitting next to. There is no sadness or plea for his mother to stop this; no, it's pure anger. Starson isn't looking at Emerial as if she is a nurturing parent, but a corrupt ruler.

Once Starson has fully risen, he bites down hard on his tongue and spits his blood out like mist. "Whatever eternity is in store for me, I want to be cleansed of your lineage." His gaze flicks to Emerials' belly, before looking up with a bloody smile. "My last breath will be for my siblings to be cleansed from you as well."

The Dragonnira's mouth wobbles for a second before she bares her fangs at Starson and lowers her arm.

Rhythmic drumming, like a strong heartbeat, echoes around the Colosseum. Chants in a tongue I don't know grow into a song that matches the deadly melody. Everyone sounds so angry that I almost start to cry from all the hate.

Major Aux steps next to Starson's side and unsheathes the blade. "Do you forgive me?"

He nods without breaking eye contact with me.

The drums' pace and the chanting start to pick up as Major Aux walks behind Starson, taking a wide stance.

With one powerful slash, a wing is severed from Starson's body with a spurt of blood that makes the crowd roar. He falls to his knees as his other wing gets cut off. Pain is etched across his face, but he doesn't scream or cry; he only keeps his eyes locked on me. I have to clench every muscle in my body to not flinch or jump to my feet in a desperate bid to stop this.

The drums are so fast, their pounding beat matches my hammering heart. The thousands of onlookers go wild with their song when Major Aux raises the blade to the back of Starson's neck.

With another swing and a grunt, the blade sails through the air, and the breath I was holding gets expelled as a scream.

Emerial ducks as the Soul Collector flies over her head, hitting the top of her chair. A hard crack tells me that the blade was now imbedded into the stone behind us. I look up, and to my astonishment Starson's head is still attached to his body.

All goes deathly silent as Starson collapses from blood loss.

Major Aux looks at Emerial with an evil grin. "The weapon you call Betrayer is for those who betray their race." His voice fills the Colosseum. "Soul Collector didn't think that Varnus was the traitor."

Is he implying that the soul-forged weapon acted out on its own?

Yes. Haidion's answer chills me down to my soul.

Emerial roars, "Seize him!"

The Wyvern guards surround Major Aux, but before they can restrain him, a flash of darkness explodes like wild flames.

Gone is the stone, and in its place is a being of shadowy darkness. Tendrils of snake-like magic come out of his back and form into wings. His body looks like it is made of cracking lava with a blazing white light underneath the surface. Smoke amasses into a cape and a crown. The only pleasant feature that is omitted from his deadly aura are his eyes, they are a purple galaxy of twinkling stars that appear almost like precious gems.

While everyone else is screaming in terror and running for their lives, I rise from my seat and start to sprint to Starson, determined to stop his bleeding.

Haidion grabs me by the waist and pulls me back. "Going to him will only make you look like a threat. See the guards?" I do; they are all dead. "Bow now or run away. I'll find you after."

I resist as he falls to his hands and knees. "Who the fuck is that?" A cold that is beyond lethal digs into my body and makes me bow against my will.

Before I can yell at Haidion for using his magic on me, he heatedly roars, "The Shadow King!"

My blood doesn't run cold. I have no reason to fear him. Instead, fire erupts from my soul, and I burn through the restraints of Haidion's magic trying to hold me down.

On my hands and knees, I crawl towards the stone slab as Haidion pleads for me to remain still.

As I reach for Starson's hand, a misty boot stomps next to my arm.

The Shadow King stares down at me, and then looks at the dragon with an evil smile. With a twirl of long, lava fingers, tendrils of smoke wrap around Starson and the chains drop from his lifeless body as it levitates in the air.

The Shadow King raises his other hand, and Soul Collector returns to him. "They are mine now." The smokiest voice I've ever heard makes me cough so hard, I start wheezing.

Maniacal laughter fills the Colosseum as the Shadow King, and all his darkness vanishes with Starson.

CHAPTER

FORTY-ONE

That's the being the Father wants me to pass the information along to about bringing restoration? Judging by how everyone reacted to his presence, it seems that he can deliver more chaos than hope. Only Haidion, Rhax, and the lords and ladies bowed while everyone else fled, including Emerial.

Haidion didn't hesitate to portal us out. "Rules be damned," he said since the Dragon Queen fled. I would argue with him about taking the blame, but instead, I'm up his ass about how to get in touch with the Shadow King.

"You have more important things to worry about." Haidion plops onto the couch in my bedroom and pulls out the gold letter. "I bet you a favor is that this is a court summons."

"Why would I be called to court?" After placing my armor on a wooden mannequin, I take the letter from him and begin pacing.

I'm unable to sit still. The fear of facing a Ghoul is nothing in comparison to meeting Rhax, the dragon who killed my brother, and then watching my friend get executed, only to find out the executioner was the Shadow King in disguise. There's so much to process; however, I don't want to. I only want to act, and the best place to start first is this letter. Having something to do keeps the pain and emotions away, and that's what I need to stay strong.

"Goddess Freyja,

For participation in the battle that occurred during the Vernal Equinox, you are hereby summoned to court.

Please report to Thunder Pass, east of Mightiarch, at Lunar Noon on the third day following the Vernal Equinox.

If you have an attorney, have them fill out their name below and arrive with you. Failure to appear will lead to your arrest.

As a defendant, you have the right to bring one being as moral support. Have them sign below and arrive with you.

Sincerely, the Lords and Ladies of Earthradon."

I hand the paper back to Haidion. "You already know I wouldn't pick anyone else."

A fancy black-and-gold pen appears in his hand. "Would you like me to ask Vahildra if he will represent you?"

"I didn't know he was a lawyer." I wring my hands together, trying to reduce the nervousness by cracking my fingers.

Haidion nods as he signs his name. "One of the best, and he can practice in Orrtiereum and on Earthradon."

"Yes, please." I clear the desperation out of my throat as shadows cover Haidion's eyes. "Why do I need representation? What am I being charged for? I lost the battle. The Unfaithful won; Thor killed the Father. If anything, the Lords and Ladies should be going after him."

The shadows clear in Haidion's eyes. "Your attorney will be here in the morning, and he just sent out his shadows to find out what they can about the court proceedings." He looks back at the paper. "They were very vague."

"How much time until Lunar Noon?"

Haidion pulls out a white pocket watch from his vest. "Twenty-four hours for us."

The cold floor numbs my bare feet as I continue to pace circles around the couch. "What am I going to do?" I mumble to myself.

Pacing for twenty-four hours is the only thing that I can think of to pass the time. Sitting still isn't an option; I'll emotionally crash. Perhaps sleep could be an option if I take the tonic Haidion gave me.

"Would you like to expel your energy some other way?"

I interlock my fingers and try to pull them apart as I keep circling. "What did you have in mind?"

Haidion gives me a grin that has some heat returning to my toes. "Many things, but how about you start with going swimming?"

"Yeah, burning some energy by swimming sounds like a good idea." It may also be calming for my nerves as well. "Are you going to join me?"

He raises his brow. "Do you want me to join you?" I'm about to nod when he adds, "Because I swim naked." Heat returns to my feet as I stumble to a stop. "Is that going to be okay?" A more vulnerable emotion flutters across his face, preventing him from forming that knowing grin.

"It's absolutely fine. Yeah. Skin. Naked. I'm perfectly cool with that." I place my hands on my hips as I try to remember how to breathe.

Haidion's smile trembles, as a warmer tone brightens his neck. "I'll give you a head start. See you down there." He exits my room with haste and fumbles to close the doors. I've never seen him so shaken before. I don't think he was even breathing.

"Skin is skin," I repeat to myself.

I recall the first time I entered Wolven territory. Seeing everyone naked was overwhelming, especially my brother. My confused feelings and insecurities settled down when I met Bralyant. After being with him, I became comfortable in my skin and seeing others comfortable in theirs. I learned that there was nothing wrong with being interested in both men and women. Being with the Wolven, it was customary to be naked. Haidion has remained clothed for the entirety of our friendship. Seeing him naked is out of the norm, which is probably why he's jittery, as am I.

Perhaps this is why he suggested swimming. The action has distracted my nerves from being anxious about one thing to another; however, this is something I'm in control of.

With each step I take to the bathroom, I drop pieces of my clothing. By the time I reach the door, I'm naked. The black stone is warm under my feet as I descend the spiral staircase.

I gasp as I take in the spring. Roots run along the floor, climb the walls, and rise through the star quartz ceiling. The light generated from the glimmering minerals in the stone makes the still and clear water appear endless. Water that is not too warm or cold envelops me like a hug as I take the last few steps. My disturbance causes the water to ripple and twinkle like I just waved a blanket of stars.

The sight of a rosy oak tree, with leaves of every color, in the middle of the spring is breathtaking. Roses bloom across the sprawling branches, giving the room a fresh, floral aroma that doesn't overpower the senses. The tree trunks splits into four boughs that weave together, creating a basin-like pool filled with water and petals in the middle.

The water is like silk on my skin as I gracefully glide through it. The sound of someone diving into the water stops me from pulling myself up to the grotto.

I peer around the tree trunk towards another spiral staircase. "The spring looks even better when night falls."

My wet hair whips Haidion in the face as I whirl around. Like me, only his neck is above the water. Against all my urges to look down, I keep my attention upwards. I can't help but laugh as the peculiar expression he makes after being struck by my hair.

"This is the type of greeting I get?" A wicked grin spreads across his handsome face.

"Serves you right for sneaking up on—" He whips his hair around, smacking me in the face.

Now it's his turn to erupt in lovely laughter, and I can't help but join him. Our laughter echoes around the room like a whimsical melody.

Before I can ask, "When does night fall?" The lights in the stone darken to obsidian. The rose petals' pastel hues darken to midnight shades. Only the stars in the quartz and the faint cracks of white light come from the tree keep the spring lit. The delicate light travels from the roots to limbs, softening the darkness and giving the colors a sensual glow.

Haidion reaches up and brushes a wet strand of hair off my face. "Would you like a drink from the grotto?" His fingers travel down my cheek to my collarbone before sliding across my arm.

His touch relaxes my muscles, and it takes all my concentration to keep breathing and wading water. "We can't go inside?"

I allow him to tangle our fingers together. "Only if the Rose Oak untangles its roots and allows you inside. If not, we can rise and take a drink from it."

Haidion brings me to a tree limb that is low enough for us to pull ourselves up by. "What are the benefits of drinking the water?"

He gives me a soft smile. "It depends on the being and what the Rose Oak is willing to bless you with. I was welcomed inside a couple of months ago. I didn't feel any different until recently. I was fighting off a powerful creature and in a dire moment of need, something inside my soul unlocked. I grew wings. There was no other influence of magic that could've done it, so I knew it had to be the grotto."

Before he can pull himself up, I grip his shoulder. "Why didn't you come and get me? I could've been there to help you, as you have done for me."

Haidion's smile drops as he takes in my worry. "I would've figured something out." A teasing grin starts to form. "I'm like you." He taps my nose. "I'm stubborn, too. Perhaps the spirit is inside me as well."

He grips the branch and pulls himself up. Water cascades down his powerful arms and tattooed, softly toned back. My mouth goes dry when his muscles ripple as he flexes to hold himself in position while he drinks.

From the strands of his drying ebony curls, I track his tattoos down his entire backside. Heat burns my body as I take in Haidion's drums of steel. His ass is both firm and round, and all I want is to sink my fingers and teeth into them. From this angle, I can't see his front, which is a good thing because I don't think I'm ready to see all of—

He turns to the side, keeping one arm on the branch and offering me his other, but it's not his arm that has my full attention. Between a pair of strong thighs is a smooth cock of significant length and unbelievable girth.

"Freyja."

My attention snaps up, and to my surprise, there isn't a knowing grin or smirk. Like before, he has a soft and sweet smile as he stares at me with loving eyes, patiently waiting for me to take his hand. I'm sure he has comments ready. Like, if you keep looking at it, it's going to wave back. But he doesn't say anything, he just keeps giving me that tender smile as he waits. He's reacting as I hoped; skin is just skin. Just because he's naked doesn't mean things have to be awkward or sexual. It's because of that unsaid understanding that I grab his hand.

Haidion helps pull me up as I grab onto another branch. "Take a sip," he fondly whispers as I gaze into the basin of starlit water with petals that dance just underneath the surface.

The smoothest water I have ever drank slides over my tongue and down my throat. My lips and body become hydrated after just one taste of the sweet floral water. *This is better than tea.*

When I look back at Haidion, I note that his face is healed; all the swelling and cuts are gone. "The grotto healed you?"

He nods and lowers us back down into the pool, keeping me close. "Do you feel anything?"

After taking a moment to assess my body, I shake my head. "Nothing spectacular, though being able to swim in such magical water is certainly a blessing."

As the words leave my mouth, rose petals of every shade of green fall. They swirl together and float down onto my head. The petals form into something I can't see, and a branch rises from the floor, creating a bench that lifts Haidion and me up until our torsos are above water.

Haidion's arm is still draped around my waist, keeping me so close that we are hip-to-hip. His skin against mine is unlike any sensation I have ever experienced before. He's so smooth; it's like no hair grows on his body.

"Beautiful," he purrs, his sensual voice a caress.

"What is it?" I look down into the water. Atop my head is a tiara weaved from green petals; my favorite color. "Oh my. It's so elegant yet so simple." I turn to the tree. "Thank you."

Haidion's fingers graze my cheek. "Your freckles are glowing, and the rosy blush of your skin is a deeper shade."

He's right; my freckles appear to be dusted by the whitest of stars. As for the deeper shade of my skin, I'm not entirely sure it's the lighting causing it.

I place my head on his shoulder. "Thank you for showing me this place."

He gives my waist a squeeze. "Come here whenever you want."

When I think he's going to pull his hand away, his fingers glide from my cheek to my chin, then brush my skin, asking a silent question.

I tilt my head back so that I can meet his eyes. "Yes, Haidion?"

A pleasurable sigh leaves his lips. "I love it when you say my name." His hand trails down my neck. "I wonder what my full name will sound like on your lips."

I lean forward, intrigued to find out. "Tell me."

"Alright, but there is an accent on it that requires the tongue to roll." He bites his bottom lip. "Perhaps I should show you first."

Show me how to roll my tongue? "How would you do that?"

He licks his lips. "Stay still."

I pinch my brows together, confused about how the action of staying still will help me learn how to roll my tongue.

My breath catches when he tightens his grip on my waist and neck. "Haidion?"

Something within him shifts from my question. His eyes are filled with uncertainty, which contrasts sharply with the confidence he had a moment ago.

He immediately drops his hand and pulls his arm out from around my waist. "Enjoy the water."

His shaky voice snatches my complete attention, but he's in the water before I can utter a word.

A moment later, he breaches the surface on the other side of the pool, and I can only watch as he climbs the stairs, disappearing from my view. A part of my chest goes with him as an ache takes its place. *Why did he leave so suddenly?*

Haidion is throwing off some very confusing signs about whether he desires me or not. Every other lover I knew made their intentions clear. Bralyant always kissed me under water or above, Vianre told me outright that she was curious to know what I tasted like, and Odin wrote me poetry about how much he admired and desired for me to be his. When it comes to Haidion, I can't tell when his tenderness is on friends only territory or moving to something else.

Maybe Haidion leaving the spring is his way of telling me where we stand. A part of me wants to cry, while the other part wants to scream for being so foolish to think I could be with my friend. The love I was trying to fill was clearly not in the friend category, but in the romantic one.

This is why I can't focus on anything but the task I must complete. I'm getting sidetracked. First, I will handle this trial, and then work on my battle plan to face Thor.

After enjoying the water for a bit, I place my tiara next to my feather on the vanity before showering. Besides not feeling up to eating, I wasn't ready to face Haidion yet. Rather than sit through an awkward dinner, I decide to go to bed. To my surprise, I slept well without the tonic, and no nightmares violently woke me.

With utter quietness, I braid my hair and pick out my own clothing. Since going to trial in armor is frowned upon, I choose an all-black outfit. Having a closet for clothes is overwhelming, but I'm able to navigate through it.

The Fate of Chance must've blessed me with luck because when I open my doors, they don't make a sound, and Haidion is nowhere to be found. It's not that I don't like him courting me downstairs, but now I know he is only doing it as my friend. It means nothing more.

Since I'm the only one walking down the hallway, the walls show my memories, but they aren't happy ones. They are filled with all my pain, guilt, and regret. The loss of my brother, taking Odin's abuse, failing to save the Father, and the image of Haidion walking away from me last night reflect back to me.

Haidion's doors open, and I'm down the stairs faster than I thought possible. Anxiety has me moving, and I pray to the Fates that the walls change before he sees my inner turmoil.

When I get to the dining room, Vahildra is already sitting there, sipping his coffee. "Freyja." He looks over my shoulder. "Is he taking longer to get ready? Typical." His silver-blue suit and trench coat make him look sharp, like a shark.

Rather than sit in my standard seat, I head towards the one Valrir sits at. I pause. "Do you know if Valrir is going to be joining us?"

"No. This breakfast is only for you, Haidion, and me." He gestures to the seat with a wave. "Please sit."

"Nine thousand years old?" Vahildra gives me a small grin and shakes his head.

A wisp of shadow mist comes out of his hand and pulls back my chair. As I sit, the wisp nudges my cheek, tickling me.

A lethal cold wind silences my giggles. Haidion is at the door, wearing all black. His hands are fists at his sides as his eyes flick between the two of us. His attention fully lands on me and softens a fraction, but his stoicism stays; I have never seen him like this.

Vahildra takes another sip of his coffee, not taking his attention off a piece of paper next to his plate. "It's rude to keep a lady waiting. I thought I taught you better."

Heated anger rises in Haidion's soul, and before he unleashes it on Vahildra, I rush to say, "I didn't want him to court me down." Both of their gazes lock on me, and everything goes deadly silent.

Haidion's cold weakens as his voice enters my mind. *Is it because of what we did last night?*

Nothing happened last night. The truth hurts, but I need to say it. "The gesture was nice when I was a guest, but now I'm going to be living here, so it's not needed."

The faintest of frowns appears on Vahildra's face before he covers it up with his mug to take another sip.

Haidion's power is pulled back into him, but he appears less poised than he normally is. "Understood." I'm hyperaware as he walks behind me, picking up the quiet sound of him running his fingers along the back of my chair. "Is there anything else I need to know moving forward?"

Only when he takes his seat am I able to take in a breath. "Don't go out of your way to be a gentleman. There is no reason for you to impress me."

A wicked smile spreads on his lips. "But I enjoy impressing you."

Rather than answer, I shrug and pile fruit, eggs, sausage, bread, and cheese on my plate. "Did you know that Major Aux was the Shadow King in disguise? He smacked you hard, and you recovered quickly, so it makes me think you knew."

Vahildra looks up. "What happened?"

Haidion doesn't answer him right away; he assesses me for a moment, and I do my best to not squirm. Rather than speak aloud, their eyes shadow over. The room is quiet for a moment as they mind speak, giving me time to devour my food.

"It appears that you need a history lesson, Freyja." Vahildra's eyes clear. "About the Shadow King."

I shake my head as I swallow a piece of melon. "I already know about him. He protects all souls from leeches and infectious magic. His territory goes beyond Earthradon. His realm is parallel to everything, even the planes. Everyone has a different opinion about him, which could sever alliances and friendships." Haidion wears his unreadable mask again. "Why was he under cover as a Wardalyrian Officer, especially a Major? No one just gains that title. He would have had to earn it over centuries of work and also be enlisted with the Guild. And why did he take Starson?"

"There is a more extensive history you need to be told. But since you know the basics, we can move on to why I'm here," Vahildra calmly interjects.

My attention stays locked on Haidion as I wait for answers.

He shrugs and piles the same food I had gone for on his plate, even taking the last of the melons. As he spears the last piece, I jab my fork with his, preventing him from moving. "Feisty this morning, or do you really like melons?"

His playful smile almost disarms me, but I remain focused. "Answer. My. Questions."

He leans in. "Will you answer mine?" *What questions does he have?*

Vahildra clears his throat, and whatever stare down Haidion and I were in breaks. He disarms me of my fork and takes the last piece of melon. A tendril of Vahildra's magic swats Haidion's hand and gives me my fork back.

"Freyja, may I suggest that we talk in private?" Glass breaks as metal snaps. Haidion's plate is broken, and his silverware is bent in half. "Is that a problem?" Vahildra glares at him.

"I don't know my own strength this morning." His eyes flick to me, and I spot a glint of desperation. "I'm anxious for you, and I would like to be a part of this conversation. Will you allow me to stay, Freyja?"

I lean in. "I'm anxious for my friend, too, but you won't give me answers."

"After," Haidion says with certainty. "Once we are done here, you and I will get the answers we want."

One question each?

I'm taken aback by his suggestion. I think I rattled off a handful of them, and now I have to pick just one. Starson's wellbeing is more important to me, so I know what question I'll be asking, but I have no idea what Haidion has to ask me.

Deal. "Yes, you can stay."

He sits back in his chair fully, his aura regaining the strength that had been absent since he entered the room.

His plate and silverware have been repaired. "Please, proceed. I'll try not to break anything while you two chat."

Vahildra takes a longer sip of his coffee and places it down with such utter gentleness that I don't even hear the glass clink against the table. Haidion appears to flinch out of the corner of my eyes, but I'm not completely sure.

"Alright." Vahildra's cooler tone gives me chills. "From what my shadows gathered, all the rulers of the races are being called to court to give a census on how many warriors they lost, along with the leaders of each army."

Odin's eyes flash in my mind. "Who was the leader of the Unfaithful?"

"That, I don't know."

"My guess is either Zeus, Odin, or Thor." Hopefully it's not Odin, but if it is Thor, then I'm one step closer to getting Faithless.

"What I do know is how the proceedings will go." He looks down at his paper. "First, since both leaders of the Tauruns are gone, and their son is too young to rule, the lords and ladies will steward the race until he becomes of age. The Vampyres are being charged with not coming to the aid of the Unfaithful, and the Spydens want justice for their Autarcha. The Sirens are being charged with treason for breaking from the United Races of Earthradon and forming the Sea Lords Alliance. If their new Kiani renounces the SLA and rejoins the URE, they will be forgiven. As for why the commanders are being called, it could be for a multitude of things.: His eyes meet mine. "Every battle or war that involves massive amounts of death results in the leaders being called."

I nod, remembering the trial after the War over the Frozen Fire Highlands. My brother was the commander, and with him dead, the lords and ladies tried to claim I was the leader until Adom stepped in to say he was. Which was the truth, he had been the second in command. There is no backing out this time; everyone elected me to be in charge.

"What should I expect?"

Vahildra puts down the piece of paper and rests his forearms on the table. "Someone made an accusation against you; that's why you are a defendant. Since no name was listed, I can only assume the lords and ladies are making the charges against you."

Haidion places down his silverware, fully engrossed in our conversation. "Against her, for what?"

"This is only a theory." Vahildra glances between Haidion and me. "Valrir told me about the chains they used on the gods to subdue them. They are the same ones the Wardalyrians use. So, someone must've given it to them. It could be the Gargoyle Guild or the Sons of Judgment. But either way, the Unfaithful have powerful allies." He takes a deep breath. "Whatever the lords and ladies will charge you with will determine if they, too, are allies with the Unfaithful."

"If the lords and ladies actually chose to side with the Unfaithful then that means..." Deep in my soul, something screams as the sensation of bars close in on me. "...they are going to be sentencing me to Wardalyn." *But why would they want to imprison me?*

"No," Haidion states with conviction. "If Vahildra plays his cards right, you won't be locked away if that is what their intentions are."

"Yes, but you need to do one thing for me, Freyja." Vahildra stares into my soul. "You need to keep your mouth shut. I'm representing you, so I'll speak for you." He leans back and gives me a little smile. "I'm not trying to stroke my own cock, but I'm one of the best lawyers in existence."

Haidion shudders like he just tasted something disgusting. "Leave your cock out of this conversation."

Vahildra's smile widens a fraction. "It doesn't seem like Freyja minds."

"Is there any other information that your shadows gathered?" Haidion stares daggers at the other Demonical, which only makes him smirk.

"No. I have nothing else. Remember, restrain your witty tongue, keep your enchanting mouth shut, and you won't face any jailtime." Vahildra rises, walks over to me, and leans down to press his cool lips against my cheek. His polite kiss tingles against my warm skin.

"I'll be back." He vanishes in a smoky mist, leaving Haidion and me alone.

I push my plate away and turn to face Haidion. "Why did the Shadow King take Starson?"

He ran his finger along the edge of his glass for a moment. "To save him." My eyes widen in surprise. "The Shadow King received a plea of desperation, and he answered. Varnus is currently being healed. It will be a long recovery, but he will make it."

I slump in my seat, relieved, and wipe away a rogue tear. "Thank you."

He gives me a warm smile. "After I was publicly smacked, the Sons of Judgment no longer suspect me. And yes, I did know that Major Aux was not who he claimed to be."

"You didn't have to tell me all that; I could only ask one question."

"I told you to trust me, and you did. It's only fair that I tell you."

Against all of my warning bells telling me not to act in a way that will cause me more emotional pain, I go to him. Haidion leaps from his seat and hugs me, flushing us together in the blink of an eye. It is more than a closeness of bodies exchanging appreciation for one another; it is an affectionate embrace as I press against his chest, and he rests his face in the crook of my neck.

I shudder when his lips tenderly brush against my skin. He drags his soft mouth up my neck until he gets to my ear. "Why are you trying to distance yourself from me?"

Haidion's breath is cool on my skin, and I melt into—*wait, what?* His question processes, and I jump out of his arms. "What makes you think that?"

He raises his brow. "Well, firstly, your reaction only confirms that I'm right. And secondly, because you aren't graceful with your steps. I heard you run down the stairs when I opened my door." My cheeks burn. "Also, I couldn't help but notice the walls before they shifted." Worry softens his features. "If you want to talk about your inner turmoil, I'm here to listen."

"Talking won't help. Action will. And as for why I ran down the stairs, it was because I was hungry. I skipped dinner and I was starting to become hangry. Also, didn't you tell me that I don't have to wait for you to head down?"

"I did, but hangry Freyja doesn't run, she stomps her feet. And the walls would've shown anger, not agony." His voice drops to a gentle whisper as he assesses me. "I wasn't talking about physical distance, and you know it. Is what you're fighting to not deal with the reason why you're pushing me away?"

I take a step back. "I gave you an answer. You can't ask another question."

Haidion tucks his hands in his pockets. "I was clarifying my question. Clearly, I didn't choose the correct wording."

"Well, that is the answer I'm giving you, and I'm not interested in doing this exchange again." I turn on my heels and storm out of the dining room, cursing myself for not being subtle with my steps, which only further proves he's right.

"We are friends, are we not?" Haidion's words make me falter before I ascend the stairs. A hurt awakens in my soul with his admission about what type of relationship we have. "It shouldn't take me withholding information for you to open up to me. In the past, we might not have had a lot of heart-to-heart conversations, but you could still talk to me. I know you're closing yourself off, and on any other day, I'd let you. But perhaps you should consider that maybe last night was hard for me."

When I turn, he's a healthy distance away, and I'm surprised that I didn't hear him approach me. "Was getting naked in front of me really that difficult?"

"Yes," he exclaims with power in his voice. It shocks my senses and knocks my stubbornness down a peg. "I didn't have the same upbringing as you. The only time that I showed another my body was when I had sex. And during those interactions, I never had an emotional connection; it was strictly a physical act. Showing my body to someone who I deeply care about was difficult for me because it was an intimacy I never had before." He pants for a second, getting his breathing under control. "Can you imagine how insecure and hurt I felt when you avoided me and ran down the stairs?"

"I didn't consider what my actions might translate as. I'm sorry; that wasn't my intention."

Haidion takes a step toward me. "I don't want your apology. I want to know why you ran."

I walk towards him until there is only a breath of space between us.

"I ran for the same reason you didn't stay in the spring with me. Because we are friends."

The admission makes me shudder, causes pain to strike my heart, and crushes my soul.

"No, Freyja. I left for an entirely different reason." He takes in a strong breath, as if he's using it to shield the tender spot of his existence. "Am I only a friend to you?"

His eyes pierce mine, and when I open my mouth to speak, I am unable to utter the word 'yes' because it is a lie.

Passionate hunger and desperate longing blaze from his soul, igniting his skin like he's burning from the inside out.

"Your hesitation speaks volumes."

A wildfire of glittering darkness surrounds us, blocking the outside world as if we were in our own pocket, where time doesn't exist and only we do.

His aura wraps around mine, fusing together into a blissful euphoria of magic and strength. There is no clashing of my heat and his cold; they blend in harmony.

I pant as the desire from the darkness in my mind tries to break free. I hold onto the last threads of strength I have, protecting me from doing something reckless like acting on my feelings that could cost me my friend.

"Haidion, what is all of this?"

He can't be shielding us away for the reasons I so desperately want. He must be doing it to help me talk to him, but still, I need to ask. I need reassurance that this doesn't mean anything more than a friend trying to help me open up.

Haidion cups my cheek and brushes his thumb over my mouth, dragging my lower lip down. "This is me showing you what would've happened last night in the spring if I had the same amount of courage as I do now."

My breath catches when he pulls my body flush to his, his hand slides to the back of my head, and his fingers tangle into my hair. "Fuck my promise," he whispers to himself before he leans in and—

"Haidion!"

The sound of Valrir's angry voice makes Haidion let out a feral snarl that I have never heard him produce before.

White mist punches through the pocket we are in, dissolving the darkness and bringing us back to reality.

Valrir stands in the doorway to Haidion's study. Her hands are balled into fists, and by the slight tremor of her chin, she's either about to send another punch of her magic at us, or she is pissed.

"Study. Now!"

Haidion's eyes darken and become flames of shadow as he stares her down. "You took control of my magic." I shrink in his arms at how deep and dominating his voice is. The one holding me isn't my friend, but an unknown monster that I immediately fear.

"Well, then you shouldn't have given me a portion of it to use." Even Valrir's tone shifts, but it is more reserved, and she takes her time to pronounce every word. My instincts warn me that getting away from her is the best option if I want to be safe.

"I'm going to go lay down for a bit." I can't hide the shakiness in my voice.

Haidion looks at me as he immediately lets go. "Freyja, I..." Worry pains his face as his eyes lighten to his natural hues.

"I'm okay." I take a step away from him, backing up the stairs.

His concern doesn't lessen as his features sadden with regret. "I'll come see you after."

"No, you won't," Valrir states. "We have matters to discuss and issues to address." She looks up at me. "I'll have him back for your trial."

She grabs his ear and drags him off towards the study. Haidion curses her name as he tries to break out of her hold.

As if my ass is on fire, I run to my room and slam the doors shut. I flood the tender spots of my existence with soul magic. But no matter how much I direct to my heart and soul to protect myself, nothing is able to stop me from feeling overwhelmed by what just occurred. Haidion disarmed me in every way possible, and I'm left in a mess of confusion. *Was he about to kiss me?*

CHAPTER

FORTY-TWO

Hours of being alone with my thoughts, analyzing, and possibly overthinking every aspect of Haidion's and my relationship have led to not only a conclusion, but a fantastic realization. "Haidion was going to kiss me."

I can't help but smile as I lounge on the couch, staring up at myself in the black mirror ceiling. Only one question arises from the depths of my mind. "What would that kiss mean for us?"

I'm failing at trying to keep my feelings for him aside so I can focus on my task. My emotions for Haidion have been all over the place ever since I arrived at his home. I've been around him more often, and he's been more sensual with me than ever before. I can only blame myself because I should tell him no, but I desire his tenderness as much as my body needs air. It's obvious that if I don't want Haidion to be a distraction, I will need to stay away from him. But I'm not ready to go home; I fear what Odin will do to me.

My options are to either tell Haidion to stop his advances and only be my friend because that is what I need right now, or I give into my wants and balance being his and going after Thor. My first dedication is to the Father and Earthradon; Haidion would be second, so he'd have to understand that this task could cost me my life. So, for the time being, do I rather keep Haidion within arm's reach and be content? Or do I allow myself to be desired the way I have dreamed about for whatever length of time my soul has left?

A knock on my door pulls me out of my thoughts. "Freyja, I thought we'd leave a little early to watch the sky come alive as the moon sets at the highest point in the sky," Haidion calls.

I'm on my feet, tripping over myself as I run to the door. I smack hard into it before yanking it open. I squeal as the door comes off its hinges and falls into my room.

Haidion wears a bemused expression that quickly turns into amusement. "Someone's eager to go. Vahildra will be joining us in a moment."

I have no words. I smile broadly as I take in Haidion, seeing him in a new light for the first time. My realization helps me to see that he is not just a friend I can rely on and make memories with, but someone whom I can trust with my heart and fall in love with. Knowing that we will always have a solid foundation of friendship makes allowing Haidion into the tender spots of my existence less scary.

The last bit of doubt gets erased from my mind as the memory of my brother's voice speaks to me, saying the words he told me during the war. *Wouldn't it be better to be with someone who is also your best friend?* I had been torn between marrying Odin and desiring to be with Bralyant. At the time, I thought he was talking about Bralyant, but now I know he wasn't; he was trying to push me in the right direction. I deserve to have a special person in my life to love and not settle for anything less.

My soul answers my brother's question for me as she burns in passionate flames, causing tears to run down my cheeks.

"Freyja?" Haidion's voice softens to a pleasurable tone that lifts me up like I'm in his arms.

I close the distance and adjust his hat the way he likes it, then whisper in his ear, "Are you ready to go, my darling?" The endearment rolls off my tongue naturally, as if I was always meant to say it to him.

Haidion stumbles back a step, his eyes wide with disbelief. He blinks for a moment, then a smile explodes on his face.

I'm tempted to say fuck it to the trial and push him against the door to finally figure out how soft his lips feel against mine.

He pulls me to him. "Yes, Freyja." His arm slides down my side, tugging on my clothes until he reaches the back of my knee. "I'm ready."

Giggles leave me as I'm lifted into his arms. His eyes blaze with purple fire, as if something within his soul is set free. When I wrap my arms around his neck, they only burn brighter.

A portal of shadow fire opens behind Haidion, and without taking his attention away from me, he walks in.

Saltwater enters my nose as a cold stone is pressed against my back. Traveling through a portal has never been that fast before; I didn't even feel my body being pulled.

I open my eyes to a muted darkness. Haidion presses his body against mine. My feet are on the ground, but having such a built body embracing me makes me feel weightless.

His arms rest over my head, against the dark rock. "If I'm your darling, are you my Freyja?" *Am I his?*

My breath catches in my throat as warmth fills my soul, soothing the ache of loneliness and agony. My soul sings the answer to me. *Yes, I am his.* "Are you mine?"

Haidion's eyes twinkle with tears. "Oh, Freyja, I've been yours."

I trail my hands up his arms, and our fingers twine together. The world fades away as the aura of his magical energy wraps around mine. They blend in harmony. It's as if darkness has found a light that won't cut through it, and light has found a darkness that won't consume it.

My mind and soul are flooded with feelings I've held back. Emotions I didn't want to experience seep into the most tender spots of my existence, and tears built up in the corners of my eyes.

Our chest press against one another as we breathe in unison like our souls are becoming one, but something is missing. I know what it is: the unsaid words that are needed to complete this joining.

I lower my attention to his mouth, wanting to show him what he means to me rather than say the words aloud. Once they are out, they hold meaning and a truth that still scares me. *What if I'm not ready?*

When I glance up, I find his eyes lowered to my lips. "I'm yours, Freyja." His loving gaze flicks up as the truth of his words sinks in. "I'll be here, no matter how long it takes for you to be mine. This I promise you." His hand squeezes my palm, emphasizing the weight of his words.

Haidion lowers our conjoined hands and brings them to his lips. With each press of his soft mouth on my knuckles, his energy pulls back. I'm able to breathe deeper, especially when he pulls away, but I instantly miss him being so close to me physically and magically.

Vahildra steps out of the portal. "Since we don't know who the leader of the Unfaithful is, it is possible that it is your ex-husband, Freyja." His words are a bucket of painful ice over my body.

I growl, "I'm aware of that."

"Can't you see that Freyja and I are busy?" Haidion says through clenched teeth as he looks over his shoulder.

"I had my shadows watch over the three potential leaders of the Unfaithful." Vahildra doesn't seem to be the least bit affected by Haidion. He comes to my side and leans against the rock wall. "Odin is fucking furious at himself for losing you."

"I hope he suffers for eternity because I'd rather die than be his." Anger rises in me and burns my skin. It makes me aware of how close the pair of them are to me. "If you both want to keep your skin attached to your body, I suggest you give me some space."

Vahildra is the first to back off, but Haidion waits a second longer before pulling away.

I don't know why Vahildra thought it was necessary to get me riled up, but doing so helped me realize that now is not the time for me to confess my feelings. I can't allow myself to be distracted.

Words aren't spoke out loud between the two men, but they are communicated through shadowed eyes.

I walk forward and lean on a stone railing. We stand on Thunder Pass, a small, rocky island with a port. The island is the waiting area to enter the caverns below the city, but most choose to wait in their ships or by the docks.

Mightiarch is before us, towering above everything with glass buildings so high they seem to touch the sky. They reflect the night, making it seem like the palace is made of shimmering clouds and twin-kling stars. The tallest buildings glow like beacons in the full moon. Only royal mortals live on Mightiarch. The rest of the mortal race are scattered throughout Earthradon in towns, either between the boarders of territories or near pantheons.

The waves gently crash on the island's rocky shore, and the wind whistles through the narrow passage. They create a mystical harmony of tranquility that helps me relax.

Haidion comes to my side and takes in the view. A second later, his voice enters my mind. *Once this trial is done, I can take care of Odin, if that is what you wish.*

I gasp in response to the sight of a rainbow bridge of light parting the dark sky. Warmth stirs in my chest as an ache pains my heart; only Heimdall could travel through light.

A familiar warrior takes shape from the rays. Eirikur forms from the colors, absorbing them into his diamond-plated armor. In the gloom, his ghostly blue eyes shine as if he were his own star. His auburn hair drapes loose over his shoulder, giving him a soft and approachable demeanor.

"Goddess Freyja," he stutters, taking me in. "Odin told us you were alive, but I had to see it for myself."

Eirikur holds out his hand to me in greeting, but I push it away and wrap my arms around his bear-like frame. He hesitates for a second before yanking me off my feet in for a suffocating hug. After a few moments, he lets me down and allows me to breathe.

"How did you get here without being called?"

Eirikur holds out his arms. "Heimdall left me a spare set of his armor, infused with his power. Anywhere light can pierce, I can travel." His attention slides to something above my head and back to me. "After the battle, Odin appeared and opened a portal. He sent the Jarls home, and us all back to Valhalla. Heimdall's armor was in my room when I returned. I wanted to find you to make sure you were alright, but the magic in the suit couldn't locate you. Wherever you're staying is either too dark or protected."

I look over my shoulder. Haidion is leaning against the railing with Vahildra at his side. Even though his eyes are shadowed over, he gives me a wink that tells me all I need to know.

"I'm staying with my friend down in Orrtiereum."

Eirikur nods. "Well, unless he lives at the lowest levels, that makes some sense. But he must have his home protected. The further down you go, the more demonic the monsters become."

I give him a reassuring smile. "He keeps me safe."

A grin wipes away his worry. "I'm glad to hear it. You look happier. You're practically glowing, or it could just be your eyes." Bells chime in the distance, signaling the time has reached the hour mark; it is now Lunar Noon. "Well, I must be getting back." Eirikur pulls me in for another hug and whispers in my ear, "I noticed Odin has one of Heimdall's axes, and when I asked about the second one, he said you had it. If you ever need me, just shine some light onto the axe until it glows and speak to it. I'll get the call."

I pull his face to mine and press our foreheads together. "I will."

His aura of strength and devotion makes me ache for my lost friend. He must sense my thoughts because his smile becomes warm. "You never lost me, Freyja. No matter the distance or time apart, you will always be my friend."

With a deep inhale, he hums a lullaby that triggers the rainbow of light to build a bridge back to Valhalla.

Once Eirikur is out of sight, I turn back to the railing, only to find Haidion lunging for me. I'm pulled into his body as Skjoldr hums in my chest. My senses tune into something extremely threatening coming my way.

Air gets kicked up and dust rushes around us as a shield of shadowy-stars covers the three of us. Haidion turns, taking the brunt of the windstorm that came out of nowhere.

A hard thump shakes the pass while a screeching roar disturbs the peaceful harmony of crashing waves. Only one being can make this kind of entrance, a fucking dragon.

Rhax stares down at me. His immense body fills the majority of the space atop the pass. I thought Starson was big, but his older brother's head is the size of my cabin. If he didn't have his neck lowered, I'd have to lay on my back to see his face. From the spikes on his tail to his crown of horns, everything about him is deadly like he was sculpted out of a mountain to be a god of war.

With a deep breath, Rhax lights his body on fire. The heat awakens the rage within my soul, along with centuries of agony. I don't know why he came here instead of his mother, but I'm taking it as a blessing from the Fates. We are no longer on his island anymore, where I had to be courteous and show restraint. Nothing is stopping me from getting my revenge.

The whirl of fire condenses, revealing Rhax's massive, broad frame. I'm twisting out of Haidion's grasp before he can stop me, and to my surprise, the shadows part like they read my intentions.

I got your back. A smoky voice enters my mind... Haidion's puppy. *Fuck him up.*

A glittering darkness coats the surrounding area, draining the natural light as if it is shielding Rhax and me from everyone else. Radiant strength fills my muscles, pumping them up as I direct soul magic into my arm and fist.

Rhax is still glowing from his shift, but that doesn't stop me as I punch him in the face.

The audible crack of bone being dislocated doesn't send me spiraling into remembering the memory of my brother dying, but it does make me realize that the impact wasn't nearly as loud as the one that came from Freyr when he was killed. Rhax has a lot more pain coming his way before I kill him.

Go for his legs.

I tuck, roll, and shoot up from the ground before plowing into Rhax's long legs to knock him on his ass.

He lands with a hard smack, and I'm on top of him, nailing his face with more punches as I let out a scream that pierces the air. Instead of trying to stop my attack, Rhax covers his ears. Something in me screams as well, begging to be let free while Skjoldr vibrates my chest to the point of making me lose my balance. She is trying to stop me but gets overpowered by a strength about to rip through my body.

Arms grab me from behind, and I'm hauled off of Rhax. My arms are pinned behind my back by an arm of solid muscle, and a gloved hand slaps over my mouth.

Cool lips graze my ear. "You will be damned to Excilum if you take his life."

I scream past Vahildra's hand, but it comes out muffled. "He killed my brother!"

I struggle in his grasp, causing myself pain as I try to break free. My movements still the instant the sensation of a blade presses against my throat. Even though adrenaline is pumping through me and I'm at the peak of physical strength, I don't dare move an inch. Nothing is there, but some force tugs on my soul, stopping me from fighting Vahildra.

I've felt this sensation before. Freyr used to do it to me all the time when I acted without thinking, and since his passing, the essence of him protecting me comes back every time I do something reckless. With Freyr making his presence known during battle, I wonder if he is here right now, and if he is, why is he preventing me from killing the being who caused his death?

Skjoldr finally overpowers me and dissipates the magic that gives me strength. The high I was on drops, leaving me physically and emotionally weak. I always step into the blade, but my stubbornness has been knocked down a couple pegs at the thought of Freyr not wanting me to avenge him. A calloused thumb wipes away tears before they can fall.

Rhax stands his face is bleeding from my punches, but it only makes him look more menacing. When he takes one step towards me, a lethal cold wind surrounds us, causing his next move to falter.

Haidion comes to my side. He doesn't move his attention from Rhax as he leans over towards my other ear. "Who did he take from you?" His words hold a deadly promise, ready to shred any soul from existence if that is what I desire.

If you want to be the one to avenge your brother, I strongly advise that you don't tell Haidion, Freyja.

I mentally snarl. *I will never tell him then.*

The smoky voice growls back. *That's not what I was suggesting. Wait until later, when Haidion isn't caught up in the heat of the moment. Trying to convince him to not act is a strenuous task, especially when it comes to you. You have no idea how much energy it took for me to persuade him to not kill Odin when he was trying to reach for you.*

"His death was not my intention, Freyja." Rhax's voice of sin and satin tries to soothe something inside of me, urging me to give him the chance to explain. Fire awakens in the depths of my soul, providing me with energy. It burns through his attempt to make me believe him. "I know you won't take my word for it, so let's try to kill each other. Release her, or I'll pry her from your arms."

When the sensation of a blade vanishes, I try to break out of Vahildra's grasp, but he won't budge.

Haidion's puppy tsks in my mind. *You don't know how to get out of that hold? It's fairly easy.*

Vahildra ignores my attempts to break free. "Failure to appear before the lords and ladies will not only penalize you, Princeling. It will affect your entire race. Are you ready to face those consequences?"

Haidion's voice enters my mind. *I hate to agree with him, but Vahildra is right. Stop fighting him, and he will let you go.*

I'm not going to submit to his control. Accepting that I can't break free means I'm giving up.

The smoky voice of Haidion's puppy chuckles. *True, but you're only going to dislocate your shoulders if you keep trying to rip yourself free. If you ask nicely, I can tell you how to get out of his hold.*

I clench my teeth in irritation. *That comment was directed at Haidion, not you.*

What makes you think you can shadow speak to him? You haven't learned shadow magic.

Laughter brings my attention out of my mind and back to Rhax. A smug grin grows on his face. "Like they have any real power over us." He takes a brave step forward. "And if you don't want the strength of your power to be humiliated, I advise you let Freyja go. She hates me more than she cares about hurting you."

I go still in Vahildra's arms as the words hit me in the chest. His blow of truth delivered more damage than my punches. I'm disarmed by the realization that I would do anything to avenge my brother, but would I stoop to hurting my friend?

A feline smile spreads Haidion's lips. "You say the lords and ladies have no power over you, yet here you are, acquiescing to their call like a loyal hound."

Steam puffs from Rhax's nostrils.

"Enough!" Vahildra's voice chills me to my bones, extinguishing my fire. "My client and I will not be late to the trial." He removes his hand from my face and waves it in dismissal. "Do with your time as you wish, but you will not be dragging Freyja down with you."

The glittering haze of darkness surrounding us dissipates as the light from the night sky illuminates the area once again.

"Soon," I spit out. "Your blood will coat my body, and your screams will soothe my soul. I give you my word."

Light surfaces in the depths of Rhax's emerald, silver-slitted eyes as if my promise pulled his soul to the surface, desperate to hear the vow for itself.

"Soon," Rhax repeats, before walking around us, not taking his eyes off me until he descends the steps.

"You're lucky the Princeling is too proud of a being to report your assault." Vahildra releases his hold on me, but he takes my hand and places it on his arm. "It will be more appropriate for me to court you inside."

Haidion glares at him. "I'm sure that Freyja doesn't want you touching her." His attention drops to me. "You don't have to listen to him, not until the trial begins, at least."

Vahildra tries to convince me with his eyes to not fight him on this, but I'm sick of his touch. When I remove my arm, Haidion steps in between us, staring the other Demonical down and daring him to argue. Vahildra takes a step back and gestures to the stairs.

Thanks for having my back.

You're welcome. Something nuzzles my hand. *It was a better option to have you release your anger before the trial rather than during.*

I mentally snarl as my irritation spikes. *That was meant for Haidion. Why would I thank you?*

With a look over my shoulder, I see a flush brighten Haidion's cheeks. I pay no mind to what made him blush; I only care if he heard my comment. If he didn't, is it because I have someone in my shadow? Why didn't Haidion tell me, and how do I direct my thoughts to him through our connection?

I'm about to ask when a wall of stone smacks into my chest, causing me to stumble and land on my ass. Nothing is there, just steps leading down to the docks.

The concerned voices of Haidion and Vahildra get drowned out by a growl that covers my body.

A radiant, masculine voice with the warmth of the sun and the calmness of the moon takes on a darker tone that has Skjoldr directing magic to protect the threads of my existence. *Are you ignorant of my aid, or are you too stubborn to admit gratitude to me?*

What exactly did you do?

What did I do? I filled you with strength because your soul magic alone wouldn't have even scratched his scaly skin, let alone break any bones. And I told you where to hit him so you could have the upper hand. You can feel it when I use my magic on you, so why are you being oblivious?

His brash tone fills my blood and tongue with venomous irritation. *I didn't need or ask for your help!* Against my instinct to not unleash my inner beast, she comes to the surface, ready to burn this presence weighing me down. *Run back to your master, you pesky beast!*

If you are going to spit fire at me, you should know exactly who you are dealing with.

A pair of mismatched eyes of vast power attached to a mountainous being with a daunting aura of life and death flashes before my eyes. He's gone before my blood can run cold. The action is too fast for air to enter my lungs and allow me to scream.

The weight keeping me down lifts as chuckles of seductive charm fill my mind. *Later, you can gawk at me. For now, you can put those luscious lips to better use and curse out my name, vixen. I'm Iraijah.*

I get to my feet as scorching heat fills my mouth. It feels like I could spit fire. *What the fuck?! You could've introduced yourself as Haidion's left hand or his friend for fate's sake. I don't care what your name is because I will only know you as Arrogant Asshole!*

I'm physically turned around to face Haidion. "Freyja, what's going on?"

Vahildra shakes his head as he walks around me, brushing dirt off my backside. "Isn't it obvious from her sudden fright a mere second ago? Your puppy made himself known."

"He's no puppy," I grumble over my shoulder.

Just like when he left me during battle, he made his absence clear. It's a gaping hole to let me know his presence was once around and partially inside of me.

Haidion clears his throat, and I swear a hint of a smile vanishes on his face. "Iraijah is one of the most loyal beings I've ever met. It's an inside joke with my royal flush of friends that we all refer to him as 'my puppy.'"

"He isn't a Cerberus like Nightnir?"

"The spirit of Iraijah's soul is that of a Cerberus, and by using his magic, he can shift into one." Haidion offers me his arm. "Remember the beast that had my back when I came to you at your call?" I nodded, recalling the terrifying monster. "That was Iraijah."

If he didn't have a hold on my arm, I would've stumbled down the stairs. Distant laughter follows us, and now I know who is lurking in the shadows.

I give them a withering stare. "If the beast who killed the gods was Iraijah, then why did the Sons of Judgment think it was Nightnir?"

He looks down to the right. If I didn't know Haidion's mannerisms, I would've assumed that he was ignoring me. But the move is a tell that he's deep in thought.

When we step off the last stair, Haidion takes a deep inhale and meets my eyes. "The universe believes that he's dead because his race was hunted to extinction." His cool aura becomes lethal as his features tighten with protective determination. "Since I have a pet Cerberus for my line of work, Iraijah takes the form of Nightnir if he wants to be out in public. If he doesn't, he will remain invisible or in the shadows. What he is exactly, is for him to tell you, not me."

I know what concern lies in the depths of his eyes, Haidion cares about Iraijah immensely. "I give you my word that I won't speak of his existence."

He blows out a sigh as if he were struggling to breathe. Some of the weight leaves his shoulders as warmth softens his features, and a grateful smile broadens his lips.

We walk the length of the dock until we reach the end, where everyone else is congregated.

I tried to talk to you earlier. But with Iraijah in my shadow, I guess that blocked me.

That's only because I haven't taught you how to navigate your mind. I'm surprised that I didn't hear you two talking. My heart warms as the glowing darkness in my mind pulsates when Haidion brushes his fingers on the back of my wrist. *Did you feel the bond beat?* I nod. *That's going to be the most direct way for you to talk to me. Your mind will reach for that connection, and your thoughts will be sent only to me. Before this, I had to listen in on your mind, like I was pressed against a window to hear you. Depending on how strong your thoughts are, sometimes you open it and I can hear you clearly. This way, it will be like you're opening the door for me to walk inside.*

Will you have to touch me every time I want to talk only to you?

He chuckles. *I wouldn't be opposed.* I clear my throat to push away the enjoyable heat trying to crawl up my neck. *But no. You need to find a way to awaken that pulsation and quell it. When I talk to you, I knock on the door, and you open it for me. That conversation is only for us. When you initiate the conversation, we remain outside, and anyone could hear it.*

I will practice then.

Don't worry about just anyone being able to listen in. I have your mind protected. And if you want Iraijah out of your shadow, just tell him.

"Shall we?" Vahildra calls.

Numerous ships are magically dry-docked as water recedes under them. A stone path and the entrance to the cave under Mightiarch is revealed as the tide heads out. Everyone takes their time to step from one moss-covered stone to the next. Like stairs, they descend to the mouth of the cave.

Before Haidion takes his first step, he brings my hand to his mouth and gives me a soft kiss, further intensifying the bond between us. Vahildra gestures for me to go before him, and the three of us make our descent.

Once we reach the end of the path, a dark barrier lifts to reveal a wall of gargoyles. Shell sconces open, illuminating the inside of the cave and beyond with pearls of light.

"No weapons are allowed in the courtroom. You are to place them in the slots in the wall. Seal it with your blood, and only you can access it. We, nor the lords and ladies, are responsible for any stolen items," the grinding voice of a gargoyle asserts. "Any use of magic is prohibited. You are all to wear stone collars for the duration of the trial. Only when you are dismissed and have exited the cave will they fall off. Present your letters as you enter."

I've been to court more times than I can count; I know the rules by heart.

After I found out that Vahildra could help the infertile, my efforts increased to get the lords and ladies to add an amendment to provide women with a higher level of treatment. Only Evasion, the daughter who ran the plane of Orrtiereum, knew what the Ancient Demonical of

Disease was capable of because he helped her. But it took my testimony that I trusted him to provide treatment for my infertility to get the lords and ladies to vote in favor of giving women governmental aid to help them conceive.

The issue of raised taxes to pay for the treatment was a hurdle. Vahildra requires funding, and the Sons of Judgment demanded compensation because a being from their plane is helping the people of Earthradon. Another issue is that the races are skeptical of how Vahildra can help since their methods aren't successful.

When we get to the Wardalyrian officers, one of them takes the letter, while another places collars around our necks. Something in my chest stirs, hating the device numbing my magic and constraining the beast of my soul.

Haidion laces our hands together. *You're not alone. We are in this cage together.*

His comforting words and touch might lessen the storm trying to brew in my soul, but they don't lessen my anxiety about what accusations have been made against me.

After walking down a hallway, we enter an open room of stone. Everything from the benches to the witness stand is stone. The same shell lights are mounted on the walls, and a chandelier of them hangs in the middle of the courtroom.

Vahildra leads us to the far-left corner, giving us a perfect view of the entire space.

Before I can take my seat, someone calls my name. Vianre picks up her floor-length red dress and runs over to me in a pair of sparkly black heels. I don't know how she can do anything else but walk in them, and I'm genuinely surprised she got across the path without falling. A small, matching top hat balances precariously on her head.

She runs up to me with a smile and tears. "I wasn't able to find you yesterday." I wrap my arms around her waist as her arms go around my neck. Before I can say a word, her lips crash to mine in a cherishing kiss. "I knew you were alive, but I had to taste it for myself. Your soul is as strong as ever."

Images of us together flash in the forefront of my mind. The last kiss we shared was just like this one, but we were naked. She was on top, her legs scissoring mine, as our sparkly bundles ground together. I blink the memory away before it can fully emerge. *Now is not the time to be aroused.*

As I set Vianre down, her attention turns to Haidion and Vahildra with interest. Gone is the flirty friend, and in her place is an overprotective one.

I clear my throat. "These are my friends. Namtar, the Ancient Demonical of Disease and my lawyer. And this is Ominous, the Demonical of Illusion." I note Haidion doesn't have a glittering aura surrounding him. I guess since he can't use magic at the moment, everyone can see the real him.

"I thought I was the only one who is friends with beings society says we shouldn't be acquainted with." Ambar walks up to us, the gold stenciling on her skin brightens when our eyes meet.

Besides the stone collar, around her neck is a piece of royal vine jewelry. Two mahogany wood beads are on either side of an aquazanite feather crystal. One bead symbolizes love and the other represents courage. The feather is engraved with a water symbol, that shows she was blessed with the power to wield the element. She is dressed in a simple white skirt of the finest cotton with a red sash around her waist. Her hair is wrapped in a green and black bandana, which towers over her head like a crown.

I drop into a bow. "Your Majesty." Vianre blinks in realization and curtseys.

Vahildra remains seated but nods while Haidion stands and offers his hand. "It's a pleasure to meet friends of Freyja." He takes each of their hands and places kisses on their knuckles.

"Oh, my. Isn't he the charmer?" Vianre takes him in from head to toe and lights up when she spots his hat.

Ambar eyes Haidion for a moment, then inclines her head towards me and whispers in her native tongue, *"Is he the better ass you've seen, or is it the other Demonical?"*

The others look at us with suspicion when we break out in laughter.

Vianre pouts, placing her hands on her hips. "Tell me, what's so funny?"

Ambar clears her throat to explain, but a familiar voice calls out my name and sours my mood.

Bralyant strides over with purpose, throwing a snarl at Haidion.

Before the Wolven King can touch me, Ambar steps in front of him. "After the stunt you pulled, Alpha, you have no right to speak to my commander."

"She is more to me than just a leader, and besides, the battle is over," he growls in her face.

Ambar lifts her chin. "But not the war." Her words settle in my soul; she is not done fighting, and I wonder if the rest of the Faithful Army thinks the same.

Hope radiates in my heart. If Ambar is still willing to fight, perhaps others are too. My plan to get Faithless from Thor hinges on gathering support to retrieve the Father's heart from Zeus. The path to restoration is being built before my eyes. I just need to get word to the Shadow King. Determination pounds in my chest, ready to come up with a plan of attack. But first, I need to get through this trial.

"Take your seats," a Wardalyrian orders from the front of the room.

"I'll find you after, Freyja." Bralyant's attention stays locked on Ambar. His passionate purple eyes darken as the gold in them sharpens. "And expect my arrival to your kingdom, Captain. We have matters to discuss, too." He whispers in an angry tone.

Ambar strains her neck to look at the Wolven King. "It's 'your Majesty.'"

Vianre goes to Ambar's side and crosses her arms with a victorious smirk. "Bow to her."

Bralyants rolls his shoulders and shifts his head down a little in a weak attempt at a bow.

A graceful voice with reserved wrath causes the air to electrify. "I suggest you kneel." Bralyant turns and comes face-to-face with Melrose Gailner, the High Queen of the Animal Spirits, and the oldest living immortal on Earthradon.

Ambar, Vianre, and I drop our heads. Out of the corner of my eye, I see Haidion and Vahildra do the same. Even though the Animal Spirits stay neutral during every battle and war, they deserve respect.

Melrose Gailner is not only the longest reigning ruler, but she was the first appointed when Earthradon came into existence just over ten thousand years ago. Rumor has it that the Animal Spirits, along with the Mages, Fae, and Dwarven, were brought over from another planet in the universe. I wouldn't believe the gossip if it hadn't been for the Mages leaving Earthradon; if they were able to leave, then they were able to come here. It makes me wonder exactly how old she is.

"Everyone, take your seats now!" The Wardalyrian yells like he plans on fusing our bodies to the stone if we don't comply.

Bralyant gives the High Queen a proper head bow before walking away. Ambar and Vianre rise, kiss the queen's hand, and retreat to their seats.

Melrose Gailner turns her attention to me and inclines her head. "Goddess Freyja." Her large, honeycomb eyes shift to the Demonicals. "May an old crone like myself join you young folk?"

Haidion tips his hat to her. "You don't look a day over eight hundred."

Her floral pink skin is pristine, as if she were a youth still going through maturity. "You flatter me."

"Of course, you may sit with us." Vahildra stands and offers her his hand, and to my shock, she takes it without hesitation. "I'd be honored by your company."

Melrose Gailner gives me a respectful nod as she passes. Her skin lights up the stone and chases away the shadows like a beacon of the strongest light. An aura of gold surrounds her opulent, curvy figure and makes her chestnut hair shimmer. Translucent, bee-like wings flutter on her back when she goes to sit. Vahildra leans forward to allow her wings room to stretch but doesn't move an inch away from her.

I catch the hint of a smile as he whispers in her ear. Melrose Gailner brings her hand to her mouth to hold back a chuckle.

After I take my seat, Haidion leans close with an intrigued, mischievous grin. *That looked more than a friendly kiss to me.*

It takes me a second to recall what he's referring to. *Vianre is just my friend.*

Does a Wiccayen normally taste someone's mouth to sense their soul's strength?

No, I mind-speak a little too loudly for my liking. *There are many ways, but lip-to-lip contact is the most effective.*

Haidion's arm slides onto the back of the stone bench, and his lips brush the shell of my ear. *Then explain to me why you were trying to hide your blush.*

I playfully push him away, but he doesn't go far. *You are lucky that I can't use my ice in here.*

What would you do, hm, freeze my cock off?

My desire for him immediately wants to answer for me, but I hold my tongue.

A Wardalyrian stands the front of the room, and with a strong flap of his wings, draws everyone's attention. "All rise for the lords and ladies."

One lady takes a seat at the judge's bench as the other sit in the jury section. All are dressed in black robes with gold collars, and adorned with their silver masks.

"You may all be seated." The lady looks at the papers in front of her. "We are going to go row by row. Those of you who were summoned, please state your title for attendance."

All the races that sit before me call out their titles as the lady checks them off the list. I tense when Drafasa and Arighness call out their names.

A disappointed huff comes from the lady. "It seems we have some beings missing." One of the Wardalyrians stationed on the edge of the courtroom walks over to her. She hands him six pieces of paper. "We are missing the leaders of the Pixies, Ghouls, Vampyres, Phantoms, and Necromancers. Along with a God."

The Wardalyrian nods, walks to the wall, and hands out the papers to his comrades. As a group, they all leave.

"While they go and fetch our other guests, we will start the proceedings. Firstly, with the death of Coalston, the Emperior of the Taurun race, and Maytower, the Emperiest, we, the lords and ladies, will steward the race until their son becomes of age." Commotion comes all from the attendants. "You all know that we were appointed to rule over the races. When one leadership fails, we step in."

The Falmenir Makuba stands. Rawldur's blonde hair falls over his sculpted, saffron-tan skin in loose waves down to his hips. He stands proudly in all his naked glory, and not an inch of him isn't covered in ripped muscles. "The leadership of the Tauruns didn't fail." His voice echoes in the courtroom.

The lady leans forward. "They both chose to fight, leaving no appointed leadership behind. They have failed to secure a leader for their race. Until the heir becomes of age, we will steward."

Rawldur approaches the judge's bench before she can lift her gavel. "The Tauruns reside in Atlantean territory, as do the Harpies, the Wiccayens, the Animal Spirits, and my people. We live and breathe as one allied nation." He turns and points to Ambar. "I might be the ruler of my race, but Ambar is my Queen, just as Adom was my King."

Vianre, Malvik, and Melrose Gailner all chant in Atlantean, "*Long live the Queen. Long soar the King.*"

Rawldur turns back to the lady. "Coalston and Maytower both believed the same way. Otherwise, they wouldn't have joined the allied army, or opened their borders to merge their lands with all of ours." He backs away but keeps his eyes on her. "They didn't fail as leaders because they knew who would be standing at their backs."

The lady sits back in her chair as the other lords and ladies on the side talk amongst each other. One lord stands and approaches the bench, handing over a piece of paper.

"Queen Ambar, approach the bench." As Rawldur and Ambar pass one another, he bows his head to her, and she returns the gesture. "We, as the lords and ladies, recognize the joining of lands that have become one, and have taken notice of who is truly ruling over them. Your cousin, Adom, was working with us to bring in mortals to live among you all."

Ambar nods. "Yes. He wanted to show everyone what the URE looks like; all races can unite and live in harmony."

"But with all the allied races seeing you as their Queen, the mortals might feel compelled to do so as well. I wouldn't want my race forced into being ruled by another monarch, especially on they don't know or trust." The lady sits up straight. "The lords and ladies have heard you, and we have come to three decisions, one of which you need to agree to. One, the lands the Tauruns did have will be boarded up; they will remain separate. We will steward, and anyone who isn't of the race living there will have to be relocated. Another option is that we can relocate the race. Or, you can choose a lord to rule at your side as King. Every century, you will choose another. I will leave the decision up to you, Queen Ambar."

Silence stills the room as a heated anger rises. Even those who aren't allied with the Atlanteans know the underlying intentions the lords and ladies have for wanting to put one of their own to rule at Ambar's side. The lords and ladies might dictate the laws, but they don't rule over the races individually. Giving them a taste of what it means to be the leaders of an immortal race will make them want to claim them all.

Ambar raises her chin. "Board up the lands." She turns to go back to her seat.

"Very well. When the sun rises on this day, the lords and ladies will work with Queen Ambar to vacate the Taurun lands and rebuild the borders." The lady raises the gavel and hits it on the sound block. "Next." The lady turns a paper over and reads another. "Since the commander of the Compassions, or as some in here have known them, the Unfaithful, isn't in attendance, the proceedings of the Vampyres betraying their leader will be moved to another day." She flips to another piece of paper. "Will the steward for the Spydens please come forth?"

A lean man in fine silk with three pairs of Spyden legs approaches the lady. His skin is milky white and has a glossy sheen, making it appear moisturized and smooth. As a male, he has a shorter pair of fang tusks than a female.

The lady leans down. "You came here today to find justice for your Autarcha. Is that correct?"

"Yes, for my sister. I have proof that the Autarch of the Scorpion race was the one who caused her death."

My eyes immediately find Drafasa. His three stinger tails tense and curl in on themselves as he stares daggers at the steward. An angry red flush makes his brass-brown skin appear to be on fire.

Another Spyden, a female, approaches the judge's bench. "I was present, along with Lanic." She inclines her head to the steward. "When the Autarch and the Autarcha fought before he left for battle, he told her, 'Staying behind only makes you look like a coward. You're a disgrace to your race, and if you decide to show up, I might try to kill you myself just to prove how weak of a being you are.'

Drafasa doesn't stand to deny her words; he only nods to himself in acceptance, as if he knows there is no hope for him.

A lead brick drops in my stomach as my blood runs cold. The realization of what will happen has my pulse racing and my heart shredding, even though it shouldn't be. Drafasa threatened to take away the one I care most deeply about. And yet, the feelings that I thought were gone rise to the surface. They are the same ones I felt when I asked Illyrical to make sure the Autarch got off the battlefield alive. No amount of love should linger; for I buried it when I said goodbye to my brother.

Lanic looks back at Drafasa, all six eyes narrowed in anger. "We heard your words, and since my sister is dead with no fatal wounds, I know that you poisoned her with your soul-burning toxin."

"Autarch, approach the bench." The lady gestures for the Spydens to take their seats as Drafasa walks up. "Do you have an alibi that can confirm your presence during the full length of the battle?"

"No, I do not. I fought with many warriors. I didn't stay with one for too long so I could help others."

The lady nods. "With the evidence piled up against you, do you, Drafasa, Autarch of the Scorpions, admit to killing your mate Ladiya, the Autarcha of the Spydens?"

My heart beats in my ears as my breathing picks up. Haidion's arm drops to wrap around my shoulders. He tries to get my attention, but I'm locked on the man I knew as my brother for the majority of my existence. He'll go to Wardalyn for who knows how long, and the image of him chained up, being broken for eternity, has me shooting up from my seat.

"I killed the Autarcha!"

All turn around to face me as Vahildra curses under his breath.

Drafasa's eyes meet mine. He's taken aback as disbelief saddens his features. With a shake of his head, he says, "She's wrong. I killed Ladiya."

"No!" I scream. "I have proof that I did."

Vahildra rises, takes my hand, and walks me to the front of the room like a disobedient child. "Only speak when I tell you to," he says over his shoulder.

Faces pale at the sight of his gloved hand holding mine. Not wanting to be close to the Ancient Demonical of Disease, everyone we pass leans away. Out of all the Demonicals, he is the most known, for all fear his purpose.

Vahildra leads me to a table and pushes me to sit as he remains standing. "My name is Namtar. I'm the Ancient Demonical of Disease, and I'm representing Freyja." He turns his attention to the steward. "It's my understanding that the Autarcha were killed during the battle, am I correct?"

Lanic's fists tighten. "Yes, but Drafasa admitted to killing her."

"But my client admits to taking her life." Vahildra turns his attention back to the lady. "And since they fought on opposite sides of the battle, the Autarcha's death is justified with or without evidence."

She nods. "Yes, it would be justified. But the Autarch admitted to killing the Autarcha. What is the proof?"

Vahildra places his hand on my shoulder before I can stand. "Just so we are in agreement, if my client proves that she killed the Autarcha, she won't be charged with her death since it occurred on the battlefield?"

"By law, yes. Goddess Freyja won't be charged." The lady turns her attention to the steward. "No justice can be found for your sister if Goddess Freyja was the one who killed her."

Judging by the shaking of his shoulders, Lanic is barely holding his anger in. I know his pain, for I wanted justice for my brother when he died, but we were in battle. Nothing can be done about it.

Vahildra looks at me. "You may speak."

My attention shifts to Drafasa as I stand. "I have a brand on my back from a deal I struck up with a Fae." Some in the audience gasp as I lift the back of my tunic. I feel their eyes on my back. "It can be read and seen."

A lord steps down from the jury section and walks over to me. Cold, prodding fingers press against my skin. Even though the lords and ladies are without magic, it doesn't mean they can't read brands. The magic is whispered into their ears, telling their instincts what is before them.

"This was made in Fanarzien," the lord announces. "I can't read it."
Fuck, he's right.

My eyes find the High Lord Fae chosen to represent his race in the trial. His leathery wings flex as a smile curves his pale, red lips. "I'd be happy to read the brand, but at a cost to you, Goddess."

Dread rolls in my stomach at what he could possibly desire in return for his help. My thoughts linger on what Illyrical's brother wanted in exchange for his "help" to free me from Odin.

"I'll read it." The smile on the Fae's cruel face shifts into a silent snarl when Melrose Gailner stands.

"Please approach the bench, Ancient One," the lady politely requests.

The lord at my back starts to walk over to the High Queen, but stops and stumbles when he spots Haidion offering his arm. The High Queen takes it gladly. The lord backs away as they walk down the aisle. Everyone in the audience, besides Ambar, eye Haidion with wariness as he guides the most respected being in existence towards me.

The Demonical bows to her when they reach the doors separating the audience from the judge's bench. When he rises, Melrose Gailner places a kiss on his cheek before turning to me. Haidion moves to sit next to Ambar in the front row, and she doesn't shift away from him, even though he is so close.

I incline my head toward the High Queen before turning around and giving her my back. Soft, dainty hands brush against the length of my brand. "Lower your shirt, my dear." After I do so, she wraps her arm around mine. "Freyja struck a deal with a Fae to protect the method of how she killed Ladiya because they witnessed it. When asked who killed the Autarcha, the Fae will only be able to state her characteristic or title."

The lady nods, dismissing the lord back to his seat. "With proof being brought forward of Goddess Freyja being the one who killed the Autarcha, no justice will be had for the death of the Spyden ruler." She hits the sound block with her gavel. "You may all return to your seats."

Lanic steps toward the judge's bench. "My race wants to part from the Arachnids. We no longer want to be joined with them if Drafasa is our ruler."

"That matter can't be discussed or dealt with today. Please see a lord or lady to start the process once this trial is over."

I step out of Melrose Gainlner's grasp and walk towards Lanic. "You only want separation now because you can't rule over the joined races yourself. Ladiya left you in charge if anything were to happen to her, just as Drafasa made his sister his stewardess. If you truly loved your sister and wanted justice, then you should've led with that!"

"You said enough, my dear." Melrose Gailner links her arm with mine and tries to escort me away, but I don't budge; I want to put the selfish and greedy being in his place.

Vahildra says my name with a stern force that would make anyone else whimper and tuck their tail between their legs, but I don't remove my gaze from the Spyden.

A chirping screech full of rage erupts out the steward as he eats up the distance between us.

Drafasa moves to stand in front of the High Queen. "I'm still your Autarch, and I order you to stand down."

Lanic's anger reaches a new height as his legs lash out, slicing through the air at me.

Melrose Gailner pulls me back with a hard tug as Drafasa moves forward to catch the legs. With a roar, he lifts the Spyden and slams him to the ground.

Before Lanic can stand, the Autarch places his foot on his back, almost squashing him. "If you dare harm Freyja, I will sever your limbs and force them so far down your throat that they come out of your ass."

"Order in the court!" The gavel is banged against the sound block multiple times. "Return to your seats, or you will be spending the next fifty-two hours in a holding cell."

Drafasa stays in between Lanic and me as he walks back to his seat. Only a couple inches of space separate the Scorpion and me when he turns in my direction; I haven't been this close to him in centuries. His aura doesn't grate against mine as I would have thought; instead, I want to be consumed by his protectiveness. Unsaid words are spoken through the cluster of his glazed black eyes. So much emotion is held back, and he doesn't let any of it out as he returns to his seat.

Before he can reach the door, Melrose Gailner holds out her hand. "May I sit with you, Autarch?" Drafasa nods and offers her his arm.

Vahildra directs me to sit in the front row. I'm too stunned to care about being manhandled. Not only was I so close to Drafasa I could smell the jasmine on his skin, but he protected me and threatened a member of his race despite me being the cause of the disturbance.

Haidion and Ambar move over for Vahildra and me. When Haidion's hand brushes against mine, I immediately grab it and hold on as if I'm about to drift off into the sea. I relish in the comfort with the same intensity. Once pain digs its sharp claws into my bones, I release. The euphoria of relief almost makes me moan. I'm anchored back to reality, and the emotions I shouldn't be feeling go back to being buried.

The lady writes some things down and flips the paper over. "Will the Mighty Kiani of the Siren race please come forward?"

A tall woman with satin-opal skin approaches the judge's bench. Just like the other beast races, she remains in her naked glory. Gills line the side of her torso; but since she is out of water, she breathes like everyone else and scales don't cover her body.

Her hips move fluidly, swaying with confidence, and her chin is held high as her coral and onyx eyes hold the lady's stare. Her movements are as elegant as her wavy platinum-purple hair. She has a lean warrior's body that can only be achieved through centuries of combat. This ruler doesn't need a crown to show that she's the leader of her race. It's obvious by the scars on her body and how she holds herself. It takes me a moment to fully realize who I'm admiring... Murrdirel's fated mate.

Dread coils in my stomach as Kailani walks past me, but her attention is on the lady. She's so focused, it's as if she were building up tension to combust the judge's bench with her mind. The determined stride of her webbed feet doesn't falter, and she doesn't even bother to lean away when she passes by Vahildra.

"You were called here today due to the rebellious acts of the Oceanic races. An alliance was formed, severing them from the URE. As the sheriff of the sea, it is your duty to use any means necessary to get them back under your control and punish them accordingly. Since you are the new leader, we, the lords and ladies, are not going to hold you accountable. But we need you to swear your oath to us."

Even looking at the lady's face, it's apparent that she is waiting expectantly for the Mighty Kiani to utter her vow so she can move on to the next order of business.

"No. I will not be swearing my allegiance to you." Gasps and growls, screeches and snarls, hisses and huffs come from the audience. "We, the Oceanic races, will no longer answer for and abide by the laws and commands to the lords and ladies. They have plagued our waters with corruption."

Kailani turns, giving her back to the lady. "But as High Lady of the Sea Lords Alliance, I give my oath to all of the races on Earthradon. We are still one." Her attention goes to Ambar. "I will not force you to be part of the SLA. Anyone who threatens you to do so will answer to me and the High King."

The lady stands. "The leaders of your race before you are the reason why greed is infesting the races of the ocean."

"The leaders before me?!" Kailani turns on her heels. "Eterna told the Unfaithful no to joining their side, and Murrdirel was influenced by a Temptational Voice from an emissary you all sent down to discuss where we stood for the upcoming battle. If he wasn't infected, then he wouldn't have killed his own mother. He wouldn't have locked up his fated mate and all the female warriors. And he wouldn't have brought the rest of our army to battle!"

"You are suggesting that a human, a mortal without magic, possessed something to influence an immortal?" The lords and ladies laugh. "Do you have any proof, either a witness to what our emissary did or Murrdirel himself to give testimony?"

A lord stands as Kailani tightens her hands into fists. "Where is the relevance of this discussion to the Siren race separating from the URE?"

The lady nods towards the lord. "True, there is no relevance. If you wish to bring your accusation to court, you may speak to one of the lords and ladies after this trial to start the process." She lifts her gavel. "Kailani, as we, the rulers of Earthradon, do not acknowledge the SLA, you and the other Oceanic races are in an open rebellion against our rule. As their leader, you are hereby arrested and sentenced to Excilum." The lady hits the sound block with a loud knock.

Before Kailani can utter a word or move, she falls to the ground as if gravity has singled her out and pushed her down. She lays lifeless with her eyes closed as the stone collar breaks.

What happened to her?

The collar tranquilized her. It only activates when a being tries to use magic.

A Wardalyrian locks a set of chains around her neck, wrists, and ankles. After he calls the broken collar to his hand, he picks the Kiani up and brings her over to the lady. He extends her right arm on the desk just as the lady places an iron block on Kailani's forearm. The Wardalyrian brings his fist down on the block, igniting the brick of metal on fire for a second.

Kailani wakes and screams. "You branded me before I was given the chance to—"

"You are in an open rebellion. You have no rights above being a prisoner of war now." The lady leans over the judge's bench. "And we are at war." She sits back down and places the iron block under her desk. "You will have one chance to tell the others to rejoin the URE. If they still don't comply, then we will use any means necessary to get them back under our rule." I swear the lady glances in our direction. More specifically, towards Vahildra. "Take her to a holding cell."

When the Wardalyrian places Kailani down, she falls to her hands and knees. "Why am I so weak?"

"You have the strength of a mortal while these chains are on." The Wardalyrian tugs on her, and when she doesn't move, he gives her a yank, making her fall flat on her face. "Crawl if you can't stand, prisoner."

A gloved hand is slapped over my mouth before I can cuss him out. An arm is draped over my shoulders, keeping me still before I rise to my feet and help.

My soul burns in my chest, causing the stone collar around my neck to heat up. When the Wardalyrian drags the Kiani with another yank, it adds more fuel to my fire.

Haidion's voice enters my mind, but I send my fire to our bond, imagining my cabin and closing all the doors and boarding up the windows so there is no way I can hear him.

Kailani is finally able to get up and walk on her hands and knees, but the sight of her arms and torso scratched from the floor has the fire rushing through my veins.

You need to calm down, vixen, Iraijah strongly pleads in my mind. *Don't make me drain you.*

If you dare take an ounce of my energy, I will never forgive you.

Freyja! If you break free from your collar, they will take you, too. That will be the least of your problems. Is that what you want?

Am I breaking free from my collar? That's not possible; he must be mistaken.

Get the fuck out of my shadow!

I'll go, but I am taking your energy with me. You can hate me all you want. I'd rather deal with your fire than see you caged.

I give him what he wants. With all my mental strength, I direct my fire to the forefront of my mind. I can't hear his howl of pain. I whimper as cold takes the place of my warmth. The sensation of being drained has me slouching against Vahildra. Only when the lady announces that we are moving forward to the last order of business does he stop restraining me. I'm released from whatever hold Iraijah had over my energy.

Haidion pulls me into his side and whispers, "We are only trying to help you, Freyja." I'm too weak to fight him at the moment, but I try anyway. "Reserve your fire for another day when you can actually make a difference and alter fate." He releases me just as I gather enough strength to push myself away from him.

Before I can get my bearings, I'm hauled to my feet by Vahildra. "If you don't stay quiet, I'm going to give you acute laryngitis," he whisper yells in my ear.

Not knowing what illness that is, I clamp my mouth shut.

Vahildra remains standing as I take my seat next to him. During the commotion of Iraijah being an asshole, I must've not heard my name being called.

"Goddess Freyja." The lady looks down at me, and I feel dozens of eyes on the back of my head. "You were called here because of your title as Commander of the Faithful Army, or as some here know it as, the Callous Army." I bite my tongue to hold back a comment about which side was truly callous. "We, the lords and ladies, are filing a charge against you for the slaughter of the twenty-two thousand, five hundred unarmed mortals you killed. As the commander, you are held responsible for their deaths."

Vahildra rests his fingertips on the table. "The army of mortals chose to fight in battle, did they not?"

A lord stands up. "That they did, and we are proud of them for it. It takes courage for a mortal to stand against powerful immortals in battle." He walks over, his steps unhurried. "They knew the cost of what partaking in that battle meant for them, death, but what they didn't expect was to be shown no mercy." He focuses on me. "After you disarmed the entire mortal army, did you not offer them a chance to have their lives spared?"

"All questions will be directed to me," Vahildra states with a level of authority that makes the lord snap his gaze to him. "My client fought under the rules of war. Nowhere does it state that mercy must be granted."

The lord takes a brave step towards my lawyer. "What kind of message do you think that sends to a non-magical race?" The lord doesn't let him answer. "The mortal warriors were unarmed and slaughtered. They were killed by a cruel goddess." A hard blow gets delivered to my soul at his words. "Testimonies from Spydens, Scorpions, and Fae were shared with our race about the level of cruelty that your client fought with." The lord's blue eyes pierce mine. "My people fear you the most among all the other gods and goddesses. That is why we, the lords and ladies, must act to deal with such a threat."

"Wouldn't you agree, Ancient Demonical, that such terror should be dealt with? Especially since the mortal race is the reason for your client's existence?" the lady asks to Vahildra, but her attention remains on me.

"What exactly are the mortals asking for you all to represent them? Because that is what you are doing, unless you have your own charges against my client." Vahildra spoke calmly, unaffected by their comments, unlike me.

I catch the lord tightening his fist before placing it behind his back. "No. We are only here to represent the mortals."

The lady turns a piece of paper over and reads, "They are wanting us to deal with the threat, known as Goddess Freyja, especially since she didn't win the battle." Her attention lifts. "It is their fear that she will call forth a counterattack."

"You say that my client is feared among all the others, but what does that say about the mortal race? Wasn't Thor the one who cut open the Great Willow Tree? Wasn't Zeus the one who took the Father's heart? Why is my client being seen as a threat when two others killed the deity that gave all of you life?" Vahildra's questions silence the room.

The lady clears her throat. "We aren't here to discuss what side the mortals chose."

The Demonical walks around the table. "It's clear which side they chose just by who they consider a threat. And if you thought differently, they would be reassured that my client has the best intentions of bringing restoration to our planet, and justice for the Father and his daughters." Before the lady can speak, he cuts her off with a wave of his hand. "But as you said, we aren't here to talk about that." He turns to the audience. "I am not only Freyja's attorney, but I am also the Governor of the Preserver Guild."

The lord finds his voice, "Where is the relevance in that statement?"

Vahildra turns on his heel and he gives the smallest of smiles. "Freyja became a member of my guild before the battle. She was tasked with retrieving Faithless, no matter the cost. Therefore, she is under the protection of the guild. If she fought on her own accord, then yes, she would need to be sentenced and punished as you all have planned. But that is not the case."

I squeeze my hands under the table and clench my jaw. Vahildra is lying. He knows I'm not fully part of the guild yet, but who can speak against him besides my own honesty? No one.

The lady lays her hands in front of her, clasping them together tightly. "We need proof, besides your word, that she is a part of the guild."

"Freyja, if you please, can you press your finger to your forehead?"

I do as I'm requested, and a hum of magic warms the skin under my finger. The lady's and lord's eyes widen.

Vahildra bows. "We are done here." He walks over to me and extends his hand.

The lady calls out, "Who was your second in command, Goddess?"

"It doesn't matter," Vahildra asserts over his shoulder. "The charges were against Freyja as a goddess, not as a commander."

I can't help my smile as I take his hand and rise, but my happiness drops at the sound of a Wardalyrian announcing, "I have brought the other leader, your honor."

Standing at the end of the aisle, I find a familiar pair of blue eyes... Thor.

FORTY-THREE

All the people in the room fade away, and in their place are the beings that were killed during the battle, regardless of what side they chose. Thor is just as responsible as I am for their deaths. But with him being the leader of the army that set out to kill the Father, my anger sways me to place the full blame on him.

If Thor hadn't led that army, everyone would still be alive. I wouldn't have had to cast Murrdirel and Adom out of the galaxy. I wouldn't have had to watch Apollo, Artemis, Heimdall, and Existence die. I wouldn't have had to hear Hel's parting goodbye by the magic of her last breath. And my final days on Earthradon would be peaceful.

You mean you were going to spend the rest of your existence being abused? The memory of Illyrical's voice pops into my mind, as if he were standing in front of me.

Before I can shake it away, another thought pops in, adding to a headache that's starting to form. *If I wasn't where I am today, my feelings for Haidion would still be buried.*

Red coats my vision as I let out a growl, and fire ignites in my soul again. I burn through the mental toil, relieving me of the pain of something trying to work against my mind. It feels like claws grasping my thoughts, actions, and existence because I plan on doing something reckless that will most likely seal my fate. It would take my brother materializing to get me to not eliminate the true threat.

Thor's over-eight-foot, ogre-sized frame is packed with so much muscle that you can't tell he has a neck. Stone runes are braided into his chest-length red hair and thick beard. His arms, and everything from the waist down, is adorned with thick leather armor. The lack of more protection allows him to have free range to swing his hammers.

My name is called out by multiple people, but all of their voices fade as I run down the aisle.

When I try to direct my soul magic, the stone collar around my neck hums, reminding me that I'm powerless. But that barrier doesn't stop my fire from spreading. As fast as water bursts from a dam, my veins are filled with blazing energy. And with each beat of my heart, my veins fill with more fire.

With the stone collar around Thor's neck, he's powerless, too. And with the chains on all his extremities, he will be too weak to fight me off.

Arms grab me from behind just as I was about to plow into Thor's legs. My arms get pinned to my sides as a pair of muscular, scaly arms wrap around me.

"Fuck, your hot," Rhax curses.

A different kind of anger awakens, making the fire become molten to the point I see steam. "Get your hands off me!" I thrash in his grip, hating how close we are and his touch.

The rest of the room finally reacts like time had slowed and is now catching up. Everyone is on their feet, shocked.

Out of the corner of my eye, Drafasa appears at my side. "My magic might be restrained, but my poison is not. Give her to me now."

Rhax growls and holds onto me tighter. "She wouldn't want you to touch her, either."

I ignore them and focus on Thor. "Where is Faithless?"

"*Where the star meets the sea.*" Thor's arrogant voice isn't filled with entitlement as it normally is; instead, he's somber as he spoke in our believers' language.

I curse Thor's name in Norliska. "*What does a childhood sailor's tale have to do with his placement?*"

Thor fights against his restraints as irritation tightens his features.

"I hid him away in a place that no man could find." His gloomy mask shatters, and the elevated voice of superior power finally comes out.

The gavel is pounded on the sound block numerous times. "Order in the court!"

"You want order, you greedy bitch?" Thor bellows, causing his stone collar to shatter. Lightning ignites in his eyes and mouth, making the lights in the courtroom flicker. "Here's your order."

The Wardalyrian behind Thor is not fast enough to grab him as he lets out another strong roar. Thunder booms as lightning explodes from his mouth.

I'm spun around, and another set of arms wrap around me before I hit the ground.

A familiar voice curses as we roll on the floor. "Close your eyes, Frizz!" The nickname is all I need to figure out who is above me.

Drafasa covers my body with his, protecting me from the explosion overhead. Even though I should heed his warning, and shield my eyes from the bright light, I keep them open.

"You lost the right to call me that name!" I bring my knees up and push him off my body.

As he flies off me, a mass of wings and scales soars through the air, hitting the judge's bench with a hard smack. At the sight of Rhax's body shaking from a lightning strike and the sound of his moans, something shifts in my soul. *Only I can cause him pain.*

While everyone stays down or tries to regain their bearings, Thor attempts to use his lightning to break his chains. This is my chance to attack, but I have nothing against his magic. My armor will be as useful as Rhax's scales at protecting me, but I only have my own two hands, and I'm not terribly skilled in hand-to-hand combat.

Considering your hands as weapons is sexy. I push the memory of Illyrical out of my mind—wait. He had given me something. I let the memory replay, pushing it forward until I reach the part where we made our deal. *The brand is removable, and can only be used by you. Just stroke a portion of it, and the weapon will come out.*

With a swipe over the back of my neck, a long handle comes out just as Illyrical said it would. I pull out a red blade that is half the length of my body. The handle is as long as my forearm with thirteen notches that I can grip, and it is covered in silver string.

I lunge forward, driving the curved sword into Thor's chest. Before his eyes widen in disbelief, I pull the blade out and swing it towards his neck.

Thor's face contorts in panic as his throat is slashed open, releasing a fountain of blood that pours down his chest. He falls to his knees as blood fills his mouth. His arm stretches towards me, and he grips my left arm before lightning explodes from his eyes.

My bones and muscles fill with radiant strenght as Skjoldr hums in my chest, alerting me to something inside my body.

Fearful screams burst out of me as a bolt of energy travels into my body, until it reaches my soul. Iraijah howls in pain bringing my attention to realize he possessed by body once again.

I'm blinded by light, and hit with a force powerful enough to make me fly backwards. Something cushiony breaks my fall as lightning crackles all over my body. I spasm, and my heart aches as if something sharp has torn it open. My throat constricts, making it hard to breathe.

A layer of coolness covers my body, soothing me from the inside out. "I've got you," Haidion whispers directly in my ear.

The courtroom comes into view a moment later. Everyone rises from their hiding spots and take in Thor's lifeless body. The crimson blood is bold against the dark stone, making me realize that I just killed Odin's first-born son. If he didn't hate me before, he's going to now.

Iraijah grunts in my mind. *Where did you get a Sihotana?*

Before I can ask him what that is, radiant energy fills my body and heals me from heart to soul.

Thank you, Iraijah. I wouldn't be alive without you.

A purr that isn't mine vibrates my chest. *I never thought I'd hear such appreciative words from your tasty tongue and luscious lips. You're sweet, after all.*

Weakened growls rumble out of me. *That doesn't mean I'm sweet. And now you have a target on your back.*

Iraijah's laughter echoes in my mind. *I can't wait.*

"Are you two having a pleasant conversation?" Haidion strokes my lip with his thumb, tracing the outline of my mouth. "Will you let me in?" The shadowy bond in the back of my mind hums.

Arighness's hiss pulls my attention away from Haidion. "*How did you conceal this blade on your person?"* The Basilisk walks over to the sword that came out of my back. It lays in Thor's blood; I must've dropped it when I got struck.

Just as his fingers graze the handle, the blade becomes a tendril of shadow and light. The strand of magic flies to me, and my skin tingles as it nestles in place.

Haidion's eyes widen, and his face pales. Everyone around me exhibits a similar expression.

Before I can ask, I'm ripped out of his arms by a Wardalyrian. "What are you doing?!"

Another Wardalyrian walks behind me and places chains on my extremities. "You are under arrest for the illegal manipulation of magical energy." His gravelly voice rakes against my skin, taking away the restoring warmth in my body, and replacing it with a hopeless cold.

To my surprise, my body doesn't weaken in the chains, even as the fire in my veins and soul vanishes. "I didn't manipulate anything. It's a brand."

"Your side of the story will be heard at your trial." The Wardalyrians take my arms to drag me down the aisle.

I look over my shoulder. Haidion is still sitting on the floor, too stunned to move.

"Ominous!" I cry out.

He blinks out of the trance he was stuck in. "Freyja!" He rushes to his feet and runs to me with determination in his eyes.

Before he can reach me, Vahildra tackles him to the ground. "You getting arrested isn't going to help her."

I turn back to the Wardalyrians and plead, "Whatever you think I'd done, I didn't do it! I didn't break any—"

Iraijah's voice silences mine. *You have proof of the illegal act on your body, Freyja.*

The memory of Illyrical's voice enters my mind. *The manipulation of magical energy is a skill that can be taught, but it's forbidden to use, like blood magic.*

Fuck, fuck, fuck. "Fuck!"

"If you make your lover your visitor request, you will see him again before you are sentenced," the Wardalyrian on my left states.

"When can I see him?" I don't bother correcting him on what Haidion is to me.

"Visiting hours are from Dawn to Solar Noon. You will give us a request, and if they aren't already here, we will find him for you. But I doubt he is going to leave. I see the love you two have."

I gasp at the sight of his familiar sapphire eyes. "You're a Wolven?"

"Guild before race. I'm Marcson. You might know my father."

The Wardalyrian on my right rumbles, "What did I say about getting personal with the prisoners?"

After a backhand smack to the head, Marcson coats his eyes with stone.

"You're the youngest son of Treason."

He confirms my statement with the smallest hint of a smile before he covers it with a thin line.

We enter the dark passageway that leads out to the ocean. *Do you know where they are going to take me?*

To the holding cells within the rock walls. My breathing becomes erratic as my heart beats in my ears. *You aren't going to be alone. With the chains on you, I can't leave your body.*

The light at the end of the tunnel comes into view, but instead of walking towards it, we turn right to face a stone wall.

With a scrap of the Wardalyrian's fingers, the wall vibrates and pushes aside, to reveal a metal door.

No matter how much I tell myself to walk, I can't. I'm dragged through into a cage of darkness.

* * *

In my panic, it took a long time for my eyes to adjust to the darkness. After who knows how long it took for Iraijah to help me calm down, I am finally able to make out my surroundings. I don't know how my eye adaptation power is still able to work, but I'm glad. Even in a stone cell with bars on one side, I'm happy I can see.

Behind me is a stone bed and a toilet. I'd sit, but I can't stop pacing. My chains were tightened so I can't reach my back, but, I have full movement of my legs to walk around. The bars have just enough space between each other to put my hand through. Iraijah said I'm lucky;

they could've hung me up like prey caught in a spider's web. I cringe at the thought.

He's been trying to distract me with knowledge about the weapon I wielded, but I can't focus on a history lesson.

For the hundredth time, I don't want to know how rare and powerful the sword I wielded was. And no, I'm not going to tell you who specifically branded me.

Rather than pass the time listening to a lecture, I talk about how I got the brand. I decide to divulge to him about my spiritual power so he can better understand why I needed to make a deal with a Fae.

Do you think my story will be good enough for them to let me go?

If you give the name of the Fae who branded you, probably. But you still had a weapon and wielded it in the courtroom. That is a ten-year sentence all by itself.

But I used it to kill Thor! With each step, the chains clank and rub against my wrists, which only heightens my anger. *Who knows what his intentions were? In the end, I stopped him. No one else but Rhax and I were injured.*

The lords and ladies were trying to imprison you. Do you think they wouldn't take full advantage of this situation, even if you saved their lives? They are corrupt. If they weren't, they would sing your praise and tell their race about you saving them. Which would ultimately make the mortals fear you less.

My pace quickens. *None of this is helping to console me.*

I'm trying to make you see the reality of what could happen, and if you don't want to end up in prison, then you need to give up the name of the Fae.

He's my friend. It has taken me this long to finally admit it to myself... I only regret not being able to tell him.

Is he important to you? The tone of his question isn't prodding because he's just curious. He wants to understand.

Even though I've only known Illyrical for a short time, I can see how our friendship would've grown. He reminds me of Haidion. I can see us having a strong connection, especially since he knows about Odin and my emotional scars.

The Fae is the reason that you're in here. While he is out there living his life, you are going to pay for his crimes.

Illyrical has been through enough, and he deserves happiness with his family. But Iraijah is right, I'm here because of him. I know deep in my soul that Illyrical didn't brand me with the intention of getting me caught. He wouldn't have told me his name if that was the case. No. Illyrical trusts me, and I'm not going to break that confidence. I'm going to have to figure out a way to escape; I need to for the sake of the Father. But first, I need to understand why the magic is forbidden.

Do you know why the manipulation of magical energy is illegal?

Iraijah lets out an annoyed huff. Perhaps he's sick of my stubbornness, but he doesn't remain silent for too long.

The magic system banned the use of manipulating magic because they couldn't understand it. Every type of magic or power has a language, like a woven tapestry. Each one is made differently, but the magic system knows all the languages. When it comes to the brand on your back, they don't know how to read the magic. They can't stop you from using it or take it away. It's beyond their control.

It was made illegal because the Queen of the Leeches ate someone who could manipulate magic, and she gained their power. The previous Shadow King prevented her from using her new magic to enter the Spirit Realm by tempting her with the Spring of Revitalization. Giving up such a sacred place cost the Shadow Realm, but once she got there, she couldn't leave. If greed enters the water, then greed will have its fill for eternity. But once they leave, it all goes away because the spring has the power to take. Ever since, the use of manipulating magic has been banned.

Now that I know the severity of the ban, it will help me figure out a way to not end up in prison. *Making a bargain is my best bet.*

Why do you think they would make a bargain with you? What are you willing to offer? Worry tinges his tone, but I don't allow it to affect me.

Before I can answer him, the sound of footsteps has me approaching the bars. A Wardalyrian holds up a torch, lighting up the dark stone hallway, and someone walks behind him.

He places the torch on the wall. "You have until the torch burns out to be in here. That includes your walk back."

"Understood." I clutch the bars at the sound of Ambar's voice.

The Wardalyrian bangs on a jail cell across from mine. "The visitor you requested is here." He turns and faces me. "Do you have a request for a visitor?"

Only one being comes to mind. "The Demonical of Illusion. Ominous."

Nodding, he turns to walk back down the hall.

A weak voice croaks out, "Ambar?"

Gasps leave Ambar and me as Kailani crawls into the light. Her satin-opal skin has lost its shine.

It's only because she's been out of water for so long. Also, gravity affects her more than us since she is an Oceanic race.

Ambar glances at me with a sad smile, but it shifts to concern as she drops to her knees and holds Kailani's webbed hands through the bars.

"You need to tell Hafgura. He was appointed High Lord after I regained order over the Oceanic races. If he hears me tell everyone to rejoin the URE, he will attack. He needs to hold off. We have time before the lords and ladies gain enough forces." Her Atlantean tongue is hard to understand given her exhausted state, but I manage to piece together what she said.

"I will find him. You have my word." Kailani gives Ambar a weak smile, then blinks in surprise as she spots me. *"Freyja?"*

A grieving pain strikes my heart. *"I'm sorry for sending Murrdirel away."*

Tears fall from Kailani's eyes as her smile becomes wobbly. *"Don't be sorry. You freed my mate; I couldn't be happier. He might be gone, but I know I will find him again. It might not be anytime soon, but love is more powerful than any kind of magic that could hold us back from being together."*

Ambar squeezes Kailani's hands, and she presses her forehead to the bars. *"If it's the will of the Fates, then it will be done. The same goes for the war that has begun."* Ambar shifts her attention to me. *"The Allied Army still stands behind you, commander."*

"As does the Oceanic races," the Great Kiani adds.

Hope swells in my chest. *"I'm honored. But until I'm able to get free, I need a second in command to see to the arrangement of our forces and establish a battle plan. I can't think of anyone else more suited for the role than you, Ambar."*

Tears follow the lines of her gold stenciling. *"I won't let you down."*

Kailani leans against the bars. *"Were you able to get a reading on the roots? Is he still alive?"*

I grip onto the bars tighter. "*The Father is alive?*"

"*I think so. The Father might've taken on a tree form, but his soul travels throughout. What I believe is that he centralized his magic in the heart. The roots are still rich with magic and move like blood in veins, but there is no longer a heart to resupply them. As we all have seen, the planet didn't die, but after a while, without the heart pumping out more magic, what's left will be used up. Perhaps then the planet will crumble,*" Ambar says.

"*Do whatever you must to see if the Father is truly alive.*"

She nods. "*I will. Since the Father is without his heart, maybe he's able to see how greed has infected him.*"

"*He does.*" I share with them the words the Father spoke to me before he left me during the battle, admitting that he was wrong about what Earthradon needed to be cleaned and how his actions have further spread greed. "*We also need to find out what Zeus's plan is for the Father's heart and where it is.*"

"*I'll figure it out. Restoring the Father's heart is our best chance to save our planet.*"

"*You need to go.*" Kailani points towards the dimming torch light.

Ambar rises, but keeps a hand on Kailani, and reaches across the space to hold mine. "*I give you both my word that I will not let either of you down.*"

Her soul burns brightly in her eyes, making the stenciling on her body glow. She might not need the torch to see her way back, but I note she still has the collar around her neck. Perhaps her soul burns like mine when I put my mind to something that can't be altered.

As she walks down the hallway with her torch, a brighter light comes closer. The two lights walk by each other, and the Wardalyrian lets out a huff. "Cutting it close." He shakes his head, and places the new torch on my wall. "You have until the torch burns out to be in here. That includes your walk back."

"Understood." At the sound of Haidion's voice, I grip the bars so tight that my knuckles turn white.

He is next to the bars in an instant. "Put your hands on mine. I don't want you to feel the metal."

He places his hands where mine were, and I place mine over his. Just his touch soothes my soul and nerves, helping me see the hope in my plan.

With bars in between us, I realize how much I crave his touch. Not just for comfort, but because I want him to touch me, to hold me, and press his body against mine. But most importantly, I want him to keep showing me how much he loves me. He wouldn't be here if he didn't care, and I don't know when I'll see him again. I press against the bars, trying to get as close to him as possible.

"Haidion," I whisper as his body presses against the bars, too.

"I'm here, Freyja. I'll always come when you call." A happy chuckle leaves me as tears fall.

We are so close that if he were to push his face forward just a little bit more, I could touch him the way that I've been desiring to for a while now. "Come closer."

Haidion doesn't hesitate to do so. "I'm going to get you out of here, Freyja."

My smile falters as sadness creeps in. "You can't. There's no way that you can."

"I need you to trust me. Trust that I will get you out."

I can't stop the cold tears. "I trust you with my life, but this you can't help me with. And don't you dare do anything reckless."

His signature smile of wicked intent forms on his lips. "Do you not know me at all?" He presses forward so much, I can't see his eyes. "Come here. Let me kiss your tears away."

I lean in and brush my nose against his. "I'd rather do this," I whisper against his mouth before I press my lips to his.

A moan escapes both of us when his soft, cushiony mouth molds against mine. Fire ignites in my soul and spreads through my veins as something deep within me sings. We feverishly move in sync with one another, just like we did in my daydream.

My mind runs wild with all the forbidden thoughts and desires I've ever had about Haidion and me, wanting to do them all, but with the bars in our way, I can't get as close to him as I want. If I had to choose just one fantasy to have, I'd want him to just hold me as we kissed. Rather than mope about what I can't do, I cherish this kiss.

His tongue licks my bottom lip, and I open for him. More moans escape me as he explores my mouth with his tongue. My own meets his, and he takes full advantage, creating a friction that has me sucking him.

Deep, animalistic growls escape him as the bars begin to shake, rattling the door.

Freyja, you need to stop. Haidion is going to draw—

A gust of wind comes down the hallway, blowing Haidion away. My teeth drag against his tongue, leaving a metallic taste in my mouth.

The torch is extinguished, and after a second of my eyes adjusting, I see a Wardalyrian stomping down the hallway.

I realize what that sound could've translated to. "He wasn't trying to break me out. We were just kissing." Admitting that out loud has butterflies fluttering in my stomach, and my cheeks warm.

"Doesn't matter. Since I wasn't here, I can only assume he was trying to." He stands over the Demonical. "Get up, or I will make you."

Haidion gets up on his own, but runs to the bars before the Wardalyrian can make a grab at him. "I will get you out of here." He is pulled back with a hard yank, but my Haidion shows no signs of pain from being handled so aggressively—wait, *my Haidion?*

"My" means I'm declaring Haidion as mine. Never have I had such strong feelings for someone that I wanted to claim them. I might not have said it aloud, but I admitted it to my heart and soul.

Haidion didn't need to get behind my shield wall, I'm allowing him in. All the barriers I've held up to prevent strong emotions that would make me vulnerable, I let down to allow the love he's been giving me in.

My heart beats strongly and sings with my soul as if the pair had finally rejoined after being separated. They mix harmoniously and overwhelm me with emotions I was too scared to feel again.

It's because of me, I kept them apart. I shielded myself after Freyr died because I never wanted to experience that hurt again. Haidion has shown me that I can trust him with my life and my heart.

He's almost out of my sight, and the reality of not being able to see him again sets in. *It's now or never, Freyja.*

"I love you!"

My words echo down the hallway, sounding foreign. I hear and feel the truth in them. I find myself crying tears of happiness and sadness after finally uttering those three words, but not knowing if I'll be able to say them to him again.

Haidion fights the Wardalyrian, but it's no use. "I love you too, Freyja. I will not let you rot in prison. You have my word."

More tears rush down my cheeks as he is picked up and carried down the hall. Why couldn't he have gone willingly? I didn't want my last memory of him to be his struggle to get to me.

I finally sit on the bed and curl into a ball.

Is there anything I can do, Freyja?

Rather than answer, I close my eyes and try to scrub away the memory of Haidion being hauled away. Instead, I replace it with more kissing like in my daydream, and saying "I love you" to him one more time.

CHAPTER
FORTY-FOUR

Light blinds me as I'm walked into the hallway leading to the courtroom. Judging by my growling stomach and exhausted state, I've been in the cell for almost a day. I couldn't sleep on the stone bed, and only water was brought to Kailani and me. With my mind not as sharp, I need to try my best to be alert and assertive. I have a deal to strike.

As I walk into the courtroom, I notice that the seats are all vacant besides the judge's bench and the jury section.

My determined features lift into a smile at the sight of Vahildra at the table in front of the judge's bench. His woodsy skin tone has a warmer shade to it than normal when his gaze meets mine. Another sharp suit, dusty black with metallic white stripes, adorns his tall, lean frame.

"May I have a moment alone with my client?" He doesn't take his eyes off me as he speaks.

"No. We shall proceed now." The lord sitting on the judge's bench flips a piece of paper on his desk.

After I'm chained to the chair, Vahildra stands next to me. He's hesitant, but when I give him a nod, he kneels and hugs me. I swear his eyes were starting to water before he leaned over.

"Ten-thousand years old?" I can't stop my voice from cracking at how happy I am to see him.

He chuckles, and I do a mental victory hoot for making him laugh. "You are a terrible guesser."

I catch a tear before it rolls down. "Where is Haidion?"

"He wasn't allowed in, so he's waiting outside." Before he pulls away, he places a cool kiss on my cheek. "I got a plan. Just stay quiet." Vahildra stands and rests his fingertips on the table. "What is my client being charged with?"

The lord folds his hands together and leans forward. "Goddess Freyja is being charged with bringing and wielding a weapon in court, the use of manipulating magic into the form of a weapon, and murdering a god without just cause."

"Without just cause?! I saved all of your lives."

"Thor was aiming his thunderbolt at you both times. You didn't do anything for us."

Growls fill my mind as Vahildra gives me a stern look before he turns back to the judge. "Unless you have reason to believe that Thor wouldn't have gone after anyone if he had successfully killed my client, then we can't assume his intentions. He did call out to the lady before he let out his first strike. For all we know, that bolt was meant for her."

The lord is quiet as he sits back in his seat. "Yes. We don't know his intentions on who he wanted to hit."

Vahildra walks around the table. "My client acted in self-defense. Thor's death wasn't without cause."

The lords and ladies murmur to one another before a lord walks over to the judge. After he quietly tells him something, he sits down again. "The jury agrees that Thor's death was with just cause. That charge will be dropped." He turns a piece of paper over. "What do you have to say for your client about the other two charges?"

Vahildra leans against the table. "Bottom line, my client used a weapon in court, knew about the brand on her back, and knew it was removable." I don't know how he guessed that because I didn't tell him. "Since we all agree that my client acted in self-defense, she should be allowed to have the brand removed before she is charged."

The lord let's out a laugh. "You expect me to allow her to leave on her word that she will get the brand removed and come back here? No."

Vahildra strides forward, making the lord lean back in his chair more. "You are putting words in my mouth, and I don't appreciate it. You are the judge, aren't you?" He doesn't give the man a chance to speak. "I ask that you tell me what it would take for her to get the brand removed because that's needed, is it not? She can't keep it. Either you act, or the magic system will. Or worse, a leech."

"She will still be sentenced for the use of manipulating magic, even if she gets the brand taken off."

Vahildra nods and takes a step back. "Yes. That was what I said earlier about her coming back to be charged. Tell me, what can we do to have her get the brand removed?"

A lady calls out, "Bring the Fae here."

The rest nod and agree while a lord adds, "He, too, should be charged. He would have the same brand."

Vahildra is too far away for me to tell him that I won't agree to those terms, so I proclaim, "I have a proposition."

My friend gives me a glare, telling me with just a look to keep my mouth shut. I don't plan on it, though. While he stares daggers at me, everyone else quiets down, waiting to hear what I have to say.

"The Father came to me before he died. He told me a message that needs to be passed along to the Shadow King." All the lords and ladies shift in their seats, clearly unsettled by me just calling out his name. "Allow me to get the message to him, and use the weapon on my back to bring restoration to our planet. Just like how I used it to defend myself against Thor, I will do the same to defend the people of Earth-radon. I'll make a vow that I will only use the weapon to defend, and then I will get rid of it after."

Without the help of Faithless, I need a strong weapon to fight against Zeus, and as Iraijah told me, the Sihotana is rare and powerful.

Underneath the judge's mask, he blinks in shock. "Are you implying that you're willing to make a bargain with us?"

"Yes, I am."

The lord leans forward, tilting his head to the side. "What are you willing to give?"

Vahildra rounds the table and smacks his hand against my mouth. "My client is not in the right frame of mind to make such vast decisions since she has been deprived of basic needs like food and light. She will get the brand removed, and—"

I slap his hand away from my mouth. "No, I won't!" I won't bring Illyrical into this.

Vahildra sits down next to me, gripping my hand tightly. "Yes, you will."

"Freyja, you have two options. One, you dismiss your lawyer, and proceed with the bargain. Or two, you spend an eternity in prison since you aren't willing to get the brand removed. Which option are you going to choose?"

A glass film coats Vahildra's eyes as he silently pleads with me. He squeezes my hand tenderly and waits patiently. Gone is the lawyer, and before me is my concerned friend.

I lean forward and place a kiss on his cheek. "I have to do this."

He pushes away from me, and I note the hurt in his eyes before he hides it behind an emotionless mask. "Then you are going to need this." With a heavy breath, he tugs off his glove.

Worried gasps come from the lords and ladies as he pulls out a gold coin layered in shadows, making it hard to discern the design and wording.

"What's that?"

If it's anything like the last coin, I'm screwed because I'm chained to a chair. I send a prayer to the Fates that Vahildra isn't going to say what I think he will.

"Freedom from the prisons in Orrtiereum." Rather than toss it, he hands it to me. "I'd feel better if you make your bargain while having this."

This was Vahildra's upper hand. Even if I got sentenced, he had a plan, and I chose not to trust him. Hurt pains my heart and saddens my soul as I look up at my friend. Rather than take the coin, I fold my hands over his.

"I choose option two. I'm keeping my lawyer."

"Then you are spending an eternity in prison." Vahildra pulls his hand away and places the coin back under his sleeve. "Charge her."

"Wait, what?!"

Chuckles fill my mind. *And you call me an asshole.*

The lord blinks in confusion. "So, you aren't going to give your client the coin? Why?"

Vahildra stands and smooths out the creases in his jacket. "My client chose not to trust me, and now she will pay the price for that." He looks at me with a wicked smile, one I'd only ever seen on Haidion's face, but on him, it's mean. "Perhaps, some more time in a cell will help you realize I hold your best interest at heart."

Chills scrape down my body as my blood freezes to the point of pain. "I thought you were my friend."

He takes a moment to fix his glove before looking at me. "I am your friend. You just haven't seen this side of me. Only when you don't listen to me or trust my word do I become a charming asshole."

"Very well." The lord raises his gavel. "Goddess Freyja, you are hereby sentenced to Excilum for your crimes."

Vahildra's attention snaps to him as the lord hits the sound block. "No. She is bound for Avokyria for the use of manipulating magic."

Avokyria?

It's the penitentiary in the Shadow Realm; a floating fortress.

The lord lifts an iron block on top of his desk. "We don't enforce the rule anymore since the Shadow King hasn't made a fuss about it. Bring her up."

Hopelessness weighs down my heart, and failure turns my stomach into knots. I failed the Father and the beings of Earthradon.

A pair of Wardalyrians come up and unchain me from the chair.

"No!" When Vahildra tries to lunge for me, another pair of Wardalyrians hold him back. "Freyja."

There is an apology in his eyes, but I don't know what he is apologizing for. He wanted me to go to prison, so why is he worried now? Rather than focus on him, I eye the block that will be brand my skin.

Even though I know this is going to happen regardless, my feet still drag across the floor, and I fight their hold as they lift my right arm to the judge.

Haidion's name is on the tip of my tongue, but calling him will only get him in trouble. I can't do that to him. This is my fate. I chose to trust Vahildra, only for him to stab me in the back.

The lord places the cold, heavy block on my forearm while the Wardalyrian balls his hand into a fist.

Haidion, I love you.

He raises his arm and slams it down.

The sound of a bone popping is audible as pain shoots to my elbow.

As Iraijah and I scream, I notice that the Wardalyrian's fist connected with my bare skin. *Where is the block?*

"You are going to pay for hurting what's mine," a smoky voice growls from behind me.

I'm released from the Wardalyrians' hold as they take a knee and bow. Vahildra and the ones who held him drop as well. But to my surprise, the lords and ladies remain upright.

At the end of the aisle, a tall being comes out of a fiery void of magnificent darkness. With each step they take, snake-like tendrils of shadow slither out of the fire. A muscular body of lava with a pair of black, flaming wings is revealed. Purple, gem-like eyes in a hidden galaxy lock onto me.

The smoldering voice of lustrous fire and treacherous seas drifts towards me. "Hello, beauty." The Shadow King grins like a predator thrilled about consuming its prey.

He tosses a block in his hand as if it were a toy, not a life sentencing tool. "I have been informed that you are in the custody of an individual who ought to be brought to my realm for punishment."

How did he know? Did Haidion tell him?

The Shadow King has eyes and ears everywhere.

The lord stammers in fear as he rises from his seat. "You have never enforced the rule before. Why now?"

"A reason is necessary?"

The lord shakes his head as he pulls out another block.

With a wave of the Shadow King's hand, the lord stops moving. "A label is unnecessary for me to know that she is mine."

He strolls down the aisle until he gets to my side, and when I start to cough from how potent the smoke is, it's immediately whisked away.

"Although I have no objection to the act of choking you, it is not appropriate for us to partake in such an activity at this time, unless you have an appetite for an audience."

Iraijah and I both let out a moan as coolness wraps around my injury. A snake-like tendril snuggles close around my forearm.

The Shadow King links my good arm with his. "What are your

thoughts on his punishment? An arm for an arm, or should I simply end his life?" Judging by how he patiently waits for me to answer, he's serious.

"Killing them is a little bit excessive." I won't take the risk if the one who hurt my arm was Treason's son.

"Not for me."

With a wink he drops the iron bar. A war hammer of shadow shoots out of his hand, and as he tightens his grip, the darkness hardens into a solid weapon.

"Present your right arm to me, and hold still."

The Wardalyrian who held my arm does as he was ordered.

The Shadow King uses little to no effort to swing the hammer. Even though it only looks like a little tap that couldn't possibly cause any damage, the Wardalyrian howls in pain. The stone shatters, revealing bruised skin.

"Now, remove her chains and collar. I intend to retain both for extracurricular use."

Another Wardalyrian rises to their feet. "You might have our respect, but you have no power to make those commands. Those items belong to the Gargoyle Guild."

"Interesting." The Shadow King twirls the hammer in his hand. "Then perhaps a trade." He offers the handle to the Wardalyrian.

Every eye in the room widens as if they can't believe what's happening. All look upon the hammer like a sacred treasure; it must be extremely powerful. The only one who isn't in the trance is Vahildra. He watches the Wardalyrian closely as if he can see into his soul.

"Yes. A trade." The man goes to take the handle, but the Shadow King pulls it back.

"First, remove her restraints."

With a firm nod, the Wardalyrian comes over to me, and scratches his nails across the collar, unlocking it. He clamps his hands over each shackle, forcing them to widen until I can pull my wrists and ankles free. From the way he removes the bindings, it makes me think that it's the magic of their guild with the power over the metal, not their position as Wardalyrians.

He holds the items toward the Shadow King, and opens his other hand to receive the hammer. One of the snake-like tendrils wraps around the chains and collar until they are gone.

As the man grasps the handle, the Shadow King's smile widens. Unhinged laughter erupts from him a second later as the Wardalyrian drops to the ground with the hammer.

The lord lets out a scream. "What have you done?" He kneels next to the fallen, unmoving Wardalyrian.

"You see, in order to wield a shadow weapon, your own shadows must be strong enough to handle it." He gestures to the fallen being. "His must have not been."

The lord looks up at the Shadow King with tears in his eyes. "What does that mean for my son?"

Vahildra places a hand on the lord's shoulder. "He's dead."

The Shadow King's laughter subsides. "I designed the weapon to be the property of the Gargoyle Guild. However, with regard to wielding it, I fervently suggest you locate an individual endowed with formidable shadows. Otherwise, the guild will lose a substantial number of members."

Vengeful fury sharpens the lord's eyes as he stands. He shows no fear as he points his finger at the Shadow King. "If I hear any word of you siring an offspring, I will take them from you as you have taken mine."

Another chuckle leaves the Shadow King as he brushes off the threat. "While I am enjoying myself, there is a greater probability that monsters will emerge the longer my portal remains open." He shifts his gaze to me. "Let's make haste. I have a bed that is eagerly awaiting your arrival."

As he turns, I tug on his arm. "Wait. Don't I get a chance to say goodbye?"

He looks me dead in the eye, an emotionless void. "No," he rumbles. "We go now."

Even though I have a message to give to him, I still fight against his hold. I want to say goodbye to Haidion before I'm sentenced to Avokyria. Iraijah tries to tell me not to struggle, but I can't. I need to see Haidion.

"Please! He's right outside."

I manage to get my arm free, but the Shadow King grabs my hand

and gives me a tug, causing me to stumble. "Either you come, or I'll make you."

"Trust me when I tell you this, just go," Vahildra urges at my back.

Even though I just witnessed the Shadow King kill someone by handing them a weapon, and his genuine amusement, I still have the courage to raise my chin. "I won't go willingly."

I should fear him, but my love for Haidion burns so strong, I'd fight the strongest being in existence in order to get to him.

With my magic flooding my body, I direct—smoke enters my lungs. Iraijah and I cough so hard that it's painful.

"Don't even think about it," the Shadow King snarls.

With a wave of his hand, the portal at the end of the aisle moves towards us. My only way to get to Haidion is to go around it and jump over the rows of seats, but the Shadow King has a death grip on my hand. I can't move. I can't breathe. I can only watch as the darkness consumes everything in its path as it closes in on us.

Memories of Haidion and me enter my mind, but I don't let them play. I send my fire to keep them back. My life will not flash before my eyes today.

Rather than take in a breath, I empty my lungs.

What are you doing? Iraijah gasps in my mind, panicked.

I'm not leaving here without seeing Haidion.

Freyja, don't—

With my fire consuming my mind to keep the memories back, Iraijah's voice gets cut off. A moment later, his radiant strength leaves me, but there is no empty ache in my chest; it is filled with the love I have for Haidion.

My fate might be tied to Avokyria and passing on the message to the merciless being that has a hold on me, but I'm forging a path that leads me to the man I love. I will see him one more time.

When the last of the air leaves my lungs, I press my injured arm to my chest and flatten my palm over my heart. The Shadow King might be commanding the portal, but I'm going to determine where we are going.

To whom is ever listening—please give me strength.

FORTY-FIVE

ALIITH

I wipe another tear away before it can land in the freshly tilled soil. Artemis's grave doesn't need my tears. She'd want me to be happy, but how can I be? She's gone, and now I'm immortal. I mean, I was before, but I had my best friend to live alongside me. A portion of myself died with her, and I don't think that part of me will ever be, filled. I don't think I'll allow it to be either.

"It's okay to cry, Ali." My gaze is watery as I lift my attention to my sister, making her a blob of sunshine.

Moriya just finished planting some luminous flare flowers for Apollo, and I'm struggling to finish doing the same for Artemis. These flowers will grow on the stones like vines, and take in the sun and moonlight so no matter what time of day it is, they will always shine with life.

I cover my sniffle with a cough and focus on placing the bulbs in the holes. "Why did we have to secretly bury them right in the middle of Animal Spirit territory instead of at home in the lands of their pantheon?"

"Avoiding your emotions doesn't mean you can make them go away," she sing-songs as she pats the soil down, not caring about the dirt on her flowy, pink dress.

My glare only makes her chuckle. This is the downside to having a sibling; they know you so well, and they are immune to your "don't fuck with me" stare. I let out a low growl and continue to fill the holes with soil.

"Ali, come on. You can talk to me." She moves to sit cross-legged while facing me. "Is it because we were on different sides of the battle or that I can't tell you who killed Artemis, Apollo, and Treason's pups?"

At the low tone of her voice, I hear the vulnerability and worry that always gets me to not be an asshole towards her.

Rather than finish my task, I sit like she is and take her hands in mine. "I'm not mad at you. I can never be because you are the ray of sunshine that can pierce through my darkness and pull me out."

A smile spreads across her face as tears slide down her golden cheeks. And being the annoying brother that I am, I lunge forward to lick her face.

"Ew! Aliith, stop!" She giggles as I lick the tears away. "It's cute when you're a puppy, not a grown ass man." She swats at me before delivering a hit to my groin.

"Fuck!" I roll over, cupping my junk. Even though I can pull my dick inside me, getting kneed in that spot still fucking hurts.

Her laughter turns into a squeal of concern. "Did I do it too hard?"

After collecting myself, I sit up, but groan from the pain. "For me, yes, but if it's for anyone else, go harder."

Ever since my sister had to fight off a troll of a man for not listening to her when she told them no, I've been training her how to defend herself. She was disappointed that she couldn't knock him out, but she was able to get away. That's the next best thing, and I was very proud of her and still am.

I tap my leg against hers. "I'm sure that my pain was only a fraction of what you felt while watching the events unfold before they happened."

She leans against me, placing her head on my shoulder. "My power is more of a curse than a blessing." Before I can catch her tear, she wipes it away. "I wish I never received it."

I wrap my arms around her to bring her close. "As long as everything happens the way it needs to, you will be shedding more tears of joy than sadness for the rest of your eternity." I lift her face up and give my sister a genuine smile. "Whatever you need, I'm here to help you."

After making a fake lunge to lick her tears again, she swats me away with a laugh. "Hearing you say it was more touching than seeing you do it."

Got it, she saw this whole occurrence happen already.

"And as for why we buried Apollo and Artemis here, in a forest and in the middle of a meadow, it is because this is one of the few pieces of land that have the most potent magic." She kneels next to me and holds my face in her hands. "Their bodies will sprout White Willow Trees."

If she wasn't holding my face, my jaw would be gaping like a fish. "What? How? That's impossible. The last sacred soul tree was used to capture the Leech Queen."

She lowers her hands and sits on her heels as rays of sunlight peek through the gloomy clouds, highlighting her curly bronze hair and caramel eyes. "They aren't like normal trees. Did you forget how they are made?"

I rest my hands behind me and cross my legs, waiting patiently for my lesson to begin. My pose earns me another smile from her, which chases away the heaviness in her aura.

"They are only made from souls who sacrifice their lives to help the betterment of magic." She bites her lower lip and rocks slightly. "Apollo and Artemis are gone, Ali. They aren't spirits."

My smile drops. "They are forever gone, then." Needing something to hold onto, I sit up and squeeze my thighs to the point of pain. I push down the heartache, focusing on my sister. "Why would they do that?"

"So they can pass on their soul magic to someone else. More specifically, the heirs that will bring restoration. They weren't the only ones either. Some of the other gods and goddesses chose to pass along their soul magic, too. From what I saw in my vision, the Father went to the gods and goddesses who died and asked if they would be willing to help. It's because of their sacrifice that we will have restoration."

"They need to be guarded." I kneel in front of Artemis's stone and finish filling the holes.

Moriya hands me a bulb I forgot to plant. "The Shadow King will send his people to guard them."

I eye her with suspicion. "Has he already done so, or are you speaking in future tense?"

"Future tense." Before I can argue, she places a finger over my lips. "Telling you won't affect the outcome. I already checked."

With a nod, I pat down the soil and shake off the dirt by wiping my hands together. "What do you need me to do?"

She gives me a smile that has her dimples showing. "Well, first, you need to stop holding back all your emotions because it's only going to make you cranky." I roll my eyes and stand, and she follows suit. "Secondly, you really need to be honest and open about your feelings towards—"

Now it's my turn to place a finger over her lips. "When I asked what you need me to do, I was talking about helping bring restoration, not what you want me to do in my personal life."

Only when she wrinkles her nose at me like a bunny, do I feel safe enough to remove my finger.

"I might be your little sister, but I'll always look out for you because you deserve happiness."

I grin. "Little is an understatement. You are a stick with rain drops on it."

She smacks me on the shoulder. "I guess my considerate brother is gone because the asshole one just arrived." After letting out a huff, she crosses her arms. "I need you to wait here."

"For how long?"

With a shrug, she starts to walk towards the forest. "I didn't see when he was going to arrive, only that he would be here when you were alone," she yells over her shoulder.

"So, you expect me to stay here for who knows how long?"

She turns around but keeps walking backwards. "If you want to help me, then yes."

I shake my head and chuckle. "That's being an asshole you know."

Her laughter is carried on the breeze. "I learned from the best." With a running start, she grows a pair of angelic wings and flies up into the cloudy sky, taking the sunshine with her.

Since I'm not one to decompress my emotions, I do the next best thing to help me, I sleep.

After shifting into my beautiful Wolven form, I curl into a ball and count my breaths. My muscles just start to relax right as I reach twenty-three, but the crack of a stick, twig, or branch has me awake and alert. There is a difference between the sound of something falling off a tree, or something being blown by the breeze, and the hard crack of wood being broken. Someone is here.

Not wanting to let the being know they alerted me, I remain still and tune into my senses. I don't smell anything different, and my ears pick up no footsteps. Either the being has light feet and messed up in their efforts to stalk me, or they can levitate off the ground, and the crack was meant to alert me to their presence.

Electrifying wind blows in my face, and I'm up on my feet in an instant. No one is around me, but a presence is. My magic tingles under my skin and in my paws, omitting my aura. If the being wants to keep their soul light, then they better not venture too close.

"It's nice to see you again, Aliith."

I turn, but only find the gravestones. Knowing that Apollo and Artemis are gone, the disembodied voice can't be them.

Since speaking is limited in this form, I let out a low growl and lower my stance, ready to attack at any moment.

"Before battle, you said you'd be willing to be Freyja's servant. Could that translate to you being interested in taking the position of her Guardian?"

Freyja's what? I know what I said to her before battle, but we were alone. Or at least, I thought we were.

I let out another growl. "Who. Are. You?"

In a flash, a broad body appears only a foot away from me. Rather than lunging forward, I stumble back, not believing my eyes. It can't be; I saw him die. I saw his ship get pushed into the water and go up in flames.

"Freyr?"

Acknowledgments

I want to express my thanks to my spouse for patiently listening to me talk endlessly about my book. I am also grateful to my parents, sister, and therapist for their unwavering support. Also, a special thanks to my editor and sensitivity reader, they have been instrumental in refining my book to its utmost potential, along with my grandmothers, who inspired me to write and be creative. I'm also grateful to my readers for taking the time to read my book.

ABOUT THE AUTHOR

My writing journey.

As a child, I had a vivid imagination when it came down to playing make-believe. I played hide-and-seek with faeries, dug up treasures to put in my treehouse, made potions from plants and flowers, and I laid in the shadowy parts of the grass, chatting with the coolness as if it were my friend.

Growing up, I had issues with speech and comprehension, which made it difficult to read books. Instead, I would write with words I understood and knew. The first story I ever wrote was when I was eight, and it was about stumbling upon a dragon in a bloody cave. Ever since then, I have loved writing my ideas on paper because it brings them to life.

With the help of a speech psychologist, more one-on-one time with my teachers, and Sylvan Learning Center, I was able to finally understand what I was reading and could expand my knowledge of words. Some of the books I remember reading on my own without any help were The Boxcar Children by Gertrude Chandler and The Chronicles of Narnia by C. S. Lewis.

When I was fourteen, it wasn't until my grandma June passed that I used writing as a coping method to deal with her loss. My writing became darker and more morbid, but it was helping me heal. Since then, writing has provided me with a sense of comfort and release.

As a teenager, I enjoyed watching Harry Potter and the Lord of the Rings movies. What got me to start writing romance into my fantasy stories was when my sister introduced me to Twilight by Stephanie Meyer. By the age of sixteen, I had written my first fantasy romance book, The Book of Nigel. I had thought to publish it, but with the darker themes, I chose to wait until I was older.

At the age of twenty-four, I picked up the book again on the ten-year anniversary of my grandmothers' death. It wasn't planned, but a coincidence. For three years, I dedicated all my free time to polish the story and made it into a series.

When I was twenty-seven, I had finished and sent my book out to Beta Readers. A couple of them made comments that my prologue could be its own book. That input got the ideas flowing and I stopped with my first series and wrote an entirely different series, Forged by Love and Sacrifice. After spending another two years developing the Forged series, I'm finally ready to share my stories with the world.

Thank you for taking the time to read about my journey on how I became an author.

instagram.com/author.k.f.lethal

tiktok.com/@author.k.f.lethal

goodreads.com/author-kf-lethal